'I have no influenc

'Ah, but when Your Majesty is Maximilian's wif

'I shall not be his wife. I don't care what he makes me suffer, I shall never give in!'

'Oh, I think you will. I think, with respect, Your Majesty, that you cannot help it. And, as your friend, I must advise you to have a care.' He sighed, dabbed his lips sorrowfully with his handkerchief, though I noticed suddenly that his eyes were hard. 'As I say, I know what Maximilian is. He will not listen to all my pleas on your behalf. He needs the treaty with Thalia. And his need for an heir is also pressing. If you continue to oppose him he will force you to comply. After all, he holds the one bargaining counter you cannot resist. He has ex-King Friedrich's life in the palm of his hand.'

The Conscience
of the King

Jane Barry

SPHERE BOOKS LIMITED

SPHERE BOOKS LTD

Published by the Penguin Group
27 Wrights Lane, London W8 5TZ, England
Viking Penguin Inc., 40 West 23rd Street, New York, New York 10010, USA
Penguin Books Australia Ltd, Ringwood, Victoria, Australia
Penguin Books Canada Ltd, 2801 John Street, Markham, Ontario, Canada L3R 1B4
Penguin Books (NZ) Ltd, 182–190 Wairau Road, Auckland 10, New Zealand

Penguin Books Ltd, Registered Offices: Harmondsworth, Middlesex, England

First published in Great Britain by Michael Joseph Ltd 1987
Published by Sphere Books Ltd 1988

Made and printed in Great Britain by
Richard Clay Ltd, Bungay, Suffolk

To Nuncs, Georgie and Osbert.
Enjoy the Mousies in the sky.

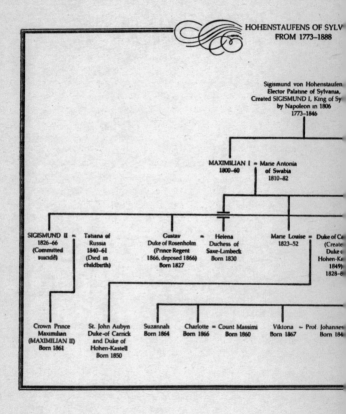

HOHENSTAUFENS OF SYLV
FROM 1773–1888

Sigismund von Hohenstaufen
Elector Palatine of Sylvania,
Created SIGISMUND I, King of Sy
by Napoleon in 1806
1773–1846

MAXIMILIAN I = Marie Antonia
1800–60   of Swabia
                         1810–82

SIGISMUND II = Tatiana of   Gustav   = Helena   Marie Louise = Duke of Ca
1826–66   Russia   Duke of Rosenholm   Duchess of   1823–52   (Create
(Committed   1840–61   (Prince Regent   Saxe-Limbeck   Duke o
suicide)   (Died in   1866, deposed 1866) Born 1830   Hohen-Ka
                 childbirth)   Born 1827   1849)
                                                                                          1828–8

Crown Prince   St. John Aubyn   Suzannah   Charlotte = Count Massimi   Viktoria ~ Prof. Johannes
Maximilian   Duke of Carrick   Born 1864   Born 1866   Born 1860   Born 1867   Born 184
(MAXIMILIAN II) and Duke of
Born 1861   Hohen-Kastell
                 Born 1850

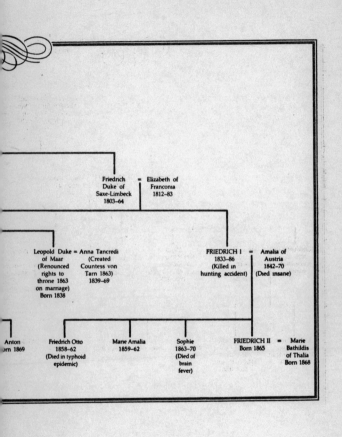

Friedrich
Duke of
Saxe-Limbeck
1803–64

= Elizabeth of
Franconia
1812–83

Leopold Duke = Anna Tancredi
of Maar   (Created
(Renounced   Countess von
rights to   Tarn 1863)
throne 1863   1839–69
on marriage)
Born 1838

FRIEDRICH I = Amalia of
1833–86   Austria
(Killed in   1842–70
hunting accident) (Died insane)

Anton
orn 1869

Friedrich Otto
1858–62
(Died in typhoid
epidemic)

Marie Amalia
1859–62

Sophie
1863–70
(Died of
brain
fever)

FRIEDRICH II
Born 1865

= Marie
Bathildis
of Thalia
Born 1868

CHAPTER ONE

Marie Bathildis

I

When it came, of course, it took us by surprise. Oh, there had been rumours ever since I could remember, rumours which had intensified in the last few months with the disturbing news Count Vielfrass's agents had brought back from Switzerland. But all the same, on that August afternoon in 1889 as we drove in our open landau along Königstrasse and across the river towards the Old Quarter, there seemed nothing out of the ordinary. The gilded spires of St Xaviersdom glinted against a cloudless sky. In Sigismundplatz a golden haze of pollen from the lime trees set my lady-in-waiting, Countess von Meltz, ashudder with a fresh onslaught of hayfever. Groups of loyal subjects waved their handkerchiefs; in the English Gardens a band played. And if there were more people in the streets than usual, and more police and soldiers lining our route, if perhaps amongst the waving crowd there were faces that stared a mute dissent, why, Baron von Schramm's iron rule had accustomed us to such shows of strength and such silent protest.

The city glided past, white and gold and green in the sunlight. The greys of our outriders kicked up little clouds of fine dust. Beside me Katerina von Meltz continued to sneeze and to apologise in succession. And I, feeling the palms of my hands grow damp beneath the kid, began bracing myself against the shyness which, even after years of governesses and Court officials trying to din it out of me, still crippled me whenever I was obliged to talk to strangers. We had always been treated as children, my husband and I; and since Schramm had used Freddy's illness to set up a Council of State – which was in truth little but a thinly-veiled regency – we knew even less of the world around us. There was nothing to tell me that afternoon, steeling myself for the ordeal of the Governors and Patrons of St Pius's Orphanage for the Daughters of Distressed Artisans, willing myself to conquer my customary inability to swallow, of that other ordeal which lay only hours ahead.

The orphans had presented their bouquets and were dancing when the young Major of the Hussars burst unceremoniously into the hall. They wore little white Grecian tunics, and wreaths of flowers in their hair, and they danced in meticulously-drilled chains and circles, faces screwed up in concentration, eyes flickering towards where the Housemother stood, stern in black serge, commanding them with her stare not to trip or falter or commit any other excess which would let down the good name of St Pius before the Royal Personage who had so charitably come to witness their performance. Pale scrubbed faces, shorn of all childhood exuberance, already tutored at six or seven in the art of concealment, disguising their fear of me as the faces of the Court Camarilla disguised their disdain, and those other faces, the silent faces of the crowd, disguised – what? Children, afraid of a twenty-one-year-old girl in a dowdy costume and last season's hat, who had only just managed to subdue her own fear sufficiently not to drop their posies. The child nearest my chair was chewing her tongue with the effort of following the piano. My heart went out to her.

It was then that I noticed the Hussars Major whisper something in the ear of the Chairman of Governors, who in turn whispered to my equerry, who whispered to the Countess von Meltz behind my chair. The Countess bent forward, shedding a drip from her nose which etiquette forbade her to wipe away; her lower lip trembled, her watery eyes bulged with consternation.

'Ma'am, a riot has broken out in the English Gardens. We must return to the Residenz at once.'

I glanced at the bobbing circles of white. The child who chewed her tongue was now irrevocably lost, scurrying to catch up with the others and somehow nudge herself back into her place. The Housemother scowled. Straight to bed, no doubt, and bread and water for the rest of the week.

'No,' I said.

'But, Ma'am, there is – shooting in the streets.'

This time the Countess's whisper was audible to everyone

in the hall. The pianist missed a beat; the circles of white hung suspended for a moment as forty garlanded heads wavered between the menacing serge figure and the direction of the whisper.

'No,' I said softly but also quite audibly. 'We will not disappoint the children by leaving before they have finished.'

The pianist turned back to the keyboard, the Housemother resumed her centurian stance, the circles hovered, jerked and began obediently to revolve again. Though behind my chair I felt my suite stiffen I stared steadfastly ahead of me, clutching the flowers in my lap.

Then, close enough to make the windows rattle, came an explosion, followed by another and another. The piano stopped mid-bar, someone screamed, someone else cried out: 'Oh my God, bombs! The anarchists are bombing us!' Suddenly everyone was shouting and screaming at once, the children broke ranks and scattered, behind me I heard Countess von Meltz burst into sobs. I thought I knew what the explosions were but did not want to form the thought that chilled me. The children were whimpering and crying, some huddled in groups, others rushing backward and forward in blind terror. Casting aside my flowers I knelt to the two nearest me and put my arms around them. 'Mama!' the smallest one was crying. 'Mama, Mama!' I stroked her hair while she buried her face in my skirt.

Suddenly I was aware of the Major of the Hussars at my side.

'Your Majesty, I beg of you – you must leave immediately.'

'Not yet. Not till I know the children are safe.'

Looking up at him I saw he was concealing his impatience with difficulty. 'The children are safe enough – I'll leave some of my men to guard them if you wish. The danger, Ma'am, the danger is to you.'

I stared at him, puzzled. The concern that threatened to push aside the constraints of protocol was real. Stripping off my gloves and giving one to each as a comforter, I reluctantly disengaged myself from the two children.

'Very well,' I said. 'But at least let us wait calmly until the poor little things can be got to their dormitories. Let us not scuttle away like frightened rabbits.'

The twin hoods of the landau had been closed and the windows drawn up and shuttered. Yet, from the way we were jolted against one another, I could tell we were passing through the cobbled, hilly streets of the Old Town, avoiding the main thoroughfares. Nevertheless from time to time we could still hear the faint rat-tat-tat of the guns. Beside me, the Countess von Meltz sobbed and sniffed. Major von Doren, my equerry, and the Major of the Hussars, who had insisted on accompanying us, held their hands grimly to their swords. Up on the box the coachman swore and cracked his whip. Then, without warning, the horses were reined in, we heaved to a stop that nearly threw me into the arms of the Major, and there came another sound, horses' hooves and a familiar, menacing rumble. The thought I had striven to push from my mind forced itself back – the memory of that day in Nordstadt, still fresh in its horror, women's faces, tiny children screaming. I could no longer contain myself. 'We must stop, go back! Oh, we must stop them! They're using cannon against our people, blowing them to bits as they did at Nordstadt. The shooting isn't rioters – it's our soldiers shooting into the crowd, shooting defenceless people! Take me back, let me stop them, I command you!'

The gun carriage and its cavalcade had passed us now and the landau jolted forward just as suddenly as it had stopped. The Major caught and steadied me. 'Your Majesty, I do not know what orders have been given—'

'You do not know?' I tore my arm free. 'I do not know, the King does not know. Yet these orders are given in our name! Sir, I do not so much command you as beg of you to let us turn back.'

'I pray that Your Majesty will not command me. My duty to protect Your Majesty's person impedes my readiness to obey.' He hesitated, cleared his throat. 'The concert in the English Gardens was a pretext for an illegal gathering of the banned Liberal League. During the meeting agitators circulated certain rumours amongst the crowd which caused it to break out in traitorous demonstrations—'

'Rumours?'

Again he made that nervous noise in his throat. Trying to discern his expression in the gloom of the carriage I thought suddenly how young he was for his rank. 'Please,' I repeated, 'tell me what rumours.'

'It was put about, Your Majesty, that the Pretender Maximilian had begun an invasion.'

There was for an instant such complete silence that even Countess von Meltz seemed to have paused mid-sob.

I attempted a laugh. 'But of course, Major, that is merely a rumour.'

A sound escaped him, a little sad sound like a sigh. 'I regret, Your Majesty . . . my commanding officer received the news not three hours ago . . . I regret to have to inform you that Maximilian's forces crossed the border this morning and are marching on Nordstadt.'

II

My second lady-in-waiting, Baroness von Lindhafen, received me tearfully in our private apartments. 'Oh, praise God you are returned us safely, Ma'am. We have all been beside ourselves with worry, ever since we heard . . .'

Looking about me at our drawing-room, Freddy's and mine, at the photographs and the cheerful cretonnes and the comfortable furniture I had had sent from Maples, from my beloved England, I felt bewildered. Everything was just as it always was, the albums set out upon the little table, the embroidered screens, the chairs placed where I had with my own hands angled them. Nothing could have changed, there could not be war, people being shot in the English Gardens. Katerina von Meltz, mopping her reddened nose, began upon a shrill and jumbled account of the afternoon's events. I silenced her, more peremptorily than I was used to.

'How is my husband?'

Mercifully Augusta von Lindhafen, taking what I hoped passed for calm in my voice, became instantly her old sensible self again. His Majesty had suffered another attack in my absence but it had only been a mild one and he was resting quietly now. Field Marshal von Falkenberg and Cabinet Treasurer Woltz were both asking for audiences but had been told His Majesty was too ill to see them and were waiting in the Audience Chamber until I returned.

I thanked her and asked her to send word to Falkenberg and Woltz that I would receive them presently. Then, without taking off my hat, I went in to see my husband.

He looked so frail and sad, my poor Freddy, propped against the bolster in his nightshirt, his round face white, his fine brown hair sticking up like a spiky crest at the crown of his head and matted, darker, where the sweat beaded his forehead, not twenty-four but a little boy, forlorn because I had deserted him. His eyes still had the cloudy, far-away look I had come to recognise so well.

'O Tilda, have they told you? Twice today. Naughty, as dear Sister Theresa says. Twice naughty.'

I kissed his forehead, then sat on the bed and took him in my arms, cradling his head against my breast, rocking him gently. 'Oh my poor Freddy. My poor, dear, beloved Freddy.' The rocking motion seemed to comfort me too; I realised for the first time how violently I had been trembling. After a while, however, my tension seemed to communicate itself in spite of me, for he pulled away and lay back upon his pillows, gazing at me questioningly.

'No gloves, Tilda? A hat but no gloves.'

'I lost them. You know how hopeless I am.'

'Something's happened, hasn't it? Something they won't tell me about.'

I hesitated.

'Oh Tilda, dear, darling Tilda, don't lie to me. They may think I'm simple, but you've always told me the truth. Please, Tilda, tell me what has happened.'

I took his hands and kissed them. Then, still with his fingers meshed tightly in mine, I told him about the Pretender Maximilian and the riot in the English Gardens, leaving out only all mention of the shooting, for I knew it would distress him pointlessly, and I had long ago understood – despite my outburst in the landau – that we had no power to change such things, had had little enough that time in Nordstadt and, with Schramm's Council of State, were utterly powerless now.

He lay for a while looking up at me in silence. Then he said, very quietly: 'So, Tilda, it's come at last.'

I stroked the hair from his forehead gently with the tips of my fingers. 'We don't know that, my dear. It may be a false alarm after all. Falkenberg and Woltz are waiting for an audience. They've probably come to tell us that the rebels have already been beaten back.'

He sighed. 'This man who says he is Maximilian, Tilda – can he really be what he claims to be?'

'The Sigismundites believe he is genuine.'

He seemed to fall for a moment into a reverie. Then, all at once, his brow was furrowed, his eyes, gazing up at me, were almost pleading. 'But even so, I don't understand – why should he want it, Tilda, why should he want all this so badly? Why should anyone want this wretchedness of ours – this prison?'

I held him to me again, stroking his hair and feeling his heart beating against mine. 'My darling, don't think about it. Try to sleep now and be well. We have each other, whatever happens. Try to be a good boy and sleep.' I began to croon to him gently, a lullaby my English nurse had taught me while my mother was still alive. His body was warm, his limbs seemed gradually to relax and grow heavy. Then, quite suddenly, he stiffened.

'Oh Tilda, I have it again. The third time today. Oh Tilda, God help me!'

I knew at once that the tingling in his left arm had begun, the aura that presaged another fit. I knew too that I had no time to comfort him, for the beginning of the aura gave me only two minutes before the fit was upon him. I pulled away the bolster and lowered him gently until he was lying flat. Then I took out my handkerchief and inserted it carefully between his tongue and his teeth so that he could not injure himself. He did not murmur or resist but simply looked up at me with his pale, sad eyes, as if this ritual we had performed together so many times imparted in itself a modicum of comfort. Pressing my fingers to my lips, I brushed his forehead with them softly. Then I sat in the chair beside the bed and waited. When the noises started and his eyes fixed and began to roll I turned my head away, putting my hands up to my face. Because he knew how it distressed me to watch him he had asked me instead to pray whenever the seizures were upon him. But I could not pray. Recently I had found it impossible to share his unshakeable belief that God, at least, watched over us and protected us; and now, as I tried to concentrate my mind, I found it filled only with a growing terror. Between the chinks of my fingers, the sight of his prie-dieu and the crucifix above it – the copper-gilt crucifix which held the relic of the True Cross – reproached me for failing him so miserably. I closed my eyes and endeavoured to shut out the Major's words, the sound of the guns, the noises from the bed, everything. Two craven tears I had been struggling with for some time oozed out from beneath my lashes.

After a while the noises ceased and there was silence. The clock on the mantelpiece told me he had been unconscious for fifteen minutes. Not good, but not the worst. Wiping my face with my hand so that he should not see I had been crying, I went over and took the handkerchief from his mouth, carrying with me the basin from the washstand, for afterwards he would always immediately be sick. The simple ritual of all these tasks, of sponging his face with a damp towel and covering him with the eiderdown so that he could get warm again, of pouring a glass of water from the carafe by the bed and holding it to his lips, helped me to pull myself together. I sat with him for a little, watching in his eyes the slow struggle back to consciousness. Once he murmured: 'Three times, Tilda, three times naughty,' and I stroked his forehead and told him what I had long since ceased to believe, that he would be better soon, that we should make the pilgrimage to Lourdes and the miracle we had prayed for together would happen. Then, kissing him and ringing for the Sister of the Good Shepherd who nursed him to come and change his linen, I went downstairs to see the Army Chief and the Cabinet Treasurer.

The two uniformed figures, one tall and glitteringly befrogged, the other hunched and birdlike in the subfusc of the Civil Service, paced the stuccoed length of the Audience Chamber in silence, as if they had during the time they had been waiting exhausted every expression of urgency they could make to each other. Watching them turn and bow as I entered, I caught again, masked by the punctiliousness of the one and the sycophancy of the other, but there nonetheless, the contempt, the intrinsic disgust of the knowing and the powerful at having to perform all the *voltes* and *terre-à-terres* of protocol before someone who had neither knowledge nor power and, were it not for an accident of birth, would not merit their smallest consideration. Swallowing hard and placing my hands together in an attempt to suggest composure, I seated myself and indicated that they might speak. As if the pressures of holding back had become intolerable, both began at once.

'Your Majesty must not be alarmed—'

'We can assure Your Majesty there is no cause for concern—'

The Cabinet Treasurer simpered. The Field Marshal glared at him. The Cabinet Treasurer, taking unfair advantage of the moment's silence, began again.

'As I say, there is no cause for concern. The er – unfortunate disturbance in the English Gardens is now completely under control.'

'How many are dead?' I asked quietly.

The Field Marshal's mustachios bristled proudly. 'Amongst His Majesty's army, I am delighted to say, there were no casualties.'

'But the women and children?'

A glance passed between them, a fleeting but impatient glance. The Cabinet Treasurer turned upon me the full force of his deprecating smile. 'Leftists, anarchists, political rabble-rousers. A symptom, merely, of our troubled times. As I have explained, Your Majesty need not be concerned—'

'Riff-raff!' said the Field Marshal. 'The army'll give 'em the medicine they deserve.'

'And Count Vielfrass's police are ever vigilant. There is, I must repeat, no reason whatever for alarm. Nevertheless, in view of the other incident, this trivial outbreak on the border,' – here the Cabinet Treasurer moistened his lips delicately with his tongue – 'in view, as I say, of this temporary ripple in our otherwise calm waters, we feel it our duty as loyal servants of the Crown to advise, to urge Your Majesties to leave the capital immediately.'

'Then there is cause for alarm,' I said.

The Field Marshal grew red behind his whiskers. 'Most certainly not, Your Majesty. The Deathwatch is quartered at the barracks at Nordstadt, the 3rd Cuirassiers are at Jedburg, only three miles away. Crack regiments, both of them. If they don't put the fear of God into the Pretender's miserable raggle-taggle—'

'Quite so,' said the Cabinet Treasurer. 'But Nordstadt is only two days' march from Rosenholm. I'm sure Their Majesties' loyal subjects would rest more easily if Their Majesties were safely ensconced in Schwanensee, in the mountains . . .'

I looked at him for a moment, at the ingratiating smile, fixed like a rictus, at the small, neat hands, palms kneaded together as if he were washing them, moving to and fro in little, exculpatory motions.

'But if there is no reason to go?' I said.

'No reason, Your Majesty. Simply, you understand, a precaution.'

'No reason at all,' said the Field Marshal, who had been containing himself with difficulty and had gone a shade redder in the attempt. 'The Herr Cabinet Treasurer is over-cautious. Untrained, undisciplined troops against the Death-watch and the Cuirassiers? You can depend on it, Maximilian won't even reach Nordstadt—'

'Nevertheless, considering everything – not least His Majesty's health – a trip to the mountains cannot but be beneficial—'

'Balderdash!' said the Field Marshal, forgetting protocol for an instant and turning directly upon Woltz. 'One sight of our troops and Maximilian's rabble will turn tail. We'll soon have him scuttling back where he came from, across the Thalian border—'

'The Thalian border?' I felt all at once cold. 'But we have a treaty with my uncle.'

Again the Cabinet Treasurer moistened his lips. His hands, I noticed, took up their work of washing more earnestly. 'The treaty, may I remind Your Majesty, operates only in the event of either sovereign state being threatened by Prussia. It does not put His Grand Ducal Highness under any obligation to help us quash internal disturbances—'

'But he's fomenting disturbance. By allowing the rebels to invade us from his territory, he's committing an act of direct aggression.'

'There have, as Your Majesty knows – notwithstanding the connection between both our Royal Houses through the

felicitous union between your own Royal Personage and His
Majesty King Friedrich – there have been areas of disagreement recently between Thalia and ourselves – the unrest on
the border, the troublesome affair concerning His Grand
Ducal Highness's projected railway. And His Highness – as
I'm sure Your Majesty will forgive me for remarking – is apt,
in any case, to be somewhat volatile.'

'But have we not made the strongest possible protest? I
demand to see my uncle's ambassador.'

'By a curious coincidence, Your Majesty, Prince von
Ansbach was recalled to Thalia on urgent business three
days ago.'

'I see.' I felt my feeble attempt at assertion crumbling. 'So
Maximilian's forces aren't just a small band of rebels. He has
the power of my uncle's army behind him.'

'Oh, it's not as bad as that. The Grand Duke hasn't gone
as far as committing troops and military equipment – that
we should interpret as an act of war. He appears simply not
to be discouraging the Pretender's activities. All in all, in
fact – ' here the hands kneaded faster, the tongue once more
explored the lips – 'all in all, we have much to be grateful
for. Prussia at least seems to be turning a blind eye to the
incident. Now if the Kaiser were to use it as an excuse to
interfere that would be a different matter, then we certainly
should have cause to worry.'

'And how long will Prussia turn a blind eye?'

'Prussia, Thalia – Herr Woltz sees threats as a small boy
sees spooks when the lights are put out,' broke in the Field
Marshal irritably. 'How often must I repeat to him, there is
no question of Maximilian getting beyond Nordstadt—'

'But I'm sure the Field Marshal agrees we must take sensible precautions.'

'Precautions be damned! All Maximilian has are Keller's
peasants and a handful of army deserters.'

The Cabinet Treasurer shot him a malign glance. 'That is,
if the rest of the army remains loyal.'

'The army is loyal, sir, loyal and willing to fight! I trust
you will vouch the same for your civilian colleagues!'

The Cabinet Treasurer's smile froze, and for an instant
there hung in the air an unpleasant silence.

'Where are Baron Schramm and Count Vielfrass?' I asked

softly. 'I should have expected them to be the first to advise us in this crisis.'

'The Minister of the Interior is at present engaged in rounding up the ringleaders of the English Gardens incident, Your Majesty.'

'And Baron Schramm?'

'The Cabinet Chief, as you know, is holidaying on his estate at Karlottenberg.'

'But he has been recalled?'

'A telegram was sent, Your Majesty, the instant we knew of the inva – er, incident. But he appears to be at one of his hunting boxes. Of course, we anticipate his return imminently.'

Karlottenberg was close to the Bohemian border, convenient for flight if things turned out badly. I felt my coldness grow. 'I see,' I said.

Another silence fell in which the Field Marshal seemed to have lost his bluster and Woltz his smile.

'So Your Majesty will understand,' said the Cabinet Treasurer, recovering, 'there is no cause whatever for alarm.'

'Absolutely none,' said the Field Marshal.

'But nevertheless we do advise . . . with all things considered . . . Schwanensee is so much pleasanter than Rosenholm at this time of year – it would inspire feelings of joy and relief throughout Sylvania if Your Majesties were to leave tomorrow morning. Or even tonight.'

I sat for a while alone in my boudoir before I returned to Freddy. I felt numb. The Field Marshal's red, blustering face and the Cabinet Treasurer's hands, washing, washing, working up a veritable lather of prevarications and excuses, continued to haunt my mind's eye. And, worst of all, there was that coldness growing within me, seeming to creep into my very bones, so that despite the evening sun slanting through the window I drew a shawl around me, shivering.

When I eventually went in to Freddy I saw to my surprise that he was up and dressed, his valet drawing on his boots.

'I couldn't leave it all to you, Tilda. You take so much upon yourself, it isn't fair to you.' Seeing the look of concern on my face, he smiled. 'Oh, I'm all right, dearest. A little weak and shaky perhaps, but all right. I thought we would have supper together, just you and I, without our suites. And afterwards you could read to me, something you like – Heine or Shakespeare perhaps. I do so love it when you read to me, Tilda.'

I took his arm so that he could lean on me and we went slowly together into the drawing-room. I did not have the heart then to repeat my conversation with Falkenberg and Woltz. Yet, as I look back, it seems as if he understood, knew better than I that this was to be the last time we should have supper together, watching the sun go down crimson and gold and aquamarine behind the spires of St Xaviersdom, lulled by the familiarity of all our modest possessions, the worn books, the favourite chairs, my canary twittering in its cage beside the piano, safe in the little island of domesticity we had carefully built for ourselves. Only later, when the blinds had been drawn and the lamps lit, did I tell him what had taken place during the audience.

He smiled wryly. His face was very white, the skin puffy round the eyes from all the tinctures and pills the doctors prescribed for him, the cheekbones, by contrast, painfully prominent. 'So they want us to run away, Tilda? At the first sign of danger they want us to pack up and run.'

'Only to Schwanensee. With the official reason that it is for your health.'

'But what would our people think? That we had deserted them, that we put ourselves and our own safety first?'

I sighed. 'The people hate us, Freddy. We must learn to accept it.'

'The people don't hate us. They hate Schramm and Vielfrass perhaps, they hate the things that are done in our name. And they think – and they're probably right – that I'm not fit to be their King. But they don't hate you, Tilda. I've watched you – with children, with the old and the sick – watched their faces light up as they see in you what I see.'

I made a restless gesture. 'Oh my dear, don't be silly. Half the time I can't manage to put two words together; I'm not clever, not even pretty—'

'Not pretty, Tilda, beautiful. Beautiful and strong and good. And they love you for it as I love you.'

His eyes were focused on me so intently, his face had such an earnest expression that although I was smiling I found my lashes were suddenly damp. 'Oh my dear, dear silly Freddy!' I threw my arms around him and hid my face in the crook of his shoulder. 'It's you who are good, my dear. You see things differently from the rest of the world, you want to find the best in everything.'

'And shall we find the best in this?' He held me away from him. 'Or do you want us to go to Schwanensee and leave our people to face the danger on their own?'

Looking at him, at my earnest, innocent Freddy, his face suffused, his pale eyes alight with the idea that he could at last perform some service which would make what we stood for meaningful, I felt myself torn between the impossibility of disappointing him and my growing fear.

'Dearest Tilda, it's not like you to give in to things without a fight, not like you at all.'

I bit my lip. 'I'm not, I don't – Oh, my dear, all I want is to be with you and look after you. If you think we should stay, then we'll stay.'

He smiled. 'That's my Tilda. After all, we're only doing what my father would have done. He wouldn't have let himself be frightened by Woltz – he'd have stuck to his guns no matter what.'

I sighed. I remembered only too well old King Friedrich's tenacity, the bull-headed persistence which had brought him to the throne after the 1866 revolution, which had held fast to the reins of power despite all the politicking of Schramm and his clique, and which had driven him to the last when, on that fateful day three years ago out hunting at Karlottenberg, he had taken the wall that was unjumpable and ended up under his horse, neck broken, leaving Freddy and myself, twenty-one and eighteen respectively, only two years married, to take on without warning a harsh world for which we were unprepared and ill-fitted.

'Besides,' Freddy was saying, 'we must listen to Falkenberg, rely on the army.'

'Yes,' I said. 'Yes, of course.'

'And whatever happens, we must put our trust in God. He will protect us. Fetch your rosary, Tilda, and let's pray to Him now for guidance.'

III

It did not surprise me that I could not sleep (I had besides grown used to sleeping shallowly, in case the nurse came to tell me that Freddy was having another fit). No, it was the dawn that was surprising, the birds singing as they always sang, the sun coming up so clear and bright and everything, as I stood before my window looking out at the dew on the lawn and the peacocks strutting in the shadows of the cedar trees, so perfectly quiet and still that it reminded me of those summers in England at Gower Castle when Mama had been alive and there had been no Court formalities, and I had got muddy and fallen out of trees and been, for the only time in my life, properly a child. Thus it was some while before my eyes travelled east, beyond the cedars and the spires of St Xaviersdom, and I saw, in the direction of the Old Town, two tall black columns of smoke.

When Rosa, my maid – the only member of my Household who had come with me from Thalia – arrived to dress me, I asked her what the fires were.

'Police headquarters, they say, Your Majesty. And the old Parliament House. Set alight by agitators during the night, demanding the constitution back. Though how setting things on fire will help I'm blessed if I know. They say the Parliament House is burnt right to the ground.'

'And what else do they say, Rosa?'

Her shrewd old eyes avoided mine in the looking glass, she bent to busy herself with a tray of hair-pins. 'You know I don't mix with the general servants, Ma'am. I've not the time for idle gossip.'

'Tell me, Rosa, what else do they say?'

'Well,' – the wrinkles deepened in her walnut face – 'there's some that say it'll be the Residenz next. But we know better, Ma'am, don't we? We know the people are loyal in their hearts, that they wouldn't touch a hair of both Your Majesties' heads. And besides, we know you'll give the order today and we'll be nice and safe up in the mountains by tomorrow night.'

I tried to smile.

'Not that I'd give two *pfennigs* for this Maximilian anyway.' She began to apply the brush to my hair with vigour, as if

her very strokes were expunging the Pretender. 'Royal blood
he may or may not have, but they say he's a great booby for
all that, brought up as a peasant with the pigs and the goats,
eating his food with his hands like a pig too, and spitting
on the floor and not even able to sign his own name. They
do say, Ma'am, that he even—'

But I was not to hear what else they said about Maximilian,
for at that moment there was a knock at my door and the
Baroness von Lindhafen appeared, still in her dressing-gown
and nightcap, looking greatly flustered.

'Herr Woltz is here again, Ma'am, begging to see you at
once.'

'But you must tell him I'm still *déshabillée*.'

'He won't be put off. He says it's of the utmost urgency.'

Yes, looking back, it was only that instant of peace when
the sun came up, the lull before the storm, that surprised
me. I was not surprised, when fifteen minutes later I received
the Cabinet Treasurer in Freddy's study, to discover that his
smile had been transformed into a sickly grimace of fear and
to learn, when I had untangled his outpouring of euphem-
isms and parentheses, that the people of Nordstadt had
welcomed Maximilian with open arms, that the Deathwatch
and the 3rd Cuirassiers had surrendered without firing a
shot, and that the Pretender, his forces considerably
augmented by wholesale desertion amongst the two regiments, was marching on Helm, where it was thought he
would encounter only token resistance. Nor was I surprised
to discover that Count Vielfrass had mysteriously gone to
ground and that Baron von Schramm, far from returning
from Karlottenberg, was thought even now to be speeding
through Bohemia into Austria, where he anticipated sanctuary in Vienna. I sat, outwardly composed, watching the
Cabinet Treasurer knead his hands till the palms were red
and waiting for the moment he would eventually cease to
speak.

'But will not someone help us? What of Austria?'

'Austria will not make any move that might be construed
as an offence to Prussia, Your Majesty.'

'Prussia, then. Surely in these exceptional circumstances
we can forget our fear of the Kaiser?'

'Your Majesty, as I have so often explained, since we

became unwilling members of the Second Reich it has been the policy of His Majesty's ministers jealously to preserve our integrity as a sovereign state. To encourage the intervention of the Kaiser would imperil our sovereignty and cannot be contemplated, whatever the cost—'

'Even if that cost is to your Sovereign himself?'

He looked down at his hands and for once said nothing.

'So,' I said softly, 'we are friendless.'

'All is not lost yet, Your Majesty. Field Marshal von Falkenberg has left for the Front to rally our forces. We have two divisions at Hohen-Kastell and the rest of the army is mobilised. We should still be able to hold off Maximilian before he reaches the capital. But, given the disturbances in the city itself, Your Majesty must take my advice – indeed, I no longer advise, I beg, I implore you to leave immediately.'

'My husband does not wish to leave,' I said.

He looked at me in astonishment. Then, just for a moment, his old, unctuous smile returned. 'But, forgive me, Your Majesty – we all know – in the light of His Majesty's regrettable indisposition – we know to whom we may look for such decisions.'

I felt myself blush angrily. 'My husband is perfectly capable of making his own decisions. And it is my duty, and my dearest wish, to abide by them.'

'But Your Majesty does not understand – I am not now merely urging Schwanensee. In view of the changed circumstances I beg both Your Majesties to leave for Austria at once.'

'As Baron Schramm has?'

'Your Majesty—'

'As you will?'

'Your Majesty must understand – forgive – I have a family to consider, and grandchildren.'

I sat at the study desk after Woltz had gone, putting off the moment when I should have to persuade Freddy into what I knew he would still see as an act of desertion. I noted impartially that, although the news of Maximilian's invasion was general and although the civic buildings of Rosenholm were burning for all to see, the newspapers laid out on Freddy's desk, faithful to Schramm's strict censorship even in his absence, made no mention of either. I heard the clock ticking on the mantelpiece and from down the corridor raised voices and someone, perhaps Katerina von Meltz, crying. But I felt nothing, as if I were wrapped all about with the cold now, frozen beyond sensation.

Then something happened which was to obliterate all other events. Sister Theresa sent to tell me that Freddy had begun another fit which appeared to be a bad one. And when I went and sat with him he did not come out of it. He seemed to pass from one fit to another without interval. His sixteenth attack in ten days became his seventeenth, then his eighteenth, while I watched helplessly, mortally afraid. His doctor, Professor Mendel, was sent for and pronounced that the patient was in *status epilepticus* and might continue in this condition for hours or days. The Professor seemed preoccupied, glancing nervously from time to time at the door or out of the window, unwilling to vouchsafe any further explanation, except to answer abruptly that yes, the convulsions could damage the brain and yes, if they were prolonged they could prove fatal. Nor could he offer any remedy beyond chloroform inhalations, which I had come to fear almost more than the fits for the terrifying interruptions they occasioned in Freddy's breathing. I stood by powerless as the chloroform was administered; twice, three times, the air seemed to clot in Freddy's lungs, so that Mendel had to resort to artificial respiration to expel it. But all the bruising and pummelling of Freddy's arms and ribs, the agonising groans as the breath was forced back into his frail body, served for nothing. The fits continued and the inhalations were abandoned.

We were obliged, Sister Theresa and I, to tie Freddy's wrists to the bedposts to prevent him from damaging himself. As the hours wore on we stripped him first of his nightgown and then of all his bedlinen down to the leather sheet beneath, to save him from being perpetually soiled by his own urine and excrement. But beyond this, beyond holding him down and stroking his brow and trying to will him back to consciousness, we were utterly helpless.

I began to pray now, in earnest, not to Freddy's God, but to one of my own who, far from being just and merciful, delighted in this suffering, gloated over the small, racked figure in the bed, ruthlessly tormented it with hidden goads, savouring each groan, each paroxysm, with a thrill of pleasure. I railed at this God, I cursed him, I wept and pleaded, venting my hate one minute, promising the next that no humiliation, no sacrifice, no abasement of myself would be too great if only he would give up his hideous sport with us. The tears poured down my cheeks until I had no more left. Day grew slowly into night. People came and went. And still in the glow of light around the bed Freddy lay, his body twisted, his eyes fixed and empty.

IV

I remember at intervals people trying to talk to me. I remember absorbing unconsciously that the army had not held Maximilian at Hohen-Kastell and that he was pressing on towards Berg, remember the combined forces of the Court Chamberlain and the Master of Horse endeavouring to persuade me that if Freddy could be carried to an ambulance and put on board the Royal Train we could still reach the Austrian border before all escape was cut off. I remember Professor Mendel stealthily evaporating and that, when Rosa had been sent to fetch another doctor, she had returned saying that there was looting in Königstrasse and that in Sigismundplatz she had seen two men put against a wall and shot. I remember it all like a strange dream in which I could have no particular interest, a trivial distraction which could only divert me from my true purpose, the concentration of my whole being upon the figure on the bed.

The new doctor, who, though a young man and not one of the Residenz physicians, seemed gentle and surprisingly capable for his years, recommended an enema of laudanum and asafoetida, to be repeated regularly until there was some change in Freddy's symptoms. I nodded blankly, too tired any longer for hope. At two in the morning Freddy's confessor gave him extreme unction and I tried again to pray, calmly, resignedly this time, as Freddy would wish me to. Rosa begged me to rest a little but though my limbs were heavy with exhaustion I dared not sleep. Beyond the sickroom I was dimly aware of voices, noise, toings and froings as if the whole Residenz were astir with anxious activity. At four o'clock the electricity failed; the men who worked the generator had apparently deserted their posts, or been killed in the street fighting which flared sporadically throughout the city. After a moment of panic candles were found and I sat watching them throw strange shadows – of Father Jacobus kneeling, of the doctor and Sister Theresa bending over the bed – feeling the darkness closing in as if the very walls of the room were stealthily advancing upon us.

Dawn came. Again Rosa bullied me take some breakfast and to rest, but I could not. My lips moved silently with the Father's prayers, but the Latin rote had no meaning, I concentrated upon it only to keep awake. Then, at ten o'clock, some twenty-six hours after they had begun, Freddy's convulsions ceased, his eyes closed, his breathing changed and he seemed to fall into an unconsciousness still more profound than that induced by the fits. The doctor had warned me that the repeated application of opium would eventually produce a prolonged narcosis, but nevertheless I found this new and deadly quiet even more difficult to bear. I was afraid that Freddy's poor worn-out body would no longer be able to resist the power of the drug, that this stupor might work more destructively upon his brain than all the storms which had battered it. I sat on the edge of the bed, I took his hand and spoke to him, but he did not stir. The doctor tried gently to reassure me, but I could only stare at Freddy and repeat his name over and over again. Yet there was nothing to do but to cover him up and wait.

We waited for eleven hours. By now the senior officers of the Household had long since abandoned their plans for our escape. Shut off behind doors barred by sentries from the Garde du Corps, Freddy's room became the totality of our existence. Dusk fell and candles were lit again. Sister Theresa, the doctor and I took it in turns to doze fitfully; and it was in one of those moments that I suddenly heard someone calling me and opened my eyes to see that the young doctor was smiling.

I went quickly over to the bed. Freddy's eyelids were quivering, his head moved slowly from side to side. The doctor took his pulse, then removed the gag from his mouth and he was instantly very sick. I thought absurdly that I had never been so relieved to see someone vomiting. But I still dreaded that these signs of awakening were only an illusion, that the Freddy I loved might now be so irrevocably damaged that he was lost to me. Sister Theresa washed his face, his eyes opened briefly but seemed unable to focus. With a shaking hand I held water to his lips, but it trickled from either side of his bruised and swollen mouth, he could not drink it. For over a day I had been unable to cry, but now I began to sob uncontrollably. Then, in a voice that was slurred but still distinguishable, he suddenly said: 'Tilda.' And, after a pause: 'Naughty, Tilda. Naughty again.' Beside me the doctor let out his breath, Sister Theresa began to pray, Father Jacobus too commenced a prayer of thanksgiving. I found myself all at once laughing crazily and, with tears that were now tears of joy, I fell across Freddy's poor broken body, pressing my face against his.

It was strange to leave Freddy's room, the room which had been my world for thirty-seven hours. The electricity was still cut off and Rosa led me across the corridor staggering beneath the weight of a massive candelabrum. I became for the first time conscious of a distant noise, a faint but distinct rumbling which appeared to transmit itself in a just-perceptible tremor throughout the building, making the window-frames rattle and the floor quiver beneath my feet. When I reached my bedroom I saw that the far horizon, beyond the city, was lit with sudden flashes of light; first a flash, then an answering boom.

'Guns, Rosa?' I asked softly.

She appeared to be absorbed in getting me out of my dress. But at last her love of drama won over her discretion.

'At Behrensdorf, Your Majesty. Our troops giving Maximilian what he deserves at last.'

'But Behrensdorf's only twenty kilometres away.'

'That's true, right enough. They say Maximilian'll put us under siege like the Prussians did Paris, and we'll end up eating the rats from the sewers just like the Frenchies. But I say twenty kilometres is twenty kilometres, Ma'am, and as long as it's not nineteen we mustn't worry.'

I yawned. I was deathly tired, too tired even for fear.

Rosa began to unlace my stays. 'There's been mortal confusion in the city all day, some getting out as fast as they

can, others coming in – hordes of them, peasants from the
countryside round and about with carts and chickens and
all their furniture piled up, and even pigs and goats. They're
afraid of Maximilian, scared out of their wits. They say there
isn't a house his soldiers don't loot or a woman that's safe,
even little children, nothing's too low for them—'

'But if that's true, Rosa, why has the Pretender met with
so little resistance?'

'I can't tell, Ma'am. Maybe he's bewitched folk. They say
he was a monk and broke his vows, and now he rides
amongst his soldiers on a big black horse, dressed all in black
like a priest but blaspheming like the Antichrist. They say
at Hohen-Kastell he forbade the taking of prisoners, and
those his officers wouldn't shoot he shot himself, without a
flicker of an eyelid. They even say . . .'

But I had fallen asleep in Rosa's arms before she had
finished buttoning my nightdress.

When Rosa shook me awake the next morning my first
fear was for Freddy, for although he had passed through
his present crisis the doctor had warned me that he was
still in danger, not only from further fits but also, in his
exhausted condition, from brain fever, which might be
brought on by the slightest disturbance. But instead she told
me that Count Vielfrass had arrived and was demanding to
see me.

'Vielfrass! At last! Oh Rosa, what time is it?'

'Ten o'clock, Your Majesty.'

Suddenly a fuller recollection of the previous night forced
itself upon me. I paused for a second to listen. 'Rosa, the
guns have stopped! And Count Vielfrass has come. That
must mean a victory!'

Her hard old eyes grew for an instant bright with tears. I
stared at her. Her lips moved as if to say something, then
she looked away.

'Well at least the Count has come to help us, to advise us
at last. Come, Rosa, I can't see him *en déshabillé*. Dress me
quickly.'

As I quitted our apartments I remember being distantly
conscious of something out of place. But it was only a
momentary sensation; as I passed through the long

succession of rooms to the State Apartments my mind was
bent upon the audience with Vielfrass.

Count Vielfrass was a man I had always instinctively
distrusted, even before I had known his full reputation as
the iron-handed master of our State Police, the manipulator
of spies and secret agents, to whom the private affairs of the
highest and lowest alike were common property. Perhaps it
was his appearance which repelled one, his foppishness, so
incongruous in a man approaching sixty, the impression he
gave of being nearly handsome and yet, missing it, not
handsome at all but curiously repugnant with his over-luxur-
iant black hair and point-device Van Dyck beard. He had a
bony face with prominent teeth which grew long and yellow
from receding gums, a feature vanity compelled him to
conceal by pressing often to his lips a lavender silk handkerchief liberally doused with cologne, and by keeping his
mouth pursed nearly shut, so that he spoke with a lisp
which, in moments when the lavender silk afforded no
protection, sprayed his listener with spittle. The lisp, the
smallness of the voice, always struck me as absurd in so tall
a man; but above the pursed lips and the waxed mustachios,
the eyes were calculating. He was, of all Freddy's ministers,
the one who made me most nervous. Nevertheless, if
Maximilian really were outside our gates, Vielfrass alone had
the skills and the power to save us.

He was seated, legs elegantly crossed, on one of the Audience Chamber's gilded sofas. I was surprised to observe that
in place of the black and yellow of his Civil uniform he wore
a frock coat and spats. And I was taken aback when, instead
of rising as I entered, he held his pose, gloved hands on
cane, with what seemed to be calculated insolence.

'Madam,' he said coldly, 'you have kept me waiting for
over an hour.'

I stared at him, not understanding his tone or his deliberate flouting of protocol, feeling my nervousness
compounded so that I was suddenly a stuttering child again.

'I know the news is bad. But His Majesty has been so ill
these past two days I hardly—'

'The news for your husband,' he said, 'is certainly most
unfavourable.'

'But we may at least put our trust in you, Count. I know

– not for my sake but for His Majesty's – we can look to you, whatever the danger, to save us.'

'Madam, you may look to me for nothing.'

I stared at him and felt as if my blood were draining away.

'I am here, not as a minister of your husband's former Cabinet, but as the representative of His Royal Highness the Crown Prince Maximilian.'

The faintness passed. I looked at him, at the yellow teeth and the moist, pursed, insolent mouth, and was suddenly ashamed that I had seemed to humble myself before him, suddenly no longer afraid but shaking with fury.

'No, Count,' I said softly. 'You're here as something even less than that. You're here as a traitor. A low, despicable, cowardly traitor!'

'Madam, when a country reaches political and economic bankruptcy as ours has, it is scarcely treachery to throw in one's lot with those who can save it. It is an act of the highest patriotism.'

The yellow teeth were bared for a moment, then veiled again by the handkerchief.

'What do you want of us?' I said.

'It is not what I want, madam, but what His Royal Highness the Crown Prince orders.' He inhaled cologne. 'The position is, quite simply, this. Nine-tenths of the country have now fallen to His Royal Highness. The majority of the army is under his command and those who are not are taken prisoner. The capital, apart from a few small pockets of resistance, has surrendered to us without the necessity for any military action. His Royal Highness is at present stationed at Marmion, four kilometres outside the city wall. But naturally he is anxious to make his triumphal progress through the city, to take up the reins of power and to establish himself here in the Residenz. It is a matter of some surprise to him – not to say annoyance – that you and your husband have chosen to stay in Rosenholm when you have had ample opportunity for flight.'

'His Majesty – as you know, as I told you – has been desperately ill – '

He laughed. 'Ill, madam? If you must so describe his attacks of feeble-mindedness, very well. But I should have thought even a simpleton would have understood—'

'God forgive you, Count! Your King has for two days been on the point of death!'

'My King no longer, madam. I have with me a Paper of Abdication. His Royal Highness the Crown Prince has graciously conceded that if your husband signs it he will be allowed twelve hours to leave Sylvania and be given safe conduct to the Austrian border, where arrangements have been made to receive him into exile. Similar arrangements will apply to any of your Household who also wish to leave. I cannot but feel His Royal Highness has been more than generous in this, but he considers it his duty, since Friedrich is his second cousin, to honour the ties of blood. He asks me to assure you that no harm will befall your husband so long as his orders are obeyed – '

'No harm?' I broke out. 'If His Majesty is moved now it will probably kill him.'

'Twelve hours, madam. Those are His Royal Highness's orders.'

'But twelve hours means now if we are to reach the Austrian border. Now, when he's too weak to travel, too weak even to sign your contemptible document.' I stared at him, for an instant speechless. All at once I felt overwhelmed with despair. 'In God's name, Count, I beg of you, if you have any compassion go back to the Pretender, tell him we will sign whatever he wishes, do whatever he wants. Only he must give us more time, a day, two days, just till Freddy is stronger – please, I'm not too proud to beg you with my tears for Freddy's life, please—'

Above the handkerchief, the cold eyes surveyed me unmoved. 'Madam, this hysteria ill becomes you. What you ask is impossible and you know it.'

My lips twisted, I felt myself grow white. Once again the anger returned, and my shame at having pleaded with him. 'Very well,' I said softly. 'But what you ask of us is impossible too.'

'His Royal Highness has been generous up to now. But I cannot answer for him if his orders are disobeyed—'

'So be it, Count. He must do with us what he will. There will be no signature to your Paper of Abdication. We will not leave the Residenz until we are ready to leave it. And if Maximilian must use force against us – as he has against our people, our cities, against everyone who still understands the meaning of the word loyalty – why then let him use it! I love my husband and I shall fight for his life with the last breath in my body. Let Maximilian fight a woman, like the coward he is!'

Count Vielfrass sniffed his handkerchief, glanced at me for an instant, then exhaled cologne slowly as if with a sigh. 'Madam, I am coming to the view that it is not only your husband who is simple-minded.' He took out his watch. 'It is now fifteen minutes past eleven. You have until eleven-fifteen tonight.'

My anger propelled me all the way to our apartments. Then on the threshold I faltered, understanding suddenly what had disturbed me before. The soldier standing to attention before our door wore, not the blue and gold uniform of the Garde du Corps, but the scarlet of the Hussars. I shivered. Beneath the plumed brass helmet the man stared mutely back at me, eyes front, impassive. I crossed the threshold and ran to a courtyard window. In the courtyard too there were more Hussars, spaced at regular intervals, arms at the ready. At some time during the night the Garde du Corps must have deserted its post without firing a shot. Now the Residenz was surrounded and the guard outside our door was stationed, not to protect us, but to hold us prisoner. All at once I regretted my angry words, wished I had tried harder to bargain with Vielfrass. But it was too late for that now. I summoned the doctor and told him what had happened. To my relief he agreed with my decision, saying that at least in twelve hours Freddy would be stronger and the risk of brain fever less: in a grim calculation of the odds, Maximilian seemed the lesser evil.

Freddy was still sleeping, and we agreed to leave him and say nothing. My next task was to summon the Court Chamberlain and, with his help, compose a speech to the Household which would set out plainly our circumstances and urge all those who could to take advantage of the Pretender's amnesty. Although many of the servants had already left in the panic of the last few days, by one o'clock everyone who remained, from footmen, cooks and stable boys to the highest officers in the Household, was assembled in the ballroom. They heard me silently, some with heads bowed, others sobbing openly, so that I too found myself fighting tears. When I had finished there was such a sudden spontaneous uproar of loyal protest that I was obliged to reiterate that it was Freddy's and my dearest wish that they should not be brought down by our misfortune, but should leave us on our own to face whatever came. It had been agreed that the only people who should stay were Rosa, Freddy's valet, Father Jacobus and the doctor. Of our retinues, Sister Theresa and Baroness von Lindhafen proved the most obstinate and could only be prevailed upon by tears to go. When I returned exhausted to our apartments, passing the same stiff, silent Hussar at the door, it was two o'clock. Only nine and a quarter more hours.

At Rosa's suggestion I tried to rest for an hour or two, but I could not sleep. Dark images kept passing through my mind: of what Rosa had said of Maximilian; of Vielfrass sneering behind his handkerchief; of old nightmares, the sound of the cannon that day at Nordstadt, and of that other day, so long ago now, in my uncle's apartments at the Winter Palace in Thalia – so long ago and yet so fresh in my mind that I put my hands to my head and squeezed my eyelids together to try to shut it out – of how his breath had smelt of peppermint and how his hands had been clammy as he touched me, and how he had laughed when he had shot Mitzi, shot my beloved, harmless little dog.

Eventually I could tolerate the nightmares, the inactivity, no longer. There were, besides, other things to be done. Getting Rosa to tighten my stays and dress me again, I went to Freddy's study. At least, though they had surrounded us with that watchful, waiting guard, they had not broken in upon us yet, searched our rooms, defiled our privacy. There were papers in Freddy's desk – not secret papers, for what secrets had we ever known? – but letters, mementoes, sentimental things which I could not bear to fall into mocking hands.

It was while I was burning our papers that I found the gun, an old pistol of Freddy's father's, wedged right at the back of a drawer. I took it out and looked at it. I had never fired a gun, but it seemed in working order, undamaged by its long sojourn in the desk, still clean and well oiled, the trigger mechanism responding surprisingly smoothly to my finger. A further hunt revealed a box of ammunition. I broke open the chamber and loaded it carefully. Then I snapped the barrel back and sat with the thing in my hands, feeling the weight and the coldness of it. I had never fired a gun but it seemed not too difficult. I took the pistol into my boudoir and laid it in my workbox on top of my embroidery. Then, carrying the box with me, I went to sit with Freddy.

V

Freddy began to stir just before the Angelus bell, and Father Jacobus was summoned to say the rosary with us. Not long after the Angelus, as the candles were being lit for our third night without electricity, the bells began to toll again, this time for the beginning of the curfew which Rosa informed me was now imposed from dusk to dawn upon the city. I saw Freddy looking at me, puzzled. The prayers had comforted him as they always did; his voice seemed stronger, his eyes clearer. I sent Rosa for the doctor and, after he had administered bromide of potassium and felt his patient's pulse, he remained in the room at my request while I told Freddy as gently as I could of Maximilian's terms, the decision I had made and the deadline which was now only two hours away.

Freddy listened in silence, seeming to understand me well enough but to register, instead of fear or surprise, only a calm resignation. When I had finished and the doctor had withdrawn he lifted his hand and touched my cheek.

'My dearest Tilda, I'm sorry you have been put in such danger for my sake.'

I pressed his fingers to my lips. 'Oh, my darling, I don't care for myself. I care for nothing so long as we are together and you are safe. I won't let them touch a hair of your head, I promise you.' I glanced across at my workbox. 'I've got your father's pistol and I'll use it if necessary.'

His eyes had followed mine, and now they took on a look of bewilderment. 'But, Tilda, you can't—'

'I can and will, Freddy ' I sprang from the bed and went

to the workbox. 'Look, it's loaded and ready. All I have to
do is release the safety catch.'

'Tilda, for Heaven's sake—!'

'I don't care what happens to me. I'm willing to die rather
than have them hurt or frighten you!'

He was struggling to sit up. For the first time his face wore
a look of blank horror. 'No, Tilda. It's you who frighten me.
Isn't it bad enough that I can't protect you, as your husband
– as any man should? Isn't it bad enough that for the last
two days I've lain here useless, nothing but a burden to you?
And now – to talk of guns and dying! No one will die for
me, Tilda, not Father Jacobus, not the doctor, not one servant
of our Household. And not you, oh my love, not you!'

He fell back, breathless. Afraid of his perturbation and of
having been the cause of it I rushed over to the bed. He
turned his head away from me.

'Please, Tilda, I can't bear to look at you with that thing
in your hands. And besides, don't you see? – that's their
way, not ours.' Now he turned back to me and his expression
was once again calm. 'Our way is to face what comes quietly
and patiently, and to learn to accept it as God's will.'

'Trust in God?' I said bitterly. 'Against that brute
Maximilian?'

His eyes filled with an infinite sadness. 'Oh, my dearest,
you have so much courage – try to learn faith as well. I need
you to pray for me. As I shall pray for you with all my heart.'

And so, when eleven-fifteen came, Father Jacobus was
with us and we were once again at prayer. I had not known
what to expect, I suppose I had imagined absurdly that they
would announce themselves, I had not bargained for them
bursting unceremoniously, not simply into our apartments,
but into the sickroom itself. I had not removed the gun from
the room but had placed it, on top of the workbox, on a
sidetable near the door where I thought I could reach it in an
instant. But everything happened so suddenly, first Rosa's
protesting voice, then the door being flung open – and then
Vielfrass and a platoon of Hussars were framed within it,
cutting me off from the gun, blinding us with their lanterns.

Father Jacobus stopped mid-phrase for a moment, then
began his litany again in an undertone. Freddy, propped
high on his pillows, with the doctor beside him, blinked at

the light but did not move. I rose from my knees and whirled towards Vielfrass.

'How dare you!' I screamed. 'How dare you enter His Majesty's bedroom without leave!'

'Please, Tilda,' said Freddy softly. 'Please, my dearest, don't.'

The tall figures of the soldiers threw menacing shadows across the bed. One of the officers, I noticed, was the Major who had raised the alarm at the orphanage. He did not meet my eyes, but looked away as if he were ashamed.

Vielfrass curled his lip above his nag's teeth. 'Madam, the time for such ceremonies is past.' He moved forward to the end of the bed. 'Friedrich Otto Wilhelm von Hohenstaufen, you are now my prisoner, by order of His Royal Highness the Crown Prince Maximilian. You will be taken under military escort to the Schloss Edelstein at Marmion, where you will sign the Paper of Abdication which has been prepared for you. I must ask you to make ready to leave now, without further delay.'

I flung my arms around Freddy's neck with my body interposed between him and Vielfrass. 'At least bring a chair or a stretcher. Can't you see he's too ill to walk?'

Freddy disengaged me gently. 'I shall walk if I can, my dear. And I should like, Count, if I may, a few moments to get dressed.'

'Very well. So long as you do so quickly and in the presence of these officers, I see no objection.'

I gasped. 'Is there nothing you will stop at, no humiliation you will spare him?'

Vielfrass smiled sarcastically. Then his hand went to my workbox and he brought out the pistol. 'Madam, I am mindful of the untimely death of King Sigismund in similar circumstances. I should not care to return to His Royal Highness empty-handed.'

There was nothing for it. Freddy must submit to the indignity of two of the Hussars accompanying him to his dressing-room while the doctor and his valet helped him into his clothes. I watched, close to tears, as he eased himself slowly down from the bed. When he tried to stand upright he staggered and I flew to him instinctively, putting my arms around his waist. His body felt pitifully thin under the nightshirt, light enough for me to support with ease, even though his whole weight was against me. Nevertheless he forced himself erect and, kissing my forehead, drew himself away.

'Please, Tilda. You must be ready too. The others will help me.'

Rosa fetched my mantle and I sat on the edge of the bed with my back to Vielfrass and the soldiers until Freddy emerged, leaning on the doctor's arm. He wore the full dress uniform of a Field Marshal in the Guard Cuirassiers, with sword and spurs but without orders. The valet, behind him, carried his helmet. The brilliance of the uniform served only to emphasise how frail he looked, how his chest seemed too shallow to bear the great gilded cuirass, how the massive epaulettes seemed to bow his shoulders. Above the gold-embroidered collar the bruises he had given himself during the fits showed livid against the pallor of his cheeks. And yet there was, too, such a quiet dignity about him that I bit my lip to keep back my tears.

The doctor led him over to the prie-dieu and he knelt, head bowed, before the Corpus Christi of the reliquary for a few moments. Then, rising with difficulty, he kissed the feet of the figure on the cross where the nail pierced them and, leaning heavily upon the doctor, turned to face Vielfrass and the officers.

'I am ready, gentlemen. Dearest Tilda, take my arm.'

I was already moving towards him. But before I could reach out to him Vielfrass had stepped between us. 'No, madam. Your husband is to go to Marmion, but you do not go with him. My orders are that you must be escorted to Schwanensee.'

I stared at him. Beyond his shoulder I saw Freddy's lips pucker as his hard-won composure deserted him. Suddenly I was blind, mad, I no longer cared what I did. I flung myself at Vielfrass with a howl, thrusting my fingers towards that pursed ugly mouth, those cold eyes, wanting to tear at them till I felt the flesh rend and my hands grow slippery with blood. But I did not even reach him. The Major caught my arms and held me pinioned. I stopped struggling and burst into helpless sobs.

Though Freddy's eyes, too, were glazed with tears, he fought to regain his control. 'Please, my dearest – if that is what must be, let us accept it. Let us try to part with dignity. Then at least, when we remember it, it won't be of ourselves that we're ashamed.'

My eyes brimmed over and for an instant I could not see him. 'Oh Freddy, I love you so. As long as we're together I can bear anything. But this – oh, my darling, this?'

'I have not been a proper husband to you, Tilda. I have failed you in – in so many ways.'

'You have been everything I ever wanted. Oh, my dear, beloved boy, who will take care of you without me, who will—?'

'Come, sir,' interjected Vielfrass harshly. 'You have had time enough for your goodbyes. It is nearly midnight and we must go.'

Freddy moved forward on the arm of the doctor. His face was ashen and as he was nearly level with me he swayed and almost fell.

'Oh no!' I screamed. 'You can't be so cruel! You can't let him go alone. Someone must be with him, someone who knows what to do when he is ill, someone who can comfort him—'

The young doctor looked at me and then at Vielfrass, and in that moment I realised I had never even known his name. 'If it is permitted I should like to go with His Majesty.'

Vielfrass hesitated for an instant before nodding his head. Freddy turned to me, his eyes glittering. 'Remember me in your prayers, Tilda. I shall never cease to pray for you.' Then, to the Major, who still held me back, he said shakily: 'Don't hurt her, I beg of you. Her Majesty is so very precious to me.'

Father Jacobus was still intoning his Latin. The room blurred so that I could no longer see Freddy as the doctor led him slowly away.

VI

I was allowed to take Rosa with me to Schwanensee. The Hussars Major, who commanded the small force that guarded us, seemed, perhaps to expiate the breaking of his oath of loyalty, disposed to be gentle towards us. But I no longer cared. For the first few days I lay in a kind of delirium, sick with fear for Freddy, tormented by all my old nightmares. I begged with tears and screams to be allowed to see my uncle's ambassador, the Cardinal Archbishop, even Vielfrass or Maximilian himself – anyone who could tell me where Freddy was, whether he was still alive, when we could be together again. I could not sleep or eat and in the end I wore myself into a state of utter exhaustion, so that I lay staring at the curtains around my bed, unable to speak, even to Rosa: until gradually, I came once more to a semblance of life, where I could sit with my embroidery in my lap and watch the mockery of the autumn sunlight dappling my walls and nod bleakly to Rosa's chatter, where I could go sometimes for hours at a time without bursting into tears.

We had never made use of Schwanensee, Freddy and I, and neither had Freddy's father before us, so that it wore a frowsy, run-down air, of silk draperies covertly rotting, of tarnished gilt and blistered wallpaper, of little piles of dust and dead insects lying in unregarded corners. It had originally been a medieval fortress and although successive generations of Hohenstaufens had build onto and modernised it, it retained, despite a spectacular view of the lake two hundred metres below, its fortress character still, stern and unbending, a prison whether we were its prisoners or not.

Of that, our status at Schwanensee, we had never received a precise definition. We had not been formally declared prisoners and yet, though the Major was lenient enough, we were not allowed to leave or even to go out riding to the villages lower down the mountain. We had few servants and received no visitors or letters. But, after the first days, perhaps because of the Major's instinctive trust in Sylvanian censorship, we were allowed newspapers. The censors, whatever political changes were afoot, had certainly remained faithful to Baron von Schramm's tradition: though Rosa and I combed every page, every day, down to the fine print, we could find no news of Freddy. But of articles laudatory to Maximilian there were plenty. I tried to close my ears as Rosa, despite my protests, insisted on reading me glowing descriptions of Maximilian's entry into Rosenholm 'leading his troops on a big black stallion, with the crowd

throwing flowers and waving banners, and looking, so it
says here, Your Majesty, every inch a King.'

'How can the people be so fickle, Rosa?'

'And when he reached St Xaviersdom, it says, he
dismounted from his horse and was blessed on the steps by
the Cardinal Archbishop – '

'The Archbishop too?'

'The Archbishop and the Bishop of Rosenholm and all the
canons. And they prayed for peace and freedom in Sylvania.
And everyone cheered as if it was a holiday. That's what it
says here.'

So it was no surprise when, one morning after we had
been at Schwanensee for a fortnight, we heard the church
bells pealing and read the next day that the Pretender had
been installed as King Maximilian II with all due ceremony in
the Throne-Room at the Residenz, amidst general rejoicing.
After taking the oath, so Rosa read, he had made a speech
promising to restore the constitution and agreeing to elections and the release of political prisoners. 'They say here,'
said Rosa, 'that he's a champion of democracy and European
Liberalism.'

'With Vielfrass as his messenger?'

'They say too that he's over six foot tall and holds himself
as straight and handsome as a Guards officer—'

'Rosa, Rosa – three weeks ago you assured me he was a
monster.'

She looked for an instant embarrassed. 'Well, they hung
out his picture in the village yesterday, and Cook showed
me the daguerreotype. I didn't want to see it, Ma'am. But –
out of politeness, you understand – I had to admit he wasn't
that ill-looking.'

I sighed impatiently. 'What does it matter whether he's a
monster or an Apollo? Our prison is his prison now. And
despite his fine words he'll have to be a brute to survive it.'

That Maximilian must indeed be a brute I received proof not
many days later. Rosa informed me with great excitement
that a landaulette had driven into the courtyard, our first
visitors since our incarceration, and some moments later
the Major begged permission to enter my boudoir. He was
accompanied by two elderly men in frock coats and he

cleared his throat in the way he had when he was embarrassed.

'Your Majesty, these two gentlemen are doctors.' They bowed and clicked their heels as he pronounced their names and I thought I detected in the muttered civilities of one a Thalian accent.

'They have come, Your Majesty – they have come to examine you.'

I reached for Rosa's hand. 'But I'm not ill,' I said. 'Apart from my misery at being separated from my husband, I am in perfect health.'

He avoided my eyes. 'They have papers authorising the examination signed by Prince von Ansbach and Count Vielfrass on behalf of the Grand Duke of Thalia and King Maximilian himself.'

I gripped Rosa's fingers more tightly. 'No,' I said.

He looked down at his boots. 'Your Majesty, forgive me. I am obliged to obey orders.' Then, turning sharply, he was gone.

I stared at the two frock-coated figures. One of them was polishing his pince-nez with his handkerchief, the other, the Thalian, had opened his carriage-bag.

'Please, Your Majesty,' said the Thalian, smiling avuncularly, 'this will take only a matter of minutes and will be quite painless.'

I held fast to Rosa. 'No,' I said.

'If you could, perhaps, retire to your bedroom,' said the pince-nez. 'And ask your maid to undress you.'

'No,' said Rosa suddenly from behind me. 'I won't do any such thing.'

The Thalian, smiling, drew off his gloves. 'Come, come, Your Majesty – Ma'am – let us not make this difficult. Just a tiny painless examination conducted according to scientific principles.'

'Just a simple matter,' said the pince-nez, 'of medical routine.'

Out of the corner of my eye I could see the door to my bedroom. I was between it and them. Though hampered by my skirts I was younger and should be quicker, provided I timed my moment correctly.

The Thalian had taken something from his bag, was

unstoppering a bottle; I smelt all at once a familiar odour.

'No!' said Rosa. 'No! I won't let you touch her!'

'No, no!' I screamed as he came towards me. And, dropping Rosa's hand, I raced for the door. But he must have been in good health for an old man, he reached it before I did, jammed his foot in it, grasped my hand as I struggled for the key. In the boudoir I heard Rosa scream. He had the key now, had wrenched it from my fingers. I tried to push the door shut, but he was stronger, pushed harder. The door suddenly gave and my strength with it. He caught me as I staggered backwards, jerking my head towards him. The chloroform gripped my throat before the pad even touched me.

When I came to myself I was lying on the bed in my drawers and chemise. My head burned, my body ached as if it were bruised, and there was another feeling too, a feeling I remembered so vividly that I began to cry before I had even understood it, a sense of having been violated, of being utterly, wretchedly degraded. And then I knew, then I was thirteen again, then I saw my uncle's face with its ugly leer and peppermint breath, and his leg was forced between mine and his trousers were open and his hand was fumbling beneath my pinafore, and I saw where his other hand was and wanted to be sick, wanted to cry out; and then Mitzi came, little white Mitzi from round the door, snarling, barking, and he gave a groan as she hurled herself upon us, and swore and let go of me. And Mitzi was still jumping and barking when he took the revolver from the desk. And then there was blood, so much blood – and I was screaming, screaming, and Rosa was holding me to her shrivelled old breast and I cried that I wanted Freddy, wanted my dear, gentle Freddy who had been able to love me without hurting me, wanted my beloved, gentle, innocent boy again.

After that, I lost the heart for anything. I would sit before the looking glass in my combing jacket, staring at my face and seeing the contamination in it. In vain did Rosa play with my hair, brushing it, coiling it, pushing it to this side and to that and telling me how becoming it would look if only I would let her dress it according to the latest fashion.

Combs and curls and pieces could not make beauty where there was none. I had grown pitiably thin since we had left Rosenholm. My skin had taken on a sickly translucence so that the veins above my jaw showed blue and my eyes appeared unnaturally large and glittering. All Rosa's rouge pots and rice-powder would never make me more than I was, a dreary, half-dead creature. I believe I might have wished for death, too, but for the thought that one day I might be reconciled with Freddy.

We had been at Schwanensee two months when the next set of carriages came. I gave a little mew of fear and ran to hide, would have locked myself in my bedroom; but Rosa, who had been tut-tutting to herself a great deal of late, spoke to me quite sternly, told me I must remember who I was and pull myself together, that I must show them what I was made of. And besides, she said, with a quiver of her old excitement, these carriages weren't like the landaulette but much grander, with crests and outriders, and one of them, she was certain, could only be . . .

I stood, listlessly, paying no attention, as she fitted me into my brown wool *Directoire* gown and fiddled with my hair and pinched my cheeks gently in a vain attempt to give me colour. The Major, with two lieutenants, was to escort me to the Marble Salon. I followed his uniformed back dutifully along the draughty stone galleries, thinking of nothing, too abject for any kind of resistance. Then, all at once, at the door of the Marble Salon, I froze; for I heard quite distinctly the booming voice of Prince von Ansbach, my uncle's ambassador.

' . . . not a beauty, you understand. Rather a mousey little creature. But brought up to it, as you might say, well-trained, biddable—'

The voice stopped as we entered the room. There was for an instant complete silence.

The Marble Salon had been, in its days of previous glory when Sigismund was alive, Schwanensee's State Dining-room. Now it had acquired the same fly-blown, faded air as the rest of the castle: footsteps echoed hollowly in it, the chipped and broken stucco work on its friezes and architraves was reflected sadly in mirrors speckled black where their silvering had perished. The great dining-table, however, bore the marks of recent occupation; chairs had been disarranged, there were papers spread out upon the mahogany, pens, an inkwell, a carafe of water. Near one of the chairs hovered Vielfrass, once again in full Civil uniform and wearing a slightly anxious air, as if he feared he was being excluded from something. The object of his concern appeared to be my uncle's ambassador who, also in uniform, stood at the far end of the room next to a tall man in black, to whom his comments had clearly been addressed. The man in black was not looking at him, but stood in the window with his back to the door, surveying the wintery view of the lake. He stood there so still that although it was only for an instant it seemed as if, until he turned, he held the room and all of us in it suspended.

Then he moved away from the window. A tall man, slim, broad-shouldered, dressed in black like a priest, with a dark, hard face and a sickle-shaped scar running up into the hairline on his left temple.

There was a clicking of heels upon marble as my escort saluted.

'Madam,' said Vielfrass, surveying me haughtily, 'is it not customary to curtsy to your King?'

I felt as if my legs would give way. The man in black looked at Vielfrass and then at me. 'Her Majesty is not our prisoner,' he said quietly. 'Will someone find her a chair.'

It was a strange voice, light, not unmusical, with traces of a foreign accent; yet there was in its quietness, in its very restraint, an innate authority, so that even Vielfrass seemed to moderate his contempt a little. He and Ansbach waited for Maximilian to sit, then they assumed their places beside him, one at each hand. The Major, having pulled out a chair for me on the opposite side of the table, took his dismissal. I stared at the three of them ranged against me; at Vielfrass with his handkerchief and supercilious eyes; at Ansbach, looking at me as my uncle always looked, a big, florid game-ster of a man like my uncle with a thick neck and meaty hands, calculating the width of my haunches and the strength of my withers and – observing nothing of the firm-fleshed, high-spirited mettle he favoured in hunters and mistresses – finding me wanting; and at Maximilian between

them, surveying me with a cool impartiality which made my
trembling increase, so that I was obliged to place my hands
on the back of the chair to steady myself. I had, I did not
quite know why, always thought of the Usurper as a man
of Vielfrass's or Ansbach's age, but this man, with his quiet
voice and cool gaze, could not be more than thirty. The
unexpectedness compounded my confusion.

'Please,' he said, 'be seated.'

My voice seemed to stick in my throat as if it were paralysed. 'I – I do not wish to sit,' I mumbled.

'We must ask you, Ma'am, to speak up,' said Ansbach.

Now the words seemed to force themselves upwards in a
shout. 'I don't wish to be seated.'

Vielfrass sniffed, Ansbach looked startled. The Usurper
continued to survey me coolly.

'I don't wish to sit, I wish for nothing. I only want to
know what, though I have begged, entreated, no one will
tell me. If you have any decency, any compassion, will one
of you tell me whether my husband is alive or dead.'

Vielfrass and Ansbach exchanged glances. Vielfrass
fiddled with his papers irritably. 'Friedrich von Hohenstaufen is being well looked after and is receiving the medical
care appropriate to his – condition.'

'Then he is ill. He's ill somewhere, suffering, alone,
perhaps even dying and I can't—'

'Ma'am,' said Ansbach, 'this is hardly the time—'

'Incurable idiocy,' said Vielfrass, 'is scarcely an illness.
And death might be considered—'

'A merciful release?' I stared at Vielfrass, then my eyes
turned in horror upon his master, Maximilian. 'Oh yes, I can
see that it would be a mercy. For you! With my husband
dead, your conscience can be easy, you can enjoy your
power, revel in everything you have stolen from him. With
His Majesty out of the way, you needn't fear that one day,
if there is any loyalty in our people, your "subjects" will
begin to feel pity and remember who was betrayed. And if
he won't, my poor husband, die of his own accord, if your
cruelty hasn't killed him, then you'll help him a little, ease
him out of life. Oh, I've learnt to understand that power
makes men vile, but I'd never known till now, never
realised—'

'I'm sure,' said Maximilian softly, that Count Vielfrass
regrets his unfortunate choice of words.' Vielfrass stiffened,
but the Usurper continued, training his eyes directly upon
me. 'I understand your very natural concern for King Friedrich, and I shall not conceal from you that he has been
gravely ill these past weeks. But he is in good hands and is
beginning to recover. Though I know it is difficult for you,
I beg you to believe that every possible care is being taken
to nurse him back to health and to find some effective treatment for his illness. Try, if you can, to trust me in this.'

I faced him squarely now, met those cool eyes of his
unflinchingly. Lifting my hands from the chair I forced
myself as tall and straight as my height would allow. 'Trust
you? You who have taken everything from me? Oh, I don't
mean position, rank – His Majesty and I cared little enough
for that – but everything we shared, our whole life together,
small things, foolish perhaps – things a man like you could
never understand. Heaven knows, I'm tired of crying and
pleading, worn down by it. I haven't the strength to fall on
my knees, humble myself before you. But if I'm to trust you,
then give me back my life, the one thing that made it worth
living, the only human comfort I've had since I was a child.
Let me join my husband and let us leave Sylvania, cease to
trouble you. Let me – oh, if you have any human feelings –
let me have that.'

There was a small silence. Maximilian's composure was,
for a second, troubled by a frown. He looked towards
Ansbach, whose bulky frame, to Vielfrass's evident pleasure,
was heaving with embarrassment.

'Hysteria, Your Majesty,' whispered Ansbach hastily. 'The
trials of the last few weeks, for a young girl – all women are
prone to it from time to time.'

'But perhaps we have not sufficiently understood . . . ?'

'Oh, I think, with respect, Your Majesty, we have the
measure of it, haven't we, Count?'

Vielfrass fingered his papers and smirked, but said
nothing.

'A small display of loyalty – not to be wondered at,' said
Ansbach bluffly, regaining confidence. 'Commendable virtue
in a woman. But at any rate, as I'm sure the Duke of Maar
has advised you, there are weightier considerations.'

'Yes,' said Maximilian, a trifle impatiently. 'You are well aware that I respect my uncle's advice.'

'She's usually such a quiet little thing. Perhaps, Your Majesty, if I could talk to her . . .' Ansbach turned to me, smiling, screwing his hawk's eyebrows and lecherous jowls into what he must have imagined was a fatherly expression. 'Ahem . . . Ma'am, my dear Marie – I hope, as one who has known you since you were a babe in arms, I may still call you that – my dear child, we are only too aware that your life so far has not been without its – disappointments. But what's past is past. What we must consider is your future happiness.'

I felt suddenly chilled. 'I have told you the only thing that will make me happy.'

'Quite so, quite so. But I'm sure you will let your elders be the judge. Even though we have, in the past, I grant you, made mistakes. Or, shall we say been misinformed.'

I stared at him.

'His Grand Ducal Highness was not made aware when he and the late King Friedrich agreed upon your marriage that the young man, the Crown Prince as he then was, had certain – defects.'

'My husband has epilepsy. If that's what you mean then say it.'

'Ah!' Ansbach's eyebrows shot up alarmingly, as if he had detected me in a false move and was swooping upon his advantage. 'But that's not all – at least, that's not what I *do* mean precisely. Marriage, my dear Marie, as you know, is no trifling matter for someone of your rank. It carries with it a burden of duty greater than that born by the ordinary man, a duty towards the whole future of the State, a duty to extend and secure the Royal line—'

'Perhaps His Highness would come to the point,' said Vielfrass tetchily. 'It's all here in the report. His Majesty hasn't got all day.'

'Please, Count!' Maximilian's voice was suddenly sharp. 'It is not I who am in need of your consideration.'

'In short,' said Ansbach, glowering at Vielfrass beneath his forked brows, 'your husband, my dear Marie, was not equal to that duty. Your marriage has never been consummated.'

I felt myself blush to the roots of my hair. 'How dare you!'

'The doctors' report sets out the case in detail,' said Vielfrass, tapping his papers. 'Her Majesty is still,' and here he masticated the words with relish, '*virgo intacta.*'

'So,' said Ansbach with his fatherly leer, 'there having been no consummation, there cannot be said to have been a marriage.'

'The Nuncio's view precisely,' said Vielfrass. 'Annulment is a pure formality.

I swayed, grasped the back of the chair again. I tried to speak but no words would come. My eyes moved helplessly, imploringly to Maximilian. He held between his fingertips the silver shaft of a pen, which he revolved for an instant before looking up. When he faced me it was with that cool, contained authority that chilled me so.

'I have need of the alliance with your uncle,' he said. 'And I must provide myself with an heir. His Highness the Grand Duke has agreed to give me your hand in marriage.'

CHAPTER TWO

Anton von Tarn

I

The night Uncle Gustav's message came from the Villa
Narzisse my father and I were in the midst of one of our
usual arguments about my career. Despite his twenty-two
years in exile he was a soldier to the very bone, my father,
and he could not comprehend that any son of his might be
otherwise; while I – well, I readily acknowledge that with
my blond hair and slim figure a uniform cannot but suit me
excessively: this, however, is definitely as far as it goes. Cold
baths, early rising, having orders shouted at me by some
frog-eyed bully who is undoubtedly my inferior in breeding
and intellect – I have never had the slightest appetite for it.
And as for shooting things – oh, I may construe Tacitus and
Catullus pretty well and my modest attempts at Petrarchian
sonnets are not without a certain elegance, though I say it
myself, but my expertise with a gun – up until that time at
least (my nineteenth birthday), it had been tested no further
than in the reluctant pursuit of chamois or capercaillie in
which I had proved myself only of danger to a couple of
unwary beaters.

No, I was adamant. My father might perceive a glorious
future for me in some Prussian cavalry regiment; I could
only envisage Heidelberg or Paris. My father might rant
about discipline and how I needed a sense of duty and a
haircut; I longed only to sit at some café table, hyacinthine
locks curling over velvet collar, expatiating to a rapt audience
of fellow students on Verlaine or Baudelaire. He might snarl,
he might threaten, he might command; my purpose was
fixed. And besides I knew eventually, when he had worked
himself to the limits of his rage, he would all at once look
at me and see in my face the image of my dead mother (an
image I had never known and had no especial feeling for,

but whose fair curls and pouting mouth he treasured senti-
mentally in miniatures and portraits on every wall of his
apartments); and then he would snort irritably and shelve
our discussion for another week.

But on this January night of 1888 we had scarce●y
concluded our first parries and thrusts when a servant
brought in the missive from Uncle Gustav. My father snatched it up and read it. A curious look came over his heavy
Roman features, a look at once doubtful and greedy, as
if he were battling to suppress some furtive desire. Then
his jaw went out, his shoulders squared, he appeared,
almost with a mental click of his heels, to reassert his
customary self-discipline. Barking at the servant to have
the sleigh harnessed immediately, he turned with a glare
upon me.

'It's a damned fine thing, Anton, to have a son and not
to be sure . . . to need to ask whether he can be trusted.'

'Forgive me, Sir,' I said. 'I admit I fail to show the mindless
obedience of a cavalry lieutenant. But until now I had not
realised that intelligence was a sign of moral turpitude.'

He looked for a moment as if he might strike me. But then
his sense of duty, or perhaps that treacherous resemblance
of mine, prevented him. He sighed. 'Come, my boy, we've
both spoken harshly. Perhaps it's true, confound it – perhaps
if I attempt to treat you like a man, you'll grow into one
in time. At any rate, I suppose there's little hope of your
understanding your obligations as a member of this family
if you are kept in ignorance of them. But if I forget you've
been an insolent puppy, if I take you with me tonight, I
require your word of honour—'

'You should not need to ask it, Sir.'

'I repeat, I require your word, as if you had sworn a
solemn oath, that nothing which passes at your uncle's will
be disclosed by you to any living soul.'

I had been used all my life to my father's cloak-and-dagger
games. They were his way of expressing his nostalgia for
the 'old country'. While my Uncle Gustav preferred to manifest his yearnings by squeezing himself into the embroidered
Lederhosen of the Sylvanian mountain people and donning a
plumed peasant's hat and slapping his little hairy thighs to

the rhythm of the traditional songs he had taught me to play on the zither, my father chose intrigue and politics to salve the pain of his exile. I was long accustomed to sudden visitors by night, to the sound of my father's study door closing furtively upon a double agent from Rosenholm or a deserting army officer, to coded messages and whispered conversations and all the melodramatic hocus pocus of his revolutionary fantasies. Old men's games. I took them no more seriously than Uncle Gustav's crocodile tears when he bemoaned the absence of good Rosenholm beer from his stein or gazed upon à water-colour of the snow-capped peaks of Schwanensee till the very gobs of sweat upon his brow, like the effusions from an over-ripe Nordstadt cheese, betokened bibulous sentimentality. I had, after all, never set foot in Sylvania but only received it second-hand, like an exhalation of stale wine. It seemed to me then merely a gingerbread and marzipan state, the stuff of biscuit tins and picture postcards, which, in adding little to the civilisation of Europe by way of painters, writers or composers, was as deserving of my complete indifference as Switzerland, my place of birth. And, besides, how could I work up even a modicum of interest in all the talk of private armies in Thalia and the resistance movement against Baron von Schramm? What did it matter to me whether King Friedrich was a half-wit and a disgrace to his throne? How could the fortunes of the Sigismundites, so long in the doldrums, change my life, even were they to rise like the phoenix of my father's imaginings from the flames? My father, by putting sentimentality before reason, had deprived me of my birthright and ensured my utter imperviousness to the fate of the whole Hohenstaufen line.

Oh, it is fair enough for a prince of the blood to engage in the occasional *divertissement* with an actress from the Volksoper – my late lamented Uncle Sigismund was renowned for such indulgences and considered the devil of a fellow. But to show such execrable taste as to become infatuated, as my father had, and not even to draw back there but to marry the woman – you may disguise it with high-flown words like 'honour' and 'true love', but such lack of fastidiousness is worthy only of contempt. He had been compelled to renounce his rights to the succession, of course. And I, only

son of that morganatic union, how did I stand as a result of
this total want of consideration? Not a Hohenstaufen prince
in my own right, son of His Royal Highness the Prince
Leopold, Duke of Maar, not a direct descendent of King
Sigismund I and third in line to the Sylvanian throne, but
the mere child of the soubrette Anna Tancredi, granted the
favour of styling myself by her courtesy title – a paltry Count,
with no more lofty destiny to look forward to than to be
gazetted into the Prussian cavalry. Was it any wonder that
night, as we drove pell-mell through the snow on our clandestine mission, that I let a small supercilious smile of
detachment play about my lips? Was it any wonder, as we
were admitted with whispers to the Villa Narzisse, that I
could barely restrain my laughter? Pathetic schoolboy stuff!
I had seen it all before and it could, or so I believed, mean
nothing to me.

My uncle, Prince Gustav, was in his laboratory with his
beloved spiders. They have always been a ruling passion,
these arachnids of his, so that I suspect, were it not for the
stern promptings of my father, he would have been happy
to obliterate all recollection of his brief regency, to live
contentedly with his memories of Schwanensee dawns and
Rosenholm *Biergartens* and leave the future of the Hohenstaufens to its fate. He has even, it seems to me, grown to
look a little like one of the hairy things, a plump black
mygalomorph perhaps, with his stumpy legs and hirsute
fingers and small, sharp, shiny-bright eyes; not in him the
aquiline dignity of the other sons of Maximilian I, not the
squareheaded Roman bulk of the younger brother, my
father, nor the flamboyant handsomeness of the elder, the
dead King Sigismund II, whose likeness, rendered by
Lenbach in the ermine cape of Grand Master of the Order
of St Xavier, hung imposingly in the Villa's ballroom; no, in
Uncle Gustav the sweep of the Hohenstaufen nose is curved
in upon itself and well-furnished with hair, the hard Hohenstaufen jaw recedes, and a foreshortened lower lip reveals a
row of broken teeth, so that one has the impression of a
proboscis, of thrusting arthropod fangs questing after prey.
On the night I refer to, when we had been conducted
stealthily into his presence, a pair of *Attulus saltators* were

due to mate and despite the imperative tone of his summons it was only with reluctance he drew himself away.

Placing a cautionary finger to his lips and casting one last regretful glance at the amorous attuli, he led us upstairs to the library, where he firmly closed the door.

'One cannot be too careful these days, Leo – even of the servants.'

'Yes, confound it! Vielfrass's damned spies are everywhere.'

Stifling a yawn, I arranged myself elegantly in a wing chair while he unlocked a bureau, sprung the concealed drawer and drew out some papers.

'You will recall old Leinsdorf, Leo?'

'He was our ambassador to the French court.'

'And remains in Paris in his retirement. Not three hours ago I received this communication from him by special courier. It contains – my dear Leo, it contains the most remarkable news.'

'Your use of our code conveyed as much.'

'Then read it, man, read it, in Heaven's name!'

My father took the papers and, jamming his eye-glass into position, settled to read while Uncle Gustav paced before the fire and I pondered the titles on the bookshelves with studied disdain. Having read the letter through, my father readjusted his eye-glass and commenced upon it a second time. The silence seemed interminable. Uncle Gustav began to suck his proboscis in and out beneath his little ragged fangs. I wondered idly whether I might resort to my cigarette-case without incurring the Paterfamilias's wrath. Then he lowered the letter and there seemed to flicker in his face once more that furtive, greedy expression. But, as before, he subdued it, drew himself up.

'Dashit, Gustav, how old is Leinsdorf? Damn near eighty, if I remember aright. This whatshisname, Miramont, probably put his nephew up to it, persuaded him to play upon poor Leinsdorf's rambling wits.'

'But why?'

'Why do any of them try it? Money, a longing for fame, downright insanity. Remember the imbecile you and I went to Brussels to see, and that other charlatan in Geneva? You summon me here as a matter of the utmost importance and now I find it's yet another fool's errand. Dammit Gustav, the boy is dead, more's the pity – and you and I must learn to accept it.'

I smiled to myself, for now I understood. Of all the Sylvanian legends I had been obliged to imbibe with my infant milk, the prize one was that the Crown Prince Maximilian, Sigismund's five-year-old heir, who had been mysteriously mislaid in the flight from Rosenholm after his father's suicide and the collapse of my uncle's regency, was in truth alive somewhere and would one day return to claim his birthright. Of all the old men's games, this was the choicest. It was played out on average every two years and I now remembered we had come round once again to the season for it.

'Fictions!' snorted my father, casting the letter aside. 'Cruel fictions, to raise our hopes in vain. Confound it, if there were any hope would we have had to wait over twenty years for it?'

'The Marquis de Miramont was an eccentric, virtually a recluse, Leinsdorf is confined to a bathchair. As he tells us, though they corresponded with each other frequently on matters of scholarship, he never visited the Hotel de Miramont until the fellow was struck by his mortal illness. He only set eyes on the nephew a year ago, and then he was sworn to secrecy until poor Miramont died.'

'So now he is dead, and Leinsdorf will foist this nephew upon us.'

'An adopted nephew, Leo.'

'Who does not even speak our language.'

'Though the boy speaks only French, he admits to being Sylvanian by birth. And then there is the mention of Mont Rémy.'

My father snorted again. 'Coincidence, my dear Gustav. That is all Leinsdorf's letter gives us – coincidences, ramblings, leaps of imagination. No doubt this adopted nephew of Miramont's can spin a yarn. But as usual, there's not one jot of proof.'

'Ah,' said Uncle Gustav, his little bright eyes glinting. 'This time, Leo, there is something closer to it.' And going once again to the bureau he came back with a small object which he pressed into the Paterfamilias's hand.

My father stared at whatever it was for a moment, transfixed. I preserved my cynical smile, for after all I had witnessed such charades before and doubtless should again. But suddenly his hand began to tremble so violently that the object fell to the floor.

Since it lay not a metre from my chair I bent casually to retrieve it and observed that it was no more than a lump of wax. But then, as I scrutinised it closely, I saw it bore the impression of a seal ring, two profiles in relief, circled by an inscription; and here I confess my smile faded a little, for a lifetime's oppressive cohabitation with family portraits had amply equipped me to recognise the heads of Sigismund and Queen Tatiana, and the words *in obedientiam gloria*, the King's motto.

My father snatched the impression back. The struggle against his hunger seemed for a moment to rack every sinew of his huge square frame.

'A sliver of wax?' he said at last. 'There must be countless craftsmen who can forge a seal. If Leinsdorf truly possessed our brother's ring he would have sent it to us.'

'He thought it too precious to risk. But the impression seems genuine enough. Look at the blurring above Tatiana's brow. That's where Sigismund chipped the stone, caught it on the mantel in his study trying to break my head, I remember, after I'd – ' Uncle Gustav's eyes suddenly lost their glitter – 'when we were having one of our rows.'

'Anyone could have come by the ring. Dieter Wolf could have sold it or pawned it.'

'Dieter Wolf is dead.'

'A body was found at Fontarelles. They said it was Dieter Wolf, but it can't be proved. Nothing, Gustav, can be proved.'

'The ring, Leo? And Leinsdorf mentions a baptismal certificate. In all the other cases nothing of the sort has come to light.'

'But it's not proof, conclusive proof.'

Uncle Gustav's furry brows narrowed. 'Perhaps not in itself. But it must bear investigating. You see, there's another element – something that's damned hard to resist . . .' He paused, sucking in his proboscis.

'Well?' said my father, impatiently.

'I am afraid for that we must join the women.'

My aunt, the Princess Helena, and her lady-in-waiting, Ursula, Baroness von Windersdorf, were poring over something together on a sofa in the Peacock Drawing-room. If Uncle Gustav is a mygalomorph, Aunt Helena is an attenuated *Pholcus phalangioides* and Ursi Windersdorf a fat oxpytila. I suppose Aunt Helena has naturally grown this way, living so long with Uncle Gustav's obsession, and Winders, in thirty years' loyal companionship, has had perforce to metamorphose too; but that evening, crouched there darkly in their weeds (the Baroness's for a long-forgotten husband, my aunt's in ill-defined memory of some secret sorrow), they had never looked so arachnidan, two females fixed upon the object between them as if they were guarding the egg-sac. Winders is somewhat over-given to dispensing motherly advice and Aunt Helena always appears slightly unhinged, though whether from the secret sorrow or from the fact she comes from the Friedrichite side of the family, which is legendary for its mental instability, it is hard to tell. Nevertheless, they are usually tractable enough old crows, gratifyingly susceptible to my winning smile and ready to offer me kisses and chocolates and defence against my father's wrath. But on this occasion they scarcely looked up as we entered, seemed indeed, insensible to our presence.

The object that held them so spellbound, I perceived with an inward groan, was a photograph. Now photographs are by way of being Aunt Helena's and Winders' particular obsession. There are always albums of them strewn about the drawing-rooms and my aunt's private apartments – Uncle Gustav rambling in the mountains at Schwanensee, my father at troop reviews, the infant Crown Prince on his first bobsleigh. But for once the albums lay disregarded; this photograph was evidently some new trophy. Aunt Helena gazed at it, rapt, occasionally plucking at the locket she always wears at her throat. Winders, by contrast, seemed almost apprehensive.

'Dearest Ma'am,' she was saying, 'we cannot be certain.'

'But I can see it, Ursi, there on his forehead. You remember, don't you, the little scar where Bobbi threw him?'

'Ma'am, forgive me—' But here, conscious of us at last,

Winders broke off, springing respectfully to her feet. Aunt Helena looked around her, dazed. Her faded eyes, as they gradually discerned us, were gleaming with a dotty radiance.

'Oh, Gustav, our prayers have been answered. We have lit so many candles, Ursi and I, and now Our Blessed Lady has taken pity on us and brought him back from the dead, may She be praised.'

'Very well, my dear. But we must guard against false hopes. Now Leo is here and you must give him the photograph.'

'Poldi, oh darling Poldi!' She turned upon my father with that same mad radiance. 'You'll see, you'll understand. You'll go to Paris and bring our dear one back for us, won't you, Poldi?'

I thought I had never heard her so loquacious. My uncle shot her a sourish look. His previous excitement seemed to have vanished; perhaps he was thinking of the attuli, legs vibrating, palps inserted; or perhaps he was merely wearied by his obligations as nominal head of the family. 'Come, my dear. Let Leo see the photograph.' And he went over and gently prised it from her grasp.

I was for an instant in a quandary. My pose of negligent cynicism required that I should hang back as the Paterfamilias examined this new object of speculation but on the other hand a pardonable curiosity made me anxious to observe what had so stirred my aunt. Curiosity gained the day and I edged up unobtrusively to peer over his shoulder.

We both peered for a moment. Then there was an audible intake of breath from my father – echoed, I am ashamed to say, by me.

It was a poor effort, amateurish and slightly out of focus; a man, I should have hazarded some ten years older than myself, posed head and shoulders before the lens, the head slightly turned. But nevertheless, despite the stiffness of the pose and the softness of the definition, there was no mistaking it: the arrogant mouth, the upper lip curved wider and narrower than the lower, the fine imperious sweep of the nose, the impression above all of a ruthless, commanding sensuality – it was there as it was in the portrait above the dais in the ballroom, confronting us as assuredly from that cheap snapshot as it did in the magnificence of Grand

Master's robes – the face of my late uncle, His Majesty King Sigismund II.

'So you see, Poldi,' crooned Aunt Helena in a far-away, sing-song voice. 'You understand now that the miracle has happened.'

'It is damned like him, Gustav,' said my father hoarsely. 'By Jupiter, it is!'

'The camera does not lie, Leo. Or so they say.'

'And yet suppose this too is some clever forgery.'

'A miracle, a miracle,' crooned Aunt Helena. 'Why, there is even the poor dear scar where his pony threw him in the Home Park.'

My father pulled himself up. 'I see no scar, Helena.' And indeed he spoke no more than the truth, for if the face in the picture bore such a mark it had been beyond the skills of the photographer to disclose it.

'Naughty Bobbi shied and threw him. Such a deep wound for a poor little boy, how he cried when they carried him in to me – '

'I see no scar,' repeated my father irritably. 'You must take a hold upon yourself, Helena. I admit in some respects the resemblance is striking. But this photograph is no more proof than the rest.'

'Proof? Oh, when one can *feel*, Poldi, one does not need proof. When one feels in one's heart as Ursi and I feel – oh Ursi, dear Ursi, you will vouch that we women can know in our hearts and souls what a man by mere reason cannot.'

Poor old Winders, constrained, with the arrival of the Paterfamilias and Uncle Gustav, by the protocol which decreed she might not speak until she was first addressed, had obviously been close to bursting-point. 'Her Royal Highness is moved as we all are by the likeness to poor King Sigismund. Why, when dear Queen Tatiana – God rest her soul – died in childbed, Her Royal Highness was a second mother to the poor little orphan prince. Oh, I have dared to express caution, have ventured to remonstrate that hopes raised so high can only cause grievous pain if they are dashed. But Her Royal Highness is so warm-hearted, Sir. And to lose a child – even though the dear Princess was not his natural mother – I know what it is myself, having lost my dear Albrecht, still-born, not ten days before our precious little Crown Prince came into the world. To lose a child you have cradled in your arms, upon whom you have lavished all a mother's tenderness and care, and suddenly to hope that child may be restored to you – is it any wonder, Sir, that the dear Princess is a little overwhelmed?'

'So, Poldi, you believe now,' crooned Aunt Helena. 'You must go to Paris and bring him back to us. You must let me see my dear one and comfort him. Such an ugly wound it was for a poor little boy, and he so handsome, just like his poor father . . .' Here, clutching her locket again, she broke suddenly into noisy sobs.

'Now Helena, Helena, you know this won't do.' The glitter had quite gone from Uncle Gustav's eyes and he seemed more than ever out of sorts with his family duties. 'Dashit, woman!' he snarled at Winders. 'Can't you take my wife away and calm her with one of your potions? If she continues like this she'll make herself ill again.'

Winders simpered and laid a hand upon Aunt Helena's arm. 'Her Royal Highness cared for me all those years ago in my trouble and you may be assured, Sir, I shall care for her in hers. Come, dearest Ma'am, lean on me.'

'Confound it, Gustav!' snorted my father when they were gone. 'Whatever possessed you to get the women involved? You know they'd fall for any likely story, you know we judged it foolhardy to take them to Brussels.'

Uncle Gustav sighed. 'My dear Leo, you will observe I know the foolishness of it even better than you. But the fact of it is that they will have to be involved sooner or later. They visited the child daily in the nursery whereas you and I – well, I cannot claim to have seen the boy above four or five times a year, and even when I did see him I'm deuced if I can remember much about it. Can you say more?'

The Paterfamilias shook his head, staring at the photograph.

'However frail Helena's wits – Leo, you've got to admit the likeness is damnable.'

My father did admit it. And, as he absorbed it, that rapacious look stole over him again. 'So, Gustav, what must we do?'

'I'm afraid, as Helena says, one of us must go to Paris.'

They surveyed each other for a moment. The Paterfamilias

possessed, in common with all good German officers, an inveterate contempt for everything about the French from their infantry drill to their courage under fire; even their language, although he had been made to construe it in the schoolroom, he had now expelled from his head as thoroughly as a priest ridding himself of a heresy. Uncle Gustav, seeming to read his mind, lowered his furry brows pleadingly.

'I realise it is my place as the elder, Leo, but, well, it must be done soon and you know I present my paper on "Courtship Rituals in the *Marpissa muscosa*" to the University Zoological Society at the end of the month.'

My father snorted. 'And how am I to interrogate the fellow if he refuses to speak our tongue?'

'Baron Leinsdorf will act as interpreter.'

'Leinsdorf is in too deep – he cannot be trusted to be impartial.'

'Then take Anton. You say his tutor spoke highly of his linguistic abilities.'

The Paterfamilias turned and stared at me as if he had utterly forgotten my existence. His eye-glass examined me for some moments with the reluctant interest he might have bestowed upon Uncle Gustav's mating attuli. 'Well, my boy?' he said eventually. 'This much-vaunted brain of yours – d'you think you could use it for something better than scribbling rhymes and sneering at your father? D'you think you're up to it, eh?'

Up to it? Paris? My heart leapt, my pose of elegant ennui deserted me instantly. 'Oh yes, Sir. Yes. You may depend on it.'

II

It is tedious to rehearse the details of the myth that has grown around Crown Prince Maximilian's disappearance, yet rehearse them my father did, over and over during the next few days, conjectures and speculations I had received at my nursemaid's knee where other more fortunate children hear fairy-tales.

The everyday care of the infant Crown Prince after his

mother's death devolved upon his wet-nurse, one Frau Wolf, to whom it seemed, although she was of peasant stock, the princeling formed an attachment which, despite the ministrations of Aunt Helena and Winders and the introduction of an English nanny, was not to be broken, so that she remained in the royal nursery long after her nursing duties had ceased. Nurse Wolf had one son, Dieter, of about the prince's age, and since there was concern that an only child, deprived of his mother's attentions by death and his father's by frequent 'diplomatic' absences, might become withdrawn and awkward, and since in any case the infant Maximilian had not yet reached the age where he must be 'Your Highnessed', prince and peasant boy were occasionally allowed to play together.

On the fateful day Uncle Gustav's regency was overthrown, it fell to Nurse Wolf in the chaos and panic of the flight to Austria to have the charge of the young Crown Prince, my father and Uncle Gustav being entirely occupied with the salvage of the family jewels and other items of Hohenstaufen wealth. The Crown Prince's carriage, containing Nurse Wolf and her own son as well as Maximilian, and escorted by outriders from the still-loyal Garde du Corps, set off *en route* for Austria with the rest, but half-way to the border was discovered to be missing. It was eventually found, not thirty kilometres out of Rosenholm, overturned in a ditch; its escort, to a man, lay dead and of the nurse and the two small boys there was no trace.

After long and fruitless searches, it was at last assumed that the nurse and her charges had perished with the rest. But then, thirteen years later, rumour began to grow that the boys had been smuggled into France and put to school in a Benedictine monastery, where they had now taken their vows. Sigismundite agents were immediately dispatched from Switzerland to find them, for if Schramm's men were to discover their hiding place first it would mean certain death for the newly-resurrected Crown Prince. But by the time our agents reached the monastery at Mont Rémy the Father Abbot was dead of typhoid fever and no amount of enquiry could elicit the whereabouts of the boys.

Three months later, however, a badly-decomposed body was found in a midden at the tiny village of Fontarelles, two hundred kilometres away. Though the skull was battered and the body unrecognisable, it bore amongst its clothing papers identifying it as the nurse's son, Dieter Wolf. If the peasant, Wolf, was dead what, then, of the Crown Prince? Once again our agents began an investigation. But no further trace of Maximilian was ever discovered.

Oh, of course there were questions, rumours. Was it not most likely that Prince Maximilian had been murdered by the same hand as his companion? But why had his body never been found? And what of the body at Fontarelles? Was it truly the corpse of Dieter Wolf? Or had the Crown Prince been murdered by Wolf's hand, and had the crafty Wolf then substituted the Prince's identity for his own and gone into hiding? The silence, the absence of all evidence of Maximilian's continued existence suggested to anyone disposed to use his common sense that Sigismund's heir was indeed long dead. But common sense has never been, it seems, a Sylvanian characteristic. The rumours persisted: gypsy women predicted that when a piebald swan was seen on the lake at Schwanensee or when the holly by the West Gate of the Residenz bore berries, or other such rot, Maximilian would return; exiles consulted the stars and saw omens in their patience cards; false claimants abounded, each with a more improbable story than the last: and on winter evenings over his brandy my father would stare into the fire as if he too saw augury there, for the idea that his nephew the Crown Prince might still be living gave substance to his fantasies, a purpose to his posturing, his private army, his talk of invasion and counter-revolution.

It was, you see, to the Paterfamilias, a simple imperative of the succession, for if the imbecile Friedrich were to be toppled, there must be a suitable Sigismundite candidate to replace him. As I have recounted, my father's sloppy romanticism had disbarred himself and his line. There was another cousin in England, son of my late aunt, Marie Louise, but he too was disqualified by his mother's marriage to an English Duke devoid of royal blood, and ranked no loftier than a Serene Highness. That left, as things stood, only Uncle Gustav, who was tarnished by his failed regency and in any case professed a vehement reluctance to return to public life; and besides, little ugly Uncle Gustav, with his furry nostrils and Gorgonzola breath and his propensity to launch into a detailed account over the *petit fours* of how his newly-hatched *Amaurobii Terrestris* had just devoured their mother, was scarcely the stuff of which my father's glorious visions were wrought. No, my father was obliged to believe in his secret heart that there was a Crown Prince, young, malleable, fit to be the figurehead of his own aspirations, for if he did not he would be compelled to recognise that his twenty-two years of plotting and planning had been no more than a senescent dream.

You could see it work on him, Leinsdorf's missive, over those days of preparation for our travels, so that he even forgot his intention to offer me up as cannon-fodder. Of course this journey might simply be a wild-goose chase like the others. But all the same you could see he was seduced by it, that image in the photograph, that apparently miraculous reincarnation of Uncle Sigismund, see the feverish expansion of thought, the appetite for power and intrigue it whetted.

As for myself, I thought only of Paris, glorious cosmopolitan Paris, of which I too had dreams. Apart from one never-to-be-referred-to experiment at the age of eleven, I had spent all my life in Switzerland, surrounded by people twice my age, whose preoccupations, cultivated like orchids in fetid seclusion, had deprived me of all intercourse with fashionable society. But now at last I should cut an elegant dash in the Champs-Elysées, drive in the Bois de Boulogne, breathe the very air which had given inspiration to Verlaine and Baudelaire and Mallarmé.

My father had begun to complain even as we reached Basle: the beer was weak, the *wagon-lit* attendant surly, the pillows hard. Not for him the thrill of travelling incognito, of emerging from the steamy cavern of the Gare de Strasbourg to the hooting of tramway cars, and the jungle chorus of an alien tribe. He was not content until his equerry, Colonel von Straubnitz, had at last located amongst the mêlée of baggage and porters the liveried carriage of the exiled Count von Hartenau, who had placed at our disposal his apartments in the Hôtel de Crécy. And, having attained this little island of the old country amidst treacherous foreign soil, having awoken unmoved to a misty January morning coming up over the rooftops of the Faubourg Saint-Germain, to all the tantalising sounds and smells of the great city stirring, he could think of nothing better than that we should attend upon Baron von Leinsdorf immediately.

Our one-time ambassador occupied an apartment just off the boulevard des Capucines in a building whose elegant proportions and balconied façade seemed quintessentially Parisian. But once a lift like a gilded birdcage had carried us unsteadily to the third floor, yes, here again was the old country, musty as a wardrobe of forgotten clothes, here were the familiar pictures, and the hunting horns and the lumbering presses hatched with crude marquetry, and all the dreary trappings of exile. The Baron received us in his study, a room littered with the scholarly papers on which he now employed his time; and though he was a cherubic little man, hairless as a baby with a face as pink as if it had been most thoroughly scrubbed, he too gave off a musty smell, as though beneath the blanket covering his useless legs he nursed twenty years of Sigismundite decay.

He began at once to retell his story. The sardonyx portrait ring was produced and yes, there was the chip Uncle Gustav had remembered above Tatiana's brow. Then papers were lifted carefully from a small wooden chest, papers tattered and yellow with age on which the seal had crumbled and the Gothic script grown faint. My father read the documents over and over, even examined them with the Baron's magnifying glass. His fingers plucked at his starched collar as if he were suffocating.

'This is remarkable, Leinsdorf. Most remarkable.'

The little Baron twinkled gleefully. He had a high voice like a cracked drum. 'Most remarkable, Sir, as you say. And to think we owe it all to Marcus Tullius Cicero. If the Marquis de Miramont had not spent a quarter-century of his life editing the great philosopher's letters and if I had not thought to consult him when I embarked upon my monograph on *De Officiis*, we should never have known of the boy's existence. Oh yes, Sir, we owe dear Marcus Tullius a great deal.'

'Quite so,' said my father impatiently.

'Of course it has taken all the strength that remains to me to keep such a secret. But young Miramont would have me

tell no one while the Marquis still lived. And besides, there
has been the boy's safety to consider. Even now I dread to
think what Schramm might do if the true purpose of your
visit were uncovered—'

'Quite, quite,' said my father. 'And when may I be
permitted to see the young man?'

'In a few minutes, Sir. I have asked him to call at eleven
to collect a parcel of books. I believe there is a way of
contriving it so that Your Royal Highness may catch your
first sight of him unobserved.'

The principal salon of the apartment was bisected by a
curtained arch. We were obliged to watch while a
manservant almost as decrepit as his master carried the
Baron from the study and parcelled him up in his blanket
again upon a low sofa. Opposite this sofa and directly facing
the curtain a chair was placed, so that we, peering through
a chink in the draperies, should be afforded a clear view of
its occupant.

The Baron rubbed his hands gleefully, glancing at the clock
on the mantel. 'This is a great moment, Sir, an historic
moment.'

'Perhaps so. But if the fellow has lied, if the papers and
the ring have come into his possession by fraudulent means,
it will be a moment he will live to regret. We'll make him
feel his damned lies like lashes, confound it if we don't!'

For the first time a frown dimmed the Baron's pink cheeks.
'Permit me, Sir – I think I must warn you – the boy is – well,
he possesses a natural independence of spirit. After M. de
Miramont passed away, he fell ill with a fever and, although
he has not yet fully recovered his strength, he has refused
all my offers of assistance, prefers to support himself by
taking a situation as tutor in the house of Weissman, the
banker. Forgive me, but I fear we must have a care—'

But what we must have a care for the Baron was not able
to divulge, since at that moment the clock began to chime
eleven and simultaneously from down the hall came the
jangling of the doorbell, obliging the Paterfamilias and
myself, like characters in some low farce, to make an undig-
nified scramble for the curtain.

We could see nothing at first, hearing, only, a soft footfall,
a quiet voice exchanging the conventional greetings. Then

suddenly my father caught his breath and, craning over his shoulder, I glimpsed a tall figure in black walking away from us in the direction of the appointed chair. The stranger reached the chair, turned; and there all at once was the face in the photograph.

I confess I experienced a sensation of anti-climax. Oh, there was still enough of the Hohenstaufen about the features if you were disposed to find it, despite the ravages of the fever; but that other quality, that brute sensuality, which Lenbach had captured so deftly in his portrait of Uncle Sigismund and which the stealthy whirring of the shutter had somehow surprised in its sitter too – of that there was no trace. Instead there was a cool, guarded look, an air almost of asceticism, echoed by the modest priestly black of the stranger's dress and the reserved posture he held in his chair. Yet I saw what made my father's hand clutch at the curtain so that I feared he would render our situation still more ridiculous by pulling it down upon us; for running up into the hairline of the stranger's left temple was the white curve of a cicatrice, like a duelling scar.

The conversation had turned towards some abstruse aspect of Leinsdorf's Ciceronian dissertation. I was amazed that the Paterfamilias's breathing remained inaudible to our quarry, but he continued calmly listening without once glancing directly at the curtain. Then, quite suddenly, in response to some utterance of the Baron's he smiled: it was an extraordinary smile, open, unforced, vividly at odds with the rest of him, illuminating the gaunt, aquiline face like sunlight pouring into a shuttered room; and in that instant we were looking at Sigismund once more, at the handsome features of the Lenbach portrait brought irresistibly to life.

The Paterfamilias, uttering something between a snort and a roar, burst out of our concealment with a screech of curtain rings. 'Who the devil are you?' he cried. 'Damn it man, who are you in hell's name?'

The stranger's smile died. He glanced first at my father and then at Leinsdorf and as he rose to his feet there flickered in his eyes an expression of – shock, recognition, anger? – I was not certain which. Then, as the Baron began upon the absurd flourishes of a formal presentation, his face seemed to close again. Despite his austere dress and haggard appearance, he showed none of the obsequiousness appropriate to a humble tutor. Indeed, his bow of acknowledgement was given with the grace of a gentleman. His eyes surveyed my father levelly. They were, like Uncle Sigismund's, a cold steel blue.

'Confound it!' roared the Paterfamilias. 'I command you to tell me who you are this instant, and what the deuce you mean by – by this damnable conjuring trick!'

Maxim de Miramont continued to return my father's stare for a moment. Though he spoke no German he could scarcely fail to take the meaning of the Paterfamilias's bulging eyes and purple visage. He turned to Leinsdorf.

'Forgive me, monsieur. I appreciate that you have acted from a concern for my interests. But you must impress upon His Royal Highness that I did not seek this meeting. I admit I have a duty to explain how I came by the ring and papers, but I am myself uncertain as to my true identity. I wish it to be understood that I make no claim upon Prince Leopold or his family whatsoever.'

III

The stranger's story, which was pieced together – or rather coerced from him – over the next week, was this.

Though he conceded he had been born in Sylvania, he professed to recall little of his early childhood. There had been a boy of his own age with whom he had been permitted to play, a nurse who had been kind to him, other women in rustling dresses whom he thought might have been his aunts; for the most part, though the detail had faded, he remembered it as a time of security and happiness. But then suddenly had come a night which had put an end to that cosy world forever, a night of noise and flashes of light and running, then mud, acres of it, tramped through painfully in the pitch darkness, with his hands, as they clung to the nurse's skirts, so cold he could not keep his grasp and was in terror she would lose him.

Afterwards he described a farmhouse kitchen he thought was in Alsace and then a much grander house in France. It seemed at about this time his nurse had suddenly acquired

money, gone up in the world. He was told he must from
henceforth call her 'Mama' and treat his playmate as a
brother. There was a new Papa too, and then another and
another, and with each one he was given a new name and
a beating if he failed to remember it. An atmosphere of guilt
and secrecy, which he began to ascribe to some defect in
himself, hung over the household. As the 'family' moved
from town to town, he sought to expiate his fault by
repressing all his memories of Sylvania, by obediently
accepting each new identity. But the beatings and the curses
and the drunken scenes continued, until finally one day he
and his playfellow were bundled into a carriage by their
latest Papa and taken on a three-day journey, at the end of
which they were deposited in a white-walled room under
the care of a monk. Both boys were eight years old and this
was the last they ever saw of the nurse. They were put to
fasting and prayers and the study of Latin as oblates in the
monastery school, taking their final vows at the age of
fifteen. The outside world was as closed to them as if they
had been entombed alive.

It had not been until his eighth year at Mont Rémy that
he had first seen the ring and papers. Although it was
forbidden for Choir monks to form associations with the lay
brothers, he had struck up a friendship with one of them
while working at the cider press and later this man, Brother
Jean, had been put to serve the Abbot himself and had begun
to hint that he knew things, secrets, about both boys. One
night, after the lights of the *Dormitorium* had been
extinguished, he had taken them to the Abbot's office and,
unlocking the chest where the baptismal certificates of all
the brothers were kept, had brought out the packet of documents their 'father' had been required to deposit in the
Abbot's care when he had made their preliminary vows.

Although the stranger had now lost almost all his German
he could easily construe the name and titles inscribed on the
parchment he was handed; but his reaction, he recalled, was
simple disbelief. He had striven so hard to erase his early
memories that his distant glimpses of another life seemed a
mere will-o'-the-wisp, a fantasy concocted to bolster him
against his subsequent deprivation. Besides, Brother Jean
could easily be mistaken – though a genial fellow, he was

virtually illiterate and somewhat partial to drink. As for the carving on the ring, monastic life had not encouraged the stranger to dwell upon his own sixteen-year-old face and it had seemed an act of imagination to draw from the comparison any but the most tenuous resemblance. Laughing, he had handed the papers back to Brother Jean and had disciplined himself to forget their existence.

Only later, during his tenth year out of the world, had he come to understand that any association with these documents could bring danger. Strange things began to happen, a rumoured attempt to break into the Enclosure, a man questioning the Brother Porter about both boys. Remembering the years of beatings and secrecy, they became filled with foreboding; both knew themselves to be without vocation, and when the Abbot's death provided the opportunity they felt it safer to steal their papers and escape.

Safer? From the stranger's account of their subsequent journey, working their way to Paris as itinerant labourers, they had thrown themselves into even greater danger, for it soon became clear they were being followed. Though time after time they believed they had shaken off their pursuers, the suspicion recurred; until finally one night on a deserted stretch of road just outside the little hamlet of Fontarelles their worst fears were confirmed, for they were suddenly set upon by four carters they had seen eyeing them in a local tavern. The stranger's description of this encounter was terse. His friend, Dieter, who was the stronger, had fought like a tiger, at one time grappling with all four assailants and shouting for him to make his escape. But as he had turned to run he had seen one of the carters rise from unconsciousness with a heavy spade in his hands. He had glimpsed the spade descend like an axe on Dieter Wolf's skull. After that he had not paused but had run until his lungs were bursting, losing his pursuers at last in the darkness.

Avoiding human habitation and living like a wild man on whatever he could come across by hunting or by stealing from outlying farms, he had eventually reached Paris, where he had been absorbed into the faceless mass of the poor. A spell in a fever hospital had enabled him to steal the papers of the dead man on the palliasse next to him and thus provide himself with yet another new identity. He had worked as a labourer, digging drains and laying cobbles, and once had even been reduced by hunger to begging; until his height and build had at last secured him employment as a footman. It was in this capacity he had entered the household of the Marquis de Miramont, who, on surprising him reading a book from his library, had not as might be expected dismissed him without a character but, astonished at such evidence of scholarship in a mere footman, had taken him up as his protégé.

Yes, the stranger admitted, there had been moments in those first years in Paris when he had thought of using the ring and papers to discover his true identity – he had once even made a vow to that effect – but poverty had deprived him of the means, and fear of the strength of purpose. And later, during his reclusive life at the Hôtel de Miramont, while his fear had been dissipated, so had his curiosity. He had spent, in all, seven years with the Marquis, who had shown him great kindness, encouraging his studies and teaching him the manners and bearing of a gentleman (for though the monastery had endowed him with scholarship it had left him in upbringing otherwise a peasant); his obligation towards such generosity had bound him more strongly than any fanciful quest for what was past. And when, at the onset of his final illness, the Marquis had insisted on bestowing upon him the protection of his name, the mystery of his identity had lost its last shred of importance. Baron Leinsdorf intended well, but the stranger could not, would not swear that the baptismal documents from Mont Rémy were his or that his likeness to the face on the seal ring was any other than coincidence. As Maxim de Miramont he at last knew certainty: he wished for nothing more.

The effect of this narrative upon my father was prodigious. If the stranger had sought to persuade he might have ranted, bullied, pursued his savage determination to root out fraud; but against Miramont's reluctance he had no weapon, still less because the extreme impartiality of the account, and its narrator's evident distaste for it, endowed it paradoxically with a curious frankness, an aura of incontrovertible truth. It was droll to watch the Paterfamilias seize upon each telling correspondence of detail – the nurse, the flight from Rosenholm, the account of the boys' life at Mont Rémy and Dieter Wolf's death – to see him weigh them all up, then founder on the stranger's refusal to draw the same conclusion. He, who was used to threaten and command, would become by turns impatient, then puzzled, then almost wheedling. But the stranger never wavered, nor sought to disguise that he had agreed to be interrogated only at the Baron's prompting. He would sit, very still and contained, repeating his answers with a weary detachment, as if he spoke of some other person with whom he recognised no connection, and though his weakness from the fever would often leave him white-lipped and hoarse, by the conclusion of these interviews there was, beneath his exhaustion, a fixity of purpose which was equal to my father's. The poor Paterfamilias! He would stare at that drawn face with its telling scar and its ghostly echoes of Uncle Sigismund, stare at it as if it mocked him. He wanted his Crown Prince so very badly; and wanting was already half-way to belief.

As for my part in these proceedings, well, it is a curious thing to become other people's voices. I would sit closeted with them every afternoon in Count von Hartenau's gloomy study while Gebhardt, my father's personal secretary, scratched away at meticulous transcripts, and feel myself battered backwards and forwards like a shuttlecock, attacked, intercepted, parried, as if I were both victim and inquisition.

Not that my performance was without merit – though for this I was grudgingly in debt to the stranger. Why was it, on that very first afternoon, when my father had unloosened his opening salvo and Gebhardt's pen was poised and the attention of the whole room was suddenly focused upon me, that I, who had always tied my servile old goat of a French tutor into the most satisfying knots, was all at once left stammering as if every word of the language had been mysteriously erased from my brain?

I could hear the clock ticking, feel the familiar purple begin to well in the Paterfamilias's jowls. But the stranger, surveying us both with raised brows, had seemed instantly to divine my difficulties and had from thenceforth confined himself to a simplicity of expression which, while it greatly assisted me, was not yet so obvious that my father could detect it. I was, of course, gratified after that first interview to receive the Paterfamilias's congratulations and to observe behind his eye-glass a sentimental glint that might even have been pride. But I could not find it in my heart to thank the stranger; his lordly supposition of my inadequacy struck me, rather, as highly disagreeable.

Indeed, on the whole, if I were to deign to take any view of the fellow, it verged upon dislike. It was not just the Paterfamilias's obsession with him or the way his modest dress and absence of gestures gave him an air of tedious virtue. There was something else about him too, something in his very self-possession which impressed me adversely. Although, as I grew more confident in my prowess as translator, my capacity to anticipate and reproduce his minutest nuances of expression forged a kind of specious intimacy between us, I was still as little able to fathom his true thoughts and emotions as I had been on the first day. There was in his reserve a quality which could not be accounted for merely by his reluctance for his task or his physical debility, a quality that reminded me of – what, I was not sure. It was as if, beneath the calm, there was a studied wariness, a sense of things compacted and hidden away, like a field telescope when it is closed up.

Still, I supposed I should in some measure be grateful to the fellow whoever he was – Crown Prince, Dieter Wolf, or simply the nonentity he proclaimed – since after all he kept us in Paris; if, that is, I were ever to see more of the city than those dreary apartments in the Hôtel de Crécy, for my father appeared anxious to protect me from foreign decadence at all costs. The opera, the theatre, the brilliance of the boulevards? In the hours left to us after questioning the stranger or reading Gebhardt's transcripts, he would insist on my accompanying him to the tedious receptions got up in his honour by fellow exiles (the ostensible reason for his visit). And as for money, if I should find the leisure to make my escape – the doddering Colonel von Straubnitz carried our currency with him always in a heavy belt beneath his tunic and could not be persuaded, even by blackmail, to part with so much as a sou.

Sometimes after the stranger had been smuggled out of the Hôtel de Crécy I would think of him with envy, absorbed without trace into the teeming life of the city, free to taste its pleasures at his will – except, of course, that Miramont with his monkish ways would make scant use of that freedom; whereas I – oh, I should rub shoulders with poets and artists yet, and savour headier conversations than the febrile small talk of the Sylvanian maidens I was nightly obliged to take in to dinner. As long as the Paterfamilias's caper continued, I had only to bide my time.

And then, as if deliberately to confound me, the stranger began to change. It seemed to happen despite all his control, as though a part of him which had been numbed was suddenly recovering sensation. One afternoon, for instance, when my father was again questioning him about that lost early childhood, he began all at once to describe furniture and rooms which, while they meant nothing to me, I could see from the Paterfamilias's face must have been in the Rosenholm Residenz. Later he was able to list (accurately, it appeared) the pet-names of various dogs and ponies in the Royal Household. He did not volunteer this information easily; on the contrary, it seemed to occasion him some fierce internal struggle. Often in the midst of embellishing detail he would break off as if he had caught himself in a betrayal; and once when, it seemed unconsciously, he had answered the Paterfamilias with three sentences of perfectly passable German, he was silent for a full quarter of an hour afterwards, staring out bleakly towards the huddled buildings in the courtyard.

Nevertheless these – admissions, confessions, call them what you will – continued. He recalled an aunt (Aunt Helena presumably) who sometimes when she came to the nursery was dressed all in white and bright with jewels which he was forbidden to clamber up and touch. He could describe details of the footmen's livery, a gardener with a port-wine stain like a star; he remembered a tall man who had slashed his cheek once with a riding crop for crying, and he reluctantly conceded that this might have been his father.

The Paterfamilias, of course, observing this development, could not prevent the little greedy sparks of hope from glittering once again in his eyes. He ceased altogether to hector, became almost genial, forbearing to interrupt the silences, even pouring water from the carafe with his own hands

when the stranger was consumed by one of his paroxysms
of coughing. Though I preserved my ironic smile, I felt with
resentment a complicity growing between them. Yes, the
stranger's inward struggle persisted; but I perceived he was
losing it little by little. Despite his holier-than-thou air, they
were taking hold, the Paterfamilias's fantasies, firing some
hidden element in him with all the heat of desire. He wanted
it to be true now, as my father wanted it; and it would be
merely a matter of time before he was forced to acknowledge
his want.

Thus it happened inevitably one afternoon a few days later
that Leinsdorf was carried up the grand staircase to Count
von Hartenau's study, while I was relegated to an anteroom
with the miserly Straubnitz; and though the stranger did not
agree at once to accompany us to Switzerland but asked
leave to consider his decision, his answer the next day was
inevitable too. The Paterfamilias, I remember, embraced him
in front of us all, pressing his whiskers in turn against both
the stranger's cheeks. And here my ironic smile faded, my
resentment rose like bile to my throat. For never once had
my father offered me such a gesture of affection, never once
in all my nineteen years had I seen such joy in his eyes. It
seemed to mark me like a criticism, to set my value – or lack
of it. And yet, were it not for the Paterfamilias's coarse
tastes, I had a stronger right in blood to be called Your Royal
Highness, to be favoured and deferred to than this unknown
man, despite his spurious resemblance to Uncle Sigismund.

And there was a further spur to my resentment. Leinsdorf
was to intercede with the banker's family to obtain the stranger's immediate release from his tutorial duties, and we were
to leave for home in three days. Paris, too, was to be lost to
me.

IV

I had tried stealing up behind Straubnitz when he was
indulging in one of his habitual dozes, but to no avail – the
wretch had woken up and squealed like a stuck pig before
I had tweaked his first button undone. In the end I had been
reduced to offering my watch to one of the Count's servants

for cash, and much of that had gone on bribing the wretch. But now at last here I was, while the Paterfamilias already snored in preparation for tomorrow's journey, rumbling through the Quartier Latin in my fiacre, with the whole giddy, glorious night ahead of me.

My banker had recommended the Closerie des Lilas, which he assured me was much frequented by students and Bohemians and where I might observe the famous cancan, and accordingly I had myself set down in the Carrefour de l'Observatoire. The people all about me, issuing from the café or promenading in the street, seemed poorly dressed, the men in rough jackets and mufflers, the women, though the night was bitter, often without cloaks, some even hatless, their mouths luridly rouged. I hesitated on the pavement, feeling suddenly uncomfortable in my sable-lined coat and evening dress, wishing I had gritted my teeth against infection and borrowed some clothes from the servant. I became aware of people staring at me, of raucous laughter, of someone jostling me so that I feared for my few sous. I turned to walk. Three women came towards me, promenading arm in arm. I heard them laughing as I passed and one of them brushed me with her boa.

And then it happened. There was a clicking of high-heeled boots behind me, a hand thrust through my arm. I shook it off, walked faster, but it came again, clutching at my elbow. A voice whispered something vile, the hand with its claw tightened, I inhaled cheap scent and a rancid body smell that made my gorge rise.

With all my force, I hurled the creature from me. I heard a screech, followed by a stream of abuse, but I walked on as fast as I could without running, head down, not looking back. There was an alleyway, stinking, unlit, but I took it, up a flight of steps, along cobblestones, stumbling blindly through puddles, slithering in mire; until at last there was nothing but the sound of my own breathing.

I stopped and found I was still shuddering. Then something scuffled in the darkness, a cat perhaps, or a rat feeding on garbage. My revulsion turned to fear; the threat of robbery came back, of footpads lurking in the shadows of the looming gables. There was a patch of light ahead, a street or a boulevard, and I made for it eagerly, not slackening my pace until I stood in a small square, opposite what seemed to be a café. Though the curtained windows did not look inviting, the square was eerily deserted and I needed to get my bearings. I took a deep breath and went inside.

As I had expected, the place was less than salubrious – zinc-topped tables, deal chairs, walls slimy with the accretions of generations of diners. But at least there were no rouged women to be seen; mercifully, apart from one old crone slumped raggedly over an empty glass, the clientele appeared exclusively male. And indeed, from the raffish mode of dress that prevailed, it seemed I had stumbled upon a hotbed of Bohemianism after all. My entrance attracted the inevitable stares as well as some whisperings, so that I cursed myself once more for not having adopted a disguise, but in an instant or two conversation and laughter became general again. The quartet at the table closest to me looked from their flowing locks and greasy velveteen collars as if they must be artists, and for one daring moment I considered approaching them. But my courage had been somewhat frayed by my earlier experience. I selected a table not far from the door, and, when a boy in a grimy apron appeared, ordered 'Absinthe!' with all the assurance I could muster.

The nectar of artists and poets arrived in a murky tumbler accompanied disconcertingly by a carafe of water and two sugar-lumps. To cover my confusion I reached for my cigarette-case and, as I drew out a cigarette, was suddenly aware of a figure looming over me. A pair of moist eyes, deeply embedded in flesh, surveyed me from under the brim of a rusty black felt hat, a voice at once resonant and honeyed addressed me in English; and without so much as a by-your-leave a portly man of my father's age pulled out the chair opposite me and sat down.

He stared at the cigarette-case for a moment where the light caught it as if he were its genie and I, by the act of touching the gold, had unwittingly summoned him up. Then he addressed me again, this time in French.

'You, monsieur, are a young milord out to taste the ineffable pleasures of this great city. And I, monsieur, am Arsène Maupin, hedonist and bon viveur, pleasure-seeker extraordinary, holder of the key to the garden of all earthly delights – at your service, monsieur.'

It was my first impulse to tell him to make himself scarce. But then I recalled my quest for Bohemian conversation. Though he was hardly prepossessing with his frayed jacket and strip of flannel that served as his necktie, there was nevertheless about his florid manner and his wide-brimmed hat (particularly his refusal to remove it) something promising. An actor, perhaps, with that booming voice. His hands, I noticed, were remarkably white and well-manicured.

I disabused him of my Englishness. He ordered more absinthe and began obligingly to make a confection of mine. It tasted disagreeably bitter, even despite the sugar, but I steeled myself not to wince. And then I made the error of proffering my cigarette case. I had no sooner opened it than a second genie, a youth of about my age, materialised in the chair next to Arsène Maupin.

'Mouche!' sighed my new acquaintance, swatting the youth playfully. 'True to his name as ever, monsieur. Always ready to settle where he perceives a tasty morsel.'

'Or a dungheap,' said Mouche, displaying a row of crooked teeth and sniggering. He was not ill-looking in that highly-coloured way that reminds one of over-ripe fruit. He appeared to be perusing my cigarette case with disquieting interest.

I proffered it to him, but Arsène Maupin laughed. 'Mouche doesn't care for cigarettes, monsieur. Only cigars.'

'Cigars, yes,' said Mouche, sniggering. 'Great big ones from Havana.' And he commenced to undulate his lips in what appeared to be a grotesque parody of his smoking one.

Arsène Maupin laughed heartily for some moments at this performance but then, perceiving me to be less entertained by it, swatted the youth again. 'Away with you, Mouche. Monsieur, as you can see, is a gentleman of sensibility and refinement. An urchin like you – how can you possibly offer monsieur what he is searching for?'

Mouche swore under his breath, helping himself from the cigarette case despite himself, and absently fondling its gold. 'So, old man!' he sneered. 'What is the monsieur searching for?'

Emboldened by the absinthe I explained, then, my desire to talk to poets and aesthetes, to escape just for one night from the intellectual desert in which I was forced to exist. Arsène Maupin listened sympathetically. He had himself, he confessed, heard the Muse in his youth, was even now considered by some to possess a certain poetical genius – here Mouche was seized by such an excessive attack of sniggers that he had to be swatted again – oh, beyond doubt, if I wished to unravel the gilded skein of Calliope, to sit at the feet of the gods, to hear the very music of the spheres, then he, Arsène Maupin, must be my mentor. And, as if to seal the compact, he ordered more absinthe.

The cloudy liquid seemed less noxious now – perhaps I was developing a palate for it. I asked him if he had ever met Baudelaire and Rimbaud and Verlaine. No, he had not actually encountered the gentlemen in person but he possessed friends who had the most intimate dealings with them (here Mouche declared he had once had dealings with Monsieur Verlaine in a pissoir, but my mentor kicked him under the table and instructed me to ignore him for the Philistine he was). In fact these friends, personages of the highest cultivation and aesthetic sense, were by chance attending a little soirée he was presiding over in his modest attic later in the evening. He would esteem it the greatest honour if I would grace his humble gathering with my presence. I said that I would, and we ordered another drink by way of celebration.

The café was filling up now and despite the bitter temperature outside it seemed to have grown abominably hot. I wished I could discard my topcoat, but dared not for fear it would be stolen. Still, it was good to unburden myself at last, to talk of things of the soul with such an understanding listener. And understanding my new acquaintance certainly was, nodding and smiling and filling my glass with rapt, even admiring attention. My heart lifted as I thought how I should spend the small hours in intimate communion with my fellow poets. I asked if they would recite any of their works; he said that they would and he hoped I should honour them with a selection of mine. I assented eagerly and, by way of practice, commenced there and then upon some particularly eloquent verses I had penned 'In Praise of Music'. It was a pity that the poem was in German, so that its finer nuances must be lost, and inconvenient too that, what with a strange buzzing in my ears and a curious thickness of my tongue, I had difficulty sometimes in mastering the words or even remembering them. But I made up for these deficiencies with the panache of my delivery, emphasising each cadence with passion and the appropriate dramatic gestures.

I was gratified at the end of my recital to find the whole café in silence. Then suddenly there was such a cheering and whistling and banging of tables that I felt quite dizzy. And I was just wondering whether I should rise to receive my applause, and Arsène Maupin was murmuring something about 'the artist's duty to disregard Philistines', when I observed that he broke off mid-sentence. Looking up I saw a tall, dark figure standing over our table.

'I regret, monsieur,' said a quiet voice, 'that it is time we took our leave.'

I stared. Though the figure seemed peculiarly indistinct there was something familiar about that voice, those dark clothes.

'But, M. le Curé,' protested Arsène Maupin, 'our young friend is enjoying himself. Besides, we saw him first.'

The voice, suddenly hard, uttered two or three short words I did not understand. Then it addressed me again. 'Forgive my being so late in keeping our appointment. But I am afraid it is now past midnight and we must leave immediately.'

I continued to stare, perplexed. The image before me wavered, grew, solidified, and all at once I was looking up into the gaunt, unsmiling face of the stranger. And I saw what had happened, saw that the Paterfamilias had discovered my escape, had arranged for me to be followed, had sent the stranger to spoil my pleasure and drag me back like a child. Well, I would not go. I had found Paris at last, and I had every intention of accompanying M. Maupin to his *atelier*, where we would recite poetry together. I tried to say as much but my tongue now seemed to fill my mouth. I turned for help to my new friend, but he merely shrugged regretfully.

'If you are engaged to say your prayers with M. le Curé tonight, so be it. I, Arsène Maupin, shall not be the wolf to steal lambs from his flock.'

The stranger had already placed a note on the table and retrieved my hat. Now, with most ungentlemanly firmness, he had me by the arm and was pulling me to my feet. I tried to resist, but for some reason my limbs would not obey my brain. And suddenly I was almost grateful to be bundled so unceremoniously towards the door; for as the night air hit me I realised I was going to be violently sick.

I woke the next morning not remembering how I had reached my bed and with a forge of satanic blacksmiths beating out horseshoes upon my skull. Later, when I was able to focus, I had the cheerful anticipation of the Paterfamilias's wrath. But it did not come. Not at breakfast, not by the time we had embarked for the Gare de Strasbourg. Even on the train the conversation in our saloon was general, the Paterfamilias's eye no more baleful than usual. Perhaps he was too preoccupied with the ordeal of the journey, perhaps he intended to save the full force of his anger until he could make me cower before his desk on the spot where so often I had stood to take the strap. Whatever the reasons, I was grateful for the respite; my face, when I examined it in the glass, was green and I was still seized with periodic fits of vomiting, so that I doubted I had the energy for lies. Nevertheless, it was unlike the Paterfamilias to stay his hand.

The stranger, too, had made no mention of my night's exploits and I had studiously avoided catching his eye. Travelling for the purposes of secrecy as my tutor, he had, of course, slipped quite naturally into the role, watching in silence my father's chess game with Straubnitz, or reading a (doubtless devotional) book. God, how I loathed his sanctimonious modesty – even his box, when it was added to our luggage, had proved smaller than most servants'. Presumably he was sitting there smugly imagining my fate when the thunderbolt eventually struck. At least, I reminded myself, the language difficulty would have prevented him from regaling the Paterfamilias with the details of my debauchery, although I supposed my drunkenness must have proved eloquent enough.

A disagreeable feature of our retiring was that, since the

stranger stood in the guise of my tutor, I was obliged to share a sleeping compartment with him. It was bad enough to share quarters with a person who had once been a footman or to think how his coughing would keep me awake; but above all I scrupled to climb into my nightshirt in full view of someone unknown to me. Mercifully, he did not object to undressing in the dark and, from his stillness, appeared soon to fall asleep.

But to me, who had longed all day for unconsciousness, sleep would not come. I would keep turning over in my mind the Paterfamilias's unexpected clemency, for it was dawning on me slowly that it was capable of only one explanation. He did not know. He had not sent the stranger to follow me, had been equally oblivious to my departure and my return. Miramont had somehow taken it upon himself to go looking for me, had smuggled me back into the Hôtel de Crécy, and bribed my valet to put me to bed, all without my father's being aware of it. But why? Out of altruism? It seemed unlikely. And how had he known where I would be when I had scarcely known myself?

And the alcoholic haze was just lifting from my brain, it was just coming to me that he could not have known, that it had all been an uncanny chance, that the stranger had been in the café for his own reasons, perhaps went there regularly, perhaps was even acquainted with Arsène Maupin, when my thoughts were interrupted by a disturbance from the bunk above.

The stranger was having a nightmare, gasping for breath, shouting out to himself. The sense was garbled at first, unconnected syllables slurred together, until the voice rose to a scream. And then quite suddenly I heard six clear, coherent words, the last of which was 'Fontarelles'.

V

Aunt Helena fainted when she saw the stranger, obliging Winders to revive her with smelling salts. In fact the joy of the two old crones was quite unbridled; their limping Court French could barely keep pace with their questions, or find sufficient interval between their tears. Only Uncle Gustav seem lugubrious and, when the ladies insisted that the stranger must indulge in the inevitable communion with the photograph albums, drew my father away to the privacy of his laboratory. And I, having, as you know, little taste for Aunt Helena's souvenirs, decided I should find it more diverting to tiptoe downstairs and apply my ear to the laboratory keyhole.

It seemed that my father's overwhelming enthusiasm must have made Uncle Gustav cautious, inclined now to take the sceptic's part. 'My dear Leo,' he was saying, 'we must have a care. We must not be too hasty.'

'Hasty? Confound it, man, I've had three long weeks to consider my decision. Miramont's probity is beyond doubt.'

'He's very convincing, I will admit. But you wanted proof, Leo. And there is still none.'

'Then look at the women, how they've taken to him. Perhaps, dashit, they're right. Perhaps there's something more than proof – a feeling, an instinct.'

'Instincts can be mistaken.'

'But he can remember it all – the White Room, the chapel garden, the Tiepolo gallery. And the rest – Mont Rémy, Fontarelles – everything fits with what our agents reported.'

'He knows nothing that Dieter Wolf could not know.'

'But the baptismal certificate, the scar . . .'

'Dieter Wolf could have stolen the papers, Leo. Dieter Wolf could have scarred himself.'

It sounded as if my father brought his fist down upon the experiment bench with a crash. 'Damn you, Gustav! Dieter Wolf was a peasant, born of generations of peasants. This man, this man is—'

'I know, Leo. But we must avoid giving way to emotion. There must be more interrogations. Others must judge, others who are not as close as we are – if it should come to it, a full Court Council.'

'Inevitably. But it won't change what stands out as plainly as the nose on my face. Miramont is Sigismund, as if we'd sat upstairs and talked to his living incarnation. Dammit, Gustav, you can't deny that!'

Uncle Gustav seemed to sigh. 'Well, let us pray he's not precisely the living incarnation. There are some aspects of our late lamented brother I shouldn't wish to—'

But here the voices approached the door and I was obliged to retreat.

In response to Aunt Helena's pleadings, the stranger was billeted at the Villa Narzisse for the next few weeks. The mountain air seemed to agree with him, for he ceased to cough and began to lose his gaunt look, growing, to everyone's satisfaction, daily more in the image of the Lenbach portrait. There were, as Uncle Gustav had predicted, further interrogations, which, though the stranger's German was slowly improving, I was still required to attend. Uncle Gustav himself worked assiduously for some days, laying snares and booby-traps; but finding his quarry easily evaded them he seemed to lose heart and withdrew to the peace of his laboratory, leaving to my father the visits of exiled notables and the other procedures of the investigation.

The stranger continued to survive these assaults unscathed. Though his internal struggle seemed to have abated, he still showed no eagerness to press his claim, still submitted to the inquisition with that unwavering detachment which, in its very refusal to persuade, gave out such a ring of truth. Even I, relaying that calm voice, was almost seduced by it. But then I knew Maxim de Miramont, knew him as no one else could.

It had, of course, begun as we had rattled towards Basle and I had caught the words of his nightmare. The next morning I had examined M. de Miramont in quite a different light. His virtue, his monkishness, was a sham; he frequented disreputable cafés, consorted with *absintheurs* and decadents amongst whom, in the stealth of the night hours, he led a mysterious other life. I even observed that the book he was reading, far from being a religious meditation, was a volume of Alfred de Musset's verses.

No wonder I had been troubled by that wariness of his, that sense of secret things carefully stowed away, for I recalled now what it brought to mind. Not so long ago there had come to my father's study a man who had spent ten years in one of Baron von Schramm's jails, alternating forced labour with prolonged spells of solitary confinement; and this man had possessed just such a still watchfulness, as if the habit of subterfuge were so ingrained in him it could never be shaken off: he had been given supper, I remember, and we had looked on astonished as, curling his hand around the bread by his plate, with a movement at once rapid and subtle he had drawn it into his palm, abstracting it instinctively from thieving eyes. Just so, I thought, had the stranger learnt to look distrustfully over his shoulder, until his control had become a habit of mind and his reserve a weapon.

His denials, his reluctance, even his apparent struggle with himself had all been part of a calculated plan, the tricks by which a consummate actor builds his performance. Oh, he might trade upon his chance likeness to Uncle Sigismund, but now when I examined his story I came upon elements I refused to believe: nothing factual, but rather instinctive doubts founded on my sudden sense of knowing him. His description of the carters attacking Dieter Wolf, for instance: 'I ran,' he had said, and then added in a low voice; 'I was afraid. I am not proud of it.' I did not believe he would ever give way to fear as he described – I might have run, but not he. He was as tall as my father and now that he was recovering his health there was little about his physical presence which suggested weakness. I did not believe Dieter Wolf had been the stronger fighter. And if I did not believe that, then I must believe he was lying.

Why did I not tell the Paterfamilias my doubts, why did I not repeat the words of the stranger's nightmare and shatter the old fool's fantasy before it was too late? Heaven knows I still resented Miramont, still could not watch without a knot in my stomach Aunt Helena and Winders lavishing upon him all the devotion they had once reserved for me.

But now, now that I suspected he was a fraud I felt for him – not admiration exactly, only fools slavishly admire others – but nevertheless a kind of kinship. That sense of intimacy I felt in being his mouthpiece, which once I had found so unwelcome, I now cultivated with postive pleasure. There was something in working with him so closely day after day, about the two of us being, as it were, an indivisible team of tongues and lips and voices, that caught me up, so that when he was threatened so was I; when he triumphed it was my triumph; so that slowly, stealthily we came together, ranged ourselves against our adversaries as one front. We had scarcely otherwise passed any but the most banal conversational exchanges (the café episode had mercifully never been mentioned); yet nevertheless a whole conspiracy of signs seemed to have grown up between us, an understanding of the smallest glance or quirk of the lips. Now, when at the conclusion of my duties he would direct at me his smile of thanks – that strange unforced smile that seemed to grant me for an instant a glimpse of his hidden persona – I did not look away disdainfully but made sure always to return it. It seemed a recognition of our secret brotherhood, in which we fought the rest of the world shoulder to shoulder.

For they had underestimated him, the Paterfamilias and his crew, just as they perpetually underestimated me. They set value on honour and duty and brute obedience, sneered at intelligence and subtlety. And now he was taking them through the hoops, this clever, calculating man, making idiots of the lot of them. The very thought of it filled me with mirth and made me his willing accessory. And besides, my knowledge was mine alone; for the first time in my life I tasted a delicious sense of power.

The day arrived inevitably for the stranger to undergo his final test, for him to be interrogated by that ultimate absurdity in my father's phantasmagoria of absurdities, the Council of the Sigismundite Court in exile. They would come, furtive and incognito, dreading the omniscience of Schramm's agents, from all the byways of Europe; General Keller from Thalia, from his post as commander of my father's private army; the English cousin, the Duke of Hohen-Kastell and Carrick, a great, lumbering doorpost of a man, who pleased my father because he wore a cavalry uniform and had seen action in the Transvaal; the exiled Bishop of Marmion; and even the Cardinal Archbishop himself, smuggled into Switzerland under cover of a journey to Rome so that his treachery to King Friedrich should not be detected. There was another traitor to Schramm's regime too, whose arrival occasioned more than the usual flourish of cloaks and daggers: my father's spy within the Rosenholm Cabinet itself, Count Vielfrass, the legendarily slippery Minister of the Interior, head of the feared State Police. The

very mention of this unexpected conspirator seemed deeply
to unsettle Uncle Gustav, who was, in name at least,
supposed to preside over the proceedings.

'For Heaven's sake, Leo, the fellow's a snake. Who's
to say he isn't in Schramm's pocket all the while, isn't
simply biding his time till he has enough evidence to betray
us—'

'My dear Gustav, we shan't succeed without his support.'

'The only cause Vielfrass supports is his own.'

'He'll support whoever wins. And he'll see now that we're
the winning side. Dashit, we have all the cards. We only
need to convince him of it.'

And convince him we should. My father, with the strength
of his own unshakeable conviction, would see to that. Apart
from Vielfrass the only other likely sceptic was thought to
be Keller, who, because of his proletarian origins, was
rumoured to harbour secret inclinations towards a republic;
but Keller possessed neither money nor influence and could
be talked round. My father's eyes already glittered with
visions of the triumphal procession through Rosenholm,
with the stranger gloriously caparisoned in all the trappings
of kingship and he himself riding just a pace behind.

In keeping with the best traditions of melodrama, the
convocation was to take place at eight in the evening, so that
the conspirators could arrive at the Villa Narzisse under
cover of darkness and depart before dawn. At seven-thirty
the rumble of carriage wheels muffled by straw began to be
heard in the courtyard, servants glided noiselessly to open
the great South doors. In the hall, beneath the Florentine
frescos, old friends met and exchanged whispered greetings
– faded dignatories plucked from obscure exile in Vienna or
Paris, the ex-Foreign Minister with his ear-trumpet, the
former Cabinet Secretary, and Baron von Leinsdorf, of
course, trundled in a bathchair by his faithful valet. Private
secretaries scuttled this way and that with folios of transcripts; in the Peacock Drawing-room Aunt Helena twittered,
with Winders loyally holding in readiness smelling salts and
eau de cologne. And through it all, in his full dress Field-
Marshal's uniform jangling with orders and decorations,
strode my father, welcoming, shepherding, drawing allies
into corners for confidential asides, his whiskers bristling

with authority, the very rigour of his cavalry corset seeming to betoken some godgiven prerogative over truth.

In the ballroom, on gilded chairs set out as if for a concert party, they began, with much clacking of canes and creaking of arthritic joints, gradually to take their places. The last to arrive was a tall man, foppishly dressed and thin as a stick insect, who from the instant of hush occasioned by his appearance – a drawing-away as if the room had suddenly been filled with a contagion – I took to be Count Vielfrass. Disdaining to exchange a word with anyone, he seated himself at the far end of the front row. He was, to be sure, an unprepossessing creature, with dyed hair and rouged lips and eyes that seemed to flicker about him with the furtive concupiscence of an elderly madame estimating trade. Several times, to my surprise, I found his glance upon me, and there was something in it, at once fishy and rapacious, which made me look away in haste.

My father, I shall give him due credit, had stage-managed the whole business admirably. At the far end of the ballroom beneath the Lenbach portrait, on either side of the dais, sat Gebhardt and I, scribe and translator. On the dais itself stood a single high-backed carved and gilded chair, one of a pair attributed to the sculptor Antonio Corradini and acquired by Sigismund during an incognito excursion to Venice. On precisely the last stroke of eight my father took his place amongst the rest of the company; the excited babble stilled and all eyes were at once focused on the empty throne with the two of us stationed like pages beneath, and the flamboyant image of the royal Grand Master towering above us. There was a moment's pause. Then the lofty double doors leading to the left-hand antechamber were opened from within and the stranger came through them.

The assembled elders seemed as a body to draw breath. The Cardinal Archbishop crossed himself, several others appeared about to rise. Even Count Vielfrass looked visibly disconcerted. The stranger mounted the dais and took his seat beneath the portrait. He was dressed, as usual, in his drab priest's black, which seemed more than ever to point up his air of asceticism. Yet there could be no mistaking the resemblance; rather, the contrast between the splendour of the painted image and the austerity of the real one seemed to heighten the effect, to emphasise the uncanny coincidence of those two dark, handsome faces.

He must have been aware of the impact he had made but he gave no sign of it. Instead, with his actor's skills, he seemed to build upon my father's *coup de théâtre*, holding the dumbfounded stare of his audience, eyes unflinching, head erect, prolonging the moment until the full measure of drama had been wrung from it. I glanced up at him for indications of nervousness, but he sat easily, his hands resting lightly on the gilt-encrusted arms of his throne.

At last, as if he sensed my eyes upon him, he turned towards me, smiling slightly, a smile, I was chagrined to observe, of encouragement, as if it were I, not he, who needed bolstering. The moment was broken. Uncle Gustav, from his table on the right of the dais, coughed uncertainly and proceeded to stumble through the notice convening the Council.

VI

It was one o'clock in the morning before they had heard all the evidence, and I had been obliged to have frequent recourse to the carafe of water at my elbow to prevent myself from losing my voice. The stranger, on the other hand, still sat calm and erect, showing no signs of fatigue. We had gone through the authentication of the seals on the Mont Rémy papers and the identification of the portrait ring; we had heard the opinion of two doctors that the scar on the stranger's forehead was not of recent origin and certainly could have been present since childhood; we had listened to Aunt Helena's fluttering recollections of the infant Crown Prince and Winders' loyal endorsement. My father had testified, and Uncle Gustav, and Baron von Leinsdorf. The stranger himself had sustained detailed questioning on the transcripts of his own statements, answering everything with his usual dispassionate frankness. He seemed unperturbed by the spasmodic aggression of Keller and the clumsy probings of the Duke of Hohen-Kastell, was easily able to extricate himself from the Foreign Minister's crude snares. You could sense the company beginning, one by one, to surrender, exhausted by the hour and the effort of concentration, unable to resist the unwavering self-possession of the man or the sheer suggestive power of the mirror-image hanging on the wall. Despite my fatigue, I experienced a growing elation, that curious feeling of kinship again, of having fought beside him and won.

Then Count Vielfrass, dabbing his lips with a silk handkerchief, rose to his feet, addressing the stranger for the first time, in a lisping, almost wheedling tone, his head cocked to one side like an elderly parakeet.

'M. de Miramont, you have been most patient with us. And most persuasive. I have seldom seen a witness give such a good account of himself under cross-examination, or so admirably convey the impression of unimpeachable integrity.'

I fancied the stranger's mouth tightened a little, but he did not answer, merely raising his eyebrows.

'Of course – as you yourself admit with such engaging frankness – you offer us no proof. But why should we doubt the word of one who is so transparently honourable and upright?'

Still the stranger did not reply. The parakeet surveyed him, bright-eyed, for an instant; then turned quite without warning into a raven.

'Of course you are aware, monsieur, that the late Marquis's surviving relatives, his sister and his niece, hold no such estimate of your character? In fact, they consider you to be the worst sort of adventurer.'

The stranger's face did not move. 'Yes,' he said quietly. 'I am aware of it.'

'They believe you endeavoured to influence the Marquis to change his will in your favour, do they not?'

'I understand so, yes.'

'And there was much at stake – three estates, apart from the house in Paris, and a fortune of some several million francs.'

'Again, yes.'

'But in the end the old man left you nothing. Only a mention in the will and a pair of antique duelling pistols of no use or value. That must have been a disappointment to you?'

'No. It happened at my insistence. I did not wish to deprive his family of what was theirs by right.'

'Oh, come now, monsieur! You had grown used to all the comforts and luxuries of an aristocrat's household. Are you now telling us you were perfectly content to give it all up and go out tutoring?'

For the first time a breach seemed to be forged in the stranger's defences. Though he remained outwardly calm, I saw his hands clench upon the arms of his throne, heard his voice all at once very low. 'I did not want the money. He had already given me his protection and his love. And no amount of money, no estates could compensate for what I had lost by his death.'

My father sprang to his feet. 'Gustav, call the Count to order! I cannot see what is to be gained by this line of questioning.'

'Very well,' said Vielfrass, suddenly the parakeet again, bill on one side, crest playfully unfurled. 'I desist. I merely ask the distinguished members of this Council, since we are all men of the world – even M. de Miramont, despite the saintly air he has acquired from the cloister – is it probable that a penniless youth, seeing the chance to lay his hands upon a very considerable fortune, would forgo such a chance on grounds of mere sentiment? However, be that as it may, let us return to the main question, the question of the substantive proof with which M. de Miramont is lamentably unable to provide us. I trust,' here he swooped upon the stranger again, 'I trust, monsieur, you would not be averse to the production of such proof, should this by some miracle be possible?'

Again I thought the stranger was taken off his guard, though he replied levelly enough. 'No, of course not. I should welcome it.'

'I am obliged to you, monsieur. I have the means, you see, to prove precisely who – and what – you are.'

With a magician's sleight of hand, as if he had been hiding it all the time in the folds of his handkerchief, Count Vielfrass produced a little bell which he rang sharply. Immediately the doors of the anteroom opened to reveal a trio of figures. Two of them I took, from the conspicuous ordinariness of their ill-fitting worsteds, to be Vielfrass's agents. But it was the third to whom all eyes were drawn, a figure so down-at-heel and shabby, so thoroughly deformed by all the degra-dations and vicissitudes of poverty that the assembly burst out into a babble of astonishment. He – for the apparition was just discernably male – bore the emaciation of a once-corpulent man, withered flesh hanging in folds beneath eyes and jowl, quivering, as he quivered, with a St Vitus tremor. His hunched frame was girt with a mangy blanket of indeter-minate colour, tied with string at the middle like a rolled-up rug. His scanty hair and beard were greasy, his nose ran, his jaw lolled, he seemed to give off, even at a distance, the whiff of a hundred low taverns. Balked of flight by his impassive escort, he turned his head this way and that with a bewildered, unfocused stare.

'This,' said Count Vielfrass, with an impresario's wave of his handkerchief, 'is Jean Marrain, formerly Brother Jean of the Benedictine community at Mont Rémy.'

Instinctively I glanced up at the stranger; this time there was no mistaking it, he had grown noticeably paler.

The Count permitted himself a smirk. 'I think, with Brother Jean's assistance, we may solve the problem of M. de Miramont's identity once and for all.'

The creature between the two policemen had continued to gaze about him blearily. Now he suddenly let out a squawk: 'Pity me, Excellency! When Dom Ignatius was chosen as the new Abbot, he expelled me from the cloister, put me out on the road. Pity a humble old man who only wants a crust of bread! Don't beat me, Excellency, don't set your dogs on me!'

Though his French was slurred, almost patois, I had begun to struggle with a translation; but the Count cut me off. 'Silence! The witness will only speak when he is addressed.'

As though obedient to a cue, the taller of the two poli-cemen raised his hand and cuffed the mendicant twice about the jowls, very neatly and precisely, as if he were dusting him. The creature let out a yelp.

'Now, Jean Marrain,' said Vielfrass, well satisfied, 'you know why you are here.'

'If you please, Excellency, they promised me soup and a bed for the night – that's all I know. Then they took me by train and carriage and brought me to this place. But I done nothing wrong, Excellency, not since I stole the chicken at Aix which, God is my witness, I wouldn't have done if hunger hadn't tempted me, hunger and cold and—'

Again the Count cut through my translation, again the mendicant was neatly dusted off. I observed that the stranger had grown even paler, that his knuckles on the arms of the chair were white.

'You are here, Jean Marrain, because during your time as a lay brother at Mont Rémy you assisted in the escape of two of your fellow monks. You knew them as Dom François and Dom Paul. But, through your sinful curiosity, you also knew the secret of their true identities—'

'Pity me, Excellency! I been punished for my sins—'

'You knew that Dom François was a worthless peasant, one Dieter Wolf. But the insignia on the papers of the other, Dom Paul, told you he was of quite a different rank.'

'Please, Excellency, pity me—'

'Dom François and Dom Paul, peasant and prince – you knew them both so well that even today you could pick out either one of them – to avoid a beating and perhaps earn a bowl of soup for your pains.'

At the mention of this gastronomic enticement the mendicant seemed to brighten. He stopped whimpering and began to sniff the air as if he could already smell the seductive aroma of the stockpot. 'Oh yes, even after all these years, Excellency, I could tell them apart for you. As different as chalk and cheese they was, Dom Paul so fond of penances and fasting and Dom François such a wicked rogue—'

The raven swooped. 'Wicked, you say? So Dom François was not in your opinion a chaste and obedient servant of God?'

'He was sometimes wild, Excellency, yes, that's true. But then they was all high-spirited when they worked in the fields with us. Boys of sixteen, seventeen, it was like a prison to them, being beaten with rods at Culps, and kneeling for hours, and licking crosses on the chapel floor for one of Dom Ignatius's penances. If they was larky now and then, sampled the cider when the Brother Workmaster wasn't looking, who's to blame them? We used to hide in the pig-shed, I remember. We'd give the old sow a drink or two to keep her quiet and she'd roll over on her side and snore fit to deafen you.'

A murmur of suppressed laughter ran through the assembly. Although the mendicant appeared in imminent danger of being dusted again, the thought of soup had apparently emboldened him, for he continued indignantly: 'They was happy times, and they was good boys. I've known brothers pray and fast till they was blue and sleep on boards with iron chains around their waists, and still not be good for all that—'

Vielfrass flapped his handkerchief impatiently. 'Enough, enough! We do not require a sermon. We require simply that you should look at the man seated over there and tell us who he is. Is he the virtuous Dom Paul? Or the sinful Dom François?'

A silence fell in which the assembly focused intently upon the stranger on his dais and the mangy figure not two metres away from him. But despite their proximity, despite the confidence of his previous assertions, the mendicant seemed to dither, casting his gaze first in Count Vielfrass's direction, then in mine, and then wildly upon the assembly at large. He shuffled his feet, began to whimper.

Count Vielfrass repeated his question. 'Tell us, please, whom you see. Dom Paul or Dom François?'

Again I was conscious of the rheumy eyes trained first towards the Count and then towards me as I translated, but obstinately refusing to fix themselves upon the face of the stranger with any spark of recognition. The silence in the body of the assembly was now intense, and I could feel geriatric bones and wasted muscles straining, willing the mendicant to utter some response. But though his whimpering grew, though there was an expression on his face as if the soup were there before him, steaming and aromatic yet just out of reach, still he said nothing.

I was aware of a stirring amongst the old men on their hard chairs, a rustle of disappointment, the first rumblings of hostility. Glancing at the stranger, I saw that his lips were bloodless, that the blanched knuckles now grasped the chair as if he held himself in it only with difficulty.

I too was overwhelmed by a huge disappointment. I had been so certain we should win. I had so looked forward to our manipulating these old men, showing them for the senile idiots they were. I could not bear to be balked of our victory now, defeated by this parvenu Vielfrass with his satyr's leer, and by a flea-bitten old tramp.

I repeated the Count's question again, this time laying delicate emphasis on the first of the two names. But though the shorter of the policemen added a kick on the shins for good measure, the mendicant continued to gaze at me confusedly, saying nothing.

Vielfrass fluttered his handkerchief reprovingly. 'Our delightful young translator must not lead the witness. I shall, however, repeat my question one last time.'

But the repetition had no effect. The mendicant seemed to struggle tragically with his fading vision of soup. Then his eyes rolled, his whimpering grew to an agonised squawk. 'I don't see no one. Please, Excellency, don't beat me! Please have pity on a humble old man—!'

A further dusting abruptly silenced him. Wheeling from the cringing form and quelling the universal murmur with one sweep of his dark wing, Count Vielfrass dived, the raven of justice, upon his audience.

'You observe, gentlemen, that Jean Marrain does not answer. But his silence, in itself, speaks volumes, does it not? More powerfully than words it condemns this man who calls himself Maxim de Miramont, who claims to be the Crown Prince Maximilian, as a despicable fraud.

'Let us consider for a moment our two young Benedictines, Dom Paul and Dom François. And let me construct for you, gentlemen, a scenario rather different from the one M. de Miramont has given us. Dom Paul is a pious and obedient servant of God. Dom François, on the other hand, is unchaste, unscrupulous and, in short, an adventurer. When he perceives his sins have found him out and he is threatened with expulsion from the monastery, he concocts a plan of survival. Convincing the innocent Dom Paul that his life is in danger, he persuades him to run away. On the road to Fontarelles he murders Dom Paul and steals his papers, thinking to claim his birthright. Why then does he not immediately do so? Because when he reaches Paris he finds an easier method of survival, a gullible nobleman whom he hopes to bleed of his fortune. But when the Marquis dies, leaving him nothing, he is thrown back on his original plan. And so, plausible as ever, he prevails upon the good Baron Leinsdorf to further his cause, insinuates himself with Their Royal Highnesses and now, at last, appears before this august assembly hoping to deceive you all. Which he might easily have done, were it not for one obstacle, the presence of this man here,' – Vielfrass wafted his handkerchief in the direction of the mendicant – 'this Jean Marrain, who, though a contemptible creature, is the one person living who can identify the true Dom Paul.

'But Jean Marrain is silent. He lies, he prevaricates, he claims to recognise no one. Your Royal Highnesses, Noble Sirs, gentlemen, do we in honesty believe that Brother Jean sees neither of the two boys in this room? Or is it more probable that he is silent because when he looks on the face of the young man before us he sees, not Dom Paul, the virtuous monk, the true Crown Prince Maximilian, but his cider-swilling companion of the pig-sty, the swindler of the Marquis de Miramont, the murderer of Maximilian, Dom François, Dieter Wolf.'

Here Count Vielfrass paused, dabbing his lips with his handkerchief and taking a small step backwards, as if better to survey the effect of his oratory. My eyes, however, were fixed upon the mendicant, noting again how his gaze seemed to travel with the pattern of our words, from Vielfrass declaiming to myself translating, as if there were no one else in the room. On occasions where our voices coincided he seemed to dither helplessly, struggling to focus on one or the other, torn between the two. I remembered his bewildered stare when he had first been thrust upon us, and all at once a thought began to take shape in my head which my father took from me, rising to his feet.

'My dear Count, it is possible this wretched man speaks nothing but the truth when he says he sees no one. Gustav, instruct my son to ask the fellow if he is blind.'

The misted eyes immediately followed the direction of my voice. 'Not blind exactly, Excellency. I can see colours, shapes of things. Cataracts, the sisters at Aix said, and nothing to be done about them – God's punishment for my sins. Oh, I can see this much.' Grotesquely, he raised one finger and, controlling its tremor with the greatest difficulty, succeeded in holding it within a few centimetres of his nose. 'I can see that all right. But faces, eyes, mouths – they're just one blur to me.'

His demonstration had been sufficiently explicit; before I had even concluded my translation uproar had broken out. While Vielfrass screamed at his agents, calling them dolts and bunglers, the assembly, led by my father, was shouting that he should withdraw his witness. The beggar squawked. Uncle Gustav called in vain for order. Even the ex-Foreign Minister thrust forward his ear-trumpet eagerly.

Vielfrass lowered his handkerchief like a flag of surrender. 'Very well, I withdraw. Throw the creature back onto the midden where he belongs!'

'No!' The voice came with the sharpness of ice cracking, turning all our eyes upon the stranger. Though he sat very straight and still, there was no mistaking the glance with which he fixed Vielfrass, and I realised that the pallor, the clenched hands upon the chair, had betokened, not fear as I had imagined, but a white-hot, scarcely-contained anger. 'I can no longer sit here and watch this poor old man bullied and frightened by your hired thugs. He has suffered sufficiently on my account. You will give him food and money and make sure he is returned safely to France. I require an undertaking from you, Count, a personal undertaking that he will come to no further harm.'

I could not help but observe the effect of these tones upon the beggar, for from the moment he heard them he appeared to undergo the most extraordinary transformation. His wattled face, his dim eyes were all at once suffused with a joyful radiance, he seemed to grow and expand with it as if he had suddenly been translated back to a younger, altogether more prepossessing version of himself. His arms jerked, his shoulders heaved, with an unexpected access of strength he tore free of his escort and staggered, arms outstretched, in the direction of the dais.

'My friend, is it you? Is it you they brought me all this way for? As God is my judge, I never expected to hear your voice again after all these years.'

Here the mendicant flung himself forward as if he would prostrate himself before the stranger, but collided with the dais instead and crashed sprawling across it. Though

Gebhardt and I sprang to our feet, the stranger was there before us, lifting Brother Jean beneath the arms until he had him upright, then holding him there, steadying him gently.

Excitement within the body of the assembly had reached fever pitch. 'Dammit, Anton,' I could my father bellowing, 'the man knows him! Ask the fellow, damn you, ask him who it is!'

'Know him? I'd know that voice anywhere. A true friend he was, when others would sooner spit on me—'

'Yes, but who is he? Dieter Wolf or Prince Maximilian?'

A suspicious look came over the mendicant's face, he turned his rheumy eyes anxiously upon the stranger. 'Are you in trouble, my friend? Is this some sort of trial?'

The stranger, smiling faintly, put his hand to the old man's cheek. 'No,' he said gently, 'I am not on trial.'

'Then what shall I tell them?'

'I think,' said the stranger gently and gravely, 'you must tell them the truth.'

I observed a curious expression pass over the mendicant's face, at once enlightened and triumphant, as if he at last perceived cabbage soup, cabbage soup with sausage and dumplings, a whole fragrant tureen of it steaming before him. He gave a lurch, staggering in a half-circle and endeavouring to face the company.

'If you want your true prince, then you have him. A prince among men, a prince by nature, who'd wake me up when I'd taken a drop or two, not kick me or piss on me like some of the Choir, because I was a lay brother and no better than a servant—'

'Is he Dom Paul, the Crown Prince Maximilian?'

'Your Royal Highness,' interjected Vielfrass waspishly, 'there is no point in pressing the witness. His testimony is already discredited.'

'He's the true Prince, before God I swear it. Find the ring that was with the papers – he's the living image of the face carved on it. But if you don't believe me, Excellency, let me swear to it, let me swear the most solemn and sacred oath!'

'Brother Jean should not be forced to swear any oath on my behalf,' said the stranger sharply. 'He has already been frightened and humiliated enough.'

Vielfrass turned away with a contemptuous shrug. 'There

is no need. It is perfectly evident he would swear his grand-mother was the Archangel Gabriel if he thought it would suit. I repeat, he is a discredited witness. Take him away!'

'Discredited, Count?' said the Cardinal Archbishop. 'I think not. Though the unfortunate man is blind, he has just described M. de Miramont to us exactly.'

'In fact, my dear Vielfrass,' said my father, 'he seems to have provided us with the very proof of identity you felt we lacked.'

There was a silence as the police agents moved to repossess their charge. But the stranger placed a hand on the beggar's arm so that they were obliged to hold back.

'I asked for a guarantee of Brother Jean's safety. I have not yet received it.'

The hostile eye of the assembly was now fixed on Vielfrass. My father and the Duke of Hohen-Kastell urged him not to prevaricate, even Keller joined his voice with theirs. The Count gave the stranger a frigid look which was answered with equal coldness. Then he curled his lip. 'Very well, monsieur. You have my guarantee.'

The leave-taking which followed was of the most touching kind. The democratic and unsparing manner in which the stranger, apparently oblivious to the filth and stench, embraced the mendicant on both cheeks, the beggar's tearful clutching of the stranger's hand, pressing it to his lips and slobbering kisses over it before he was led away, could not but move the company to fellow feeling. You could hear the rustle of relief, the stiffened limbs stretching themselves now doubt had been dispelled, the little coughs and croaks of appreciation.

Glancing at Count Vielfrass, I thought he was only too aware of the effect of this farewell scene and how it served to augment the hostility towards him. Not only had he failed to win his point, he had succeeded in polarising in the stranger's favour whatever last vestiges of sympathy might previously have remained unengaged. No longer the raven, he gave the impression now of a vulture who has just been unseasonably deprived of a particularly juicy corpse. And I was wondering how he would recover himself when, with another of his lightning metamorphoses, he confounded us all by turning back into the parakeet, head cocked, voice lisping, favouring his audience with his most ingratiating of smiles.

'Well, gentlemen, I have played devil's advocate and I have satisfied myself of any lingering doubt, as I hope I have satisfied you. I offer no further challenge to the manifest probity of the man before us.'

'Thank you, my dear Count,' said my father, casting his glance in the direction of the portrait. 'May we commend your courage in challenging what to the rest of us is already patent from the evidence of our own eyes.'

Sneaking a sideways look at the stranger, I saw he seemed suddenly tired as if, at last, he felt able to relax his guard. 'Gentlemen,' he said quietly, 'you will forgive me, but I feel I have now answered all the questions it is in my power to answer.'

Then he rose from his chair and walked slowly down the steps of the dais and out of the ballroom.

I was in the antechamber almost before I knew I had followed him. It had seemed natural, fitting somehow, that I, his voice, his alter ego, his fellow warrior, should join him in victory. Oh, they would spend another two or three hours deliberating, old codgers chewing things over with their toothless gums. But the outcome was inevitable. I felt light-headed, felt an overwhelming impulse to burst into peals of exultant laughter.

Though I soon caught up with him, he did not turn until we were out of the anteroom and into the hall.

'Congratulations, Your Royal Highness!' I said.

He smiled wryly. 'My dear Tarn, don't you think that's a trifle premature?'

'Not a bit of it,' I said. 'The whole performance was wonderful. I've never seen anything so pleasing as the dreadful Count Vielfrass discovering he was the last rat aboard his own sinking ship.'

Suddenly we were standing there, the two of us, laughing, and his hand was resting lightly on my shoulder; and I was struck by the realisation that in all our hours together, in all the subtleties of our curious intimacy, this was the only time, apart from the night in the café, that there had ever been any physical contact between us. I found myself staring into his handsome, inscrutable face, grateful for our proximity, yet also made uneasy by it.

He smiled and squeezed my shoulder gently. 'Thank you, Tarn, for being my voice so skilfully and patiently these past weeks.' Then he turned towards the staircase.

I don't know why – perhaps I wanted to cement our kinship, to prove to him, if he still doubted it, that I was clever too, of a more exalted species than the likes of my father – or perhaps I quite simply wanted to call him back – but it came upon me all at once to test my power, the knowledge that set me apart from the others, the memory of the words he had uttered in the darkness of our sleeping compartment.

'Tell me, Sir,' I called after him, 'who was the devil you met and fought at Fontarelles?'

I had caught him off balance, there was no mistaking it. The set of his shoulders perceptibly changed, he paused with his hand upon the marble of the balustrade. But when he turned back, he was still smiling, unperturbed.

'A personal devil. One of my own conjuring,' he said. Then he began to ascend the stairs.

CHAPTER THREE

Marie Bathildis

I

'I won't,' I cried. 'King Friedrich is still my husband, in my eyes and in the eyes of God.'

Prince von Ansbach once more assayed his avuncular expression. 'My dear Marie, the annulment is proceeding without a hitch. So far as the Almighty is concerned, the unfortunate Friedrich might never have existed.'

'If God appears to have so much regard for the powerful and so little for the weak I'm afraid I must begin to question His existence—'

'Child!' The Prince's hawk brows shot upwards and he abandoned all attempt at conciliation. 'A show of spirit in a woman can be a fine thing – for certain women and on certain occasions. You are not one of those women. You have been brought up to know your duty and to be obedient to it. If His Grand Ducal Highness could observe you now, defying his express wishes, descending even to blasphemy—'

'My uncle blasphemes everything I hold sacred!'

'Marriage to a drooling idiot who hasn't even the spunk to take his rights? By God, at least Maximilian is a proper man!'

'A man who preys upon the weak and innocent, a man who cares for nothing but power?'

'A man with red blood in his veins, who'll beat this nonsense out of you, my girl, who'll teach you what it is to be a woman!'

Once again, as on numberless occasions during the bitter winter weeks since Maximilian's visit, I felt my eyes burn. 'Sir, you presume upon the years you have known me. You are not the Grand Duke, but his servant. You will remember to whom you are speaking and show the respect due to my rank. And you will refer to His Majesty King Friedrich with respect too.'

He stared at me for a moment, his crimson cheeks swelling as if he were gargling corked wine. I could not bear him to see my tears and turned my head away.

'Please,' I said eventually, 'could you not explain to my uncle how wretched this makes me? Could you not beg him to show some mercy?'

'His Highness does not regard it as unmerciful to expect Your Majesty to understand her duty.'

'Oh, I know he always hated my mother, that he despises me. But, all the same, if he realised how repugnant Maximilian was to me – if Maximilian himself knew. There must be several princesses, Hapsburgs, Hesses, who are beautiful and clever and would suit him far better than I.'

'There are no suitable princesses who are also Catholic. And besides there is the question of the treaty between our two countries.'

'My uncle, it seems, has scant respect for that!'

'On the contrary, Your Majesty, Sylvania's new situation makes him value it highly. The Thalian-Sylvanian railway link with Austro-Hungary has, as you know, always been a project dear to His Grand Ducal Highness' heart.'

I stared at him. 'Do you mean His Majesty has been betrayed, I am to be sold for – for a railway?'

'Trade links, Your Majesty. His Highness is most enthusiastic. He has even ordered the construction of a new royal train to make the inaugural run, has sketched out the designs himself.'

I continued to stare at him for a moment. He had laced his fingers together, thick fingers, meaty as blood sausages, and was contemplating the effect.

'I won't!' I burst out. 'Maximilian is a monster. I won't marry him, I won't!'

'My dear Marie' – he had returned to his avuncular manner, yet there glinted in his bulging eyes a flash of menace – 'my dear girl, I fear you have no choice. In a few weeks' time you and your precious Friedrich will cease to be man and wife, even in name. And if you don't marry Maximilian you'll have no income and nowhere to go. The

Grand Duke, you know, won't, under any circumstances, take you back.'

'I don't want to go back to Thalia anyway,' I said. 'And I wouldn't take a *pfennig* from Uncle Berthold, even if he tried to force it on me.'

'Hush, Ma'am,' said Rosa, settling me back on my pillows. 'You're wearing yourself to a shadow with all this crying and carrying on.'

'I only want to be with my husband. If Maximilian would have some pity, if he'd let us go into exile, go to England, anywhere . . .'

'I swear,' said Rosa, clicking her tongue reprovingly, 'the pillowcase was wet enough this morning to give Your Majesty pneumonia – or a nasty bout of neuralgia at the very least.'

'We don't need money, His Majesty and I. I'm used to nursing him. And I'm strong, I could work.'

There was, I thought, the fleeting trace of a smile on Rosa's face as she handed me the cup of camomile tea she had made me.

'But I could!' I said, wiping my eyes and sitting up indignantly. 'I can sew, I could get work as a seamstress.'

'Poverty, Ma'am, is only romantic to them who've never tried it.'

'If His Majesty and I were together we could bear anything—'

'One room to sleep and eat in, with the cowshed next door and both sluiced out into the yard from the same bucket? Potatoes and cabbage soup and a bit of sausage in the soup once a week if you're lucky? Oh, I know Ma'am, believe me. There was a time before I went into service with His Grand Ducal Highness . . ' Her peasant face broadened gently as she shook her head. 'You can't just take up poverty on a fancy, Ma'am, you've got to be bred for it. And besides, His Majesty needs doctors and medicines. Who'd pay for that?'

'My English relations will help us. My mother's cousins. They'd never let us starve.'

She sighed as she took the teacup from me. 'I don't mean to meddle, Ma'am, and I don't mean any disrespect - you

know I don't – and far be it from me to speak ill of His
Majesty King Friedrich, him always so sick and suffering it
like a very saint, with never anything but a kind word for
everyone – but . . .'

I glanced at her suspiciously. 'But what, Rosa?'

'Well, as I say, Ma'am, King Friedrich was a saint, a true
Christian—'

'The past tense, Rosa?'

'Thank God, His Majesty still lives, may Our Blessed Lady
watch over him. But as a husband – for a pretty young
girl—'

'I am not pretty. Don't say such things.'

'For a girl with spirit, in the first bloom of her youth –
Your Majesty needs a man who is strong, who can protect
her and love her as a man should.'

I stared at her, shocked. 'You too, Rosa? Even you?'

'They say there's many at Court who envy Your Majesty.
They say King Maximilian's set all the ladies' hearts aflutter.'

'Aflutter for the rank, the position, no doubt. While I, who
once possessed it, know it is nothing.'

'But he's handsome, Your Majesty. You can't deny that.'

'To those harpies at Court an unmarried king is always
handsome.'

'Handsome and strong with a clever head on his shoulders
– his own man, so they say. And, begging your pardon,
Ma'am, there's some who might say, too, that it's not healthy
for Your Majesty to spend her life like a nun in the cloister,
that it's high time she had a good man to show her – well,
those things that turn a girl into a woman.'

Christmas passed, a bleak and lonely time, with no visitors,
and still no news of Freddy. Schwanensee, in winter, took
on its most forbidding aspect. The lake froze and our view
of it, and of the mountains beyond, was obscured for days
by snowstorms, so that all sense of a world outside was lost
to us, smothered in a thick, impenetrable blanket of grey
which, deadening sound and sight, made us feel we had
been deprived of every faculty save one, the capacity to
suffer cold. For, muffle ourselves as we might in shawls
and mittens, the bitter wind, sweeping from the mountains
across the lake, sending the snowflakes whirling and spat-

tering against our window-panes, seemed to creep in every-where, through floorboards and ill-fitting sashes, through the very stone itself, so that the water in my bedside carafe was frozen by morning, the milk grew a crust of ice on the long journey upstairs from the kitchens and even the locks and hinges on the doors were stiff with tiny icicles.

Towards the end of January men were sent with spades and chains to channel out a passage for a sleigh, and Count Vielfrass was announced.

As I faced him across the icy wastes of the Marble Salon I found that cold and desperation had crushed my fear of him, that for once I was not stammering and gauche. I seated myself, but did not give him permission to follow suit.

When I spoke my breath was visible on the frosty air. 'So, Count! Not content with having brought me as low as anyone can be brought, you come now to gloat over your achievement. It is my misfortune that since I live here under guard at all your mercies I do not possess the power to have you thrown out.'

He bared his yellow fangs, giving in turn a frosty exhalation. 'I come, Your Majesty, on behalf of His Majesty King Maximilian.'

His use of the correct form of address and the fact that he had not, regardless of me, seated himself, took me aback for a moment. 'I see,' I said, recovering. 'Once again he uses you to do his dirty work.'

'His Majesty is much occupied with the drafting of our new constitution, as indeed, being one of his chief advisors, am I.'

'In that case, Count, since your time is precious, I shall ask you to spare me no more of it.'

The lavender handkerchief fluttered. 'Your Majesty would not dismiss me so abruptly if she knew the true purpose of my visit. I come, on explicit instructions from King Maximilian, to give you a letter from Frie – from ex-King Friedrich.'

I could not help myself. In an instant I had forgotten my anger and had started from my seat. Before I knew it I was across the waste of marble that lay between us and had almost ripped the proffered envelope from his hand.

The letter was sealed with Freddy's ring, though not addressed. My numbed fingers fumbled with it, could not tear it open fast enough. But the writing, as I unfolded the paper, was a stranger's.

My beloved Tilda,

I pray that you are well and not grieving too much. I beg you not to worry about me, since I am being well cared for and am getting stronger day by day, though I am still not able to hold a pen for any length of time, which is why I have been obliged to dictate this letter.

I wanted to write, my dearest Tilda, because I know very well your strength of mind and your great loyalty and I do not wish the love you have always so generously given me to stand in the way of your true interests.

Maximilian is a good and upright man and will make you the husband I have never been able to be to you. I implore you not to stand out against his offer of marriage but to accept it, both for yourself and for our people. You have so much to give, my dearest, so much that is strong and joyful and alive which could not be fully given while you were tied to me.

Do not believe that I have ceased to love you, for that could never be. But my love is not, should not be, enough for you – indeed, if I care for you at all I must have the strength to give you up. All these months we have been parted I have prayed unceasingly to Our Father in Heaven for guidance and He has made me understand that this is His will.

I pray also for you, Tilda, that God in His infinite wisdom will help you to see the right way. I long only for your happiness, for it is my happiness too.

Remember me in your prayers, dearest, as you will always be remembered in mine.

Freddy.

My vision blurred, the paper fell from my hands, I must have swayed for Vielfrass suddenly stepped forward. I recoiled from him, groping for a chair.

Then all at once my eyes were clear again. I remembered the letters Freddy had written me on the rare occasions we had been parted or during the long hours when duties of State had forced me from his side, letters scrawled in a round, free, almost childish hand, the margins decorated with little pen and ink sketches and caricatures. I remembered every line and contour of his signature and the kisses that always followed it, loved, familiar marks to which the formless scribble at the bottom of this letter bore not a jot of resemblance. I stared hard at Vielfrass and then at the sheet of paper on the floor between us.

'I trust you will pick it up and take it away with you, Count,' I said. 'I believe it is not mine, but yours.'

His neatly-etched eyebrows feigned a puzzled frown. 'Your Majesty has begged all these weeks for some communication from King Friedrich. Forgive me, but I was not aware—'

'Oh Count, I think you are well aware of every word in that letter. After all, your lackeys concocted it, no doubt to your dictation. It's nothing but a forgery, and an incompetent one at that. You didn't even think it worth attempting a passable imitation of His Majesty's handwriting.'

'Friedrich is too weak to write. The letter says so.'

'The letter says many things and all of them are untrue. His Majesty would never leave me, abandon me to Maximilian. He loves me, he needs me, he hates Maximilian as I do. No, Count. You think me a silly little fool, and perhaps you have good reason. But I am not quite so foolish. Take your contemptible piece of paper, take it back to Maximilian and tell him that if he wishes to win me over he must find some more convincing ploy. Take it now! Go back to Rosenholm and leave me alone with my grief!'

I was almost at the door when suddenly he spoke. 'Your Majesty, forgive me, but you are mistaken—'

I turned angrily, for I had so clearly ended the interview and protocol forbade his addressing me further. But when I saw him I paused, astonished. He had bent to pick up the letter, and it was as if, in the act of bending, he had contrived by some illusionist's trick to change himself, so that he went down one person and came up another. Gone was the hauteur, the supercilious sneer; now the moist lips drew back in a humble, self-deprecating smile, now the cold fishy eyes seemed to glisten with some secret grief, now even the carefully-waxed mustachios seemed to droop ingratiatingly. His voice, when he spoke again, was changed too, its lisp softer and more pronounced, its tone cloying, almost flirtatious; his head was cocked to one side in a way which, so strikingly incongruous with his beard and bony cheeks, appeared curiously girlish.

'With respect, Your Majesty is mistaken in me. I am Your Majesty's friend, not her enemy.'

A fresh gust of his breath overpowered me. I took a step backwards. This change in him frightened me more than the cold, calculating Vielfrass I had always known, not only because there was in it a repellent intimacy like a revelation, but because it was impossible to tell which was the real man, this or the other, or whether in fact both disguised a third, entirely different person.

I forced a scornful laugh. 'My friend? You, Count?'

'Oh, I know Your Majesty does not like me, perhaps could never bring herself to.' There was a pathos, almost, in his frankness, in the little sad moue of the lips which accompanied it.

'You betrayed me, betrayed my husband.'

'I acted at the time, Your Majesty, for the sake of my country. How was I to know that my country's interests would not be best served . . . ?'

I stared at him, surprised. 'But you are Maximilian's creature.'

'I am obliged, yes, to obey his commands. God knows, I have begged him often enough not to force you, Heaven will attest that I implored him not to send you that wicked letter – and yet it is I in the end who must be the messenger, the one to bring you pain. Maximilian will not listen to me, Your Majesty, or respect my judgement. You see' – here the lavender handkerchief was raised momentarily to his lips – 'he too dislikes me.'

It was ludicrous, this pathetic appeal for sympathy; and yet in its very ridiculousness there seemed something ominous.

'Your Majesty may reject my friendship. Heaven knows, I cannot blame her. A man whose fate it is to serve the great and powerful, who is not the architect of the design but merely the humble stonemason sent to hew it from the rock, such a man will always have his detractors. Who knows, who cares what struggles of conscience may send him sleepless to his bed at night, what conflicts between his loyalty and his honour. Whoever dreams that, far from longing for a place close to the seat of power, he may value it as nothing, simply because he values his integrity more—'

'Please, Count!' I said impatiently.

'Maximilian is ruthless, Your Majesty. Selfish, ruthless and cold.'

I attempted a laugh. 'But everyone tells me what a paragon he is, everyone from Prince von Ansbach to my maid.'

'They do not understand him, Your Majesty. They do not see him as Your Majesty and I see him. The people hail him as their saviour because he has a soldierly seat on a horse. The Camarilla twitter admiringly because he cuts a dash in uniform. But you and I, Your Majesty – we, we alone it seems, understand him for what he is. The Sigismundites have made a rod for their own backs. Even the Duke of Maar cannot control him. Why, in this matter of the constitution—'

I sighed. 'The constitution?'

The scarlet lips gave a deprecatory grimace. 'Your Majesty loves this country, that I know, even though it is only your country by adoption. Maximilian would throw it over to the mercies of Keller and his crew, the Liberals, the revolutionaries, the rabble-rousers. Oh, let him hold elections by all means if the people require a sop, let him set up some sort of token Assembly. But universal suffrage, the power taken from the aristocrats and landowners who for centuries have exercised it by right, that power, that sacred responsibility, to be snatched from them and given to the peasants—!'

'Please, Count,' I said, 'I scarcely see what all this signifies.'

He moved closer to me, so close that I could feel the spray of his spittle freezing in little sharp spikes as it met the air. 'It signifies,' he lisped, 'it signifies, Your Majesty, that Maximilian intends to weaken the proper power of the Right so that he may consolidate his own position. It signifies that those of us who love Sylvania must stand together to protect her interests, to protect the true interests of her people before, to serve Maximilian's ends, they are sold to the anarchists. You may not value my friendship now, Your Majesty, but you will have need of it, we shall both have need of each other. It will, you see, be up to us, we who know, we who understand, to work together, to use what influence we have with Maximilian in order to save our beloved country from an autocracy more oppressive and terrible than Baron Schramm's.'

The lisp had become a hiss now. A great gob of saliva, impelled by the force of it, splattered, on his last words, directly into my face just below my right eye. I wiped it sharply away before it froze upon my skin.

'I have no influence with Maximilian.'

The yellow teeth were bared, the head was once more girlishly cocked to one side. 'Ah, but when Your Majesty is Maximilian's wife . . .'

'I shall not be his wife. I don't care what he makes me suffer, I shall never give in!'

'Oh, I think you will. I think, with respect, Your Majesty, that you cannot help it. And, as your friend, I must advise you to have a care.' He sighed, dabbed his lips sorrowfully with his handkerchief, though I noticed suddenly that his eyes were hard. 'As I say, I know what Maximilian is. He will not listen to all my pleas on your behalf. He needs the treaty with Thalia. And his need for an heir is also pressing. If you continue to oppose him he will force you to comply. After all, he holds the one bargaining counter you cannot resist. He has ex-King Friedrich's life in the palm of his hand.'

II

I tried to persuade myself that it was only Vielfrass, in this new and sinister guise of his, adding subtle refinement to my torture. But, though his protested friendship might be spurious, what reason could he have to lie? I knew Maximilian to be brutal – what care had he shown for Freddy's life so far? I had seen for myself that he was cold-blooded – how else could he press this marriage upon me, even send me that cruel forgery to make me believe Freddy had forgotten me? But this? Perhaps, after all, it was only a trick, meant to play upon my fear. Surely no one, not even Maximilian, would force me to put the life of the only person I loved in the balance? I had called Maximilian a monster, but surely he must possess some ordinary human feeling? Yet I remembered the hard, dark face, the hands gently revolving the silver pen, the chill of that quiet voice. Yes, it seemed to me, here was a man without mercy, a man who could, who would kill to get what he wanted. And I, by resisting him, was every day strengthening his determination, every day playing a terrible game of chance with my beloved Freddy's life.

I was sitting alone in my boudoir by the fire, my handkerchief knotted in my mittened fingers, my body hunched and shivering, no longer merely with cold, when I was all at once startled by a noise, a little cough like someone nervously clearing his throat. I looked up and saw the Major who commanded my guard standing hesitantly in the doorway.

'Your Majesty, I know – forgive me – I should not intrude without permission, without observing the proper form. I . . .'

I stared at him abstractedly.

'Your Majesty will pardon me, but I could not, could no longer—' He broke off suddenly, and to my great alarm came pell-mell across the room and threw himself on one knee at my feet.

'Your Majesty, I can no longer live with the dishonour of what I have been forced – no, what I myself have so cravenly done. I have broken my oath of allegiance to the Crown, to Your Majesty and to His Majesty King Friedrich, my sacred oath by which it was my duty as a soldier in His Majesty's army to be bound at all times. It does not matter that I followed the orders of my superior officers. I knew – knew then – that it was dishonourable, that it violated every code I must uphold as a soldier and a loyal subject – and as a man. And when they took His Majesty to Marmion – all these weeks I've watched Your Majesty here, suffering – been ordered to guard Your Majesty as if Your Majesty were a common criminal, instead of someone I have so despicably betrayed – Oh, Ma'am, on my knees before you I most humbly beg your pardon, and if you can find it in you ever to forgive my treachery, I solemnly vow that I shall dedicate myself to serve you in every way within my power.'

I continued to stare at him. I thought again, absurdly, that he was young to be a Major, probably not much older than I was. Behind the inevitable moustache he had a pleasant, open face – the face of a landowner's son from the East, brought up to clear, uncomplicated ideals, not equipped for the exigencies of politics and Court intrigue.

'Your Majesty, if you cannot forgive me I shall understand that it is no more than I deserve. Believe me, I do not wish to intrude upon Your Majesty, only to—'

I roused myself. 'Please. There is really no need . . .'

'But, Ma'am—'

'There is no need. Things are,' – looking down at my fingers, I slowly unwound my handkerchief – 'well, they are as they are. You have done your duty, it is merely that circumstances have changed what that duty requires. Of course I forgive you.'

'Your Majesty – oh, Your Majesty, may I be honoured enough to kiss your hand?'

He had seized my fingers and pressed them to his lips before I could prevent him. I looked down, bewildered, at his blond bent head, at his eyes, when he raised them to meet mine, shining with joy and enthusiasm.

'Oh, Your Majesty, if you will only permit me to serve you again – serve you as I ought, with my life if necessary!'

I smiled faintly. 'Major, I am grateful for your loyalty. But that you should offer your life, or even risk the danger in which this conversation places you – you must understand, your oath is to Maximilian now. There is no longer any way in which you can serve me.'

'Oh, but Your Majesty, there is.' Forgetting protocol, he seized my hand again. 'I know, you see, where they have taken King Friedrich. And I think I know how he can be got free.'

I hesitated. But there could be no suspicion of a trick in his open, eager face. 'You know? Oh, tell me, tell me!' Suddenly I had grasped his hands in mine, was holding them fast as if the very pressure of my fingers would wring the words from him. 'Tell me how he is, how they're treating him! Oh, have you seen him, my darling Freddy, did you speak to him, did he give you any message for me? Will they let him have books and a proper doctor, do they—?'

The Major interrupted me, laughing. 'Your Majesty, forgive me, but I cannot tell you all at once, much as I would wish to.'

So I sat silent while he explained what he knew. It seemed that after Freddy's abdication at Marmion they had taken him to the Schloss Schwarzteufel near Waldheim, where he remained under close guard – not that such precautions appeared necessary, for in the first weeks he had suffered another crisis and had twice been on the point of death. However, the Major assured me, thanks to the ministrations of a doctor who understood his case, he was now out of danger, the frequency of his fits had decreased and he was recovering, albeit slowly. His guard consisted of a battalion of the 4th Cuirassiers, one of whose officers, a lieutenant, had been a friend of the Major's younger brother at cadet school. It appeared that during his Christmas leave in Rosenholm the Major had coincidentally met this lieutenant, also on leave, and over a bottle of brandy they had fallen to discussing their respective parts in Maximilian's coup, discovering that both were affected with the same sense of shame and dishonour. It was when the bottle had been drained that the lieutenant had finally admitted what he was under strict orders never to reveal: that he not only knew the secret of Freddy's whereabouts but was also compelled to carry out the distasteful task of being his rightful sovereign's jailer. There and then he and the Major had sworn a solemn vow, which they had sealed with drops of their own blood, that if they could not restore Freddy to his throne they would, at all cost, liberate him from Maximilian, for it was the very least their duty owed.

The lieutenant commanded a platoon and naturally knew every detail of the guard: how often it was changed, how its duties were ordered, where every man was posted. It only remained for him to discover how many officers in his company would throw in their lot with him; then he and the Major could lay their plans to rescue Freddy and to convey us both to the safety of Austria.

I listened incredulously, at first hardly daring to hope. But the Major's dedication, his zeal for the task, the enthusiasm that shone in his eyes, were infectious.

'When?' I asked, clasping his hand once more. 'Oh please, my dear friend, let it be soon. I miss His Majesty so much, and besides – well, you know what that brute Maximilian requires of me.'

A frown clouded his enthusiasm for a moment. 'Your Majesty, it will happen, we shall succeed, you have my solemn promise on it. But it cannot be soon, not as soon as you would wish. My friend and I must plan carefully – we shan't be permitted any second chances. And His Majesty is still weak. In his present condition the journey from Waldheim to the border would certainly kill him, particularly in this weather. We must bide our time until the snows have melted and he is stronger.'

I felt my lightheartedness vanish. 'But I can't wait. Don't you understand what Maximilian means to do, don't you see that His Majesty is already in the most terrible danger?'

He looked at me, puzzled. As I recounted my conversation with Vielfrass I saw his frown become thoughtful. 'Perhaps, Ma'am, you could temporise with them. After all, there are advantages. I should not suggest it if it could be avoided, but – supposing you were to agree to what Maximilian asks?'

I grew all at once white. 'No!'

'But, Your Majesty—'

'No! How can you even bring yourself to say it? I believed you were my friend, Major, believed you sincerely wished to help me, and yet you suggest that I . . . that I give in, lower myself, offer myself up to a man who . . .' I tailed off, choking with angry tears.

'Your Majesty,' he said gently, 'pardon me if I have offended you, but I meant it for the best. Do you not see? It is not a question of your marrying Maximilian, merely of agreeing to a betrothal. Don't you see how this will give us the time we need?'

I glanced up at him through my tears. The fire had returned to his eyes again, his honest face was once more suffused with dedicated fervour.

'If you agree to the marriage, Ma'am, His Majesty will no longer be in any danger. And besides, think of all the other advantages it gives us. Any suspicions Maximilian might have will be lulled and we can proceed with our plans more easily. You will be freed – if he thinks you've come round he will treat you more gently, and in any case he can scarcely continue to keep his fiancée a prisoner. We'll have a great deal more room in which to manoeuvre. And, above all, we'll have the time to wait till spring, when everything will be in our favour. Oh, Your Majesty, forgive me but you must see what we gain by it.'

I looked up at him for some while in silence. 'Supposing,' I said eventually, 'supposing, Major, that it is not time enough? What happens, what must I do then?'

'It will be, Ma'am, I promise you. I promise that you will be united with His Majesty and that both Your Majesties will be safely in Austria before the day comes for your marriage.' He dropped suddenly on one knee again, with his hand pressed to his heart. 'I swear it, Ma'am, on my honour – and my life!'

When he had gone I sat for a long, long while before I could bring myself to go to the bureau and pick up my pen. But at last I dipped the nib in the freezing ink and wrote, in a shaky hand that was quite unlike my own, my letter of consent to Maximilian.

III

I am not sure quite what I had expected in response. I dreaded another meeting with Maximilian, dreaded it more now that I had a part which, for Freddy's life and for both our futures, I must somehow learn to play. And when, three days later, men were once again dispatched to dig out the road up the mountain, I was thrown immediately into a panic, uncertain as to how much my new role should force me to concede, unsure that I should be able to repress my loathing for my future 'husband'. So why was it that when the Major announced to me, not Maximilian, but His Serene Highness the Duke of Hohen-Kastell and Carrick, I felt, instead of relief, a sudden anger as if I had been insulted?

He stood before the feeble fire in the Marble Salon, a tall man, taller even than Maximilian, in General's uniform, with the snow still crusted on his boots. When he saw me he moved aside to allow me the fire, bowing respectfully.

I had chosen, despite Rosa's mutterings, to appear veiled and in black, as if I had been recently widowed (for was this not miserably close to the truth?). The rustle of crape as I seated myself was for the moment the only sound that broke the silence between us. Both of us stirred uneasily, seeming uncertain where to look, and I all at once realised that despite his height and his ramrod bearing the stranger was as much discomposed by our situation as I. With a small gesture of my head I motioned him to speak.

'You do not know me, Ma'am, although we shall soon be cousins. I'm His Majesty's cousin, you understand, on his father's side, through his aunt, the late Princess Marie Louise.' His speech was clipped, with undertones of what I was certain was an English accent. He stood very stiff with his hands behind his back, inclining the upper half of his body as he spoke, as if his head, neck and shoulders were welded together. Seeing that I made no move to respond, he continued, flushing slightly, 'I – well, since His Majesty was unable to respond to your letter in person, he sent me along in his stead.'

'Unable?' I said softly.

'He's been kept pretty busy with the Season, of course. And he leaves tomorrow on a State visit to Prussia.'

Again that inexplicable anger. 'I see,' I said.

My tone seemed further to discomfort him, for he became even stiffer. 'He sends his apologies of course, Ma'am. And he's given me a letter for you – there, you see – a letter and the documents from Monsignor Scarlatti, the Nuncio, setting out His Holiness's consent to the annullment.'

I did not move to take the papers he proffered me.

'And he asks me to find out whether you are in need of anything.'

'I am in need of nothing,' I said.

This time he was definitely taken aback. 'Well, Ma'am, there must be things, arrangements – a young girl getting betrothed and all that . . .'

I was jolted back to the part I must play, the need to gain time. 'Yes, of course, the betrothal. I should be grateful – it's only the sudden change in my circumstances, you understand – I must have a period to adjust, consider,' – my words sounded unconvincing even to myself – 'I shall need at least a month or two before we are officially betrothed.'

He smiled. 'Naturally, Ma'am. Quite understandable. And it'll suit His Majesty, too. He won't want the celebrations before the constitution is ratified and the elections have taken place.'

'Of course,' I said tightly. 'The elections.'

The anger that I could not comprehend was now so clear in my voice that another silence fell between us.

He advanced a few steps towards me. 'Please,' he said, 'let me give you the letters.'

I took them and stared at them without speaking for some moments. Finally I forced myself to open the envelope from Maximilian. His letter was brief and businesslike, formally thanking me for my acceptance of his offer and rehearsing the conventional phrases of solicitude for my happiness and well-being. He acknowledged that ours could never by any means be described as a love match, yet hoped that our mutual love for Sylvania would unite us in a partnership which, though it were no more than a marriage of convenience, would prove satisfying to us both in its dedication to the people and to the State. Though his writing was difficult to construe, closed in upon itself like the writer, the words 'no more than a marriage of convenience' flashed before my eyes several times. I thought again how much I hated him, hated that hard, closed face, hated even his handwriting. I thrust the letter aside. But the second envelope, the parchment that contained the official end to my marriage to Freddy, that sought to wipe out my few precious years of happiness as if they had never existed, I could not bring myself to open. I stared at it numbly and tears I could not suppress began to fall in great damp splotches on the paper.

I could feel the Duke shifting uncomfortably but I could not move or speak. I sat there with the envelope between my fingers, crying uncontrollably.

He came hesitantly towards me. 'I say, Ma'am, please don't. You don't know how it confuses a fellow to see the fair sex cry. Please, if it's anything I've said . . .'

I shook my head mutely.

'Look here, I know I'm not much of a substitute for Max, I know a girl wants to see the man she's going to marry, not some other duffer sent along as a pretty poor sort of Cupid—'

His misunderstanding made me cry all the harder.

'I say, you really mustn't, y'know. Max would be most distressed. He doesn't mean to neglect you, but these are difficult times – the political situation – he's still got his work cut out—' He was standing beside me now, bending over me, proffering a large white handkerchief almost in desperation. 'Look, Marie – perhaps I may call you that since we're to be cousins – this isn't like the girl Princess Vicky and Lady Alice described to me, the girl who was up and down trees like a regular little monkey and made her pony take five-barred gates—'

I stopped, mid-sob, to stare at him in astonishment. 'You know my mother's family? You know Aunt Victoria and my cousin Alice?'

'Indeed I do.'

'And you've been to Gower Castle?'

'Was there the summer before last. Went to say goodbye before I left my regiment and joined Max in Thalia. Lady Alice and I were once – well, but that's by the by.'

I raised my veil and looked at him, taking him in properly for the first time. He was a great, sturdy column of a man, built true as a mast of oak, with sandy hair and a sandy moustache and a great many freckles on his hands and on his large, pinkish face. His features – snub nose, solid jaw – bore no particular marks of distinction; it was a face which, had you been absent from it for any length of time, you would have been hard-pressed to describe, though the deepset eyes were surprisingly gentle, for all the military rigour of the rest. He must have been twenty years older than I, yet now, as he hovered uncertainly over me, his general's bearing unbending into a sort of gruff fatherliness, he seemed suddenly to share my shyness.

I took the handkerchief and dabbed at my nose.

He smiled. 'There,' he said, in English. 'That's the ticket.'

I found myself smiling too, despite myself. 'You'll have to forgive me,' I said. 'I haven't spoken English for so long I think I've forgotten every word I knew.'

But I had not forgotten, and for the next hour we sat together by the fire while I questioned him eagerly about England and Gower Castle and all my mother's family, every aunt, every cousin twice-removed, until I was once again transported back to that green, rolling paradise of my childhood and Maximilian's letter and the Papal document seemed part of another far-distant world.

When he left, promising to come again as soon as he could, I felt suddenly full of hope. In the Major I had my chevalier, my brave and loyal knight, sworn to serve me; and in St John Aubyn, Duke of Hohen-Kastell and Carrick, I had, for the first time, found a friend.

IV

After Aubyn's visit everything seemed to change. The snow stopped falling and a sharp clear sunlight descended upon the white of the mountains and the blue of the lake. Then the snow on the lowlands melted, carriages began to come daily up the winding pass from the village and Schwanensee began to hum with a life it had not known since Sigismund's time.

Though I was now to be styled by my maiden rank as Princess of Thalia, I was to retain my former place in the order of precedence, second only to the King himself, and to have restored to me all the honours and entitlements of my position. A Riding Master and a Major Domo, equerries, French ladies' maids, a hairdresser, even a small, excitable artist from Vienna to paint my portrait – gradually a full household began once again to be assembled around me. Dust was swept away from corners, chandeliers were refurbished, mouldering draperies renewed, so that everything in the State apartments seemed to smell suddenly of fresh paint and lavender wax. Clearly Maximilian, though he was not prepared to honour his future bride with his presence, was anxious that she should be spared no material comfort, albeit that I noticed there was no talk of my guard being withdrawn.

Then there were the visitors: the Cardinal Archbishop to counsel me on the annulment; the Princess Helena who, as

Maximilian's aunt and nearest female relative, would stand
in place of his mother at the wedding ceremony; Prince
Gustav, her husband, and the grizzled imposing Duke of
Maar, who intimidated me with his fierce side-whiskers and
jangling spurs – they all came to inspect me, my future
Sigismundite relations, to weigh me up and make sure that
I appeared capable of providing their much-needed heir.

As part of my new household I had acquired two replacement ladies-in-waiting, the Baroness von Windersdorf and
the Countess von Tarn. Ursula von Windersdorf had been
bestowed upon me from her own household by the Princess
Helena because, as she murmured in her vague, discon-
nected way, 'Ursi will look after you, my dear – poor mother-
less girl – though I shall miss her, dear Ursi – let her be your
mother, for darling Max's sake.' And motherly the Baroness
certainly was, a rotund, jolly woman with haphazard hair,
endless advice, and a herbal *tisane* for every ailment from
toothache to the vapours. But, despite my initial distrust of
anyone who, standing in such close relation to Maximilian's
family, must clearly be encouraged to observe me and report
upon my behaviour (a subtle reminder, like the guard, that
my period of imprisonment was not entirely a thing of the
past) I could see that she was kind and, for all her chatter
and inquisitiveness, well-intentioned. Of my second lady-
in-waiting I was by no means so sure. Suzannah von Tarn,
morganatic daughter of the Duke of Maar, was an ungainly,
sallow-faced girl four years my senior, who seldom spoke
unless she was spoken to and appeared to carry in her every
movement a sullen defiance. There was, too, something
furtive in her, so that occasionally when I looked up from
my embroidery or glanced round in conversation I would be
sure that she was watching me, intent on seeing through
my pretended good spirits. The reason for her behaviour I
was to discover quite by chance, though this was by no
means to allay my disquiet.

One afternoon when the first almond blossom was out
and a few crocuses had begun timorously to unfurl their
stars in the scrubby flowerbeds that bordered the castle wall
along the South ramparts, Baroness von Windersdorf and I,
well-muffled against the cold, were taking in the brisk air
from the lake when, rounding the buttress which obscured

from our view the far end of the South wall, we were
surprised to see two figures deep in conversation within the
shadow of the Eagle Tower. They sprang apart as they heard
our footsteps on the gravel and I perceived that the woman
was Suzannah von Tarn. The other, a young man I had
never seen before, I assumed from the expression on Suzannah's face, at once furtive and inimical, to be a secret
admirer, so I was much surprised when she introduced me
to him, curtly, as her brother.

Removing his hat, the young man bowed very low, and
we exchanged a few formal pleasantries. He was of medium
height, slim and about my age, perhaps even younger, and
there was something in the cut of his fur-collared coat, in
his clean-shaven upper lip, in the elegant langour of his
gestures, which contrived to suggest at one and the same
time the ultimate refinement of fashion and a *dégagé* Bohemianism. But the most striking aspect of his appearance derived
from his being side by side with Suzannah. For, though the
mould which had formed both of them was recognisably the
same, I should never have taken them for brother and sister.
Where she was plain and heavy-set, he was quicksilver;
where her high cheekbones and narrow jaw suggested only
stolid gloom, his gave him a feline handsomeness that was
almost feminine in its delicacy; the lips that drooped with
perpetual disappointment in her curved with an agreeable
insouciance in him, the colourless hair became a radiant
gold: it was as if nature out of sheer perversity had deprived
the sister of all the qualities most highly praised in a woman
in order to lavish them on the brother.

I felt, with embarrassment, that I was staring at him, and
noticed that he too seemed to be examining me with
disquieting interest. Indeed, as we turned to retrace our
steps towards the West Gate, it was he who fell in beside
me, Ursula von Windersdorf dropping back to join his sister.
But, despite a certain almost impudent ease of manner – I
was surprised, for instance, that such a junior and low-
ranking member of the family should permit himself to refer
to his King with such familiarity – he had a charm which
soon made me forget my shyness, so that by the time we
had regained the hall I was laughing at his caricatures of
members of the new Court at Rosenholm as if our twenty-

minute acquaintance had grown into an established friendship.

Since Ursula von Windersdorf appeared to be on the best of terms with him, ruffling his hair and calling him 'a wicked spoilt boy', and since I hoped at least to please Suzannah, I suggested that his servant and luggage should be sent for from the village. But, though we spent a livelier evening than any since my incarceration, with Anton von Tarn playing the out-of-tune music-room piano for us and singing folksongs, Suzannah continued obstinately silent and morose, until eventually she begged to be allowed to retire, pleading a headache.

When she had gone and Ursula von Windersdorf was rummaging in her workbasket out of earshot for a moment, the Count raised his eyebrows in an expression of elaborate despair.

'My poor dear sister! There are some people who simply shouldn't be permitted to fall in love.'

'Suzannah's in love?' I asked, astonished.

'Oh, blindly, insanely. But it doesn't suit her. She hasn't the face or the figure for it. She'd be much better off with a nice sensible bout of religious mania.'

'But who is she in love with?' I said.

The eyebrows swept upwards, then narrowed into a little frown of dismayed concern. 'Do you mean you don't know, that she hasn't confessed to you? Why, with Max, of course.'

I stared at him.

'Oh, she's been mooning after him like a cow with the colic ever since she first clapped eyes on him. Not, mind you, that Max has noticed. Men seldom notice poor Suzannah.'

'But it must be dreadful for her,' I said. 'Being here with me – thinking that I shall marry him.'

Count von Tarn gestured airily. 'Oh, I've no doubt she imagines it's better than nothing. After all, she has her rival in her sights. And she can devote herself to Max from a distance, indulge in a veritable orgy of unrequited passion.'

'No wonder she hates me,' I said.

He laughed. 'Oh, I shouldn't concern myself if I were you. When one sees what love does to the poor creature, one finds her hatred a positive blessing.'

But the Count's laughter did not console me. Not only

was I forced to play a part it took me the utmost effort to sustain, not only was I, with the advent of my new household, seldom alone, compelled always to be on my guard; but now I knew I had an enemy close by, an enemy who would watch and wait until, inevitably, I betrayed myself.

In Rosenholm the constitution was finally ratified, elections were called, and, Right and Left gaining seats in the new Parliament in almost equal numbers, Maximilian took what was generally viewed as the wisest course in the interests of peace, appointing Vielfrass as Chancellor, with Keller and the Left as the official Opposition and the Duke of Maar remaining as Chief of the King's own personal Cabinet of advisors. Aubyn replaced Keller as Army Chief, which occasioned me some sadness, for it decreased the frequency of his visits, although Count von Tarn, on the pretext of seeing Suzannah, had now become a regular visitor in his stead.

And all the time 23rd April drew nearer, the day Maximilian and I were to be officially betrothed.

I had begged the Major to spare me, if he could, the betrothal ceremonies, for as yet Maximilian's continued absence on matters of State had saved me from the need directly to lie; but still the Major asked for more time, still he talked of the strict security at Schloss Schwarzteufel, still he urged me to consider Freddy's condition which, though he continued to show improvement, was not yet stable enough for him to travel. And so, as April passed, I began to steel myself to the unavoidable ordeal to come.

The morning of the 23rd dawned very clear and bright. In Rosenholm the bunting already proclaimed the start of four days' official celebration. At Schwanensee the castle buzzed with the preparations required to accommodate all the Sigismundite relations with their separate suites, servants and horses. My dress was in readiness, lilac mousseline de soie and tulle, starred with lace marguerites and embroidered with seed-pearls; I had been apprised of my timetable by my Major Domo, from the moment of His Majesty's arrival with his retinue in my apartments to the formal family dinner at 5pm: when, after an early luncheon which I could not eat, I went down to the music-room for a final sitting for my portrait, I was trembling so much that, despite all the beseechings of the excitable little artist, I could not keep my head or hands still.

It was Aubyn who saved me, appearing suddenly and without ceremony, clutching a wicker basket. In our conversation about England we had, of course, touched often upon English horses and English dogs. Now, opening Aubyn's basket, I saw, huddled together for security, their noses quivering, their black eyes gazing in trepidation up at me, two eight-week-old golden labrador puppies.

I threw my arms around Aubyn and kissed him, I gathered the dogs to me in a squirming confusion of tails and legs and kissed them too. The portrait was forgotten, the little artist waved his brushes in vain. Aubyn stood laughing by as I burbled with pleasure, as I begged him to admit that the pups had the softest mouths, the sweetest expressions, the funniest baggy stockings above their oversized paws. And somehow, while we were watching them get their bearings, while we were having our noses licked and our fingers chewed and were rescuing one small adventurer from Ursula von Windersdorf's workbasket, we did not notice that the other, the sturdier of the two, had climbed into the tray of paints and was savaging a tube of ultramarine – whereupon the culprit promptly made off with his trophy, shedding a thin trail of blue in his wake. Chaos ensued: Aubyn leapt into pursuit, Ursula von Windersdorf shouted encouragement, the little artist jumped up and down hysterically; and it was while Aubyn was on hands and knees beneath a chiffonier endeavouring to extract the offender, and while Ursula was holding her sides with laughter and while I, doubled up with laughter too, was attempting to stop the second pup from emulating her brother's example with the yellow ochre, that we suddenly became aware of a figure in the doorway – a tall, still figure in black.

V

Nothing you have rehearsed over and over in your head is ever the same when it happens. I had become engaged to Freddy by proxy and had thus no preconception of him beyond what the miniature of a rather stiff, pale young man would allow. But my image of Maximilian had grown rather than diminished in clarity during the months since our meeting. Many was the time I had struggled to shut out the memory of that dark face with its sinister scar, many the time I had shuddered to think of him impartially contemplating Freddy's destruction. So why, when I knew Maximilian to be the embodiment of everything brutal and heartless, did the man at the door, taking in with one glance Aubyn grovelling under the chiffonier and the Viennese gesticulating and me with my hands full of paint and struggling puppy, throw back his head in a great peal of unrestrained and perfectly human laughter? Why, when in my consternation I lost my hold on the dog, did he bend and catch it by the scruff of the neck, cradling it in the palm of his hand and tickling it behind the ears with every appearance of gentleness? In all my imaginings of this encounter I had sworn, as far as my pretence would allow, to hold myself in proud defiance, yielding nothing, setting out precisely the distance between us. Yet now all I could do was stutter and look awkwardly down at my hands while he, surveying the artist's doll-like travesty of a portrait and complimenting both myself and the painting in elegant terms which signalled our dismissal, clapped his hand warmly upon Aubyn's shoulder and took him off to discuss army reforms. I despised myself for blushing, was chagrined by the satirical glimmer I thought I detected in his gaze. And my confusion was complete when Ursula pointed out what must have been the reason for his amusement – that I had all the time sported a large blob of ochre paint on the side of my nose.

It was unjust, his catching me off my guard, his showing signs of humanity where I knew there could be none, for it made me more than ever a prey to my wretched nervousness. By rights it should be I who had the upper hand, since I knew that everything which was to pass between us was to be no more than a charade. He could mock or be dismissive as he pleased. I had my secret tokens of defiance – the lilac dress chosen because mauve could also serve as mourning; Freddy's ring, transferred to my left hand but worn proudly nonetheless, concealed beneath my glove. Yet now I was filled with a sense of dislocation, as if far from controlling the charade I was caught up in it, was myself being manipulated. Even my reflection in the looking glass, as maids and hairdresser tweaked me into some approximation to modishness, looked unfamiliar beneath its fashionable curls. An oval face, trimmed now by the months of my incarceration of all its girlish plumpness, so that it seemed to have taken on the fragility of china. A pale doll's face with a neat doll's mouth and dark eyes, glazed and inexpressive with panic; a china doll like the creature in the portrait, who, in the unaccustomed finery of Maximilian's couturiers, was as much a thing created to his commission as the painting itself. When the moment came for me to go into the drawing-room to receive him, I tried to hold my chin high, I clenched my hand determinedly on Freddy's ring. But as I performed my clumsy curtsy I was overwhelmed by a feeling of powerlessness, an abiding sense of my own unreality.

He wore the dress uniform of the Deathwatch with Field Marshal's distinctions, with the crimson sash of the order of St Othmar across his breast and the collar of the Order of the Golden Spur. He appeared once again to be inspecting me as if this time he wished to ensure his creation was not marred by smudges of paint or other signs of human carelessness. Then he took my hand and raised it to his lips.

Though he held my fingers lightly, though his lips scarcely brushed my skin, the effort of not flinching made me tremble so much I could hardly stand. A new dread filled me, that he would take it as his right as my fiancé to kiss and paw me. I could not look at him. Out of the corner of my eye I could see two adjutants move to flank him, each bearing a crimson velvet cushion.

Maximilian took my right hand again, holding it gently but firmly to still its trembling, and I felt the ring, his ring, the huge cabochon sapphire set with diamonds, slide into place where not two hours previously Freddy's wedding band had been. It hung a little loose as if, in all the organisation which had gone into this moment, no one had remembered I had lost weight. I forced myself to look at it in order that I might contrive to avoid facing him directly; but, taking my chin between his fingers and thumb, he tilted my head upwards so that I was compelled to look into his dark, conquistador's face, so that I met his eyes for an instant and saw that they were a clear, disconcerting blue. I was once again assailed by my own powerlessness, for I knew that this was the moment when he must inevitably kiss me, knew that for Freddy's sake I must not protest or wrench my head away. I closed my eyes. But his lips avoided mine, imprinting themselves softly upon my forehead. 'There, my dear child. It is done, over with. You may stop shivering and open your eyes. There is a debt of honour I must also repay.'

The second adjutant moved forward with his velvet cushion, on which was displayed a heavy antique parure of brilliants and crysoberyls – the Maria Antonia parure made by Castellani for Maximilian I and traditionally worn by every Sylvanian Queen at her wedding. I had heard of it but never seen it, for it had been part of the priceless hoard of jewellery and works of art smuggled into Switzerland by the Sigismundites when they fled.

'My family stole it. But it was yours by right when you married King Friedrich. I simply return it to you.'

I stared at the jewels. They seemed to wink back at me where the light struck their myriad facets, as impervious as the clear blue eyes I strove to avoid. It did not matter that I knew my head would never be bowed with the weight of that massive diadem, that I should never feel the chill burden of that necklace on my skin. I could not bear to hear Freddy's name on his lips at this moment of all moments, and suddenly I was struggling against my caution, unable to contain myself.

'It is impossible . . . I must . . . Give me leave, Sir, to speak to you privately.'

He motioned our suites to withdraw to the far end of the room.

'I cannot pretend,' I said, managing to keep my voice low only with effort. 'I cannot love you.'

He looked at me for a moment, then to my surprise he smiled. 'My dear, fierce little Marie, we shall not pretend. We do not love each other and were our circumstances different we should both order our lives very differently. Our marriage is forced upon us by duty. And I thank you for understanding that duty, at least with your head if not with your heart.'

'You can expect nothing of me,' I said.

'I expect no more, child, than you can give – which is to be very beautiful and to work, as you have always done, for our country and our people. And since we speak of work,' – again he smiled – 'we have four exceedingly hard days ahead of us which we must begin upon now by demonstrating to my family what a splendidly well-matched and promising couple we are.'

I fell silent, my protest stilled, the sense of my own unreality surging over me again. For, though he took my arm to lead me down to the State Apartments where the Sigismundite relations waited in the Throne-Room to kiss my hand, though he smiled and his tone was light, there was, in the smile, in the irony, just as there had been in his expression in the music-room, a detachment which appeared to indicate nothing so much as my dismissal.

It is, after all, expected that a good-looking and unmarried King shall have – as well as his horses, his guns, his handsome retinue of tall young aides-de-camp – a suitable woman to flourish on his arm. I was, it seemed, in the architecture of Maximilian's public persona, merely a boss or cartouche, scarcely structural, but necessary to complete the symmetry.

It had begun at the stiff formal dinner with the Sigismundite relations, when I had been seated between Maximilian and the Duke of Maar. I could not talk, I could not eat, but no one remarked upon it or even seemed to notice. Yes, of course Aubyn, dear kind Aubyn, had smiled warmly as he kissed my hand and murmured that 'old Max was a damnably lucky fellow', but Aubyn was too far away for conversation, on the opposite side of the table. And my only other ally, Count von Tarn, seemed to change in Maximilian's presence, to become the assiduous courtier, reserving his repartee and his spiky stories for the King alone. Oh, Maximilian, when he condescended to notice me, was immaculately polite, gentle even – with that impartial gentleness which so carefully abstracted personal heat from any contact between us – but he did not seem to care that I was pale and spiritless and could not make small talk, as if, when he had said he expected no more from me than I could give, it was a matter of indifference to him whether he were given anything. I sat as silent and stiff as the footman behind my chair, realising that in these ceremonies, of which I had supposed I was the centre, my role was little different from that of the footman himself, to be extravagantly, splendidly got up and discreetly invisible.

Oh, I was useful, for I did not require instruction in my part: I knew how to stand for hours in the pouring rain or stifling heat without fainting or complaining; I knew that I must try to smile at all times and endeavour to look interested when asking unimportant questions of self-important people; I knew not to count the miles I had walked or the times I had permitted my hand to be kissed or the bouquets I had graciously accepted. But my usefulness consisted in my being quiet and neat and obedient, in my understanding that I was after all only one more complication in a timetable, one more body in a seating plan, one more name to be considered in lists of precedence.

How I began to hate that courteous detachment of Maximilian's over the following three days in Rosenholm, to hate it more than I should have loathed roughness or brutality. Against brutality you can rebel, your gestures of defiance and plans of escape have meaning. But against indifference, particularly when it is charmingly, smilingly expressed, there are no weapons. My feeling of not existing grew, as if someone were slowly erasing my image with strokes of an indiarubber. I had always dreaded my public duties, the more so since Freddy's illness meant I must usually perform them alone, but at least my gaucheness had been a badge of identity. Now, caught up in the relentless efficiency that attended Maximilian's honeymoon with his subjects, politely exclaiming at the firework display given in our honour, holding my *cercle* at the endless receptions, receiving yet more posies from curtsying schoolchildren, I found even this token of my humanity was taken from me, disguised, accommodated by Maximilian's own unfaltering competence. I had been ashamed that I had appeared plain, dumpy, so lacking in regal glamour, but at least I had been perceived for what I was. Now, though the people's curiosity about me was, of course, at fever pitch, though they took in every detail from the angle of my hat to the seams in my gloves, they saw me, the real me, not at all. If I coughed or rubbed my nose or accidentally stubbed my toe it was instantly interpreted as evidence of my feelings for Maximilian. It was all there, in the coy postcards made of our betrothal photographs where the obligation to pose had forced us into a glazed parody of intimacy, in the speculations of our less reputable newspapers which Rosa insisted on reading out to me – 'a *coup de foudre*', 'a couple so evidently headlong in love' – I was a fiction invented for Maximilian's benefit to rally the people and achieve his political ends. In the new Court, where so many familiar faces were missing, replaced by younger, more fashionable elements, scions of Sigismundite houses returned from exile, I began to search for my old enemies, for the Baroness von Bad-Blixen with her savage *lorgnette* and belladonna tongue, for the vixenish Countess von Kleist, as if the sting of their contempt would restore me to a proper sense of myself again.

There grew in me a desperate longing to break through Maximilian's infuriating detachment, to scream, shout, force him to acknowledge something in me beyond the marionette he had created. But, apart from the fact that my inability to talk to him seemed to increase with our propinquity, we were seldom alone together and then only ever for a few moments. I was not staying in the Residenz, but with Prince Gustav and Princess Helena in the Rosenpalast nearby, and in those brief periods when we were not forced into each other's company by our official engagements, Maximilian was busy with his advisors and his dispatch boxes while I was left to the Princess Helena's haphazard attempts at motherly duty. On my third morning in Rosenholm she took me to inspect the apartments in the Residenz I should occupy after my wedding, where, on Maximilian's instructions, extensive redecoration had already begun. They were in the East Wing, on the opposite side of the courtyard to the rooms I had shared with Freddy, and as I stared apathetically at the lavish hangings, the gorgeously embossed wallpapers, the elegant splendour of the Louis-XVI furniture, remembering bitterly my old simple, cosy home, something jarred – the absence of a study or any other obvious concession to masculine tastes; whereupon Princess Helena revealed – with some surprise for she had assumed in her vague way that Maximilian and I must have discussed such things – that he and I were to live in separate apartments, his being on the floor directly above. This new proof of my inconsequence, this physical embodiment of it in plaster and stone, stung me all at once with the same fierce anger I had felt when Maximilian had sent Aubyn to reply to my letter. No matter how I reminded myself that I should never live in these apartments, that I should soon be sharing my old peaceful domestic routine with my beloved Freddy, the insult rankled, and in its wake came a curious sense of guilt, as if, in allowing myself to feel this humiliation, I was yielding somehow, betraying Freddy.

After all, I should be grateful to Maximilian for his neglect. I should be glad he did not seek to force commitments from me, glad he evinced no desire to touch or kiss me, glad that he remained unalterably a stranger. I had come through these four dreadful days with all but my pride unscathed, I could return safely to Schwanensee in the knowledge that in weeks, perhaps days, I should be free. If he had not been as I had expected it did not change things. I disliked him, loathed him more than ever. And at least I knew that when he found me gone it would occasion no more than an irritating blow to his dignity. So why, that night, at the Gala performance of *Tristan und Isolde*, as I sat stiffly beside him trying to ignore a thousand pairs of opera-glasses trained not on the stage but on us, did I find myself covertly studying him, wondering what thoughts that cold Roman profile concealed? And why did I once again feel crushed by the sheer weight of his indifference?

The following morning, presumably because he thought it was required of him, he came to see me off at the station and while my baggage was being installed on the Royal Train both our suites withdrew tactfully from our private waiting-room, leaving us, for once, inescapably alone. I should have been amused at the farce of our situation, at our being so obviously expected to exchange the sighs and regrets of parting lovers; but instead I found myself, shut in this small room with him, overwhelmed by my usual confusion. He, on the other hand, stared out of the window at the rain sleeting across the platform as if he were perfectly comfortable with his own thoughts.

Suddenly I could bear his disregard no longer.

'I apologise, Sir,' I said. 'I've never had the slightest talent for making conversation. It's one of my many faults – they should have told you. I'm not clever or accomplished, I can't discourse on music or literature or politics. And I've never been able just to talk about nothing.'

He turned from the window with that inevitable, faintly amused smile. 'My dear child, I like your silence. In a life where everyone seems to have something pressing to say to me every minute of the day, it has the miraculous quality of peace.'

I felt the anger rise in me again. 'I still love Freddy,' I said. 'I can't just stop it, snuff it out.'

'Yes,' he said softly. 'I understand that.'

'No! You don't understand, however can you? Just because he has epilepsy – he isn't simple, despite what they all say. He can paint and draw, he loves poetry, he has a good mind—'

'I know,' he said.

'He's good and kind, and he needs me – needed me . . .' I scarcely knew what I was saying now, had forgotten caution, felt as if I were losing the power ever to save Freddy or myself, that only some reaction from Maximilian, some crack in his reasonableness, some tiny spark of conflict between us would bring it back.

'Please,' I said. 'Let me see him. Let me see him just once before – before . . .'

He came over to me and, resting his hands lightly on my shoulders, looked down at me. Then he gently touched my cheek, just at the side of my nose, as if he were wiping away a speck of paint which still lingered invisibly.

'No, Marie. Not now. Not, anyway, until after we are married.'

I felt a great surge of relief as if my lungs were suddenly filling with fresh clear air. He had given it to me, given me back my reason to fight him, made himself once again the brute I had imagined, the ruthless calculator of Vielfrass's disloyal whisperings. I should return to Schwanensee free.

VI

'But how much longer, Major? How much longer do you imagine I can stand this waiting?'

It was an airless day, and the walk I had taken to ease my restlessness had merely left me prickly with exhaustion, so that my voice was sharper than I had intended. The Major's devoted face creased in alarm.

'Please, Ma'am! I beg of you, remember the risk.'

I looked back down the South Walk, but Ursula and Suzannah, languid with the heat, trailed behind us, well out of earshot.

'The risks, the waiting! Is it any wonder my nerves are jangling? It's been six months now, Major – and still nothing.'

He sighed. 'I know, Ma'am. I've explained how strict the security is at Schwarzteufel. We must continue to wait until they decide to move His Majesty.'

'You said they would move him last month.'

'But then His Majesty suffered a series of attacks and the doctors advised them to delay.'

I flicked my fan disconsolately. 'My poor, dear Freddy. Perhaps they've changed their minds, perhaps they don't intend to move him at all.'

'Oh no, Ma'am. Lieutenant Kessler assures me it's been decided. He's to be sent to the Benedictine monastery at Freischutz to convalesce. Apparently the monks in the hospital there have a long tradition of caring for the sick.'

'And presumably also of being efficient jailers.' I jabbed at the gravel with the toe of my boot. 'Major, we are now near the end of June. The wedding is barely three weeks away.'

I heard the little nervous tickle rise to his throat. 'His Majesty hasn't had an attack for ten days now. They'll move him soon, Ma'am, depend on it.'

I turned and looked up at him. 'But supposing, Major, it is not soon enough?'

'Your Majesty, I swore that we should free King Friedrich before you were obliged to marry Maximilian. I swore it on my life.'

His eyes burned so zealously, his face was such a picture

of distress that I was instantly ashamed of doubting him. 'Forgive me,' I said. 'It is only the waiting. It has made me so low-spirited lately.'

Low-spirited I had certainly been since my return from Rosenholm. Perhaps it was Schwanensee, which, obdurately dank in the winter, became in the heat oppressive with the pervading smell of drains. Perhaps it was that, with Aubyn away on manoeuvres and Anton von Tarn reluctantly knuckling under to examinations at the Military Academy, life had become irredeemably dull. In spite of Rosa's scolding, I could no longer make even a pretence of enthusiasm for the wedding arrangements.

I had been separated from Freddy for nine months now and I found I was beginning to forget what he looked like, so that I was obliged to consult faded photographs to reassemble a clear image of his features, to conjure up his gentle voice and all his beloved gestures and expressions. Of Maximilian's face, the cool eyes, the dismissive curve of the arrogant mouth, I had a precise picture which would wake me often in the night like a haunting. But though I wore Freddy's ring still, wound round with a curl of his hair and concealed in a tiny chamois bag where my chemise met my stays, his presence seemed to be drifting away from me. I remembered, on a morning in the depth of winter, seeing one of the black swans which had given Schwanensee its name pecking vainly at the lake, and being told by Rosa that it was trying to free its mate, trapped beneath the surface; now it seemed to me that Freddy, too, was separated from me by just such an impenetrable barrier, his beloved face immobile, blurred by the fissures and whorls in the opaque surface of the ice.

Four days after my conversation with the Major, Count von Tarn arrived unexpectedly. Usually his malicious chatter made me smile in spite of myself, but that afternoon he too seemed despondent and as we began the inevitable promenade of the South Walk his descriptions of the horrors of the Military Academy and his complaints about his father's refusal to let him leave the army and become Maximilian's private secretary grated on me. No longer bothering to listen, I stooped to pet the dogs and let them off the leash.

'I see,' he said, pouting with mock affront as I caught him up again. 'I come here hoping to lay my head in the lap of my dear soon-to-be-cousin Marie and let her sooth my fevered brow, and now I find she has an attack of the Suzannahs.'

I looked at him blankly.

'The gloom, the sighs, the complete lack of appreciation for any intelligent conversation. You must be in love. A royal bride in love with her royal bridegroom – it's scarcely the *soignée* thing, you know.'

I was suddenly annoyed by the latitude he presumed. 'Really, Anton, you are most impertinent!'

'Then you are in love with Max?' He seemed so uncharacteristically serious that I wondered for an instant whether this was a trap, whether like Suzannah he was spying on me.

'When I am married,' I said carefully, 'it will be my duty to love my husband. And, like Maximilian, I also have a duty to strengthen the treaty and continue the line.'

His expression lightened, almost as if he were relieved. 'Dear Max!' he said, with a curious little laugh. 'He does carry tedious words like "duty" and "honour" round with him like an infection, as if he expected us to catch the horrid things and give up everything important in life.' His smile broadened to the customary teasing grin. 'Well, if it's not Max you love, then who is it? Aubyn? Aubyn's beastly dogs? Or is it that splendid Hussar up ahead who seems to be waiting for you so devotedly?'

I had been gazing absently out across the lake. Now, with a start, I looked towards the end of the South Walk and saw the Major standing in the shadow of the Eagle Tower, staring so intently in my direction that he might have been beckoning to me. Beatrice and Benedict bounded towards him, yelping gleefully. I called them back and restored them to the leash, using the action to cover my sudden trembling, caused by a mixture of excitement at something I had detected in his stance and anger that he should be so indiscreet. Though I was burning to find out the reason for his foolhardiness, I decided that I had no choice but to ignore him. And when I looked up from the dogs I saw with relief that he was gone.

I assayed a laugh. 'My loyal guard! They protect me so assiduously you might mistake them for my jailers.'

But Count von Tarn's momentary interest in the Major also seemed to have vanished, and now he stood, elbows on the parapet, head bowed, gazing down into the waters of the lake. His air of dejection surprised me.

'It seems to me, Anton,' I said, attempting to imitate his own teasing tone, 'it is you, not I, who are suffering from the Suzannahs.'

He looked up with a wry smile, suddenly no longer the cynical poseur, but very much the boy he still was. 'Does it, Marie? Well, I suppose I am. And confoundedly, stupidly painful it is too.'

'May I know who she is?'

He gave me a strange look and then, to my amazement, burst out laughing. 'No, dear Marie. You may not.'

'Does your father disapprove?'

His laughter redoubled, and I was all at once disturbed by the bitterness of it, wondered suddenly if his questions, his despondency, meant that he thought of me as – but no, that was absurd!

'My father? Disapprove? He would die of apoplexy if he knew. Or horsewhip me. Or both. So you see, Marie, I'm entitled to my Suzannahs, I—'

But I was no longer listening, for I had felt Beatrice and Benedict tug at the leash and had seen out of the corner of my eye the flash of a scarlet tunic reappear by the Eagle Tower. This time I could stand it no longer. Thrusting the dogs' leash into Anton's hand, and giving the feeble pretext that I would reprimand the Major for being so tactlessly intrusive, I hurried towards him.

We did not speak till we were out of sight beyond the tower and skirting the East ramparts in the direction of the chapel.

'You must be mad!' I said.

'I'm on leave tonight for four days. I couldn't go, Ma'am, without speaking to you. You wouldn't have wished it.'

We slid into the shadows of the chapel porch, crossing ourselves with holy water from the stoup. In the emptiness of the nave our whispers echoed alarmingly; the candles beneath the statue of Our Lady flickered in our faces.

'They'll move His Majesty to Freischutz on the 22nd July. I got word of it this morning.'

'But that's impossible! It's the day before the wedding.'

'There is no other way, Ma'am. My friend has only three fellow officers to rely on. They can't overpower a whole battalion.'

I looked at him helplessly. In the candlelight his eyes seemed to glitter, pleading with me. 'Don't you see, Ma'am, it makes everything easier. You will be in Rosenholm, the distance we shall have to travel to meet up with the party from Waldheim will be much shorter. Your Majesties will have the best possible chance of reaching the border safely.'

I sighed, but I knew in my heart that, even though it meant going through more ceremonies, more pretences, if it were our only chance I must take it. We left the chapel separately. I stayed behind for a moment to light a candle for Freddy, for both of us. Then I went to rejoin Count von Tarn.

He was still gazing gloomily out across the lake, and though I did not know which I feared most, an embarrassing declaration or an inquisition, he merely asked mischievously what I would give him not to tell Maximilian that I was conducting a disgraceful flirtation with the commander of my guard.

VII

'If you ask me, Ma'am,' said Rosa, clicking her tongue irritatingly, 'you're stark mad.'

'I didn't ask you, Rosa.'

'But having gone so far with it – the foreign Families all here, the souvenirs in the shops, the trousseau ready to be displayed – you may just as well put a good face on it and swallow the rest of the medicine.'

I made no reply other than to pull off Maximilian's sapphire and cast it into the hairpin tray.

'Think how His Majesty will feel.'

Putting Freddy's ring back in its rightful place I offered

her my hands for her to draw on my gloves. 'I am doing it
for His Majesty, Rosa.'

'But His other Majesty – think of the scandal! He'll never
be able to show his head in any of the Courts of Europe
again, let alone in Rosenholm.'

'Perhaps he should have considered that while he was
sending me forged letters and threatening me with King
Friedrich's life. Besides, he wants this marriage as little as I
do. In a couple of days he won't give a fig.'

She turned away shaking her head and, muttering, began
to drag the big wicker skip into the centre of the dressing-
room.

Had I not, I thought as I watched her, been forced to go
through enough as it was? I had made for the second time
my formal entry as a bride into the city, in the great glass
State Coach with its panels by Rubens and its ostrich-plumed
greys; I had dutifully waved my handkerchief at the crowds
along the troop-lined route, at the schoolgirls who threw rose
petals and the tradesmen proudly displaying my portrait and
the flag wavers brandishing the green and white of Thalia
and Sylvania's scarlet and black. I had been blessed by the
Cardinal Archbishop in St Xaviersdom and welcomed officially to the Residenz by a guard of honour of the Deathwatch
and the traditional offering of bread and salt; I had comforted
Princess Helena who, accompanying me in her role as
Maximilian's substitute mother, seemed more terrified and
bemused that I was; and I had done my best to smile at
Maximilian himself, and not to flinch when he had taken my
arm to conduct me on an inspection of the wedding presents,
the porcelains and rare enamels sent by foreign dignatories,
the toilet sets and ink stands encrusted with gold and lapis
lazuli, the embroidered pen-wipers and firescreens lovingly
crafted by schoolchildren and peasant grandmothers.

The three-day retreat required of me before the ceremony
was, by contrast, a blessed relief. Tradition permitted me to
meet Maximilian only once a day at communion and then
we were forbidden to speak. Daring to look sideways at him
as we knelt together at the altar rail, I thought with surprise
that he appeared tired and uneasy, and I observed that on
each occasion he refused the sacraments, remaining instead
with his head bowed in prayer.

The retreat, of course, had its other advantages. Using the excuse of piety, I was able to rid myself for much of the time of Ursula and Suzannah, so that I could be alone with Rosa to rehearse every step of our plan. And now, on this last evening, I had announced that in order to compose myself I should retire early. I had said my paternoster with Maximilian's chaplain and made my confession. No one would disturb me until the next morning – when they would find me gone.

I considered myself in the glass with satisfaction. I was wearing a drab grey travelling cloak resurrected from my old wardrobe and at least three years out of fashion. With my hair simply done and with the addition of a hat with a heavy veil, I should pass very well as a poor-genteel burgher's wife – I should scarcely merit a glance, let alone recognition.

Dusk was falling over the unfamiliar view of the English Church and the Opera House. Nine o'clock. At Aveling, exactly half-way between Waldheim and Freischutz, the citizens, the mayor, even the local police, would be carousing in the taverns and beer-gardens in anticipation of the next day's festive dinner and dancing in the streets. And in the gathering shadows outside the town the four horsemen would be waiting, their pistols concealed beneath their capes, listening for the rumble of wheels on the deserted road, for Freddy's closed carriage with its military escort. I looked about me for the last time. I should miss Aubyn – if I felt I was betraying anyone it was he, with his bluff good nature and his unfailing kindness. And I should dreadfully miss Aubyn's dogs, slumbering now in their baskets in the boudoir, drugged with a mild opiate by Rosa so that they should not signal my absence by howling. But, for the rest, I felt only elation that the moment of freedom had come at last.

Darting me a final acid look, Rosa flung open the lid of the skip and with her assistance I climbed into it, deploring the need for so many skirts and petticoats. When at last I was installed, foetuslike, upon the cushions she had thoughtfully placed in the bottom, she handed me in my hat and draped a layer of crêpe-de-chine chemises and bloomers over me. Then she closed the lid.

Though she had torn out the oilskin lining so that the

weave of the wickerwork would allow me a small supply of air and even minuscule glimpses of my surroundings, the confined space, with the weight of material on top of me, was decidedly claustrophobic. I should only be imprisoned thus for half an hour but I knew I should measure every minute of my captivity. I cursed the obligation to wear stays, feeling whalebone dig into my hips, my armpits, all the soft and vulnerable parts of my body.

But there was worse to come. I heard Rosa admit the footmen, heard her caution them not to wake me, then grumble on about the whims of young girls, and how she couldn't see that Valenciennes lace wasn't just as good an edging to lingerie as Point d'Alençon, she couldn't indeed, but it was my wedding and the trousseau would go on display to all the nobility in a day's time, so if it meant unfortunate girls sewing through the night, spoiling their poor eyes and working their fingers to the bone – well, that was Royalty for you and what was there to be done about it?

The basket lurched as they picked me up, lurched and swayed abominably, through the door and along the corridor, so that I was afraid I should sneeze or be sick. Then came the ordeal of the back stairs, three rickety flights with the wicker bottom bumping against every step on the way down. The man in front swore at the weight and his companion replied with a lewd joke about the intimate nature of their burden. Then I was flung down unceremoniously and pushed and shoved and jarred against a gatepost, until suddenly I could feel the shock of the cool night air and smell horses. The cart to take me to Amdorskis, the lacemakers in Schneiderstrasse. I was jolted onto it so violently that I was certain my head must be bleeding where it had been hurled against the lid of the basket. I heard one of the men give the driver instructions to take special care of his load – Their Majesties' honeymoon depended on it – and more obscenities and laughter followed. Then the whip cracked and we were off.

Though it was dark inside the cart I had the sense, once we had passed the guard at the South Gate, of people thronging the streets, laughing, singing, enjoying the fine night and the promise of tomorrow's holiday. I smiled to

myself wryly, trying to take my mind off my pins and
needles and my ever-increasing collection of bruises. By now
Rosa would have arranged the bolster in my bed with the
false pieces to look like a glimpse of my hair upon the pillow.
By now the troops of Freddy's escort would be lying gagged
and bound in some unsuspecting Aveling farmer's cornfield,
while three of my loyal officers, discarding their capes to
reveal their uniforms, rode in their place, and on the box the
fourth guided Freddy's carriage off the Freischutz road and
due south towards the mountains and the railway halt at
Marienberg.

After a while the increase in our jolting told me we had
reached the cobbles of the Old Town. The festive noises died
away. Everyone in the garment quarter would have shut
up shop and migrated to the centre of the city to join the
merriment. The narrow streets here would be dark and
deserted. The cart stopped, I heard the driver climb down
whistling, heard the bolts being drawn back in response to
his knocking and then, with joy, the Major's voice.

I bore with fortitude my last banging and shaking up the
stairs to the rooms over the Amdorskis' shop. The lid of my
prison was unfastened and I saw the Major's face looking
down at me with concern. My legs and arms had lost all
feeling and he had to lift me out and prop me in a sitting
position against the wall until I could chafe the blood back
into them. My hair had come unpinned, my hat was
crushed, and my travelling cape was creased almost beyond
recovery. I groped my way across the landing to the nearest
door in search of a looking-glass.

The Major stopped me. 'No, Ma'am. The old couple are
tied up in there. I'd rather they didn't see Your Majesty,
rather they stayed as much in ignorance as possible.'

'But I must look a fright,' I said. 'People will notice.'

'It's dark, Ma'am,' he replied, in a voice too grim for
gallantry. 'And there'll be no one at Marienberg except the
station porters.'

He looked, by the light of the lantern, in his civilian
clothes, younger than ever. His face wore a worried frown
and his hand shook slightly as he picked up his pistol. While
I smoothed myself down as best I could and pinned on my
hat, he went to the landing window, drew up the sash a

few inches and gave a low whistle. Almost immediately there came the answering rattle of wheels upon the cobbles outside. Extinguishing the lantern, he led me downstairs. The carriage stood, blinds drawn, waiting for us before the Amdorskis' shuttered shop-front.

We did not speak a great deal on the two-hour journey to Marienberg. I passed the time with thoughts of Rosa and Freddy. I knew it would be no challenge to Rosa's native cunning to persuade the guard at the South Gate of the Residenz into conspiring to her truancy: 'Her Royal Highness, bless her, sleeping like a baby, ready for the Great Day – and me, well, Sergeant, you know how it is, with everyone else in the city enjoying themselves, I fancied a spot of fresh air and maybe a glass of *Apfelwein* – if you, naughty boy, won't tell on me.' By now Rosa would be on the night train to Austria, chugging steadily towards Marienberg. And Freddy – fear of discovery had prevented me sending any message to him, we had been obliged to leave him in ignorance; my heart pounded as I imagined what must now be going through my astonished, happy Freddy's mind.

Beside me the Major sat very stiff and upright, with his pistol – rather melodramatically, I thought – cradled on his knee. Occasionally he made the little nervous noise in his throat, covering it with a pretence of coughing. He seemed completely given over to the tension of the moment, his reflexes tuned, his concentration absolute, as if he were about to go into action. And I knew too that he was calculating the speed of the horses, trying to estimate the distance we had covered, for the night train drew in to Marienberg station precisely at 12.14am, stopping only for a few minutes to pick up mail, and it was too dark to consult his watch to see what progress we were making.

After a while the horses slowed as we began to climb and I felt the cooler air of the mountains. In a nearby hamlet the church clock struck the half hour. Eleven-thirty. The Major seemed to subside slightly with relief. On the road into Marienberg we encountered several parties of revellers who passed close by our wheels catchcalling drunkenly, but the station was a kilometre further up the pass and as we rounded the bend and the horse's hooves crunched upon the gravel of the forecourt there was silence – nothing but the distant chink of cowbells.

The Major pulled up his blind a whisker and peered at his watch by the moonlight. Five to twelve – we had made good time. Freddy's carriage should be here by now, hidden in a deserted barn five hundred metres up the pass. At twelve o'clock precisely one of the officers would ride into the forecourt, ask the Major the way to St Kuno and be directed back along the road by which he had come. Carrying the travelling rug which the Major had so solicitously spread over my knees, I should then descend from our carriage, and the Major and I should walk onto the platform to wait for the train. At ten minutes past twelve Freddy's carriage would draw up and he too would make his way onto the platform. Though we should board the nearly-empty train separately, the three of us would meet up in the same second-class carriage and four minutes later we should pull out of Marienberg on our way to Austria. Once we were moving I should strap the travelling rug around my waist with a strip torn from my petticoat so that beneath my voluminous travelling cape I should appear in an advanced state of pregnancy. Freddy would simulate sleep, his head buried in my shoulder to disguise his face from any railway official who ventured to penetrate the drawn blinds of our compartment. We were ready then to prepare ourselves for the most dangerous point in our journey, the stopping of the train at the Sylvanian side of the border.

We had considered the train our safest form of travel since it was the most obvious and public and therefore arguably the least likely choice we should make, but we needed to take some precautions for a police search at the border. Here again we should rely upon being as obvious as possible. Assisted by Freddy, keeping his head well down, I should leave the train and, feigning the first stages of labour, ask to be conducted to a waiting room and given smelling salts. The Major would stride up to us, saying he was a doctor and offering to be of help, and between the three of us we should create a pandemonium of our own while the police were combing the train, a pandemonium which, we prayed, would be so delicate in its cause as to leave us undisturbed except by well-meant offers of assistance. At the first signs

of the train's departure we should, of course, be hurried
back to our compartment, the Sylvanian railway officials not
wishing to burden themselves with the bother of a happy
event which could just as well occur in Austria; and in five
more minutes we should have travelled over the border to
freedom, to be joined by Rosa, who had all the time stayed
where she was, in the anonymous squalor of chickens and
cloth bundles in the third class.

It was risky, but I was heavily-veiled, no one was looking
for a pregnant woman, and my histrionics would draw attention away from Freddy, who could keep his head averted in
his attempts to loosen the neck of my dress and show
husbandly concern. If for some reason we were unable to
carry out our stratagem the Major had bravely sworn to
create a diversion, using his pistol if need be to draw the
police away from the train, but I prayed his gallantry would
not be tested.

Somewhere in Marienberg a clock began to chime twelve.
The Major stiffened as if he had received the order to
advance. Concealing his pistol in the breast of his jacket and
commanding me somewhat peremptorily to remain where I
was with the blinds drawn, he jumped down from the
carriage. I listened expectantly for the sound of hooves. Only
a nightjar churring, a drunk maundering further down the
pass, cowbells. I waited. A minute. Five minutes. Supposing
they had met with some unforeseen delay, supposing overpowering the guards had taken longer than they'd planned?
I could hear the Major clear the nervous tickle in his throat.
Suddenly I could no longer stand not seeing, not knowing.
I flung open the carriage door and though he shook his
head, motioning me back, I climbed down to join him.

The moon, which had been obscured by cloud earlier, was
now very bright, so that the little rustic station-hut cast
deep shadows across the gravel. It seemed desolate as if the
station manager, in holiday mood like everyone else, were
sleeping off a night in the *Bierkeller*. There was nothing, no
one; only the majestic sweep of mountains soaring into cloud
on one side and the dark chasm of the gorge on the other.
Then, simultaneously, I heard the steady chug-chug of the
night-train grinding towards Marienberg and the pounding
of hooves at the gallop coming down the pass.

I could have laughed with relief. The horseman rounded the bend into the forecourt, I half-turned to smile at the Major – and then I saw the flying cape, the ashen face, the forehead caked with blood. Scarcely reining in his horse, the man screamed: 'Get away, Siegfried! We were betrayed! They moved him yesterday! Get back!' Then several things seemed to happen at once. A voice behind us bellowed: 'State police! Halt! You are under arrest,' I spun round, a lantern flared, a shot sounded. The horse thundered past us, riderless, still at the gallop and instantly there seemed to be shooting from everywhere. The Major hurled himself in front of me screaming: 'Get into the carriage! For God's sake, get into the carriage!' He aimed his pistol. It roared. There was an answering roar. And I saw, as if in slow motion, the Major lifted off his feet, jerked upwards, then falling, falling, a dark stain spreading in his back. It seemed an eternity before he hit the gravel, crumpling awkwardly. Then everything was very quiet.

I stared at the Major lying at my feet. The stain was spreading beneath him now, wider and wider. I bent down and touched his head. His mouth was open and I could see both rows of his very even white teeth. Siegfried. I thought absurdly that I had never once asked his Christian name. '*I will serve you, Your Majesty. With my life, if necessary.*' I put my arm around his shoulders and tried to draw his head into my lap. The lantern shone suddenly into my eyes and five or six men seemed to materialise from the shadows. I was conscious of a thin rodent face behind the lantern and then of someone pulling me by the arm, trying to drag me to my feet. I looked about me bewildered. Our cabman had climbed down from his box and was held between two of the police agents in a posture of abject surrender. On the gravel a few metres from the Major was another dark bundle, lying in another dark stain.

The hand tugged at my arm again and a voice said: 'You will oblige us by not resisting, Ma'am. We have orders to take you back to Rosenholm immediately.'

There was a whistle and a belch of steam; the night train to Austria, pulling away from the station.

VIII

They had smuggled me into the Residenz through the little
door at the side of the chapel, over the roof and down the
back stairs to Maximilian's gun-room, the route Sigismund's
mistresses from the Volksoper had been said once to take.
There was no sign of the guards on the East Gate and our
progress had been unobserved and unobstructed. Though
the two agents who had escorted me back from Marienberg
had treated me peremptorily – not roughly, but without due
respect for my rank or concession to my tears – once we
were inside Maximilian's apartments the awesomeness of
where they were seemed to impress them, to bring them
back to a sense of the proper formalities. Rodent-face was
summoned into Maximilian's presence to make his report
and I was left in the morning-room with the other man as
my guard.

Maximilian's apartments, as did mine, led off a long
central corridor and, though it was now nearly four in the
morning, every light seemed still to be ablaze and I could
hear a constant bustle, the duty adjutant delivering and
sending telegrams, doors opening and closing, voices. I
froze. The voices of Vielfrass and the new Chief of Police,
Weber. Yes, of course – though Vielfrass was Chancellor
now, Weber was only a cypher; the control of the secret
police was too vital an asset to be surrendered, where police
agents were involved Vielfrass was bound to know. My eyes
began to sting again. I had not thought that things could be
any worse.

We seemed to wait for ever, the policeman and I. I began
gradually to become conscious of my surroundings and as I
did so I felt a growing perplexity. For, in marked contrast
with the splendour of my new apartments, Maximilian's
rooms were spartan. I looked around me at the distempered
walls, unadorned apart from a small portrait of Sigismund
and Tatiana above the mantelpiece, at the plain, utilitarian
furniture, the sparse rugs upon the polished floor. In its total
absence of ornament or luxury, even the trivial clutter of
ordinary life, the room was like a blank page waiting for the
handwriting of possession, as if its occupant were merely

passing through and had not thought it worth bothering to unpack.

And yet, at a second glance, it was there after all, the handwriting, impossible to construe, like Maximilian himself. I remembered now passing a bedroom, white like a cell, with an iron bedstead, remembered the fanciful rumours that he had once been a monk, and found it suddenly strange that I had been told scarcely anything about his past life. I became aware that my surroundings were not uncomfortable or stark; rather, there was something fitting in their functional cleanness, a harmonious feeling of light and space, of pleasing textures and simple things well-made. There was a faint aroma too, an admixture of worn leather, furniture wax and Turkish tobacco which, far from betokening stern self-denial, came agreeably upon the senses. I realised with a start that the opulent décor of my apartments, which I had taken as yet another indication of Maximilian's desire to coerce me into his image, had been decreed because it was thought I would expect it.

The rodent-faced agent put his head round the door and, with a nod to my guard, motioned to us to follow him. The bustle in the corridor had ceased, the adjutants, the secretaries had all quite suddenly vanished. We passed through an empty antechamber and came to the half-open door of what, presumably, was Maximilian's study. I paused. But when I looked round for my escort it too had suddenly melted away. I took a deep breath and pushed the door open.

The room in which I found myself was as spartan as the first, except for the addition of a great many books and papers. There was a tiled stove at one end, a few hard upright chairs, a chess-board with the pieces set out, another portrait of Sigismund and a desk. At the desk, amongst a welter of papers, Maximilian sat, reading a telegram. He glanced up as I entered, cast the telegram aside and pushed back his chair. He wore a black single-breasted Litewka – the undress he presumably favoured for work – as if this evening he had not taken dinner. His hair was dishevelled and there was the beginning of a shadow about his jaw. But there was nothing in his drawn face of weakness or exhaustion, or even of his customary dismissiveness, only a cold, implacable anger. I avoided his eyes.

'You may sit down,' he said very quietly.

'I think I should prefer to—'

'Sit down!' he said.

He had scarcely raised his voice, but in spite of myself I obeyed immediately. He stood before the stove, beneath the portrait of Sigismund, surveying me in silence with a curious expression which might have been contempt or even pity. I had not imagined that his anger would frighten me so much. I found my eyes, in order not to meet his, settling on the portrait of Sigismund, found myself thinking how alike they were, father and son, menacingly imperious and tall. I could feel his immobility like a force, sense, in the discipline of it, what was contained, as if a wrong movement on my part, the merest start, would suddenly unleash something ungovernable and terrifying. His silence seemed interminable.

'So,' he said eventually in that quiet, icy voice, 'I see I should have accepted your own estimate of your intelligence. I see I should have understood that your head was filled with romantic twaddle, that you based your life on the fatuous extravagances of cheap novelettes.'

I stared at him, not comprehending. 'What have you done with my husband?' I said. 'I want Freddy, I want to know that he's safe.'

'Friedrich is perfectly safe at the monastery at Freischutz. And that is considerably more than could have been hoped for if your little escapade had come off. Have you any idea what gallivanting round half Sylvania in the dead of night would have done to him? Have you any conception of what would have happened if he'd had another fit? Well, tell me, have you?'

'Don't shout at me,' I said.

He had not shouted, but he had taken a step towards me so that I suddenly felt trapped in my chair.

'Shout at you?' he said. 'Dear God, when I think of the cost of tonight's stupidity I have some difficulty in restraining myself from breaking your neck.'

'I can see that it has cost you your pride,' I said.

He took another step towards me, then his jaw muscles

tightened, he turned away. Going to his desk he took a cigarette from a silver box, tapped the tobacco tight and lit it. I had never seen him smoke before.

When he spoke, his voice was even again. 'My dear, pretty, brainless Marie, when you embarked upon this adventure of yours did you not think, just once, of the consequences? Apart, that is, from half killing the man you profess to love?'

'I thought we should be free. We should have been if your vile secret police hadn't tricked us.'

'Oh? And what, pray, would you have done when you were apprehended at the border?'

I told him. He stared at me for a moment, then threw back his head in a long sarcastic laugh.

'So, child, in order that you could indulge your highly-coloured fantasies, I now have three promising officers under arrest, one policeman and one soldier injured, and one man dead.'

I was conscious with horror of the blood on my clothes. 'The Major?'

'No. I received a telegram from the hospital at St Kuno half an hour ago informing me that though Major von Pallandt is gravely wounded he is likely to survive. Lieutenant Kessler, however, has shot himself. I understand that was the shot which triggered off the police fire at Marienberg.'

The relief at his news of the Major went through me in a great sigh. Then I remembered the other dark heap on the gravel. I felt the blood on my cloak like a taint.

'Of course,' he continued, drawing on his cigarette, 'Major von Pallandt's survival could be argued to be somewhat academic. He and his three fellow conspirators face charges of high treason. And the penalty for that, as I'm sure even you can remember, is the firing squad.'

I stared at the hem of my cloak. I felt suddenly sick.

'And then there is the matter of your maid.'

'Oh no, not Rosa!'

'She was arrested at the border and is also under a charge of treason.'

'Oh please, not Rosa! She's the only person who came with me from Thalia, she's not just my maid, she's my friend.'

'Then she has good reason to regret your singularly selfish notion of friendship.'

Oh Rosa, Rosa! The tears began to ooze slowly down my cheeks.

'Your maid will be sent back to Thalia where I shall ask your uncle to show clemency towards her. Friedrich has begged me to spare the four officers' lives and I shall do so, principally for your sake – it seems to me you have enough to reproach yourself with already. But the waste still remains, the stupid, futile waste of it! All four men were career officers – I gather Major von Pallandt in particular was marked out for an exceptionally brilliant future. Now they will be court-martialled, discharged with ignominy and given long terms of imprisonment, probably with hard labour. And for what? So that you could have your pathetic little adventure!'

I hung my head abjectly, wanting to hide myself. He moved away from me with an impatient sigh.

'Don't you see, Marie? Don't you understand your responsibilities? You have only to flutter your lashes and there will always be some impressionable young man consumed with lofty ideals and ready to serve you – simply because of who you are. Don't you see that it gives you an extra burden, a duty to think most scrupulously before you act? You're not in a position to indulge in flights of melodrama like any other stupid woman brought up on a diet of romances. You – both of us – have an absolute duty to measure the consequences of our actions and to know that one wrongly-made decision can put at risk reputations, futures, lives.'

I looked up. 'And I suppose you considered all that most scrupulously before you plunged us into war, before you set my people, Freddy's people, to kill one another and betray their King?'

He returned my look coldly, steadily. 'Yes, child, I did consider it. I consider it still. I am precisely aware of my duty to Sylvania and of the fact that it is my responsibility to prevent any further blood being shed.'

'Then why did you allow what happened tonight? Why, if you knew our plans, as you obviously did, did you lead us on, let us fall into your vile trap? Why didn't you stop us?'

'Because I need the loyalty of the army, because I cannot allow the smallest seeds of revolt to go unpunished. And to act, I needed evidence. Oh, Lieutenant Kessler had been under suspicion for some time. Vielfrass's men had been watching both him and Pallandt – watching you too, Marie, and your maid. But there was no concrete evidence against you, only surmise. So we brought forward our plans for Friedrich by a day, set up a fake escort party and waited.' He bent to throw the stub of his cigarette into the stove and suddenly there was a note of weariness in his voice. 'I suppose I hoped, even at the last moment, you would draw back. I suppose I hoped you, of all people, would realise the foolishness of it, that it wasn't an interesting garden party you were planning. I held – I had been encouraged to hold – a higher estimate of your good sense and understanding.'

He turned towards the window and a silence fell. Beyond the spires and domes of the city the sky was shot with pink and gold, the first glimmerings of dawn.

'What will you do with me?' I asked softly.

'I have managed with considerable difficulty to conceal your part in tonight's affair. There has been a trivial incident, that is all, involving a few young army hotheads. The men who brought you back will hardly find it worth their while to talk. And I think you can rely upon the honourable instincts of your fellow conspirators to protect the name of their Queen at all costs.'

'But Vielfrass knows,' I said.

He gave a bitter laugh. 'Yes, Vielfrass knows. And I must say I don't thank you for it. I most particularly don't require to be in our esteemed Chancellor's debt at the moment.' He sighed, moved towards his desk where the lamp was still burning. His anger seemed spent now, he ran his fingers through his hair as if my inadequacies had fatigued him. 'Marie, we have nothing further to say to each other and it is now nearly half-past four. You will find that there is temporarily no guard outside your apartments. I suggest you return to them quietly before anyone wakes. You will need to sleep if you can manage it. We have a difficult day ahead of us.'

I stared at him, thinking I must have misunderstood. He had picked up a handful of papers from his desk and was leafing through them, not looking at me, assuming my dismissal.

'But you can't . . .' I said. 'You can't still be expecting me to . . . that we should still be married?'

He glanced round from the desk with his eyebrows raised. 'What else should I expect?'

I continued to stare at him unbelievingly. 'No,' I said. 'Oh please, no!'

'It's peculiarly unsatisfactory to both of us, I agree. But it's somewhat late, don't you think, for us to have any choice in the matter?'

I got up from my chair and went unsteadily towards him. 'Oh please, I know there'll be a scandal, I know what I'm asking will damage your self-esteem – but please, if you can bring yourself to have any feeling for me, if you possess one ounce of compassion, please, please . . .'

He put the papers down with irritation and surveyed me for a moment as if I were a small and recalcitrant child. 'My dear Marie, I have a hung parliament with Keller, justifiably, believing the Liberals should have more influence, and Vielfrass threatening to stage a revolt if I give it to them. I have a people who are so used to brutality and persecution that injustice has become a premise of their existence. I have men out of work and families going hungry, industrial collapse in Nordstadt, and on top of that I'm told the harvest is likely to fail in this drought. Today's elaborate pantomime is one of the few ways I can make Sylvania appear united for once, one of the dismally few means at my disposal to convey to the people that there is something solid in all the chaos, some other force above the squabbling of their politicians which they can look to for hope. I cannot, however much I might wish to, cancel our pretty little pageant. My personal feelings, and yours, are immaterial.'

I had been about to put my hand pleadingly on his arm, but now I drew back. How I hated his coldness, his cynicism, his refusal to recognise me as anything more than a necessary piece in his grubby political game!

'I won't marry you!' I screamed. 'I'm married to Freddy, before God! I won't marry you, I'd rather die first!'

I saw for an instant all the anger come back into his eyes, thought he would strike me, put my hand up to protect myself. But instead he turned away with a gesture of impatience.

'Why?' he said at length, in a voice that was tight with the effort of control. 'Why have we gone so far with what appears to be a ludicrous charade? I understood that you could not love me, that the idea of our marriage was displeasing to you. But then, when you wrote giving your consent, I was persuaded that you saw, as I did, a responsibility, a duty, that you put your feeling for Sylvania above yourself. I have tried as far as possible to respect the difficulty of your decision, to leave you alone to come to terms with it. But, God knows, you have always been free to choose, God knows I have never forced you—'

'Not forced me?' I stared at him contemptuously. 'You, who sent your minions to blackmail and threaten me, who even stooped to forgery, who held me to ransom with my husband's life? I knew you would get your way somehow, I knew that a man like you wouldn't be restrained by conscience or pity. I lived every day in terror for Freddy and what you would do to him. What other choice had I but to write that letter? It was the only way I could think of saving Freddy, my only defence against your blackmail. And now I have no defences, nothing . . . and you may be as heartless and sadistic as you like . . .' I tailed away into impotent sobbing, crying noisily where I stood, covering my face with my hands.

There was a long silence. I was conscious of him watching me, conscious of a change in him. When he eventually spoke his voice was a whisper.

'My poor dear child, if that is your estimation of me I am not surprised our marriage is repugnant to you or that you tried to run away.' He paused as if he were thinking. Then he came over to me and lowered my hands from my face, slowly, carefully, as if he were touching something fragile. I was suddenly exhausted, too drained and defeated to tear myself away. I stood with my hands in his, compelled to gaze up at him. Blurrily I saw that he too now wore a look of utter exhaustion.

'I could have stopped it,' he said. 'Even two months ago – if I had sufficiently understood. But I cannot stop the wedding now. However, I shall make you a promise. It was always my intention that we should live as separately as our official duties would allow. Once you have given me an heir I shall hold you to nothing but the strict formalities of our marriage. We shall live discreetly and permanently apart. You may go where you please, do what you wish – so long as our obligations to Sylvania are fulfilled I shall not question you or make demands of you. We shall have, in every sense, the purely business arrangement we have talked of. But now,' – letting go of my hands, he brushed my cheek with his fingers for an instant – 'now it is light and you must return to your apartments. Please try to sleep a little and prepare yourself for this afternoon. I am afraid there is no escape.'

CHAPTER FOUR

Anton von Tarn

I

It was judged by the elders of the Council, in their wisdom, that His Royal Highness Crown Prince Maximilian Eugen Sigismund Otto Lothar von Hohenstaufen, Duke of Rosenholm, Elector of Nordstadt, direct blood descendant of Friedrich Barbarossa and putative heir to the Emperor Charlemagne, should, for reasons of security and so that he might better benefit from my father's political tutelage, forthwith take up residence with us at the Schloss Beauregard.

This arrangement filled me with mixed feelings: on the one hand, suspicious as I was of His newly-elevated Highness, it would enable me to enjoy daily the spectacle of my father being most thoroughly gulled; on the other, it threatened to subject me to discomforts and humiliations of a hitherto unprecedented nature. I might chuckle to consider my father's dilemma – unthinkable, indeed, that he should surrender his *droit de seigneur* over his own household, yet this was precisely what the rules of precedence for which he was such a stickler decreed; I did not, however, smile so unrestrainedly when I contemplated the indignities which would be inflicted upon my own person, along with everyone else who was not of the blood: the loathsome straitjacket of waiting to be addressed before speaking, the seesaw of sitting and standing in tune with the Royal Personage's movements, the ludicrous possibility that rooms I had freely strolled in and out of ever since I was a child I should now be obliged to quit backwards, bowing.

And then there was my position as only son of the household: my father, after all, scarcely disguised his preference for his protégé. I should be displaced, become, in my own family circle, a hanger-on, a mere equerry like the moribund Straubnitz. Worst of all, the Paterfamilias, in mapping out a regime to equip His Royal Highness for his future career, with tuition in politics, economics, protocol, military strategy and Hohenstaufen tradition, had found a new means of tormenting me. The afternoons were to be set aside for the acquisition of those skills he considered fundamental to the proper conduct of the monarch – riding, fencing, pistol and rifle practice – and while, by nature of my cadet status, I was summarily to be excluded from any subject I might have found intellectually stimulating, it was decreed that I too should benefit from these afternoons of 'character-building'.

It is not hard to imagine my suffering at the prospect of this indignity. To be obliged to spend valuable hours away from my books, rushing about in a lather pretending to terrorise inanimate objects with swords or guns, or engaging in disagreeable intimacies with man's most treacherous servant, the horse – well, as I have already made clear, I had up until then viewed a talent for such pursuits to be incompatible with any degree of intelligence. And yet, before we had even begun, I had a presentiment that the new Crown Prince, despite his cleverness, would not require his character built, that he would have found, in the refining influences of the Hotel de Miramont, the means to acquire a good seat on a horse, that he would possess a natural eye and an athletic prowess far beyond mine. And I discovered unworthily that it mattered, that I could not pass the whole thing off with my usual disdain, that the memory of the café incident was enough – I now passionately desired not to appear foolish in front of him.

In the event, when His Royal Highness arrived at the beginning of that May 1888, most of my problems simply evaporated. Whether reluctant or not to tempt fate now he had so successfully pulled the wool over everyone's eyes, he contrived to behave with modest restraint, submitting to my father's authority as his senior in age and his mentor and still addressing him as 'Sir', which delighted the old fool mightily. He refused the accumulation of his own personal suite, contenting himself with the part-time services of Straubnitz, persisted in wearing his priest's black and, on his own insistence, was moved into a very ordinary set of rooms not far from mine, which maintained a chill simplicity throughout his occupation. And as for his relations with myself, well, though I confess it was to be some time before I was to use the '*du*' form towards him, since we were to be thrown much together and were, after a manner, old acquaintances, we fell very naturally and easily into addressing each other by our Christian names.

Even my physical sufferings were not as intense as I had anticipated. His months of illness and inactivity inevitably held him back at first, and besides I had arrived at a stratagem which, though it involved compromise, at least saved my pride. Since I must display my incompetence before him, I should work upon it, hone it, bring to it all the flair and hyperbole of a dramatic statement. Though it was difficult to appear witty when entangled in one's own rapier and even harder to fall off a horse with any degree of panache, I endeavoured to accomplish these things as amusingly and gracefully as I could, endowing my lack of brilliance with a rare brilliance of its own. In short, I became Court Jester. And there was a surprising compensation in this. My abiding fear of things equine and explosive began to diminish; I began to discover in myself a certain competence after all. True, I should never be able to persuade any quadruped into the finer points of dressage or fire a rifle without seeing my own reflection in the sights, but I might make a swordsman yet, and even derive some enjoyment from it.

There were other compensations too. My father was delighted with his protégé's progress. Max had used his seven years' unlimited access to M. de Miramont's library to good effect, and was widely-read in philosophy, history and political theory. Once his German was equal to it, his morning sessions in my father's study soon spilled over to the luncheon-table, transforming themselves from a pupil-teacher catechism to the enthusiastic debate of two like minds. You could see my father, finding such an accommodating audience, responding with the pathetic eagerness of a suddenly-requited lover. And his fondness for Max made him altogether more lenient towards me. It was not only that, having ensured at least four hours of my day were employed in sweaty masculinity, he ceased to mention my military career (perhaps, in his preoccupation, he had simply forgotten it). Max liked music, so for the first time, instead of being compelled to endure my sister Suzannah's nightly war with the pianoforte, I was permitted publicly to indulge my own 'unmanly' talents for the guitar and zither. Max could and did talk of poetry and plays as unashamedly as he discussed politics and history, so literature too was rehabilitated from forbidden feminine territory.

I was all but overwhelmed by this sudden, unlooked for freedom. After supper, if Max had finished working and we were not afflicted with *émigré* visitors, I would try to inveigle him into my study, where I would keep him up talking, just the two of us, into the small hours. I told him of my burning ambition for a university life and how, of course, my father implacably opposed it. I found myself talking of all kinds of things I had never been able to mention to anyone before: my hopes, my expectations, my constant battle with frustration and despair. The most extraordinary thing was that he listened – didn't tell me to take a cold bath or square my shoulders, but actually listened as if he understood.

One night after we had both retired and I found myself still restless and excited, unable to sleep, I began to reflect upon this curious phenomenon, this kinship I felt for him, which he perhaps even reciprocated.

The circumstances of my childhood have conditioned me to caution. My father had always doted on my three sisters, but I, who with characteristic lack of consideration had contrived to kill my mother at the moment of my birth, what room had I ever found in his affections? It did not help that Aunt Helena and Winders would pat my curls and point out that I was a very pretty child – prettiness was scarcely an attribute my father found commendable in a son. Then there was the business of growing up with so many girl-children. In order that I should not be contaminated by such excesses of femininity, I was given separate tutors, set to separate studies. Not that I was permitted the companionship of boys of my own age, either. The peculiar circumstances of our existence, my rank, which was too lowly for distinction yet too grand for ordinariness, a sort of genealogical no man's land, did not allow me to mix with the middle-class bankers' and merchants' sons who were the best our canton could yield for such a purpose. Up till now my only experience of affection had been the abstracted effusions of my Aunt Helena, and my closest male companion Uncle Gustav, who left me in no doubt, were it to be between me and the spiders, where his choice would lie.

Max, though eight years my senior, was the first person I had ever met who shared at least some of my interests. It was such a curious, beguiling experience to have someone to laugh with, someone who put their arm around your shoulders as though you were an equal, someone who addressed you as a human being, not a recalcitrant second lieutenant or a phenomenon considerably less interesting than a mating tarantula.

Sitting there that night, drawing upon the last of a great deal too many cigarettes, I made an extraordinary discovery. I admired Max. This was extraordinary not because of my suspicions about him – certainly, if, as was not improbable, the mendicant had lied and Max was Dieter Wolf, that made him, given the body at Fontarelles, not merely a fraud but a murderer; yet there was an excitement in this, in contemplating that this daring companion of mine had savoured the juices of the forbidden fruit, had, with godlike dispassion, taken life. No, what was curious in my feeling for Max was that I despised the very notion of one human being slavishly adulating another, considered it as much an aberration as my sisters' repulsive spooning with their suitors. Yet admiration was the word that came closest to encompassing my emotions. Max was handsome, clever, even rather better at some things than I was (albeit that since these things were in the main to do with guns and horses they did not qualify in any proper sense). Why not admire him? (I threw the remains of my cigarette into the embers.) Because after admiration came words like friendship, trust and loyalty, words of which I had learned justifiably to be cautious. And after all, my common sense told me that anyone who draws you out does so for a reason – human-beings are not given to listening to their fellows simply for the joy of it, but rather because any ordinary mortal talking unrestrainedly about himself will eventually reveal weaknesses which can be exploited. If Max had succeeded in drawing me, had I met with equal success? While he had talked freely of literature and music he had never once ceased to be his wary, infinitely inaccessible self, had never once spoken of the Marquis de Miramont or his time in the

Enclosure, no matter how I had sidled up in ambush. No, I would do better to steer clear of words like trust and friendship.

Yet even as I delivered myself of this caution I found my eyes hot with entirely unsoldierly tears at the thought of how I must stand deprived of both these rarities before I had ever enjoyed them.

The next night (perhaps unconsciously I wished to test him) I drank far too much brandy; and I told him something I have, for reasons which will become obvious, never told anyone, even when I was afterwards interrogated by my doltish English cousin and bullied by my father.

By the time I was eleven the Paterfamilias, observing that no amount of beating and cold baths would din the poetry or the prettiness out of me, had conceived a drastic plan. We had recently been visited by my Aunt Louise's son, the aforementioned doorpost, St John Aubyn, Duke of Hohen-Kastell and Carrick, who had forsworn family custom and gone away to school, to an English institution of military traditions, after which he had duly passed out of Sandhurst and been gazetted to the Guards. Accordingly my father decided that there was nothing for it but that I should be packed off to this English military school.

Imagine being suddenly transported to a country where there is neither winter nor summer but a perpetual dank, soupy inbetweenness in which your head is thick and your nose runs and your very bones feel damp. Imagine how I, a foreigner, unsuitably pretty and ineffectual at dangerous exercises on draughty playing fields, was teased. One night the senior boy in the dormitory, one of the bloods – Effingham I remember his name was – tied me face down upon my iron bedstead with the help of his cronies and, taking the point of his compass, proceeded to drill into each of my buttocks an extensive pattern of small holes which he then studiously filled in with ink. How long I lay there while he refined his handiwork, how long I sobbed into my pillow while they all gathered round, sniggering, with their candles, I do not know. When at last they untied me I went to the sluice and scrubbed my skin till it was raw. Then, tearing my towel into strips, I attempted to hang myself from the window-frame. And so, a week later, I was collected by my stiff-upper-lipped, stiff-brained cousin, and dispatched upon the packet-steamer to Boulogne.

Other people's humiliations are always amusing. I waited for Max to laugh. But perhaps he knew, perhaps he truly had been made to lick crosses on the floor of the monastery chapel and sleep with chains around his waist. He merely listened gravely with his eyebrows slightly raised.

By the time I had reached the end of my narrative I could feel my chin trembling treacherously. 'I should have preserved the pattern for my father,' I said. 'He could have construed some moral significance from it – joined up the scars, perhaps, and made a map of Friedrich the Great's campaigns.'

'Whereas in reality,' said Max lightly, 'they made several sonnets and the start of a novel.'

I stared at him. Then, despite myself, it was I who began to laugh. 'That's right!' I said. 'I'll show them! I'll write, I'll work until my brain is numb. I'll be another Kleist, another Schiller. I'll prove my genius to the dear Paterfamilias. And then we'll see – oh, indeed we shall – just who despises whom!'

Of course the next morning I was horrified by my confession. Certain he would hold me in contempt, I took the precaution of remaining pointedly aloof for a couple of days. But, as with our Montparnasse encounter, he never once referred to the episode, even obliquely; indeed, so far as my withdrawal would allow, his manner towards me continued unchanged. And when, a few days later, my father knocked me completely off balance by referring to Heidelberg in a tone almost devoid of his usual sneer I knew that Max had begun to press my case for me, that I was perhaps, for the first time in my life, allowed the unimaginable luxury of friendship.

II

I have said that Max was good at everything, and so he was, abominably, infuriatingly good. As well as being formidably intelligent he was, as my father would say, a man's man – a superb horseman, an elegant duellist, rapidly on the way to becoming a crack shot. In fact, when you looked at him you could scarcely believe my father's good fortune in having supplied himself with such a Crown Prince. There was, on top of everything, that mysterious presence of his, which came not simply from his being tall and straight and handsome, but from the sense he gave of being somehow subtly, silently in control. Even his irritating austerity of dress served to remind you how splendid he would look in all the glamour of a uniform, the black and brocaded silver of the Deathwatch or the scarlet of the Hussars.

However, I would observe that consummate ability is not necessarily the characteristic a man looks for in a friend. Rather he desires friendship to be the discreet setting for the gems of his own accomplishment. Max must somehow, in spite of everything, possess an Achilles heel; and so he did, though its precise nature I could then only imperfectly define.

It was, if you like, the Sigismund in him – not the face, but the nature, captured to such perfection in the Lenbach portrait. I had from the first noticed that when Max spontaneously laughed or smiled it was as if the door to a forbidden room had suddenly been opened, affording the fleeting glimpse of another person. As the summer wore on and he succumbed to the pleasures of his temporary freedom, I was increasingly vouchsafed these glimpses. And I would watch him smelling a rose in the garden, or giving his horse full rein in open country, or lying, eyes closed, upon the sofa in my study listening to me play the guitar, and think that he liked these things – passionately, indulgently he liked them. Oh, it was not that the control was not there, or the asceticism, but rather that they existed, had to exist, because perhaps he liked such things too well.

One glorious afternoon we had slipped away from the two servants my father had bestowed upon us as watchdogs and were riding through a pine-wood when we came upon a clearing with a small, waterlily-covered lake. Dismounting, we both decided to swim. I am not a strong swimmer and came out of the water first, drying myself with my under-linen and dressing immediately. When I turned round to look for Max I saw that he had flung himself down in the lush grass at the water's edge and was letting his body dry in the warmth of the sun. He lay on his back with his arms outstretched and, watching him, I had the sense of every muscle and sinew, every naked inch of him luxuriating expansively in the brilliant heat, unfolding to the touch of it upon his breast, his shoulders, his thighs, to the scent of the grass and the little muzzy sounds of grasshoppers and the birds singing far away in the wood, drinking it all in, intoxicated.

I stared with fascination at this unselfconscious nakedness, at the water glistening on his chest and belly and in the black hair above the thick stub of his cock, suddenly abjectly aware of my own boyishness; and as I stood looking at him I saw with a mixture of awe and embarrassment that he had begun to be aroused.

I must have betrayed myself somehow. All at once he was conscious of my presence, opened his eyes, rolled over abruptly onto his belly. I turned away, flushing to the roots of my hair.

'Do you know,' I said, in a voice that sounded brittle, 'I sometimes find it quite impossible to imagine your life at Mont Rémy. How you must have hated it!'

He looked at me for a moment. Then he smiled. 'There were compensations. When the Father Librarian had taken too much wine in the refrectory we could always steal his keys and open the closet where the evil books were kept.'

Reaching towards his heap of clothes, he found his ciga-rette-case and lit one of his rare cigarettes. I too took out my case and sat down on a large stone a few feet away by a clump of fritillaries. I smoked looking out towards the lake, still acutely aware of his nakedness.

'These books,' I asked, 'were they really lewdly, lasciv-iously, disgustingly evil?'

He laughed. 'They were mostly books on heresies – rather interesting on the whole. But we were told they were evil, so evil they were.'

'You weren't allowed to make your own judgement?'

'Good Lord, no. Critical thinking prevents obedience and the surrender of the individual will.'

'Ugh!' I said. 'It sounds exactly like the army. One for all and all for one, and that sort of rot.'

Again he laughed. 'Perhaps not precisely. But in that respect, yes.'

'Well, up with the individual will, I say. Let it reign gloriously, egocentrically supreme. And let us rejoice that you have been given back yours, splendidly and irrevocably.'

'I'm not sure,' he said dryly, 'that I have been given it back irrevocably.'

I glanced round at him astonished.

'If your father's plans come to fruition I may find myself obliged to submit my will to rather more general considerations.'

'But power *is* the exercise of the individual will.'

'Power, my dear Anton, is the responsibility to exercise authority fairly and wisely.'

'Oh bosh!' I said. 'You sound like the Pater. I don't believe in honour and duty and *noblesse oblige* and all that claptrap. They're just words to provide a spendidly high-minded disguise for the fact that the world is run by individual will, and the more wilful the individual the greater his part in running it. It simply isn't possible to sweep all the untidy bits of humanity under a nice clean carpet of justice and reason! Man is a supremely selfish creature and his prime impulse is to gratify that selfishness, whatever platitudes he may mouth about the general good.'

He shook his head, laughing. 'My dear Anton, your idealism is occasionally quite overwhelming.'

'I prefer cynicism – it saves one from disappointment. Of course Pater says it wears off with age, gets replaced, apparently, by something he calls "The Pragmatism of Maturity".' I threw my cigarette into the lake. 'Anyway, I'll bet you there isn't a man alive who can truly subdue his individual inclinations – not for anybody's good.'

'Perhaps not,' he said, rising and turning his back on me in one single movement, then reaching for his clothes. 'But it may still be his duty to try.' And I had a curious feeling we were suddenly talking at cross purposes.

III

It came to be remarked upon amongst my family circle that I was manifesting a change altogether for the better. I am sure my father put this down to the many hours I now spent in virile pursuits, but he also attributed it to Max's influence, and in this he was to some degree correct. Max might be a liar and a murderer, but he had used his actor's skills to enter most thoroughly – even over-extravagantly – into his part, not only professing to share the Paterfamilias's archaic code of honour, but also on occasion rehearsing its hackneyed notions to me without so much as a hint of mockery.

I have omitted so far to mention in this narrative an irritation which, though ludicrous in its nature, had plagued our household since Max's arrival. Of my three sisters, the younger two had mercifully by this time been married off, but this left the eldest, Suzannah, still at home without a suitor on the horizon. I have never, since being surrounded by them in my childhood – petulant, hysterical, bossy creatures – been able to observe much use for women. Oh, perhaps they have certain advantages when they are old and inclined to view one's youth with indulgence, even stumping up a note or two in times of pecuniary extremis. But what use is a young woman unless she is at least decorative? And Suzannah is most positively not that. She combines a stultifying aridity of mind (she was as a child, I remember, obsessed with the martyrdom of St Theresa) with everything that is physically offensive in womankind – in short, with her sour armpits and heaving bosom, she gives the impression that all the trickery of perfumes and powder, the intricate confections of lace and silk, are but a means to disguise the unwholesome mystery of female biology.

Yet for all that, for all that she was even then a spinster well beyond marriageable age, and carries, as I do, the morganatic taint, you could see her commence to preen herself in that irritating way girls have, whispering with her maid and flaunting her most elaborate *toilettes* and staring at poor old Max over dinner in a manner which was calculated, even more than Uncle Gustav and his spiders, to put any sensitive person off food altogether. It did not seem to matter to her that, since he had taken his final vows at Mont Rémy, he was still technically bound by the rule of celibacy and would remain so except in the unlikely event he became King (in which case the Nuncio could be empowered to absolve him for the sake of continuing the line). Rather, it appeared to encourage her – the lure of clerical black perhaps, for all dessicated spinsters.

You might imagine that a person of Max's intellect would easily be able to ignore this pathetic spooning – the little walks round the garden, the vibrato twitterings at the piano – it wasted, after all, time which could have been spent in intelligent conversation with me. But no, if he did not precisely encourage the creature, he would nevertheless persist in treating her with the utmost politeness. And when early in our friendship I attempted to amuse him with several wittily-turned epigrams on the subject I found they fell on decidedly stony ground. The same was true of my more passionate imprecations against my father. On these occasions, Max had the capacity to switch from detachment to an icy sarcasm which left me on the one hand angry that the justice of my cause was not recognised but on the other wretched, ignobly afraid I had forfeited his respect. And so I was obliged to blunt my wit and to vent my sense of injustice before the more amenable audience of my looking-glass. After all, he was endeavouring to persuade my father to send me to Heidelberg. And – then there was this other thing I felt for him, admiration, kinship, or whatever it was. Oh, I heartily disliked it when Winders was so good as to point out some little mannerism of Max's she perceived I had adopted and I cringed when Aunt Helena in a mystical voice proclaimed us to be 'David and Jonathan'. But it also gave me a *frisson*, as if I had been obscurely honoured.

I cannot put my finger on the exact moment that I too began to enter into the dream. Perhaps it was General Keller's visit, or what I gleaned of it from the conversation at table, which was my only source of information. Max had been exhaustively briefed on his meeting with Keller for, if there was a tension always in his encounters with Vielfrass, Keller was considered by my father to represent the greater problem – a man of peasant stock, sceptical about the monarchy, a good soldier perhaps but ideologically unsound. And indeed

on that first day there was a discernable edginess, with Keller
suspicious, Max quiet. Yet the more I observed them the
more I was conscious of a surprising similarity. Oh, Keller
was an ugly enough brute of a man, a good foot shorter than
any Hohenstaufen, with a leonine head too big for his body,
bad teeth and atrocious table-manners – but in his wary
determination there was nevertheless an echo of Max's, as
if they had both been tested in a harder school than the rest
of us.

What was even more surprising was the debate which
continued, like intermittent sniper fire, through luncheon
the next day. The subject was social reform and my father
had taken his usual antagonistic stance towards Keller's
liberalism – and Max, though more moderate and more
rational, stood with Keller! The Paterfamilias might rail about
the realities of Sylvanian politics and the divinely-ordained
differences between the Three Estates; Max politely, yet with
the same quiet tenacity he had shown during his interrogation, dissected his arguments one by one and laid them
aside, like so many stray fishbones at the rim of his plate.

It was the first time I had ever heard Max express opinions
which did not coincide with my father's, but it made me
wonder suddenly whether the Paterfamilias would be able
to guide his protégé as much as he hoped, or even control
him at all. And it was then I became aware that a turning
point had been reached, that Max, as Crown Prince, was no
longer my father's toy, the ultimate embellishment of the
dream. He stood outside the dream, informing it with a
dedication of his own. He had taken my father's nostalgic
longings and his fantastic cloak-and-dagger paraphernalia
and as though by a subtle and complex trick of the mind
had cajoled them into reality. Then it dawned on me that it
would happen, that we should invade Sylvania, that Max
might eventually become King. I began, amazedly, to feel
the inevitability of it – we all felt it, Aunt Helena with her
prophetic gaze, our ever-increasing flow of visiting dignatories, and even my father who, after an amusing spell of
puzzlement, seemed either through The Pragmatism of
Maturity or through his respect for Max, to become
reconciled to his altered role of *éminence grise*. Only Uncle

Gustav remained strangely lugubrious and increasingly closeted in his laboratory.

It will already be apparent to you that I am not a great believer in the nobility of my fellow man. This does not however mean that I disdain the concept itself (I remember at an early age being moved to tears by the heroism of Sir Lancelot); it is simply that I recognise we are unworthy of it. Now, with the thought of troops massing, of battle standards, of pistol and sword not as the instruments of moral correction but as weapons of war, I found myself revisiting Chrétien de Troyes and Gottfried von Strassburg, steeping myself in the *Niebelungenlied*, poring over the *Odyssey* and the *Iliad* for ever more extravagant descriptions of gallantry and valour. I was Galahad and Siegfried, I was Achilles mourning Patroclus, I was Nisus dying sword in hand to avenge the death of his friend Euryalus. My daily torture in the gym and the rifle range became the training of the youthful Tristan in chivalry and all the courtly arts, my nightly conversations with Max the last precious confidences of friendship before the din and mire of the battle. Sometimes, indeed, as we rode out together through the castle gate or feinted and parried beneath the eye of our fencing master, it was easy to imagine that comradeship between us, that sense of doing battle together against my father and his cohorts, transformed literally into the Dorian warrior bond, two friends fighting selflessly, shoulder to shoulder on some unnamed battlefield, against the Peloponnesian hordes of Friedrich and Schramm. I began to have absurd dreams from which I would wake with a feeling of elation: Max surrounded by spears and lances, on the point of death, and me rushing in to save him; Max with his horse expiring under him and me selflessly giving him mine in the thick of the fighting; Max mortally wounded and dying in my arms (though sometimes this last took place the other way round). I resolved to set aside my novel and begin upon a poetic drama based on Plutarch's sacred brotherhood of Thebes, one hundred and fifty pairs of friends formed into an heroic regiment.

Oh, my suspicions about Max still lingered. And yes, the resentment was there too, fierce as ever when I considered my displacement, so that I alternately chafed at being in Max's shadow and bemoaned the fact that my new respectability was merely a reflection of his light. But set against this were the inestimable joys of friendship. I found myself wrapped in an unfamiliar warmth which, when I examined it, I discovered to be happiness. You may easily guess that this sensation was to be short-lived.

Max's valet, Beck, had been specially selected for him by my father because, as the son of one of our oldest and most trustworthy servants, his discretion and loyalty could be relied upon at all times. Despite this, he was still a young man, no more than four or five years older than me, and good-looking in a brutal, peasant sort of way, with blond hair, a powerful physique and startlingly white teeth – good NCO material is how my father would have described him. Apart from noticing his looks I had, of course, paid scant attention to him; but recently I had formed the habit of dressing for dinner early and going along the corridor to visit Max for a smoke and a chat as he dressed, on which occasions Beck was often in evidence, laying out clean linen and sorting collar-studs; and I could not think why, but I began to dislike the fellow intensely. Though he always remained in the background, always kept his place, somehow his presence was intrusive, offensively so – perhaps it was just the rude musculature of the man, or those irritatingly perfect teeth.

On this particular evening I had strolled along to Max's rooms with a book I intended to lend him, August von Platen's sonnets on Pindar's death in the arms of Theoxenos. Pausing only to deposit the volume on the sofa table, I passed on through the sitting-room. But at the bedroom door I froze.

That afternoon, while we had been duelling with rapiers, Max had slipped and wrenched a muscle in his shoulder and now he was lying stretched out on the bed and the valet Beck was massaging the injury. From where I stood I could see the whole length of Max's naked body except where Beck, working, from time to time obscured it, the forceful muscles of the shoulders, the long sweep of the back tapering down to the lean pelvis and buttocks and the hard, well-knit thighs. There is an elegance and grace about Max's body despite his disdain for personal ornament, a natural fluidity of movement that emanates from the perfect co-ordination of muscle, tendon and sinew and conveys nothing so much as power. Beck was rubbing in oil as he worked so that every cord and curve of the tawny skin glistened, as if the whole, like the figure of some Doric athlete, had been miraculously cast in bronze. It was both beautiful and sickening. For I was aware as I watched, in the way that Max lay, head to one side, eyes closed, every nerve relaxed, and in the way that those other strong fore-arms kneaded and coaxed and caressed the anointed skin, that there was a dreadful familiarity, an ease of relationship between master and servant which suggested that this was not the first but the hundredth time they had been together thus, fair skin working on dark, pleasurably, wordlessly engrossed in the strength of each other's body.

My eyes all at once were burning. I turned and went silently back through the sitting-room and out into the corridor.

I possessed in my bedroom an atrocious copy of Honthorst's St Sebastian, filched from the schoolroom when I was thirteen. The painting depicts the saint as the perfect victim, a fair-skinned young man clad only in a loin-cloth, a little flabby in the thigh perhaps but suitably broad in shoulder and torso and tastefully pierced with the arrows of martyrdom, from which piercings run discreetly tantilising rivulets of blood. My attachment to this work of art was construed at the time to be, as with my sister's fondness for St Theresa, a sign of piety, a hopeful indication of my moral awakening. In reality I had conceived that it would answer a somewhat less elevated need. And so it had, night after night, though I was obliged to lie rigid with my mouth clamped shut, in mortal dread that my father would wake and hear the bedsprings, even despite his apartments being in the opposite wing.

Now I fell upon this picture, crouched before it abjectly. I was aware of a mixture of sensations, rage and despair and the misery of betrayal and intense physical pain. I hated Max, hated Beck with his hefty forearms and his shiny teeth. How could he, how could Max besmirch our friendship so, how could he so lower himself, demean my respect for him, my affection, my trust? I stared at the face of St Sebastian, but he continued to gaze down at the bloody badges of his martyrdom, lids lowered, mouth rapt. Not so with the arrows which pierced me – I reeled from the pain of them. For I knew, no matter how I tried to shut it out, that it was not just the betrayal, not just that odious complicity between them, not just that the man Beck was a servant, a peasant, the lowest of the low; I had felt this pain before, that day at the lake.

Tearing off my clothes, I rushed to the cheval-glass in my dressing-room. I had often had occasion to study myself in it with pleasure, to feel pride at that beauty of mine which my father found so unforgiveable. Now I cursed this perfection, this prettiness, now I execrated my slight figure and hairless chest; for I could see, from my faintly sloping shoulders to my narrow pelvis and willowy, girlish legs, that I was inferior in every respect, that while they, the two of them in Max's bedroom, had been absorbed in the celebration of their manhood, I was in comparison a contemptible boy.

From that day the pain never left me, but lingered on drably, contaminating everything. Naturally I could no longer bear the sight of Beck, could not abide even to be in a room with him, and spent many of my morning hours when I should have been working at my play concocting elaborate schemes for getting rid of him, from somehow slipping one of my diamond necktie pins into his pocket and accusing him of the theft, to luring him to the rifle range when I was due to display my woefully inaccurate aim. My agony also infected every moment of my daily contact with Max, so that what had seemed so easy and delightful now became an excruciating effort. It was as if I had suddenly begun to see everything from another perspective where there was only ugliness and suspicion. I found myself examining his every word, his every smile and the direction of his eyes, for signs of duplicity and hidden meaning. Even inanimate objects where he touched them seemed to taunt me with a secret from which I was excluded. The Marquis de Miramont's old flintlock pistols in their battered case habitually lay on the shelf above Max's writing desk, forming, apart from the books, the only decoration to his sitting-room. I remembered I had taken them down one day and had laughingly brandished them about, striking a highwayman's pose, and I was not sure, but I had the sense that he had somehow disapproved, as if I had blundered in through that forbidden door of his, violated something. Now, as I looked at the pistols lying antiquated and useless in their worn velvet casing, a host of unformed questions jostled in my mind and I found the pain reasserting itself with a new intensity.

I hated them all. Yes, I hated Beck. But I hated my father too, for keeping Max so many hours in his study and monopolising conversation with him and even for clapping him on the shoulder to give emphasis to a joke. I hated Suzannah for taking Max away to scrutinise her tawdry watercolours. I hated Aunt Helena and Winders for ceaselessly adoring him with their eyes. I hated the riding master and the fencing master and the shooting instructor and the deceased Marquis de Miramont and the footman who cleaned Max's boots and any number of other nameless persons who peopled my imagination in shadowy configurations of sin. Even when my father quite suddenly announced that he would agree to my studying at Heidelberg the following year, my heart did not lift, and the casualness with which I received his concession sent him into such a paroxysm of fury that he almost withdrew it. I spent considerable time before my looking-glass experimenting with exercises to toughen my shoulders and the set of my jaw. Gloomily, I contemplated growing a moustache.

And then, to cap it all, my father announced that my English cousin, St John Aubyn, was to spend a month with us.

IV

It had never occurred to me that Max would actually like Aubyn. After all, he preferred amusing, intelligent people – why else had we become friends? And anyway Aubyn, apart from being an insufferable thick who had probably never read a book all the way through in his life (unless it were on bog spavin or some other equally fascinating topic) was of another generation, nearly forty and closer to the old men than to us.

But there he came, with his freckles and his plain manner and his even plainer face, His Serene Highness St John Aubyn, Duke of Hohen-Kastell and Carrick; and there was Max, to my horror, talking to him, riding with him, holding competitions of marksmanship with him. I might try to interest him in the latest verses of my play or in Pindar and August von Platen and he would give me a half-pretence of paying attention; but the other half was listening to Aubyn.

What made it worse was that Aubyn was bereft of all sensitivity. When Max and I went for fencing practice he came too. When we gathered after supper for our nightly conversations Aubyn joined in, even suggested we play backgammon or cards. There was never a moment free of his loutish presence and his everlasting talk of horses and military derring-do. I could have borne it even then perhaps if Max had given any indication that he knew how he had betrayed me, how this new faithlessness was added to the accumulation of his treachery; but he did not. Rather, he seemed to assume that I would manifest the same predeliction for Aubyn's company.

But how could I, when the man demeaned everything so? Max appeared, for instance, positively enthralled by his descriptions of military manoeuvres and his speculations about Friedrich's army; but their talk of war was not of Siegfried or sacred brotherhoods or glorious deeds: no, it was dry-as-dust stuff about the disposition of regiments and the relative merits of the Gatling versus the Nordenfeldt gun.

It was as if I had suddenly become to Max a tiresome younger brother who was to be tolerated and allowed to join in every so often simply because I was there. True, his manner seemed outwardly to not have changed towards me; yet there was something in Aubyn's very dullness, his Philistinism, his indiscriminate jolliness, which he seemed to embrace gladly, as if he were starved of it, as if the fellow's arrival had come as a relief. It had ceased to occur to me that twenty-seven was very much older than nineteen; but now, watching the two of them together absorbed in their military

speculations or laughing over some chance of fate on the
rifle range, it struck me that they possessed in common a
whole universe from which I was excluded – the comradeship, as my father would say, of two 'men's men'.

And then I began to notice other things too: how Max was
different when Aubyn rode with us, testing his horse's
mettle and his own skill to the limits in the knowledge that
Aubyn would follow or even outstrip him, so that they had
to rein in every so often and wait for me to catch up; how,
when we were fencing in the gym, Max would thrust and
parry against Aubyn with a concentrated determination he
never used against me nor even our fencing master, and
how when they had finished the bout, whoever was the
victor, they would come away laughing with their arms
around each other's shoulders, dissecting the finer points of
it as if they had not so much been opponents but had fought
together against some arcane force. And with a churning
sense of humiliation I began to realise that Max had always
held back with me – oh, not obviously, perhaps not even
consciously, but nevertheless consistently, with the instinctive allowance the strong make for the weak.

My rage knew no bounds. I abandoned the Court Jester,
approached every afternoon's athleticism with a new and
deadly seriousness, determined to show that I was a force
to be reckoned with. The more determined I became, the
more incompetently I acquitted myself. Oh, they were not
unkind; they even encouraged me, tried to teach me the
finer points of technique. But I felt all the same that when I
was not there they would ridicule my inadequacy, that
Aubyn, though he kept up his cheerful duffer's façade, was
remembering the compass episode and sniggering, and that
Max – oh, God help me – Max was joining in.

I gave up reading, gave up writing. I mooned about
smoking cigarettes, and in the evenings began to drink too
much, thereby making even more of an idiot of myself. I
could feel every day Max withdrawing from me further: he
had ceased entirely to put his arm about me or ruffle my
hair when he found me stretched out in an armchair reading;
the lightness of his voice when he deigned to address me
now had a deliberateness about it; and sometimes when I
glanced round I would find that he was surveying me

covertly with a thoughtful, almost troubled expression. I was lonely now as I had never been in a lifetime of loneliness.

When, at the beginning of November, Aubyn at last returned to England, I felt no respite, for now there was a further prospect of wretchedness. From certain remarks Aubyn and Max had thrown out, I gathered it had been judged appropriate that Max should spend an extended period with Keller and the army in Thalia, and that he was likely to take his departure some time in the spring.

V

A few days later my father suggested we should go hunting on Uncle Gustav's estate. It was a half-hearted affair: Uncle Gustav does not shoot, I cannot, and, though Max, my father and Colonel von Straubnitz bagged a few chamois, none of us seemed to be able to raise enough enthusiasm to keep out the cold. In the evening, around the tiled stove in the dusty billiard room of Uncle Gustav's hunting lodge, the conversation was desultory. When the old men rose to retire I thought at first Max would follow their example, but then he seemed to think twice about it, unusually, for him, helping himself from the brandy decanter instead.

We sat together in silence for a few minutes, staring at the stove. I could not think of anything to say that would not end up as an imprecation against Aubyn, or the detestable Beck, or against the execrable nature of the human race in general. In the end it seemed that we would both try to speak at once. He paused and I said, with an unsuccessful attempt to rid my voice of rancour: 'I suppose you miss our delightful cousin?'

He seemed to ignore my tone. 'Oh, I shall see a good deal of Aubyn in Thalia. He's to resign his commission in the English army and become Keller's second-in-command.'

Perhaps it was the brandy, but his mention of Thalia once again brought the shaming tears to my eyes. 'I hate Aubyn,' I said. 'Not only is he a clod and a bore, but underneath that infuriating English politeness of his I always get the impression he thinks I'm an insufferable brat.'

He looked up from his brandy glass with a dry smile. 'And

you don't, my dear Anton, have it in you to be such a thing?
Particularly not in the last few weeks?'

I could no longer suppress my rage. 'I wanted a friend,' I
said, 'not an elder brother! If I'd wanted someone to
patronise me and tell me how to behave I'd have made that
perfectly clear.'

He put aside his glass with a sigh. 'Oh God, Anton, don't
be such an idiot! And for Heaven's sake, don't sulk! There's
been enough thunder these last weeks to deafen us. Poor
Uncle Leo, who's become so proud of you, can't understand
why you've suddenly turned into a schoolboy again.'

'I don't care a damn for my father,' I said. 'It's you, Max,
you who treat me like a schoolboy, you who've desecrated
everything there was between us!'

'Oh, for God's sake, Anton! Please try to be no more
ridiculous than you absolutely must.' He paused, and when
he continued his voice had softened, as if he regretted his
harshness. 'I very much wish that I could – that I was able
to help you understand . . .'

He paused again, and I found myself hanging on the
silence, wondering if he were about to give me an opening,
an opportunity at last to confide the full extent of my
suffering. But he checked himself, as if he had thought better
of whatever it was.

I was almost relieved, for how could I have explained to
him? Oh, I could have pointed out how Aubyn had clod-
hoppered in upon our private moments, I could have
reproached him for not taking my athletic endeavours seriously, I could have implored him to get rid of the hateful
Beck. But how could I have described to him succinctly the
nature of my affliction when I was not even sure I could
define it for myself? And besides I was shocked that during
all the time I thought I had been keeping my wretchedness
secret I had apparently been so utterly transparent.

I looked at him sitting in the dull light of the spirit-lamp,
his face half in shadow, its private thoughts carefully
compartmentalised and packed away. He seemed older
suddenly and harder, the man who now debated with my
father as an equal, the Crown Prince who would review
Keller's troops in Thalia and discuss fire power and the
commissariat and approve the finer details of invasion plans.

I took a large gulp of my brandy. 'Why do you want it, Max? Why do you want it all so very badly?'

He glanced up abruptly. Then his expression cleared as if he had been thinking of something else and had taken a moment to understand me. He raised his eyebrows, but did not reply.

'The power or whatever it is? You're clever enough to have been anything you chose. But you chose this. Why?'

'I think I prefer to believe that I did not choose it, that from the moment of my leaving Mont Rémy it simply became inevitable.'

'Oh bosh, Max! Such sophistry is unworthy of you. You chose to come here. You could have been free for the rest of your life, not as you are now, chained to the destinies of a gingerbread country and the moonstruck plots of senile old men. But you chose – even after ten years – you chose to come.'

The eyebrows were sardonic. 'And are we not to suppose that any man would have chosen as I did?'

'No, most men wouldn't. Most men would be afraid. But you long for power, don't you Max? You enjoy controlling things – yourself, others. God, sometimes I feel you control us all.'

His laughter was unforced, apparently without anger. 'My dear Anton, you give me credit for Machiavellian skills I'm afraid I do not possess. If I must explain myself, then I can only say that I wish to try to do well what others have done badly.'

'But they won't let you, don't you see? This power, this control you want so much – they won't let you have it. Oh, you may talk about duty and the general good and sometimes I believe you almost mean those things. But the others – my father, Keller, Vielfrass and a thousand people you haven't even met yet – they'll all have little, individual, selfish reasons for wanting their own way, supporting their own interests. It isn't the Holy Grail you're in pursuit of, Max, but a grubby swill-bucket filled with the mish-mash of other people's greed and prejudice and fear.'

'And you believe I'm unaware of it?'

'I believe – oh God, I believe you're strong and clever and I know you have the capacity to be ruthless – perhaps even more than that. But it seems, oh, it seems such an appalling waste! What's Sylvania to you? A lunatic glimmer in the Pater's addled brain? Uncle Gustav expatiating on Nordstadt cheese? You're like me, you've never known it, you can't really care for it, not in your heart of hearts. Oh, please, Max,' – I took another gulp of brandy – 'don't go to join Keller. Wait, come to Heidelberg with me next autumn. You could take up your studies again, read for a doctorate. My allowance won't precisely keep us in caviar but we could both exist on it until we were established. I beg of you, Max – come to Heidelberg!'

Though his voice was surprisingly gentle, I knew before he spoke what his answer would be. 'My dear, idiotically-generous friend, I don't need to tell you that even if I wanted to I couldn't. I am much too far in.'

I thought then of asking him again about the words of his nightmare, of forcing him to tell me that he was really Dieter Wolf and that he had killed the Crown Prince at Fontarelles. But I knew I should not receive a proper answer; and in any case I discovered to my amazement that I had ceased to want one, that I no longer cared, beyond his presence there in that room, who he might be.

I helped myself to more brandy and lit another cigarette. 'Very well. Then I won't go to Heidelberg either. I'll come to Thalia with you.'

He lowered his glass. 'Anton, that's perfectly absurd.'

'Not in the least. Sylvania is supposed to be my mother-land. Why shouldn't I fight for it? Why shouldn't I, Max, fight for your cause?'

'Because you loathe the idea of the army. Because Heidelberg has been your burning ambition ever since you can recall.'

'Then I've changed. I'm surely allowed, in my pitiable immaturity, to change my mind. I'm sick to death of books. I've lived, breathed, slept books ever since I can remember. I read them, I write them, the only life I've ever known has been utterly and entirely lived out of them. You can burn every book in Switzerland so far as I'm concerned. I want action, I want to fight glorious battles and earn medals and be honourably wounded. I want to ride on a splendid horse in a splendid uniform and strike terror into the hearts of

Friedrich's cavalry. I want the Pater, when I have died my noble death, to take laurel wreaths to my sepulchre and weep for gratitude that he had such a son.'

'Oh, for Heaven's sake, Anton—'

'Or, on second thoughts, perhaps I'll moulder away in some forgotten shell hole, in an unmarked grave. And the Paterfamilias will search the battlefields of Sylvania to bring the hero home, and Aunt Helena and Winders will send up Ave Marias for my unshriven soul and Uncle Gustav will probably name a new and particularly noxious species of spider after me . . .' I paused to take more brandy, surveyed Max over the rim of my glass, observed that he seemed undecided between laughter and impatience. 'Oh, you needn't think I'm not perfectly serious, that this is all a lot of bibulous tosh. I never was in more deadly earnest. And there'll be no trouble with the Pater. You managed so admirably with Heidelberg it should be the work of a moment to persuade him of this.'

He set aside his glass again and it was clear that impatience had won. 'Anton, the notion is ridiculous and I will not permit it. Now for Heaven's sake let us talk of something else.'

'*You'll* not permit it? I'm not one of your subjects yet. I'm of age and I'll do as I please. Just think how overjoyed the dear Paterfamilias will be when I tell him!'

He was angry now, I could see. Though he strove to conceal it as he always did, it was there all the same in the set of his mouth. 'Anton, this is not a foolish game, whatever you may imagine. We're talking of an invasion, civil war. Not shooting at clay pigeons and paper targets, but men being killed, perhaps, if we fail, all of us.'

'Do you think I don't know that? God, Max, how you patronise me! Real guns, real killing! Do you think I'm so useless, so weak, so inferior that I can't even come to grips with . . .' Here I found the brandy had gone to my eyes again. 'Oh Max, don't you see that I can't bear it? When you go there won't be anything. Nothing. Nothing at all.'

Swallowing hard, I fumbled for a cigarette. I thought he stirred in his chair as if he would come over to me but then, once more, he appeared to check himself. When I looked up, though his face was now against the light, it seemed to wear that uncharacteristic troubled expression I had observed before.

'I'm sorry,' I said, assaying a laugh. 'It's the bloody drink. I'm evidently intent on proving that the dear Paterfamilias is right about me after all.'

'Anton,' he said softly, 'you know my affection for you is not in question—'

'Except when I'm an insufferable brat.'

'Except for then, of course.' He smiled, but I was aware of having interrupted him, as if he had been choosing his words with particular care. 'But out of my affection – because of it – I must ask you to promise you'll forget this whole absurd idea. Our friendship gives me a responsibility—'

'To take care of me as if I were some sort of subhuman species without a functioning brain of my own? Damn you, Max, you hold no responsibility towards me of any kind!'

'Towards your father, then. And on my own account – perhaps that most of all.'

'In God's name, for what? What responsibility? Oh come, Max, you owe it to me to explain.'

He fingered the rim of his glass as if he were again thinking carefully before he spoke. 'Not to impose upon our friendship, my dear Anton, more than it will bear.'

'Not to impose? But, merciful Heaven, what else is friendship for? Why else above everything is it sacred? What is there that trust and loyalty and heartfelt affection cannot bear? I want to fight for you, Max, I want to go into battle beside you. Don't you see it's the natural expression of everything I feel for you, the only truly noble expression of it? Damn you, Max, you're the one who places such stress on honour and duty. Don't you see that this is the way I can make myself worthy of you, don't you see how glorious it would be – all the noble traditions of chivalry and honour reaffirmed, brought to a new flower? Think, Max, think of us truly as David and Jonathan, Achilles and Patroclus, Gawain and Galahad—'

'I thought we had agreed this was not a quest for the Holy Grail?'

'Then think of trust and loyalty and two hearts inextricably bound by the sacred vows of comradeship. God, Max, with Keller and Vielfrass and all the rest you'll need someone you can trust, someone you know will never betray you, someone who'll serve you willingly through thick and thin. Or do you, perhaps, think I'm not up to it? Do you think I'm not strong enough, that I haven't the courage or the firmness of purpose, that I'll let you down? Dear God, what must I do to prove my determination? Must I swear a solemn and chilling oath, must I open a vein and write my name in blood, must I put my hand in the fire to prove that I would gladly die for you? Tell me, Max, and whatever it is, even if it's storming Rosenholm with only ten men or charging alone against a whole regiment of Friedrich's cavalry, I'll undertake it!'

I paused. Usually my dramatic excesses amused him, but now he contrived to look firm and grave.

'Very well,' I finished lamely. 'I know you don't hold my military prowess in high esteem. But you could always find me a job on your staff, carrying messages and running errands and that sort of thing.'

Still serious, he put aside his empty glass and stood up. 'I ask you for only one undertaking, Anton – that whatever you and I – whatever happens – you will go to Heidelberg as your father has agreed.'

That night I could not sleep for sheer rage that I had such little control over my own life, so little power. And also I was afflicted by a sense of there being something else, something in all my eloquence and rhetoric I had left unsaid. To console myself I concentrated my ire upon the loathsome Beck, like a gypsy woman sticking pins into a wax image willing him to come to some unspeakably painful end. And it seemed I was not, after all, completely without power, for two days later he tripped on the back stairs and fractured his collar bone. I only grieved it was not his neck.

CHAPTER FIVE

Marie Bathildis

I

The marriage was to take place according to custom at five o'clock. No one appeared to have been woken by the events of the previous night, or even to remark upon the absence of Rosa. It was as if it had all been a dream; only my bloody travelling cloak, hidden beneath my bed until it could be burned, remained to testify that I had not imagined everything.

When I had married Freddy he had been too ill to stand and we had gone through a simple ceremony in his bedroom with only his father and members of the Court Cabinet in attendance. But now, in order that Maximilian should give the people 'their pretty little pageant', I must submit to the whole elaborate tradition of a Sylvanian Royal Marriage. I sat, weak and dazed, in my combing jacket while the golden *toilette* service given to Sigismund I's Queen by Napoleon was laid out in preparation for the Mistress of the Robes to dress me before Princess Helena and the ladies of my Household. Outside in the courtyard, the Garde du Corps were already assembling their gun carriages to ride out to the parade-ground; a soft haze hung upon the steeple of the English Church and the domes of the Opera, muting sound, as if the whole city were held in suspense, waiting on tenterhooks for the hundred-and-one gun salute which would announce the exchange of rings, the inescapable culmination of my misery.

I stared at myself in the looking glass. My maids, without comment, had daubed the bruises on my neck and shoulders with camomile so that they should not mar the splendour of my antique lace and silver tissue. My face was a mask of *poudre de riz* and geranium petal – tradition forbade it the concealment of a veil, but it was in any case bereft of emotion. I was no longer conscious of any sensation except a persistent nausea. I turned obediently this way and that, allowing the ladies to adjust my orders, direct my four pages, spread out the five-metre length of my silver train, clasp my numbed hands around the huge shower bouquet of myrtle and Maréchal Niel roses. As the Mistress of the Robes lowered the heavy Maria Antonia crown onto my garland of orange blossom I caught sight of Suzannah von Tarn's face in the glass holding back laughable tears of envy. I emptied my mind of thought. I should not faint, I should try to smile, because that was what I had been trained all my life to do, because that – the mindless discipline of nodding and smiling – was the last reserve left to me. I took the Princess Helena's trembling arm and, like two automata, we began our progress through the State Apartments to the chapel.

It is strange, but I remember little of it now, now when I so badly want to, as if I really had been in a trance. I remember feeling glad I had been spared Uncle Berthold, who had pleaded gout and sent Ansbach in his place. I remember glancing about for my English relations and seeing no one I knew, not one aunt or cousin. I remember him, of course, standing at the altar rail in his white and gold gala uniform, his breast heavy with orders and decorations, his dark face very calm and composed, and I remember that I could not look at him when he took my hand to lead me to my prie-dieu and that when I touched the place in my *décolletage* where Freddy's ring still rested it no longer seemed like a talisman, as if everything tender and joyful had from that moment deserted me. And yet I recall now, despite his composure, there were things about Maximilian which surprised me; that his hand too shook a little as he placed the ring in turn on each of my fingers, that, as the church bells pealed out and the salvos of the Garde du Corps resounded, he was careful as ever to avoid my lips, merely kissing me lightly on the cheek; and that when it was over and we were processing down the Picture Gallery to the blare of trumpets and the rattle of kettle-drums, past the throng of Residenz servants surging against their cordon of footmen to snatch a first look at us, his arm seemed to hold up my fainting steps as, bending his head to me for an instant, he whispered that I had been brave and he was proud of me.

But for the rest, it all blurs into a succession of standing, sitting, walking, smiling: standing for the Cardinal Archbishop's interminable address; sitting to have my hand kissed in the Throne-Room by an unending procession of foreign royalty, ministers and diplomats; sitting again for the dinner I could not eat, course upon course of it, while the Duke of Maar growled and Anton played courtier and Aubyn seemed surprisingly quiet and glum; then walking, walking to the White Room for the Torch Dance, with all the Cabinet Ministers processing round and round to the strains of military marches, and Maximilian and I following them, all of us with torches, and us handing out the Sigismundite relations and the foreign dignitaries, two by two in order of precedence, handing them all out, walking endlessly round and round, till the walls of the White Room, the stucco, the tapestries, seemed to rock with it and our eyes were seared with candle smoke and our noses filled with the stench of wax. Standing, sitting, walking, smiling, till my aching head could no longer bear the burden of the great diamond and crysoberyl crown, till my train and jewels seemed to crush me with their weight so that every movement was an agony of effort. Then it was nine-thirty, time for my Garter, the white ribbons embroidered with my cypher, to be distributed to the dancers; time for Maximilian and myself to retire. And suddenly my trance was broken.

I had never been in the bridal suite of the Residenz before, for Freddy's illness had precluded the need for it, and it was otherwise always kept locked and sealed. It consisted of a single vast bedroom, served through connecting doors by a dressing-room on either side, the whole lavishly ornamented with stucco, gilt and frescos of Cupid, Venus and attendant putti, and carpeted throughout in a design of orange blossom and myrtle entwined with white ribbons. I was preceded there by six pages carrying golden candelabra, and escorted by Princess Helena and my ladies-in-waiting. In the right-hand dressing-room I was put into my négligé by my maids, and my hair was taken down, while Suzannah, face empty now, laid all my jewellery and orders carefully in a rosewood and gilded-bronze chest which she carried away on a velvet cushion. Then Princess Helena and Ursula followed me into the bedroom, where a white silk nightgown was eased carefully over my head, and my stockings, my stays and the rest of my underthings were removed from beneath it. I watched the maids gather up and fold everything, saw with dismay the little chamois bag containing Freddy's ring swept away with the rest. When every item of my clothing had been accounted for, the maids, carrying their burden as reverently as if it had been precious metal, curtsied and departed with it. Princess Helena and Ursula curtsied too, Ursula with a maternal simper, the Princess gravely, as if the occasion brought to mind some personal sadness. Then they went out, and I heard the key to the connecting door turn behind them.

My first reaction was to run to the other door, but that too, though I rattled and pulled at it, was locked on the outside. The sashes of the double windows proved equally obstinate, and besides I was on the third floor, though I considered briefly throwing myself out nonetheless. I looked about my prison wildly; there was not even a bell, all means of summoning servants, summoning anyone, being presumably locked away with everything else behind the dressing-room doors. The huge bed on its dais, canopied in rose-pink brocade and encrusted with gilded flowers, love-knots and putti, confronted me mockingly, its silk sheets neatly turned back on either side, waiting.

I sank into the sofa at the foot of the bed and considered my final stratagem. I had not until the instant of my being conducted away from the White Room brought myself to contemplate this moment, had anaesthetised myself against it, so that even my fleeting thoughts of Uncle Berthold had not had the power to admit it to consciousness. The horror had come to me slowly in the dressing-room after the first relief of having the train lifted from my shoulders, the great ugly Castellani diadem taken from my burning head. It was as if following the numbness that first attends a wound, the pain had started, stealthily, pervasively, making my throat constrict and my stomach hollow. And then I had seen, amongst my brushes and powder pots laid out for the next day, the pin for the pink hat I should wear to morning Mass.

I had not paused, I had scarcely even thought what I was doing before I had placed my hand over it and slid it into my palm, point upwards against my wrist. It had remained there while my hair was brushed and I was undressed, and now it was lodged in the sleeve of my nightgown just above the cuff. I pulled it out and examined it; beneath its pearl and diamond haft its spike was a good nine centimetres long and stiletto-sharp.

I was still pondering it nervously when there was a knock on the dressing-room door and then the sound of the key turning. Holding the pin in front of me with both hands I sprang to my feet. But the head which came round the door was Ursula von Windersdorf's. Hurriedly I pushed my weapon back into my sleeve.

She was still in Court dress and she tiptoed in clutching her train, holding one finger conspiratorially to her lips.

'I shouldn't be here, Ma'am – it's against all the rules, all the tradition. But – well, His Majesty hasn't come up yet, and I remember my own wedding night. I've brought Your Majesty something, something that might be of help.'

Though she talked of help I noticed she locked the door behind her and put the key safely in her bosom.

I sat down on the sofa again. The fright she had given me had set my legs shaking so that they would no longer hold me. She seated herself beside me and took my hand.

'Your Majesty – my dear – poor Princess Helena should have spoken to you but, perhaps as an old widow woman, God rest dear Albrecht's soul, I might be permitted instead to give you some advice.' She lowered her voice delicately. 'Men, dearest Ma'am, cannot help themselves, it is in their natures just as it is not in ours. Which is why we must submit to our duty, so that we may use our moral influence to moderate their animal passions, to keep their brute instincts within proper bounds—'

I felt the saliva rise in my throat. 'Please, Ursi – please don't!'

She patted my hand. 'I know you are thinking of the pain, dear Ma'am, but if you are brave and simply let him have his way it won't be so bad. And to keep your courage up – there, I've brought you a little Dutch courage too.' Whereupon she disclosed from the folds of her train a silver-topped hunting flask.

I stared at it, thinking it was one of her concoctions of ipecacuanha or rosehips.

'Try a little now, Ma'am,' she said, unscrewing the cup. 'I've brought some violet cachous so His Majesty won't smell anything on your breath.'

The substance looked like water. I put the flask to my nose for an instant, then reeled back choking.

She laughed. 'It's only Aquavit, Ma'am. It won't hurt you.'

I thrust the flask away from me. 'But that's what the peasants drink in the taverns in the Old Town.'

'And excellent it is too, in an emergency. Two or three good draughts of that and you'll scarcely be conscious when – well, why should we women suffer more than we need, eh?'

'No!' I said. 'Please, no!'

Shrugging her shoulders, she put the flask aside. 'I shall leave it for you, Ma'am, in case you change your mind. And now – His Majesty will be on his way, and I mustn't be caught here, must I?'

'Oh please, Ursi, don't leave me!'

She shook her head reprovingly. 'Alas, we women have our duty. But think – though you may not expect any pleasure from it yourself – just think of the pleasure of being a good wife to His Majesty, of bearing him children.'

'Oh no, no! Don't lock the door! Ursi, I forbid you to lock me in!'

But the key was already turning.

I sat for a long time staring blindly after her. Now images I could not shut out thrust themselves at me, of Uncle Berthold with his hand working, working, and white fur sticky with blood, and that dreadful day at Schwanensee when I woke and knew they had touched me. I put my hand to my mouth, biting the flesh to keep back my nausea. Oh Rosa, Rosa! How I longed for her to be there cradling me in her arms, how I longed for my dear gentle Freddy. I felt for the hat-pin again, wondering whether I had sufficient strength to use it.

And yet perhaps it would not prove necessary. After all, Maximilian did not love me – I aroused no appetite in him, he had never looked at me in that way my uncle or Prince von Ansbach had, as if I were butcher's meat. Perhaps if I were to plead exhaustion . . . He could scarcely have slept himself, and besides, it was true, I was near collapse, my legs weak, my body aching as though my very bones were bruised. I had only to get between the sheets and feign sleep and perhaps he would return to his own apartments.

But no, that was no good. So great was my exhaustion that I might, even despite my terror, sleep; and then I should leave myself vulnerable, past defence. No, I must keep myself awake somehow so that I could reason with him. Staring dazedly at the door through which Ursula had departed I realised suddenly that it was not by this door he would enter, that his dressing-room was to the left, behind me. I swung round quickly, my heart thumping, my eyes fixed on that left-hand door. I strained my ears for any warning sound from the room beyond. Sliding the hat-pin down into my palm again, I sat bolt upright, waiting.

My fatigue or my faintness must have got the better of me for he was in the room, turning the key on the inside, almost before I was aware of him. I sprang to my feet, staring at him in horror, for I could see in an instant that he would not have any pity for me.

He was bareheaded without a nightcap and wearing a long midnight-blue silk dressing-gown with great sweeping quilted lapels, tied at the waist like a smoking jacket. But beneath the silk robe there was no nightshirt; he was naked, like a peasant. Though his expression was impenetrable, there was in his bearing, not desire, but something more frightening – a discipline of purpose which would not brook deflection. His nakedness seemed to fill the room. The scar at his temple showed very white.

He moved towards me, his Turkish slippers making no sound on the carpet. I seized the hat-pin in both hands again, edging away.

'Don't come near me! Don't touch me!'

He paused, observing my weapon with mild surprise. 'My dear sweet Marie, I thought we were finished with histrionics?'

The unconcern in his voice maddened me. 'I mean it!' I said. 'I won't let you touch me.'

'Yes,' he said softly, still moving towards me, 'I'm sure, Marie, that you do.'

I darted away from him, off the dais and round the other side of the bed. Still he came after me, slowly, silently across the carpet. My hands were beginning to tremble and my teeth were chattering.

'Don't you see! I'm not your wife. Not before God. You have no right to anything from me!'

He was almost level with me. Now that I had lost even the advantage of high heels he towered over me, a full foot taller, lean and straight and hard. I could see the corded sinews of his neck, measure the broadness of his shoulders, see the contours of his pectoral muscles where the silk fell open across his chest. My futile weapon would only glance off that hard complexity of muscle. I dared not lower my eyes below his waist, yet that was where I must strike if my stiletto were to have any effect. Only I could not. Still he came closer and I could not.

I was cornered now between a commode and the night table, my back against the wall. He was barely three paces away from me so that I felt his nakedness, every taut muscle of it, like a crushing force.

'You're stronger than I am,' I said. 'You could take what you want, make me submit. But I'll fight you. You'll have to break every bone in my body first!'

The irony had gone from his eyes, his face was grave. 'I should altogether prefer not to. I should much prefer you handed me that pin.'

He could have taken it, reached out and pulled it from my trembling fingers. But he stayed where he was, very quiet and still. I could strike him now, he was close enough, open to me. But I could not strike unless he made some movement. Oh, if he would only please try to take it!

'Don't you see that I can't!' The hat-pin began to quiver uncontrollably. 'Don't you see that I can't give in!'

There was an expression in his eyes, a tension suddenly that I did not understand. I looked about me wildly. I could not strike him. I wondered briefly whether I could hurl myself at the commode, topple the candelabra, use the

flames as my escape, but I was too far away. I glanced back
at the hat-pin. My palms were damp with sweat, the haft
slithered in my grasp.

'Don't you understand?' I said again in a whisper. 'I can't
let you, I can't. I'd rather die!'

I closed my fingers with all my remaining strength around
the pin and jerked its stiletto up hard towards my windpipe.
He was on me in an instant as if he had known, seizing me
by the wrists, slamming my hands against the wall. I
screamed as the pain ran down my arms, I felt the pin drop
from my grasp. Then slowly, slowly, I sank to the floor, my
knees buckling, my head falling forwards, my hands sliding
gradually down after me.

'Oh, please understand that I can't, I can't! You all believe
it was Freddy, that his epilepsy stopped him being a man.
But it was only that he was gentle and kind and wouldn't
make me do what I couldn't. I couldn't let him touch me –
like that. Oh please, try to understand.'

Burying my face in the carpet, I began to sob convulsively.
I heard him bend to pick up the hat-pin. Then he came
over and knelt beside me and very gently lifted me by the
shoulders until my weight was against him and my head
was supported in the crook of his neck.

'My poor sad lunatic child. You may stick me with as
many hat-pins as you please so long as you never try again
what you tried just now.'

I felt his hand in the small of my back, felt him softly
stroking my hair. It was strange, half-lying, half-kneeling
against him like that, feeling his arms around me, feeling
myself enfolded by the solid strength of his body, not like
being held by Freddy, but just as gentle, just as comforting.
I became conscious of the warmth of him, of the little pulse
throbbing at the base of his throat, of the scent of his skin.

After a while, when I had ceased to sob with quite such
force, he wrapped my arms around his shoulders and,
picking me up, carried me over to the bed and propped me
against the pillows; and I told him then what I had never
been able to bear telling anyone, not even Freddy – about
Uncle Berthold and his 'touching games' after my mother
died. He listened in silence, his eyes grave, and when I had
told him as much as my feeling of shame would let me I was

filled all at once with a sense of lightness, as if he had taken some of the burden from me. Lying back on the pillows with my fingertips resting in his, I began deliciously, peacefully to drift into sleep; until I was suddenly aware of his hand being withdrawn.

I opened my eyes. He had picked up the flask of Aquavit from the commode. He sniffed it experimentally, then poured a measure. I blinked sleepily as he brought the cup over to me.

'It will taste like firewater. But see if you can manage a few sips.'

I looked up at him in surprise.

'Oh, I agree it's a curiously earthy substance to find in this meringue of a room.'

'Baroness Windersdorf brought it,' I said. 'She thought it would—' I stopped short, suddenly bolt upright and wide awake. 'No!' I said unbelievingly. 'No! I've explained to you, I thought you understood!'

'I understand how difficult it is for you. I shall try to be as gentle as I can.'

Though his voice was soft, his look of purpose had returned. While his arm, spanning my body across the waist, touched me nowhere, I felt suddenly imprisoned by it, felt the last traces of comfort I had found in his proximity ebb away.

'Oh no, please! You can't be so cruel, so inhuman. I've explained that it's impossible, that I can't, I can't . . .' I paused, choking, waiting in vain for his expression to soften. 'Oh please, not tonight, not now, not after everything that's happened. Please have some mercy for me tonight.'

His lips curved regretfully, but the intent look in his eyes remained. 'My dear child, if it is impossible tonight it will be still more impossible tomorrow, and the night after.'

My throat constricted. I held myself back against the pillow, tried to draw away from him as far as I could, from the overpowering animal sense of him I had once more, the pervasive sense of his nakedness.

'You said – you promised you would not force me.'

'I said I should prefer not to.'

'But now, when you understand my disgust, my revulsion – oh why, please, why, why?'

'Because, Marie, we neither of us enjoy the luxury of choice.'

'Because you must have an heir?'

'Yes.' He sighed as if he too were suddenly filled with distaste. 'Because I must have an heir.'

I began to cry again, limply, helplessly. He put up his hand to touch my hair but I turned my face aside, burying it in the pillow. There was nowhere I could escape, nothing left to me, no strength, no means any more to resist him. I turned back from the pillow, seeing him indistinctly through my tears.

'Please, whatever you must do, let it be over with as soon as possible. Please don't make me suffer more than you must.'

He did not speak, but merely touched my hand very lightly. Then he offered me the cup of Aquavit again, wrapping my fingers around it because I was trembling so much. But it seared my throat, I could not take more than a sip of it before I felt the saliva well up beneath my tongue and turned aside, trying not to retch. He took the cup from me and put it on the night-table, waited till I had stopped choking and had wiped my eyes. Then he stood up.

'Please, child, take off your nightgown.'

My hands went to the ribbons at my throat in horror. I had never once seen my own body naked, it was unthinkable that I should expose it to him, unimaginable that I should lie there displayed indecently to those cool, hard eyes.

'Not like this,' I said. 'Not in the light.'

I watched as, one by one, he snuffed out the candles. 'Please, everything – the night-light too.'

As the night-light dimmed, the room was plunged into utter darkness. I could not see him, I should not be able to tell when he was close to me. But no, I could sense him on the far side of the room, sense his silent tread upon the carpet. I flung off my nightdress and scrambled into the bed, pulling the sheets up to my chin. I heard a rustling sound, the swish of silk, and realised he had taken off the dressing-gown. Biting my lip so that I should not whimper, I lay on my back, every fibre stiffened, my eyes closed. There was a pause that seemed to last an eternity. Then I felt a counter-acting pull on the left-hand side of the sheet.

I held my breath. The contact with his skin came suddenly, so that I felt the warmth of it, the pressure of his shoulder, his thigh against mine before I had time to jerk myself away. I lay rigid, willing myself separate, willing that no part of his body should touch me again. Then I felt his hand move softly downwards across my belly, felt to my horror his lips touch my breast. I let out a cry, began to struggle. He stopped, withdrew his hand. His voice came very quietly out of the darkness.

'Dear child, don't fight me. It makes it impossible to avoid hurting you.'

Then he replaced his hand gently, this time between my legs.

I reared up with a strangled sob. 'Please, only do what you must do. Don't touch me anywhere unless – unless you absolutely have to. Please!'

There was a pause. I heard him sigh. The springs creaked as he sat up and in one sharp, violent action stripped off the sheets. Next he took a pillow from his side of the bed and, lifting me by the waist, slid it under my hips. There was nothing gentle in his movements now, only a clinical determination. I lay rigid, too frightened to protest, paralysed with terror as he knelt over me, spreading apart my legs.

I closed my eyes, but I could still sense him kneeling, towering over me, as vividly as if I could see his shadow in the darkness. Then all at once an impression grew upon me of his abstracting himself, interposing something between us, of his drawing away behind whatever it was into a great, focused, impenetrable detachment, as if he had rid his mind of my body on the bed, the sound of my breathing, the room itself, as cleanly as though they had altogether ceased to exist.

I remembered screaming when he entered me, screaming and screaming. When it was over he lay very still for a few seconds, then he levered the weight of his body off me and sat up. He must have been aware of the tears squirting from beneath my tightly-closed lids, for he seemed about to touch my face. Then, as if he thought better of it, he drew back and I heard him swear softly to himself.

I did not open my eyes until long after the sound of the

key turning in the lock, long after the dressing-room bell had shrilled, a far door had closed and there was silence.

The palms of my hands burned where I had dug my fingernails into them and my lips were cracked and dry. And there was another pain, too, which I could not think about, and a stickiness between my legs, a dampness on the sheet beneath me. I lurched across the bed and was violently sick into the basin in the night-table. When my stomach was empty and I could do no more than retch convulsively, I groped for the quilt, wrapping it tightly around my nakedness. Then, unable for a second longer to bear the contamination of the bed, I stretched myself out on the carpet, sobbing.

II

It was customary, after Mass on the first morning of the honeymoon, for the bridal couple to attend a full Court Breakfast, where the Cabinet, the Camarilla and the *Corps Diplomatique* might feast their eyes upon the spectacle of newly-wedded bliss. I sat, in my pink hat with the traditional spray of orange blossom not yet in flower pinned to the bodice of my pink silk dress, unable to touch the champagne or to eat, yet unable to lift my eyes from my plate. I could not bring myself to look at the women, who I knew must be gossiping, whispering to one another, and to look at the men, even dear, decent Aubyn, was impossible. I imagined Prince von Ansbach speculating with relish about the blood-stained sheets, Vielfrass with his moist lips pursed in an arch little smile, and once, when I glanced up, I was sure I detected even Anton von Tarn surveying me with unusual interest. Beside me Maximilian sat, a charming, polite, infinitely distant stranger. When he had come to my apartments to take me down to Mass he had lifted my chin in his hand for a moment, compelled me to look at him, parted his lips to speak; but then, reading my eyes, he had turned away, and ever since, despite his taking my arm as carefully as if I were cut crystal, despite his showing me every courtesy, I had felt an immeasurable space between us, as if he had once again withdrawn into that abstraction I had sensed in the bedroom. Yet, nevertheless, whenever I walked or sat, there were reminders of the obscene intimacy between us, and I was obliged to focus my eyes on the tablecloth to keep myself from crying.

The ritual of my public humiliation was not to stop with the Court Breakfast but was laid out before me in carefully calculated segments of time: receptions in the morning for delegations from every region of Sylvania, civic dignitaries and their wives in the ribbons and embroidery of their local costume presenting their felicitations and endless bouquets of flowers; a formal luncheon, followed by an appearance on the Residenz balcony to acknowledge the cheering of the crowd; and then a Gala night at the opera, and a Court Ball. The rigour of our schedule made me fear that my strength would give out, for I had not eaten for a day, nor slept for two, but at least it precluded conversation of an intimate nature with anyone, and in our only free moments, the two hours before the opera set aside for us to rest and dress, I was relieved that Maximilian retired to his own apartments to work, while Ursula shepherded me, half-fainting, to lie down for a while.

A vinegar compress had been applied to my forehead and I was stretched out in my chemise beneath my quilt when I heard the voices of my two ladies-in-waiting, carrying from my boudoir as Ursula was gently closing the bedroom door.

'There,' said Ursula. 'Her poor Majesty's done up, dear thing. And His Majesty too, by the looks of the shadows under his eyes. Oh well, there's nothing like a wedding to exhaust everyone.'

'That's not why His Majesty is exhausted.' Suzannah spoke so seldom that her voice always surprised me; it was so very clear and precise, almost melodious, quite unlike the rest of her.

'Oh?' said Ursula.

'I thought you would have heard. He woke the Riding Master at half past one this morning to take out that black stallion of his—'

'That horrid temperamental Balthazaar the poor Princess swears will break his neck?'

'He had it taken to the covered riding stables and rode it round and round putting it through *levades* and *caprioles* until the horse was in a lather and it was nearly four in the morning. One of the adjutants told my brother.'

Ursula clicked her tongue. 'Men! Who's to account for their strange ways! Still, my dear, we mustn't stand here chattering. We'll wake Her Majesty. And who's to know if there isn't already a baby on the way?'

These last words filled me with a new access of horror. It was bad enough no longer to be oblivious of my body, to be suddenly aware of every contaminated centimetre of it so that I could not shift my legs or put my arm across my breasts without feeling shame; but to think of this contamination taking hold upon me irrevocably, bloating me with the gross evidence of its invasion, was repugnant beyond words. Then it occurred to me that if it were possible, as Ursula had said, for me to be impregnated in just one night, perhaps he would feel there was no need for a second. Suzannah's story of his nocturnal activities showed how distasteful he too found our honeymoon rites. Perhaps once the letter of his duty were fulfilled, once he had so brutally established his possession, he would leave me be.

I prayed for it as we held the public scrutiny from our opera box, as we sat beside each other on the Throne-Room dais watching the dancing. That on our retiring he left me immediately to work on his dispatch boxes made me almost certain of it. But I was not so easily to be spared.

This time I knew the futility of resistance, only struggling when I felt his hands upon me in the darkness, otherwise merely biting my lip and willing it to be over quickly. He seemed soon to understand the impossibility of coaxing any response from my rigid body, for I sensed him once again remove himself, retreat an infinite distance, expelling my very identity from his mind. As before, he left me immediately he had finished, and as before I wrapped the quilt around me and stretched out brokenly on the carpet. I wished profoundly that my maids did not now, presumably on his instructions, remove from my access everything, even my little manicure set, which might prove in moments of solitude temptingly sharp.

The next day we were finally to embark on our honeymoon trip. Both our suites, under the command of the Master of the Horse, would travel to the Summer Palace, just outside

Helsingbad, then Maximilian and I should continue on to the Turkish Hunting Box seven kilometres away. Apart from the necessary horses, stable boys, cooks and bodyguards, Maximilian would take with him only his Private Secretary and his valet, while I should take two personal maids and one lady-in-waiting, whom I had inevitably decided should be Ursula. The arrangement was convenient for Maximilian since it meant he could have his dispatch boxes delivered to the hunting lodge and yet still consult with his advisors in the formal surroundings of the Summer Palace. Indeed the Duke of Maar and Aubyn were to travel down on the train with us so that last-minute briefings could take place before Maximilian's three-week absence from the capital.

I was glad of the businesslike atmosphere in the blue and gold Royal Saloon as we embarked, for it gave me the excuse to retire to my own compartment. My inability to eat was beginning to make me faint and, though it was another blazing day, somehow I could not get warm even with my sable cloak pulled about me. Yet I could not stomach the sight or smell of food and when luncheon was announced just after Behrensdorf I pleaded train-sickness and remained on my bunk. As I tossed to and fro, searching for some yielding spot in the rock-hard pillow, it occurred to me that I might never be able to eat again. I viewed the prospect with equanimity.

I had never stayed at the Turkish Hunting Box before. It had been a conceit of Sigismund II's, a discreet trysting place in which to conduct his various liaisons, and was in fact a very ordinary hotch-potch of buildings – stables, tea pavilion, church, rifle alley, a small farm – though the lodge itself had been fancifully decorated in the Eastern manner, with the drawing-room done out as an Ottoman Sultan's tent and other rooms poaching their style less discriminately from other parts of the Orient. Its primitiveness dismayed me – there was no gas or electric light and no running water, baths being taken in wooden tubs filled from copper cans carried up from the kitchens. My bedroom, which boasted a great deal of japanning and lacquer, was on the first floor overlooking the garden, opposite Ursula's and above Maximilian's, which was connected with mine by a spiral staircase giving off the anteroom. I had retired to bed before my maids had finished unpacking, had even missed bidding goodbye to Aubyn, who, still strangely gloomy and uncommunicative, had excused himself from joining Anton and the Duke of Maar in staying for dinner. Though vague enquiries were made after my health no one seemed to object to my absence, apart from Ursula, who clucked about something on a tray. Even if my bedroom smelt musty with disuse, even if the *chinoiserie* bed was hard and lumpy, there was, I thought, lying in my nightgown looking up at the fusty draperies of the tester, at least some feeling of sanctuary there. Except that there was no sanctuary, no privacy, no room of my own that could not be invaded, I realised with a start. I got up from the bed and went to the door to lock myself in. The key was jammed and the lock broken.

That night a new dimension was added to my horror. When his hand touched my thighs in the darkness I found myself yielding to it, opening myself to him with a weak little moan, as if my body, conditioned by the assaults upon it, had taken on its own volition. Only when his lips, encouraged by my surrender, began gently to explore my breasts was I recalled to a proper sense of myself. I reared up, arching my back, and when he did not immediately desist I sank my teeth into his shoulder. He pulled away with a muffled exclamation.

'No more!' I said. 'No more than you have to.'

He did not speak, and I could sense him kneeling over me, very still, in the darkness. Then he gave a sigh and there followed a long pause in which I could feel him begin upon that ritual going-away. I lay rigid, shocked beyond measure that I should have allowed my enfeebled condition to betray me, to betray Freddy so shamefully.

The next night and thereafter he gave up any attempt to arouse me. We exchanged no words and I had the impression of him striving to reach the necessary conclusion as quickly as possible, the sooner to leave my bed. Afterwards, as I lay alone in the darkness, I would hear him calling down the spiral staircase for his valet to draw him a bath, and then half an hour or so later I would hear the clop-clop of a horse being led up the drive from the stables to the South Gate, and then the retreating of hooves at the gallop in the direction of the Helsingbad road and the Summer

Palace. If I could not sleep I would hear the hooves returning again, often at four or five in the morning when the light was beginning to come up.

I wondered if this was how men went with prostitutes, this perfunctory coupling in the dark with every element abstracted beyond crude biological fact. I found myself trying to imagine his face when he uttered that low drawn-out sigh which heralded my release – a sound, not of pain or pleasure, but perhaps of relief. Was he already thinking that he would soon be able to wash away all traces of me, just as I was longing for first light when I could ring for the maid to change the sheets? What was in his mind as he rode towards the blazing lights of the Summer Palace? Did he console himself with the assurance that I was, after all, his property, that he had merely claimed what was his right? I did not care, for I had won my victory too; I had set, at least, a limit to my suffering.

Besides, I never saw him. Waking that first morning at the hunting lodge, I found myself too weak to leave my bed. Apart from his nightly visits in darkness he did not choose to intrude on me, preferring apparently to busy himself with the day's schedule of work. As I lay with the blinds drawn I would hear the sound of horses and dogs, of voices on the stairs, but my own room and the antechamber beyond remained sepulchrally quiet. Ursula, who must perforce, if I remained shut up, share my isolation, came to sit with me for hours at a time, working at her needlepoint and trying to entertain me with books or chatter; but though I was grateful for her patience when she must secretly be longing for walks in the sun, there was nothing I wanted, nothing that would console me.

As the third day at the hunting lodge drew into the fourth and I still had not eaten anything, had taken nothing for a week beyond glasses of seltzer water, I lay half-waking, half-sleeping, too enervated even to raise my head from the pillow. I had bade a tearful goodbye to Beatrice and Benedict on leaving Rosenholm, but I was glad now that I had been dissuaded from bringing them with me; I could not have walked them or even found the energy to pet them. It was a curious feeling, this drawing away from life, even from the few things I loved in it, debilitating, numbing, but not disagreeable. I found a certain satisfaction in observing the shallowness of the depression my body made in the bed, the way my hip-bones jutted out sharply above my concave stomach; with the slightest careless movement Maximilian's rings slid off my finger.

'Your Majesty, this cannot continue,' said Ursula for the hundredth time, putting aside her needlepoint. 'You must allow me to tell His Majesty, ask him to send for Dr Seisser from the Summer Palace.'

'Oh Ursi,' I said feebly, 'you know I've forbidden you to bother him. It's nothing, nothing at all. I shall get up when I don't feel quite so faint.'

'You feel faint because you won't eat, Ma'am. And what will His Majesty say if you drive yourself into a consumption and I don't tell him?'

'I shall eat soon. It's only that everything makes me feel so sick. You must on no account tell His Majesty. I don't wish him to be worried.'

'He ought to be worried. You should be taking healthy walks in the fresh air and eating enough for two. That's what's needed for making babies.'

Babies, babies! If I were dying would they cease to see me as a machine for turning out Maximilian's progeny? I pulled the sheets up to my chin and closed my eyes.

Ursula paused. Then she adopted her coaxing, confidential tone. 'Your Majesty – dearest Ma'am – you mustn't take it all so hard.'

I pretended not to hear her.

'We women must do our duty, as I've said. But God gives us the strength to rise above it. And besides, I'm sure His Majesty will be most considerate, once there's a happy event to look forward to.'

I sat up indignantly. 'Baroness, I have a bilious attack, no more. It has nothing to do with His Majesty! And now I should be grateful if I might be left alone to sleep.'

The effort of anger had so exhausted me that I did doze for a while after she had gone. The sounds of horses returning from the Summer Palace and the gong for luncheon woke me. I lay back and closed my eyes again; at least if they were all at table I should be left in peace.

I was woken again by the creak of the blind being raised.

I sat up, blinking stupidly at the brightness of the sunlight. Then I gasped, put my arms protectively across my breasts; for I saw that the figure in the window was Maximilian.

'Forgive me,' he said quietly. 'I didn't mean to frighten you, but I'm tired of darkness. And besides I need to look at you properly.'

For a moment the light behind him prevented me from seeing his face. Then he moved out of the brightness and came round to the chair beside the bed. He was wearing a loden jacket and high tanned leather boots and he too, I thought suddenly, looked drawn and weary. Though I fell back on the pillows, averting my face, he sat for some moments looking at me in silence. I felt him pick up my hand, measuring the thinness of my wrist, turning it so that he could see how close the veins were to the surface of the skin and how the movement made his rings slide up and down my finger. He leant over and very gently turned my face towards him.

'My dear Marie, I had understood only that you wished to be left alone. But now Ursi Windersdorf tells me you are genuinely ill, that you have eaten nothing for a week.'

I looked up at him, at the face that was usually hidden from me by the darkness. It was, I thought, paradoxical that this face, with its sardonic mouth and haughty precision of feature, should be, in spite of our hideous intimacy, even more the face of a stranger. 'She should not have told you,' I said. 'In any case, it doesn't matter.'

'No, of course it matters not at all. To a blackmailer, a forger and the potential murderer of your former husband, it matters very little that his wife is attempting to starve herself to death.'

His irony annoyed me. 'I don't care if I do die.'

'Mmm, yes – you are all of twenty-two. It's a fine age for romantic deathbed scenes.'

'Anything,' I said angrily, 'would be better than this.'

'As it happens, child, I agree with you.' He rose and, to my surprise, rang the bell. Almost immediately two footmen appeared with a laden trolley. I stared in silence as they ceremoniously lifted the covers so that I could inspect what was beneath. Beluga caviar, oysters, smoked salmon, sea-gulls' eggs served in a napkin with fresh butter, peaches, wild strawberries, a cream cheese from the mountains crusted with juniper berries; when they had finished their display they bowed silently and left.

'I see,' I said wearily. 'On top of everything else you are now going to force me to eat.'

'No, Marie.' His voice was suddenly without a trace of irony. 'No, I don't think I can bear to force you to anything, ever again.' He came and sat on the edge of the bed and took my hand, and I noticed again the lines of exhaustion around his eyes. 'You may leave the food – look at it, consider it, then ring for it to be taken away if you wish. But, before you do, I have something else which may help bring back your appetite.'

He took from his pocket a sealed envelope. I stared at it unbelievingly. 'A letter from Freddy?' My hands went out to take it, then drew back. 'It's only another forgery.'

'Perhaps you would care to open it and see.'

I wrenched at the sheets of paper, almost tearing them in my impatience. My eyes swam as I saw the familiar round scrawl, the little pen-and-ink sketches filling the headings and margins. I glanced up at Maximilian. And all at once I was laughing and crying for joy and my arms were round his neck and my head was buried in his shoulder. I hung there, feeling his hand in the small of my back through the silk of my nightdress, feeling, as I had when he had comforted me that first night, the warmth and strength of him, the faint throbbing of his heart and all the smaller pulses of nerve and sinew, sensing the proximity of his lips to my hair. But after a minute or two he disentangled me and laid me carefully back upon the pillows.

'My poor lunatic little Mouse,' he said softly. 'Try at least to manage the strawberries.' Then he was gone.

I propped myself up to devour Freddy's letter. But, though it covered several sides of paper, though I delighted in the drawings of the cloisters and the monastery garden which spilled over in places exuberantly into the text, I found it left me with a puzzling feeling of dissatisfaction. So much of it seemed preoccupied with monastery routine or the expression of religious sentiment: there was little mention of his feelings for me beyond the odd formality of his conclusion, which, while telling me he loved me and commending me to God, also congratulated me on my marriage to Maximilian. I supposed I was selfish to be searching for comfort when I should be glad that he was happy and appeared to be suffering fewer fits. Then I remembered Vielfrass's rigid censorship: of course, if Freddy were at last permitted to send me a letter he would be severely limited in what he could write; I must read between the lines for his true feelings.

Nevertheless, the letter consoled me. I lay back in the sunlight, feeling for the first time in days a genuine pleasure in its warmth. My eyes wandered to Maximilian's food-trolley; prolonged starvation had removed my appetite but the luscious scarlet of the strawberries, the dewy beads of moisture caught in the fur of the peaches looked tempting – perhaps a tiny morsel of something would not hurt me. I ate a peach, and a sliver of cheese on a hunk of warm, crusty bread and three of the oysters. My feeling of well-being increased and after a while I thought I might try a spell out of bed.

As I was attempting a few experimental steps, Ursula knocked. She was so profuse in her pleasure at my small inroads into the food that I did not have the heart to scold her for betraying me. Indeed, I felt unaccountably light-headed and cheerful.

'I think I shall send for someone to dress me,' I said. 'What time is His Majesty expected to take dinner?'

Ursula looked at me with surprise. 'Did he not tell you, Ma'am? Count Tarn came down from the Summer Palace and he and His Majesty have gone off deer-hunting at Falkenwald. They won't be back for three days – longer if the sport is good.'

III

How could I explain to Ursula why my new-found good spirits drained away as suddenly as if the sun had gone in? I could not begin to explain it to myself. Abandoning my plans to dress, I collapsed back into bed, feeling the sting of completely irrational tears. Three days without his mentioning a word to me, though I suppose I could have adduced the significance of the jacket and the hunting boots. Three days stretched limitlessly ahead with no one but Ursula and her *petit point* and her French novels, nothing but empty chatter and loneliness.

And yet I had wanted to be alone, I had taken pleasure in it. Why, when I could now rest safe in the knowledge that he would not intrude upon me, did I feel bereft, as if the sense of his being somewhere present, working below or returning from the Summer Palace, had constituted a positive force in my existence? Why, when I so loathed our nightly encounters that they had made me ill, did I suddenly feel a panic akin to despair that he had decided to relinquish them? I had told him that he could expect nothing of me and I had at last made him understand that I had meant it. My victory was complete; why, oh why did I feel this choking misery?

After all, I knew what Maximilian was – one letter from Freddy did not change that, make him any the less calculating and ruthless. Yet he had always been gentle with me, as gentle as I would allow. If he had been angry, hard in his judgements, it was only because my foolishness had provoked him. If he had hurt me it was because I had given him no choice. There was nothing in his manner of the villain Vielfrass had painted, and so many others, even Rosa, had spoken well of him. Could dear, upright Aubyn, for instance, cherish any friendship for a man who was capable of half the evil I had supposed, would Ursula and Princess Helena and even Anton von Tarn virtually worship such a man? Should I have been able to tell him about my uncle – unspeakable things it shamed me to mention – and should I have seen in his eyes the look of shock and anger if he were really incapable of decent feeling?

I found myself of a sudden longing for that dark face in all its contradictions, for the imperious sweep of its profile, for its distances and its ironies, for the way the small lines at the edges of his mouth were etched deeper when he smiled, for how, smiling, laughing, he somehow looked younger and less formidable. And yet I had never come near to penetrating that invincible armour of his, I understood nothing of what moved him or gave him joy. I longed now – as I longed perversely to feel the still warm impression of his body in the bed, to smell the sweetness of his skin – I longed just once to have lifted the darkness, to have looked into his face at the conclusion of our love-making, to have seen him in the one instant he was unguarded.

I lay on the bed in a kind of fever. My body burned so that I could be comfortable nowhere, as if it were asserting a consciousness, a virulent demand of its own. Pulling up my nightgown to my armpits, I stared tentatively down at myself, at the pallor of my skin and the flatness of my breasts and stomach, at the little mound of brownish fuzz rising at the cleft of my legs. Experimentally I put one hand to my right breast, drew up the other hand slowly between my thighs; and suddenly my stomach was hollow, I felt myself grow wet and open, felt the beginnings of a rapacious pain. Ashamedly, I dragged down my nightgown, flung myself onto my belly with my thighs clamped together; but the hollowness persisted, my legs trembled uncontrollably with it. I buried my face in the pillow, moaning wretchedly for him.

I sat up abruptly, biting the back of my hand. Was this febrile hunger love? Did I then love Maximilian? But I loved Freddy, I had sworn to love only Freddy: from so many small betrayals was I now to come to betray him utterly? Yet there was nothing of my feeling for Maximilian in my love for Freddy. I loved him, yes, for his goodness, his innocence, his childlike vulnerability; but not like this, with this importunate hunger that refused to be subdued. I had worried about Freddy, fretted inconsolably for him, but I had never felt a three-day absence from him as something my body could not contain. When I thought of Freddy I thought of peace, of companionship, of simple duties and services which brought contentment. But when I thought of Maximilian – when? When had I not thought of him? Had not his very existence informed my thoughts, my actions, like an obsession, ever since our first encounter? Did not I cling now to the precise tones and shades of him as if to hold his image fast were a physical imperative?

I fell back in the bed suddenly with my hands over my face. For if I loved Maximilian it came home to me with force that he did not, could not, love me. He had said as much several times: ours was a marriage of convenience, a working

partnership in which we should live our separate lives. His
gentleness had never been of the sort which stems from any
degree of passion, but rather the impartial kindness one
shows a small child. And had I tried to change this, tried
in some way to deserve his acknowledgement? No, I had
repeatedly opposed him and let him down. My failure of
duty, my irresponsible involvement of the Major and Rosa
and everyone else in my futile escape plan, my exploiting of
their loyalty and good will, had earned me his justifiable
contempt. And then the wedding, the few short days of our
abandoned honeymoon – why had I fought him, rejected
him, turned what might have been the beginnings of tenderness into a degrading ritual of punishment? I shivered as I
recalled his silence, his ridding himself of me in the darkness, his careful replacement of me with something –
someone – else. How could I call him back from that infinite
distance once I had forced him to set it between us? And
there were other things too. I remembered how he had
looked drawn and exhausted before he had gone away, but
I had made no concession to it nor asked the cause; I had
simply persisted in my own selfish histrionics. I remembered
how he had talked the night before the wedding of Sylvania's
problems and the atmosphere of political unrest; yet,
although I knew the fierce demands he made upon himself,
I had not respected his burden but had merely added to it.
Why, I was even incapable of proper conversation with him,
incapable of uttering anything that was not a reproach or a
complaint. I had been selfish, stupid, cruel and thoughtless
– and yet now I demanded that he should love me, must
love me if I were not to wither and die.

I jumped out of bed and rushed to the glass. I had never
been beautiful, but now even the china-doll illusion of prettiness created by my maids and my *coiffeuse*, had gone. I saw
a little pale girl in braids with a pinched face and an
expression of plaintive discontent, nothing that would
provoke, even in a well-disposed heart, the faintest glimmerings of desire.

After a while, however, I began to wonder what would
happen if I tried – started afresh. The problem was that I
did not know how. Oh, I supposed I could begin to eat
again; then I should not look quite such a scarecrow. And I

could do my best to smile and seem happy with my lot and chatter prettily, as far as my shyness would allow. But somehow, against the weight of Maximilian's indifference, these things seemed of little avail. Yet try I must, for after the second day, and night, of his absence, I was more hungry and hollow and wretched than ever.

When Ursula began one of her cluckings about my failure to rise from my bed, I found myself suddenly interrupting her. 'Ursi, did your husband love you?'

She looked up from her *petit point*, astonished. 'Well, Ma'am, of course, ours was an arranged marriage, as it is with Your Majesties, with most people of rank. But yes, it was Albrecht's duty to love me, just as it was mine to love him.'

'But wasn't there – didn't there ever grow to be anything more?'

'More, Ma'am?' She seemed imperfectly to understand me. 'He was a good man, he didn't keep a mistress or shame me with actresses – though of course the smallpox took him from me after barely a year. But he respected my position. I had nothing to complain of.'

'Oh,' I said bleakly.

She smiled at me over the top of her close-work spectacles. 'And you'll have nothing to complain of either, Ma'am. His Majesty is a good man too, with all his father's strengths – and none of the late King Sigismund's sad little weaknesses. His Majesty will stand by his duty to you, so long, dear Majesty,' and here she wagged her finger in teasing reproof, 'so long as you also fulfil yours.'

I could scarcely conceal my dissatisfaction with Ursula's answers. A sense of duty I knew Maximilian possessed in abundance. But it was not duty I wanted. I fell to thinking about the early days of my marriage to Freddy. We had not always loved each other – indeed, when I had arrived from Thalia and had been shown the sickly, bedridden young man I was to marry, when I had learnt what it had pleased everyone to conceal from me, that he suffered from fits, I had locked myself in my bedroom and howled with despair. But then, gradually, as I had come to discover that he was not, after all, simple-minded, as I found out how to nurse him and comfort him, a bond had grown up between us as if he were my child. Perhaps there were little services I could perform for Maximilian – soothing his brow when he was tired, shielding him from small irritations and inconveniences – which would somehow establish a similar bond. It was an indefinite plan, hazy in its detail but so sound in its intent that it filled me with encouragement. I should make myself necessary somehow to Maximilian. I should start the moment he returned.

But the third day became the fourth and then the fifth and still there was no sign of him. Even Ursula seemed to wilt, exhausted now of all stratagems to revive me. Then suddenly, at about six o'clock, there were horses at the South Gate and a commotion in the garden beneath our windows, the *Jägers* laying out the carcasses of the stags for the customary ceremony of celebration. Ursula and I rushed to my writing room to get a better view. I could see Anton von Tarn amongst the huntsmen but alas Maximilian was hidden from me by the gables. I waited till the *Jägers* had sounded the traditional call on their hunting horns, then I raced back to my bedroom, heart pounding.

It seemed to take forever for the bath to be drawn, my stays to be laced and my hair dressed. I had chosen a gown of buttercup peau-de-soie with feather trimmings, but with my invalid's pallor it made me look too sallow and I was obliged to settle for my blue shagreen. As for jewellery, I had determined upon the diamond and pearl choker, and the diamond stars for my hair which had been part of Maximilian's wedding present to me. But when I surveyed myself in the glass I saw how sharply the bones at my shoulders stood out, spoiling my *décolletage*, how the dusting of geranium petal scarcely heightened my pale cheeks; even my diamonds seemed to glimmer wanly.

The curtains of the Turkish Saloon were already closed and the candles lit in the heavy chased-brass *torchères*. The room, with its extravagance of pattern and texture, its preponderance of deep blues and crimsons, its fantastical ornaments crowned with feathers, gave off an equivocal atmosphere, an impression at once opulent and decadent, of light passing suddenly into mysterious shadow, of candle-flame glinting on a scimitar or a jewelled dagger, of strange shapes thrown upon walls and ceiling by the flying eagle cresting the great appliquéd canopy of the Sultan's tent. A sense of dark, unspoken things hung in the recess that held the opium couch carved for a Grand Vizier; the air was pungent with amber and camphorwood.

There were three of them apart from Maximilian, Count von Tarn and two young adjutants from Maximilian's retinue. They had abandoned the formalities of dress in favour of smoking jackets and Anton, lounging upon the cushions of the opium couch, was drawing deep upon the pipe of a silver-mounted hookah. Evidently the four of them had been expecting to spend a convivial evening unfettered by the company of women; and now Ursula and I had broken in upon their intimacy; had obliged them to jump to their feet and apologise for their dress and for the tobacco smoke, had quenched their conversation with a constraint like a cold douche. It was not that the two young officers were not respectful of protocol; they were, immaculately so. It was not that Maximilian did not come forward and take my hand and looking me up and down, eyebrows raised, for a moment, say that he was glad to see me recovered, or that Anton von Tarn did not immediately extinguish the hookah and become the courtier again. But I had such a sharp sense of not belonging, of being, in my full *toilette* and diamonds, as fanciful and out of place as Sigismund's Turkish ornaments, that I imagined a coldness settling around me, so that even Anton seemed to fix me with a resentful look. As for Maximilian, though he appeared unusually open and relaxed, none of his smiles was for me, nor his laughter; during the whole evening he scarcely looked at me, as if it were an effort for him to recall my existence. I was not sorry when the brandy arrived and Ursula and I could make our excuses. At least Maximilian would be obliged to remember me when he came to retire.

It appeared that our honeymoon seclusion was to be preserved no further for our three visitors had been offered guest-rooms, so that the company was unlikely to break up early. But I consoled myself with the thought that it gave me more time for my preparations. I had the maid dress me in one of my prettiest nightgowns, with blue ribbons and a froth of lace at the neck. I scented myself liberally and made

the girl pay special attention to my hair. I lay on my bed
with the night-light burning and waited.

I waited long after everywhere was wrapped in silence
and darkness.

IV

I would make him notice me, understand that I had changed.
Though I had scarcely slept, I rang for the maid early to lay
out my riding habit. He always rode in the mornings; I
should ride with him.

I fidgeted with impatience as I was buttoned into my
serge bodice. Apparently His Majesty had not yet finished
breakfasting. I was still drawing on my gloves as I strode
into the dining-room.

Anton von Tarn, attired for shooting, was perusing the
morning paper, one of the adjutants was helping himself
from the dishes sizzling over the spirit stove. They both
glanced up in astonishment as I entered.

'If you're looking for Max,' said Anton, suppressing a
yawn, 'you've missed him, I'm afraid. Doubtless fearing
Count Vielfrass has staged a revolution in his absence, he
rode off for the Summer Palace about ten minutes ago.'

I whirled round without a word and made for the stairs.
In the vestibule I found a footman to send to the stables; if
they could saddle me a mount and find me a groom I might
catch him at the gallop.

But, after some interval, the footman returned looking
sheepish. 'I regret, Your Majesty, but the Saddle Master is
unable to provide Your Majesty with a mount this morning.'

'That's absurd! Tell him I order him to – no, I shall go and
speak to him myself.'

I stormed back through the vestibule and out through the
garden door down the drive. In the stable yard the cobbles
and mud slowed my progress. A boy appeared carrying
harness and tack. I bearded him instantly.

'B-b-b-ut, Your Majesty,' – he was stuttering, bowing and
walking backwards simultaneously – 'they give us a special
order, Your Majesty, not to—'

The Saddle Master appeared behind him, a bullfrog of a

man, portentous in his cocked hat and embroidered uniform.
He bowed as low as his bulk would permit.

'Your Majesty is deeply gracious to honour us with her
presence, ah, deeply gracious . . . but we regret we have
no mount . . . no horse, ah, suitable for Your Majesty at
present—'

'Any horse will do,' I said icily. 'And you will be so good
as to find me a groom.'

'No mount, Your Majesty – and, ah, no suitable groom.'

'Herr Sattelmeister, you forget yourself. I order you to
saddle me a horse and find me a groom immediately.'

He took a deep gulp of air into his gills. 'We regret – Your
Majesty will be so generous as to forgive – we, ah, already
have our orders.'

I stared at him. 'Whose orders?' But even as I said the
words I knew the question was superfluous. How dare
Maximilian humiliate me like this! Or was it perhaps that he
merely considered it sensible, in view of my neurasthenic
behaviour, that I should not be allowed out riding alone? I
flushed. For a moment I hung between the impossibility of
retreating and the sense that my humiliation was just. Then,
ahead of me, past the Saddle Master's bulk, I saw one of the
boys leading out a black stallion already saddled and bridled.
I recognised it as the great black brute that was one of
Maximilian's favourite mounts. The animal had his ears laid
back and was jerking his proud head up and down, chafing
against the bit; but at least it would only take a few minutes
to put the side-saddle on him.

'I am countermanding your orders. I shall ride Balthazaar.'

As if understanding me the horse reared up, straining
against the leading rein and snorting its disapproval.

'My dear Marie,' said a quiet voice behind me, 'I see there
is no end to your determination to break your neck.'

I whirled round. Maximilian stood about ten paces away
surveying me with mild amusement. 'Very well, Sattelmeister. Since Her Majesty has evidently recovered from her
indisposition you may saddle her the bay. And I suppose,
in the absence of a groom, I may persuade her to make do
with me.'

I opened my mouth for some suitable retort but he had
turned away, had taken Balthazaar's reins and was stroking

the great beast's neck companionably. Although I had achieved my object I felt deflated, felt suddenly the futility of all my resolutions, the impossibility of equalling even Balthazaar's place in his affections.

The bay was led out and Maximilian himself placed me carefully in the saddle, looking to the bit and curb before giving me the reins. Then he mounted Balthazaar and we trotted out in silence towards the Helsingbad road. We were about ten minutes' canter from the hunting lodge when he suddenly glanced back over his shoulder. 'Damn!' he said. 'I thought I had lost them.'

I turned the bay's head and noticed two horsemen some distance behind us, who, seeing that they were observed, reined in their mounts and attempted unsuccessfully to conceal themselves in the shade of a tree.

'Detectives,' he said, with a curl of his lips. 'They must have caught my trail again when the saddle-girth broke and I had to double back.' Seeing my astonished expression, he laughed. 'Oh, not my idea, I assure you. Uncle Leo has been as nervous as a cat ever since he got it into his head that someone was taking pot-shots at me in Switzerland. But, you know, if there is one thing about this extraordinary new life of mine I find insupportable, it is never being able to be alone – not even to be able to go out riding by myself. I'll tell you what, child, if you are really so anxious to put your neck at risk why don't we see if we can make a better job of shaking them off this time?'

I had barely the space to nod before he had given Balthazaar his head and we were off the road and galloping across country, describing a bewildering course of circles and zig-zags, past outlying hamlets and coppices, through a small wood dodging perilous overhanging branches, over dykes and walls, careering headlong down banks and through watersplashes, until I had utterly lost my sense of direction. Maximilian scarcely had to use his spurs on Balthazaar but, though the bay had little of the stallion's mettle, I somehow managed by judicious cuts of the whip to keep up. I had not ridden so hard since I had last been hunting and I cursed my foolish sojourn in bed, for my back began to ache and my arms to feel they would be wrenched from their sockets. But I was nonetheless exhilarated, for I was aware that, apart from taking the jumps first, he was making no concession to me, was treating me for once not as a necessary encumbrance but as an equal. When we finally reined in the horses and I saw that we had travelled in a semi-circle to the perimeter of the Home Park (without a detective anywhere in view), though my hands were burning I felt elated.

The Summer Palace had been built on simple, classical lines at the beginning of the century by Sigismund I, but had been substantially augmented in imitation of Versailles by his namesake, with the addition of two new wings including a hall of mirrors, and extensive vistas of lakes, lawns, Italian statuary and geometric box-tree. We had approached it from the west end and now, distances made deceptive by the morning heat-haze, it seemed to rise up out of the water before us, shimmering in the spray of the fountains. Maximilian suggested that we skirt the lake and walk to the terrace through the garden, and we dismounted at the West Gate, waving back the guard to excuse them from a formal turn-out.

He smiled as he helped me down from the saddle. 'Aubyn was right. You ride very well.'

I blushed stupidly. 'We went out once or twice when he was at Schwanensee. But otherwise I'm afraid I'm horribly out of practice.'

'You and Aubyn get on well. I'm glad.'

'We have England in common and my English relations. And he seems to share my interests in so many ways, it makes him very easy to talk to —' I stopped, blushing more deeply, realising the implicit comparison in my remark, wondering if Maximilian, too, saw it.

We walked on without speaking for a few minutes, he looking straight ahead, flicking his riding crop from time to time against his top boots, I trailing a little, dumbly. Apart from the whir of dragonfly wings above the waterlilies and the steady chatter of the fountains, the silence was absolute. I was aware of him deliberately slackening his pace so that I could keep up, and felt the sense of equal companionship drain away.

'Please,' I said, 'teach me how to be a good wife to you.'

'My dear Marie, if I had believed I should need to teach

you that I should not have asked the Grand Duke for your hand.'

I paused, struggling once again with the impossibility of expanding any conversation with him. 'But I want so much to – Oh, I know everything has gone badly so far, but I want to change that, be a proper wife, do things for you, take care of you . . .'

He laughed. 'Dear child, on present form I think it would be better, don't you, if I were the one who took care of you.'

Though his laughter was not unkind I felt momentarily close to tears, for I had only to glance up at him to recognise the absurdity of my suggestion.

'I know I have been stupid,' I said. 'I know I've behaved abominably, let you down, been petty and obstinate and childish. But I'm truly sorry, truly ashamed. I want so much to make things up to you – if only you'd let me, give me the chance. I know you say you expect nothing of me—'

'I said I expected no more than you could give.'

'I know all I've done so far is to demonstrate how little I'm capable of. I'm not even good at the things women are supposed to be good at, like painting water-colours and singing duets. But there must be something, some way I may be useful to you. Perhaps I could – well, arrange things, make things prettier and pleasanter for you. I could have the State Apartments at the Residenz redecorated, for instance – I'm sure I could manage that.'

He laughed again. 'No.'

'But I—'

'My dear Marie, I don't suppose you have any conception of our financial situation – there's no reason on earth why you should. But Baron Schramm left Sylvania stone broke, in hock to half the bankers in Europe. To raise money I've had to dispose of all our estates in Thalia and Prussia, every single one of our assets abroad. There's our personal fortune, of course, the money my uncles smuggled into Switzerland – at least that has helped me meet the cost of the wedding celebrations. But the wedding will be our one and only glorious extravagance. From now on any public money that's spent will go where it's badly needed – to start up new industries, to compensate the farmers if the crop fails, to help the people in this country who are quite simply

starving. And you and I, I'm afraid, must set an example –
which we certainly shan't by having the Residenz redecorated from top to bottom.'

I stared up at him in silence for a moment. 'But there must
be something I can do,' I said desperately. 'Something more
than – than just duty. I can't bear this being shut out, this
uselessness. I want to be allowed to share your life. Please,
I know if you treat me like a schoolgirl it's because I deserve
it, but please, tell me there is something.'

He stopped suddenly, turned, put his hands on my shoulders. 'Dear little Mouse, of course there is. I want from you
what I've always wanted – a working partnership.'

A marriage of convenience, separate lives. My desolation
must have shown in my face, for his brows narrowed. 'But,
dear child, don't you see that is what you can give me? I'm
not remotely interested in your merits as a water-colourist.
I want from you what you have always excelled at – your
natural, instinctive touch with the people.'

I stared at him. 'But I'm too shy and awkward, I've never
been any good—'

He smiled. 'No good? Then it was not you they always
wanted to see in the hospitals and orphanages, not you who
insisted on visiting the children with typhoid and diptheria
because you thought the comfort it would bring them
outweighed the risk to yourself?'

'Who told you that? Aubyn again?'

'No. But I trust my source.'

'You don't understand. I did those things because Freddy
couldn't, because I had to be Freddy as well as myself. I
didn't do anything Freddy wouldn't have done if he hadn't
been ill.'

'And what of Nordstadt?'

The name made me shudder. I turned away.

'When you went to Nordstadt on your tour of the region
there had been a bread shortage and a spate of political
arrests. There was a crowd of demonstrators outside the
Rathaus waiting for you to arrive. It was a large crowd, but
it was peaceful – a great many women and children, and
nobody armed. But the police mounted a baton charge to
break it up, and when that didn't succeed they brought in
the 4th Fusiliers with a cannon.'

I put my hand over my eyes for a moment. 'I didn't know.
I was powerless, I couldn't stop it!'

'But you did stop it. You insisted on driving into the
square, getting down from your carriage and walking into
the thick of it. You could have been hit yourself or torn apart
by the crowd. But no one could stop you and the army was
obliged to hold its fire. And afterwards you stayed to comfort
the victims, you covered one poor woman who had lost an
arm with your cloak—'

'Please!' I said. 'I don't want to remember. It was horrible.
And it was done in our name.'

'It was done in Schramm's name. The people understood
your courage in defying him. And they saw your horror.
Just in that moment they saw there might be something
beside the Baron von Schramm, some hope of deliverance.'

'But there never was. After that he set up the Council of
State and Freddy and I could do nothing, we lost what little
power we had.'

'But there are things you can do now to make sure what
happened at Nordstadt can never happen again.' He was
walking faster so that I had trouble in keeping up, and his
face was animated with a warmth I had never observed in
it before. 'Don't you see? There is so much for both of us to
do. And you – you must teach me. There are things I am
only just discovering that you, who have been brought up
to this, understand without the need for thinking. Dear God,
there is so much in the past to be made up for, so much in
Sylvania still to be put right. You may give a man the vote,
but what good is it if he sees that nothing is changed by it,
that the political wrangling still continues, that no one truly
seems to have his interests at heart? And you can't eat a
vote, it doesn't automatically entitle you to a job. Because
there are no longer so many political prisoners in our jails,
because we have stopped shooting people in the streets, it
doesn't necessarily follow that there is more stability, more
hope of work.' He slackened his pace, paused. 'We shall go
to the North in two months' time, Marie, you and I together.
We shall talk to the people there, try to show them there is
something beyond Vielfrass and his crew of reactionaries
that they can depend upon and trust.'

His enthusiasm frightened me, I felt inadequate, as

distanced by it as I was by his coolness. 'But I'm not clever,' I said. 'I've never known anything about politics, I don't understand them.'

'My dear child, I'm not asking you to read Hegel or Marx. Politics are no more than instinct and common sense. Your instinct at Nordstadt was immaculate—'

'And my common sense?' I asked. 'You don't seem to think very highly of that.'

He smiled. 'I'm sure if your energies were directed less singlemindedly into fighting me you would recover it. But in any case I must accept a great deal of the blame. I have left you too much alone, I see that now. I'm afraid I don't possess Aubyn's happy knack of understanding.'

Though he was smiling his mention of Aubyn for some reason embarrassed me, and we walked on towards the terrace for a minute or two in silence. I felt more than ever the impossibility of getting close to him, felt that he had overestimated me, that the one part of himself he held out for me to share was an abstraction with which I should never come to grips.

'I'll try,' I said quietly. 'I'll try very hard to be what you want of me. But you must help me. If I seem like a child it's because Freddy and I were treated like children – nothing important was ever explained to us. I don't even understand now why you're so concerned about Vielfrass. I know he's vile, but I've seen the people cheering you in the streets, I've seen their loyalty. Surely that counts for more?'

'It does today, Marie. But it may not tomorrow.'

I shivered suddenly, remembering the events of last summer. 'But now that there's a constitution, now that Vielfrass is accountable—?'

'My dear child, Sylvania is a powder keg, a backward country with a history of oppression, a bankrupt budget and no economic future to speak of. In one sense Vielfrass is right. A little freedom can be dangerous, raise the people's expectations, cause more riots and unrest, make Prussia think we're rather too risky a neighbour. Bring back the oppression, Vielfrass would say, and you have control, you're not inviting Prussia to help you keep the peace with a tactical invasion.'

'And is that why you need the treaty with my uncle so badly? To assist you against Prussia?'

'Yes. But even more I need the Thalia-Sylvania railway.'

I laughed. 'Uncle Berthold's toy?'

'You would adore his designs for the Royal Saloon – somewhere between the Taj Mahal and a Viennese bordello. But it's not a toy to me, it's a weapon of survival.'

'Because Vielfrass wants it?'

'It's Keller who wants it. So Vielfrass, of course, is mortally opposed to it.'

I shook my head, bewildered. 'There you are. I shall never understand.'

He laughed. 'It is perfectly simple, truly. Vielfrass believes you can't fulfil the people's expectations so you may as well crush them. Keller and I believe the opposite, that if the country is to have a future at all we must set up some workable industry in the North to create jobs and earn foreign currency. And in order to do that we need to . . .'

He had tailed off because we had reached the colonnaded French doors at the top of the terrace steps. I was suddenly uncomfortably aware that he had not expected me to accompany him, that he had come to the Summer Palace to work and that this would be the parting of our ways.

'I should like you to go on explaining,' I said. 'You were wrong when you said I could teach you things. I've been trained, yes, to perform certain duties, but I've never understood properly why there was a need for them – beyond my position, the fact of what I am. I should like to understand, I'd like your working partnership if you still think I'm capable of it. And I'd like you to explain it all when you can find the time.'

He stood for a moment surveying me with his detached, half-amused look, tapping his riding crop thoughtfully against his boot. Then his face softened, an expression came into his eyes I did not perfectly understand.

'Why not now?' he asked softly.

'But your work . . . ?'

'I think for once it may wait.'

We passed through the vestibule and into a lofty hall columned in red marble and sombre with the busts of dead Hohenstaufens cast in bronze as Imperial Caesars. He strode on but I found it easier to keep up with him now, found myself suddenly lighthearted as if, in some indefinite way, a pact had sprung up between us.

'But why a railway?' I said.

'Because there is no earthly point my bringing in advisors from England and France to establish modern industries if I can't find a market for what those industries make. And to do that I need efficient transport. Come into the library, I can explain better with a map.'

The library led off the hall through a pair of vast chased-silver doors. It too was a high cavern of a room which amply merited the fire that, even in summer, blazed in the grate at its far end. Huge leather globes stood in the window recesses, architecturally-framed bookshelves lined the walls with a gallery running three sides of their perimeter taking a second storey of books up to the cornice. Yet, despite its imposing proportions, the fire, the warmth of leather and carved wood, gave the room an amenable nut-brown glow.

Maximilian, instructing the footman outside the door that we were on no account to be disturbed, went to the bookshelves and, taking down maps and atlases, began to explain about the Thalian railway link and how, though we had an ample railway network in the wealthier South giving us access to Austria, we had no rail connection with France and Southern Europe, and no modern transport system in all the poorer regions of the North around Nordstadt, merely the slow and unwieldy means of the river barge. He talked lucidly and concisely, yet as I listened, trying to understand about steel-mills and enamel factories and Vielfrass's alliance with the aristocracy and the *Landgrafs*, which compelled him to be protective of the present rural economy and implacably opposed to any industrial expansion, I found myself aware, no longer of a feeling of happy complicity, but of a growing tension between us. Though Maximilian did not stumble or search for words, he had lost the heat he had shown in the garden, as if some part of him were engaged elsewhere. In the garden too, when we had first begun to talk properly, he had put his hands lightly on my shoulders, but now, though in bending over the atlases we were forced into each other's proximity, heads bowed together as we traced routes and boundaries across the pages, arms, shoulders, hands

nearly touching, he seemed scrupulously to avoid all contact
with me. With the unnaturalness of our holding ourselves
so carefully separate I found that even my breathing had
become a conscious effort.

When he moved to turn the page I started clumsily and
my fingers collided with his. He withdrew as if from the
force of an electric shock. Then suddenly his hand came
down on mine so hard that it hurt me. I gasped. The pressure
of his hand intensified. I stared up at him. His eyes were
trained upon my face, no longer with amused indifference,
but with a fierce concentration. I tried to turn my head away
but his grip on my hand tightened again, compelling me to
look at him. Then suddenly he released his hold and, still
with his eyes on my face but smiling slightly, a curious, half-
questioning smile, he drew something from his pocket. It
fell with a sharp sound upon the page and rolled into the
channel of the binding. I looked down and saw my diamond
and pearl hat-pin.

There was a moment of utter silence. When I lifted my
eyes I saw the question in his, saw his brows drawn, his
mouth intent with it. I picked up the hat-pin and very slowly
raised it to my lips, pressing the point against my lower lip
until I had drawn blood. Then I turned and threw it in the
fire.

I could hear the flames spit as they rose to take it, then I
was conscious only of his arms hard about me, of the taste
of his mouth mingling with the metallic sweetness of my
blood.

When I opened my eyes I was still shivering with him, my
lips still parted with the echoes of a cry. He stirred, then,
sighing reluctantly, came out of me and lay for a moment
with his head between my breasts. An awareness of my
surroundings stole upon me slowly like a gradual coming to
consciousness: the disordered tangle of our clothes upon the
floor, the heat of the fire upon my right flank, the long, lean
weight of his body stretched between my legs. I gazed down
at him, taking in the curve of his shoulders and the sweep
of his back, the whole fine-tuned, powerful beauty of him,
wanting to touch him, wanting to touch the place where the
tiny hairs curled into the nape of his neck, but almost not

daring to. He sighed again, shifted and, kissing each of my breasts in turn, rolled off me onto the rug and, scooping me up into the crook of his shoulder, laid me very gently across him so that my head was pillowed on his chest and my right leg rested lightly between his.

'My dear, dear little Mouse,' he said, burying his lips in my hair. 'My very dear, beautiful child.'

I lay for a while feeling his hand caressing my neck and shoulders, thinking how strange it was to be so utterly consumed by him, to be stretched out passive and sleepy and unashamed while the daylight streamed in through the tall windows and the flames danced brightly upon our nakedness and shelf upon shelf of books stared down at us like so many scholarly eyes sitting in judgement. The thought made me self-conscious and I moved my leg awkwardly from its resting place.

'My dear child, what's the matter? Are you cold?'

I explained about the books. He laughed uproariously. 'Caesar, Cicero, Tacitus . . .' he read from the shelf closest in view. 'A warlord, an orator and an historian. They all have considerably more to be ashamed of than you, my funny, prudish, passionate little Mouse.'

'Don't call me that. Please.'

'Mouse? But that, dear Mouse, is what you are.'

'I know what I am. It's horrible – and mocking.'

'Is it? It's certainly not intended to be. At least, it's not you who are mocked.' He sat up, lifting me with him and, propping himself against one of the great wing chairs, turned me so that I was cradled in his arms.

'I know how they described me to you,' I said. 'I heard Prince von Ansbach say it.'

'That you were a mousey little thing?' He kissed the place on my lip where the hat-pin had broken it. 'So he did. And then I was confronted with a beautiful spitfire of a creature with great wide eyes who blazed at us, defied us, poured upon us the contempt for our treatment of her that we entirely deserved.' He kissed me again lightly. 'Yet you are a mouse, nonetheless, with your silky brown hair and your big, bright brown eyes – little and quivering and delicately perfect, timid one minute and wild the next. And very, very beautiful.'

I felt my usual embarrassment, the suspicion of insincerity that gallantry always provoked in me. 'Please,' I said, 'you need not pay me compliments.'

He held me for an instant at arm's length with a little dry smile. 'Not clever? Not beautiful? Oh, dear child, if you will believe nothing else, will you believe this?' And he began to kiss me again harder, my eyes, my hair and then my mouth. After a while he drew back to rearrange me carefully upon the rug. 'Will you believe,' he said very softly, 'that now I am not obliged to rape you in darkness I want you to distraction?'

I was not sure why he had chosen the Private Bedroom built for Sigismund II instead of his own apartments, except perhaps for some ironic amusement it afforded him. It was a room more overblown even than the Bridal Suite at the Residenz, draped entirely from ceiling to floor in primrose silk, except where gilded nymphs, bare-breasted, held aloft swags of drapery or cavorted licentiously with putti above Venitian mirrors. The massive bed, more beswagged and befringed than all the rest, held centre place behind a gilded balustrade flanked by two enormous *torchères* each entwined wantonly with cupids and nymphs. I span round bewildered, seeing in glass reflected in glass swathe upon primrose swathe, nymph upon nymph, and in their midst myself, pale, dwarfed, insignificantly human.

We waited until a fire had been lit and a meal – luncheon or dinner, who knew which? – laid for us in the antechamber. Then he began for the second time, very slowly, the complicated process of undressing me, kissing each new area of my body he exposed; until at last we both stood together naked.

He gazed at me smiling for a moment, then turned me round so that I was suddenly confronted with myself in one of the glasses.

'Look, little Mouse,' he said. 'Look very carefully and try for once to understand how beautiful you are.'

He held me against him with his arms tight about me and I was obliged to look at the pale naked figure with the mass of heavy hair tumbling over its adolescent breasts. I hardly thought I could discern beauty; instead I saw how dark his

skin was against mine, how small and frail his embrace made
me, how his eyes were clouded with a mixture of amusement
and desire. Then I saw blurrily, for he moved his hands to
my breasts, then slowly down over my belly until my head
was thrown back and my body was arched against his. He
turned me round and entered me standing and, with my
legs locked around his waist, carried me thus to the bed.

Later, as we lay drowsily in each other's arms I felt him grow
serious, as if without taking his head from my breast or his
thigh from where it paralleled mine, he had moved away
from me again. I looked up, touched his face. His eyes
changed, his lips broadened into a smile.

'Tell me what you were thinking?' I said.

'Oh, only that of all the monstrous rooms in all the royal
palaces of Sylvania, this is undoubtedly the most
monstrous.'

'And you possess every one of them,' I said with a laugh.
'Monster upon monster.'

He raised his eyebrows in mock horror. 'Thank God, I do
not. I hold them mercifully only in trust.'

'But they are yours now. Your castles, your palaces, your
estates.'

'The country's palaces, the country's estates. Dear God,
child, until recently my possessions numbered one or two
books, a pair of aged duelling pistols – and a ring which I
do not wear. I should hardly wish to be encumbered with
all this grandeur.'

It was the most he had ever said about his past. I waited
for a second as if I were afraid of breaking a spell. Then I
said softly: 'But it was your father's.'

The thought seemed to make him serious again. 'Yes, it
was Sigismund's.' He lay silent for a moment, gently
stroking my hair. Then he said: 'According to Aunt Helena,
Crown Prince Maximilian Eugen Sigismund Otto Lothar von
Hohenstaufen was conceived in this bed.'

I had started to laugh, but I stopped short, thinking
suddenly that I understood his seriousness.

'I want very much to have your child,' I said.

To my surprise he stopped stroking my hair as if his train
of thought had been sharply broken. 'Oh, Mouse,' he said

softly, lifting my face to his, 'of course I want that too – I
am obliged to want it. But we have time enough, we have
only just begun upon – everything. And besides,' he was
laughing now, his eyes teasing, 'you have been quite
sufficiently dutiful for one day in remaining awake
throughout my discourse on Sylvanian railway systems.'

V

Afterwards, nonetheless, I was convinced I had conceived
that day at the Summer Palace, convinced of it by a curious
feeling I had two days later of something in my belly shifting,
falling into place, so that, even though the absence of my
monthly bleeding might have been purely the result of my
attempt at starving myself, even though it was altogether
too early in any case to tell, I kept the certainty with me as
a secret extension of my happiness.

When we returned to the hunting lodge there were no
more shooting parties and we were able to devote ourselves
assiduously to the remaining days of our honeymoon.
Maximilian continued, too, in intervals between our love-
making, with my political instruction, the two activities
merging quite naturally and fluently into one, so that I
remember those weeks as a flurry of creased papers and
disordered clothes, and laughter, and sunlight warm upon
my naked body. I discovered to my surprise that once I had
overcome my fear of my own dullness I began to learn
quickly and with enjoyment, as if a source, not of drudgery,
but of pleasure and stimulation had been opened up to
me. When we returned to Rosenholm I began to sit with
Maximilian every morning as he went through his dispatch
boxes, taking in the minutiae of the day's business, glowing
with a feeling of usefulness – though whether he allowed
me in his study because I really was useful, or whether it
was that we should otherwise be prevented by his rigorous
daily routine from appeasing our limitless hunger to touch
and kiss each other, I was never quite certain.

Though Maximilian had judged it better, in view of the
likely failure of the harvest, not to extend our honeymoon
with the traditional European trip, we spent September very

pleasantly in the capital with few formal engagements and little enough social obligation of any kind. Prince Gustav and Princess Helena were in Zurich for a scientific congress, the Duke of Maar was on a diplomatic mission to Austria and Thalia, even Vielfrass, with the summer vacation of the Assembly, had retired to his country estate. Anton too had ceased to visit, although I gathered he still paid duty calls on his sister. He had been ordered by his father to knuckle down to military life, so Ursi said, and was training with his regiment for November's manoeuvres at Jedburg. I thought sometimes of our conversation at Schwanensee, when it seemed I had only narrowly been saved from a declaration of love, and wondered whether that were the explanation for his resentment; but the boy would soon see his feelings were hopeless and we should become friends again. About his sister, alas, I cherished no such optimism; during those weeks in Rosenholm her sour face was the one blight. Yet was it my fault that I was now so gloriously, deliriously happy? Was I to be held just as guilty for loving as I had been for my failure to love?

One visitor who was frequent and thoroughly welcome, however, was Aubyn. The constitution, though it gave the final sanction on all other financial expenditure to the elected Assembly, still left Maximilian in control of the vital army budget, and he and Aubyn, and Leopold von Maar on his return, occupied many hours discussing the modernisation and re-equipment of our forces within the slender means available. And Aubyn, of course, would not let these meetings pass without afterwards coming to my apartments to spend a further hour or so chatting. Indeed, on our first day back in the Residenz he and I had strolled together in the gardens, marvelling at how unruly Beatrice and Benedict had become during my absence.

We had been watching the dogs squabbling over a stick when he had suddenly surprised me by taking both my hands and gazing at me full in the face.

'By God, Marie, to say you look well wouldn't be to do it justice – you look absolutely cracking. And Max, too. I've never seen him quite so chipper.'

I squeezed his hands. 'Oh Aubyn, we're so happy.'

'I'm glad, my dear. Truly glad of it.' He frowned suddenly.

'D'you know, there was a time . . . Well, tricky things weddings, get everyone on edge. But I don't think I could have borne – a fellow likes to feel his friends are happy, don't y'know.'

I smiled. 'Sometimes I'm so happy I think I must be dreaming.'

'Excellent. Capital. All I wanted to hear, really. Max is a thoroughly fine chap – and your happiness is mine, you know, always will be.'

He had looked so very solemn as he had pronounced these last words that I had wondered for a moment if there were something still troubling him; but then he had taken my arm in his usual comfortable way and we had gone to disentangle the dogs.

My happiness in those weeks did, indeed, seem boundless. In the sharing of his work, in the infinite pleasures of our love-making, I felt myself drawing ever closer to Maximilian. It was true that there were still some things he would not let me share: oh, certainly I now possessed the accepted knowledge of his past, the monastery, the years in Paris, the time in Switzerland; but when I pressed him further he was always reticent, would never expand upon it. Oh, he seemed genuinely to wish me to share every aspect of his working routine; yet twice he was suddenly called away from Rosenholm for two days with scant announcement of his departure and no explanation on his return. And other intimacies, too, were curiously refused me: though we worked daily in his study it was to my apartments that we always retired for the night and I had never once set foot in his bedroom, so that I found myself longing sometimes, when he left my bed at dawn, to see from the inside that cell-like room, to experience all the tiny details of living with him that were still mysterious to me, the sight of his hair entwined in his brushes, the way he looked in the glass when he fastened his collar-stud, the scents of his tooth-powder and shaving-pot. Sometimes when I observed him far away in thought I would wonder whether I should ever know him as I had known Freddy.

But then, I would remind myself, Freddy's illness had fined down his life, simplified his relationship with the world, made issues clear-cut and judgements absolute. To

Maximilian on the other hand, pondering the financial deficit and the failure of the harvest, struggling to hold the balance between Right and Left, working with Vielfrass, a man he disliked and distrusted yet was obliged to conciliate in order to keep the peace, everything was shifting, relative, every decision a means to an end, not an end in itself. If there were areas of Maximilian I might not know, secret places where I might not tread, if I might never understand why, for instance, he refused the sacraments unless public duty made receiving them unavoidable, or why sometimes, even in the midst of laughter, his eyes would darken momentarily as if with pain, it mattered only fleetingly; for I after all, who watched him sleeping, who held him at the climax of making love, surely knew him better than anyone, knew as much as he would ever allow to be known.

It frightened me sometimes that my happiness often obliterated all thought of Freddy. I still kept his ring in its chamois bag hidden in the depths of my workbox and his letters, tied with pink ribbon, in one of the pigeon-holes of my bureau. The letters came regularly now, often six or seven pages long, affectionate, detailed, though still with that puzzling lack of intimate reference I had noticed in the first. Nevertheless he continued well and surprisingly happy, so happy that I might even suppose he was not suffering by my absence as greatly as I had feared. But when I thought this I would instantly reprove myself for too easily trying to excuse my own neglect, and I would suddenly experience a foolish chill, like an omen.

In October we went as we had planned on a tour first of the areas most devastated by the failure of the harvest and then of the North. Though it pierced my heart to see the pinched faces of the peasant women, the children with running noses and rickets and no shoes, everyone welcomed us ecstatically wherever we went, fêting us with flowers and deafening cheers, so that sometimes I doubted Maximilian's estimation of the difficulties ahead. Nevertheless, I noticed that the loyal subjects carefully assembled to bow and kiss my hand, the people we were allowed to talk to at dinners and receptions, were always the well-fed burghers and land-owners of the region, people with correct conversation and unimpeachably conservative views. Much to the consternation of our suite, Maximilian began to demand sudden changes in our schedule so that we could show ourselves to the grimy girls who worked the pit brow of the near-exhausted mine at Nordstadt, and the bargees and fishermen at Andershaven, and the men, bleak with long despair of work, at the brickfields of Helm.

Throughout the tour my admiration for Maximilian grew. He, who claimed not to have the knack of understanding, seemed endlessly ready with the right word of sympathy, the appropriate gesture, seemed to possess unbounded reserves of patience, tact and charm. I loved the look of respect on the tough faces of the miners, the devotion of the old women reaching out their hands to him, their adoration echoing mine. I felt myself drawn beneath the spell he cast so that my duties no longer seemed onerous and even my shyness seemed to disappear. It was so novel to share, to know that when I felt pain at the poverty around me he felt it too, to catch his eye in the midst of a particularly pompous civic speech and see that he too was carefully restraining the quirks of incipient laughter. We worked unremittingly, often from nine in the morning till ten or eleven at night, but for the first time I understood the usefulness of it, and the satisfaction. I no longer cared about the sugared romances written daily in the popular press for I suddenly felt they were all true; we *were* idyllically happy, we *were* head over heels in love, and the radiance of it seemed to be projected back at us from the faces of everyone we met. Though I was not, despite Maximilian, beautiful, I began to understand how it might feel to be so, and to realise that beauty and happiness in themselves bestowed a gift.

My joy was increased too by my pregnancy. I had not seen a doctor – I had no need to – so that the secret was still entirely mine. I bubbled with it, longed for the moment I should tell Maximilian and yet, perhaps because of his words at the Summer Palace, his apparent desire that we should first have space to know and enjoy each other, I kept putting it off. Yet I must tell him before the tour was over, for after it we should suffer our first real separation, he to go on to Jedburg to observe the manoeuvres, I to return to Rosenholm. And besides, though I had found myself surprisingly well, not gaining weight and very little sick, I had begun to fall prey to a debilitating tiredness which, after day upon day of factory and hospital visits, of the unveiling of monuments and the pinning on of medals and the consecration of churches and regimental flags, threatened to overwhelm me.

On our last day, after reviewing the garrison at Nordstadt, we were returning to the Schloss Sonnentau where we were guests of Count and Countess von Spitze when, climbing down from our open landau, I was suddenly seized by an attack of dizziness, so that Maximilian, who had my hand, was obliged to hold me tightly against him to stop me from falling. Supporting me up the steps and into the vestibule somehow, he lowered me into a chair and was on the point of summoning our doctor when I prevented him.

'It's nothing, I promise you. Just tiredness.'

He surveyed me with concern for a moment, then he lifted me in his arms and carried me up the Grand Staircase to our apartments, where he laid me on the bed. I was indeed so exhausted that my eyes began to close immediately with the sheer relief of lying down. Though we were supposed to dress in a hour's time for a dinner and ball at the Rathaus, he would not hear of my getting up. He offered once more to send for the doctor and for Ursula to come and sit with me, but again I dissuaded him.

'Please, my darling, there's no need to fuss. I shall be perfectly well once I've slept.'

He stroked my hair, his eyes thoughtful. 'You're sure, Mouse, certain it's nothing?'

I could have told him about the baby then, even began to assemble the words for it, but my eyelids were heavy, I was already drifting deliciously into sleep.

I must have slept for hours, was only woken by the sense of someone softly touching my cheek. When I opened my eyes he was bending over me, still wearing his dress uniform and orders, his expression, in the flicker of the night-light, unexpectedly transparent and tender.

'Forgive me,' he said. 'I could not go to bed without looking at you, and then I could not resist the temptation of just one kiss.'

I smiled lazily. 'Did they mind very badly my not being there?'

'My dear child, it was you they had all come agog to see. They were quite put out to discover they should have to make do with your poor clod of a husband.'

'Oh Max, I didn't wish to disappoint them.'

He laughed. 'I can assure you, Mousie, not one of them can possibly have felt as bereft as I. How I shall manage without you for the next three weeks I am not at all certain.'

I put my hand up to his face, traced with a loving finger the sickle shape of the scar at his temple. My adoration for him seemed to rise in a great wave and fill me so that I felt I should burst with it, and with the pain of our coming parting.

'Are you better, little Mouse?' he asked softly.

I nodded. 'But please – before you go to bed – will you come and put your arms around me for a while?'

He smiled, touched my lips with his. Then I heard him go into his dressing-room. I lay with my eyes shut until I felt his naked body slide between the sheets next to me and I was folded into his arms. We lay, not moving, not speaking, buried in the warmth of each other. Then his lips came down upon mine and he shifted his body so that his pelvis was pressed hard against my belly.

His hand shook slightly as he stroked my cheek. 'Oh, my darling child, I am afraid I am incapable of simply lying here and holding you.'

Afterwards as we lay dazed and tangled together, he gave a long, spent sigh. 'Oh Mouse. Dear, dear beautiful Mouse.'

I thought, then, that I would tell him about the baby. I moved so that I lay across him with my arms about his neck and my eyes looking down directly into his. But first there was something else still unspoken between us, something else I longed inordinately to put into words.

'Oh Maxim,' I said softly. 'I love you. I love you so very, very much.'

His eyes flickered suddenly as if with a momentary access of pain, his hand, which had been lazily caressing my breast, withdrew. He moved so that we lay side by side facing each other, and his expression was all at once perfectly opaque, as closed and distant as I had ever seen it.

'My dear child,' he said very quietly, brushing a strand of hair from my forehead, 'you do not love me, must not think anything so foolish. We have an arrangement, a working partnership. Though it may have turned out, for both of us, better than we thought, please – for your own sake – remember that is all.'

I stared at him for an instant, but his eyes had moved, he was turning away. I turned too, feeling a constriction in my throat. I lay for some moments with my back to him and my face buried in the pillow, praying that I should not choke or scream. I could feel him very still, scarcely breathing. After a few minutes, with a small sound that might have been either a cough or a sigh, he climbed out of bed. Though he touched my hair softly as he left me I did not acknowledge it or lift my head, for I was by now too consumed with silent tears.

VI

It was as if my whole world had, in that moment, been reversed upon its axis. What I had longed for now filled me only with a corrosive fear. I could have told him about my pregnancy at any time during that last day before he went to Jedburg, but I did not. The day itself, a day of freedom which we had so planned, so looked forward to, we spent in a kind of quiet dullness, not speaking very much, not making love, but treating each other with a sorrowful consideration, as if someone close to both of us had just died. When he finally parted from me he kissed me with great tenderness but without passion and I held him mutely, unable even to say goodbye.

I did not tell him about the baby, I could not, for obliterating all thought was his promise the night before the wedding: 'Once you have given me an heir I shall hold you to nothing but the formalities of our marriage, we shall live discreetly and permanently apart.' A business arrangement, a working partnership – with his tenderness, his pretended passion, merely a means of coaxing me into fulfilling its conditions. And now that they were fulfilled, now that I had accomplished my duty, he would, as Ursi had said, be 'considerate'. After all, he had not changed; he had not loved me then, he did not love me now. It was only I who had been inconsistent, altering my view of our agreement, foolishly wanting, assuming more.

Oh, it was idiotic, of course. I must accept things as they were, as I should always have understood them to be. A baby was not, after all, something I could keep secret indefinitely. I should write a letter while he was at Jedburg; that would be easier, take the emotion out of it, avoid my having to be present when my sentence was pronounced. And yet I could not bring myself to do it immediately, kept stealing a little more time as if I were secretly hoping for a reprieve.

I began, instead of longing for the child inside me, to loathe its secret presence. And it, seeming to sense my revulsion, began stealthily and inexorably to make that presence felt. I had congratulated myself on remaining so well; now, when by my calculations any suffering on that score should be gradually abating, I started to succumb to paroxysms of sickness which were increasingly difficult to conceal. One morning I was out exercising the dogs with Suzannah when I was attacked with such suddenness I barely had time to fly into hiding, and when I returned I could see the unspoken question rising in her eyes. Though she made me sit down on one of the rustic benches in the cypress walk and offered to run and fetch a doctor and administered smelling salts from her reticule with, for her, surprising kindness, I cursed the fact that it was she who had caught me out. While I managed to pass the episode off as a bilious attack I could see she remained unconvinced and ever afterwards I seemed to feel her eyeing me sideways with a malicious look, inspecting my waistline for tell-tale signs.

The incubus in my belly, of course, obliged. Where I had gained no weight before, except a little swelling and sensitivity of my breasts, suddenly almost overnight my waist thickened, my breasts burgeoned, so that every day there was a gown I could not wear, a *décolletage* that was too revealing. My maids, of course, dressing and undressing me, letting out seams and powdering me ever more heavily to disguise my pallor, could not but know my condition, but I thanked Heaven that, although they might chatter amongst themselves, they were not Rosa and their position forbade them to comment. I had them lace me tighter and tighter each day, and I flattered myself that the agony was worth it, for, discreetly dressed and after an hour of such effort, I seemed no more than a little plumper, as if I were regaining my girlhood podginess. And still I could not, would not tell Maximilian in my letters.

One afternoon when his three weeks of absence were nearly over, Ursula was reading to me in my boudoir when I was suddenly so overwhelmed by the discomfort of my stays that I found myself struggling for breath. She lowered the book, staring at me reprovingly.

'Dear Majesty, it's a wicked thing, you know, this fashion for tight-lacing – particularly for a young lady in your condition.'

I tried to outstare her but found myself blushing. 'I must take myself in hand, Ursi. One minute I'm starving myself and the next I'm getting fat.'

'Nonsense, Ma'am. Forgive me, but you can't fool an old woman. Why, I've known for weeks there was a baby on the way.'

My hand had gone defensively to my stomach. 'Oh Ursi, don't tell anyone – I forbid you.'

'Dear Majesty, it won't be up to me one way or the other soon. You must be well into your fourth month.'

'But I must tell His Majesty first, before anyone else knows.'

'I can't think,' she said, taking off her spectacles, 'why you haven't told him long before this.'

'Because – because . . .' Suddenly I found myself collapsing into one of the spells of weeping that came to me so easily nowadays. 'Because he won't want me any more.'

She came instantly and put her arm around me, crushing me against the stray pins slotted for safekeeping into her bosom. 'Oh, but dear Majesty, dearest Ma'am, that's such a silly fancy. Of course he will. Why, he adores you, and now he'll be so pleased and proud of you, you'll see.'

I gazed up at her through my tears. 'Just a fancy? Oh Ursi, do you really think so?'

She laughed, patted my shoulder, stroked my hair. 'Of course it is. All young ladies in your condition have fancies

– I certainly remember I did, wanting to eat goat's cheese of all things, and dreaming every night of snakes.'

'I didn't know you'd had a baby, Ursi.'

'Well, it was after Albrecht had passed on and – he died at birth, poor mite.' Her voice assumed a resolute cheerfulness which made me ashamed. 'He's buried up in the mountains, at Schwanensee, so his journey to his dear Papa was only a short one, thanks be to God. And – well, let it be a lesson, dear Ma'am, and don't cramp our next King with tight-lacing before the little angel's even had a chance to draw breath.'

I made Ursula swear that she would not break her promise and talk to Maximilian as she had the last time. But all the same she had encouraged me. Perhaps it was just a fancy. Maximilian had been so tender, so loving – it had not been self-deception, I had felt it. Perhaps he had not really meant what he had said. Perhaps it had been merely part of that closed, unfathomable area of him, an involuntary response born out of his unwillingness ever to talk about his feelings. Why, even now he might be regretting his words, longing to retract them, as he could not in a letter, with smiles and tenderness and kisses. It was too late for me to write to him, for he would be home in two days, but was it not better anyway that I should give him my news in person?

And then, just as I had allowed myself the joy of imagining his arms about me once more, just as I had surrendered to it so that I was feverishly counting the hours until his return, I received word that he had decided to break his journey at the Saxe-Limbecks' hunting box near Freischutz, to delay his arrival for another two days. His telegram was short, almost abrupt, giving no explanation for his altered plans, as if I should understand, however much I might long to see him, that a day's shooting must necessarily come first. What was the point of deceiving myself? How could I continue to buoy myself up with false hopes when my importance to him had once again been so cruelly and precisely defined?

Nevertheless, on the afternoon of his return, I dressed carefully and made the *coiffeuse* take great pains with my hair, determined that my anger and disappointment should not spoil our reunion. I remember, before I went into my boudoir, thinking how I should compose myself so that I appeared tranquil and busy, the picture of unconcern. I remember, too, on opening the door, an eerie sensation, the consciousness of a flurry of skirts, of a faint draught, as if, though the room was empty, someone had left by the other door the moment I entered. I picked up my workbox and saw to my surprise an envelope nestling amongst the skeins of thread. It bore my name, but in an unfamiliar hand. Puzzled, I broke the seal and pulled out a single sheet of paper. Though the writing here was different, familiar, my first thought was that there had been some mistake, for the letter was addressed, not to me, but to Maximilian. But by then it was too late. My eye had already taken in words, phrases, so that I was compelled to continue reading.

CHAPTER SIX

Anton von Tarn

I

Languidly I watched through the haze of my cigarette as the little fencing master, conceding to Max for the final time that afternoon, took off his helmet, clicked his heels, bowed, shook hands, clicked his heels again. Negligently I uncurled myself from my pose of elegant ennui as glossy pate, glossy imperial and little glossy boots clattered over the wooden floor to engage me in the same salute. Nonchalantly I affected a yawn as Max, likewise divesting himself of his helmet, came to sit beside me on the bench; determinedly I ignored the fact that the hand which held the cigarette seemed to be shaking.

'So,' I said casually, 'poor Maître Gérard is dispatched yet again as if he were a bluebottle parrying a fly whisk. No doubt you are thirsty for a more stimulating opponent?'

He paused in the midst of pulling off his gauntlets, raising an eyebrow. Unlike Maître Gérard, he had not a bead of perspiration on him.

'Oh, never fear,' I said, exhaling smoke with magnificent insouciance. 'I think you'll find me worthy. Since you last condescended to engage me I've put in a little practice.' (I dared not admit how much practice, how many hours in the mornings when he had believed me to be writing I had been down here in this wretched gymnasium working blindfold on my arm and hand, cutting and lunging like a madman at the sawdust sack in the corner.)

He smiled. 'Forgive me, Anton, I'm afraid I promised to talk to your father about this morning's dispatch from Thalia.'

'I observe you're sceptical. You don't believe in my miraculous improvement?'

'I believe it and I should like nothing better than to test it. But, alas, tomorrow.'

I stared at him. I had abandoned *The Sacred Brotherhood of Thebes*, given up my life's work for this moment, and I was not now to be cheated of it. Snatching one of his gauntlets from his hands, I struck myself lightly across the cheek with it, then hurled it to the floor.

'You dog, you cur!' I shouted. 'How dare you, sir, strike a gentleman and your equal! I demand satisfaction this instant.'

He seemed unimpressed by my thespian abilities, merely turning away, smiling.

'Damn you, sir!' I cried, pointing at the gauntlet. 'My challenge lies there. Do you so far demean your rank as to spurn it? Do you deny me the right, the right of any man of breeding, to avenge my honour?'

He was laughing. 'My dear Anton, your father has news from the Grand Duke—'

'To hell with the Grand Duke, scurvy knave that he is! Will you condemn yourself for evermore as an arrant coward or do you accept the quarrel?'

Still laughing, he bent and picked up the glove.

'Very well, sir,' I said. 'Choose your weapons.'

He glanced at the sword beside him. 'Sabres, my dear Count.'

(I was secretly relieved at this, for I am like a butcher's apprentice with a duelling sword, and foils present too narrow a *place d'armes*, hits only counting on a precisely-agreed area of the breast.) 'My seconds shall attend Your Highness.'

'Are your seconds instructed as to the exact terms of combat?'

'Oh, I think to the death, don't you?'

'Or failing that, the best of three hits.'

'The best of five.'

'My seconds find their principal adamant. Letters from the Grand Duke usually render Uncle Leo apoplectic.'

. 'Very well. The best of three.'

We shook hands upon it and I went to the stand to select my weapon. I swished the curved blade flamboyantly once or twice, felt its unhoned foible, not sharp enough through padding perhaps to kill, but sufficiently dangerous, so Maître Gérard was fond of cautioning me, to inflict unpleasant damage if wielded injudiciously. My appearance in my leather fencing-tunic always satisfied me; I assuredly looked the part whenever I picked up a sword, slender, patrician, elegant, the heavily padded shoulders and arm-guards adding to the whole effect a deceptive suggestion of brawn. I strapped on my leg-pads – Max always disdained to wear them, saying they restricted his freedom of movement – and fetched my helmet.

Max was waiting, idly adjusting the wrist-bands of his gauntlets. Taking our distance we saluted each other with all due forms of ceremony, left, right and centre, tapped our crossed blades smartly together twice and came to guard.

Owing to Maître Gérard's perverse preference for being demolished by his brilliant pupil I, his dunce, had been allowed ample opportunity to study my adversary's form. If he had a weakness in all the crisp wristwork and mercurial slipping and redoubling it was, I thought, that he occasionally laid himself open recovering from *quarte*; for the rest he had the advantage over me in height and reach, he was the master of the dazzling *riposte* and his feet worked economically and to a purpose, while mine, though they covered the ground gracefully enough, might just as well be performing a waltz or a polka for their relationship to the endeavours of my arm. My only real chance was to get in *corps à corpse*, where he disliked to fight, preferring to achieve his hits by virtuosity rather than brute force.

I hung back out of measure for some moments, trying accurately to assess his state of mind. True, my passivity had forced him to take the initiative of a few half lunges; but I felt nevertheless that he was toying with me, extending the invitation out of politeness, as if his fire had been damped after all by Maître Gérard's exertions or, as was more probable, he were merely bored. Then it occurred to me that I did indeed have one real advantage, that he was never able when fighting with me to maintain full concentration, that my sheer lack of challenge as an opponent slackened his hold upon it whether he would or no. If I could concentrate myself I could catch him out, surprise him, perhaps even force him into a transverse, back him up against the bench or the sword stand where his agility could not help him and the last light of the winter afternoon would shine straight into his eyes. I willed the whole concentration of my being upon him, screwed up my brows with it. If I kept myself out of measure long enough, if I retired when he challenged me, his boredom and my advantage would ever be increased; and then I should strike.

I chose the moment when I felt I had tried his patience to the limits, launching my attack with a series of brisk feints at his left arm, driving my cut towards his right. He parried, took guard; but I knew I had caught him off balance and must pursue my onslaught before he recovered. I took guard, came off immediately with a feint and then a miraculous double feint, lunged, was parried, felt him annoyed at being forced on the defensive, narrowly dodged a retaliatory thrust at my shoulder, took guard, lunged again, met his blade, parried it and then – incredible, for I had never once managed it before – came back with the *riposte*, elegantly, effortlessly, without so much as shifting my feet or body, finding my target just above his heart.

I was astonished with myself, unable to conceal my jubilation. 'First blood I think to me, Your Royal Highness.'

'Nicely done, my dear Count.' He extended his right palm in formal acknowledgement of the hit. 'I observe I must look to my laurels.'

Yet, when we came off guard and engaged again, I felt he was no more with me than before, that, despite his obligingly adopting the ceremony of my little *pièce de théâtre*, despite a note of genuine praise in his voice, he still held back from my challenge with a mannerly detachment, as if even now he could not take me seriously. I knew I had gained my point by stylish swordsmanship, yet all the same I felt somehow that he had made a concession, would not have left the opportunity open to Aubyn or even to Gérard. An angry sense took root in me of having been cheated, I flung myself with redoubled effort into lunges and feints and cuts but still my anger mounted. I saw now that while I danced and *volted* enough for two he had scarcely to move to hold his ground, that while I exhausted myself with flourishes which, as my emotion got the better of my judgement, became increasingly rash and out of control, he simply

worked me like a puppet, directing with his own blade
where and how he would have me go. By rights it was I,
not he, who should have been backed up against the wall
with the light in my eyes, by rights he should have easily
achieved his equalising hit ten or fifteen sword-strokes ago.
Oh, to be fair he left me no obviously contrived chances, he
tested and probed all my newly-acquired skills in his calm,
crisp, workmanlike way; but I could not resist the thought
that he was merely giving me a run for my money, and that
when he felt his failure to hit had ceased to be credible he
would skin and fillet me as cleanly as a master chef.

The moment came a second or two later when, merely by
taking a step sideways, he carefully removed his left arm
from the direction of one of my wilder cuts, surprised me
hopelessly undefended and caught me on the right shoulder.
I, however, taken off balance, sword arm out of control, hit
him in the same instant just above the left elbow with my
flailing blade.

He paused, waiting for me to acknowledge the hit.

'May I remind Your Royal Highness,' I said, 'that simul-
taneous hits count for neither party.'

I was in the wrong and I knew it. The rule in sabre fighting
only applies if both hits are made on the lunge whereas, if
one man lunges and not the other, the hit on the lunge still
carries the point. I had made nothing that could be construed
even as a pass but had got home by cloddishly tripping
over my own feet. Nevertheless I stood in silence, resolutely
refusing to concede the point.

He laughed – good-humouredly, I will admit. 'Your Excellency does not do himself justice. Before he unaccountably
lost his temper his swordsmanship was quite adept enough
not to require any revision of the rules.'

I suddenly could not bear that he should mock me or that
he should always be so unassailably in the right. He was
standing with his sabre lowered and the pommel resting
lightly on his thigh. Without retiring out of distance or taking
guard or any of the expected formalities, I charged him. He
had his blade up in an instant, delivering the point to my
mask while he dodged out of measure, then returning at
once for the attack.

I saw that he was at last angry, would no longer hold

back, would punish my foul in the sharpest, most expedient way by going immediately for the decisive hit. His anger exhilarated me, and his seriousness and the sense that with every cut I now had the full magnificent force of his body bearing down on me. I fought back feverishly, thrusting and slashing, throwing form and technique to the winds. When I stupidly laid myself open by trying two cuts in one lunge I did not want it to end, could not bear it should stop when we had only just started, failed once more to acknowledge the hit, paid no attention when he hit me again seconds later. He shouted at me to halt, that it was my third, disqualifying foul, but I only screamed back: 'Your Royal Highness may go to the devil! There are no fouls in the game of life and death!'

I thought I saw his mouth tighten and his eyes grow dark behind the ironwork of his mask. I rushed at him, trying to strike aside his blade, but he beat me back. I hurled myself at him, howling like a savage, slashing, stabbing, hacking, forgetting that to use the point is forbidden, not caring, striking anyhow, not just at his head and torso but beneath his padding, wielding my blade like a meat cleaver, chopping below his waist at his thighs and calves. Damn the rules, damn convention, this wasn't sport, a gentleman's game, this was a fight, a test of strength, an exhilarating madness where nothing counted but the fire of the moment, where I should drive him, force him to submit. Striking two-handed I carved my path towards him, got within measure, suddenly was grappling with him, swords locked at the hilt. I was soaked in sweat, I could hear my breath coming at a distance, my arms ached, my chest felt as if it were clamped in a vice. I knew he was stronger but I had the daring, the glorious, intoxicating madness on my side. And then I felt him push against me with all his might and our weapons unlocked and I was flung away, staggering.

He came on slowly then, slowly, relentlessly, leaving me no chance to run or throw down my sword, slowly, inescapably, not with my heat but with that cold, white anger of his, cold, expert, implacable, beating me back towards the wall, driving me further with every finely-judged cut, making me feel the strength in each blow so that my arm, my whole body was jarred. I thought suddenly that he would kill me, thought it with a lurch of my stomach, with excitement, with desire, knew he could kill, that it was in him, there beneath that cold efficiency, like an arcane power; then my excitement turned to fear, I remembered the body at Fontarelles, stepped back too quickly, met the wall, stumbled, saw too late how he switched his sword to his left hand, saw it only as he was making the *volte*. I recall bellowing from the depths of my lungs. But even before I had uttered a sound his right hand was across my body, my wrist was scorching in his grip and I felt the point of his blade at my throat.

The sabre clattered from my useless fingers. Releasing me, he bent to pick it up, turning away. My arm felt as if it had been jolted from its socket, my wrist was on fire. I let out a great howl of rage and frustration. Then with my one sound hand I tore off my helmet and hurled it across the room.

'Damn you, Max! Damn you to hell! Why can't we ever just fight? Why must you hang back one minute, then try to kill me the next? Why must you always control things, have it all your way, never give the other fellow a chance? I wanted once, just once to win. Oh God, it's so unfair, so wretchedly, damnably, humiliatingly unfair!'

He had replaced the two sabres in the sword stand and removed his helmet and gauntlets. Though he was unsmiling, he surveyed me with apparent detachment, all trace of anger gone.

'My dear Anton, I understood it was you who had decided to dispense with fair play.'

'Very well,' I said. 'I acknowledge the fouls. But was there a need nearly to break my arm and half murder me into the bargain?'

His lips twisted wryly. 'I apologise for hurting you. A certain reluctance to be castrated may have made me go too far.'

I stared at him and saw for the first time the neatly-edged rent in his breeches, slicing the inside of his left thigh some five or six centimetres from his groin.

'Oh hell,' I said softly. 'Hell, hell, hell!'

He laughed. 'For God's sake, it's no more than a scratch.'

St Sebastian's wounds bled tidily, with all the discretion of art. No so the 'scratch' which from its uppermost point was already seeping into the torn cloth.

'Oh, hell!' I shouted. 'Hell and eternal damnation!' Flinging myself at the wall I beat my open palms, wrists foremost, again and again upon the dado, finally crashing my forehead to rest against its icy tiles.

'I wish to God I could explain, say something, anything that would – oh, it's not enough to ask you to forgive me, to agree that of all the insufferable brats I'm the worst, the most insufferable, the veritable lowest depths – it's not enough, damnably it isn't. And even if I could explain – well, you wouldn't think more ighly of me, most assuredly not, in fact you'd probably agree with my father, agree the horsewhip was too lenient. Yet I value your friendship, Max, and your good opinion, more than anything else in the world. It's just that this other thing takes me over, confound it, so that I can't prevent myself, can't seem to manage . . . can't feel anything but the pain, this wretched, sickening bloody pain . . .'

I tailed off miserably. He said nothing, but then I heard, felt him cross the room towards me. Silently he put his hand on my shoulder so that his fingers rested lightly on the nape of my neck. I drew in my breath, feeling at once the familiar constriction, the blinding, urgent access of my pain. For a second or two I dared not move, dared not turn towards him lest he should see what was in my face. But the pressure of his fingers increased, there was a tension communicating itself through his arm, through the propinquity of his body, that made me arch my neck with a moan.

'Damn you, Max!' I said, turning. 'I'm sinking, drowning – for God's sake, save me.'

'Damn you, Anton,' he said in a voice I had never heard before. 'How, when I have ceased any longer to be able to save myself?'

CHAPTER SEVEN

Marie Bathildis

I

When he came into the room his arms were outstretched to embrace me, his lips parted in a smile, his eyes filled with undisguised joy at our reunion.

I stared at him. I suppose I had expected him to have changed somehow, or at least that I should see him differently. But he looked as he had always looked, a very tall, well-made, broad-shouldered man with a hard, handsome face and a commanding aura of dignity and strength. I searched in vain for traces of effeminacy, for some obvious mark of his corruption. I felt sick and bewildered.

Reading my face, he stopped short, lowered his arms. 'Dear Mouse, what is it? Are you ill? Oh, my darling, it is not the—?'

I cut him off by silently holding out the letter.

He stared at it, perplexed, then took it from me and began to read it. I watched his face change, saw the perplexity grow into horror and then into an ice-cold anger.

'Dear God, how could he have so forgotten himself as to – and who, in Heaven's name? – Marie, where did you get this? Who sent it to you?'

'It doesn't matter. Nothing matters so long as you say it isn't true. Oh please Maxim, tell me it's just wickedness, tell me there's no truth in it.'

I watched the anger die in his face and any hope I had possessed died suddenly with it. He stood perfectly still looking at me in silence, and there was for a moment a tightening of the muscles around his mouth as if he were struggling with something. Then his eyes seemed to grow cold, his expression stiffened, I had the sense of every line and contour of his face hardening against me.

'Oh no,' I said. 'Oh no. Please, no!'

'My dear child, I beg of you, there is no point—'

'No point?' I screamed. 'Oh please, have some mercy, tell me anything, lie to me even, only please deny it!'

His lips twisted wearily. 'Marie, I could not deny it even if I wished to. The letter is perfectly explicit and its signature entirely legible.'

'A love letter!'

He sighed. 'Yes. I suppose that is one description of it.'

'And how long have you and he . . . ?' I could not bring myself to say the words, make it real. 'How long? Before we were married?'

'Marie, I repeat, there is no point—'

'Before we were married?'

'Yes.'

'And afterwards? After you took me as your wife?'

He looked at me and for a fleeting moment his face seemed once more taut, embattled. Then steadily he levelled his eyes with mine as if he were aiming a gun.

'Yes,' he said very softly. 'If you must have it all. Afterwards too.'

I felt the sickness rise in my throat and threaten to choke me. I thought I could have born anything but this, could have understood lies, excuses, would have been comforted by any sign of cravenness in him. But this quiet dignity of his, not excusing, not evading – this unsparing truthfulness was more than I could stand.

'Oh, tell me, please! What is wrong with me? What is it that I lack, Maximilian, that you have to – have to . . . ?'

'My dear child, nothing. You are very beautiful and very desirable. It is no fault in you that makes me what I am. I beg of you to understand that.'

'Understand?' Oh, if I were to understand, it meant I must accept that this man who stood before me seemingly unchanged, this man the scent, the touch of whose body I had loved, was capable of – I sank into a chair, cramming my handkerchief into my mouth to subdue my nausea.

I felt him move towards me, prayed he would not try to touch me.

'And do you love him?' I said. 'Do you love him more than you love me? Oh, but of course I was forgetting, you do not love me, you cannot love me and I was too stupid, too innocent to comprehend why. You love him and you cannot love me – cannot love – cannot . . .' I tailed away in a paroxysm of sobbing.

'I think,' he said quietly, 'I should have done almost anything to spare you the pain of this. But now you know you must not torture yourself with questions. You must please, dear, sweet child, accept that there is no lack in you, accept that it is I who—'

'Accept? But I am your wife. How can I accept that you have lied to me, deceived me—?'

'I have tried never to lie to you, either before or now.'

'But you married me. You married me and did not tell me.'

His lips curved mordantly. 'My dear Marie, I scarcely see how I could have told you. Perhaps it was wrong of me to marry you. It seems now that it was, criminally wrong. But at the time there appeared no reason why you should ever be touched by it. If I had little enough inclination for the marriage, you had even less. We were joined together only by duty, were to live in all other respects apart. Neither of us could have been prepared for—'

'For my falling in love with you. Oh Maxim, you will never know how I loved you, how much I loved . . .' The past tense brought me to a fresh tumult of sobbing. I buried my face in my hands.

He made a little uneven sound in his throat. 'Dear Mouse,' he said very softly, 'I am sorry that such a precious gift has been squandered in vain.'

I could feel him close to me, bending over me. I wanted to cry out at the tenderness in his voice, wanted perversely to feel his lips in my hair, his arms around me, longed for an instant in desperation for that comfort which would now forever be denied to me, as if there were magic in it, as if this moment could be obliterated, our words made as though they had remained unsaid. I gazed up at him, seeing him indistinctly through my tears.

'But it was Anton,' I said pleading, 'Anton who wanted it, not you, wasn't it? If it had not been for him, you would never have – couldn't have brought yourself . . .'

'No, Marie. I wanted it too.'

'Then there have been others?'

He sighed, turned away. 'Yes. Of course there have been others.'

'How many others? How often – when did you – how many more?'

'Stop it, Marie!' His voice was suddenly sharp. 'Stop it, I beg of you.'

I stared at him. From somewhere deep inside me there grew a high-pitched animal wail which burst from my open lips involuntarily. I clasped my belly as if I could hold the sound within me but it poured out, rising, falling, in wave after anguished wave until IIwas bent double with it, rocking backwards and forwards, hearing the noise from afar as if itt were no longer part of me but possessed a force of its own, an independent existence from which Ihad become inexplicably detached.

He came over and knelt beside me. 'Please, little Mouse. Not now, when you know at last that I'm not worth loving. Please, dear child, you'll make yourself ill.'

He touched me then, very gently on the shoulder, and suddenly I could no longer bear his truthfulness, that cruel impartial tenderness of his, suddenly the wail became a scream of rage.

'Don't touch me! Don't come near me. Don't you understand how you disgust me? To think that I ever – ever wanted you to – and you're not even ashamed!'

He gave an acrid little laugh. 'Not ashamed of hurting you, of that letter and the squalid intrigue your being sent it suggests, of the fact that I laid you open to it, put you in a position where you could be made the victim of any filthy scheme evil-minded people can concoct? Oh, my dear Marie, shame seems rather too mild a word for it, don't you think?'

'But of the other? Of this other vile, repulsive thing – this sickness of yours?'

'Of this sickness, as you call it, I am neither ashamed nor proud. Perhaps if I could have chosen I should have wished to live differently. But since I could not I am obliged to accept what I am.'

I stared at him, still not believing. As if it were my only means of holding on to reality, my only weapon, my rage rose up and overmastered me. 'Accept, again? You seem inordinately fond of that word, Maximilian. You set it high, as if there were some moral tone to it. Yet what are you? What is it you accept, as though unlike the rest of us you had no obligation to struggle with what is evil? An offence against God, against nature itself, something so degrading, so bestial even the filthiest beggar in the gutter would be disgusted by it. Merciful Heaven, and they said Freddy, my darling Freddy was not a man! He had more manhood in one drop of his blood than there is flowing in your veins. And I must remember that I let you touch me, kiss me – that I allowed myself to be contaminated by your filth, that I listened to your lies and your deceit? You, Maximilian, who have lost all title to call yourself a man, who are lower and viler than the lowest animal!'

I pursed my lips and spat with force into his face. He did not move, not even to wipe my spittle from his cheek. When he eventually spoke his voice was deadly quiet, as if he were endeavouring to rid it of all inflection.

'If omission is deceit, Marie, then it appears we are both guilty of it. Why must I find out from the women of your household that you are with child? Did you not think to tell me of it? Or were you perhaps anxious to hide your condition for as long as possible lest it should prove repugnant to your lover Aubyn?'

I was already reeling from the violence of my own words. Now I gazed at him with blank shock.

'Well,' he said, with a small shrug of his shoulders, half turning away, 'as it transpires your pregnancy is fortuitous. I realise, of course, that there is no question of your maintaining even the formalities of a marriage which is in all respects repulsive to you, nor shall I ask it. We may use your condition as an excuse for you to retire to Schwanensee or the Summer Palace, wherever you choose. We shall have our arrangement as we planned it. And after the child is born – then I shall do everything in my power to set you free.'

I chose the Summer Palace and left the next morning. The church bells were already pealing their joy at the Court Physician's announcement that Sylvania might expect a happy event in May. As my carriage drew out of the West Gate a crowd shouted: 'Long live Maximilian and Marie!'

CHAPTER EIGHT

Anton von Tarn

I

The house of Mme Zelenska is an eminently respectable house. It sits very stiff and square behind respectable wrought-iron gates in a respectable bourgeois suburb of Rosenholm just beyond the Old Town, and even its lowered blinds give it the demure air of a burgher's daughter casting down her eyes at some over-familiar swain. Its steps are always scrubbed to a pure and stainless white, its brass door-knocker twinkles virtuously, and in summer the serried ranks of its flowering borders stand primly to attention as if proclaiming an irreproachable order and rectitude – not that Mme Zelenska's visitors are given to noticing such horticultural niceties, for they usually arrive by night, entering quickly and looking neither to right nor left, bent on floribunda of a more exotic kind.

Paying off my hackney carriage and drawing the collar of my overcoat closer about my face, although it was a mild enough night for early autumn, I gained the door and gave the requisite three knocks. They were answered, not by the maid, but by the Dusky Maiden, who seemed to have added this ceremony to her other duties for the evening. She wore, indeed, full parlour maid's uniform, neat black stretched tight at her haunches, neat little apron and little frilled cap perched provocatively in her frizz of hair. I muttered the password. Giggling, she dropped me a curtsy and ushered me in.

'Good evening, Excellency.' Glancing sideways at me, she performed a pirouette to show off her costume. 'You like, yes? I wear it tonight just for a fancy – with you aristocratic gentlemen it make always big success.'

Irritated by her familiarity, I pulled the brim of my opera hat a little lower.

She giggled, unabashed. 'You come into the drawing-room? You will enjoy! Some of the gentlemen are making charades.'

'Not tonight. I'm here on a piece of private business.'

'Oh very well,' she said, still flashing her eyes at me and running her tongue over her lips. 'One day I tempt you, Excellency. But now I fetch Madame.'

I thrust some coins into her hand and, blowing me a kiss, she disappeared with a flash of shapely ankle in the direction of the drawing-room. She did not offer to take my hat; Mme Zelenska's callers often manifest a well-nigh umbilical attachment to their head-coverings, even indoors.

She reappeared a few moments later in Madame's stately wake. From the open double doors to the drawing-room came sounds of music and merriment. I could imagine the scene: the room, though spacious, rendered claustrophobic by the genteel profusion of Madame's treasures, the Meissen dogs and the souvenirs from Baden Baden, the alabaster Apollo donated by a French nobleman and the stuffed badger, trophy of an English milord, the palms and the plush and the shawls and the fringes, and the firescreens embroidered by Madame's own needle – only the conventional plethora of photographs is strangely missing. At the piano sits the frail old fellow who, it is rumoured, was once a prosperous merchant in rubber galoshes, and on *chaises* and sofas the faithful recline, smoking and waiting for their fancies to be tickled; at the centre – an empty space amidst the acolytes – the high-backed chair from which Madame habitually holds court; and over all, a heady miasma of cigar smoke and cheap scent and other more subtle, cabalistic perfumes.

The Dusky Maiden had scarcely exaggerated the uproarious nature of this evening's entertainment: above the pianist's doddering strains bellows of laughter echoed down the hall, and through the open doors I glimpsed a stalwart figure in a tutu from the Volksoper attempting to execute a *fouetté* on points. I thought I recognised him as a particularly ramrod Major in the Garde du Corps; the effect of his performance was somewhat marred by his eyeglass, which remained resolutely in place.

'Ah, Herr Sebastian. Such a pleasure,' said Mme Zelenska,

extending her gloved hand. 'The other gentleman has not arrived yet. Perhaps you would prefer to wait for him upstairs?'

I attended her progress up the staircase and along a corridor until we came to a room dark with gargantuan furniture and hung with portraits of past military heroes. At least half its length was filled by an oval table covered with green baize.

'The officers like it for cards,' she said. 'But for – er, business purposes it is also very discreet. Having, you understand, a door through to the back stairs.'

She tapped her nose lightly with her folded fan. I nodded and, unbuttoning my overcoat and slinging off my hat, drew out two banknotes which I placed, half-covered by my hand, in the middle of the green baize table. She smiled. I removed my hand and she withdrew the notes softly, not with greed but with a long-acquired prudence.

No one knows whether Mme Zelenska is really Russian, or whether she started life straightforwardly as a Bauer or a Schmidt. Certainly she appears the very epitome of the middle-class Teutonic matron, as respectable and squarely-built as her house. She looks exactly what, to all intents and purposes, she truly is; a pillar of the social order, an upholder of the sterling values of commerce, a thoroughly respectable citizen in whose broad bosom state secrets could safely be kept – as indeed it is rumoured they from time to time are, deposited there by a high-up civil servant or even, some say, by a Cabinet Minister. Thus, although certain aspects of her business affairs are not precisely congruent with Article 175 of the Imperial Criminal Code (an absurdity by which we Sylvanians, as members of a state within the Prussian Reich, are supposedly bound) she has run her nice respectable house profitably and without interruption since anyone can remember, while other less fortunate practitioners of her trade have been obliged to take frequent sabbaticals in Rosenholm's jail.

This evening she was, as ever, very much the *grande dame* in a magnificent *toilette* of bottle-green velvet encrusted with lace and jet *passementerie*, more jet glittering at her throat and falling in shiny streams over her imposing embonpoint, while in the coils of her iron-grey hair two dark ostrich feathers nodded like the plumes upon an undertaker's horse. Only her gruff base and the shadow about her heavy jaw, which no amount of powdering can entirely conceal, served to flaw the impression of matriarchal virtue.

The Dusky Maiden had brought my pipe of hashish but I waved it away, ordering instead a bottle of Moët – when my companion arrived I should need all my wits about me. Surveying the Dusky Maiden as she disappeared with further provocative flashes of ankles and rump I raised my eyebrows questioningly. Though I suspected even then that Mme Zelenska had long seen through my incognito, I knew her sturdy business principles deserved absolute trust. Of the Dusky Maiden I was by no means so sure.

The Dusky Maiden is the jewel in Mme Zelenska's crown, the spice in the recipe which sets the delicacies offered by the establishment far above other more homely fare. Many cultures and races appear to commingle in this extravagant concoction, although it is said her country of origin is Portugal and that she began her career at the age of twelve as a cabin boy. Since then she has moved across Europe, ever further from the sea, ever closer to the ungentle attentions of the law, refining and perfecting her effeminate arts, so that the scions of several aristocratic houses are purported to deluge her with furs and diamonds, and one retired General has three times threatened to shoot himself dead at her feet. Although I am bound to admire the flair with which she has brought herself to this veritable apotheosis of femininity, it is not, of course, to my particular taste. Yet I am frequently the unwilling subject of her attentions; even now, reappearing with my champagne, she endeavoured to inflect the simple removal of the cork with all the overtones of a Bacchanalian orgy. I sat back, expelling disdainful smoke from my nostrils.

'Ooof!' she flounced. 'His Excellency is the most handsome man I ever see. But he is also the most cruel!'

Mme Zelenska shook her head, laughing, after the Maiden's retreating wiggle. 'Your Excellency need not worry. She's a good girl at heart – and besides, she's seen the inside of enough prisons to know the price of exercising her tongue. Nevertheless I shall make sure when the gentleman arrives that you are attended by no one but me.

Discretion, Herr Sebastian,' and here she once again tapped her nose with the fan, 'discretion, we know, is all.' Then she left me to speculate unpleasantly about my tardy companion and our forthcoming interview.

My detractors will undoubtedly assert that I am incapable of any creditable emotion, much less love. And I shall not deny that in my feeling for Max there is everything carnal, that it consumes me with its heat. But from this very heat comes a chastening flame, a fine, high spirituality which is beyond the comprehension of Philistines.

Dear God, those first short winter months before we left Switzerland – I remember how I chafed against the constraints imposed by our necessary deception (though I must smile ironically when I consider how things stand with us now). Yet the constraints fuelled our heat too, the free-masonry of signs and codes, the exquisite agony endured through poverty of time and opportunity, the minute preoccupations of a secret life, which foster a skill in sounding out the thickness of walls, in creeping noiselessly down darkened corridors, in cultivating a tidiness proof against the scrutiny of the most observant domestic. There was the delectable savour of the stolen apple in it. And Max too – it was as if, after his months of scrupulous control, he was now taken over by that fatal twinship with the Lenbach portrait, by all the importunate Sigismund appetites, so that I would know, as I suffered the daily torture of our restraint, that he was tortured in equal measure, that he would come with the same perfervid urgency to the moment of our relief.

Out of this, out of my new understanding of my true nature, I acquired an Olympian exhilaration. It is undeniable that for two or three days I was oppressed by guilt for what had followed the sabre fight, as if I had simply confirmed all my father's worst suspicions. But the absurdity of my shame soon overtook me, the preposterousness of resisting what my body had craved in agony for. And besides there was nothing sissyish or effete in my relations with Max, none of the obnoxious effeminacy I have observed to be engendered in most men by a predilection for what they are pleased to call 'the fair sex', the repulsive spooniness, the facile emotional outpourings, the complete abnegation of all intellectual rigour. Rather, our feelings for each other, since they were neither dragged down by the dead-weight of female ignorance, nor degraded by the primitive female urge towards parturition, were able to ascend to a higher plane where the virtues of masculine friendship, masculine intellect and masculine ardour could combine unalloyed. When I thought of Max, magnificent, powerful Max, physically perfect as a Michelangelo god, aroused, urgently desiring me, I could not doubt – I still cannot – that we had been granted, through the special individuality of our natures, the glimpse of a sublime aesthetic, a divine throwback to the consummate nobility of the Ancient Greeks.

I began again upon my play about the Theban Brotherhood, rendering up the legend of the warrior lovers as a glorious hymn to my own revelation. When the odious Beck, returning, shoulder mended, was granted my father's permission to continue his service to Max from the ranks in Thalia, my joy grew unbounded. I exulted in my sense of my own exclusivity, even went so far as to look indulgently on lesser mortals whose lives and aspirations were fettered by the earth-bound, the 'normal'. I could observe the Paterfamilias noting with surprise this new generosity of mine, the small brotherly gestures towards Suzannah, the offers to fetch and carry for Aunt Helena, could observe that he took it as evidence that my improvement of character, which had seemed to falter during Aubyn's visit, now resumed apace. And you may imagine how the exquisite irony of this delighted me, for I knew it was Max's influence to which he once again attributed my reform.

Max, alas, appeared to find the irony of our situation less entrancing. It is a curious contradiction in old Max that though he accepts his nature without guilt he seems reluctant to accept its consequences, which must of necessity in an earth-bound world be deception and lies. I was aware, though he never expressed it, that he cherished the absurd notion of having betrayed my father's trust, and that this troubled him. About me, too, he continued to retain some ridiculous scruples, which irritated me not a little, particularly since they once again brought the matter of Heidelberg to a head.

*

Towards the end of February 1889 two incidents occurred which convinced my father that Max would be safer if his departure for Thalia took place forthwith: one was the avalanche which brought to light the skeleton of a man, unidentifiable except, to Max's distress, by the still-preserved fragments of a mangy brown blanket tied with rope; the second, two shots fired in the path of our sleigh – the work of a haphazard poacher we were certain, although my father inevitably believed the worst.

I had assumed as a matter of course that when Max left I should now accompany him, so that I was astounded, on casually mentioning the subject, to be told that I must honour my promise to read for my degree. And when I objected, accurately, that I had never given him such an undertaking, he grew all at once like his old self, very cool, very grave.

'Anton, we have both always known our time together was circumscribed. It helps neither of us to question that now – you, most particularly, must not.'

'Not question it? Stand by while you discuss our separation as coolly as a surgeon deciding to amputate a limb?' I sought refuge in laughter. 'My dear old Max, you've been overworking, allowing the Paterfamilias to drive you too hard. I'm not, may I remind you, some trifling pastime like philately or alpine rambling to be taken up or dropped at will. I'm your comrade at arms, your blood brother, the one person in the world who would cheerfully give his life for you—'

'Try, my dear Anton, not to drown us in a tide of words. I don't ask for your life. On the contrary, I wish to give it back to you unencumbered.'

'By taking from me its sole purpose?'

'By taking no more than I have wantonly, stupidly taken already. Dear God, do you imagine I should forgive myself if I permitted you to pass up Heidelberg, squander your ambitions, your dreams, your entire future?'

'But you are my future, Max. You and I are bound together, irrevocably. Cut yourself – I bleed. Breathe and I feel the air in my lungs too. Leave me and you kill me as assuredly as if you had put your hands about my throat.'

I carried on in this vein for some time, working myself

into a frenzy with my own oratory. I screamed, I flung myself face down on various items of furniture, I even contemplated seizing the paper-knife from my study desk and doing away with us both there and then in spectacular consummation of my passion. But I had learned by now that my turns of melodrama, while they might sometimes in lighter moments amuse Max, could never move him. No, if I wished to sway him I had much better work upon his guilt.

Accordingly, I quieted myself and said, very softly: 'I realise you are incapable of love, Max. But don't despise me for loving you. I am your creature, your creation after all. I am only what you have made me.'

He had been on the point of quitting the room but I saw him pause with his hand on the door-knob, saw, despite his unrelenting expression, that I had got home. I buried my face in the cushions of the sofa.

He came over after some moments and, gently ruffling my hair, found a cigarette and lit it for me.

'I don't deny my cruelty,' he said quietly. 'I don't deny the selfishness of giving way, taking what I wanted, when I always knew it would bring us to this point. But in Sylvania I should not be able to avoid hurting you further. You must try to understand that I shall no longer be governed solely by what I want, there will be duties, obligations—'

'Oh?' I said sourly. 'Our old friend The Common Good again? All that claptrap about the subjugation of the individual will?'

'You forget, Anton, that I shall almost certainly be required to marry.'

At the time, while I found this notion both disgusting and laughable, I was not disposed to take particular account of it. Indeed my mind was focused elsewhere and, though he remained obdurate, I listened to him quite calmly. For I had, of course, perceived that I could frustrate his opposition easily by calling on the aid of one obvious and powerful ally.

II

It is my observation that while the baser human impulses like jealousy and greed usually awaken in man a sound instinct for self-protection, love, on the other hand, drives him inevitably to acts of indescribable folly.

The Paterfamilias, while he had embraced wholeheartedly my sudden dedication to a military career, while he had even permitted himself a sentimental tear that his despaired-of son should now be so ready to comply with his wishes, had stipulated one condition; I should take no advantage of my lineage or my friendship with Max, but should serve my three months of cadet training like any other raw recruit. And so, in March 1889, I found myself under canvas with twenty-nine fellow nincompoops, being bludgeoned into officer material for Keller's much-vaunted army.

I shall not dwell upon my sufferings during this period. Suffice it to say that love did not ease my hard mattress, nor render the peasant diet of beans and noodles more palatable, nor bestow upon me, along with my makeshift volunteer's uniform, a uniform mind. I could not, as my swinish comrades did, bend my pride to the unrelenting boorishness of my so-called superiors, could not slavishly obey commands that were an insult both to my breeding and intellect, with the result that I spent many hours in extra drill, days confined to barracks or in solitary, as if, to justify their own inferiority, they must somehow torture me into their mould. And as for my fellow volunteers, stamping their clodhopper boots, and drilling like happy sheep – well, I made it my practice, so far as our total lack of privacy would allow, to hold myself at the dignified distance befitting my rank; while they, jealous no doubt of my influence with their future King, showed their respect for my reserve by hurling derisive epithets at me and by playing such sophisticated tricks upon my person as putting dead rats in my bed and filling my boots with urine.

And Max – whose silent displeasure I had been obliged to suffer, for whom, indeed, I endured all this? Yes, his prognostications had been correct: from the moment of our arrival in Thalia I scarcely saw him. While my sleeping quarters were a dank tent smelling vilely of the socks, the armpits, the bodily excreta of five other 'comrades-in-arms', he lived in luxury six kilometres away at Elfinsberg, an elegant eighteenth-century palace lent by the Grand Duke as his headquarters. Oh, he was frequently conjured up as a threatening presence whose attendance at troop reviews or manoeuvres required even those of us who were far from the scene to clean already gleaming bayonets and polish mirror-glass boots. Sometimes, digging shelter trenches or throwing up field works, we even glimpsed him at a distance, riding a big black horse with Aubyn or Keller at his side. And on the rare occasions when I was not on duty or sweating beneath the bestial eye of the Sergeant Major, I was permitted one concession to my rank, that I might be allowed to dine at Elfinsberg; but even then there were always ten or twelve at table and I was never alone with Max. For the rest, the only tangible proof I received of his existence was the black Sigismundite eagle which flew on crimson from the flagstaff on our parade ground, and the coroneted eagle with four crimson roses, his personal standard, which fluttered alongside it.

It is not true that suffering is enobling. I began to feel almost glad I was so little in Max's company, for I found a resurgence in me of all the bitterness and cynicism he professed to disapprove of, as if, like its scratchy blankets, the army clung to me, chafing me into resentment, leaving me with dehumanising weals and mutilations. My resentment of Max himself, for instance, began to boil again so that at times I hated him. Why was it that I should have to bear persecution and ridicule and the abuse of mediocre minds while he received nothing but respect and admiration? I might curse my ambiguous rank, which did not allow me the reverence due to royalty, yet held me at a height above the common herd from whence I could observe what a brutish mass it was. But at least, though my blood was morganatic, no one could doubt its authenticity. I found my suspicions of Max had not died, but had merely been buried and now began to surface and fester once more, so that I would dwell upon Brother Jean's testimony and the body at Fontarelles with an obsessive hunger.

And then there was my jealousy, which, as I lay wakeful, listening to the porcine symphony of snorts and grunts all around me, was the blanket triumphant, rough and amorphous and itchy, encompassing me with its harsh embrace until my skin, my eyes, my very brain were raw. I began to see rivals in every corridor of Elfinsberg, the willowy blond intelligence officer I had met at dinner, the duty adjutant with the provoking mole on his upper lip who had seemed to smile at me so superciliously. And then there was Beck, subsumed anonymously within the ranks of the infantry, yet emerging in his off-duty hours perhaps to bestow God knew what favours upon his lord and master.

Even when my training was at last over and I was gazetted a lieutenant and sent to Elfinsberg to join the Mole as one of Max's personal adjutants, I took my tetchy blanket with me. The Theban Brotherhood of Lovers? When I thought of them now they were blanketed too, scratching waspishly at one another in a tangle of suspicion and deceit.

Then, at the end of the summer, we went to war. Not much of Dorian nobility here either, but noise and mud and a futile, milling confusion, wagons of wounded stuck in cart-tracks one way, troops trying to move another, peasants fleeing with furniture and cattle moronically impeding both. Mercifully, since my job was to run errands for Max, I spent my time behind the lines, never entering the battle zone (usually some dismal *petit-bourgeois* town of surpassing ugliness) until the firing had ceased and we were firmly in possession of it. And I cannot say that I felt cheated of glory, for there was something in the squalor of it all – in the men, not dying tight-lipped and defiant, but lying with their legs shot off screaming for their mothers; in the stench of death, not on a wide and magnificent plain but lingering around the doors of a provincial Rathaus; in the dreary sycophancy of turncoat officials and the grasping meanness of the peasants who supplied our commissariat and the eagerness of the oppressed Sylvanian people to finish the business of looting their compatriots before they spared time to acknowledge they had been freed – there was in all this something which took me beyond fear to a desperation lest my life, my intelligence, my talent should be squandered for such ignominious gains.

That was our war then, the war my father had schemed twenty years for, a war of liberation on behalf of a people who appeared most justly to deserve every indignity slavery can impose. In its drab little tapestry of horrors only two details strike me as being of any significance. One was the death of Beck at Jedburg – I saw him myself, spreadeagled across the base of the equestrian statue in the main square, his shoulders just as powerful, his teeth just as perfect but with butcher's meat where his stomach should have been. And the other – well, perhaps it was a judgement on me for the instinctive feeling of triumph when I saw those perfect teeth smiling their death's head smile – but though what happened at Behrensdorf was an accident, a misjudgement anyone could have made, it sent me a new tormentor of a very different kind.

Behrensdorf was only twenty kilometres or so from our goal of Rosenholm and the fighting there had been the heaviest of the whole campaign. When we had at last taken the town there had been nowhere suitable for our headquarters, so we had moved on eight kilometres to the West, to Bad Gottfriedsburg, once a prosperous spa town until the waters, like everything else in Sylvania, had drained themselves dry. There we were able to establish ourselves in a ramshackle fashion within the crumbling portals of the Grand Hotel. As luck would have it, however, a sizeable group of refugees, mostly women and children, were discovered to be sheltering in the pavilion built around the now-defunct wells, and since they had been without food for three days Max, who was inclined to be over-particular about these details, decided their hunger should be relieved from our commissariat. It was to me, of course, that the task fell of riding back into Behrensdorf, where GHQ was, to deliver these instructions, even though there were still pockets of resistance remaining in some of the outlying hamlets.

Taking with me a corporal who, though he was an ugly, unpleasant fellow, was reassuringly a crack shot, I started off well enough, delivering my message without event. But on my way back, in the outskirts of a village two kilometres from Bad Gottfriedsburg, I rode suddenly into sniper fire. I did not stop to think as one bullet clipped my left epaulette and another passed inches from my nose but, forgetting the corporal, forgetting everything save my desire not to die a futile death, I flung myself upon my horse's neck and, jabbing my spurs into her flanks, gave her full rein.

Beyond my need to escape from the bullets and find shelter somewhere in what was now open country, I had no idea where I was going. Presently I came upon a road bounded by a high picket fence and, seeing an open gateway, galloped straight through it. I was aware of being in an ornamental garden and that there were people, civilians, milling about in a disorganised straggle, flinging themselves out of my path. I was dimly conscious too, as I thundered past them, of a strange noise, a babel of chanting and muttering that was not quite human. Before me loomed a red-brick hulk of a building, hideously turreted and spired, with row upon row of mean windows staring blankly in the shadow of the afternoon sun. The mummers' troupe in the grounds were far behind me now and the immediate environs of the building seemed deserted. Cautiously I reined in my horse.

It was a monstrous pile of a place, which I seemed, from its bleak and unornamented walls, to have approached from the rear. It might have been some trading baron's gothic fantasy of grandeur except for something stark and institutional in its brick which was more suggestive of a barracks or a prison. By contrast the grounds, which stretched as far as the eye could travel, were lush and green and meticulously tended, not a blade of grass out of place in the satin-smooth lawns, not a ragged edge to the manicured flower-beds. Yet there was in this contrast a dissonance, indeed something about the whole place which disturbed me.

Nothing stirred except for a bird singing lustily in a cedar close by. The sound of my horse's hooves upon the gravel seemed to ring out like a warning bell. To my left a side door hung open above a small flight of stone steps. Dismounting and drawing my revolver, I tethered my horse to a post beside a clump of bushes and glanced nervously in through the doorway. It gave onto a flagstoned hall and then a long, pictureless, windowless corridor with grey walls and a high, vaulted ceiling. Both hall and corridor were devoid of any sign of human occupation and there was again, in their starkness, their emptiness, that dissonant, repellent feeling. I stood listening to the silence, undecided what to do, whether to ride back in the direction I had come and risk stumbling into the line of fire once more, or to seek shelter here, forbidding though the prospect might be. While the sun blazed over the verdant lawns it was cold in the shadow of the building, so that I found myself shivering.

And as I stared up indecisively at the looming brick I saw suddenly what had disturbed me; there were bars on the windows, every last one of them, not only on the outside but on the inside too.

I was turning to go. And then, out of the bushes, something sprang at me. I heard the howl, saw the arms raised with the hands like claws, saw blood-streaked eyes and a leering mouth spumed with saliva. Almost before I knew what I was doing, without thinking even to use my revolver, I was up the steps and through the door, fumbling with its great bolts, shooting them fast, turning the lock for extra measure. I leant for a while, quaking, with my back against the heavy oak. I was soaked in sweat and I realised, with shame, that I was whimpering. Grasping my revolver with both hands, I looked about me. After the brilliance of the sunshine my eyes accustomed themselves slowly to the windowless gloom. The thing, whatever it was, appeared to be making no assault against the door and so far as I could hear there seemed once again to be perfect silence. But there was no question of my returning outside and making my escape. I should have to find some hiding place until it was safe to open the door. I began to edge myself along the corridor flat against the wall, my gun at the ready.

I was aware now of a droning, muffled sound that seemed to come from somewhere deep within the building, a human sound, yet with a discordant animal quality like the chanting I had heard in the garden. I began to quake uncontrollably. I was trapped between the sound and the thing outside the door, my only hope lay in finding a place to hide until someone, Corporal Grüber perhaps, if he were still alive, came to rescue me. The revolver in my hand lent me some reassurance, but, given the general inaccuracy of my aim, it was only a small comfort. If I were set upon violently by more than one assailant I should soon be overpowered before I could even put my weapon to use.

Groping my way along the corridor I came to a heavy door, steel-plated and bolted on the outside. In the top half was a square sliding panel. Still trembling, I reached up and drew it open.

The steam hit me first, full in the face through the steel grating like the explosion of a geyser, then the stench and the din, so that I momentarily reeled backwards. It was a long room with small barred windows placed well out of human reach just below the ceiling. In its far corner, some twelve feet above the floor, jutted a pipe from which there fell a continuous douche of water, and in a trough beneath, manacled to the wall at ankles and wrists so that even by kneeling, head forwards, he was unable to avoid the impact of the torrent, was tethered a naked man. Flanking the walls, packed close together like beds in a dormitory, were iron bathtubs, wooden-lidded and secured by heavy padlocks; and in these bathtubs were also men, some old, some young, about twenty in all, with only their heads protruding. The man beneath the douche writhed, the heads in the bathtubs lolled and rolled, great gobs of condensation dripped from the ceiling and ran in murky streams down the walls. And through the thick air, drowning even the machine-gun roar of the douche, came a monstrous cacophony of sound, wailing, yowling, sobbing, screaming, high-pitched cackling laughter. Suddenly the occupant of the bathtub nearest the door noticed my face at the grating and began to howl expectantly, suddenly they all saw me and set up a great rapacious baying. The man beneath the douche began to urinate from excitement, mixing his stream with the cascading water. I shut the grating hurriedly and leant against the wall, gasping for breath.

So I had, indeed, stumbled not into shelter but into the local madhouse, left open and unguarded by its attendants, who had presumably fled before the advance of our troops. I felt for a moment that I should weep from terror. My only recourse was to brave the thing at the door with my revolver. But what of the creatures I had seen in the grounds, who, I now realised, must have been inmates making good their escape? Supposing some of them had returned, supposing there was not one madman outside the door but a whole mob of them? And what of the gunfire from which I had originally fled? At least inside the building the corridors were empty, suggesting that the only lunatics who remained were like those I had just glimpsed, too heavily restrained to wander at will. But supposing some of the craftier inhabitants had not left but were crouching in the shadows, biding their time, waiting to attack, supposing they were watching me at this moment? My racing brain seemed suddenly incapable of thought. I only knew that, standing like this in the corridor, in the open, I must inevitably be in danger, that I must find somewhere to hide until I could take hold of myself, work out a proper plan for escape.

Across the corridor was another door which, although fitted with plates and bolts like the first, stood ajar and silent. I flung myself to the opposite wall, edged up to the door and, levelling my revolver, pushed it with my foot so that it creaked open. I braced myself. But there was nothing, no one.

It seemed to be the laundry-room. In the centre of the stone floor was a huge cement vat supplied by flowing water from a sluice, while around the perimeter was a motley collection of mangling machines. Here again the atmosphere was dense and clammy. From wooden hoists high in the ceiling, sheets thick as barge sails dripped a steady rain which splashed upon ironing tables, plopped into piles of folded clothing and pattered into the trough like spray from a fountain. The place seemed to have been deserted hurriedly for everywhere were signs of labour cast aside, a sheet stuck, half-digested, between the rollers of a mangle, a petticoat draped across the margin of the trough with the soap still lying where it had been dropped.

I stood very still for a moment, searching for a cupboard or a piece of machinery big enough to provide a hiding place, trying to attune my ears to cut out the sound of the water and detect other sounds beneath. There was a door to the left of the one by which I had entered, presumably leading to a sluice or a linen room. It too stood half open and I was just about to approach it when I thought I heard a stirring within. Then I saw something which turned my blood cold. The door, which opened inwards, moved slightly and on the wall beyond there was all at once a shadow, a long thin shadow the shape of a bayonet.

In my fear of the lunatics it had never once occurred to me that they might not be the only occupants of the asylum, that it might have become a refuge for enemy troops. There was someone there, hiding behind the door, I could hear their breathing. And that someone – maniac or soldier – was armed, waiting to surprise me, to leap out and kill me as I crossed the threshold.

I began to shake so violently that I could hardly raise my revolver. Trying to swivel my body noiselessly, holding the gun in both hands, I managed finally to train the barrel at the gap in the door. The sweat was pouring off me, running down from my armpits inside my tunic, dripping saltily into my eyes. My fingers were so wet that the revolver felt slippery and when I went to release the safety-catch it took me some seconds before I could make the mechanism work. It slid back at last with a click that must have been audible to my assailant behind the door. But the shadow on the wall stayed steady.

'Come out!' I said. 'I am armed and I have you covered. I shall not hesitate to shoot!'

Even to me my voice sounded squeaky with panic. The bayonet shadow never wavered but continued to cast its poised and lethal shaft across the wall.

'Come out!' I repeated. 'I am an officer in Crown Prince Maximilian's army. We have taken Behrensdorf and Bad Gottfriedsburg and your forces there have surrendered. Throw down your weapon and come out unarmed. Otherwise I shall shoot.'

Still nothing. Only the faint sound of breathing and that shadow on the wall. I was shaking so convulsively that, though I tried to tighten my finger on the trigger, I doubted very much I could fulfil my threat.

'Come out,' I said, almost sobbing. 'Do you hear, damn you? Throw down your arms and come out of there. Or I'll kill you!'

There was a moment of absolute silence. Then a sound half-way between a snuffle and a snigger. And the shadow on the wall was lowered, lowered – and manifested itself in the gap in the doorway as – a broomhandle.

I thought for an instant I should faint. Then the door gradually swung fully open and a woman came out, a big woman, middle-aged, in a shapeless blue serge dress and wooden shoes. She still held the broom in one hand, bristles uppermost, but in a practical, matter-of-fact way, more like a staff than a weapon. She had a broad face, crimson with broken veins, that registered neither fear nor hostility but rather a kind of condescending, motherly amusement. Her hair was neat and her ample person seemed relatively clean. She did not look like a dangerous lunatic, indeed she appeared no different from innumerable placid peasant women I had seen on cottage doorsteps or working in the fields. All the same, I could not be sure.

'Don't come any closer,' I said, 'or I'll fire.'

She grinned. 'Oh, the little schoolboys playing at being soldiers. Bang, bang, I'll shoot you dead with my great big gun.'

'I mean it,' I said. 'I shall shoot if I have to.'

She was still smiling, did not even seem to be listening. Her eyes were not on the barrel of the revolver but had moved downwards and were trained on my breeches. And I felt suddenly with horror what she saw, that I had wet myself.

She threw back her head and let out a great, gusty bellow of laughter. She laughed and laughed, and in her laughter was the sniggering of an English dormitory long ago, and the mocking titters of three elder sisters and the guffawing of my so-called comrades at training camp and every derisive, sneering laugh that had ever been directed at belittling me. And I do not know what happened – it was an accident, I swear it – the safety-catch was off and my fingers were slippery, I was not even aware of pressing the trigger until I heard the roar and felt the recoil, it was an accident, an accident that could have happened to anyone.

I watched astonished as she and her broom parted company, travelling upwards and sideways in opposite directions, then downwards again to the floor, the broom first with a clatter, then she with a thud. She seemed to be just as much taken aback as she clutched the spreading stain at her bosom. Her wide-open eyes continued to register amazement long after she had twitched a couple of times and was still, her gaping mouth seemed to go on emitting gales of incredulous laughter. Only the stain had ceased to spread, a small stain considering, barely the circumference of a coffee saucer.

I stared at the revolver, which was still hot and smoking. I had never been able to use it before on anything but a practice target. It had only been a split second – if I could

take that second back, start again from the second before . . .
I felt profoundly puzzled as if I were suddenly faced with
an impenetrable conundrum. How could a second alter your
whole life, an unplanned, unconsidered, accidental second?

'Well, well, Lieutenant,' said a voice behind me. 'We've
got ourselves into a teeny-weeny bit of a mess, haven't we,
sir?'

I spun round in horror. Corporal Grüber must have
followed me after all, must have found his way into the
asylum by another door. He was a bull-necked brute of a
man, his coarse proletarian face so badly ravaged by acne
that it reminded one of minced beef. This livid infection of
flesh was now seared with a smile like an open wound, a
crafty, contemptuous smile that took in the body on the floor
and the revolver in my hand and the stench of cordite and
the dreadful, humiliating stain at my crotch, took them all
in and weighed them up like a usurer computing interest.

'She was a maniac,' I said. 'She attacked me. She tried to
kill me.'

'With a broom, sir? What was she trying to do – sweep
you to death?'

'She came at me like a wild animal. I had no choice, I was
obliged to shoot.'

'Shooting an unarmed civilian in cold blood – and a
woman at that? You know as well as I do, sir, that's one for
the firing squad.'

'Corporal, I have told you, she was a dangerous lunatic,
she tried to kill me—'

He shook his head as if with a sudden access of sorrow.
'You can't come it with me, Lieutenant. I'm afraid it won't
wash. I saw it, you see, saw the whole thing from just where
I'm standing now. She caught on you'd pissed yourself and
started laughing. So you shot her. I can't deny the evidence
of my own eyes, now can I, sir?'

The gun was all at once so heavy in my hand that I thought
my legs would buckle. I understood with sudden terrible
precision the enormity of my situation, saw my father's face,
thought of Max – God, Max!

'Please,' I said, 'it was an accident! I didn't mean – didn't
know what I was doing. It was an accident, an accident I
tell you!'

He continued to shake his head sorrowfully. 'An accident maybe, sir. That's for a court martial to find out. I can only tell what I saw, can't I? I can only state the plain facts like any honest man.'

The tears had come to compound my shame. 'Please, Grüber, try to understand, please – have some mercy!'

'Of course, you being who you are – related to our future King and all that – things won't go so badly for you, not like us ordinary poor sods who has to take what's coming. They won't fancy the scandal, will they? They'll most likely pull a few strings, hush things up . . .'

Hush things up? The firing squad was preferable to my father's anger. And as for Max – knowing his ridiculous pretence of moral scruples, I understood it would not matter how I was punished. The revolver slid from my fingers. I wanted to be sick.

'On the other hand,' – he wiped his nose thoughtfully between thumb and forefinger and the slit eyes were once again illuminated with a crafty gleam – 'on the other hand, there is what you might call my patriotic duty. I mean, there's the truth, isn't there? And then there's my duty to Sylvania. I mean, I could stand up and swear on oath what I seen like an honest man. But if that brings scandal on my future King and his relatives, where's the good in it, who'd thank me?'

I gaped at him, scarcely comprehending.

'Whereas if I was to keep quiet, considering there's no other witnesses and once both of us gets clear of this place who's to know, who's to care about one dead loony? – if, as I say, I was to keep my trap shut – well, you could take the opinion I was serving the motherland better.'

I continued to stare at him, not daring to hope.

'You could say the motherland would be grateful. The motherland and my future King . . .'

'Yes. Oh yes, Grüber, yes.'

'Of course it would mean sacrificing my honesty. And what's an ordinary sod got but his honesty?'

'Please, Grüber—'

'But if the sacrifice was appreciated – by those who knew about it – '

'It would be, I swear it would.'

'Then I've got nothing to fear, have I? Because I know you'll protect me, won't you Lieutenant? I know you'll show your gratitude. You being such a wealthy young gentleman and so closely related to the Crown Prince.'

'Oh, thank you. Thank you, Grüber.' I was so overcome with relief that I barely took in the significance of the leer which once again split the chancrous face, almost went to pump the hand he proffered me. Then a noise like the cawing of a raven made me start in terror.

'The Crown Prince! The Crown Prince! Let me curtsy to His Royal Highness the Crown Prince!'

Grüber too span round. Behind him in the doorway stood an aged crone, dressed like the woman with the broom, in shapeless blue. But this woman was tiny, no higher than Grüber's elbow, as slatternly as the other had been well-scrubbed, as shrivelled and deformed by Heaven knows what corrupt appetites as the other had been rosy-cheeked and healthy. Her matted hair hung upon her crooked shoulders, she shuffled tipsily in her clogs, there was a stench about her, even from where I stood, of putrescence. It seemed to me, though I tried frantically to interpose myself between her line of vision and the body on the floor, that she could not fail to see it, nor the tell-tale saucer of crimson. Yet, to the astonishment of both of us, she appeared blind to everything but our presence, suiting her action to her words and dropping us a lavish if unsteady curtsy.

'Cut along, mother!' said Grüber savagely. 'There's no Prince here.'

But she grabbed at his arm as if she would engage him in conversation. 'My son was a Prince, you know. My son was a Prince and Princesses and fine Court Ladies used to bow down to me – '

'You heard what I said, mother. Bugger off!' He tried to shake himself free, but in doing so occasioned what I had been dreading – her eye was suddenly caught by the bundle on the floor.

'What's Ilse doing down there?'

'Having a little nap. Now do a scoot like I told you!'

The old crow gave a self-righteous sniff. 'Just like that Ilse, always sleeping when she should be working. The company I'm forced to keep! Not like the old days when they all came to see me, Majesties and Royal Highnesses and Excellencies bowing and giving me money and jewels. 'Cause,' – here she tried to stretch up and whisper in his ear – ''cause I done them a favour, you see. And they was grateful, so grateful they'd give me anything. But then the men came and put the bells in my head, clang, clang all day long, and tortured me with snakes and spiders and took away my diamonds and put me in here with these common sluts, these prostitutes, these poxy whores—'

She seemed suddenly overcome, swaying drunkenly, no longer aware of us.

'Come on,' said Grüber. 'Let's cut it while the going's good.'

'But she's seen,' I said. 'She knows.'

Grüber guffawed unpleasantly. 'She knows nothing! You heard her – Kings and Princesses and diamonds! She's as daft as that bloody brush over there.'

And indeed, as I followed him out, obeying his order meekly as though I, not he, were the common soldier, I could still hear her moaning to herself: 'My son was a Prince, a Prince I tell you . . .'

III

God, how this mean hole stifles me – my motherland, the 'old country', with its frowsy peasant hovels and its garbled dialects and its contemptible poverty. Oh, it is true the mountain people are rosy-cheeked and healthy enough – I saw a village elder on my last trip to Schwanensee whose skin was stretched so tight he would have made ample sausage-meat for half the starving brats in Nordstadt. But they are smug too, swilling beer in their *Lederhosen* and recounting their folk superstitions beneath marzipan gables, as mean-spirited in their way as any northerner, so that despite the natural magnificence which surrounds them their world takes on the cramped perspectives of a doll's house.

Rosenholm, I admit, owes to the architectural mania of the first Sigismund a certain classical elegance. But the sweeping proportions of Königsplatz, the grandeur of St Xaviersdom and the Opera cannot disguise its resolute provincialism.

And I, who dreamed of Paris or Heidelberg, am suffocated by it.

After the revolution my life was perhaps at first not so intolerable. Though my father insisted I should spend a year at the Military Academy, I was allowed to maintain my own apartments in the wing of the Rosenpalast he and I shared; and since he was now preoccupied with diplomatic missions and affairs of State he left me largely to my own devices. Max too was kept constantly busy with his official duties, but nevertheless he would find the time after supper or the opera to walk through the Residenz gardens to the Rosen-palast and much of our previous intimacy returned.

It is true he was different now, obsessively discreet and often immersed in his own thoughts, much more the old, prison-wary Max, so that the infectious smile, the door opening brilliantly upon his other self had become a rare occurrence. It is true that while he had never discussed politics with me he now seemed little disposed even to talk about the subjects which had been meat and drink in our Schloss Beauregard days, as if art and poetry had suddenly vanished from his horizon. But then, of course, this was no more than the actor manifesting itself in him again, that uncanny knack he had of subsuming his other self, the fraud, the liar, the debauchee, of playing his role as wholeheartedly as if his nature had been translated by it. Vain for me to point out that now he had actually made himself King he had no need to take the wretched performance so seriously, that he could, in common with most of the reigning monarchs in history, use his wealth and power to indulge his own personal pleasures – he would merely become more impervious and aloof.

There is a portrait done of him at about this time by one of our native artists which shows very well how, as with the last stage of a metamorphosis, he had evolved into the kingship so that it fitted him seamlessly. It depicts him in the uniform of the Deathwatch, mounted on his charger Balthazaar, and it provides an interesting contrast with the Lenbach portrait. While Sigismund is shown as eminently human in all his arrogance and dissipation, our Sylvanian portraitist has seized upon his commission to give vent to the full flood of his patriotism, so that from Max, the mirror image, there shines an almost inhuman nobility and grace. With every brushstroke of the handsome profile, the proudly-carried head, the dauber has sought to convey not so much a man as an ideal; even the silver cuirass and the sweep of the sword strike a chivalric note. Late at night, lying smoking amidst my rumpled sheets, the smell of his sweat still on my skin, I would think often of this portrait, think with infinite pleasure that I alone knew the canker in the rose. And it seemed to me there was a power in this knowledge which, even more than love, bound us inextricably together.

Then came that dreadful night at the end of the year, bursting upon me with the shock of shellfire.

Despite my father's ambition that I should serve in the Hussars or the Deathwatch for two years and then enter Staff College, I had been for some time canvassing the idea that I should resign my commission and become Max's Personal Secretary, an appointment so eminently sensible, so transparent in its convenience that I was astonished to find Max himself lukewarm to it. Yet I remained confident of eventual success and when my man brought in the urgent message from the Residenz I concluded no more than that Max had recovered his senses and succumbed to the inevitable change of heart.

I remember a feeling of satisfaction as I surveyed my quarters, the first on which I have been permitted to imprint the refinements of my own taste, remember adjusting a jade figurine here, plumping a cushion there, before pouring another measure of brandy and disposing myself elegantly on the sofa with a novel by Pierre Loti.

Max's appearance when he was announced cut through my feeling of well-being like the North wind whipping across the snow in the Residenz gardens. He still wore the Litewka in which he attended to his dispatch boxes and the frozen crystals glittering in his hair suggested he had braved his walk bareheaded, oblivious of the temperature. Whether because of the cold, his face had such a glacial, sick look that, though I had moved towards him to exchange our usual embrace, I instinctively drew back.

'My dear, you look as if you had spent the whole day

closeted with our delightful friend Vielfrass – or possibly the whole week.'

His expression tightened into that regal stoniness of his. 'Please Anton, don't be flippant – not for the moment, at least.'

I watched him take a cigarette from the box on the mantel, light it and throw the spent match on the fire. He smoked in silence for a moment, half turned away from me, appearing to stare at his own image in the mantelpiece glass as if he disliked what he saw. I allowed my uneasiness to dissipate itself in a little laugh. But when he turned his face was still unsmiling.

'My dear Anton, you are aware of the talk some months ago concerning the possibility of my marriage—'

'The dear Paterfamilias's plan to marry you off to a treaty so that you could beget railway lines? Why, yes of course. But mercifully the Treaty herself would not oblige.'

'It seems Her Highness of Thalia has changed her mind. I'm afraid I must tell you that I received her letter of consent today.'

'You poor dear thing,' I said, raising my glass. 'Please accept my heart-felt commiserations.'

He surveyed me for a moment. Then he flung his cigarette on the fire. 'For God's sake, Anton! You won't make this in the slightest bit less painful by obstinately refusing to understand.'

'Oh, I understand, my dear old Max. And I can't pretend to undivided joy, as you may imagine. I'm simply resolved to be noble and forgiving about it. After all, the presence of the Little Treaty and the patter of tiny railways, disagreeable though they might be, can't change anything that's truly important – they can't change our friendship or our love.'

He was silent for an instant, and when he spoke his voice was very quiet. 'My dear Anton, you will always have my affection and my friendship – I give you my promise on it. But from today that is all there may be between us.'

My hand lowered the brandy glass slowly. I felt, despite the heat of the fire, a coldness as if the wind had suddenly blasted its way beneath the door. The sensation only lasted for a moment, then I laughed. 'Oh come, come, Max. I admit the prospect of the Little Treaty is infinitely depressing. But surely there is no reason for both of us to lose our heads. Sit down, won't you? Take some brandy – it's excellent cognac *mousseux* my cellerer imports from Rheims—'

He was all at once as close to normal uncontrolled anger as I had ever seen him. 'In Heaven's name, Anton, try just for this evening to refrain from playing childish games! I have endeavoured from the first to explain this to you. God help me, I had even, by some curious feat of self-deception, persuaded myself you had accepted it.'

'What should I accept?'

'That in honour this is the only course I may take.'

'Honour? My dear old Max, there's no honour involved, only a preposterous treaty and the Grand Duke's obsession with narrow gauge and bogie carriages. If you must marry then it will be for show, for appearance's sake, a marriage in name only—'

'It cannot be a marriage only in name. One of its purposes is to provide me with an heir.'

'My dear, if you are obliged to endure such indignities you have all the more need of your friends. Oh, for Heaven's sake, Max, you are being perfectly absurd. My Uncle Sigismund, your father,' – I could not help giving an edge to the word – 'your father was renowned for his indiscretions, half the Court keeps mistresses. Oh, I admit bourgeois morality might not regard our pleasures quite as sanguinely as it condones their grubby little antics, but the principle's the same. There's no reason on earth why anything between us should change.'

He sighed, and the sick look came into his eyes again. 'My dear Anton, you must face the inevitability of this somehow – I must compel you to face it. I don't give a damn for the Camarilla or for fashion. I know only what I myself must do. And I am afraid I do not believe I can make marriage vows and then cynically break them, I do not believe, when Princess Marie is prepared to sacrifice what she holds dear, that I can ignore my own obligations. Heaven knows, I expect little enough from this marriage, but I cannot deny that it is a marriage, or that when the Princess is my wife she must become my first care—'

'And what about me? I suppose I've sacrificed nothing, have no claim on you! Oh, you can't permit yourself to deceive the Little Treaty, yet you can cast me aside like a spent cigarette – I who've served you, fought for you, I who was compelled to forego Heidelberg, made to throw away my career as a writer, give up everything for you.'

He seemed indisposed to reply to this. I poured myself more brandy, forced the laughter back into my voice. 'And why today? In all this tomfoolery, that's the greatest absurdity of the lot. You're not married yet, not even betrothed. If you're hell-bent on destroying me why must it be now, why choose this moment when there are weeks, months before this pathetic pretence of yours even begins?'

'It begins now. From the instant I received her letter it began. And in any case, what difference can it make – a few weeks, a day here or there? Would there ever be a date that miraculously diminished your unhappiness – or my wretched responsibility for it?'

I watched him turn away towards the mantelpiece, tried to extract hope from the excruciated note in his voice, endeavoured to keep the little, cynical, unconcerned smile playing upon my lips. But when he turned back he had regained every last atom of his control.

'God in Heaven!' I broke out. 'I wish I knew what sin I have committed, what I have done to deserve this from you. I am your willing slave, Max. I can only assume you take pleasure in testing me, that you derive some perverse delight from pushing me to the very limit!'

'You cannot truly believe I have ever wished for this. Or that to see you suffering costs me nothing.'

'Then you must be mad. That's it – the constitution and Vielfrass, and Keller drivelling on about democracy – they've all finally turned you looney. Faithful to the Treaty? For the rest of your life! Why, they say even for a woman she's unspeakably dull, not beautiful, not even charming, as plain and dreary as a Sunday in Nordstadt—'

'She is a child, Anton. A pretty, sad, frightened child.'

The sudden gentleness in his voice deepened my horror. 'Oh, so you defend her now, do you? Perhaps after all you secretly want her, perhaps you imagine you'll enjoy procreating in the mire with her like a couple of farm animals. Is that it, Max? You want her, you're in love with her?'

'My dear Anton, I have only seen her once.'

'Then she's in love with you?'

'She too consents to this marriage out of duty.'

'Duty?' I took my brandy glass and hurled it into the fire. The glass shattered, spitting blue flame. I turned upon him savagely. 'Duty, honour? Damn you, Max, let's cease this pretence. I know you, know what you are. You no more care about duty or honour than I do. God, how I've come to hate those mean little words, words which have no significance for men like us – we, who know our very nature sets us apart, who glory in our uniqueness, our individuality. If you have any duty, Max, any duty at all, it's to preserve what's fine and high, to be faithful to your true self, not to wallow in the ordure of earthbound men. You have no duty to this woman beyond what appearances require. Duty can't send you eagerly to her bed, smother your deepest instincts, crush appetites that grow ever more consuming the more they are starved. These precious vows of yours, how long do you think you will keep them? Do you seriously imagine you can deny your true inclinations for the rest of your life?'

'I don't pretend it will be particularly easy. But I am resolved to try.'

'A vow of chastity? You will become a monk again?'

He surveyed me for a second. Then he favoured me with an acrid smile. 'My monastic vows were made for me by my so-called guardian when I was eight. These at least, since I take them consciously and willingly, I shall have the strength to keep.'

'I pray so, Max. I pray that your admirable self-control will not desert you, that God, before whom you make your promises, will not see fit to test you again.' I began, very slowly, to move towards him. 'Oh Max – my dear old hypocritical Max – God's obedient servant! Have you forgotten I know the Godhead you've served since your twelve-year-old self succumbed to Brother Ignatius? Have you forgotten that I know what drives you, know it as only a lover knows it? Or will you deny all we are to each other, not just in friendship or affection, but above all in this?' Seizing his hand, I pressed it hard against my fly. 'Do you feel, Max, do you feel that you have only to touch me to arouse me? And you – with your twisted pretence at scruples, your miserable lip-service to honour and duty – does your body deny me? Damn you, Max, does it, can it?'

I kissed him then, full on the lips. I felt for a few seconds his instinctive response. Then determinedly he freed himself.

'Damn you to hell, Max! If it isn't me, it'll be your valet or your groom or some new adjutant who catches your eye. Your marriage will be a farce in three months. You can't obliterate the nature you were born with, all the self-control in the world won't change what you are.'

He looked at me in silence for a moment or two, then he smiled dryly. 'Perhaps so, Anton. But nothing can alter the fact that I am obliged to try.'

IV

In our Schloss Beauregard days I should probably have attempted to shoot myself. But now I knew at first hand the power of firearms I had, not unnaturally, lost all inclination for such spectacular gestures. Instead, after an initial period of ignominious despair, I began more calmly to consider my situation. And the further I considered it, the further I became convinced that everything I had asserted was true: he could not deny the imperatives of his nature. Whatever platitudes he might mouth about Sylvania and The Common Good, however much he endeavoured to imitate the wretched creature in the equestrian portrait, he could not obliterate the Max I knew, the sensualist, the Machiavelli, the Olympian disdainer of good and evil. His true self would understand that I was the only one worthy of him, would be drawn back to me irresistibly. I had only to stay calm and wait.

Accordingly, I set out to make myself agreeable, as if I had accepted my lot. I even went to inspect the Little Treaty and found her quite as satisfyingly dull as rumour had proclaimed. There was not the slightest possibility – there never will be – of Max finding her anything but repugnant; indeed my careful study of her revealed at each meeting new deficiencies of intellect and spirit, while she, poor bovine creature, appeared utterly to succumb to my flattery to the point where I almost feared she had formed an attachment for me.

Though he kept me at arm's length, never seeing me except when there were others present, Max seemed impressed by my exemplary behaviour, was charming, even affectionate. And then came the wedding, the exquisitely dreadful wedding, which exceeded even my predictions of disaster – and oh God, I had hope again, no, not just hope, but positive proof of my power. I renewed my campaign for the Personal Secretaryship. I perceived at last a fixed limit to my suffering, I stood possessed of the certainty that he would cast the Little Treaty off as soon as she was declared *enceinte*.

And yet it had drawn into October, and I was still waiting. I might view with amusement Max's public performance as doting husband, but my secret knowledge did not protect me from the fact that his efforts to beget an heir had kept him from me for weeks. Oh, there had been rumours enough, ever since the honeymoon, to raise my hopes time after time; but still the confirmation had failed to materialise. And now he was away on this wretched tour of the North. I sat at Mme Zelenska's card salon, staring sourly at the military heroes and reflecting that I could not be asked to bear much more.

It would have been easier if my life had not become so uncomfortable in other respects. There was Grüber, for instance. He had been cashiered from the army after the revolution for raping a peasant woman during the capture of Marmion, but it had not been long before he had reappeared in Rosenholm with the first of his demands upon my 'gratitude'. Now he pursued me so that I was seldom free of him, and I was beginning to fear my chronic lack of funds would soon be drawn to my father's attention. There was the regiment, of course, and the appalling prospect of spending most of next month in some provincial hell-hole on manoeuvres. And then there was that other affliction which always attended Max's absence, my mortifying jealousy. Oh, I could assuage my sexual hunger easily enough – my looks assured that there would always be some strapping captain or major to attend to that – but the jealousy still

burned as fiercely as ever, so that on some nights the waiting
seemed to erode my certainty and I sank into bleak despair.

And now there was this – this sinister assignation at Mme
Zelenska's. No explanation, just a note so brief it was almost
a command. Was there a sexual motive? Did it presage
more blackmail? Whatever the reason behind it, the signature alone declared that the meeting could scarcely
favour my interests. And he was late, damn him! I paced
the stuffy card salon, my nervousness and my impatience
mounting.

He came ten minutes after, heavily cloaked and ushered in
by Mme Zelenska herself as she had promised, by the back-
stairs door.

'Apologies for my unpunctuality, dear boy. Affairs of
State, as I'm sure you'll understand. The government of the
country does not grind to a halt simply because His Majesty
is away from Rosenholm.'

Even in the levelling uniform of white tie and tails, I
reflected, Count Vielfrass was still a parvenu, with his
raven's-wing hair and his manicured beard and his osten-
tatious aura of cologne. I did not return the little bow he gave
me or the honeyed smile. His very friendliness redoubled
my suspicions, and besides I objected profoundly to the
familiarity of his address, his apparent disregard for the fact
that, though our titles might suggest equality, he was the
son of a tradesman while my father was a Hohenstaufen
Prince.

He seemed not a whit disconcerted by my studied disdain,
merely divesting himself of his cloak and dabbing his lips
once or twice with the inevitable lavender handkerchief. 'Ah
yes, His Majesty. First reports of the Royal Tour say he is
taking the North by storm. And Her Majesty too. Such
charming simplicity of manner, don't you think? The
people's adoration is unqualified – and it will know no
bounds now she is with child.'

I would not have him, of all people, taunt me with false
hopes. 'Mere tittle-tattle,' I said languidly.

'On the contrary, dear boy, I have it from an unimpeachable source.'

I affected a yawn. 'Come Count, I scarcely believe you

have brought me here to discuss the more elaborate embroideries of our Court gossips.'

'You were surprised to receive my note?'

'Most surprised, both by the note and Your Excellency's suggestion that we should meet in this house. I should hardly have thought our Chancellor would wish to risk the scandal of being discovered in such an – unusual establishment. And I, as well you know, am confined by my soldier's code of honour to the company of my fellow officers in our regimental *Kasino* – to be apprehended here would be to disgrace the whole regiment.'

He bestowed upon me another of his moist smiles. 'Dear boy, my heavy burden of responsibility does indeed, as you so rightly point out, dictate the need for the utmost discretion. But I am told there is no house more reliably discreet in the whole of Rosenholm. And I am also informed that you, despite your admirable concern for the honour of the Hussars, are not unacquainted with it.'

In spite of myself, I flushed. How could I forget that Vielfrass's spies were everywhere, how could I allow myself in the very first cuts of our encounter to be riposted so neatly? The pause that accompanied Mme Zelenska's bringing a second bottle of champagne permitted me to recover my negligent air. I watched him take a little mincing sip of the wine as if he somehow suspected poison, then smack his lips and nod to Mme Zelenska. Why had he summoned me here? Perhaps I had been correct in surmising some sexual intention. Certainly when our hostess had departed and I found him gazing coquettishly over the rim of his glass, head on one side, eyelids batting, for all the world like an ancient whore, my fears on this score redoubled.

'My dear Tarn,' he lisped, 'I detect a certain hostility in your manner, and it grieves me. I have invited you here out of friendship, to be of help to you. I should be most distressed if I felt you disliked me, indeed I should.'

I did not deign to respond.

'Oh, it is yet another burden of high office. If one is the humble servant of the public good one cannot be always courting popularity. But nevertheless I feel it at times quite deeply. His Majesty, you know, dislikes me too.'

I stared at him. In the twinkling of an eye he had ceased to be the coquette, had transformed himself into a maudlin drunkard anxious to confess his secret soul, although to my certain knowledge he had taken no more than two sips of champagne. These transformations of his, like the changes in one of Uncle Gustav's poisonous familiars, altering colour with the flutter of a leaf or a shift in the sun, disconcerted me profoundly. One could not help but fear, however carefully one charted all the shades of his various mutations, that he might suddenly take on some altogether unexpected camouflage which left one prey to his fangs.

'Yes,' said the drunkard with a weary wave of the handkerchief and a blurry gesture to his brow, 'His Majesty, I'm afraid, does not care for me at all. Oh, it is not his fault, I do not criticise him for it. He is influenced, you understand, by hostile voices. They pour the toxins of liberalism in his ear, men like Keller and His Highness of Hohen-Kastell. Even your noble father – pray forgive me – pays lip-service to their doctrines. I warn His Majesty constantly of the dangers, of course – but will he listen to me? I do not have the glamour of popular appeal on my side, I am a reactionary perhaps, a stick-in-the-mud, all I care for is to safeguard the glorious institution of the monarchy, to preserve His Majesty's position as Head of our beloved State. But forgive me, dear boy, I see I bore you. I know you have not the slightest taste for politics. In fact, that is one of the characteristics in you which most commends itself to me.'

Here he favoured me with yet another sickly leer but did not wait for me to break my silence. 'Yes, I wish with all my heart that I possessed some influence with His Majesty, the influence you, dear boy, exercise – or, should we say, used to? – the privileged position of confidence vouchsafed to one who is His Majesty's cousin and his friend. His most particularly intimate friend.'

I drew in my breath. So that was it – blackmail after all. 'I do not comprehend Your Excellency.'

Instantly the drunkard was gone and the interrogator faced me over the rim of the wineglass, eyes fish-cold, voice like a rapier. 'Come, come, my dear Tarn, we know His Majesty's predilections. Our investigations into his life in Paris show little reason to doubt the view of the Marquis's family that he was Miramont's catamite. Of course there is no firm evidence – His Majesty is exceptionally discreet. You, sir, alas, are not.'

I stared aghast as he drew out a sheet of paper upon which, even from a distance, I could recognise my own handwriting. Count Vielfrass's spies were truly everywhere. I had not for one moment been aware of my desk having been entered or my papers rifled.

I cast the document aside, affecting nonchalance as best I could. 'I fear Your Excellency is mistaken. This is simply a passage from my play *The Sacred Brotherhood of Thebes*. It is my hero Pythias's eulogy to his comrade Damon, spoken on the eve of the battle of Leuctra – you may observe the name Pythias at the top of the page.'

The fish eyes of the interrogator did not waver. 'It is a document which would outrage the moral decency and religious sentiments of any respectable Sylvanian.'

'It is, I admit, a trifle florid in style. But then I was obliged to make several drafts before it would come right. Your agents, with characteristic lack of discrimination, have stolen an early and inferior version.'

'Whatever the version, it contains descriptions of acts which contravene the criminal code of the Reich, which carry as their penalty both imprisonment and loss of civil rights.'

I was sweating profusely now under that icy stare. 'What will you do?' I said. 'Is it your intention to have me arrested?'

To my astonishment the interrogator vanished just as suddenly as he had appeared, the coquette returned, fish eyes twinkling, saffron fangs bared in a hideously suggestive smirk. 'Good Heavens, dear boy, how you mistrust me. Did I not make clear at the outset that my one desire is to help you, to be your friend?'

Try as I might, I could not find myself consoled by this. 'Help me, Count? How?'

For answer he rose and rang the bell, and when Mme Zelenska appeared I saw she was carrying an inkwell and a blotter. The ink was of precisely the colour I favoured, the paper my chosen quality and texture and the pen on the blotter one of my own which I had assumed I had merely mislaid.

He came over to my chair and laid his claw on my

shoulder. 'My dear boy, I have observed you have not been your usual delightful self of late. Something has made you depressed, discontented—'

'On the contrary, I am in the best of spirits.'

'Ah, how I admire you noble young military types, so gallant, so tight-lipped in adversity! But I must confess that if I were you, dear boy, I should take His Majesty's cruelty much harder, I should feel very deeply the lack of compunction with which he has cast off old friends, thrown his heart into this marriage—'

'His Majesty's marriage is scarcely a proper subject of conversation between us.'

'Perhaps not. What business is it of ours that His Majesty seems quite intoxicated by the charms of his new wife, that he is wretched unless she is at his side at all times, that his dedicated pursuance of his marital duties is said to make Don Juan appear something of a slouch?'

My control deserted me. 'That's not true!'

'Tush, tush, dear boy – unimpeachable sources. They say he takes her into his confidence in everything, even goes through his dispatch boxes with her. Enchanting, don't you agree? Enchanting, but perhaps also, to us men of affairs, a trifle concerning. Her Majesty, like all women, has a tendency to be sentimental. Unlike yourself, who hold no views other than those dictated by a perfectly proper self-interest, Her Majesty inclines to the liberalism of Keller and the Duke of Hohen-Kastell and thus, I am afraid, exacerbates their dangerous influence. Ah, but what price our concerns, our anxieties, where Their Majesties' happiness is at stake, eh? Love – such a transitory emotion – we must marvel at its flowering while the blooms still last. Her Majesty is, as we should expect, as deeply attached to our beloved King as he to her. But she is also a lady of high moral principles – not to say a trifle prudish.'

Stomaching my revulsion, I looked up at him. 'What is it, Count, that you want from me?'

'I should like you to make a fair copy of Pythias's eulogy, amending none of its content except to set it out in the form of a letter and to substitute, wherever you use the name Damon, the terms of endearment by which you habitually address His Majesty.'

His face was now so close to me I could feel his spittle on my cheek, smell the gusts of decay beneath the cologne.

'What if I refuse?'

'Refuse the chance to recover His Majesty's favour? I doubt, dear boy, that you will. But in that unlikely circumstance, I should of course be obliged to remind you of your relationship with a certain ex-Corporal Grüber.'

I started so violently I nearly knocked over the inkwell.

'However,' he said with a little laugh, tightening his grip on my shoulder, 'I'm sure it won't come to that. An intelligent young man like yourself would wish, at all costs, to save your father the distress of knowing you had paid a convicted criminal large sums of money to conspire with you in the practice of unnatural vices.'

So Vielfrass's spies were not infallible after all. To conceal my relief, I reached for my glass and pretended to be preoccupied with refilling it. Yet I had only in part been spared, the blackmail still held even if he had mistaken the nature of my relationship with Grüber. My father would still find out about the money, and it was even possible that the true reason for the payments would emerge. And besides, though I loathed and detested Vielfrass, though I deeply distrusted the motives for his 'help' and utterly disbelieved his estimate of Max's attachment to the Little Treaty, I was tired of misery and loneliness. Why should I obstruct the means when it could only hasten the one end I had desired so impatiently all these weeks?

I lit a cigarette and took a deep draught of it. 'Very well,' I said. 'Hand me the pen.'

He stood over me as I worked, exhaling scent and corruption. When I had finished and he had sealed the envelope, he astonished me by handing it back to me. 'Yours shall be the choice of place, dear boy. You have more ready access to Her Majesty's household than any of my agents – your sister, after all, is one of her ladies-in-waiting. I shall be the judge of time. We need reasonable confirmation of this pregnancy. It is certainly not in either of our interests to deprive Sylvania of an heir to the throne – that would truly be to court anarchy.'

Our business being concluded, he rang the bell. I waited for him to drain his glass and put on his cloak and hat but he seemed, rather, to settle himself, reaching indeed for the champagne bottle as if it were I, not he, who was expected to take a judicious departure.

'Your Excellency should have a care,' I said dryly. 'This house may be discreet but it is still subject to Article 175. It would distress me to hear you had been apprehended by one of your own agents.'

He drew a cigarette from his case and was all at once no longer the coquette, nor the interrogator, nor the all-confiding sot, but the debonair man of the world, urbane, expansive, infinitely relaxed. 'Dear boy, you are naive. My people have greater interests than the trivial pecadillos of a few cavalry officers – or at least they are trained to respect that wise old saying about giving a man enough rope. And besides,' – here the saffron smirk appeared again – 'why should we destroy the excellent source of information we have taken such pains to create?'

I experienced the chill of revelation, was still experiencing it when Mme Zelenska returned. And suddenly it was no surprise that it was not she who escorted me downstairs but the Dusky Maiden, nor that as the door closed upon the card salon I thought I heard skittish giggles.

I did not doubt that there would be a price to pay for Count Vielfrass's friendly assistance. Oh, he might for his own ends expedite my reconciliation with Max, but he would tighten his hold, make sure that this was added to the force of the other blackmail, until I was required to perform more and more little tasks for him – in my own interests, of course. I had no intention of becoming Vielfrass's servant; rather, I thought it behoved me to find a lever of my own, a source of power even the Count could not share. I pondered my Olympian kinship with Max, my secret knowledge of his true nature. It seemed to me that when dear old Max returned I should no longer rely upon his understanding of how inextricably we were bound, but should put myself in the way of demonstrating, if need be, the strength of the shackles. In these past wretched weeks a plan had been forming in the back of my mind to make use of certain information, to prove a hypothesis I had speculatively put together. Now I revolved this plan again, saw it assume a sudden and pleasing clarity. Max would assure my future, Max would protect me against Vielfrass; I should make perfectly certain he was left with no other alternative.

There were three days' leave due to me before I went on manoeuvres. What could be more appropriate than that I should pay a call on Aunt Helena before I left Rosenholm, poor vague, lonely Aunt Helena, with only Uncle Gustav for company now that Winders was pressed into Her Majesty's service? I knew the contents of those dreary photograph albums by heart – she even assisted me by leaving the drawing-room for a moment to fetch Winders's latest missive from Nordstadt – and it was the work of seconds to locate the photograph I needed, substituting one of the loose snapshots in the back of the album so that the gap would not be noticed.

Next morning, with the photograph safely tucked into my letter case, I set off for Schwanensee and the Austrian border.

CHAPTER NINE

Marie Bathildis

I

I stood beneath the Christmas tree at the Summer Palace and saw, beyond the glow of its tapers, another tree, brighter, set up in the Golden Drawing-room at Schwanensee, with all the family and their suites around it and Maximilian in their midst, smiling. And somewhere would be Anton von Tarn, smiling too, a small, significant, exclusive smile, caught in the flicker of a taper, caught and returned and gone in a moment, a signal between two conspirators who are confident they are neither observed nor understood.

How many times had they smiled thus, secure in their certainty of my obtuse innocence? At my wedding? On that night of my honeymoon at the Turkish Hunting Box? At their secret meeting on the journey home from Jedburg when I had foolishly longed for him so? How they must have laughed as they rehearsed their lies and organised their fictitious shooting trips. I had learned to love Maximilian, I had excused his evasions, his unaccountable absences as tokens of some hidden care whose burden I must respect; now it seemed my first judgement of him had come closer to the mark all along, had been deficient only in its mildness. A monster? Was he not worse? Was he not capable of a degree of depravity that exceeded anything my dull brain could comprehend? And how he had played upon my dullness, twisting every detail of our life together into his evil deception, every loving gesture, every moment shared, every sweet and passionate yielding of flesh, so that I should never again contemplate such joys without suspecting their treachery.

Well, my innocence was gone now, gone for ever. It was as if the existence of a secret society had been revealed to me which had subtly changed my perception of the world so that I saw its caballistic signs in the most ordinary events, the most trivial nuances of voice and gesture, saw its membership extending in every direction, weaving its influence insidiously into the very fabric of normal life. He had said there had been others – how many others who, like Anton, had smiled, pretended friendship and mocked me behind my back? To my jaundiced eye even my dear Aubyn could now no longer be taken on trust. Indeed, could I trust anyone? Perhaps they had all known, even those who were not part of it – Ursi, the spiteful Suzannah – had known the truth and joined with pleasure in the laughter.

A secret society whose members were everywhere, yet whose membership was closed to me – that was the horror of it. To have discovered Maximilian unfaithful with another woman would have been pain enough, but at least I could have hoped; at least to inveigle him back I could have tried to make myself more attractive, more compliant, more loving than my rival. But against this unimaginable thing I was powerless. I might change my *toilettes* or the way my hair was dressed but I could not alter the one thing that exiled me from Maximilian forever – my sex.

Oh, it hurt when I sought to conjure up that image which was beyond my conjuring, that abhorrent intimacy of lips and skin and flesh, lips I had kissed so rapturously, skin whose warmth was even now palpable to me. I hated Anton von Tarn, hated Maximilian, could find no words that properly expressed my repugnance for them. And yet what hurt me most was my own overpowering burden of guilt.

So unnatural, so utterly beyond comprehension was this love of Maximilian's that I could not help feeling I had driven him to it. If I had not sought to punish him during that first week of our honeymoon (oh, how well I remembered his drawing away from me and saw the significance of it now), if I had from the first been a good wife to him, perhaps he would not have felt the need for this other monstrous thing. It was I who had brought this horror upon myself, by failing him, by being the stupid, dull little mouse I was. Not clever, not understanding – not even beautiful, that was part and parcel of the lie – I could see, could prove to myself simply by looking in the mirror that Prince von Ansbach and my uncle were right, and there was nothing in me for a man to find worthy of even passing interest.

Indeed I had never felt my unattractiveness as keenly as I did now. My hair was lank, I was costive, my back ached abominably and the growing burden of my belly sat ill upon my small frame. I might once have longed passionately for this child, but I did not want it now, it reminded me only of all the horror.

As my belly was a constant reminder of Maximilian, so Suzannah's ugly features recalled at every moment she was in my presence their beautiful counterpart, the mocking face of her brother. Small wonder this alone had the power to turn my dislike of her into an obsession, so that I was endlessly inventing pretexts to keep her from my sight. But worse still was the conviction I had that the flurried skirts I had sensed leaving my boudoir the instant before I had found the letter could only have been hers, that she it was who had seen fit to enlighten my innocence. Passionately, desperately, I wanted her sent away, back to Rosenholm, anywhere that would relieve me of her; but that would mean demanding her removal of Maximilian, who would probably dismiss my request as a petty attempt to exact revenge upon his lover; and besides I could not bring myself to write to him.

His silence too was absolute. No visitors came from Rosenholm. The Summer Palace, blanketed in snow, seemed as remote as if it were on another continent. I kept to my apartments, huddled before the fire. Even Ursi appeared uncharacteristically subdued and was twice confined to her bed with chilblains. I seized upon the days of solitude with relief, grateful that her indisposition made her disinclined to question our sudden exile or our exclusion from the Christmas festivities.

And then, two days before Christmas Eve, Aubyn arrived unheralded. I thought I had never been so pleased to see anyone in my life. One glance at his broad, transparently-honest face told me how absurd my suspicions had been. Forgetting my ugliness, forgetting everything save the delight of seeing him, I flung my arms about his neck. But his gruff: 'Whoa there, old girl, steady!', his diffident drawing away, reminded me all at once of Maximilian's unkind accusation and I too fell back shyly.

Maximilian's shadow could not, however, cloud my happiness for long. In my shifting world of doubt and suspicion, Aubyn seemed more than ever a rock, solid, reliable, unchanging. When Aubyn told me I was looking 'corking, don't y'know,' I forgave the lie, sensing the good-natured desire to please, feeling his inherent gentleness and taking comfort from it.

Oh, it was a joy simply to talk to someone freely and openly again. He was full of admiration for the way Beatrice and Benedict had grown and complimented me extensively on my training of them. He talked to me of Rosenholm and politics, of how the reorganisation and re-equipment of the army was proceeding apace and of the new poor relief measures, and of how Vielfrass, having blocked the Bill on the Sylvanian-Thalian railway for months, had been obliged for the sake of the Treaty to put it to the Assembly, suffering a revolt in the extreme right wing of his party and escaping defeat only with the help of the Opposition; and I felt a sudden ache despite myself, felt for the first time how my exile deprived me, that my return to the routine feminine occupations of reading and needlepoint did little to assuage the hunger for constructive work which my partnership with Maximilian had awakened.

Over dinner, which we took alone together in my apartments, I brought up the subject of Suzannah, not particularising my reasons for wanting her removal – how could I? – but simply saying she was surly and disobliging and did not suit me. To my surprise, Aubyn frowned and looked almost disapproving. 'Mmm, well – I should hold hard if I were you, my dear, not be too hasty. You ladies fall in and out with one another, y'know. In a month or two you may be bosom pals again. No sense in hurting the girl, or giving offence—'

'To Count Tarn?' I said sharply.

'To Uncle Leo, my dear. She is his favourite daughter.'

'The Duke of Maar is not my concern. I must have the choice of my own ladies-in-waiting.'

'Nevertheless, Suzannah von Tarn's a good-hearted girl and quite devoted to you.'

I let out a sour laugh. How Aubyn, like Freddy, always allowed his own good nature to deceive him into thinking better of everyone than they deserved! But he was not to be put off, was looking at me, indeed, most gravely.

'But then, my dear Marie, so are we all – devoted to you, I mean. And none of us likes to see things as they are.'

I lowered my eyes to my plate. I had prayed so hard that he would not try to discuss my situation.

'D'you know, you haven't once asked after him.'

'I assume His Majesty is well.'

'Oh Marie, my dear girl – ' I could feel him carefully editing the reproach from his voice. 'Yes, I suppose poor old Max is well enough for a man who drives himself like the devil, working night and day, hardly bothering to eat or sleep, till I'm damned if I've ever seen him so exhausted.'

'Maximilian is never happier than when he is shut away with his dispatch boxes.'

'Dashit, Marie, he's worried sick! That infernal scoundrel Vielfrass wants revenge for his humiliation over the Railway Bill. He's insisting he must pacify the Right by tabling tax concessions for the *Landgrafs*. He hasn't the majority to prevent Keller defeating him and the government will fall. Which means there'll have to be elections.'

'But perhaps this time the Liberals will be returned.'

'Under the new constitution there's a damned good chance of Keller gaining enough seats to form a government. Whereupon our friend Vielfrass, confound him, will more than likely stage a coup and overthrow the constitution. And I need not point out to you how dangerous that would be for Max.'

'But the people love him. I know he's pessimistic about their loyalty, but I've seen them – only two months ago in Nordstadt they were hailing him as if he were a god.'

'Max is no friend to the old guard of the Right. And if they decide to stir things up the people won't stick. Even now there are ugly rumours about you and he, that your condition is merely an excuse for your absence, that you've quarrelled irreconcilably and decided on a permanent separation.'

'I hardly believe,' I said coldly, 'that His Majesty's popularity depends on my constant presence.'

'Oh Marie, Marie,' – for a second he seemed about to slam his hand down upon the table in sheer exasperation – 'you know how popular you are in your own right, you know dashed well that any rift between you can only help to undermine his position. But besides, there's more than the blasted political mess. He's lost without you, y'know, misses you wretchedly—'

'He has told you as much?'

'Not in so many words – you know old Max. But I sense, I understand from my own . . . Confound it, no one who felt any glimmering of fondness for you could abide this strain between the two of you, this sudden falling out, whatever it is! Oh, I'm a pretty poor sort of chap when it comes to dealing with the human emotions, but if there has been a quarrel, if you were to bring yourself to tell me about it, then I'd do my level best to help, you know I should.'

He meant it so generously, he offered me such a longed-for means of sharing my burden of guilt and shame, that I nearly told him then, all of it. But I could imagine the shocked disbelief spreading over his decent face, imagine his revulsion shattering in an instant his friendship for Maximilian, and I could not bear to destroy his illusions so brutally.

Instead I attempted to brush away his concern. 'Truly, dearest Aubyn, there has been no quarrel. I am simply obliged to conserve my health and strength, which I shall do better here than in Rosenholm.'

'But you're as downright miserable as he is. A fellow need not be a genius to tell that.'

'It's my wretched condition. Ursi says it makes most women querulous and nervy. You must not be concerned for me – please, dear friend.' Here I put out my hand to touch his great comforting paw but, suddenly recalling Maximilian's accusation, drew back. 'Please, if you have a concern, let it be for yourself. Don't out of generous impulses towards me, lay yourself open to . . .'

He had observed the withdrawal of my hand, was staring at me with alarm. 'To what, dear girl? To what may I lay myself open?'

'To nothing.' I stumbled, aware that I was blushing. 'Merely that Maximilian is your friend and so – and so your first loyalty must be to him. I am sure he would not look favourably upon our discussing him in his absence, or even that you had come here on your own account, without his knowledge.'

He threw back his head in laughter. 'But, my dear Marie, he asked me to come – not that I did not most heartily wish to – but he requested it, urged me to it.'

Now it was I who was astounded. 'To persuade me back to Rosenholm?'

'To deliver his Christmas presents, find out how you were, to . . .' Here his laughter died, as if my surprise, my previous entreaties, my incoherence had all at once coalesced into an unpleasant revelation. 'But hold hard, dear girl, you can't mean – Oh Lord, if it is I who have somehow – by something I stupidly did or said . . . Please God, it's not I who have caused you and Max to quarrel, compromised you like a dashed idiot in some thoughtless way—'

I too, from his eyes, from his stricken expression, received enlightenment. I did not, could no longer take his hand. But I said, very gently, what was no more than the truth. 'No, dear friend. It is nothing that you have done. I promise you that.'

So Aubyn loved me. No, it could not be true, it was merely another hysterical fancy brought on by my tiresome condition; not even his compassionate heart could open to one who offered so little in return. And yet, when I thought back, when I remembered – perhaps I had been blind all along, as I had to the monstrous thing in the letter, perhaps he had always loved me, even before I married Maximilian. And supposing I had known then, had understood?

It dogged me, that thought, would not let me rest. Supposing I had married Aubyn? On Christmas Eve, as Suzannah scowled and Ursi twittered, trying to make light of our lonely celebrations, I seemed to see his face still, to see the gentleness concealed in the deepset eyes. Oh, he was not handsome, his stiffness of bearing was sometimes disconcerting, perhaps even a little ridiculous, and he was nearly twenty years older than me; but I perceived with an ache how he would cherish a wife, be to her in all things loving and straight and honourable. And how we understood each other, he and I, who shared so much in common, our fondness for England and dogs and horses, for the smaller, ordinary pleasures in life. Aubyn was not ruthless, cynical, obsessed with power; beneath Aubyn's clumsy exterior beat a simple heart whose demands were small, whose only desires were generous. I could see it now, set out before me on my present table. Of Maximilian's gifts, the principal offering was a spray of roses, the blooms wrought in rubies, the leaves in emeralds, the stems in diamonds and white gold; it glittered up at me by the flickering light of the Christmas tree tapers, this triumph of the jeweller's art, as brilliant and cold and hard as Maximilian himself. Aubyn's presents were small and insignificant beside such a spectacle, yet they were chosen with infinite regard for their precise appeal: books, a cashmere shawl, a little travelling clock, handsome new collars for Beatrice and Benedict and – my favourite of all this little accumulation of treasures – a gilded cage with a pair of bright-eyed finches in residence. Their plumage was more dazzling than any gemstone, their soft throats and cheekily-cocked heads more perfect than any artifice of man, their fluttering and chattering filled, unlike Maximilian's counterfeits, with the joyous warmth of life.

And then, even as I was cooing at them through the bars, ignoring Ursi's exclamations over the jewellery, offering my fingertips to be pecked, I saw that it would not do. I loved Aubyn's simplicity, his directness, loved them as one cherishes these things in a friend; but I was not, could not ever be in love with Aubyn. In life with Aubyn there would be happiness, yes, the undemanding tranquillity of routine, of feeding his pretty little finches every morning and knowing that they and I were safe, cut off from the world's uncertainties. In the jewelled flowers, as they sparkled from their bed of velvet, was an exotic, impervious beauty that was unapproachable, even repellent; and yet, despite their artifice, their conscious and intricate refinement, there was something fired by the candle-flame, here in the sudden flare of a diamond, there glowing fiercely in the blood-red depths of a ruby, something that both chilled and fascinated. Maximilian did not love me, had killed the love I felt for him; yet I still longed for him as I could never long for

Aubyn. Maximilian was alien, depraved, cruel; yet still I saw that dark face and desired to touch it, to watch it melt in tenderness, to have bestowed upon me the rare brilliance of his smile, to feel his head heavy on my breast in the aftermath of love-making. I tried to tell myself that the tenderness, the smile, even the love-making, were all a pretence, that the gifts I thought I had been vouchsafed were mere illusions. But even as I did so I wanted him again, more fiercely than I had ever wanted him. Abruptly I ordered Ursi to close the jewel-case. There was no joy in my discovery, only a sense of my own weakness and a pain worse than any I had suffered before.

Staring through tears at the Christmas tree, I saw that other tree at Schwanensee again, saw Maximilian returning Anton's smile. And I saw Aubyn, too, for the first time, set a little apart from the others, he with his own secret. I had lost Maximilian and now I must lose Aubyn as well, for I could not allow him to continue to love me when there was no hope, must henceforth discourage his visits, cease my selfish dependance on his friendship. Oh, that even this last comfort should be taken from me, that I should be left with nothing!

I struggled through the ordeal of Midnight Mass, fighting the self-pity that came upon me in great waves, feeling faint with the effort of holding back my tears. Then as we were leaving the chapel I experienced such a curious sensation, disturbing yet not quite painful, that I seized hold of Ursula's arm with a gasp.

She smiled indulgently. 'It's His dear little Highness quickening, Ma'am. No cause for alarm, simply his way of telling you he's alive and well.'

I put a tentative hand to my belly. Alive? I had not once in these weeks of wanting to hide myself, praying for a miscarriage, thought of this deformity as life. A child, Maximilian's child, small, curled, helpless and human, already perhaps beginning to take on Maximilian's beauty – and Maximilian's taint?

I moved my hand protectively. The child was mine now, only mine. I would see that he grew straight and upright and honourable, make sure that no blemish marred his beauty, fight for him, endure for him, defend him against the world. He was mine. I was not after all completely bereft.

II

I retreated into my new-found sense of peace as one might into a great feather bed, wrapping my entirety in it, pulling it up over my ears. I would not think of Maximilian or Rosenholm or even of Aubyn, but only of the child. So when, one morning a fortnight later as I was breakfasting late in my boudoir, Ursi appeared in a great flutter to tell me that His Majesty had arrived unexpectedly and was on his way up to my apartments, I was seized with confusion. But even as I stood there trembling, wondering whether there was time to summon a maid to squeeze me into my stays, the dogs had already bounded from my side, I could see them dancing at the heels of the tall black figure who strode towards me through the open succession of connecting doors.

I curtsied, and there was an awkward silence while Ursula and Suzannah gathered up the dogs and withdrew. He wore his service uniform and his top boots were still crusted with snow. He seemed more than ever to fill the room with that commanding presence of his so that again I searched vainly for some weakness, some physical evidence of his monstrous secret. Instead I saw only the hard, handsome face that haunted me, the conquistador's profile, the determined line of the jaw. And yet perhaps Aubyn had not exaggerated the burden of his work, perhaps there was a strain there too, around the eyes, in the set of the mouth, a haggard look he had not worn before.

I felt him studying me just as closely, felt him taking in every detail of my face, my hair, my figure beneath the cambric morning-gown. I hung my head, mortified.

'Aubyn was right,' he said softly. 'You are more beautiful than ever.'

The lie again. My blush deepened and I did not raise my head.

'Your doctors report that you are in good health and progressing excellently – physically, at least.'

I looked up. 'I have nothing to complain of. But I shall be glad when it is over.'

I was aware of something in his eyes which, as I spoke, vanished, as if with an imperceptible shift of the light. 'Of course,' he said. 'I understand how difficult this time must be for you.'

It was there in his voice too, that subtle shift, a note, not of anger or reproach, but of a sudden weariness, as though what I had seen might almost have been regret. All at once I wanted to cry out that I was sorry I had spat at him, reviled him, that I forgave him, would forgive him anything so long as he came back to me. But though I opened my mouth, some other part of me, pride or morality or fear of being injured again, prevented me from finding the words. I stood gazing at him helplessly, feeling the moment pass.

When he continued his tone was merely businesslike. 'Marie, while I am advised by your doctors that your physical health is excellent, they tell me that they have some concern — Good Heavens, little Mouse, whatever is it? Are you in pain?'

I looked at him astonished for a moment. Then, following his eyes to where my hand had instinctively travelled, I found myself laughing despite myself. 'Oh, my dear, it is nothing – only the child kicking me.' On impulse I reached out and placed his hand beneath mine. 'There. Do you feel him? Your son.'

I saw in his face the wonder that had at first dazed me, saw it gradually merge into a look of infinite tenderness. Then his eyes moved upwards to meet mine, so that I was acutely conscious of our two hands resting together on my belly, of how close he was, of how much I wanted to put up my other hand and touch his lips. And in that instant his mouth tightened, he withdrew his hand abruptly.

'Let us pray, Marie, that it is a son. Then I shall be able to release you from any further obligation to me.'

I could not help myself. I burst suddenly into wretched, disappointed tears.

'Oh my dear child, don't cry. I know the waiting is hard, but once it is over I shall keep my promise. I am unable to free you from your public duties, but at least in private you shall have as much freedom as you wish, travel when it is possible—'

Though his voice was gentle his misunderstanding made me cry all the harder. I covered my face with my hands.

'You shall live as you please, and, within the obvious bounds of discretion, with whom you please. If there is someone you can love, though we may not be divorced, I promise you I shall not stand in your way—'

'No!' I could not bear this obvious reference to Aubyn. 'No, I want no one, nothing.'

He sighed, and I was aware of him close to me but carefully not touching me. 'Little Mouse, your doctors are concerned for your mental well-being. It shames me that I have brought you so much suffering, and I should like to find some means of making you happier. You say there is nothing you want – yet perhaps there is one thing that may cheer you a little. Shouldn't you care to see Freddy again?'

Freddy? I was overwhelmed by the now familiar sense of guilt. So obsessed was I with my own selfish concerns that even Freddy's letters had lost the power to hold me to my duty to him. 'But I . . . Perhaps he isn't well enough, won't forgive me for . . .'

'He is now quite well enough and is longing to see you.'

'And you'll permit me to go – you'll let me visit him at last? Then yes, oh yes, I should like to very much. Is he still at the monastery? May I go to him immediately? Oh, Maximilian, may I go to him tomorrow—?'

He laughed. 'Thank God, at least you are smiling again. Yes, Marie, he is still at Freischutz and yes, you may go to him as soon as you please – provided, of course, that your doctors agree to your travelling. And when you make your journey you may also, if you will, perform a favour for me.'

He rang the bell and a footman appeared with a small parcel. 'He has asked often for this. I feared it had been lost, stolen by my troops when they took over the Residenz, but it came to light the other day. Please,' – he gestured at the wrapping – 'open it if you care to.'

I pulled back the paper and saw a familiar wooden case, ornamented at the corners with chased silver and gilt. Unfastening its clasps, I drew aside the two halves of the lid to form the wings of the miniature triptych, worn panels of crimson velvet embroidered with seraphim on a background of stars, flanking the gilt and enamel cross which bore the image of the Corpus Christi and contained the sliver of wood from Calvary; Freddy's precious reliquary of the True Cross. I gazed down at the closed eyes of the dead Christ, at the place where the feet were pierced by a single square-headed gilt nail. The reliquary had been a present from Freddy's mother, Queen Amalia, on the occasion of his First Communion, and was said to date back to the sixteenth century; it must have been of inestimable value yet to me it was an object as everyday and familiar as Freddy's brushes or the water carafe on his night-table. How often had I seen him kneel and kiss the feet of the Christ where the nail transfixed them. I recalled with a sudden blurring of vision the last time I had watched him perform this quiet act of devotion, the night Vielfrass had come with his detachment of Hussars to take him away. I felt all at once a passionate longing for his innocence, his simplicity, his goodness, together with a sense of my own utter unworthiness.

'If you would restore the crucifix to Freddy I should be most grateful. And now, dear child, I understand how painful this intrusion of mine has been for you – I shall try to content myself in future with your doctors' reports and intrude on you no further.'

Recollecting myself, glancing up, I thought I again saw that odd sad look cloud his eyes. But perhaps I only saw what I wished to see, for even before I was fully conscious of it he had turned away to ring for the footman and was in a moment as cool and indifferent as his parting words had been.

The night before we set out on the journey to Freischutz I could not sleep. Though I tried to summon up all the joyous anticipation I must surely feel at seeing Freddy, I could not rid myself of Maximilian, or the bleak disappointment I had felt at our interview. I was certain now that I had imagined his look of regret. Oh, he had been moved by the child, but then he needed the child, it was the only element of my existence which retained any importance for him. As to the rest, he had been with me less than half an hour and had made it clear he would deign to pay me no further visits.

Yet how weak to permit myself this wretchedness. I knew what he was, and if I were in danger of forgetting it I had only to remind myself of his treatment of Freddy, the forged letter, the threats to Freddy's life, the endless period of my darling's imprisonment and the blank refusal, until now, to let me once see him. And why had Maximilian relented so suddenly after all this time, what was his motive? Surely not the straightforward need to restore Freddy's relic of the True Cross? He had never cared for Freddy, had trampled on him just as heartlessly as he had deceived me. Was not this merely some new device to manipulate us both for his own ends? Once again, I felt angry with myself, angry and ashamed that I had succumbed so foolishly to Maximilian's spurious brilliance when Freddy's goodness should have remained my guiding light.

I was angry too that I had failed to mention Suzannah's removal to Maximilian, that he had allowed me no opportunity to discuss the matter with him. Yet I knew in my heart how impossible such a discussion would be. If even Aubyn had resisted it, how much more Maximilian, who would protect Anton's interest at all costs? I supposed grimly that I should never be rid of Suzannah. Why, I should even be tormented by her presence during my visit to Freischutz, for the doctors had decreed, given the length of the journey, that it would be prudent to keep both my ladies in attendance.

The baby's kicking had aggravated my sleeplessness and, wrapping myself in a shawl and a heavy dressing-gown, I had left my bed and settled in a chair by the window where I could look out over the blighted vista of the West Gardens. It was a clear night, bright with moonlight reflected in the glimmering expanse of snow and the rimed crust of the frozen lake. Then I saw, or thought I saw, something move in the shadow of the orangery wall. It was gone in a moment, or perhaps it had only been a trick of the moonlight. But no, there was something, someone there, I noticed for the first time a single track of footprints on the path to the orangery coming from beyond my vision but from the unmistakeable direction of the West Door. Yet who could be out in the gardens at this time of the morning, when the cold was so bitter that simply to remove one's gloves was to risk frostbite? I felt suddenly afraid. No one would brave such conditions unless they had some sinister imperative for silence and darkness. Perhaps after all I had been mistaken. I stared fascinated at the shadow by the orangery. The snow glittered, no sound came through the clear air, everything was still.

Then suddenly a shadow detached itself from the darkness of the orangery wall, began to run, black against white, down the path, back to the West Door. It was heavily muffled, a black shape running, feet crunching softly in the snow, muffled, unrecognisable; only the heavy skirts, impeding the progress of those running feet, betrayed it as a woman. I held my breath, feeling myself beginning to shiver, I almost looked away. But then, in that instant, I saw another shadow, a man's this time, a man in what seemed to be a fur cap and service greatcoat, standing at the far end of the wall, closest to the orangery. He paused for a moment, silhouetted distinctly against the white of the snow, seeming to turn and look back towards the terrace. I drew breath sharply. For suddenly my fear was tangible, suddenly I was certain both from something in the stance of that figure and from the brief glimpse I had caught of the face, that the man beside the orangery wall was Anton von Tarn, and that the muffled woman could therefore only have been his sister, Suzannah.

III

The Father Abbot and the Guest Master, bowing low at the knee, had met our carriage in the courtyard, and now the heavy oak doors of the guest wing had creaked shut behind us and we were in a tiled hall with limed walls leading to a long, tiled, unadorned corridor. I was aware of a church smell, part wax, part incense and yet with another note to it too, a sour indefinable something which had greeted me before on countless visits to hospitals and orphanages and which now filled me with a strange apprehension, as if I should be called upon to perform some onerous duty and be found unequal. The Brother Porter was walking backwards before us, bowing. At the end of the corridor I glimpsed an oak door with the single word *Enclosure* inscribed above the lintel. We were shown into a small parlour to the right of the corridor and the Abbot left us, again bowing low.

The parlour was limed like the hall, without carpets, curtains or pictures, apart from an engraving of Our Lady and the Christ Child in a rough wooden frame. The chairs too were plain deal, straight-backed and hard as if any concession to comfort would only prolong a visitor's stay unsuitably, and the door, presumably for similar reasons, was of glass. I felt repelled by so much unbending cleanliness and denial. How Freddy, ill as he was and used to my homely chintzes and soft chairs, must have suffered in his months here. Of course in his letters he had accepted it with equanimity, had even shown enthusiasm for his incarceration – but was it not altogether typical of Freddy that he should make the best of whatever befell him? How I longed to embrace him, to show him all the warmth and tenderness he had lacked. And yet – and yet this spare little room with its scrubbed tiles and plain furniture reminded me suddenly of Maximilian's apartments in the Residenz, of the white-painted bedroom I had never been allowed to enter. I pushed the image of Maximilian away angrily. My apprehension obscurely increased.

Aware that I was preventing my ladies from being seated, I sank heavily onto one of the unwelcoming chairs. Ursula immediately reached for the Berlin work from her basket, rummaging for wool and beads. Suzannah, inevitably, sat staring dumbly at her gloves.

After some minutes the Abbot and the Guest Master returned, bowed once more and led me alone down the corridor to another glass door exactly like the first. I paused on the threshold, all of a sudden trembling; for there, at the far end of the room, was Freddy.

I could scarcely believe how greatly he had changed. There were roses in his round cheeks, his eyes seemed to shine, he was sturdier, almost strong-looking, even his spiky brown hair appeared somehow smoother and glossier. I had always imagined myself running to him, flinging my arms about him protectively, but now it was he who bounded towards me, arms outstretched, his boy's face split with a great, joyous, beaming smile.

'Oh Tilda, Tilda! How wonderful to see you at last. Oh, my dearest! Oh, may God be praised!'

I found myself instinctively holding back from his embrace, afraid that he would be hurt by the sight of me big with another man's child. But he paid no heed to my resistance, clasping me to him and looking into my face with unaffected delight.

'Oh Tilda, you are so lovely. I have prayed every day that God would protect you and keep you, and He has answered my prayers. Oh, you were born to be a mother, Tilda. It makes you lovelier than ever.'

I smiled through my embarrassment. 'And you, Freddy, you look so well – even in this place.'

'Even in this place, Tilda? Dearest, it is because of this place, as you call it, this miraculous Holy place, that I have a life again, a body that serves me, serves God, instead of my serving it. Do you know, I have not been naughty, not had a single fit for three whole months?'

I touched his cheek with my fingertips. 'Oh my love, my darling boy, I am so glad.'

'The brothers prayed for me, Tilda, that I might be released from my infirmity. And Our Heavenly Father answered, showed that the purpose in my suffering was at an end, so that through His mercy I might be granted another, higher purpose.'

'Then you may leave here at last? If Maximilian will also show some mercy, you may be free to live as you like?'

I thought suddenly of Maximilian's promise to let me lead my own life once the child was born, to let me travel, be with whom I pleased. I thought of England once again, of the happy existence I had imagined for Freddy and myself, peaceful country walks, soft English twilights, a little house somewhere with lawns and a limewalk and espaliered plum trees in a walled garden. Freddy was my peace, my happiness, and now that he was well . . . But I saw an expression of complete astonishment transform his face, saw him look at me almost reproachfully.

'Leave here? Dearest girl, has he not told you – ? Oh, my darling Tilda, one of my most pressing reasons for seeing you is that in four days' time I shall be admitted to this cloister as a postulant.'

I let my arms fall from his shoulders. I felt again the repulsion I had experienced in that first tiled parlour, image of this one, with its sour smell and its punishing chairs.

'Oh no, Freddy. No, please—'

'But my dearest, it has been my deepest wish for many months now. It has only rested on the question of whether I should ever be well enough—'

'And now that you are well, now that the monks here have nursed you back to health – you have no need to repay them, they have been your jailers as well as your nurses, you need not sacrifice any more of your life—'

'Dearest, I repay no one. It is simply God's wish.'

I stared at him. His round face was calm, seraphic. He touched my hand as if willing me gently to understand. I had suffered so much and now even Freddy was deserting me. I turned away.

'Oh my darling Tilda, you are so generous, so good. Yet you sometimes try so hard to close your mind to Our Heavenly Father, even though he is always there, watching over you. Don't you see? Oh, how can I make you understand? Dearest Tilda, come with me now, let us walk in the garden if you are well enough to bear the cold, and let me show you!'

Fresh snow had fallen during the night and my galoshes sank into it nearly up to the ankle. Though there was no wind and the sun was shining, the air nipped my nose and ears so that I drew the hood of my travelling cloak close around me, buried my hands deep in my muff. Freddy, however, seemed braced by the cold, strode a pace ahead of me in his overcoat and comforter chattering excitedly, his pale eyes glittering, the frost and his excitement combining to heighten his colour till his cheeks glowed apple-red.

'Freddy, my darling, where are we going?'

He stopped, turned back, grasped my arm. 'But we're here, Tilda. Don't you see? The miracle of God is all around us.'

I looked about me, confused, seeing only the great, obliterating blanket of snow which wrapped the garden in its stillness, eliding paths and lawns and flowerbeds into a

featureless wilderness. Snow clung in drifts to the arches of
the cloister, buried the roots of the gaunt birch trees, levelled
the grave mounds in the little cemetery near the high wall.
There was no sign of any human presence for, according to
Freddy, it was the hour for the brothers to study in their
cells or in the library; no footprints marred the pristine white-
ness, no sound came to break its dense hush. I shivered,
perceiving nothing miraculous in this eerie, inhuman silence.

'But don't you see, Tilda? Look upwards – look, where
the branches of that tree meet the sky.'

I raised my eyes and saw against the blue the fine lattice
of the birch branches rimed in every cleft, on every bough
to the tip of the slenderest twig with pure crystalline white,
fragile and delicate as guipure lace, incandescent where the
sun was here and there caught in the minute facets of each
perfect crystal.

'There, Tilda. There you see the miraculous perfection of
Our Heavenly Father. No mere man could create such
beauty. And when I stand in this garden I long so earnestly
to be at one with it – or, if as a humble sinner I cannot, then
to give myself to Him so that He will teach me, so that I may
come a little closer to such wonder, to the infinite mystery of
His divine presence.'

I stared at his shining eyes, his flushed cheeks, looked
away without speaking.

'Oh Tilda, please understand, I have not come to this point
easily. I have had my enemies, my temptations – my illness,
for one, and the selfish *accidie* it often brings me. And you,
Tilda – it has not been easy to give you up, my heart has
often been selfish there too. Sinner that I am, I doubt that I
shall ever be equal to loving God truly, unselfishly, but at
least in His infinite wisdom he will guide me. You, Tilda, I
could never love as you deserve, not as a man should love
a woman—'

'You have loved me, Freddy, better than anyone has ever
loved me.'

'But as a brother, as a friend. Not as a husband. My body
has always been a burden to myself and to others, I have
never understood physical passions well enough to overcome your – doubts. But Maximilian is understanding and

strong, he has been able to give you the happiness you
deserve.'

I whirled round upon him. 'Maximilian? My dear Freddy,
sometimes you take Christian charity too far. How can you
speak well of the man who forced you to abdicate, threw
you into prison, left you here to die?'

He gazed at me with utter astonishment. 'But I have
received nothing but kindness from Maximilian. Far from
leaving me to die, he has taken the utmost trouble to find
me specialists from Berlin and Vienna, and expert nurses
and the blessed peace and tranquillity that has done me so
much good here – in fact, had it not been for Maximilian I
should probably have died at Marmion, or Schwarzteufel or
in the escape plot I was told some poor misguided officers
hatched for me out of misplaced loyalty.'

I bit my lip.

'And as for being forced to abdicate, my dearest Tilda,
how could I not give up willingly what my infirmity made
me so ill-fitted for, what I had scarcely even, in truth,
possessed? I should have been blind had I not seen at once
that Maximilian, with his authority and his intelligence and
his understanding of the world, was a thousand times better
suited to the Kingship than I. He is strong enough to stand
up to the Schramms and the Vielfrasses, he can give our
people the freedom and justice they have been denied. He
is like you, Tilda, he knows his duty to Sylvania and he has
that touch you have, that precious gift of making the people
trust and love him. That is why, when I understood you
were adamant in your refusal to marry him, I wrote to you
absolving you from any obligation towards me.'

I stared at him aghast. 'You wrote? You wrote that
dreadful letter I received at Schwanensee?'

'I explained to you that I'd had to dictate it to my chaplain
at Schwarzteufel because I was so weak. But I knew I must
write, I knew you and your great sense of loyalty and –
forgive me, my darling – your obstinacy at times, and I
knew I must persuade you that in denying this marriage you
denied your own happiness. Oh, I prayed to Our Heavenly
Father for guidance every moment I had the strength. But I
knew in my heart that the marriage was His will. After all,
I had talked so much about you to Maximilian, about your

beauty and your goodness and your sense of duty, that he almost loved you before he ever saw you. I knew he would care for you and protect you as I had never been able to, and that you and he would be a partnership, working together for the good of our people, as you and I had never been. For you, for Sylvania, it seemed so much for the best.'

I continued to stare at him incredulously. So that was it. When Maximilian had forced me by threats to accept his proposal, it was Freddy – Freddy whom I had believed threatened – who had been his staunchest ally. When Maximilian had spoken of his knowledge of my dedication and sense of duty it was Freddy who had been his source. Freddy had given me up without a thought, without regret, as he had the throne and his freedom and all other despised 'worldly things'. I had felt angry and deserted when he told me he intended to enter the cloister. But this was nothing to the sense of betrayal I experienced now.

'I see,' I said. 'I was in the way of your new-found vocation. So you decided to dispose of me – as one might a worn rug or a pair of old gloves.'

'Oh Tilda, Tilda.' He grasped my hands inside the muff, gazing at me so earnestly that I was almost ashamed of my bitterness. 'Dearest Tilda, I have said it was not easy. Setting aside my duty to God, you are the one person in the world I love. I was so wretchedly lonely and miserable without you in those months at Schwartzteufel. But I knew if I saw you there was a danger that, out of foolish loyalty to me, you would change your mind about the marriage. And after you were married, I had to leave you free to learn to love Maximilian. But oh, my dearest, it has been hard – not to see your beautiful smile, not even to be able to write to you properly at first. I did not want to lose you, Tilda. But I knew if I really loved you I had no other course. And truly it has been for the best. I can see it in your face, Tilda, in the way you have come into your beauty, the way it shines out of you where it was hidden away shyly before. The people love you more than ever. And there is the baby – and oh, Tilda, he loves you so very much.'

I released my hands coldly. 'You need not comfort yourself with fictions, Freddy. Maximilian does not love me.'

It was his turn to stare at me. His round boy's face became

creased with dismay. 'But, my dearest Tilda, how could you believe such a thing? Since your marriage he has talked of you constantly – indeed, if it were not my greatest pleasure to talk of you too, I should say he finds it difficult to avoid mentioning you on the slightest pretext—'

'You have seen him then? He visits you here?'

'Of course he visits me. Apart from during your honeymoon and your tour of the North, he has come regularly. Indeed, with his experience of monastic life and the failure of his own vocation, he has been most generous in talking with me about my doubts, even when it must have been painful for him. Why, when I had finally come to my decision and the Father Abbot accepted me as a postulant, he broke his journey from the troop manoeuvres at Jedburg, postponed his return to you for two days, just to come and give thanks with me.'

I felt bewildered. But had not Maximilian delayed in order to meet Anton? Or was this true, and could Maximilian's other absences have a similarly innocent explanation?

'Oh Tilda, you must see how he loves you. And you must love him too. You should not cling, however well-meaningly, to your old loyalties to me – and you should not feel that I have forgotten you, discarded you, as you said. You will always be in my prayers. And this place is not the prison you seem to imagine. Even when I am professed you will be able to visit me – I hope and pray that you will and that I may see the baby when he is born. Oh Tilda, Tilda, don't run away from me so coldly. Is there something wrong between you and Maximilian? Have you quarrelled?'

I tried to ignore the distress in his eyes, the way his face, always so patent of its emotions, seemed to crumple like a child's. 'You must understand,' I said icily, 'that I cannot ever love Maximilian – even to ease your conscience. I cannot now, I cannot ever.'

'Then there is something wrong. I wondered, when he was here last week – he seemed suddenly so . . . Oh, but Tilda, Maximilian is a good man, and he badly needs you.'

I laughed bitterly.

He seized my hands again beneath the muff. 'My dearest, please – you must know as well as I that there is something deeply troubling him. In spite of his reticence, I have often felt it – as you must have. He refuses the sacrament, denies himself the Grace of God, in our conversations about Mont Rémy I have always sensed an unspoken sorrow. If he has not altogether lost his faith, Tilda, he is exiled from it. And without God's help his earthly duties must be an unimaginable burden. Oh my darling you must love him, help him. His nature is so instinctively inclined towards what is just and good.'

He had forced me to meet his eyes and I could not avoid being touched by the look of pleading in them, as if he had taken Maximilian's supposed sorrow upon himself and bore in proxy every twinge of it. I wanted to scream at the cruel irony. But, if it had been impossible to admit the truth to Aubyn, it was unthinkable to tell Freddy. Poor, simple, unworldly Freddy, who saw the workings of God in everything, who would always believe good of his fellow man despite all evidence to the contrary – how could I find the words that might begin to explain to someone of his innocence the full extent of Maximilian's depravity? And yet, looking into those guileless eyes, intent now with entreaty, I wished so much for a spell to be laid upon me, some magic suspension of reality, so that I might succumb to all his dreams of goodness and happiness, see Maximilian as he saw him. Was he not so certain, had he not confounded so many of my beliefs? Maximilian had not threatened him, had not ill-treated him, had not been to the Saxe-Limbecks' hunting box with Anton von Tarn. But the other remained, the monstrous indecency set out in the letter. No entreaty of Freddy's, no excruciated twist of that beloved face could change it. I stared at him, confused, still wanting to cry out, still hardening my voice to scream that I could never, never love Maximilian. My mouth opened, but no words came: instead I was suddenly shaken with angry sobbing.

It was strange, when I had so often held and comforted him, to feel Freddy's arm supporting me while his other hand held my face to his chest. It was strange walking back towards the monastery building with the weight of my body buttressed against his and my head on his shoulder. I was shivering and the austere parlour with its bare walls and lack of a fire seemed scarcely warmer than the garden. He was unstintingly kind, fussing about the baby, scolding himself for having been thoughtless, drawing my furs closer around me. We sat without speaking, my hand in his, and I could tell after some moments from the intensity of his expression and the furrows in his brow that, with the silent concentration of his entire being, he was praying for me. I tried to sustain my anger, tried to feel affronted by this unsolicited gift of prayer, but it was impossible to perceive the sincerity in his face and not be mollified by it. And, in some mysterious way, after a while I did begin to feel more tranquil, as if without my knowing it we had come obscurely to a reconciliation.

Then I remembered the reliquary.

There being no bells to ring, I was obliged to go myself into the other parlour to fetch it. Suzannah and Ursula sat as before, Suzannah in doltish silence, Ursi, who had borrowed her workbasket, sorting skeins of green wool. Though they both immediately rose it was Suzannah who came forward with the precious parcel, I remember that well – had cause vividly to remember it afterwards a thousand times.

The look on Freddy's face once he had broken the sealing wax and undone the wrapping was one of ecstasy. Tears sprang to his eyes. 'Oh, my darling, that it should be found at last, restored to me after all this time!'

'You may thank Maximilian,' I said quietly.

'I cannot keep it, of course, for I shall be allowed only a few personal possessions and, after my final vows, none. But *we* shall have it with us – all my brothers in Christ. It shall be part of our daily communion with Our Heavenly Father, our offering to him.' He began to pray again, moving his lips silently. Then he bent forward and kissed the cross as he always did, where the nail pierced the feet.

There was an instant of silence into which fell – or did I only imagine it afterwards? – a scarcely perceptible sound, a dull click like the single tick of a clock. Then he let out a cry, half surprised, half anguished, and the wooden box clattered to the floor. I saw his face raised towards me, saw blood pouring from his lower lip. His mouth was suddenly spumed with a great gush of saliva, a creaking, grinding sound came from his throat as if, though he tried to speak, the muscles were frozen. His eyes rolled, he doubled up retching. Then his arms began to flail, tearing at his chest as if he were suffocating.

My shock left me. I knew what to do, I had done it countless times. I must get him to the floor, support his head, force some object into his mouth to stop him choking. I tore off my cape for a pillow, found a handkerchief from my reticule; but though I flung myself upon him he bucked against me, retching, struggling, making that strange whining sound. A gush of bile mingled suddenly with the froth of saliva. He fell, I fell on top of him, fighting to hold him down. I got my hands to his mouth, tore at his lips, but his teeth were locked fast, the tip of his tongue almost severed by them. I screamed. Ursi and Suzannah and the Brother Porter came running. I was aware of their clamour as I lay across Freddy, tossing and pitching with the movements of his body. I knew he could not hear me but I pleaded with him, implored him to let me help him. I had seen him so often in the grips of strong convulsions, but this was different; I had never experienced such impenetrable locking of the jaws, I had never seen his face growing blue like this as if the air were being forced from his body. And now the rhythm of his breathing changed to a hoarse gasping followed by a long, tearing sigh, and there was a smell, a strange smell which, in all my intimacy with Freddy's bodily secretions, I did not recognise.

Hands pulled at my arms and shoulders, trying to tear me off him. I fought savagely against this intervention, still pleading with Freddy, clinging to him with all my strength. Despite my tenacity they prised me away. And then as I writhed and sobbed, I saw the black figures of the monks dragging Freddy's body onto a stretcher, two of them lying across him to hold him down, and I heard Ursi's voice begging me to calm myself and I was forced to watch helplessly as they lifted him up, still pinioned, and bore him away.

Bewildered, I allowed Ursi and Suzannah to wipe the blood from my hands. Then they half carried me upstairs to the guest-room where the monks had laid him. A doctor, Ursi assured me, had been sent for and must be by this time on his way. Meanwhile one of the brothers struggled to wash

the vomit and blood from Freddy's face as two others lashed
him to the iron bedstead. They had not covered him, for the
convulsions rendered this impossible, and he thrashed from
side to side upon the white coverlet, his face greyish-blue,
his eyes glassy and dilated, his mouth, despite the efforts of
the monks, still frothing with bloody foam. Around his bed
in a circle, intoning psalms, stood the rest of the brotherhood, black cowls over their black habits and scapulars,
while a server lit a candle on a small table and the Father
Abbot set out the Holy Oil. Freddy had received Extreme
Unction before, it was only a sensible precaution, nothing
more. Yet those calm voices chanting the Miserere made
me shudder. In the torchbearer's flickering light, the circle
of pointed hoods seemed to shadow the walls with
predatory menace, like the Hounds of Hell.

I screwed my eyes tight and tried to pray. But I could not
shut out the sound from the bed, that agonised gasping as
if each time the effort tore vital tissues asunder, followed by
the wrenching sigh. The noise of it seemed louder than the
chanting, louder than any sound I had ever heard. The
intervals between gasp and sigh seemed each time more
protracted, so that I strained forward, willing the next breath
out of him, holding my own breath till it came.

The Father Abbot had begun upon the prayers preceding
the anointing. Half way through the Indulgentiam, his
voice changed, took on a quiet urgency. I opened my eyes
and saw Freddy's body arched and rigid above the bed.
Then the convulsions ceased, dark bile spurted through
his clenched teeth, a stain began to spread between his
legs. The Father Abbot leant forward hastily and anointed his forehead. Freddy gave one infinitely protracted sigh.
I waited for the gasp to follow it, heard the Abbot cut
off the ritual with a last amen, heard the ensuing silence
with disbelief.

IV

The doctor had arrived and would give me a sedative, Ursi
said, but I would not see him, nor would I be persuaded to
leave the room so that the brothers could begin the laying-

out. I sat, frozen with disbelief, staring at the bed. Freddy's eyes had rolled upwards so that only the whites were visible, his mouth was fixed in a grisly rictus. Though the Father Abbot had talked of the glories of Paradise and the triumph of death, he looked as if he had stared upon some unimaginable horror. His forehead and cheeks were livid with bruises and his lower lip was grotesquely swollen and caked with blood. Yet even now, as I gazed upon this disfigured mask and heard the tolling of the passing bell, I still expected the body on the bed to give some sign of life, to rise up, speak to me, confound the message of that remorseless tolling. He had been so well, so full of hope and energy, better in health and spirit than I had ever seen him. And he had survived worse fits, had been unconscious for hours and still come through at the end of it. My beloved Freddy, the new strong Freddy with the shining eyes and pink cheeks who had comforted me in the garden, could not be dead, could not have been snuffed out so brutally.

There grew out of my disbelief a profound and puzzling sense of unease. It was all wrong; I had seen the effects of his epilepsy too often not to feel that something this time had been strange, different. His warning aura, for instance, the tingling in his left arm that always gave me a minute or two to settle him; this time there had been no aura – from the moment he had cried out to the onset of the fit had been no longer than ten or twelve seconds. Then there had been the vomiting, successive and violent, even before the start of his convulsions; Freddy never vomited during a fit, only at the end, just as he recovered consciousness. The impenetrable fastness of the jaws, the bluish tinge to his skin, the rasping sound in his throat as if the muscles had been paralysed – they were all new and unexpected terrors. He had kissed the feet of the cross, then he had cried out and turned to me, his lip pouring blood as if he had bitten it – and then, in the space of three-quarters of an hour, convulsed, vomiting, breathing as if his chest were slowly being crushed in a vice, he had died.

With an effort I roused myself and went over to the bed. Fighting a sudden revulsion for the bared teeth and blotched skin, I bent to kiss him; but my throat constricted, I had to turn my head aside hurriedly. It was the smell again, not the smell of vomit or the evacuations occasioned by the violent conclusion of his spasms, but another sharper, over-riding odour emanating from his twisted lips, the faint but pervasive scent of bitter almonds.

I took a deep breath and forced myself to look again. There had been a great deal of blood from the injuries to his tongue and lip, but its flow had ceased with death and it had begun to clot. I stared at the wound in the lower lip, which seemed to penetrate the tissue completely as if, like his tongue, he had bitten through it. Taking the edge of the coverlet in my fingers, I gingerly wiped away some of the blood. The puncture thus revealed was smaller than I had expected and very deep, as though it might even carry through into the gum; but that was not what transfixed me. A tear made by teeth would surely be oblong, jagged: this mark was precise and clean and round.

I started, aware of someone else in the room. Ursula stood at my shoulder, waiting for the sign to speak.

'Where is the crucifix?' I said sharply. 'What have they done with it?'

'Dear Majesty, the doctor is waiting. Forgive me, but Your Majesty must rest, must think of the baby—'

'I want the crucifix, Freddy's relic of the True Cross. Where is it?'

'Your Majesty, I beg you—'

'I want it, Ursi! Fetch it for me.'

Clearly believing it was wiser to humour me, she left the room, returning a few minutes later with the wooden case. I snatched it from her. Both case and crucifix had sustained some damage as they had crashed to the floor. The left wing of the triptych hung loose upon one hinge, the enamel of the Saviour's halo was cracked, two of the bloodstones set at each point of the cross were badly chipped; but it was when I looked at the feet that my fingers began to tremble. Where the single square-headed nail had been there was now a small hole, two or three millimetres in diameter, piercing the gilt and appearing to penetrate the wood beneath.

I stared for a moment at the puncture in Freddy's lip. Then I swung round upon Ursi. 'Someone has tampered with the image of Our Saviour. Someone has removed the nail from His feet.'

'Your Majesty can see how His poor Majesty damaged the blessed relic himself when he fell – though God will surely pardon him. If a nail is missing it must have broken off then.'

I looked again at the nail's empty socket. I thought I could discern two or three fine scratches in the surrounding gilt, bright and clean as though they had been made recently. The hole in the wood, too, was the colour of sawdust, again suggesting it had been freshly bored.

'The nail did not break,' I said grimly, 'any more than His Majesty died of epilepsy.'

Ursi's frown deepened. 'You have suffered a terrible loss, Ma'am, enough to make anyone overwrought. But at all costs we must think of the poor baby. Let me bring the doctor to you now so that he can give you something to make you sleep. Then you won't need to worry yourself about one little nail—'

'One little nail? If it has broken or fallen out, it will still be downstairs in the parlour, will it not?'

'Ma'am, I implore you, the risk in your condition—'

'Then if it is downstairs, I should like it found. You will instruct the brothers to go down on their hands and knees and not rest until they have found it. And while they are searching you will be so good as to summon the Father Abbot to my presence.'

They had tricked me. I had allowed myself to be led to another room, the better to conduct my interview with the Abbot, and while I waited for him I had been persuaded by Ursula to stretch myself out on the bed and to try a cup of herb tea, which she assured me she had prepared herself. But I should have heeded my suspicions; the tea was the doctor's handiwork, within a few minutes my limbs felt leaden and my eyes would not focus. I battled against the drowsiness for now, of all times, I needed my mind clear. Maximilian had brought me the reliquary to take to Freddy and I had given it into Ursi's safekeeping – or was it Suzannah's? But it had been Suzannah who had taken care of the parcel and had placed it in my hands in the parlour,

Suzannah who had rushed in with Ursi when Freddy had been seized with convulsions, Suzannah who could so easily have used the confusion to remove from the feet of the Christ whatever device had made the tiny click.

But had I really heard a click? The nail had been in its place when Maximilian had given me the reliquary, what evidence had I, apart from surmise, that Suzannah or anyone had tampered with it? And what motive could Suzannah have for murdering Freddy?

My eyelids dropped. Yet out of the darkness images still loomed: Freddy's face, covered in blood; the ghostly black circle round his bed, Hounds of Hell willing his destruction; and another ghostly figure by the orangery at the Summer Palace, silhouetted against the snow, stealing away from a secret assignation. The images blurred, shifting, distorting, until I felt I would smother in their teeming darkness, rose up shrieking from my pillow; and found myself caught in someone's arms, with someone's lips pressed to my hair.

I opened my eyes and saw the confusion of my nightmare coalesce into – Maximilian.

'My dear little Mouse, I set out as soon as I received the Father Abbot's telegram. I could not leave you to suffer this alone.'

There were dark marks under his eyes and he wore a gaunt look as if he had not slept. From the sharp light filtering through the mullions of my cell I saw that while I had lain in my drugged stupor night must have fallen and been succeeded by another day.

'Dearest child, I wish I had some means to comfort you, lessen the shock. Dear God, I too could scarcely believe – I knew he could not be cured completely, yet all the same he seemed so much stronger, there seemed so much reason to hope.'

My face was still held gently between his hands. A good man, Freddy had said, whose nature tended instinctively to what was right and just. But Freddy, in his own goodness, could be so easily deceived. My bewilderment vanished, the shadows of the nightmare dissolved back into a clear continuation of my thoughts the day before. Suzannah herself had no motive, yes, that was true, but Anton von Tarn was her brother, Anton von Tarn had met her secretly the night before our journey to Freischutz, Anton was the creature of the man Suzannah loved, whose instrument she would willingly become; and that man, too, was the only person who had a motive for killing Freddy, the clear motive that his power and position could never be secure as long as the deposed King of Sylvania remained alive.

I hurled myself away from Maximilian, face down upon the pillow. 'Don't touch me, don't come near me! Get out of my sight!'

I felt his hand still on the nape of my neck. 'Little Mouse, I know his death was ugly and painful. But please – he is at rest now and you must try to calm yourself—'

'Oh yes, Maximilian, you know!' I reared bolt upright, facing him squarely. 'You know precisely how Freddy died and just how much I watched him suffer. You know every last hideous detail – because it all occurred exactly as you planned it!'

Apologising to the Father Abbot for receiving him lying down, I gestured at my one hard little chair to indicate that he might be seated. He was a man of perhaps any age from forty to sixty, with a raw-boned, wasted look; and yet, despite his haggard appearance, I observed on closer inspection that his face was unlined, the colour and texture of wax, as if the hollows beneath his cheekbones and the spare contours of his jaw were merely the refinements of fasting and meditation, a deliberate economy of flesh that left only what was strictly necessary for obedience. Ignoring my instruction to sit, he remained at the foot of my bed with his hands folded inside his sleeves and his eyes slightly lowered.

'I understand it is intended that King Friedrich's funeral should take place here tomorrow?'

'Although His Majesty was called to his Almighty Father before he was able to test his vocation, he often expressed the wish to be buried here, Ma'am, and the Cardinal Archbishop has granted a special dispensation for him to be interred in our garden, close to our little cemetery.'

'I forbid this funeral. I forbid it absolutely until a proper medical examination has been carried out.'

Although the Abbot raised his eyes, there was no

expression of surprise or alarm in them, no obvious disturbance of his composure. 'Forgive me, Your Majesty, but the doctor has already examined His Majesty's body. I am afraid, despite his suffering, there was little unexpected in the fit that killed him.'

'King Friedrich did not die of a fit. I intend to prove – a proper examination will prove – that he was murdered.'

Again there was no perceptible change in the creaseless face. 'God's will seems on occasion harsh. But we must learn to submit to it, Ma'am, and to hold fast to our faith in His infinite mercy.'

Suddenly I feared and distrusted that quiet voice, that inhuman composure which reminded me so inescapably of Maximilian. 'Pray don't delude yourself, Father. This was not God's work but the work of man. King Friedrich was murdered. My husband murdered him!'

'You must forgive me, Ma'am, but I—'

'But you know King Maximilian to be good, fair, honourable? Oh Father, beneath that plausible exterior, my husband is capable of more evil, more hideous refinements of sin than you, sheltered here in your cloister, could ever begin to comprehend.'

'We are all sinners, Your Majesty. It is true that His Majesty broke our Rule in France, but His Holiness himself has pardoned him and absolved him from his vows. And what was wanting in his obedience then, he endeavours to expiate by his devotion to duty now. He has been unstinting in his care for his cousin since King Friedrich has been on retreat here, most generous in his benefactions to our community—'

'I see. So you are in his pay, frightened of offending him?'

A certain hardness entered for the first time into the Abbot's voice. 'I fear no one, Your Majesty, but God.'

'Then you will help me, Father, help me find justice?'

The hardness melted into a look of grave pity. 'We shall all try to help you, Ma'am, by keeping you ceaselessly in our prayers. As we have offered intercessions for the soul of our dear Brother in Christ, Friedrich, so we shall pray that the Almighty Father will see fit, in his infinite wisdom, to lift the burden of your suffering and restore you to health and tranquillity of spirit.'

*

I had never seen Aubyn angry before. When he had entered
my cell his brow had been furrowed with concern; but now
his face was scarlet beneath his freckles, his jaw jutted with
the effort of control, he had drawn himself up so ramrod-
stiff that I was forcibly aware of the difference in our ages
and of his Field Marshal's epaulettes.

'Dashit, Marie, I won't have it, won't listen to another
word of this cock-and-bull story! For pity's sake – I know
you've had the devil of a time, that you loved the poor fellow
– but if you expect me to believe this preposterous rot about
booby-trapped crucifixes and poisoned needles—'

'A spike on a spring fitted into the feet where the nail
should be, looking enough like the original nail for Freddy
not to notice when he kissed it and triggered off the mechanism. Freddy always kissed Our Lord's feet in that
particular spot, it could be relied upon to work. And after-
ward his convulsions would draw attention away from
anyone covertly removing the spring – perhaps it was even
part of the plan to replace the nail but for some reason it
wasn't possible. Oh God, Aubyn, you must believe me. You
can see the wound in his lip.'

'The poor chap bit himself when the seizure took him.'

'It wasn't a seizure, it was—'

'Yes, I know, I heard you perfectly well. It was cold-
blooded murder, plotted by poor old Max to secure his
throne and carried out by person or persons unknown.'

'Suzannah von Tarn is scarcely unknown.'

'Now hold hard, Marie—'

'She had ample opportunity. She's in love with Maximilian
and she hates me. And the night before we left the Summer
Palace she—'

'Dashit, Marie, I won't listen! She's Uncle Leo's favourite
daughter, my cousin, yours too by marriage. She's devoted
both to Maximilian and to you and anything else is simply
wicked tittle-tattle. She's a dear, honest, good-natured girl,
unlike that puppy of a brother of hers—'

'But Aubyn, that's what I'm endeavouring to explain, that
she's under the influence—'

His hand thundered upon the iron bedstead so that the
whole structure vibrated. 'I tell you, Marie, I won't hear any
more! If that's your estimation of poor Suzannah then yes,

you are right, she should leave your household immediately. And as for Max – God, I was aware of the strain between you, but not that things had come to this pass. Dammit, I was with him when he saw the body. He has a proper command of his feelings like any grown man. But – well, he was obviously thunderstruck. The idea that he'd callously do away with the poor chap, his own flesh and blood – it's not just preposterous, it's downright offensive and I won't have you repeat it to anyone outside this room.'

'I have already told the Father Abbot.'

'Well, at least he can be counted on to button up. My dear girl, have you no idea, no inkling of the damage these accusations could do to Max if they became public knowledge?'

'Because people would begin to see Maximilian as he truly is?'

'No, dammit! Because they're not true, because Max is incapable of any part of it.'

'I think I know him better, perhaps, than you.'

'I know him as a friend, as a man I've fought alongside, as a damned fine King. I know he's decent and honourable, as upright a chap as you could hope to find.'

I smiled bitterly. 'You're a hypocrite, Aubyn. If you truly cared about decency and honour you would listen to me. But no, like everyone else you'll protect Maximilian because you know your position and power depend on it. Anyway, you need not be concerned about the Father Abbot. He won't bring your house down. Maximilian has been sufficiently prodigal with his donations to guarantee his silence.'

He appeared once again to be about to savage the bedframe but his hand paused in mid-air, was lowered slowly as he looked at me instead. He continued to look at me for what seemed a long while, till his freckles were once again detectable above the fading scarlet, and his fierce brows had contracted to a frown.

'My dear Marie, you are a beautiful, intelligent woman. I have admired you, respected you, always, as you know, been fond of you. But if there is any poison to be found in this place, it is only the poison spread by your absurd fantasy. Dear God, I know you have suffered, I make allowances for that – but you must take a grip on yourself, otherwise you will damage Max, damage your child, end up, as your ladies fear, dead of brain fever or in an asylum.'

With all their talk of illness, they could not stop me attending the Requiem Mass the next day, or following my beloved Freddy's coffin to its last resting place. I remember that I felt very calm, though I was obliged to watch Maximilian's stony counterfeit of grief and though I had glimpsed, as the procession formed, those two corresponding faces, one plain, one beautiful, Suzannah and Anton von Tarn, not speaking, not appearing even to see each other, yet bound together by their complicity, two sides of the same false coin. Yes, I was calm enough, concentrating my being upon the coffin and the simple black cloth that covered it, unadorned by any trappings of worldly rank, as if Freddy had indeed died the humble Benedictine he had wished.

It was only when they thrust into my hands the silver bowl of earth to cast upon the lid that I knew I could no longer bear it. I threw myself forward into the mouth of the grave but Maximilian was too quick for me, catching me up in his arms, holding me so tightly that though my feet slid on the frozen earth I was hauled clear. I grappled with him, tried to bite his hand, screamed from the depth of my lungs: 'Murderer!' Then someone else, Aubyn perhaps, took my weight from him, lifted me up, I do not remember distinctly; but it must have been Aubyn for when I came slowly back to consciousness he was sitting beside my bed, his hand in mine, his angry look replaced by an expression of great sadness.

My eyelids were so heavy that I could scarcely lift them and the closed shutters made the light dim, so it was some while before I was aware of the other figure, motionless at the foot of the bed. I heard Aubyn whisper: 'It's all right, my dear fellow. I think she's beginning to come round.' The dark head bowed for an instant, then the figure moved silently, seemed on the point of bending over my pillow, hesitated, placed his hand on Aubyn's shoulder.

'Stay with her as long as you can. Look after her for me, as I know you will – and as I, God help me, may not.'

CHAPTER TEN

Anton von Tarn

I

Though the mountain air was sharp with the first autumn snows, the sun, as my four-in-hand had crossed the Austrian border and begun its lumbering ascent of the pass, had dazzled. But now, in this paved chamber with its mildewed rush matting and inevitable tawdry Virgin and Child, there was no sun; only the rankness of women shut away with other women to wrinkle and decay together. I felt suddenly exultant in my healthy flesh, almost vented my disdain in laughter. But then I remembered my errand still hung in the balance. Crossing myself with water from the stoup, I assumed an appropriately devout expression.

The ancient eye had surveyed me warily from its loophole as I had explained my need: a simple desire to correct an injustice, right old wrongs, a secular matter, yes, but in its purpose imbued with Godly intent. Even when the shutter had been finally drawn aside to reveal the veiled face I had stood for a while in doubt as to whether the documents I carried, impressively endorsed with my father's name and seal, would procure the required dispensation. But now, having submitted the photograph to be passed through ahead of me in the revolving cupboard usually reserved for relatives' gifts, I waited expectantly before the curtain in the visitors' parlour.

I seemed to be kept waiting an unconscionable time. Then at last I heard a scraping behind the curtain, the shutter in the iron grille being drawn back. There was a shuffling followed by muttered words of prayer. I composed my face carefully.

'Praise be to Jesus our Lord.'

'Now and forever more, amen.'

It was a quavering voice, muffled by the heavy curtain. I

addressed it with the eloquent speech of gratitude I had prepared, then, receiving no response, asked: 'You are apprised of the nature of my errand, Mother Abbess?'

Again silence.

Inwardly cursing the curtain, I went on hurriedly: 'The year I am enjoined to enquire about on behalf of His Royal Highness Prince Leopold is 1861. In May of that year Her Royal Highness the Princess Helena, His Royal Highness's cousin, entered into retreat in this convent, accompanied by her lady-in-waiting, Baroness von Windersdorf. In June, the Baroness, who had been seven months a widow, was confined. The confinement proved no better starred than the marriage for, although on 3rd June the Baroness was delivered of a son, two days later the child was called to join his father. I must ask you if your records confirm these facts?'

Another silence. Then quietly the voice behind the curtain said: 'No, my son.'

My pulse was suddenly racing. 'Permit me, Reverend Mother – in what way do your records differ?'

'No child was born within these walls on the date you mention.'

It was scarcely the answer I had been expecting. I rocked with it. For two pins I would have torn down that wretched curtain. 'Then the Baroness was not confined?'

'Baroness von Windersdorf was confined a fortnight later, on June the seventeenth.'

So they had even lied about the date. Was not this proof – the proof positive I had hardly dared hope for – that my theory was founded on more than idle speculation? I composed myself for my next and all-important question.

'And on what date, then, did the child die? Was it the nineteenth?'

I dared not breathe.

'We have no record of a death, my son.'

I could have shouted and danced in jubilation. Now there was only one further fact that remained to be established.

'Reverend Mother, you have very graciously consented to examine a photograph with which His Royal Highness has entrusted me. It was taken only a year after the Princess and her lady-in-waiting were on retreat here. Permit me to ask if you are able to identify Baroness von Windersdorf from this picture?'

There was a long pause. Then, very slowly, the purple curtain was drawn back and through the spiked mesh of the grille a tiny head was visible, hunched in its shoulders like a tortoise in its shell. Behind the thick veil I sensed reptilian eyes surveying me critically, so that I was again conscious of a certain over-eagerness in my manner which I should do well to restrain.

I lowered my eyelids piously. 'The Mother Abbess is most forebearing. His Royal Highness has empowered me to make some tangible recognition of his gratitude should my mission prove successful.'

The photograph was raised to the grille so that its face was visible to me. Then a scaly finger came up and, hovering for an instant between the two crinolined figures, settled decisively on one.

ALBRECHT LOUIS VIKTOR VON WINDERSDORF
3rd – 5th June, 1861.
Though his span was but a short one,
his loving mother remembers him always
in her prayers.

Not precisely Winders' style – one would have expected something altogether more florid, with at least a mention of dear, deceased Albrecht senior and some effusion about their both being joined together in the Almighty's bosom. But then one would also have assumed the last male of the Windersdorf line to have merited the family mausoleum at Meldingen, not this paltry grave without even a coronet or a crest in the draughty little cemetery behind the chapel at Schwanensee. Altogether, poor Albrecht Louis Vicktor had received small honours, despite his having accomplished the quite remarkable feat of dying before he was born.

II

So the Little Treaty had departed in high dudgeon to the Summer Palace and now here was the long-awaited summons from Max. I must, however, be sure to tread carefully. I knew old Max quite well enough to anticipate that he would require an explanation of how Pythias's eulogy to Damon had found its way into the Little Treaty's workbasket, and that he would probably make some ritual show of anger before he brought himself to acknowledge the felicity of his release.

Dear old Max. How superlatively he has learnt to put on that regal frost of his. Having come not twenty minutes before from the investiture ceremonies of the Order of St Othmar he still wore full dress with the star of the order and his other decorations, which served magnificently to enhance the effect. I was almost moved to smile at the way he had unconsciously positioned himself beneath the portrait of Uncle Sigismund which hangs in his study, so that one was yet again forcibly reminded of the visible proof of his lineage. Poor Max. If he knew what irony his play-acting provoked in me now . . .

Nevertheless the set of his jaw confirmed my need for caution. He did not offer me any greeting nor even indicate that I might speak but merely picked up the letter from his desk, handing it to me in silence. I read it slowly, taking care that my face should register the requisite surprise and shock.

'Well?' he said at last, in a voice which would have made a glacier seem warming. 'What explanation can you offer for the existence of this document?'

'I – I don't understand.' The tremor that caused the paper to shake in my hand was not entirely due to my thespian abilities, but I knew what I must do, had even taken the precaution of rehearsing my performance before the glass. First, feign astonishment that the letter had found its way into his possession; next establish that it had been intended for no one's eyes but mine, had been written indeed as the only means by which I could relieve the suffering he had caused me; and finally, pose the question: if I had not sent it, who . . . ?

Vielfrass! That I should have, by my foolishness, exposed him to Vielfrass's spies! God in Heaven, I would rather die, rather have my heart torn out than put him in such danger,

I who loved him, served him, would give my right arm for
him . . . !

I was able to continue in this vein for quite some time. I
should have preferred in the latter stages to have flung
myself into the nearest chair and plunged my head in my
hands, thus both enhancing the dramatic effect and avoiding
his scrutiny. Deprived of this stratagem, however, by his
stony refusal to grant me permission to sit, I managed
instead to squeeze out a few tears, which I hoped gave me
a suitably pathetic appearance.

Nevertheless as, finally exhausted of breath, I hung my
head abjectly, I could tell he was still unmoved. True, he
had not admitted how he had come by the letter and in this
there was comfort, for it meant, despite his anger, that he
entertained some element of doubt. But if I were to bring
him over completely I must do more; I must, as always,
work upon his conscience.

'Forgive me!' I said in muffled tones. 'Forgive my piping
the eye like some snivelling schoolboy. But I have not your
self-discipline, Max, I feel pain so deeply. Oh, if I had not
been in despair, not been so crushed by my loneliness—'

'Don't, Anton, begin again. I want the truth, not an
avalanche of words.'

'Words, yes, words will be my undoing. But at least this
abominable letter is from my pen, in my hand. If Vielfrass
decides to use it against us it condemns me utterly. You,
mercifully, may plead ignorance, may put the whole business down to my moral deficiency. I shall take the blame for
everything. But I embrace the sacrifice gladly, Max, if I make
it to spare you—'

'I do not require sacrifices, merely the truth.'

'As long as you are safe, Vielfrass may do with me as
he pleases – if only, oh God, if only he does not tell the
Paterfamilias! And yet, as I say, what more do I deserve,
what else matters so long as you are protected from
scandal—?'

'Anton, I give you warning—!'

'But supposing he should tell my father – the power of
your rank protects you, Max, whereas I have nothing, no
prospect but ruin, and even that would be preferable to the
Paterfamilias's wrath. Oh, forgive me, I do not regret our

love, I do not regret that in my innocence I allowed you to seduce me or that for what we both did I must now take the sole blame. But please, oh please, Max, don't let Vielfrass tell my father!'

I stood there, allowing my tears to fall copiously now upon the crumpled sheet of paper. Though he maintained his icy reserve I thought I could detect a shift in him, as though he were calculating his suspicions against the pitiable spectacle I presented, perhaps even regretting the humiliation he had forced me to endure.

'I shall ask you Anton, one last time. Did you send this letter to me – or to anyone?'

'Oh, Christ in Heaven, do you think so little of me?'

'Do I have your word?'

'Yes, I swear it.'

'And it is the truth?'

'On my honour, Max. On my honour, before God!'

He paused, surveying me for a moment. 'Very well. I suppose it is possible I have misjudged you.'

'Then you will help me? You will use your power to protect me against Vielfrass?'

'My dear Anton, I am no more immune than you to the consequences of your damnable stupidity. But yes, if you have told me the truth I am bound by my responsibility towards you.'

I smiled through my tears, began upon a lavish speech of thanks, but he cut me short, commanding me to put the letter on the fire, and when I straightened up from the stove I saw that he had returned to his desk as if he considered our interview concluded.

I stared at him incredulously. 'And is that all I may expect?'

He glanced up, eyebrows raised. It was as though I were one of his adjutants or some other person of no significance. I knew I stood in danger of undoing all I had achieved, but I was seized by a sudden incontinent fury.

'The letter is burnt, Max. But every word of it still stands. I haven't ceased to love you or to suffer daily from your cruelty. You can't turn off love like water from a tap. If it requires two to begin a love affair, then two must end it, and I have not ended it. It will not, cannot end, until I choose that it should—'

'My dear Anton, don't be preposterous.'

'No, Max, it is you who are preposterous! You have done your duty, got the Little Treaty with child, she has even been considerate enough to retire into purdah. There can be no possible reason to continue this accursed abstinence.'

He sighed. 'If you are unhappy – and I accept that you are – you must consider whether some of that unhappiness is not of your own making. And now I have work to attend to, and I believe we have in any case said all we may usefully say to each other.'

I stared at him for a moment. Then I laughed. 'Oh, my dear old Max! So you still cling hypocritically to your vow? It rings a little hollow, don't you think – since it is already broken!'

I watched with amusement his expression change. I should not forget that first night of the honeymoon trip to the Turkish Hunting Lodge, nor the violence with which he had at last given way to his need, as if he had sought the extinction of both of us. It was what had nurtured my hope all these months, what had made me so certain he would eventually be true to his nature.

'I am not proud of it,' he said quietly. 'If ever I have been guilty of abject folly it was that night.'

'A vow once broken is so much easier to break again.'

'No, Anton. A vow broken with such appalling consequences is infinitely easier to keep in future.'

'But my dear old Max, let us not forget I was there that night, that I saw how she disgusted you, watched the extraordinary spectacle of you trying to get drunk to forget it. And now she awaits her accouchement – my dear, every sensibility revolts against anything so abhorrently reminiscent of the cowshed—'

He took two steps towards me, and I was all at once reminded that he was capable of killing. 'You will never,' he said, in a voice barely above a whisper, 'either to me or to anyone else, speak of Her Majesty in such a way again. Is that clear to you? Or do you compel me to make it clearer?'

Involuntarily, I had backed away. I found to my chagrin that my legs were shaking. 'Dear God, Max! You slight me, you abuse me, but you are always so ready to defend her!'

'Her Majesty is both your Queen and my wife. You will remember your honour and control your tongue.'

'Was I supposed to remember my honour that night at the Summer Palace? Damn you, Max, we were lovers then. We are lovers still.'

'You deceive yourself Anton, if you continue to entertain any such hope.'

'So you love her? The delights of fatherhood have so far addled your brain that you have persuaded yourself you love the Little Treaty?'

There was a silence. Then he turned aside. 'I think,' he said softly, 'that I long ago forfeited the right to love anyone.'

The silence grew, and with it my sense of the cruel indignity of my position. 'You can't!' I burst out. 'I've sacrificed everything for you Max – Heidelberg, my writing, my every hope of happiness. Oh, if you hadn't seduced me I might have been different, my whole life might have taken an altogether more fortunate course. But it is too late even to contemplate that now. I am what you have made me, Max. I have nothing else!'

I heard him sigh. Then he said wearily: 'I accept my obligation towards you. I have promised you my friendship and protection and I shall honour my promise. Beyond that, Anton, there is no further recompense I can make.'

No further recompense? Oh, my dear old Max, we should see about that, we should indeed.

III

'Her Excellency will receive you now, sir. She conveys her apologies that she is too unwell to observe the customary formalities.'

The apartment was dark and fusty. As the nurse led me down a narrow corridor my foot squelched in something on the parquet and a pungent smell arose, attaching itself to my wake like a familiar. I suppressed a shiver of disgust. Here was I, impatient to commit my incognito to the delights of Vienna, and I must perforce surrender the morning to business. Still, if I were fortunate there might yet be time before luncheon to brave the December air with a stroll along the Corso; and after that, a leisurely repast at the Sacher, followed later perhaps by the opera, and supper with some strapping cavalry officer who had returned my glance.

The nurse paused before a door at the end of the corridor. Discreetly, I wiped the edge of my shoe upon the rug. And then, all at once – pandemonium. I was aware of a vast coroneted bed, heavy with draperies, and of a stench so appalling that I reached for my handkerchief. But it was the noise which assailed me first: a yapping, yelping cacophany, a flurry of fur, a row of little sharp pink mouths strident with malice. Two of the creatures no bigger than rats launched themselves from the bed on a direct course for my ankles. From amidst the draperies a yap came, higher and more piercing than the rest. The noise ceased abruptly, my two assailants retreated, twitching their muzzles with disappointment. The nurse stood aside, announcing me in a tone which admitted nothing untoward, and I was obliged to pass into the room and suffer the door to be closed behind me.

Wallowing amongst the pillows lay the largest woman I have ever seen. Her bosom heaved like a monstrous bellows, her neck shook with blubber, her face was the size of a dinner plate and smooth as the bladder of a well-stuffed liver sausage. The papillons, cheated of my ankles, had disposed themselves in the nooks and crannies of this vast edifice – two upon the mound of the belly, two more on the pillow and another nuzzling between the prodigious breasts – from where they viewed me with unconcealed disdain.

Stomaching my revulsion, I clicked my heels and bowed, and with a gracious wobble of her dewlap Countess von Blankenberg indicated I might sit – an activity that involved the eviction of two more diminutive beasts from the only chair on which rapid scrutiny suggested I might risk my pearl-grey trousers. One dog wandered off to cock its leg against the foot of the bed, the other remained, sniffing my shoes. The Countess considered my ginger perch on the edge of my seat with impassive detachment.

'Well, Herr Sebastian,' she snapped. 'Prince Leopold has been content to leave me forgotten in exile for thirty years. To what do I owe his sudden regard for me?'

'You were, I believe, madam, lady-in-waiting to the late Queen Tatiana?'

She let out a little high-pitched laugh. 'Myself, and Marie Hoffmannstahl-Linz and the Countess Czernitz. And much honour and reward it brought us all, I must say!'

Her bitterness surprised me. 'Her Majesty's death was indeed a tragic misfortune.'

'Many women die in childbirth. And Tatiana was a frail, neurasthenic creature. She had the full attention of all three Court Physicians and they couldn't save her. If Prince Leopold still wishes to cast the blame upon me after all these years then you may go back to Sylvania at once and tell him I won't stand for it. You may tell His Royal Highness that it's time he had the grace to stop tormenting a poor sick old woman.'

I was profoundly puzzled, for this was not at all a turn I had expected in the conversation. She had seized a confectioner's box from the bedside table and was angrily cramming pieces of crystallised violet into her mouth. Thinking to conciliate her, I bent down to pat the dog snuffling at my trouserleg; it promptly bit me.

My cry of pain seemed to mollify her somewhat. 'Well,' she said between mouthfuls, 'isn't that why he sent you?'

'Most assuredly not, madam. His Royal Highness holds you in the greatest esteem. My mission is – in strictest confidence – to elicit your assistance in tracing the wet-nurse Wolf.'

'Wolf?' The name prompted a fresh assault upon the chocolate box. 'And why should he wish to find her? An uncouth, illiterate peasant with ideas above her station?'

'A question of reward, madam. An expression of gratitude that His Majesty King Maximilian has been so miraculously restored to us.'

'Apparently Nurse Wolf has received her just reward. They say she's dead.' The Countess paused to feed crystallised violet to a papillon which was licking her ear. 'Besides, if His Royal Highness truly wishes to know about the woman he need not bother me. He should direct his questions at Baroness Windersdorf.'

My ears pricked up. 'Ah?' I said encouragingly.

'Baroness Windersdorf recommended the creature and forced her upon us.'

'Was that not a trifle unusual? After all, the Baroness

was a member of Princess Helena's Household, not Queen Tatiana's.'

She sighed impatiently. 'But it was Princess Helena who had the ear of the King. Tell me, young man, has Prince Leopold grown feeble-minded?'

'N-no. Not at all. But perhaps if you explained everything from the beginning it would be of assistance – assist me, you understand, in representing your case to His Royal Highness.'

The huge breasts heaved. 'Oh, very well. Yet I should hardly have thought it requires much explaining. Princess Helena was of the Family, the King's cousin, not to mention his sister-in-law. Whereas Tatiana was an outsider, with no English or German and precious little French, and for all she was cousin to His Imperial Majesty of Russia, she bored Sigismund to distraction. The Princess used to intercede with him on Tatiana's behalf, so naturally Tatiana followed any course she advised.'

I raised my eyebrows.

'Oh, I know they say the Princess lost her wits after the revolution. But in those days if anyone was head of our Household it was she. Or rather, her creature, Baroness Windersdorf. It was even Windersdorf they sent to dismiss us the night after Tatiana died.'

'Dismiss you?' I was again puzzled.

'The Court Physicians and all three ladies-in-waiting. Naturally Tatiana's Household was disbanded in due course. Princess Helena took charge of the orphan Crown Prince and her Household replaced ours. But while everyone else was permitted to stay on at Schwanensee until they had been given other positions at Court we were not even allowed to wait for the funeral. We were instructed to leave the very next day.'

'Forgive me, madam – that strikes me as exceedingly strange.'

'Strange? Young man, we found it scandalous! I was sufficiently astonished at the arrival of the Baroness, since after all she'd only a fortnight previously been brought to bed of her own stillborn child. We'd even attended the funeral out of courtesy, and a very perfunctory affair it had turned out to be, with the coffin brought across the border the day after the death and committed to the earth straight away, before any members of the late Baron's family could attend. And now here she was, a woman of inferior rank to all of us, handing out our dismissal as if we were domestic servants. She was acting on Princess Helena's authority, of course. It was said King Sigismund blamed us for Her Majesty's death, so everyone who had attended Tatiana during her confinement was sent packing. Even the nursery maids had to go. The only person in the nursery who kept her place was that woman, Wolf.'

'Nurse Wolf?' It was not now the presence of the dogs that held me tense on the edge of my chair.

'By the time King Sigismund arrived at Schwanensee to see his son and heir the infant Crown Prince was in the sole charge of Baroness Windersdorf and an ignorant peasant wet-nurse.'

'Then His Majesty did not attend the birth?'

'I explained to you, young man – King Sigismund preferred the attentions of *demi-mondaines* from the Volksoper to the company of his wife. Her Majesty's confinement took place three weeks earlier than anticipated, when the King was holidaying incognito in Venice. Of course, the Cabinet Secretary was present in the anteroom and was shown the new-born infant, as is the custom. But the King himself was not there. Not one member of the Royal Family was with the Queen when she died – not even Princess Helena. Yet they blamed us, we who had been closest to Tatiana and had cared for her and her child in her last hours, they blamed us, young man, and banished us from Court in disgrace—'

I cut her short. 'The Crown Prince was born on 19th June, so you must have left Schwanensee on the 21st? Presumably, therefore, King Sigismund cannot have returned from Venice until the 22nd at the earliest?'

'Yes, yes. What do dates matter? It's the ingratitude, the injustice that matters – a life wasted in obscurity and exile. But Prince Leopold knows all that. Why should he send you here to torment me by going over the whole wretched affair?'

I doubted the Paterfamilias did know the exact circum-stances of Countess von Blankenberg's fall from favour, or that even if he had he would have attributed much importance to it. Assuredly it would not have made his brain race and his heart pound as mine pounded now.

'Nurse Wolf had a child,' I said. 'Did you ever see it?'

'Most certainly not, young man. Why should I have had the slightest interest in it?'

'Do you remember where she came from, where Baroness Windersdorf found her?'

'I think she was from a village on the Windersdorfs' estate. How should I know? It could scarcely concern me.'

IV

My father's study; a panelled room like his sanctum in the Schloss Beauregard, where my boyhood had endured so many indignities; a panelled room hung with banners and insignia and other trumpery trophies, and he, behind his desk in his cavalry corset, puffing up his chest to flourish the braid upon it, wearing even the crape armband of King Friedrich's mourning as if it were some portentous badge of dignity.

Like Max, he forbore to indicate that I might sit. Instead he flared his nostrils and adjusted his eyeglass to a suitably belligerent angle.

'I am sure you are aware, sir, why I have summoned you here. I should have taken action a damned sight sooner had not the death of poor King Friedrich prevented me. But now that the funeral is over and we are back in Rosenholm, I can defer this interview no longer. I have received the most displeasing report from your commanding officer.'

So far as King Friedrich's obsequies were concerned, I was primarily conscious that they had afforded me a week's compassionate leave, the three remaining days of which I could not permit to be wasted. Accordingly I found myself surreptitiously consulting my fob-watch.

His hand came thundering down upon the desk, setting the trinkets upon it aquiver. 'Damn you, boy! You will listen to your father when he addresses you!'

'Forgive me,' I said, smiling sweetly, 'but I must ask you to be brief. I have ordered my landau to be ready in ten minutes to take me to Behrensdorf.'

'Dear God, boy! Have you no respect? You are in mourning for a king of Sylvania and a cousin.'

'An ex-king, as a matter of fact. And a second cousin. Besides, I am perfectly sure I may mourn a man I have never met just as satisfactorily at my friend Messinger's hunting box as I may in this waxworks.'

His eyeglass juddered. 'I repeat, you will listen to me, sir. And you will show respect. I have received a most shaming report of your conduct from Colonel Arendt. He informs me that on no less than three occasions you have wilfully absconded from your regimental duties. The first two incidents, after the manoeuvres at Jedburg and then again for three days in December, he saw fit most unwisely to keep from me, preferring no doubt to spare me the disgrace. But this last absence of yours, not a week ago, has been the final straw. He does not wish to see you cashiered – your kinship with me precludes such public dishonour. But he despairs of disciplining you, not merely because the privileges accorded to you as my son render effective punishment well-nigh impossible, but because whatever measures he has so far taken you have greeted with signal contempt. Confound you, boy! You are not some burgher's lad from the North. You are the son of a Hohenstaufen prince and cousin to the King. If your code of honour as an officer did not require the highest standards of duty and obedience, your blood alone would demand them. How dare you behave like some insolent puppy playing hookey from the schoolroom! How dare you disgrace your father and every noble tradition of service this family holds dear! I require an explanation for your behaviour and you will not leave this room until I have received it!'

He had gone an exquisite shade of crimson during this monologue. I paused for a moment. Then I said lightly: 'I suppose, dear Paterfamilias, that I was bored.'

'Bored! You arrogant little whippersnapper! I should have taken the strap to you more often when you were a boy!'

'My dear Papa, I know these images of violence always excite you, but you should have a care or you will do yourself an injury. I have repeatedly suggested I should be better employed as Max's Personal Secretary and you have repeatedly blocked my appointment. You can scarcely blame me if I am a trifle disaffected.'

'His Majesty and I have discussed your request at some length. He agrees with me that it would not be a suitable appointment.'

'I see.' I too was suddenly angry. 'So that's how far dear Max's friendship extends – to indulging in squalid little plots behind my back.'

'His Majesty has always been the first to defend you – has come to your defence, in my opinion, a damned sight more often than you deserve. You will not use the kindness he has shown you as an excuse for familiarity. When you speak of your King you will speak with respect!'

'Respect, duty, honour! Good Lord, and you wonder why I am bored.'

He mastered himself with difficulty, his crimson gills graduating in the process to a most interesting shade of puce. 'Perhaps Maximilian is right. He has always been of the view that you are ill-fitted for the army. He suggests I take the course I first decided upon and send you to Heidelberg.'

'Does he now? Well, I don't wish to go to Heidelberg. I'm not some parcel that you may wrap up with string and sealing wax and send hither and thither at will. Damn Colonel Arendt. I'll stay in Rosenholm with my beastly regiment.'

'Very well. Then you remain in the Hussars on these conditions. The privileges you were granted as my son are now revoked. Unless you are on leave, you will cease to occupy your apartments here – you will be billeted in the Maria-Antonienburg with the other junior officers. Like them, you will restrict your off-duty hours to the regimental *Kasino* where you may benefit from the influence of your seniors. And when your present leave is up, you will be confined to barracks under close arrest for twenty-eight days. If, in spite of all this, you remain insubordinate, you will be forced to resign your commission and take an ignominious discharge. I shall steel myself to such a disgrace. It will be less than the shame of allowing your behaviour to continue as a stain upon the honour of our family.'

I groaned inwardly. To be confined to barracks for a month

hardly sorted with my plans. To conceal my annoyance I consulted my watch again. 'I am afraid, dear Father, I have given you every second I can spare. My horses will be playing up like the devil. I trust, in any case, that is all.'

'No, it is not all!' He seized a bundle of flimsy-looking papers and, rounding his desk, began to advance upon me. 'What do you imagine these are?'

'My dear Paterfamilias, I am not yet possessed of psychic powers. Since I haven't the slightest idea, why don't you tell me.'

'Bills. From your wine-merchant, your tailor, from art galleries in the Lindenplatz, from at least four jewellers—'

'No gentleman settles his bills instantly. That would give the tradesmen quite the wrong idea.'

'Confound you, boy, most of these accounts have been outstanding for well over a year. They have been presented to my Comptroller as a last resort. Dear God, there's even an IOU for gambling debts written out to a fellow officer in your regiment!'

Curse Grüber and his everlasting desire for gratitude. 'They must have slipped my mind, Papa. Or perhaps the fault lies with the scope of my allowance.'

He was assuming that remarkable puce tinge once more. 'You urged me, sir, to treat you as a grown man. I agreed that you might occupy your own apartments. I endowed you with a sizeable – a damned generous allowance. I permitted you privileges and freedoms I never had as a boy, that most youths of twenty-two could not begin to dream of. I did it because you are my only son – and because, God help me, you are the child of mine who, in looks at least, most reminds me of your dear mother. And in return you have abused my trust, exploited my generosity and poured contempt on any notion of honour I have tried to instill in you. A gentleman does not pay his bills? In the name of Heaven, how many times must I din into that much-vaunted brain of yours that you are not some *Landgraf's* brat! You are King Maximilian's cousin.'

He was flourishing the bills in my face. I brushed them aside. 'You think very highly of dear old Max, don't you, Pater?'

'He understands his duty and obeys it unswervingly. In

all the time I have known him he has never been less than honourable, never less in his relations with me than—'

'Than a son, Father? A better son than I am?'

'If Maximilian were my son I should not now be standing here wondering how he had been so misbegotten, I should not receive daily reports of his gambling and his drinking and his fondness for low places and low people—'

'Dear old Max. Such a paragon of virtue. Yet I might tell you things about him, Pater, that would—'

I thought he would strike me, I even ducked to avoid the blow. But, though he raised his hand, it was as with all the quarrels we had ever had. He paused, his eyeglass glittering, little beads of sweat occasioned by the restriction of his corset bedewing the deep magenta of his brow.

'You will cease, sir, to imagine there is any friendship between you and His Majesty. I have heard things of you which I will not sully my lips by repeating, things which the very fact of my being your father forbids me to believe. You are not fit to be in His Majesty's company and you will affront him with your presence no further. You will cease to importune him about the Private Secretaryship, or to claim any connection with him beyond the tie of blood which regrettably exists between you. I do not merely express a wish, Sir, I do not urge or advise. You will from now on refrain from any contact with His Majesty other than that which family duty renders unavoidable. And this, damn you, is an order!'

I surveyed him coldly for a moment. A sentimental old man, cherishing the tawdry gold cast of my mother's hand upon his desk and all his other cloying memorabilia. A foolish old man, who believed he had power yet could not comprehend those things in which power consisted. An old man who credited age with some curious intrinsic virtue. I smiled.

'You castigate me, dear Pater, for my moral turpitude. You talk grandiloquently of respect and honour and family duty. But, if I may be permitted to say so, I find the whole thing somewhat rich. I must think of my Hohenstaufen blood, must I? Honour all it stands for? Well, what does it stand for, Pater, diluted and defiled in my veins as it is? You lecture me on morality, you hand out orders as to how I must behave. But where was your fine moral sensibility, tell me, when you threw away my birthright by marrying a whore?'

He struck me then, before I was even aware of the movement. The blow shook my teeth and left me for a second groggy. When my vision cleared I saw he was gazing at me stupidly, as if he were as shocked as I. Tasting blood, I put up my hand and found my left nostril was streaming. I took out my handkerchief and carefully wiped my upper lip. Then, still holding his gaze, I said softly: 'You will regret that. Oh yes, dear Paterfamilias, you will come most assuredly to regret it.'

V

'Wolf, you say? Well, there is Karl Wolf, the blacksmith, and his family and some cousins of his at Überberg, and I believe there was another family Wolf in the mill-house although they moved away after the father died—'

'Annelise Gertrude Wolf. She left the district some thirty years ago. She may have been in service with Baron von Windersdorf.'

The parish priest at Meldingen was a rickety terrier of a man who, weighing up his worn soutane against my elegant Homburg and sable-lined coat, seemed eager to please. He had swallowed without demur my touching story of a consumptive waif, taken in out of charity and craving to see her last living relative, an aunt on her father's side, whom I had nobly promised to attempt to trace. The churchyard, of course, was useless, gravestones sunk beneath drifts of snow, but there were the Parish Registers – he had tended his little flock at Meldingen for nigh on forty years and had chronicled every eddy in the passage of the souls in his charge.

Despite the stove sputtering in one corner it was almost as cold in the vestry as it had been in the church itself. I watched impatiently, sunk in my collar, as he rubbed his mittened fingers and, exhaling gusts of steam, struggled to heave a pile of mouldering tomes onto the ramshackle table. At last, when he had settled me in front of them, he took the hint and withdrew.

I searched for some while fruitlessly. There were Wolfs in plenty, marrying, dying, giving birth, but no Annelise Wolf, at least not with the particular qualifications I required. Sighing, I lit a cigarette and began upon a different tack. This time, thank God, I was rewarded. Annelise Gertrude Baumgärdt, married to Gregor Hans Stroop in 1855, delivered of five children between 1856 and 1860. Nothing remarkable in this perhaps – except that every one of Annelise Stroop's children had died shortly after birth, the sturdiest surviving three short months and the least fortunate a mere day.

I started. The little priest had appeared at my elbow with a steaming bowl of noodle soup. As I took it in my gloved hands I was aware of his eyes straying inquisitively over the open page, calculating where my glance had fixed upon it.

'Annelise Stroop?' he said thoughtfully. Then all at once he clasped his mittens in excitement. 'Do you know, Herr Sebastian, I believe you may have come upon something! Annelise Stroop was indeed in service with the Windersdorfs. In fact, she was wet-nurse to Baroness von Klaar's children – Baron Albrecht's sister – when the Klaars used to live up at the Schloss with the late Baron before he was married.'

'She seems,' I said, glancing back at the register, 'to have had superlative qualifications for a wet-nurse.'

'The poor infants, gathered so early to their Maker? Ah, Herr Sebastian, it is sometimes hard for a simple priest to explain why God, who is Love, should single out certain of his children to be tested so painfully. And sometimes, poor sinful mortals that they are, they prove unequal to the test.'

'Then Annelise Stroop went to the bad?'

'One must reprove sin, but one may also forgive it. It seems she blamed poor Gregor Stroop for the taint which blighted their offspring. But the Stroops have lived in this village and begotten healthy children for generations, while she was an outsider – from Behrensdorf, I think. I urged her to accept it was God's will. But she, poor soul, would have none of it.'

'She was driven to betray her marriage vows?'

'One hesitates, Herr Sebastian, to rake over what is best

forgotten. But yes, it was common knowledge at the time. The fifth child. It died just the same.'

'And after that, presumably, she abandoned her husband and left the district?'

'It seemed to turn her brain. I was unable to give her comfort. And then she began to get strange notions which set the other women against her – that she had powerful friends who would advance her in life, that she was a cut above the rest of them, too good for the village. She left quite suddenly, I recall – it must have been nearly a year later.'

'And was she – forgive me, Father – was she again in a delicate condition?'

He paused as if I had sparked off some train of thought. Then once more he wrung his mittens ecstatically. 'My goodness! Why, I believe you truly have come across something. The father was rumoured to be Hanno Wolf the joiner, cousin of the Karl Wolf I mentioned earlier.'

'So when she left she took his name?'

'She may have preferred it to Stroop. My housekeeper tells me young women who are – shall we say, on the slippery slope – quite often change their names if their own is not euphonious.'

The chill in my bones overcoming my distaste, I took a gulp of the soup. The Father, who had been watching with solicitude my initiation to this gastronomic experience, appeared to drift away on some fresh river of thought. He shook his head sadly. 'But, your poor orphan charge . . . it is not a happy tale to tell of her last living relative.'

'And it is the end of the tale, I assume. You never saw Annelise Stroop again?'

'Oh, but I did, sir, I did. Not four years ago.'

I put down the soup bowl. 'Here? In Meldingen?'

'In Übersberg, five kilometres away. She was found in the Jessners' barn, far gone in drink, poor woman, destitute and starving.'

'And you recognised her?'

'I should not have, no, but when I heard her confession she told me who she was. That was as much as I could understand, I am afraid, for otherwise she was quite delirious, poor soul, raving about palaces and princes and diamonds. She was unconscious by the time I administered the last rites.'

The surge of excitement I had felt ebbed abruptly. 'Then she is dead.'

'Oh no. God in His wisdom saw fit to spare her. But she was stark mad with the drink, alas. Dr Strauss had her taken to the asylum for the insane at Bad Gottfriedsburg, where as far as I know she has been confined ever since.'

CHAPTER ELEVEN

Marie Bathildis

I

'You have repeatedly petitioned to see me, Count, and have been repeatedly told I am in deep mourning for King Friedrich and will see no one. Yet you now have the impertinence to present yourself here at the Summer Palace. I grant you this audience in the hope that my personal expression of displeasure will succeed with your obstinacy where protocol and simple good manners have failed.'

His shoulders drooping, his nag's teeth bared in a servile smile, Count Vielfrass presented the very picture of humility; yet I thought I detected the lowered eyes examining me covertly, all the same, for signs of hysteria, reminding me that this was Vielfrass at his most dangerous. No matter. I felt I had grown in the last six weeks preternaturally old and withered, too desiccated for any emotion, even fear.

Though the Audience Chamber doors had been closed upon us, I did not indicate he might approach my chair, merely giving him the sign to speak.

'Permit me to express on behalf of the Cabinet, indeed the whole Assembly, our heartfelt relief that Your Majesty's health is improving and that there is now no further danger to our unborn Prince.'

I surveyed him stonily. The doctors might claim the child was unharmed but I had felt no movement from it since Freddy's death and was convinced it had died with him. However, that too was no longer of any consequence.

He gave a cough and I observed him encroach a little, as if his respectful distance handicapped him. 'You are justly harsh, Ma'am, and I admit my impertinence. But I came – I felt obliged to come – to reassure you that you are not alone.'

'You are obscure, Count. Please speak to your point.'

'You will recall a conversation before Your Majesties were

even betrothed, a conversation in which I endeavoured to
assure you of my friendship, even ventured to suggest you
might one day have need of my services. I extend that friendship, those services to Your Majesty now.' Observing that
I did not respond he dabbed his lips with the inevitable
handkerchief. 'No friend, Ma'am, could stand by and hear
you accused of neurasthenia when you alone have had the
courage to name poor King Friedrich's murderer, to shout
that name from the housetops so that, were not all around
you unaccountably deaf, justice might be done.'

'No one else believes King Friedrich was murdered,
Count. Why should you?'

'Then you have indeed forgotten our conversation at
Schwanensee, Ma'am. I told you then – I too know what
Maximilian really is.'

There was such a degree of insinuation in those fluttering
eyelids, that honeyed lisp, that I shuddered. So Vielfrass
had always known my marriage would be a mockery. I felt
at once an obscene intimacy with him, a craven desire to
unburden myself of all I had suffered, together with loathing
for Maximilian that he should have driven me to this hideous
fellowship.

'The laws of morality, Ma'am, are sacred. They bind us
all, however highly we are placed. Once His Majesty has
decided he is above those laws – well, who can say what he
may be capable of? Besides, I deal in facts. My agents give
me to understand that the community at Freischutz has
received a further and most substantial donation – anonymous, of course, but I believe we shall have little trouble in
tracing its source to His Majesty's exchequer.'

The dull ache of my hatred flared suddenly into pain.
'Well, Count, what do you offer me? Will you give me justice
for King Friedrich?'

'I fear,' – here again the handkerchief obscured the pursed
lips for a moment – 'I fear, Ma'am, however diligently
my agents work, His Majesty still has the power to evade
us.'

'Oh, of course, Count, how foolish of me! How foolish of
me to ask for justice in this benighted country of ours when
everything, the Church, the army, your precious State
Police, even the monarchy itself is rotten to the core. There

is no justice any more, we have poisoned it, murdered it, there is no justice left to us but the justice of death—'

'Death, Ma'am?'

'Death, when we shall all be judged. Except that I wonder sometimes whether even God has deserted us, or whether indeed there is a God at all.'

He coughed again, and I saw that while I had been caught up in my misery he had seized the chance to sidle across the carpet, so that he stood distanced only by the marble table between us.

'Your Majesty should not despair. Maximilian may evade the law, but he cannot evade the people.'

I stared at him.

'The people have remarked upon your absence from Rosenholm and expressed their discontent at it. They observe that, while His Majesty presents a fine enough figure, he can be – shall we say, somewhat aloof. They take your absence from his side not as neglect in you but as a criticism of him. And now, when they hear these rumours about King Friedrich's death, hear tell of the strange scenes that occurred at his funeral, they are naturally . . .'

He had paused to take refuge in the handkerchief. 'Well?' I said.

'They are naturally stirred up. There have been riots, Ma'am, in both Helm and Nordstadt.'

'I have not read of any riots.'

'Oh, you would not, Ma'am. The press has been subject to the most rigid censorship. But the rioting has occurred all the same – indeed at Helm the situation was so grave the army had to be called in.'

'Censorship? Cannon? I see it has not taken my husband long to fall back on Baron Schramm's methods.'

'Precisely, Ma'am. And the people do not care for it, most decidedly they don't. They see how the new order is no different from the old and they are disillusioned. Indeed, they fear things may be even worse, that Maximilian's fondness for so-called Liberalism may have threatened the very foundations of the state. At Helm, Ma'am, there were Socialists in the mob inciting the rabble to support a Republic. The threat to our institutions, our whole way of life, not to mention the possibility of a Prussian invasion if this unrest

continues – the people are understandably alarmed, Ma'am.
And in some quarters they are saying there is only one way
to safeguard the monarchy, to restore our beloved Sylvania
to peace again . . .'

He was leaning across the table now, his yellow fangs
bared, his eyes mesmerically intent upon mine. 'In some
quarters the people are saying they must look to you, Ma'am,
and the child you are carrying, that Maximilian should be
deposed and a Council of State or a Regency set up, that
Your Majesty is our only hope of stability and a return to
the rule of law.'

I had been staring at him, fascinated, but suddenly I no
longer heard him. For I felt the child, the child I had thought
dead, quite distinctly kick me. I put my hand to my belly in
disbelief. But no, there it was, boisterous, healthy, insistent.
I was flooded with a great warmth, as though the blood
were all at once racing in my veins, prickling in every toe
and finger, bringing me joyously back to life. And in that
moment I saw Maximilian's face as he too had felt the child,
saw suddenly the man I had known when I had permitted
myself to love him.

'What is it, Ma'am? Are you taken ill? Shall I call for a
servant to fetch some water?'

I had forgotten Vielfrass. I looked up and perceived him
with that same immaculate clarity. 'How dare you!' I said.
'How dare you, Count, come here and say such things to
me.'

'Ma'am, I report to you only what the people are saying.'

'Then the people are talking treason, and to repeat their
words is also treason. Your audience, Count, is at an end.'

I remained in the Audience Chamber for some time staring
ahead of me as if I had been stunned. For with my new and
terrible clarity of vision I saw myself, above all, most
perfectly. I had indeed since Freddy's death, since perhaps
the moment of reading Anton von Tarn's letter, been gripped
by a kind of insanity. I had so often cautioned Freddy for
being too simple in his judgements, but it was I who had
persisted in seeing everything in black and white. Freddy,
detecting what he had described as Maximilian's 'exile from
God', could perceive it in the context of the man as a whole,

could allow himself to make concessions for it; I, confronted with Anton's letter, would have nothing but that this one fault should stand for Maximilian's entire character, obliterating all its strengths and virtues. Freddy had understood that it was possible to love two things differently but equally and that love itself sometimes involved self-denial; I understood love only in terms of my own blinkered demands.

I saw now that, whatever it was in Maximilian's nature that compelled him to desire Anton von Tarn, he had also tried, with great patience and forbearing, to love me. Oh, perhaps this twist in his nature would have prevented his ever succeeding, but how much more had I prevented it by my utter rejection of him. He had said so often that he expected no more from me than I could give – and I had at last proved I was capable of giving nothing. Well, he could not love me now. Yet that need not prevent me from starting properly to love him, from making for myself a new construction of love that did not consist in demands and payments. I might see what compassion and generosity might do, I might try, although I was exiled from his thoughts, to keep him always in mine, so that, if the will had any power of transmission, he might feel, even at a distance, a little of my tenderness for him and take warmth from it. And warmth, tenderness, loyalty he would certainly require in good measure; for I understood to what dangers my hysterical behaviour had exposed him. I could still hear Vielfrass's seditious words. But I could also see, from the painful vantage of my new perspective, what I had obtusely ignored before: the image of Count Vielfrass that night he had come with his detachment of Hussars, watching, waiting in Freddy's bedroom, watching Freddy kneel at his prie-dieu and kiss the nail in the feet of the cross.

I was grateful Aubyn had responded so promptly to my telegram, although I was conscious that he viewed with apprehension my agitated manner and my insistence on checking that there was no one listening at the door. Indeed, though he had been the soul of kindness these last weeks, always finding time from his duties when I needed him, I was aware that there was in his manner towards me a new constraint, as though he would never truly forgive me for what had happened at Freischutz.

'Well, dear girl, I am at your service. So long as you don't require me to enter into yet another discussion about poor Suzannah.'

'No, my dear Aubyn. I have changed my mind about the Countess. I wish her to remain in my household for the time being.' And so, indeed, I did, for it had come to me, in my newly-practical frame of mind, that I was much better off having Suzannah where I could watch her just as closely as she watched me. I had even tried altering my manner towards her and had found my advances rewarded, astonishingly, with the occasional smile – though she could scarcely be so credulous as to believe my friendship genuine.

'No, Aubyn. I asked you to come because I think I know who murdered Freddy and I need your help.'

He sighed deeply. 'Dashit, Marie – and I, like a damned fool, thought you were looking a little more chipper, had some colour in your cheeks at last. Don't you think you've persecuted poor old Max enough?'

'Oh please, Aubyn, listen to me!' I described my encounter with Vielfrass and what I had remembered about him.

Aubyn snorted. 'My dear girl, the fellow's a viper. But what you've told me is hardly proof of anything.'

'What he suggested was treason.'

'In a private audience with no witnesses? Marie, you know the man as well as I. He'll wriggle out of it, deny the conversation, twist your own words against you, like as not. And why should he want to murder poor Friedrich?'

'To hurt me. To hurt Maximilian by turning the people against him. Aubyn, were there riots?'

'Oh yes, there were riots all right – fomented by the scoundrel himself for his own nefarious purposes. Vielfrass knows he'll have to go to the country soon, so he's doing his level best to make the forces of the Left look as terrifying as possible in the hope that the voters will be put off supporting Keller. At Nordstadt several of the principal agitators were recognised as notorious Right-wingers and at Helm there's even a suspicion one or two Prussians were involved. But of course we don't have a shred of real evidence – Weber may be nominally in control of the police, but they're still in

Vielfrass's pocket, every man jack of them. That's why Max ordered me to bring in the army at Helm, and why he and Uncle Leo persuaded the Minister of the Interior to impose censorship – at least it has stopped the poison spreading. Max hates himself for both, of course. But in a dirty game both sides have to play dirty.'

'Is there no way of stopping Vielfrass, or at least controlling him?'

'My dear, you know we rely on him to conciliate the *Landgrafs*. Max would have to be pretty damned sure of his ground to act against him. And unless the blackguard properly oversteps the limits, decides he's strong enough for a *coup d'état* for instance, we've got no proof, nothing we could make stand up.'

'But if I could find proof, prove it was he who had Freddy murdered?'

He turned away with a laugh. 'And how do you propose to do that, dear girl? Even supposing the poor boy didn't die quite naturally of a fit – and I'm by no means convinced that he didn't – how do you propose persuading our loyal State Police to raise the view halloo against their master?'

'But you could find me someone, someone who wasn't one of Vielfrass's agents. Oh Aubyn, you know you could.'

He tugged at his moustache. 'Marie, if you're in earnest, if you must persist with this damn fool notion, why don't you talk to Max about it?'

'How can I? After all that's been said, all the terrible things . . . Please, Aubyn, we must be as secret as possible, you must not tell anyone, not even Maximilian. Please, my dear friend, promise me solemnly that you won't.' For I had remembered that I could not secure my evidence against Vielfrass without also implicating Anton von Tarn.

He sighed. 'Dammit, I don't care for the business, Marie. I suppose I could send you someone, some trustworthy young officer – Heaven knows, there are enough who'd leap at the chance of doing special service for their Queen. But I still don't care for it.'

'Oh Aubyn, if it's to help me, to help Maximilian—'

'My dear, I know you've chosen widow's mourning for Friedrich. But if you truly wish to help Max then the best thing you can do is cast off this wretched seclusion of yours and go back to Rosenholm.'

I felt my eyes suddenly burning. 'I can't. Oh, if only – but I can't, I can't!'

II

Perhaps Aubyn had, after all, decided I had simply taken another of my hysterical fancies, for the first week of March went by without a word from him. I contained my impatience with difficulty; yet fear that my correspondence did not escape the eyes of Vielfrass's agents prevented me from writing to him and I could not, without confirming his belief in my hysteria, summon him from his duties again. No, I must somehow send a messenger to him, but who? Suzannah was there, watching me always, making me suspicious of everyone about me, for I saw now that I had no means of knowing how far Vielfrass's network of spies extended, whether it had drawn in other officers of my Household or perhaps some of the servants. There seemed only one person I could safely confide in – Ursi Windersdorf, who in addition to being trustworthy could also claim a visit to Princess Helena as a convincing pretext, even to Suzannah, for making the journey to Rosenholm.

Accordingly I dashed off my note to Aubyn.

8th March 1891

My dearest A.,

While I understand your reluctance, I am still determined to carry out my plan. I crave justice for my beloved F. And besides, how can we live in peace when we know the man who has been the cause of so much wickedness remains unpunished? Please send me the reliable person you promised. I am prepared to pay him 5,000 florins for his pains, half now and half upon the completion of his task. It is impossible, as you will readily understand, to discuss such matters further in a letter, so please arrange that he and I may meet confidentially. I long to hear from you, dear friend, and beg you to commit this note to the fire once you have read it.

Your affectionate cousin,

M.B.

I sealed this with my ring. Then, taking Ursi no further into my confidence than to instruct her to tell no one of her mission, I made her promise that she would only surrender my letter to Aubyn in person. The three days of her absence seemed endless. Yet Aubyn's reply, when she brought it to me in my boudoir, was more than I could have hoped for.

11th March 1891

My dear Marie,
I see you still persist in this cloak and dagger business so it seems I must humour you, much, I may say, against my better judgement. The man I am sending you is Captain Rohrbach of the Intelligence Corps, who has been highly recommended to me through General Stahl by his commanding officer, Colonel von Leitwitz. Your emissary may meet him at 9 pm on 19th March in one of the private rooms of the Mayerhof, Helsingbad, where he will be waiting to receive your instructions. Please, my dear cousin, now Captain Rohrbach is able to relieve you of your anxiety in this matter, try to preserve your health and strength so that all those who care for you may rejoice in your complete recovery.

Your devoted servant,

St John Aubyn.

Memorising the time and place of the meeting, I put a taper to the letter and watched it shrivel to ashes in the grate. Yet I was nevertheless faced with a problem. I had no emissary to send to Helsingbad, I was still unprepared to risk explaining the full implications of Freddy's death to anyone in my Household. But it was unthinkable that, even incognito, I should go to a public place alone and unprotected to meet a man I did not know. There seemed no alternative but to confide more fully in Ursi.

She listened to me gravely. Indeed, she had become very grave and doleful of late, no longer the fussing, clucking Ursi, but a crestfallen mother-hen with dull eyes and draggled feathers. Her chilblains were troubling her still, she said, and she had broken out in an eczema on her hands and face, which added to the impression of her having imperfectly moulted. I told her only of my suspicions of Vielfrass, mentioning nothing of Suzannah's and Anton's part in the affair. When I had finished she heaved a deep sigh and looked down for a while at her reddened fingers.

'Forgive me, Ma'am – of course I can only be glad that your suspicions no longer rest upon His Majesty – but is this wise? The doctor could find nothing untoward about dear King Friedrich's death.'

'The doctor was mistaken, Ursi. Or bribed to be so.'

'But would it not be better to let things lie? To go chasing about in Helsingbad at all hours of the night, and you, Ma'am, in such a delicate state of health—'

'Ursi, I am not mad, however much you and His Highness of Hohen-Kastell may try to persuade me into it. I wish to do this for Sylvania, for King Friedrich, and above all for my dearest – for His Majesty, whom I have so much wronged. Now, are you for me or against me?'

My first concern was, of course, to conceal our nocturnal excursion from Suzannah. I announced that I intended to remove myself to the Turkish Hunting Lodge for a change of scene: Suzannah was to go ahead of me to ensure that the housekeeper had completed all the necessary preparations, spending the night of the 19th there in expectation of my arrival the following morning. My heart lifted the instant she departed, I felt a thrill of excitement as Ursi and I, in the greatest secrecy, climbed into our unliveried coupé. It was agreed that I should present myself to Captain Rohrbach as one of the ladies of my Household; for the rest, my deep mourning with its heavy veil would suffice to preserve my incognito. But as our distance from the Summer Palace increased so did my apprehension. After all, Aubyn's objections had been grounded in truth. I had no firm basis for my suspicions, only a memory of seemingly unconnected incidents; the figures by the orangery wall, Suzannah handing me the reliquary, Vielfrass's brutal treatment of Freddy. I began to doubt I should be able to explain myself clearly enough to Captain Rohrbach to prevent him too from concluding I was mad. And what if, despite all our precautions, we were followed? What if I were recognised, discovered in such a compromising situation? By the time we drew to a halt outside the Mayerhof I was trembling, and as I stepped down onto the cobbles the crowded street filled me for an instant with unreasoning panic.

I had never been amongst the people like this, not on my ill-judged excursion to Marienberg nor even on that terrible day in Nordstadt. Oh, I had always known that what I saw – the scrubbed faces in their Sunday clothes, the neatness, the order – I'd known that was not reality. But this, the noise, the men spilling out of the beer-hall opposite or loitering in groups on the pavement – it left me momentarily weak and dazed. Through the open doors of the beer-hall I could see the drinkers in their *Lederhosen* beating the tables to the rhythm of the accordion, while between the benches women with trays struggled in a thicket of bawdy hands. Outside two peasants seemed to be trying to sober a drunken comrade by holding his head beneath the water of the horse-trough. Another drunkard brushed so close to me that I looked round instinctively for my guard; but there was no guard, no protection, only Ursi behind me, picking her way through the puddles and whispering that we must make for the hotel quickly as our presence was attracting glances.

At least within the Mayerhof there was a reassuring calm, the respectability of faded plush and heavy draperies. I tried to compose myself as we were conducted upstairs to the private dining-rooms and at last to a door at the end of the passage, where I settled Ursi in a chair, on guard. I bit my lips as my fingers turned the doorknob. At a chenille-covered table a man sat with a meerschaum between his teeth and a stein at his elbow. It was an ordinary enough room, furnished with the same faded gentility as the lobby, and the officer rose politely enough as I entered, extinguishing his pipe and bowing low. Yet there was a clandestine air about the dimmed gas-light and smokey atmosphere which seemed to bring in upon me the impropriety of this meeting, and something too in the man's manner which, had he not introduced himself as Captain Rohrbach, would have made me retreat, believing I had been directed to the wrong door.

It was not simply his unprepossessing appearance – though he was tall and well-built and carried himself with a proper military stiffness, his face was so badly affected with a skin eruption that it looked as if it had been flayed; there was a coarseness in his glance, an insolent lingering on my veil and figure which left me feeling obscurely humiliated, despite his most respectfully helping me to a chair. However, Aubyn had recommended him, Aubyn trusted him. Nevertheless, I felt vulnerable in my incognito, bereft of authority, reluctant to expose my difficulties to such a man.

'Well, Ma'am, to business. And may I say how deeply honoured I am to be chosen to serve Her Majesty – even though I do not have the privilege of addressing Her Majesty in person.'

Again I had the feeling of that brazen glance insinuating itself beneath my veil. Yet there was nothing for it: I had pleaded with Aubyn, caused him to take trouble for me, dragged Ursi and myself through the dangers of keeping this rendezvous. I began falteringly to recount my story.

It was not easy to remember to use the third person and, conscious of those eyes fixed upon me, I stumbled sometimes. Yet I got through it all, Freddy's curious symptoms, the puncture in his lip, the missing nail, the smell of bitter almonds, my suspicion of a plot which spread beyond the monastery, perhaps to the highest echelons of government. A smirk seemed to play on his lips when I mentioned Count Vielfrass and how even the State Police could not be trusted to handle so confidential a matter. But when I came to recount my suspicions of the Tarns I seemed to produce an even more singular effect. His crooked mouth broke into a lurid grin.

'Count Tarn, eh? I had the honour to serve alongside His Excellency the Count in the war of liberation. And a very brave, gallant gentleman – oh, a very brave soldier he is!' Indeed, the thought of Anton's bravery seemed to amuse him so exceedingly that he burst out in a roar of laughter, which subsided only in the fit of coughing that attended it.

'Well, Ma'am, I'll see to your business – Her Majesty's business – don't you fear. Only one small point to clarify and we can be taking our leave of each other. One small point.'

I stared at him puzzled.

'The money, Ma'am. Half now, half later. Two thousand five hundred florins.'

Aubyn's letter had mentioned nothing about the money. Thankful we had taken the precaution of bringing it, I sent him to the door for Ursi, who drew the bundle of notes from her reticule; as we watched him count it I could not help noticing his fingernails were dirty. After he had finished he pocketed the bundle carefully, then looked up at me. I had such a strong sense this time of his eyes piercing the veil, calmly, insolently perusing my face, that I glanced away abruptly. When I brought myself to look at him again his lips were fixed in an ingratiating smile.

'I'm a sentimental man, Ma'am. Pressed into Her Majesty's special personal service – it's an honour for a poor, ordinary fellow like me. Would you give me something to remember the occasion by, something Her Majesty might have touched – one of your gloves, Ma'am, or a handkerchief . . . ?'

'Captain Rohrbach, I—'

'Just as a keepsake, Ma'am. Something to make an honest man feel proud.'

I felt suddenly that I would answer his request, give him anything, simply to bring our interview to a close. But not a glove, not any personal article which I might imagine him fondling as if his fingers crept upon my skin. Ursi always carried in her reticule one or two silver card- and cigarette-cases engraved with my cypher, for just such an eventuality. I presented him with a cigarette-case on behalf of Her Majesty, then we departed hastily to find our carriage.

I was still trembling as, with curtains drawn, we rumbled away from the Mayerhof. 'Oh Ursi, you saw how disagreeable he was! How can His Highness be so certain we can trust such a man?'

'From what you say, Ma'am, His Highness of Hohen-Kastell has never met Captain Rohrbach in person. Did you not tell me he was recommended by General Stahl?'

'Yes, but – oh goodness, Ursi, what's that noise?'

From ahead of us came the sound of voices raised in a

jeering chant. We lurched suddenly as our coachman
swerved the horses to the right. Struggling to pull the
curtains I saw we had entered the main square of
Helsingbad, where the statue of Maximilian I stood before
the Rathaus. Out of the darkness I could discern a crowd
around the base of the statue with torches and banners. The
flames danced, the shouting grew. And before we turned
into Königen Amaliastrasse I was just able to make out the
words on the placard being strung around the statue's neck:
'Communes not Kings! Let the People Rule!'

III

I could not sleep, no matter how Ursi might ply me with
rosehip tea and chloral mixture. It was as if what we had
seen, coming so close upon my meeting with Captain
Rohrbach, was somehow a sign, a mocking gesture from
Count Vielfrass to let us know we were detected. I felt now
how foolish I had been to risk such an expedition for, even
if the Captain's distasteful exterior belied his loyalty, it would
take him weeks, months, to piece together the circumstances
of Freddy's death and provide us with the watertight
evidence we needed. And with open revolution in the
streets, whoever the instigators, there was no time. As long
as the violence and the intrigues persisted Maximilian could
only find himself in ever-increasing danger.

'Oh Ursi, Ursi! I wish I were not so powerless. I wish
there were something, now, this moment, I could do.'

She hesitated. 'Dearest Ma'am – I trust you'll not think
me impertinent – but you could return to Rosenholm, go
back to His Majesty.'

'That is what His Highness of Hohen-Kastell urged me to
do. But Ursi, how can I? After all my cruelty, all the hurt I
have caused His Majesty . . . Oh Ursi, I've been so selfish
and disloyal. If he's in danger then so much of it is my fault,
as if I'd deliberately surrendered him up to his enemies.
How can I expect him to take me back now?'

'His Majesty is a proud man, Ma'am, but he is not stony-
hearted. Surely he could not look at Your Majesty, big as

you are with the dear baby, and refuse to find in himself any forgiveness?'

'No, Ursi. Even if he could forgive me there is more, there are – other things.' I saw with chill clarity Anton von Tarn smiling that exclusive, conspiratorial smile and fought suddenly to repress my tears. 'It is impossible that His Majesty can ever want me as his wife again. And if I wish to undo some of the pain my selfishness has caused him I must simply accept it. If I truly love him I cannot go back, don't you see? To do so would be to demand that he love me too, to try to force from him what I do not deserve and he is unable to give.'

'But dearest Ma'am – though I do not know what is in His Majesty's heart, God forbid that I should – it is not a question of love but of duty. If you were to appear at His Majesty's side these rumours that are the cause of all our troubles would cease instantly. His Majesty would not perceive it as a demand upon him but as the simple fulfilment of your duty as his wife, something above and beyond your feelings for each other or any misunderstanding that has occurred between you.'

I stared at her. What she said was so eminently right and sensible that I could not imagine why I had not considered it before, was shocked to realise that in all my thoughts of Maximilian, all my plans to make reparation, I had still been too selfish to consider the one thing which should have been paramount.

She meanwhile was expanding on her theme with an almost feverish excitement, her bosom heaving, her hand clutching at mine with such eagerness that I could not but observe her with astonishment.

'You cannot have forgotten, dearest Ma'am, that next week is Holy Week. If you were to accompany His Majesty when he goes to St Xaviersdom on Easter Day, if your subjects could see you there together giving thanks for Our Risen Lord, then there could be no more rumours of a quarrel between you. Oh Ma'am, I beg of you, it is the only way, you are the only one who has the power to stop what they – to stop this discontent, these intrigues against His Majesty.'

I bent forward and kissed her cheek. 'Very well, Ursi. I shall take your advice gladly. But we won't wait until next week. We'll leave for Rosenholm early tomorrow morning, while Countess von Tarn is at the Hunting Lodge and cannot report our movements.'

This first voicing of my distrust of Suzannah seemed to strike her like a blow. She drew back from me, averted her eyes with a sudden look of anguish.

'Oh Ma'am, forgive me for being direct, but you cannot believe the poor Countess is guilty of anything underhand. I can assure you she is entirely above suspicion.'

'Not you too, Ursi? I hear the same view endlessly from His Highness of Hohen-Kastell, yet I cannot see how either of you have the slightest reason to be so certain.'

'I have known Suzannah all her life, Ma'am. During my time in the Princess Helena's household I watched her grow up—'

'Into the surly, silent, disagreeable creature she is now?'

'You are too hard on her, Ma'am. It is never easy for a shy girl to whom nature has denied the superficial physical qualities so many young men mistake for marriageable virtues. Our faces do not always indicate our characters. If they did her brother would be a veritable saint, instead of . . .'

I gazed at her in surprise. 'Why, Ursi, I thought Count Tarn was your "wicked spoilt boy", your most particular favourite?'

She bit her lip. 'Yes, so he is, Ma'am. It – it is only as I told you, that he has fallen amongst bad company of late and Prince Leopold has had occasion to be displeased with him.'

Though the journey from the Summer Palace to Rosenholm took less than a day by train, secrecy was vital, for if Vielfrass had spent so much effort in separating me from Maximilian he would surely not take lightly the news of our imminent reunion. I decided it would be safer, therefore, to make the distance in two days by road, in the same plain coupé which had taken us to the Mayerhof. Ursi protested, reminding me of the discomfort in such a protracted journey now I had grown heavy with child, but I was adamant. On the road we should be our own masters and could alter our route to shake off any pursuers.

I telegramed Suzannah at the Hunting Lodge, informing her that I had decided to go instead to Schwanensee and ordering her to return to the Summer Palace where she was to superintend the packing and transportation of my boxes. Then, with two of my guards, armed but in civilian dress, accompanying us as outriders, we set off for Rosenholm.

I look back on those two days as an interlude of peace, in whose simple and unexpected pleasures there was no whisper of what was to come. The sun shone gloriously, the countryside was sharp with spring. In towns and villages old women took the air on their doorsteps, dogs lazed in the dust, children bowled hoops, the daily round of herding cows and buying bread and drinking *Apfelwein* under the lime-trees seemed to continue in its untroubled way as if no one in Sylvania had heard of riots or elections.

We spent the first night comfortably in Friedrichsberg, where we were treated with all the courtesy and discretion due to our deep mourning. We were not followed, nothing untoward occurred to alarm us and I found I was beginning to enjoy my incognito, felt childishly pleased with the lack of ceremony and timetables, as if I had been transported back to the days in England when my mother was alive. There was such satisfaction, too, in knowing that at last I had chosen the correct path, and happiness in counting the hours until I should see Maximilian, even though the meeting, when it came, must of necessity be distant and formal. Ursi, also, seemed quite her old self, clucking and flapping and bolstering my aching back with cushions. At Marmion we put up at the Hotel Angleterre and the next morning, Palm Sunday, began upon the short distance into Rosenholm.

We had been late starting out, owing to my exhaustion and to some delay with the horses, and by the time we reached the Old Town it was already the hour at which the Palm Sunday procession would be in progress. As we drove over the river our carriage was obliged to slow, and just past the English Gardens we drew to a halt, one of our outriders coming to the window to inform us that, the streets around St Xaviersdom being closed, access to the Residenz was impossible from this direction other than on foot. Ursula was all for us taking another route, but I still had my holiday mood upon me. 'No, Ursi. We've preserved our incognito for two whole days. Let's make it last half an hour longer. The Kirchengasse is only a few metres from here. Let's step down and watch the procession.'

It had been the custom, which Maximilian had reinstated, for the male members of the family to follow the palm-decked cross from the cathedral to the shrine of St Aloysius at the Jesuit Church in Sigismundplatz and then, after prayers, back to St Xaviersdom. Now my heart leapt at the thought of watching Maximilian as if I were merely another of his subjects, of catching just one glimpse of that dear, longed-for face before I should be obliged to confront it with apologies and explanations. Despite Ursi's protests we joined the crowd lining the Kirchengasse and, after two elderly burghers had gallantly given way for us, were afforded an excellent view.

The Kirchengasse, predating Sigismund I's classical restoration of the city, is narrower than the elegant thoroughfares surrounding the Residenz and the Opera and hemmed in on either side by tall gabled houses. From where we stood, twenty metres or so from the cathedral square, the crowd would be pressed so close to the procession that, were it not for the cordon of infantry keeping us firmly to the pavement, those near the front would be able to reach out and touch the participants. The mood seemed thoroughly amiable, however – old women chatting to the soldiers, sweethearts arm-in-arm, tradesmen in their fob-watches and Sunday waistcoats. In front of me three children giggled and whispered while their mother tried to restrain their excitement. It was difficult to imagine a more law-abiding, good-natured gathering, so that the crowd outside the beerhall in Helsingbad and the scenes afterwards seemed figments of a nightmare.

Now singing could be heard from the direction of Sigis-mundplatz and an expectant whisper rippled up the street, rolling over us in its wake a respectful hush. The cross came into sight decked with its beribboned palm of pussywillow and after it the servers, their lanterns jingling with bells. A pungent cloud of incense filled the narrow gully of the Kirchengasse and through it, as through a mist, I saw the choir pass and the banners, the dove and the lion, and the lilies for Our Lady, and the effigy of Judas Iscariot. The chanting of the singers echoed from the high walls around us, the bells clanged, the incense swirled, I craned my neck to catch sight of Maximilian. The Cardinal Archbishop came into view with two acolytes bearing his scarlet train, and the Canons of the Chapter in their violet chasubles and the Bishop of Rosenholm, who would celebrate the Mass. And then there was another ripple in the crowd, an excited murmuring, and I saw at last, following the carved figure of Christ on the donkey, the family group bearing its palms, with Maximilian at its head.

The procession stopped. Carried on the breeze came the faint sound of the *Gloria laus et honor* sung behind the closed cathedral doors, then the clearer tones of the processional choir chanting their answering Hosannas. The Bishop of Rosenholm had drawn to a halt level with us, by straining on tiptoe I had an almost clear view of Maximilian, bare-headed and in uniform, flanked by two Garde du Corps officers and followed by Prince Gustav and the Duke of Maar, with Aubyn and Anton von Tarn bringing up the rear. I felt the crowd with all eyes upon the tall, composed figure of their King, felt my heart join with theirs in a great wave of love. Then the singing ceased, there was silence while in the square the cross-bearer struck the closed cathedral doors with his staff and they were drawn open. Suddenly 'Hosanna in the Highest' burst out, the procession prepared to move. And there was a bang like a firecracker. And another and another.

What happened next seemed for some seconds devoid of all reality. I saw Maximilian and the Duke of Maar both fall. Then there were more shots, I was dimly aware of glass splintering in the window of a house on the opposite side of the street. I opened my mouth, could find no sound, then all at once seemed to utter a scream that filled the Kirchengasse. It took an instant before I understood that everyone else was screaming too. 'The King, they've shot the King! Oh God, they've killed the King!'

I could not see, he was on the ground and I could not see, the crowd closed in front of me. I had to reach him somehow but procession, crowd, soldiers all seemed to flow together in a powerful current that beat me back. I struck out with my arms; behind me I heard Ursi screaming, felt her pulling at my cloak, tugging, shouting. People seemed to press in on us from all sides, pushing from the direction of Sigismundplatz, heaving from behind me, pouring in an overwhelming tide towards us from St Xaviersdom. Then there were hooves, the clash of sabres. The conflicting tides seemed to whirl and eddy together in a maelstrom. I glimpsed the woman with the children who had stood in front of me lashing out several heads away, howling, shrieking. There was a space, a gap in the sea of heads as if someone had fallen, then she fell too, and the man and woman beside her. I found myself moved forward, no longer of my own volition, my arms pinioned, my body pressed by that swirling tide till I felt the breath being crushed out of me. I saw an officer on horseback with his sabre raised about seven or eight metres ahead, I heard Ursi scream: 'Oh dear Lord, the baby, the baby!' Then I fell, and she fell in the same instant, spreadeagled on top of me.

When I came to I was gradually aware of a noise, hooves and shouting, and beneath the shouts a low unearthly keening. I remembered that sound; the crowd had made it after the army had fired the cannon at Nordstadt. I tried to rise, felt arms thrust beneath me, heard Ursi's voice above the din, commanding and peremptory: 'A carriage, my man! We must get her away from here. For pity's sake, find some horses and a carriage!'

A man's face was looking down at me, a man in police uniform. His expression changed from concern to horrified astonishment and I realised my hat had fallen away, dislodging my veil.

'Now you see who she is help us quickly. For pity's sake man, get your wits about you!'

With his aid and the assistance of one of the young officers who had ridden with us from the Summer Palace, I was raised to my feet. I seemed able to stand, although I rocked, bewildered, for a moment. Then I remembered.

'Oh, dear God! I must go to him! No, let me go! I must see him, I must—'

'No, Ma'am,' came Ursi's voice firmly. 'These gentlemen are taking us somewhere we'll be safe. We'll go with them to the Residenz. Come along, Ma'am. Take my arm and don't look back.'

'But Ursi, oh merciful Heaven, Ursi—!'

I glanced wildly down the Kirchengasse and saw that a wine-merchant's van had been slewed across the street to block it. In front of the van stood a cordon of infantrymen, arms at the ready, and drawing alongside was a military ambulance. I gaped at the ambulance, at the silent, ominous barricade. Slowly I grew conscious of the other bodies scattered in the Kirchengasse, piled sometimes in twos and threes where they had fallen, a heap of worsted here moaning, a child's hat, a young boy pulling vainly at the limp arm of a woman.

'Don't look, Ma'am. I beg you, come away!'

They had commandeered a private omnibus in one of the side-streets near the cathedral square. We were bundled into it and, with the blinds drawn, set off immediately at high speed. I clung to Ursi, too dazed even to cry.

'Please, please Ursi, tell me he's not dead.'

'I don't know, Ma'am. We'll know everything when we're safely at the Residenz.'

There was suddenly a strange inflection to her voice, as if her power of command were draining away. I felt something sticky on my cheek and drew back. She was hatless and her hair was matted with blood; more blood was beginning to trickle in a steady stream from her nose.

'Oh Ursi, oh my dear, what have they done to you?'

'Someone must have kicked me when we were on the ground, Ma'am. I thought if I covered your body with mine, held them off—'

'Oh Ursi, my darling Ursi—'

'We were saved by the Hussars driving the crowd back towards St Xaviersdom. I thought if I could protect you till it was over, protect the dear baby . . .'

She slumped sideways, her face ashen. I struggled against the swaying of the omnibus to lay her out full upon the seat, but her head seemed to pain her too much, I had finally to prop her upright as best I could. I was dimly conscious of my own injuries, a graze on my left cheek, bruising to my knees and to my hands and forearms, which seemed to have taken the greatest impact of my fall where I had instinctively sought to shield my belly; but the pain scarcely mattered. She had an ugly gash in the back of her head near her right ear and the blood streamed so copiously from her nostrils that, though I tore strips from my petticoat in an attempt to staunch it, I was hard put to prevent it choking her.

She had saved my life, saved the baby, with supreme presence of mind had hastened me away from danger, but now the control she had shown in those first terrible moments disintegrated as she succumbed to shock and to the severity of her injuries. It was as if I were watching her age before my eyes; her mouth grew slack, her grasp feeble, her skin grey and loose upon her bones like a wrinkled stocking. Once she raised her lids and gasped: 'But they couldn't – they can't have killed him!' Then she burst out in a paroxysm of sobbing, her chin dripping with blood and saliva, so that my makeshift compresses were drenched.

It was during the onset of this crying fit that the omnibus stopped, apparently at a road-block, and I heard unfamiliar voices and what seemed to be an argument between the officer of my guard on the roof and the police agent on the box beside the driver. The omnibus afforded no communication with the box and the drawn blinds prevented me from seeing anything. After some moments our carriage gave a shudder that sent us both sprawling and we set off again. I did not think, I was too preoccupied with Ursi, too afraid of her grey skin and the bleeding that seemed as though it would never stop, too dazed with terror for Maximilian; some time had passed before it was forced in upon me that we had turned and were travelling in the opposite direction, that the cobbles meant we were back in the Old Town, that every turn of our wheels, every lurch and shudder, was taking us further and further away from the Residenz. We stopped again and, letting go of Ursi, I clambered onto the facing seat and raised the blind.

What I saw made my scalp prickle. For though it was the one Sylvanian institution I had never been called upon to visit, I recognised that drawbridge, the portcullis that was even now being winched open for us, those invincible walls of medieval granite.

I flung myself upon Ursi, trying to shake her to consciousness. 'They've brought us to the Schloss Eisen! Ursi, they've brought us to the city jail!'

The Governor of the Schloss Eisen was a small man with a pallid look, like a plant that has been kept too long away from the light. He demurred gently as I stormed at him, from time to time passing his hand over his forehead with an agitated sigh.

'Your Majesty, I wish you would permit me . . . your lady-in-waiting is in the care of our doctor and I should feel so much more comfortable if you would consent to his attending you as well.'

Though I was giddy from exhaustion and my wrists and fingers were now so swollen I could no longer wear my gloves, I brushed his solicitude aside. 'You have had the impertinence, sir, to keep me here against my will and without explanation for over two hours. How dare you show such disrespect, such absence of consideration for the fact that I am distracted with anxiety for my husband!'

'Your Majesty, it was with great relief that I was able to read you the telegram we received an hour ago informing us that His Majesty has mercifully escaped serious injury.'

'But I must go to him. It is beyond all reason that you should presume to keep me here!'

'I cannot but agree, Your Majesty. It is most puzzling and unfortunate. But I am afraid I have been given my orders.'

'From Count Vielfrass, I suppose.'

'I am not at liberty to say, Ma'am. I only wish—' Here he was interrupted by a knock at the door. Going to it and opening it the merest crack so I could not be seen, he returned with some papers which, begging that I would excuse him, he began to read. I observed him pause, feel for the arm of his chair, then, remembering that my refusal to sit precluded his doing so, continue to read where he stood.

Eventually he put the papers down carefully on his desk and surveyed me for a moment, smoothing his moustache in embarrassment.

'Most unfortunate news, Ma'am. I am afraid I am obliged to . . . I must beg your forbearance a while longer.'

I stared at him. 'What are you saying, sir? Are you attempting to tell me I am under arrest?'

'Er, no . . . well, not exactly . . . that is to say, it is not absolutely clear.'

'But it is clear that you are forbidden to let me leave here and go to my husband. On whose instructions are you acting? Tell me once and for all – is it Count Vielfrass?'

'The orders I have just received are from Herr Commissioner Weber, the Chief of Police. But,' – here he licked his lips as if to continue profoundly distressed him – 'the paper is countersigned by His Majesty.'

IV

The brilliance of the White Room's chandeliers made me blink. Though I had at length been persuaded to rest and had permitted the prison doctor to attend to my cuts and bruises, I was still befuddled with the shock of the Governor's words.

Three figures confronted me in the White Room; Count Vielfrass, Commissioner Weber – an insignificant man nervously clutching a dossier – and Maximilian, who stood before the mantelpiece a little apart from the others with his back turned to me. I was reminded, as my guard clicked their heels to attention, of the night I had been brought to his study after the incident at Marienberg. I waited for him to turn, suddenly dreading what might be in his face, but he remained quite still, with his eyes apparently fixed upon the fire. Then I saw that while his right hand rested lightly on the mantel his left hung at his side, the shoulder held awkwardly and the arm stiff and useless.

'Oh my darling, you are hurt! They told me you were safe, that the bullets hadn't touched you—'

I had made instinctively to go to him but my guards restrained me, both Vielfrass and Weber stepped forward as if they would interpose their bodies between us. Only Maximilian remained motionless, his hand on the mantel, his head averted, as though I had never spoken, were not even in the room. There was a pause. Then he raised his eyes from the fire and said, still without looking at me: 'I have no more than a flesh wound. Uncle Leo is dead.'

He turned then, very slowly, letting his hand fall, stiffening his back, continuing to hold his eyes carefully away from me until he could no longer postpone the instant they must acknowledge my presence. The scar at his temple gleamed white, his lips were bloodless, his face rigid with a bleak determination to suppress all feeling. He surveyed me in silence for a moment as if he were uncertain what he saw. Then his glance seemed gradually to take in the cut on my cheek.

'I instructed you that Her Majesty should not be harmed, that she should be treated gently for the sake of the child.'

Vielfrass simpered. 'You forget, Sir, Her Majesty – for reasons which are now abundantly clear – took a fancy to watch the procession. The Schloss Eisen doctor reports, however, that she has sustained no serious injury. Shall we—' he dabbed his lips—'will you give us leave, Sir, to proceed with our business?'

Nodding wearily, Maximilian seated himself. A chair was brought forward for me and my escort took their dismissal. There was a pause while Weber, sitting at a small table, fumbled through his dossier. Then, without looking up, he read in a high, uncertain voice: 'Marie Bathildis von Hohenstaufen, you are charged that together with St John Aubyn, Duke of Hohen-Kastell, you did treasonously conspire to bring about the death of your husband, His Majesty King Maximilian II of Sylvania, and that as a consequence of this conspiracy you did on the twenty-second day of March in this year of Our Lord eighteen hundred and ninety-one occasion injury to His Majesty's person and cause His Royal Highness the Prince Leopold, Duke of Maar, to be most brutally murdered. Have you anything to say in answer to these charges?'

I was conscious of Count Vielfrass watching me with a barely-disguised smirk on his lips, but I no longer had eyes for him or for Weber. Maximilian sat apart from us in the furthest corner of the room, his body slewed sideways to avoid the pressure of the chair upon his injured shoulder, his chin supported in the palm of his right hand so that his face was masked. I waited for him to look up, to say something.

Vielfrass' voice cut through the silence. 'It appears we

must ask her Majesty a second time – does she offer any answer to the charges against her?'

I continued to gaze at Maximilian, willing him to look at me, pleading wordlessly with him to understand that these accusations were absurd, that this was another of the Count's plots in which we were all caught up, he as well as I. But he did not move or turn his head, remained fixed in his awkward pose with granite immobility.

The heat in the room seemed fierce, the silence thick with it, so that tiny noises, the crackle of the fire, the ticking of a clock, came distantly, as if through fog; it seemed to gather in upon me, this heavy blanket of heat and stillness, bearing me down with its weight. I remembered Marienberg once more, and how I had spat in his face when I had confronted him with the letter, and my screams at Freddy's funeral and all my other foolish accusations. His image, immobile, frigid, wavered for an instant, was swallowed by the fog, returned only blurrily. Oh, if he could not believe my innocence, if I justly deserved such cruel judgement, could he not at least bring himself to shout, curse, sneer at me as Vielfrass did, offer me anything but this unrelenting rejection?

The lavender handkerchief fluttered. 'Well, Sir, since Her Majesty offers no defence against the charges, may I suggest we proceed as you have determined. The Duke of Hohen-Kastell, as you know, is already being transported under guard to his Friedrichsberg estate.'

I had scarcely heard Vielfrass's words but now Aubyn's name filtered slowly through the haze, assuming a sudden dreadful clarity. I struggled with my exhaustion. My tongue seemed swollen and ungainly, when I found my voice it would not rise above a whisper. 'Please, not Aubyn. If you must believe this of me – please Maximilian, not Aubyn.'

Count Vielfrass whirled round in triumph. 'Aha! So Her Majesty deigns to answer us at last – and her first words are to beg mercy for her lover! Do you deny then, Ma'am, that, for motives of revenge and the better to further your adulterous liaison with the Duke of Hohen-Kastell, you enlisted his help to hire the assassin who committed the treacherous and bloody assault upon His Majesty's person this morning?'

'Yes. Yes, of course I deny it.'

'Even, Ma'am, against the overwhelming evidence?'

'Evidence?' I felt the room recede again. 'There cannot be any evidence.'

Count Vielfrass's fangs were bared for an instant in an ugly little smile. 'Weber, if you please, the letter.'

Weber fumbled in his dossier again, extracting after a few seconds a sheet of paper, which he carried over to my chair. He held it with a shaky hand a little away from me, too far away for me to take it from him, yet close enough for me to read what was written on it and to observe that the lower left corner was charred, as if someone had made a half-hearted attempt at putting a taper to it.

The Count advanced upon me. 'Do you deny, Ma'am, that this letter is in your hand and bears your seal?'

'No, but—'

'Then I am sure you will oblige us by reading aloud its contents. Or perhaps you will permit me to read it for you. "My dearest A., While I understand your reluctance I am still determined to carry out my plan. I crave justice for my beloved F. And besides, how can we live in peace when we know the man who has been the cause of so much wickedness remain unpunished . . . ?" The letter goes on, does it not, Ma'am, to request that the Duke of Hohen-Kastell recruit an assassin, to whom you promise blood money of 5,000 florins. Although you urge His Serene Highness to burn this interesting document, he seems, alas, to have been somewhat lackadaisical in obeying your instructions, and so it remains to incriminate both of you.' He paused, the better to register his effect. With his glossy head and his tongue flickering over his moist lips he seemed at that moment like a sleek, black snake. I fought my lassitude, discovered at last the desperate energy that would shake me free.

'If that is all your evidence, Count, then your plot has failed. I wrote to the Duke begging him to find me an agent who would help me convict King Friedrich's murderer.'

'And we all know, Ma'am, whom you took that to be. Oh, come now, you surely won't disown that you publicly proclaimed His Majesty's guilt, poured out your hysterical suspicions to anyone who would listen?'

'I was wrong, foolishly, terribly wrong—'

'Indeed you were, Ma'am, for you seem to neglect that most of us have excellent memories. I, myself, though I should not wish to vaunt it immodestly, possess a certain capacity to retain salient detail. You write: "I crave justice for my beloved F." Did you not use those very same words to me twelve days earlier when you received me in audience at the Summer Palace? Did you not demand of me, as you demand in this letter to the Duke of Hohen-Kastell, that I should bring His Majesty to justice?'

'No, Count. On the contrary, I—'

'Tush, Ma'am! I shall quote your exact words. "Will you give me justice for King Friedrich?" Then you went on to say there was no justice left in Sylvania except the justice of death.'

'Count, you take these phrases out of context, twist them against me—'

'So you will admit you used those words, admit in the presence of His Majesty that you said them to me?'

'I may have used such words, yes, but you, Count, know only too well—'

'She confesses to it!' Whirling away from me, he began to advance on Maximilian. 'She confesses that she told me the only proper punishment for Friedrich's murderer was death. And if we were to press her further she might also admit that she blasphemed, denied the existence of God, and that the rest of our interview was spent in speculation about her popularity with the people and whether, in the event of Your Majesty's overthrow, it would give her sufficient power to seize the throne for her unborn child. May God forgive me, I kept silent about this conversation at the time. We are all apprised of the unfortunate effect Her Majesty's delicate condition has had upon her mental state, and I heard her more in pity than in anger. If I could only have known, understood the extent and force of her delusion – but I did not predict that, when I could not be prevailed upon to help her, she would look elsewhere for assistance, turn to her lover on whose absolute obedience she could rely, her lover whom she would at last be free to marry once King Friedrich was avenged and "this man who is the cause of so much wickedness" lay dead!'

He paused again to assess the effect of his words, remained with arms outstretched in mute appeal, letter in one hand, lavender silk fluttering like a banner of victory in the other. Maximilian had not moved or glanced up during the Count's tirade but now his control seemed for an instant to waver, there flickered in his face a look of pungent distaste.

'There is no need to persist, Count. The charges have been laid and it is agreed how you will act. Let that be the end of it.'

Vielfrass stepped back a pace, dabbed his lips as though momentarily affronted. 'Your Majesty will forgive me – since it was yourself, Sir, who expressed doubts, wished Her Majesty to be cross-examined so that she might defend herself—'

'Defend myself?' The Count's words and the undertone of pain in Maximilian's voice gave me sudden encouragement. 'I have no need of any defence. It is you, Count, who must summon every treacherous excuse, every lying word your silver tongue can command.' Staggering slightly, I rose from my chair, addressing myself directly to Maximilian. 'Oh, Sir, I have been wrong, stupid, cruel, guilty, but please, I beg of you, believe me now. It is this man who engineered King Friedrich's death, this man to whom I referred in my letter, this man who spoke treason to me at the Summer Palace, who suggested I might give support to your overthrow. Maximilian, you must believe me. Today he might have killed you if somehow his plans had not gone awry. And Heaven knows what fate he schemes in future for both you and Sylvania.'

Maximilian looked at me, his face opaque. Then his eyes moved slowly to Vielfrass. I had expected a further burst of oratory, a rush of eloquent disclaimers embellished with flourishing silk, but now to my amazement I saw the Count transformed into the humble courtier once more, shoulders deferentially stooped, head bowed as if in sorrow. There was silence for a moment. Then the head began to shake, the shoulders heaved with a lugubrious sigh. 'Your Majesty, if the Queen sees fit to transfer her sad delusions from your person to mine, then as a devoted servant of the Crown I can only welcome the burden, since it takes a little from Your Majesty's heavy cross. But as for the rest,' – here the head shook sorrowfully once again – 'even my most pitiless detractors will admit I have as little interest in damaging the

monarchy, in laying the way open for Socialist vultures to
feast upon its carcass, as I ever had in destroying poor feeble
King Friedrich. Few today can have felt more fear than I
when I heard the sound of the assassin's shots and saw the
spectre of an empty throne, of anarchy and revolution. For
– as Her Majesty appeared to forget during my audience –
Sylvania's constitution disbars an unborn child from inherit-
ance. And were that not so, it grieves me to say I should in
any case have been filled with dread that my beloved country's fate should be entrusted to someone of Her
Majesty's . . . ahem . . . uncertain mental stability.'

I stared at Vielfrass in perplexity. I knew he was lying,
knew he was guilty. Yet what he said was undeniable: he,
the leader of the Right, the fanatical opponent of all Liberalism, had nothing to gain from an assassination plot. I
swayed, groped blindly for the support of my chair. 'But
you must believe – oh, Maximilian, you must see that you
have only the Count's word against mine, that these charges
are nothing more than an evil fiction.'

Maximilian's face had resumed its bleak mask. 'Marie, it
is not only that the Duke of Maar is dead. Seven others,
some of them women and children, were crushed to death
in the confusion afterwards. I cannot ignore the weight of
the evidence against you.'

'But these lies are not evidence. You cannot condemn us,
condemn the Duke of Hohen-Kastell, merely on the strength
of one misreported conversation and one misinterpreted
letter.'

Count Vielfrass gave a little cough. 'Perhaps, then, Her
Majesty would be so good as to furnish us with some explanation for her dealings with a certain ex-Corporal Grüber?'

'I know no one of that name. How could I?'

'On the contrary, Ma'am, I have positive proof that you
did know this man and indeed that you and one of your
ladies kept an assignation with him not three days ago at an
hotel in Helsingbad.'

I stared at him.

'Come, come, Ma'am. Do you deny your visit to
Helsingbad? You were observed to enter and leave the
Mayerhof by two of my most reliable men.'

'I met no one called Grüber there.'

'But you did have an assignation?'

'I had an appointment, yes, with a certain Captain Rohrbach.'

'Rohrbach, Grüber – a man who is a rapist, a thief and a known political agitator usually furnishes himself with several aliases. Would you care to elaborate for His Majesty upon your reasons for meeting such a disreputable person in such curious and clandestine circumstances?'

'I met no Corporal Grüber. I met a Captain Rohrbach from Military Intelligence who had been recommended to me by—' Too late, I bit my lip. The Count's yellow fangs were bared triumphantly.

'So the Duke of Hohen-Kastell had loyally answered your request, as you knew he would.'

The room was swimming. I remembered my instinctive distrust of the man at the Mayerhof and felt suddenly sick. 'I met Captain Rohrbach,' I repeated foolishly. 'Rohrbach, Rohrbach! I asked him to investigate King Friedrich's death—'

'The under-manager of the Mayerhof will testify that the man who booked the room was Grüber. Furthermore, when my men raided Grüber's lodgings this afternoon they found amongst his effects a silver cigarette-case engraved with your cypher and a bundle of notes – some eighteen hundred florins – which appear to correspond with notes you drew in a total sum of two thousand five hundred from your personal exchequer four days ago. As for the true nature of your conversation with Grüber only the facts can now speak. We could, of course, have interrogated the man and made him confess your complicity. But, owing to the considerable presence of mind of Count Tarn, who alerted His Majesty's escort to the rifle barrel at the Kirchengasse window, the assassin Grüber was eliminated by the marksmanship of the Garde du Corps only seconds after he had fired the shots which injured His Majesty and left Count Tarn's own father, the Duke of Maar, pumping out his life's blood upon the cobbles.'

I sank slowly into my seat. 'It's not true,' I said. 'You have twisted it all. If you don't believe me, ask Baroness Windersdorf. She knew why I went to the Mayerhof, why I gave Rohrbach – Grüber – the money. She knows the Duke of Hohen-Kastell and I are innocent. If you want the truth you have only to ask her.'

Vielfrass dabbed his lips. 'I can assure you, Ma'am, we should most certainly have questioned the Baroness by now as an essential witness. But she is, alas, lying unconscious and despaired of by the doctors, injured, I believe, while endeavouring to save your life. However, I have little doubt that could she speak she would merely reiterate what the rest of your household can tell us – that you repeatedly accused His Majesty of the death of King Friedrich, thus establishing your motive for your vile and seditious crime.'

The room span, the fog swirled in upon me, pressing me in its clammy folds. I heard Maximilian bark out an order for someone to fetch water. My fingers were by now so swollen they could scarcely contain the glass and I spilt it freely on my bosom and chin. When the fog cleared Maximilian was standing over me, a few paces from my chair. Carefully, or so it seemed to me, avoiding any contact between our hands, he took the glass and placed it on the mantelpiece. From somewhere behind me, Vielfrass's voice came: 'Her Majesty has heard the case against her. Is there anything further she wishes to say?'

However little Maximilian's death might serve his interests, it was he who had contrived this plot, I was certain of it. He had coolly, calculatingly measured out the moves which would implicate Aubyn and myself. As to why or how, what he stood to gain from his machinations, my numbed brain refused any longer to hazard. I only knew that he had set the trap and that I, in my stupidity, had rushed us headlong into it. Nothing less than Maximilian's instinctive belief and trust would save us now. But Maximilian had no reason to believe or trust me. I hung my head in silence.

Maximilian had remained by the mantelpiece as if he desired to re-establish the distance between us. Now he turned full towards me and, though he drew himself up, battling visibly against the pain in his shoulder, there was in his face, his whole bearing, a sudden desperate weariness.

'Marie, you must understand that if I wish this country to recover its respect for the rule of law I must see that justice is done. Oh, you will not be condemned out of hand on the basis of this cursory examination – there will be a full judicial enquiry and neither you nor Hohen-Kastell will be publicly charged before that enquiry is concluded. But I have been obliged to relieve Hohen-Kastell of his command and to place him under arrest. You too will remain under guard at the Summer Palace until the enquiry is over. I have given orders that all due allowance should be made for your condition and that you should be treated as leniently as possible. But I am afraid I must inform you that, should you be confined before the enquiry brings in its verdict, your child will be immediately taken from you and placed under my protection. You will leave for the Summer Palace at first light tomorrow morning.'

He had turned away, Weber was attempting to gather together his dossier, Vielfrass had moved to the door to summon my guard. I made one final struggle against the all-enveloping fog.

'I should like, before I am sent away, to speak to my husband alone.'

Weber started, spilling a pile of documents. 'Your Majesty, I should hardly advise—'

'In view of what we have heard, Sir,' said Vielfrass sharply, 'it would be most imprudent of Your Majesty to lay yourself open to so great a risk.'

Maximilian's voice was suddenly raw. 'Damn you, look at your Queen for a moment! She is bruised, shocked, seven months great with child, and it is only by the utmost effort of endurance that she has prevented herself from collapsing. What possible harm do you consider, even in your wildest imaginings, she could be capable of doing me?'

When they had gone he stood surveying me for a while in silence and, as though his strength were deserting him, there grew in his eyes a stricken look, an accumulation of pain and despair which mirrored my own.

He turned abruptly away. 'I care nothing for myself, Marie. If it were simply for me, if it were not for this accursed responsibility to remain alive, I think I should view death with positive indifference. But Uncle Leo, who was my tutor, my friend, who so generously trusted me . . .' He gripped the edge of the mantel with his one good hand, seemed to focus for a moment intently upon the fire. 'I held his head. It was all over in a matter of minutes. He looked surprised, nothing more – just taken unawares. It was over before the surgeon even reached him. And there was nothing, stupidly, hopelessly, damnably nothing I could do!'

I wanted to go to him, to put my arms around him. But the impossibility of it held me to my chair, the sense that my touch was vilely tainted. And, indeed, when he looked up from the fire his mouth was tight and his eyes were hard with anger.

'There was nothing I could do. And so, Marie, I must do what I can now, so far as the moribund law of this luckless country will serve me, to make sure that if Leo Maar died squalidly, pointlessly in my place he shall at least not die unpunished.'

The intensity of his anger frightened me, I could not look at him. I struggled for words of sympathy but they froze on my lips, as inadequate, as offensive as my embrace would have been. After some moments I said quietly: 'I too care nothing for myself. I have lost the right, thrown away everything I was given. But Aubyn – please, when the pain is less, think clearly and carefully of Aubyn. He has never been anything but your loyal friend, he would sooner die himself than conspire with anyone to kill you. And as for our being lovers – oh, you hinted at it once, perhaps in part even wished for it – but it has never been so, nor ever could be. Every kindness Aubyn has shown me, every comforting word, every visit to the Summer Palace, has sprung from loyalty and friendship to you. How can you doubt him, how can you, who know him so well, question even for an instant his steadfastness and honour? If Aubyn is guilty of anything it is simply of being too good-natured, of pandering to my foolishness. And so I have led him to this, betrayed him, just as I have brought pain and destruction to everyone who is good to me, to Freddy, to Ursi, to you . . .'

I tailed away in an access of wretchedness. He was silent for some while. Then, without turning from the fire, he asked abruptly: 'Why did you come back, Marie?'

'Come back?'

'Yes. Why did you return here to Rosenholm instead of going directly to Schwanensee as your Major Domo informed me? You presumably had some reason, after all these weeks of refusing to leave the Summer Palace. Or perhaps it is as Vielfrass says – you wished to watch the culmination of your handiwork?'

I hung my head miserably. 'I came back because it was my duty.'

'I see.'

His coldness crushed me, I searched in vain for the last remnants of my self-control. 'I wanted – I have failed you so badly – I knew, if I could make no other reparation, that it was my duty to be at your side – that you would need that, expect it, even if it was too late for me ever to ask . . .'

He seemed to start, to turn suddenly towards me, but I blundered on, scarcely knowing what I was saying. 'I have been so afraid. When I heard the shots and saw you fall – I could not bear . . . Oh, I have learnt too late, understood too late – in spite of the child, if you had died I should not have wished to continue living.'

There was a silence. Then I heard him whisper: 'My dear, dear little Mouse.'

I looked up and saw with surprise that his uninjured hand was clenched upon the edge of the mantel and that he was trembling. He seemed to struggle to hold himself where he stood, his knuckles grew white with the effort of it. Then I saw slowly return to his face the set, impervious look. His hand dropped from the mantel, he moved away.

'It is no use,' he said, in a voice devoid of expression. 'I am obliged to see that justice is done. I am obliged to act on the evidence against you.'

CHAPTER TWELVE

Anton von Tarn

I

'I must say,' murmured Count Vielfrass, sipping his champagne, 'one does rather tire of this perpetual mourning. It seems we had only just put it off for ex-King Friedrich, and now we must needs put it on again for your late lamented father. But to you, dear boy, it is less of an imposition. Black is always so much more becoming to the young.'

I did not reply and Mme Zelenska's card salon, its blinds drawn as much for discretion as against the April afternoon sun, assumed a subaquatic hush in which, above looming reefs of furniture, the pale faces of the military heroes glimmered like so many ancient, predatory fish. I thought of Nurse Wolf and cursed myself. We had stood in a room with her, Grüber and I, that day of my accident, had stood beside her and spoken to her and then shooed her away. If I were to bind Max to me with hoops of steel she was the final proof I needed, the ultimate glorious confirmation of my power. But we had let her elude us and later she had followed the other inmates of the asylum and made her escape. Finding her now, without a clue to her whereabouts and the whole length and breadth of Sylvania to choose from, would be an impossible task.

'As your father's sole male heir, you are now, of course,' said Vielfrass, 'an extremely wealthy young man. I take it you will give up the army. What a pity it is that your birth precludes your succeeding to the Dukedom.'

'I have already resigned my commission. And as for the title, let us not be so hasty. I have every reason to suppose that His Majesty, in his beneficence, will make a special dispensation. He feels as keenly as I do the injustice of my position.'

'Ah,' said Vielfrass sagely into his wineglass.

I forbore to mention that, while Max had been quite his

old, sympathetic self immediately after the Paterfamilias's death, he had been curiously unresponsive when I had broached the matter of the Dukedom, and had subsequently allowed his time to be monopolised by Suzannah, who was no doubt pressing interests of her own. However, he would soon come to see the logic of it – I need not be anxious on that score. Indeed, on the whole my life had much improved since the Pater's untimely demise. An advance from the estate had gone some way to solving the problems of my exchequer and, besides, Grüber's demands upon my gratitude were now most fortuitously stilled. If only, if only I could find Nurse Wolf.

Vielfrass was surveying me, parakeet's head cocked. 'Dear boy, I realise you have suffered a tragic loss. But you do seem – forgive me for mentioning it – not quite yourself today.'

I drew upon my cigarette, staring at him coldly through the smoke. 'Why, Count, are you having me followed?'

'I, dear boy? Good Heavens, whatever put that idea into your head?'

'A scruffy individual in a vile-looking bowler who nearly bumped into me twice in the Lindenplatz yesterday. And another fellow of the same ilk who would probably even now be clipping his fingernails in Madame's shrubbery, had not my hansom shaken him off.'

'Not mine, dear boy. If I were to set watchdogs upon you I should do you the honour of selecting thoroughbreds, not the mongrels you describe.'

'Who else, if not you?'

'One of your creditors? Or perhaps, for some reason, you are suffering the hallucinations of a guilty conscience.'

'If I am being followed, Vielfrass, you are responsible. There isn't a spy in Sylvania who hasn't sold you his soul.'

'Precisely. Which is why I may put my hand on my heart and say that these hallucinations of yours are not of my creation. Besides, dear boy, why should I waste good men trailing you? I trust you implicitly – you have, after all, tendered me such excellent securities.'

How deeply I resented his assumption that he had the power to control me, and how immensely I should relish it when he discovered that it was he, not I, who was expendable. Meanwhile, as to this matter of my shadows, I did not believe him for an instant.

As though he read my last thoughts, he took a little, affronted sniff of his handkerchief. 'My dear Tarn, you distress me. I thought we had become such friends over the past months. It would cut me to the quick, I assure you it would, if I found you regarded me in no higher light than suspicion.'

He put out a claw towards my arm, but I was spared his clasp by the timely entrance of the Dusky Maiden with my hookah.

Poor Maiden. Instead of the abundant frizz which had been her crowning glory she wore now one of Mme Zelenska's wigs, a little too large and dressed in a shamingly *démodé* fashion. It had hardly, I suppose, been her fault that the retired General had chosen at last to carry out his threat and shoot himself dead at her feet – or that he had selected the night before the assassination attempt for this romantic gesture, a thoughtlessness of timing which had resulted in the Maiden being rounded up with every other suspicious character in Rosenholm and transported to the Schloss Eisen. Although the influence of her many admirers had eventually secured her release, help had come too late to prevent the prison authorities from shaving her head in a manner quite brutally masculine – I had seen it. I had heard the story of her incarceration, too, many times, but that did not discourage her from regaling us with it once more as she lit the hookah.

'Oouf, Herr Sebastian! You are so handsome and so cruel. Your dear friend suffers and you curl your lip. When I tell you about this stinking prison of yours – first they put me in a cell with all these stinking old women – the lice, the stink, you cannot believe! So I tell them – I do not wish to be with these stinking bitches, I wish to be with the men. So they laugh and they say "We know your sort!" So I say "You know from nothing!" So they laugh again. So I lift my petticoats. Then they laugh on the other side of their stinking faces—!'

'Yes, yes—'

'So they put me in a cell with the men and shave my head.

But we play nice games. I show you games we play, maybe?
You give me a kiss, Herr Sebastian, for all my suffering?'

'My friend and I have business to discuss. Make yourself
scarce, damn you!'

At which point, mercifully, she did; but not before she
had clasped her lips round the mouthpiece of the pipe,
taking a long, langorous draught, then offering the wood to
me glutinous with her saliva.

The heavy perfume of the hashish clouded the air, and
through it Count Vielfrass's face began to assume a new and
interesting clarity, as if, like a surgeon, I were whittling away
the goatee beard, flaying the skin from lips and cheeks,
peeling it back with infinite care to reveal the vulnerable
tissue beneath.

I leant back in my chair with a sigh of satisfaction. 'So
what will happen now, Count – now that His Majesty has
been deprived of my poor deceased father's services as his
Cabinet Chief?'

'In my capacity as Chancellor I have been able to make a
suitable recommendation. His Majesty will find Baron
Menken most able and assiduous – although he may be
somewhat disappointed that the Baron does not incline to
his liberal views.'

'And the army?'

'It will be announced tomorrow that General von Olendorf
will replace the Duke of Hohen-Kastell. I experienced some
difficulty with His Majesty at first – he believes Olendorf
unsympathetic to his democratisation of the army. But the
General, though something of a reactionary, is a professional
officer through and through. And it is high time His Majesty
stopped playing tin soldiers.'

'So now you control both the army and the State Police.'

'Oh, I shouldn't put it like that, dear boy. Let us say it is
simply a return to the old order, an affirmation of the ruling
class's natural right to rule and a triumph for political
stability.'

His smugness irritated me. 'How much for the old order
if Keller defeats you on the Land Tax Bill?'

'To be defeated by His Majesty's Opposition when His
Majesty's Opposition no longer speaks with the voice of
its voters? To be obliged to go to the country and turn a

negligible majority into a landslide? I scarcely think that can
be counted a defeat.'

I laughed. 'You seem so very certain of yourself, Count.
But can you truly predict the mood of the people? His
Majesty, for instance, has never been more popular than
since the attempt on his life.'

'And so he should be, dear boy, so he should be. The
person of the monarch is sacrosanct – at least until Her
Majesty provides us with the succession. The people have
been shaken to the core by these anarchist disturbances in
the North. And now they have witnessed their beloved King
narrowly escape death at the hands of a Left wing fanatic.
They will rejoice, with us, at a speedy return to conservatism
and the old values.'

'Then it is to be a Liberal plot, the whole affair?'

'Oh, I think so, don't you? At least, in public.'

'And our two conspirators?'

'The tribunal that judges them will be somewhat less
public. His Majesty will, after all, wish to avoid the scandal.
I fancy His Highness of Hohen-Kastell will eventually be
acquitted. He scarcely possesses the intelligence to be a credible malefactor. And besides, now that he has been removed
from his post and a rift has developed between himself
and the King, he really need not be considered with any
seriousness at all.'

'Which leaves Her Majesty.'

'Ah yes.' He gazed lugubriously into the bottom of his
glass and heaved a sigh. 'I fear the tribunal will feel obliged
to deal more harshly with her. His Majesty, of course, will
be highly resistant to any public punishment, even a discreet
exile, and I must say I agree with him there – the open
disgrace of our Queen would hardly serve anyone's interests. No, the matter will require the most tactful handling.'

I raised my eyebrows.

He sighed again. 'A difficult and dangerous business,
childbirth. Queen Tatiana, despite the finest physicians in
the land, died of puerperal fever – as indeed did your own
dear mother when you were born. It is, alas, so often a
woman's lot – the sacrifice they make for us mere men.'

I remained for a while after he had gone, allowing the fumes of my pipe to play over my senses. An agreeable drowziness stole upon me, in which I felt at once bathed in tranquillity and possessed of infinite clarity of mind – a sensation abruptly banished by the realisation that the Dusky Maiden had tip-toed up behind me and was nibbling my ear.

'Oh, Herr Sebastian! Just one kiss. One kiss, eh, for all I suffer?'

I pushed her away. She giggled and fastened her arms about my neck.

'I do not tell you, in the prison there is a strange rumour the day they take me in. They say Her Majesty visits – they say some trusty see her in the Governor's office. I do not believe, of course. Her Majesty visit stinking prisoners? Never! But these stinking old bitches who are in my cell, they make a big noise about it—'

'Cut along, damn you!'

'A great noise these women make, Excellency, you will not believe. And one of them – she is the rottenest, stink-ingest one of all – she begin to carry on like Her Majesty is a close relation—'

'I said, cut along!'

'She raves on about palaces and diamonds, all kinds of stories, tells us her son even is a Prince—'

The hashish haze left me instantly. Seizing the Maiden by the wrists I forced her round till she was facing me.

'What did you say?'

'I say – ' she giggled uncertainly, taken aback – 'I say there is this old bitch in prison who talks about palaces and diamonds and—'

'A small woman, all skin and bone?'

'Excellency, you bruise my arm!'

'A filthy creature, half-mad and far gone in drink?'

'I tell you, of all of them she is the stinkingest. And she says Princesses bow down to her, she even says, you will not believe—'

'That her son is a Prince?' I sprang from my chair. 'Oh yes, yes, my dear, I do believe! Indeed, I believe so much I shall give you that kiss you are eternally pestering for.' And I promptly clamped my lips upon hers.

She responded with a sigh of delight. I let her work upon my mouth until she was quite frenzied with excitement.

Then, exploring the flimsy sateen of her skirt until my hand was at her groin, I grasped my target and wrenched smartly twice, sideways and down. I was rewarded by a howl of pain and rage which echoed satisfyingly after me, even when I had reached the staircase.

CHAPTER THIRTEEN

Marie Bathildis

I

The news that Aubyn was free, that he was here at the Summer Palace asking me to receive him, filled me for an instant with vain hope. But I had only to look at his face to understand that it was no accident the strength of my guard had been doubled in the past week. I quickly composed myself. If nothing could save me now, at least my joy at his freedom should not be marred by any twinges of self-pity.

Perhaps I had at last learnt resignation in those long weeks of waiting, although at the start I had fretted in confusion. Oh, I had understood my helplessness; Ursi, who alone might have testified for me, had suffered a stroke and now lay in the Rosenpalast, paralysed and bereft of speech – poor Ursi, I owed her dearly for her sacrifice. But even her loyalty would have been of little avail. I had confided in her no more than to confess my belief that Vielfrass was Freddy's murderer; she was ignorant of the true contents of my letter to Aubyn and had not been present during the interview with Grüber; by clever cross-examination the Count would have found a way to twist her evidence against me.

No, it was not my helplessness that racked me nor even the matter of how I had been left so defenceless – by now it seemed no more than inevitable that Vielfrass's spies should have rifled Aubyn's study, followed me to Helsingbad, somehow substituted Grüber for Rohrbach. It was the who and the why which troubled me. Vielfrass hated Maximilian and might, despite his denials, nurse some complex motive for the assassination attempt, but what of his fellow conspirators? If the Tarns had been involved in Freddy's murder I must believe they had been part of this conspiracy too. And yet it was unthinkable, however much Anton wished to harm Aubyn and myself, that he would plot

Maximilian's death. Suzannah, too, loved Maximilian. And, besides, the botched attempt in the Kirchengasse had ended in the death of their own father.

Sometimes I began to believe I had imagined everything, that the letter had come by coincidence into my workbasket, that Freddy after all had died of natural causes, that I truly was neurasthenic and the malice and intrigue I saw all about me were no more than an hysterical delusion. Perhaps it was only my jealousy of Anton which had made me suspect him, perhaps I was jealous of Suzannah's feelings for Maximilian too, perhaps if I could perform some trick of the mind I should perceive the world clearly and sensibly again. How often I wished it were so, wished for the comforting dawn that would chase away these months of darkness, wished to wake with my head pillowed in the hollow of Maximilian's shoulder, feeling his breath gently stirring my hair.

Yet my imprisonment in the Summer Palace, the guards, the accusations, the tribunal were real enough. Perhaps my only delusion was that my suffering was unique, that I was the centre of the plot. I was reminded of the folklore of the mountain people, of how, according to the legend, a vast dragon had once slumbered across the south of Sylvania, its head in the east and its tail curled at the westernmost tip, a dragon so large its nostrils were taken for volcanoes, its outspread claws for lowlands and the fins on its spine for distant peaks. The people, building their hamlets within the interstices of its scales, saw their crops devastated and their population scourged by plagues; yet they were unable to divine the cause of these calamities, since the sheer vastness of the monster was beyond the scope of their comprehension. Thus it seemed with Sylvania now, with her poverty and discontent, her quarrels between Left and Right, her pervasive corruption. In Schramm's time I had believed it was my ignorance which prevented my understanding, more recently I had come to think that every unexplained evil was part of a plan conceived solely to torment me; but now I saw that the extent of the malady was simply beyond my grasp. And I shivered for Maximilian, who must grasp it, who must somehow exorcise the demon which possessed us. For I well remembered the end of the mountain people's fable, how one day a knight chanced upon the eye of the dragon and, recognising it for what it was, ordered a huge bolt to be made, which the people by means of a vast bow, drawn taut by a thousand horses, fired into the epicentre of the monster's pupil. But in its death agonies the dragon tore at the earth, gouging out lakes and throwing up mountains, and from the contamination of its rotting flesh came yet more noxious plagues, so that where it had slept there remained for many years afterwards only chaos and desolation.

From fear then, and from sheer exhaustion, I gradually abandoned my futile speculations. I was, besides, in almost total ignorance of how matters stood in Rosenholm, for until this sudden appearance of Aubyn's I had been permitted no visitors and although I was allowed newspapers they remained bound by rigid censorship. Aubyn's fall from grace had been explained by a disagreement over army reforms, while my condition precluded the need to elaborate upon my continued absence from public life. Vielfrass, of course, had succeeded in blaming left-wing fanaticism for the assassination attempt; but though he might be skilfully manipulating the press he had achieved less success in the Parliament House. His expected defeat over the Land Tax reforms had come about in the middle of April and the election date of 21st May was now a mere ten days away, three days after I was due to be confined.

Without even Ursi's chatter to distract me, I spent my days in lethargy, beyond thought or hope. Only the life within me proclaimed a purpose, and I was glad of my increasing need to centre myself upon it as if nothing else existed. The baby kicked constantly now, so that my nights were often sleepless and my back ached abominably; but on it I could lavish all the tenderness and love I should never be permitted to bestow upon Maximilian, to that tiny, miraculous, impatient creature I might turn during my long days of solitude, so that I should never feel myself entirely alone.

Not that I was ever far from the prying eyes of my jailer. Suzannah von Tarn had departed to the family estate for the funeral of her father and I had expected, given the charges against me, that she would be removed from my household. But no, with an exquisite cruelty that could only be of Vielfrass's devising, she had been sent back as my guard to continue her work of spying. And spy she was, I was certain of that, whatever might be her knowledge of the assassination plot. A few weeks ago I had surprised her in the Italian Garden taking leave of a shifty-looking man in a rusty bowler. He had made off behind the box hedge, of course, the moment I had turned into the walk towards them; but I had glimpsed her with him again, had caught sight of a sharp rodent's face which had seemed somehow familiar. It had taken several hours, but I had placed that face eventually – my police escort on the journey back from Marienberg. I supposed I should not be surprised to find Vielfrass's agents now showing themselves openly at the Summer Palace or to discover Suzannah in direct communication with one of them, but this confirmation of her guilt made the daily cruelty of her presence ever more unbearable. Even now, as she preceded Aubyn into my drawing-room, I felt a shiver of revulsion, almost hated Aubyn for smiling warmly at her and for his courteous little bow as she withdrew.

He looked older, I thought, so that I was forcibly reminded of the years that stood between us; old and tired and, despite the habitual rigour of his bearing, depleted somehow, as if the trials of the past two months had taken their toll in ways far beyond the loss of his office. Yes, his face was grim with the unhappy news he was obliged to bring me, but there was more, an extinction of warmth in the deepset eyes, a jaded, bitter set to his lips; although every button and medal on his uniform gleamed with their usual brilliance, you felt he carried them as if he believed they were secretly tarnished.

I listened to him in silence while he recounted the verdict of the tribunal. His words came haltingly as he struggled with his anger.

'It was a sham, of course, from beginning to end. There was no letter. I burnt the confounded thing, threw it in the fire as soon as I'd read it.'

'It didn't burn,' I said gently. 'They showed me when they confronted me with the charges. It was only singed at one corner.'

'I destroyed the wretched thing, I tell you, watched it turn to ash. What they showed you was a forgery.'

'I'd recognise my hand and my seal, however tired I was.'

'Then it's just more of their damnable jiggery-pokery. God

knows what limits that devil Vielfrass recognises. I heard only yesterday about Captain Rohrbach. Fished out of the river six weeks ago at Behrensdorf. Suicide by drowning, according to our esteemed State Police.'

I drew in my breath. For I remembered suddenly the street outside the beer-hall, the two men holding the struggling figure head down in the water of the horse trough. But what of that now, or of the mystery of the letter? Captain Rohrbach was beyond our help, and there was nothing, as ever, we could prove.

'My dear friend,' I said softly, 'there is no purpose in turning these things over and over. At least Count Vielfrass has not been entirely victorious. You, thank Heaven, are safe.'

'And you, Marie? Am I supposed to stand back and let them do with you what they please?'

I paused for a second. Then I said: 'Do you know what they have decided?'

'They will stay their hand until after the child is born. Or so Max, at any rate, informs me.'

'Maximilian? Then you have seen him, talked to him recently?'

He gave a curious frown, a grimace, almost, of distaste. 'I should hardly be here without his permission. I was summoned to present myself the day before yesterday.'

'And how was he? Oh, Aubyn, tell me? How does he look, how do you think he seems?'

'Confoundedly cool and calm as he always is. Tired, perhaps – they say he sleeps no more than two or three hours a night these days. But all the same remarkably cool for a man who has the whole dashed country ready to tumble about his ears.'

'The elections? But perhaps, despite Vielfrass, Keller can still win.'

'Keller?' Aubyn snorted disgustedly. 'Keller, my dear Marie, is dished – him and his whole wretched party. It seems Corporal Grüber was one of Keller's original volunteers in Thalia, was even a member of his bodyguard for some time. Oh, Vielfrass won't come out with it in the press and risk a libel suit, but it's the rumour in every tavern in Sylvania for all that – the assassination attempt wasn't simply an extremist plot but carried out on Keller's personal instructions so that he could stage a coup and set up a republic. Vielfrass can count on a landslide on the twenty-first of May. Then he can overthrow the constitution and claim it's the will of the people. And Max won't have a leg to stand on if he tries to resist. Oh, our friend the Count has had deucedly good value from his bloody little drama in the Kirchengasse, make no mistake.'

I sighed. 'Then let us pray he sees no further need to threaten Maximilian's life.'

'My dear Marie, there's little fear of that. He has Max in checkmate. You're awaiting sentence for high treason, Leo is dead, Keller is discredited, and I'm to have no more than a sinecure, the Governorship of Rosenholm – everyone Max trusted has somehow been pushed aside or eliminated. He can't even rely on the army now – Field Marshal von Olendorf is one of the old school with a nostalgia for the days of Baron Schramm, he'll make it his business to rally the generals to Vielfrass's standard. No, Max must dance to Vielfrass's tune. Not, I may say, that he appears to care any longer. God, I can remember when he professed to have ideals, principles. But now he seems perfectly content to be that blackguard's puppet – either from expediency or simple cowardice.'

I stared at Aubyn, shocked. 'Maximilian has never been a coward.'

'Has he not? Then why did he allow the whole cock-and-bull story against us to go unchallenged? God in Heaven, I could come to terms with my own disgrace, even forgive the fact that my loyalty, my kinship with him could all so suddenly count for nothing. But you, Marie – how could he stand by without a murmur and let this happen to you?'

'He had no choice. Vielfrass placed him in a position that obliged him to act as he did. If he cared for justice he had to be seen to let justice be done—'

'If he cared for justice? What justice is there in allowing your conviction on charges even a congenital idiot could see were a tissue of lies? You, his wife, the woman who is about to bear his child? But then I suppose that wouldn't sway him as it would any normal man. I suppose in his particular scheme of morality it counts for as pathetically little as every-thing else!'

I gazed at him with dawning horror. For suddenly I under-stood his defeated look, saw why he wore his uniform as if what it stood for shamed him.

'Oh, our dear friend Vielfrass spared me nothing during my interrogation. It was, after all, what drove you into my arms, was it not? – the reason we were supposed to have become lovers. And I, blind idiot – I could never understand Max's affection for the boy, could never comprehend why he defended him to Leo, but, by God, how could I have dreamed that a man I respected, a man who seemed in every way so such a man, could stoop to – could be capable of . . .'

He struggled with himself, brought his great fist crashing down upon his open palm in the powerlessness of his anger.

'And you, Marie! When I think how often I accused you of disloyalty, criticised you for deserting him, lectured you like a smug old fool – was there any wonder you came to hate him, any wonder he was insupportable to you as a husband? And what could I offer you, in all your suffering? What did I do, insensitive dolt that I am, but sit in judgement on you, turn the knife in the wound?'

'My suffering,' I said softly, 'was often of my own making.'

'I couldn't begin to grasp it, you see. Couldn't make out what was there before my eyes. Couldn't or didn't wish to. My cousin, my closest friend, the man I believed could save this country, the man I might once have said I loved – if he hadn't, curse him, debased the word beyond use!'

'My dear Aubyn,' I whispered, 'can you truly have ceased to love him?'

'Can I truly, Marie, feel anything but the revulsion any normal man would feel?'

'But when you saw him had he changed? Did he not appear in every respect exactly the man you always knew? And was not this always in him, even when you thought him fine and honourable? Oh, dear Aubyn, I beg of you, do not make the mistake I made. If he was honourable then, he is still honourable – it is you who have changed, not he.'

'You defend him? Dear God, Marie, you of anyone have the least cause!'

'But I do defend him. And I love him, too, with all my

heart. Oh Aubyn, please, my dear friend, think! Except in not revealing to you this one aspect of his nature has he ever lied to you or deceived you? Has he ever wavered in his duty to Sylvania, in his compassion for the people and his determination to uphold their rights? When you fought beside him did he ever betray the slightest sign of cowardice or did he not, as you yourself told me, ride into the lines to encourage his troops, regardless of the risk to himself? When he had Freddy at his mercy did he ever offer him anything but kindness and friendship? Oh, my dear Aubyn, don't let this single – fault, flaw, whatever you choose to call it – stand in the way of all the other things Maximilian is – is now, when you know about Anton, just as much as when you did not.'

He remained averted from me, his shoulders stiff, his hands knotted behind his back, as if by this obdurate rigour he might render himself deaf. 'You love him? When he's abandoned you, surrendered you up to Vielfrass and his carrion?'

'But, my dear Aubyn, I repeat, he has no other choice. He might wish me innocent, might even believe it. But I have been found guilty. He cannot ignore that without making a nonsense of every principle he holds. He cannot confound every hope he has of freedom and justice for Sylvania merely to save me. And I should not be worth saving if I demanded it of him.'

The muscles worked in the back of his neck. He turned slowly towards me with a look of puzzlement. 'My dear Marie, this is most unlike you. You have always been so fiercely determined, so—'

'Wilful?' I smiled. 'Then perhaps I understand what my duty is at last. Perhaps, too late, Maximilian has succeeded in teaching me that no part of me is free, that the forfeit I pay for my privilege and rank is higher than the hours of discomfort and boredom, the smiling and the standing and the endless *cercles* asking dull questions of dull people, that my personal wishes must be subject always to my obligation, not to who but to what I am. Oh, dearest Aubyn, it is hard, very hard when you are as selfish and obstinate as I. But then perhaps you understand, for it touches you also. And Maximilian too – his forfeit is so much the greater than ours.

Does he not, on that count alone, whatever your private feelings, deserve your loyalty and your support?'

It seemed to me that his expression had softened a little, but I was suddenly unable to look at him for I found my eyes were burning.

'Please, Aubyn, try to love him as you used to. I am so afraid for him. And you still have the power to help him. I now have none.'

II

Whatever I had said to Aubyn, I felt less equanimity about my fate when he had gone. The sight from my drawing-room window of the scarlet ranks of my guard drilling in the parade-ground beyond the Aphrodite fountain made me shiver. Though I retired to my boudoir I paced the carpet restlessly, unable to settle to anything. Suzannah offered to sit with me, no doubt hoping to glean some information about the interview with Aubyn; I dispatched her immediately to walk the dogs. Yet still I was fidgety, incapable, even on the chaise, of lodging my bulk in any comfortable position. Desultorily I picked up my embroidery frame, then discovered I had mislaid my thimble.

Suzannah, with characteristic lack of order, had forgotten to carry her workbasket away. I began to rummage through the tangled skeins of silk, pricking my fingers on stray needles and muttering irritably about her slovenliness. A tin of beads spilled, reels of cotton skittled to the floor, but of a thimble there was no sign. My irritation grew savage. I emptied the contents of the basket onto the rug and there, close to one of the corner pockets, easily detectable beneath the silk of the lining, was a small thimble-shaped lump. I had no difficulty in finding where the object had made its escape – a tear along the stitching inside the pocket had turned, from neglect, into a sizeable rent – but, scrabble for my quarry as I might, it eluded me, I seemed only to push it further away. Then my fingers touched a smaller object wedged into the kapok of the quilted base – something hard, a fragment of broken jewellery perhaps, or the shaft of a bodkin. I drew it out, rolled it into the palm of my hand;

and stared. A gilt stud, square-headed, with the pin slightly twisted as if someone, having wrenched it from its setting by force, had endeavoured to straighten it again. A square-headed gilt stud like a nail.

I gazed at it, first incredulously, then in horror, and then in triumphant fury. And as I stood with the nail from Freddy's reliquary in my hand, as I looked up wildly from it, the door to my boudoir opened and there was Suzannah.

'Forgive me for disturbing you, Ma'am, but I have just received grave news from Rosenholm—'

I screamed. If my heaviness had not prevented me I would have flown at her. I hissed, I raved, I thrust the evidence of her guilt into her face, forced her to look at it so that she could not evade me. I screamed and raged until my heart was thumping so wildly that I found myself fighting for breath.

I was aware when my vision cleared that she was looking at the nail with a curious expression, first of perplexity and then as if with some slow dawning of enlightenment.

'Well?' I gasped. 'What lies will you tell me now? Or will you have the courage to admit you are not only a spy but a murderer?'

Her eyes moved to the scattered jumble on the rug. She had turned very pale. 'I remember now – she emptied it too. I came into my sitting-room and she was there. She said she wanted to borrow my needlecase and she had upset my workbasket by accident. It didn't occur to me, I never connected it with . . .'

Her strangeness confused me. 'She? What game is this? I order you to answer me!'

'It cannot have been more than a week after King Friedrich's death. She must have given up in the end, assumed that because I am not very tidy I must have lost it without knowing.'

'I demand you answer me. Or do you now even deny that this is your workbasket?'

'No, I do not deny it.' That clear, musical voice seemed more than ever incongruous in its illusion of frankness. 'I do not deny it, Ma'am. But the day King Friedrich died I lent my workbasket to Baroness Windersdorf.'

'Ursi Windersdorf? You dare to save yourself by accusing her?'

'She wanted emerald wool for her Berlin work. She must have found the opportunity to remove whatever killed King Friedrich from the cross but not to replace the nail. Then later when she tried, someone – perhaps it was me – disturbed her. My workbasket must have been the nearest hiding-place.'

Green wool. I remembered now, remembered entering that chill little parlour to fetch the reliquary and hearing Ursi chattering about green wool. But it could not be possible. Suzannah von Tarn had always been my enemy. Ursi had sacrificed her health to save my life.

'How dare you! How dare you slander Baroness Windersdorf to save your own contemptible neck! Is there not something repugnant even to your conscience in accusing a person too ill and helpless to defend herself?'

She stood there, that stolid, sullen woman, in whose down-turned mouth and heavy brows seemed to be written every grudging and spiteful emotion, stood and held my eyes without wavering. I began, despite myself, to be disconcerted by her composure.

'It is not my pleasure to cast suspicion upon the Baroness, Ma'am,' she said gravely. 'I should wish to speak otherwise of her, particularly at this moment. I came to tell you that we have just received news from Rosenholm that Baroness Windersdorf is dead.'

'Oh no. Oh, poor Ursi!'

'It happened the day before yesterday, very suddenly, Ma'am. They say it was another stroke.'

I felt myself swaying, saw her hand go out to support me, pulled myself abruptly away. 'And you accuse the poor woman of killing King Friedrich, knowing that she is dead? You are worse even than I thought!'

'I do not accuse her to save myself, Ma'am. On the contrary – although I cannot expect you to believe me – it is Your Majesty's safety that is my concern. There is a gentleman downstairs who begs to be admitted to your presence. He carries a letter addressed to you which was found amongst Baroness Windersdorf's effects. I implore you,

Ma'am, if you are strong enough, to receive him immediately.'

Quietly, firmly, she seemed to deflect my hostility, as if she had taken charge of me, were coaxing a fractious child. A footman was dispatched to fetch the mysterious emissary to my drawing-room. I sat with the incriminating nail still clenched in my hand, staring at her, bewildered. My enemy, my jailer? Suddenly I was no longer certain, suddenly her calm, the note of gentleness in her voice confounded me. But when the messenger from Rosenholm was announced I saw my instant of doubt had been too generous. There, in his shabby worsteds, was the sharp-faced agent I had first encountered at Marienberg.

'So, Countess, you are not content with lies and treachery and murder! You are determined, I see, to insult me too. This man is one of Count Vielfrass's creatures!'

'I beg you, Ma'am, give him permission to speak. Then he may tell you whose creature he is.'

I felt suddenly exhausted. The tribunal had found me guilty, I was powerless now against all their schemes. I gazed at the shabby man with his pinched nose and rodent's eyes and wished profoundly to be by myself, stretched out peacefully on my bed absorbing the rhythms of my belly. I sighed. 'Very well. But you will be brief. I am so tired of lies.'

He clicked his heels together with surprising punctiliousness. 'Captain Radek, Your Majesty. Formerly of the State Police. Now under orders directly to His Majesty King Maximilian.'

I gazed at him, felt once again dizzy. 'No. I have told you – I am tired of lies.'

'Please, Ma'am,' came Suzannah's voice gently, 'please – take the Baroness's letter.'

It was a long, incoherent and detailed letter, dated three days before Ursi's death, in which she confessed to delivering the mysterious document which had estranged me from Maximilian, to poisoning Freddy and to implicating me in the assassination attempt. She had opened and read my note to Aubyn, allowing a forged copy to be made which she had presented to him in its place. She had abused her position

as my confidante further by divulging information which had
enabled the substitution of Grüber for Captain Rohrbach. It
had even been part of the plan that she should give false
evidence as to my motives and my relations with Aubyn,
but she had been mercifully spared by her illness. Her
conscience had always weighed upon her unendurably and
now, when she was close to death, she could no longer
remain silent. She begged me with many professions of
repentance and piety to forgive her. 'I was not, I think, in
the beginning, dearest Ma'am, a bad woman, although for
many years I have existed in a condition of mortal sin. It
was fear of the consequences of that sin which drove me to
act as I did, not for myself but to protect others. Yet I should
have forseen that one wickedness spawns another and
another until, though I sought to prevent misfortune, I found
myself steeped in the most terrible evil. I blame no one but
myself for the crimes I have committed. I embrace willingly
the complete and unconditional responsibility for my sins,
as I must before Almighty God in that last and eternal judgement. If you can find any forgiveness in your heart, I beg
you, Ma'am, pray for my immortal soul.'

I read the words but could not take them in, at first even
refused to believe that the characters which hobbled so
uncertainly across the paper were inscribed by Ursi's hand.
Yet it was her seal I had broken, her voice which spoke to
me from the scrawled foolscap.

'But she was my friend,' I whispered. 'Ursi was my friend.'

Suzannah von Tarn asked if she might look at the letter
and, unresisting, I let her take it from me. She persued it
for some minutes, then handed it to Captain Radek.

'You may tell His Majesty we both witnessed Her Majesty
break the seal. There can be no doubt that it is genuine.'

I stared at her wonderingly. Her composure had not been
shaken, her face, when she had examined the letter, had
registered no emotion, merely a cool and careful appraisal.

'You knew,' I said. 'You knew all along.'

'No, Ma'am. I know nothing even now of the document
the Baroness mentions, and until you discovered the nail I
am afraid I inclined to Aubyn's belief that King Friedrich had
died of epilepsy. But I realised the false evidence against
you could only have been concocted by someone in your

Household. Naturally that led me to suspect Ursula
Windersdorf.'

'Naturally? Oh yes, it seems so obvious now. It could only
have been Ursi. But why was it not clear to me before, why
could I not see it?'

She gave one of her rare and curiously-luminous smiles.
'Because, Ma'am, you could not believe the traitor was
anyone else but me.'

III

Later as, at my insistence, we dined alone together, I looked
at Suzannah von Tarn and thought that I had never met her
before, never indeed even seen her properly. Perhaps it was
merely that our afternoon's experiences had crushed with
one blow the mighty defences we had erected between us,
but her down-turned lips, parted, smiling, seemed all at
once softer, her eyes disclosed an unexpected capacity for
sympathy. Even her manner, which I had thought morose,
appeared now to emanate from a simple disinclination
towards small talk; she combined a careful formality of
speech with moments of disconcerting directness that were
almost masculine and which reminded me of Aubyn or the
gruff ways of her father.

But then, if I had never seen Suzannah before, what had
I to blame but my own blindness? If she had not smiled it
was because I had not, if she had seemed terse it was because
of my own churlishness, if there had never been any friendship or intimacy between us it was because I had abused her
and treated her with open contempt.

I reached across the table to take her hand. 'My dear
Suzannah, why is it that you do not hate me?'

She responded with that disturbing frankness of hers. 'But
I think I did hate you a little, Ma'am, certainly at first. You
were so fortunate, yet you seemed to have small appreciation
of it. You were young, still of an age where a woman is
regarded as valuable currency, not a worn coin to be tossed
into a drawer and forgotten. You were about to marry a man
I – a man any woman would have been proud to honour
and love. And – oh, it was no more than my own foolish

envy – you possessed the good luck to have been born pretty—'

'You must not say that, Suzannah. I know I am not . . .' I paused, suddenly remembering Rosa and her lectures. Had I, perhaps, through my unease with myself, transferred the blame for my failings to Suzannah, hating her plainness because I hated my own?

She smiled. 'I did not understand you very well then, Ma'am, or – forgive me – your shyness. I thought several times of asking my father to intercede for my removal from your household. But he saw my position as a signal honour in view of my morganatic blood. And besides he would have been bitterly disappointed if I had failed in my duty.'

'But when he died – you were free at last to escape my unkindness. Why did you choose to come back to me?'

'Because His Majesty asked me to. He was very good to me after Papa was killed, listening patiently while I raged and cried and made wild promises of revenge. Then later he told me about the secret charges against you and asked if I would help him prove you innocent and convict the real assassins.'

'I think if I had been you I should have found it all too easy to believe me guilty.'

'But I knew you could not be, Ma'am, because of Aubyn. Dear Aubyn – he would not hurt a fly, still less plot to kill his best friend and take his friend's wife as his mistress.' The warmth in her eyes flared for an instant into a flame I could not avoid noticing. She blushed, continuing hastily. 'Besides, His Majesty believed in both of you. He said that if I returned here I should be in a good position not only to report anything suspicious but also to protect you in case Count Vielfrass was planning to harm you further. I knew you would not be greatly pleased with this arrangement, but there was no one else at Court His Majesty would trust and I saw it was for the best, despite the difficulties. I was introduced to Captain Radek and told him my suspicions of Baroness Windersdorf, which he began to investigate. You know the rest.'

I gazed at her wonderingly. 'And I never so much as guessed at it . . .'

'Oh, Ma'am, but you must have known His Majesty would

do something. You surely cannot have believed he would simply surrender you up to the mercies of Count Vielfrass?'

I flushed and looked away, embarrassed that her faith in Maximilian seemed so much greater than mine.

'Poor Ursi,' I said softly. 'She seemed my friend, she saved me, saved the baby. I still cannot understand how she brought herself to do such terrible things.'

'I have known the Baroness all my life and though she was given to interference and gossip I have never until now heard of her harming anyone. She speaks of committing some mortal sin, of people she must protect – it seems evident she was in the grip of a blackmailer.'

'And have you any notion who these people are, what guilty secret she was hiding?'

She frowned and I noticed her animated look had vanished. 'No, Ma'am. The pity of it is her confession takes everything upon herself. She does not even name her accomplices.'

'Yet why? She must have hated them and longed to see them brought to justice.'

'She appears to have been very frightened, Ma'am. Fortunately Captain Radek was able to search her body before the women began the laying-out, for she carried your letter hidden on her person, between her chemise and her stays.'

'But death would free her from fear. Why should she continue to protect, even from the grave, the man who had brought her so much misery? Why should she not spell out directly the name we have little need to guess at? – for her blackmailer must certainly have been Count Vielfrass.'

Instead of answering me she looked away. Then I remembered the figures I had seen by the orangery wall the night before we had set out for Freischutz, the woman's, which I now knew to be Ursi's, and the man's. I opened my mouth to frame a further question but at that moment Suzannah met my eyes again and I suddenly had no need to ask it. When Anton von Tarn had paid his calls upon my household the presence of his sister had merely provided a convenient pretext.

Suzannah must have read my face too, for she fixed her eyes steadfastly on her plate and seemed to assume all her former reticence. I was touched with anguish for her, wished

I had not so stupidly made patent my understanding, for
how could she, for all her courage, be expected voluntarily
to betray her brother. But, though I tried to smooth out the
constraint between us, carrying the conversation to other
topics, talking of Aubyn in a vain attempt to draw her out
again, it was useless. The unspoken subject of Anton now
hung oppressively over us so that she remained quiet and
gloomy and I, despite myself, found I was inescapably
reminded of her likeness to him.

When I suggested we should retire she hesitated,
appeared to struggle with herself, hesitated again, then
said abruptly, 'Anton never knew our mother, and perhaps
Papa was too hard on him. Perhaps I am hard on him as
well.'

She paused, licked her lips, seemed so uneasy that I was
about to dissuade her from continuing when she said in a
sudden rush: 'It worries me that he is so close to His Majesty.
In Switzerland, before we returned here, His Majesty
showed him great kindness and now Anton seems to take
advantage of it, as if he believed it gave him some sort of
power. I have several times thought to speak of it to His
Majesty, but it is difficult – not just because Anton is my
brother, but – because I cannot, I do not, dare.' And she
turned her eyes on me with a look of fierce entreaty.

While my maids were braiding my hair for bed I stared into
the glass and tried to suppress a shudder. It was as if all my
distrust and fear of Anton von Tarn, my sense of loss, were
fresh again, the wound unhealed, the pain undiminished by
the passing of these long months. Suzannah did not know
the nature of her brother's advantage with Maximilian and
I should take pains to spare her enlightenment. But as for
what she asked of me, that I should warn Maximilian against
him – if it was impossible for her was it not doubly impossible for me? Yes, I suspected Anton, perhaps of much worse
than she, but I had no proof, nothing that would confirm
even to myself that my suspicions were more than jealous
inventions. I had been so wrong before – about Ursi, about
Suzannah, about Maximilian himself. I saw suddenly that
cold, closed look of Maximilian's, the mouth hard, the eyes
carefully veiling their contempt for my jealous outpourings.

Suzannah must confide in someone else, I could not do what she asked of me.

I recoiled with pain from the thought, for it seemed to set out anew the division between myself and Maximilian, a division which even Ursi Windersdorf's confession had no power to heal. Oh, he had done all he could to protect me from Count Vielfrass, he would be relieved when Captain Radek reported the contents of the Baroness's letter. But none of this would alter the fact of our estrangement. We should resume the appearance of a marriage, perhaps after the baby was born I should even return to Rosenholm; but Maximilian would remain just as irretrievably lost to me.

IV

And then, late the next afternoon, taking the sun on the West Terrace, we saw something moving beyond the lake, a speck that grew and gradually resolved itself into a horseman. Suzannah and I were strolling together, a footman with the dogs on a leash a few paces behind. We all stopped simultaneously in astonishment. The rider, with fine disregard for the labours of the palace gardeners, was pounding up the walk towards us at the gallop, leaping outcrops of lawn and box-tree, sending the gravel flying beneath his hooves. He skirted the fountain, was lost for a moment behind the corner of the orangery wall, then reappeared galloping across the lawn, his course set directly for where we stood on the terrace. A rider in a black and silver uniform, a tall man on a strong black horse. I gasped, groped involuntarily for Suzannah's arm.

At the terrace steps he drew in his reins abruptly. Suzannah assumed charge of the dogs as the footman rushed down to seize the stallion's head while he dismounted. He paused for an instant to look up at me. Then, taking the steps two and three at a time, he reached out, grasped my hand and fell on one knee at my feet.

'My dear, dear little Mouse. Will you forgive me?'

I felt, in a daze, his lips touch my hand, looked down wonderingly at his bent head, at the place at the nape of his neck where the fine hairs curled gently above his collar.

'Please,' I whispered, 'please, Maximilian, you should not kneel to me.'

'You must have believed I was utterly heartless. Or that I had lost my wits.'

'Maxim, there is no need—'

'The day Leo was killed— Oh God, I was blind with pain and rage, I could not bear that you should be guilty, yet for one insane moment I lost faith. But then you, quietly, lovingly, brought me back to my senses.'

'It does not matter now. Suzannah has explained. There is nothing – nothing to forgive.'

He rose with my fingers still pressed in his. For some moments his eyes searched my face intently. Then, in a voice that was barely audible, he said: 'And for the rest?'

'I was a child. Perhaps if I had tried to understand – will you forgive me, too, for that?'

His eyes remained fixed upon mine, he seemed to catch his breath. Then the pressure of his fingers increased, his other hand came up, as if with disbelief, to touch my cheek. He held me thus for some time, very still, not speaking, though his lips were parted and his face was all at once vividly naked. At last, gathering me into his arms, he began to kiss me, lightly as though he feared me fragile, then, as my lips responded, harder, deeper, until I felt him tremble. His hand was still trembling after our mouths had drawn apart. 'Oh, my darling Mouse, whatever else I am, whatever I may have done, never doubt that I love you. Never doubt that I love you so that I ache with it.'

His fingers cupped my chin, holding my face up to his. I gazed at him, almost could not find the words, so long had I struggled not to say them. And then, when they came, it seemed they could not be stopped, so that he began to laugh, kissed my lips to silence me, my lips, my eyes, my throat, my hair.

'Dear lunatic child! You remind me that there has been a notable deficiency of laughter recently. These months of pretence, thinking of you locked up here on my orders, wanting to come and hammer on the gates and proclaim your innocence to the world, yet knowing I could not without sacrificing the chance to prove it – God, sometimes it has all seemed so hopeless. Even when I thought of risking a message by Suzannah or Radek what could I have told you? The tribunal might yield up Aubyn but I knew it would cling remorselessly to you. When Radek found the letter, when he arrived in the dead of night to confirm that it was a confession, I could have wept with joy. But even then I – I was not certain whether you could – oh, let me look at you again to reassure myself I am not delirious, my lovely, generous, sweet little Mouse.'

The concentration of his gaze, the intensity of its appraisal, brought back all my self-consciousness. 'No longer little,' I said ruefully.

He smiled, took my hands and laid them beneath his where my waist had once been. 'But never, never more beautiful.'

For a while we remained with our hands folded together on my belly, silently taking stock of each other, joyously retrieving every minute detail that memory and distance might have mislaid. I was dimly aware that Suzannah and the footman had somehow melted away, that all around us, too, was silence, the deep, heavy stillness of the afternoon sun. I watched his smile broaden as he felt the movement of the baby, thought how it changed him, that smile, made him younger, boyish, given over suddenly, unashamedly, to delight. And yet I also saw what the smile could not obscure: that he was thinner, that for all the commanding handsomeness of that hawk's face the marks of strain and fatigue were now etched harshly upon it. I found myself wondering whether it was true, as Aubyn had said, that he had forsworn sleep, whether sometimes in the solitary darkness of his study his mastery of himself had faltered before the depredations of pain and grief.

'Aubyn gave me the news from Rosenholm,' I said. 'Is the situation truly as dangerous as he says?'

The smile twisted, his finger came up gently to seal my lips. 'Not now, Mouse. Or at least not yet. I have missed you so wretchedly and we have such little time together.'

'Then you cannot stay?'

'Only for a few hours. And even to risk that is probably madness.'

'But is it not over at last?'

'Over? My dear Mouse, it is only just beginning. But – oh,

my darling, don't look so disconsolate. You, at least, are
safe. And later yes, of course I shall tell you everything. But
let us, just for now, forget politics. Let us indulge in the
blessed luxury of being mere frail human-beings.'

His arms encircled me once more, his mouth found mine.
We continued for some while dizzily engrossed in each
other, our lips increasingly feverish and urgent. His hand
moved upwards to my breasts, I sighed, began instinctively
to trace the line of his backbone down to the hard muscle at
its base. He shuddered, drew his mouth away, buried his
lips in my hair. His voice, when he spoke at last, shook with
the effort of control.

'Oh dear God, Mouse! I cannot touch you without wanting
you. But I am afraid of hurting you or the child.'

Though he was infinitely gentle, I could feel in every sinew
of his body how much his gentleness cost him; his cry, when
at last hunger overmastered him, seemed less of pleasure
than of relief from pain. He lay for a while separated from
me and silent until, no longer able to bear not seeing his
face, I turned and laid my cheek against his. His hand came
up to stroke my hair. 'Oh my dear little one, I have never
possessed much talent for chastity, and these months
without you have turned me into a selfish brute.'

I brushed his lips softly with mine. 'You are not selfish.
You are as Freddy always said you were – honourable and
generous and good.'

To my dismay he burst out in sardonic laughter. 'Mouse,
Mouse, what a catalogue of virtues! When did this noble
ambition to canonise me set in?' Then, seeing I was offended,
he kissed the tip of my nose. 'Frail humans, Mousie. I do
not mean to mock you but we must understand that if we
are intent on being happy together.'

'Then I may never praise what I love in you?'

'You must see me for what I am, if I am not to make you
wretched again. I am scarcely a paragon, Marie.'

There was a mordant note to his voice. I stared at him,
not understanding. He had said that I must know him and
yet this bitter self-disgust frightened me, reminded me
suddenly of his silences, his evasions, of all the inner territory he kept so impregnably guarded. The thought of Anton

came unbidden, and with it promptings of the unwelcome duty Suzannah had laid upon me. If I were truly to know him, must we not talk of Anton, must I not be forced to listen while he gave his account of their love? And then – then I should have to find the words somehow that would outline my suspicions, destroy his trust in me, shatter this unhoped-for, unimagineable happiness before I had even felt wholly possessed of it. All at once it seemed that nothing had changed, that the subject of Anton still hung between us, as inimical and dangerous as ever. My throat constricted.

But then, before I could turn my head away, he caught me gently and I saw that the expression in his eyes had shifted, that his face was empty now of everything but tenderness. Wrapping my arms softly about his neck, I kissed his eyelids, each in turn, and the tired lines beneath them. Then I drew him down until his head was cradled on my bosom.

The last rays of the sun filtering through the blinds gave the room a subtle fluidity, a sense, in the stealthily shifting patterns of light and shade, of distances changing, of objects imperceptibly set adrift and floating. Beneath the high, swagged canopy of the bed we drifted too, spent, indolent, lapped in each other's warmth, half way between sleeping and waking.

He stirred, liberating himself from a tendril of my hair which had strayed across his lips. 'Dear child, how long, how very long I seem to have loved you and thought it hopeless. Now I find I am to have hope again I think I am quite drunk with it.'

Laughing, I snuggled closer to the crook of his shoulder. 'How long, exactly, Maxim, have you loved me?'

'Oh, absurdly much longer than I have had the grace to admit to myself. But then I think I have always been chary of loving. For all the years of my youth I was obliged to hold it indistinguishable from sin.'

He had never before spoken of his time in the monastery. I glanced up, wished I could more distinctly see his face through the twilight. 'It must have been so hard,' I said unwarily, 'to renounce all human love.'

'I was, my dear Mouse, sufficiently content with sin. I

think if I had troubled to draw the distinction I should merely have dismissed it as a blight upon pleasure. And when at last I found it out I did not believe I should ever love again.'

Suddenly I was no longer warm in the crook of his shoulder. I had not thought – I had been sleepy, intoxicated, oblivious to danger. But now, coolly and deliberately, he had brought me to the moment when we must speak of Anton. I struggled for some way to evade him, for words that might take us on some other course, but in the end I only said weakly: 'Then you have loved a great many people?'

'No, Mousie. Only one other.'

Thought his tone was still light I could feel he hesitated, so that my mouth was dry. 'Another woman?'

This time there was no doubt of his pause. I screwed my lids tight. I did not want to hear it, this confession of love that would bring home my obligation to Suzannah, my duty to explain that the man he had adored might be guilty of deception, even of murder. I felt the full force of my jealousy again and knew it was useless – I should never find the right words. I buried my face in his shoulder, almost fought him when, gently dislodging me, he shifted me upon the pillow until I could not avoid his eyes.

'Armand de Miramont was father to me, Mouse, and mentor and guardian and friend – and sometimes also a formidable adversary. But then I was an unpromising youth, wild, ambitious, bitter with my lot and not over-given to scruples. If there is any good in me now it is because he drew it out of me, if I have any notion of duty it is because he, against all the odds, instilled it. We were only lovers for three years – he was too ill and I too consistently unfaithful for that part of things to have continued longer. But in our seven years together I learnt what love is, the receiving of it and at last, in the end, the giving.' He sighed and there seemed to flicker in his face once more that mordant look. 'I think if he had lived I might have been stronger, he might perhaps have saved me from – but still, no matter. That was four years ago. And now by some miracle I love you, my dear sweet Marie, and you, yet more miraculously, love me.'

I was overwhelmed by a tide of selfish relief. 'Then you have not – could not love in that way again?'

I was unable to tell whether he deliberately misunderstood my question. 'Oh, my darling Mouse, of course my love for you is different. You are my wife, about to be the mother of my child. But the difference, little one, is not in strength.' He kissed my forehead. 'I have told you of Armand de Miramont simply because I wish you to understand that I cannot, however much the strictures of morality demand it, be ashamed of my love for him. I beg you, if you can, somehow to accept that.'

'Oh Maxim, with all my heart I will try.'

'You will be obliged, sweet child, to try harder than you know. My feeling for you may make me struggle with my nature, but it will not change it. You may wish in time you had not been so ready to forgive.'

'But if you love me, only keep loving me . . .'

He smiled dryly. 'Then that will be sufficient for happiness? I pray so, Mouse. Oh, my darling, I do not know whether I can ever be the husband I should, ever remain faithful to you, but I swear I am resolved to it with all the strength I possess.'

It seemed now that I might speak to him of Anton, that the moment had arrived, as perhaps it never should again, where I might admit my suspicions without any taint of jealously or revenge. And yet I hesitated, still stupified with relief, still too much in dread of forfeiting everything I had been given. I opened my mouth, my lips tried to frame the words. But then, lifting my face to his, he began at leisure to kiss me, and when we at last drew apart I asked only: 'And the others – apart from the Marquis de Miramont – did you never feel anything for them?'

He laughed. 'Oh, my darling Mouse, you surely cannot require a chronicle of my whole disreputable life?'

It had grown so nearly dark that I could no longer read his eyes. 'Has it really, Maxim, been very disreputable?'

'When I was eighteen, Mouse, and in the world at last, I was not mightily concerned for my immortal soul.'

'And were they all – were there women before me?'

'The duties of a footman can be extremely arduous in a house where Madame has long been a widow.'

'Maxim, I cannot believe—'

'As I have said, I was never endowed with an instinctive

preference for chastity. And I had little interest in starving.'

'Maxim, you are teasing me!'

'Not a bit. I have warned you that your capacity for forgiveness may be stretched to its limits. It was probably quite wrong of me not to have stood aside decently and left you free to marry Aubyn.'

'Now I know you are teasing.' I put my hands to his face, searched its shadows anxiously. 'My darling, you cannot truly have ever believed I was in love with Aubyn?'

'He is all the things you wish to perceive in me – upright, generous, honourable. And I think he has for a long time secretly loved you.'

'If he cared for me once, he has not your patience – my foolishness soon restored him to sense. And besides,' – I revolved my pleasure in the thought – 'I should not be surprised if he reaches an understanding with Suzannah. She would certainly not be averse to it.'

We made a light supper of plovers' eggs and lobster mayonnaise washed down with champagne, and I thought that food had never tasted so good. He was so very tender, adjusting my pillows and finding cushions to ease the discomfort of my back and belly, so altogether gentle and concerned and loving that I still caught myself staring at him from time to time, bedazzled. And yet there were moments now too when I looked at the dark head on the pillow beside me and felt stupidly close to tears. Our few hours together were slipping away remorselessly. At first light he and his adjutants would board the Royal Train en route to Nordstadt, where he would join Uncle Berthold in laying the first sleeper of the Sylvanian-Thalian railway. Afterwards the elections would take him back to Rosenholm and I should not know when I might next see him.

I drew his arms more tightly around me. 'Please, my darling, let me come with you tomorrow.'

'My dearest Mouse, though it tortures me to leave you again, you know that is not possible.'

'Because of the baby?'

'Apart from the baby, apart from the danger to you, the risk to everything is too immense.'

'But now Ursi has made her confession the tribunal will

be forced to reverse their verdict. There is no further reason for our separation.'

'Baroness Windersdorf's letter will remain our secret for the moment.'

I stared at him, astonished. 'But it is evidence against Count Vielfrass. There can be no question that she was acting under his orders. Surely the letter at last gives you some ammunition against him?'

'Since she does not name him, I doubt it. And in any case I am not prepared to put it to the test. The fellow is so damnably ingenious at covering his tracks. In all Captain Radek's investigations he has scarcely come close to him. Forged documents, bribery, twisted police evidence – we know Captain Rohrbach was murdered, yet we can't attach it to him, we know a large anonymous donation was made to the Benedictines at Freischutz but we cannot trace it to its source. Ursula Windersdorf was – apart from one other possibility – our only hope. And even there we had achieved little progress until fate made its timely intervention.'

'I cannot help but feel sorry for Ursi,' I said quietly.

'Do you, my love? Well, I do not. You may add to my catalogue of sins that when I think of Freddy and Leo and of all you and Aubyn have suffered, I am inclined to be most unforgiving.'

'But you will let Count Vielfrass slip away from you?'

'By no means. But I have no wish simply to wing him. When he is brought down it must be clean, efficient and permanent. And to succeed in that I must force him to declare himself. Until then I am obliged to allay his suspicions by behaving as if I accept that I am powerless. That is why Ursula Windersdorf's confession must remain a secret.'

'But he will know that you came here, you cannot avoid him knowing.'

He smiled. 'I confess to the insanity of it, Mouse, but I am not made of iron. And perhaps, after all, the risk is not so great. He will know that I have visited you, but he will not know why. When he arrives from his electioneering in Karlottenberg to observe the inauguration of the railway he will perceive nothing from my demeanour but that I was taken with a sentimental urge to see my wife one last time before the tribunal passes sentence. He will consider it a weakness, but with luck he will suspect nothing more. He is by now so perfectly confident he has me trapped.'

Though his voice was light, the very thought of Vielfrass made me shiver. Maximilian stroked my cheek. 'Oh Mouse, it will be all over soon one way or another. And you are safe here – at least I have been able to use the excuse of your imprisonment to turn this place into a fortress for you. Your guard has been doubled and if you look about you – at the boy who attends to your dogs, at the footman behind your chair at dinner – you will see Radek's men, not Vielfrass's. Suzannah will keep you company. And if my plans do chance to go awry, the proof of your innocence is securely locked away in Aubyn's office in the Maria-Antonienburg.'

I paused. 'Then Aubyn knows we are reunited? You have told him of Ursi's letter?'

'Radek arrived while I was in the midst of explaining to him that the governorship of Rosenholm will be far from a sinecure during the next few weeks. He knows everything, and I must say I have never seen any news give him more pleasure – he seemed almost as insane with joy as I was.'

'And did he – have you both . . . ?' Remembering my last conversation with Aubyn I scarcely knew how to frame the question.

'Has he forgiven me for Palm Sunday? Thank God for his generosity – once he realised I had not simply abandoned you he seemed prepared to forgive me anything.'

So, after all, Aubyn had listened to my pleas, pushed aside what Vielfrass had told him and rediscovered his old openness of heart. The thought warmed me, though its comfort was short-lived. I could not find myself deceived by Maximilian's careful lightness or consoled by his hints at a plan to deliver us. The contest with Vielfrass seemed too unequal, he had been forced to concede too much already. From the West Gate, the clock began to chime eleven; another hour gone. I touched the scar on his shoulder, a fresh scar still purple and angry, indented a little in the surrounding muscle where the knife had probed for the bullet. 'I am so afraid for you, Maxim.'

Turning over onto his back, he worked his arm around

me. 'You should not be, Mouse. If the fates are not entirely opposed to us we shall win in the end.'

'They have not favoured us greatly thus far.'

'We must win, Mouse, I cannot countenance that we should not. It is the only way in which I may atone—' He broke off abruptly, lay for an instant staring up at the tester and, though by the glimmer of the nightlight his face was opaque, I could feel the sudden tension in him, thought I had heard in his voice the bitterness that had frightened me earlier. 'Oh, I was so ambitious for this, Mousie. Even in Paris when Uncle Leo lectured me about duty and I tried to persuade both of us that I did not want it, I wanted it so. I justified my ambition, as all men do, by telling myself I should be better, fairer, that it was not simply for my own self-esteem I wanted it, but for justice, for peace, to put paid to oppression and poverty and suffering.' He gave a savage little laugh. 'Justice? Peace? An end to oppression? Now I censor the press, send the army against civilians, order the arrests of the innocent to appease the guilty – and all this so that I may preserve my own position. I am obliged at last to recognise my ambition for what it is – simply and nakedly, ambition.'

I stared at him puzzled. His eyes were still focused on the tester and his mouth was set hard. I found his hand and pressed it tentatively. 'But you do serve justice and freedom. It is merely that others work against you.'

'Do I, Mouse? I pray so. But it is a curse I have brought down upon myself that when I look into my heart I can never be sure. Count Vielfrass too cloaks his self-interest in grand words – tradition, order, the sacred privileges of land and birth. Perhaps we are not so very different, Vielfrass and I.'

'You must not say such a thing, must not even begin to think it.'

'My hunger for control is no less than his.'

'But what you have is yours by right, what you were born to. Whereas Vielfrass is a liar and a cheat and a murderer.'

He turned to me for a second. Then he laughed that acrid laugh again. 'And I am not quite all those things, Mouse – not yet. But since I see most perfectly the things I am, since I see now that it is his ambition against mine, see it stripped bare of all high-sounding ideals, let ideals be damned. Damn honour if it means this perpetual squalid compromise with what is right! I shall fight him at his own game, by his own rules, I shall arm justice and freedom with a few of his chosen weapons. And I will win, Mouse, I must. For justice and freedom. As the occasion for my hunger, not the contemptible excuse.'

I lay for a while in silence beside him, bewildered by his heat and the pain in his voice, conscious once again of the territory I might not enter, yet feeling he was struggling to open some part of it to me. But I was helpless, bereft of the words that would give me passage. Instead I asked gently: 'Yet can you win? If you cannot use the letter, if Captain Radek has no evidence, can you even begin the fight?'

He ceased his grim contemplation of the tester, his face softened into a smile. 'The elections, Mouse, will be the turning point.'

'But Aubyn says he is bound to gain a large majority and that he will claim his victory as a mandate to cancel the constitution.'

'That is why I must pray he loses. Then he will be driven into the open at last.'

'A *coup d'état*?'

'He will believe he has no choice. He must compel me by force of arms to repudiate the elections and concede the constitution – either that or depose me for a baby not a week old.'

'You are saying – he would take my baby?'

He circled his arms protectively around my belly. 'No, little one. I trust the loyalty of the Hussars while you remain here. And my orders are that at the first sign of real danger you must be moved to Schwanensee so that you are close to the Austrian border. Whatever happens, you and the child will be safe.'

'But you, Maxim? What if he succeeds?'

'He will certainly retain the support of those *Landgrafs* who believe Keller to be the devil incarnate. And he may count on Menken and the other reactionaries he has infiltrated into my cabinet, as well as a certain element in the army. There is even some suspicion that he has had secret dealings with Berlin, may threaten Prussian intervention to bring me to heel. But I have certain forces on my side, too. The loyalty of the army is not entirely lost to me – Vielfrass may repose his faith in Olendorf but Olendorf is a soldier first and foremost and I believe he will place his oath to his sovereign higher than his political convictions if he is compelled to make the choice. Aubyn will travel unofficially to Berlin directly after the inauguration of the railway, while I shall put your uncle's presence in Nordstadt to excellent use. And – if I may admit to any good from the bloody business in the Kirchengasse – the people at least are well disposed to me at the moment. Oh, it will be touch and go. There will inevitably be fighting, more Sylvanian blood shed wretchedly by Sylvanians. But I believe in the end Vielfrass will be defeated and exposed as the traitor he is.'

I put my hand up to his face. 'But at such risk – at such terrifying risk to you.'

Again the heat came into his eyes. 'I will not live with this craven compromise, Mousie. I will have hope for this country at last. And besides, the risk is nothing so long as I know you and the child are protected.'

'Yet everything depends on Keller gaining a majority. And, as Aubyn says, Keller is dished.'

I saw that his lips had curved in a curious smile. 'My dear child, I shouldn't at this stage be quite so certain of that.'

'But Aubyn says Vielfrass has made it certain—'

'And has taught me a few of his skills in the process. Captain Radek has not come away from his endeavours entirely empty-handed. And at Nordstadt I am due to grant a private audience to Drexler, the editor of *Der Freie* – an excellent man whose goodwill I have come to trust. Oh yes, I am learning to play quite adroitly by Count Vielfrass's rules.'

It was dawn so soon. I had tried not to sleep, tried not to deprive myself of a moment of him, but my exhaustion had defeated me and now, waking with the first notes of birdsong, I could feel him alert and watchful beside me and knew that he had succeeded where I had failed, that his eyes had not closed all night.

His hands moved to feel the kicking of the baby. 'Another week, little Mouse. Only another week.'

I smiled. 'Perhaps. Ursi says – said – first babies are often late.'

'And shall you mind waiting longer?'

'I shall mind nothing so long as you come back to us safely. The waiting is tedious, but then I—'

He turned me gently so that he could see my face. 'Then – what, Mousie? Oh, my dear child, are you frightened?'

'Of my confinement? No, no, of course not. Suzannah will be with me and—'

'And so, too, Mousie, shall I.'

'But it isn't possible, how can you?'

He took my hand, the hand on which his rings no longer slid perilously. 'Whatever happens, wherever I am, I shall try to come to you. You have my firm and solemn promise of that, little Mouse.'

He kissed me so long and with such tenderness that neither then, nor later when, dressed, he came to say goodbye and I made my parting picture of his face, did I remember that I had still not spoken to him of Anton. Or, if I remembered, once again my cowardice stealthily pushed the thought aside.

CHAPTER FOURTEEN

Anton von Tarn

I

It was just after half-past ten when, taking my keys to the double doors which partitioned off the Paterfamilias's old living quarters, I stole quietly into Aunt Helena's and Uncle Gustav's apartments in the East Wing. This section of the Rosenpalast was almost in darkness for, my aunt and uncle being away on some arachnidophiles' conference in America, their residence was virtually shut up, empty apart from a few servants – and the one other occupant who occasioned my errand. The shadows, the dimmed gas brackets, the ghostly silence in the corridors dismayed me not at all, however. True, I was a familiar enough visitor, the dutiful nephew who came and went at will – should I bump into a wandering footman I could always plead insomnia and the need to borrow a book from Uncle Gustav's library; but if the darkness hid my presence on this particular May night so much the better. My footsteps muffled by the carpet, I ascended to the second floor and, making my way past Aunt Helena's rooms, paused outside the door I wanted.

There was little question of my being disturbed; the nun who acted as nurse would already be snoring peacefully in the maid's room at the end of the corridor, and old Winders herself would even now be sitting in the Blue Drawing-room surrounded by all those treacherous photograph albums, waiting for me to keep our assignation. Nevertheless, I listened for a second or two to make quite sure before I turned the knob and entered her sitting-room.

Here I set down my lamp on a table and put a match to the wick. I had, I calculated, about fifteen minutes before my absence would begin to seem suspicious. Commencing my search with the bureau I moved through the sitting-room systematically, taking care to replace everything where I had found it. Then on to the bedroom; a vile smell of medicines and sickness but nothing here either, not in the jewel-box, nor amongst the folded underthings, nor even beneath the mattress; no letters, no diaries, no notes stuffed into secret drawers or other evidence of betrayal. Extinguishing my lamp, I stole downstairs to the Blue Drawing-room as silently as I had come.

She was not there. The lamps were lit, one of the albums even lay open on a low table beside a sofa. But of old Winders there was no sign. I cursed her under my breath. The other drawing-rooms were in darkness, so was the music room, the library . . . and yet she could not have gone far, an old woman with a stick and a dragging leg, she could not have followed me in my quest upstairs without my hearing her. Then, as I hesitated in the library doorway, I was aware of a faint but insistent whine, the sound of the electric generator from Uncle Gustav's laboratory.

Though the rest of the Rosenpalast is lit by gas, the generator is my uncle's special luxury, and feeds the ultimate apotheosis of his obsession, a row of oblong boxes, glass-fronted like fish-tanks, extending from his workbench the length of one wall. Illuminated from within and kept at carefully regulated temperatures, these tanks display like so many *objets d'art* the prime specimens of his live collection.

I have always been repelled by this garish shrine to the creatures and by the way Uncle Gustav has of sitting in front of it for hours, watching for furtive scuttlings. I have remained unconvinced by his reassurances that the gauge of the ventilation grills renders it impossible for the beasts to escape, and I have only to see a twig quiver or a quartet of furry legs stretched out laconically towards the glass to feel my skin crawl. Now, as I stood in the doorway, I had within my direct line of vision Uncle Gustav's prize exhibit, a pair of Black Widows presented to him on his last trip to America, a species so poisonous it is said they can kill with one bite. As if to confound all my uncle's reassurances, they had been allotted special strictures of confinement, a cage within a cage, a wooden box about twenty-five by eighteen centimetres with glass back and front, which was propped against the glass of the exterior tank. I did not need to advance closer to be conscious of them, one in each corner above their branching twig, two mature females, their bulbous bodies supported on legs of deceptive frailty, drab, motionless and deadly.

Repressing a shiver, I crossed the threshold. The blinds were down and the light from the tanks was the only illumination in the room. Tall shadows crept upon the walls; in cabinets, on shelves, rows of glass tubes – the pickled trophies of a lifetime's collecting – winked where the half-light caught them. On Uncle Gustav's workbench his microscope, his boxes of slides, his dissecting needles and bottles of preserving fluid stood neatly laid out to await his home-coming; and, sitting on his high wooden chair, hidden from me at first by the door, there was Winders, just like a fat black spider herself – but an old spider, powerless now to bite, limbs on the left side flaccid and useless, scuttling days gone.

On the inside, the door was hung with a heavy curtain to exclude winter draughts. Despite the mildness of the night, I slid the drapery across the lintel, would have turned the lock too, had not the key been unaccountably missing. I could not tell if she were afraid. The winking eye and twisted mouth admitted of no variation upon the ludicrous come-hither gaze that was now her permanent expression.

'Why here, Winders?' I asked. 'The drawing-room is somewhat more hospitable.'

'Had g-g-given you up,' she said in her querulous drunkard's voice. 'Fancied . . . l-l-looking at the creatures.'

Whatever her fancy, it was deucedly inconvenient. In the plush and velvet of the Blue Drawing-room it would have been the work of a few moments to pin a feeble half-paralysed old woman to her chair and press a cushion over her face. But here, in Uncle Gustav's laboratory with its marble floor and wooden stools, there was little to assist me in counterfeiting the second stroke that would appear no more than inevitable.

'T-t-tired,' she whined. 'Why so late? No consideration for a s-s-sick old woman.'

My handkerchief? No, that would not do. There was a towel, I noticed, hanging on the washstand in the corner. I could cram one end in her mouth while I blocked her nostrils with the other. But it would be a messy and distasteful business and although what servants there were had mostly retired by now I should risk alerting someone by a prolonged struggle.

'My dear old Winders, we must, as ever, be discreet. It wouldn't do at all if it were to be noised abroad that you had recovered the use of your tongue, would it now? Someone would be bound to insist that you testified at the tribunal – and we both know in your present state of mind you're scarcely up to such exertions.'

'What you want?' A pendulum of spittle swung from her lower lip. 'Won't do any more of your vile work! Won't do it, d-d-do you hear?'

'Oh Winders, Winders, tush, tush! A few little tasks here and there, a few tiny favours—'

'You said . . . said the l-l-letter was a little thing. But evil . . . brought evil to Her M-m-majesty . . . whatever was in it.'

'Her Majesty? May I remind you that you held the Little Treaty in no higher regard than I. You told me yourself that she would never love His Majesty as he deserved, that she was thoroughly peevish and self-centred.'

'Evil! And then more evil! Our Blessed Lady forgive . . . to k-k-kill King Friedrich—!'

'A congenital idiot with one foot in the grave? You may think of our assisting the other foot as a simple act of mercy.'

'They say he was strong . . . would have r-r-recovered. Their M-m-majesties loved him.'

'Some small sacrifices are necessary when the objectives are glorious. The letter had done its work but old Max was still inclined to be sentimental, further measures were required if the Little Treaty were to remain permanently alienated. When you reported the gift of the reliquary the course was obvious – we believed she would accuse him and she amply rewarded our expectations, did she not?'

'And then this last . . . this terrible wickedness. Not to tell me. Let me run errands, open her letters, report to your spies, let her meet . . . vile person in the M-m-mayerhof. Never guessed . . . may I burn in hellfire! . . . never guessed you and that wicked Vielfrass . . . plotting to k-k-kill His Majesty!'

I sighed. 'My dear old Winders, I begin to tire a little of

your hellfire – and of your stupidity. I am the last person to wish Max dead.'

'Murder your King, murder the man who has been a f-f-friend to you. David and J-j-jonathan, Her Highness and I used to say . . .'

'In Heaven's name, woman, stop snivelling and exercise what is left of your brain. The odious Grüber was a crack shot. If old Max hadn't suffered a foolish attack of gallantry and thrown himself into the line of fire when the Paterfamilias was hit he'd have escaped without a scratch.'

She appeared to gape at me with her one eye. Her lopsided mouth worked soundlessly.

'And you, you old fool, you had your bout of heroics too, didn't you? Getting your head kicked in to save the Little Treaty. And what reward came to you from it, eh? Nothing but to end up more senile and ugly and useless than you were before. I'm surprised at you, Winders, truly I am.'

She was whimpering now, the saliva frothing on her lips and drooling down her chin. 'Murder your f-f-father! Things you made me do . . . But not evil in my heart . . . Not like you, wicked boy! Murder your own father!'

'Oh tush!'

'I saved Her Majesty . . . for his sake . . . for His M-m-majesty. She learned her duty, learned to l-l-love him. Saved her for his sake . . . and the dear b-b-baby.'

I could not suppress a little moue of disgust.

'Oh, you mock me! Foolish old Winders. Threaten those she loves . . . make her your servant, kick her, abuse her . . . But you will be punished . . . if not in this world, in the next . . . You will be punished with all the agonies of h-h-hell!'

Here the effort of speech became too much for her and she was obliged to splutter impotently as she fought for breath.

I smiled. 'You're very free with your talk of hell, Winders, and of how you were my mere servant, of how I played upon your innocence and virtue. But have you not forgotten one small but salient detail? Yours was the wickedness that began the whole business.'

She was mopping her chin with her handkerchief. 'I

regret . . . God is my witness . . . Wrong, great wrong . . . but d-d-done from love.'

'And who is to say I do not act for love's sake too?'

'Love? You?' She gave a sudden snuffling laugh. 'No love in you. Not one ounce. Only evil. Evil! You are a w-w-w—'

'A wicked, wicked boy? But not so wicked as you, old Winders. Not by a long chalk. I have the full measure of you now, you see. I know it all at last. Everything.'

Her single eye goggled at me. In the silence I fancied I heard the spiders scraping and scuttling in their cages.

I smiled. 'I'd only guessed the half of it, hadn't I? Enough to drop a hint about my visit to the convent and throw you into the most spectacular funk. Enough to persuade you that if you didn't do what I required you would put at risk those persons you so mawkishly claim to love – not to mention the whole Hohenstaufen line. But I hadn't got quite all of it, had I, dear old Winders? I'd underestimated the sheer extent of your cunning.

'Oh, it seemed simple at first. Aunt Helena's great secret sorrow, the locket she wears with the twist of dark hair in it, the widow's weeds. Being married to Uncle Gustav can't have been entirely jolly – no one cares to play second fiddle to a roomful of spiders. And Uncle Sigismund, with his legendary appetites – my dear old Winders, it was all so obvious. Uncle Sigismund was easily bored, wasn't he? – had turned his attention to the ladies of the Volksoper even before Aunt Helena realised she was *enceinte*. Uncle Gustav was unlikely to accept the child and although the crinoline hoops of those days hid a multitude of sins the truth could scarcely be concealed indefinitely.

'So you, old Winders, hit upon the most ingenious plan to save your friend from dishonour. You would claim to be with child by your dear departed Albrecht and Aunt Helena would graciously offer to attend you during the confinement. A retreat to a convent across the border a month before the birth and who would be the wiser? It happens from time to time, I am told, in most of the highest families in Europe. The child, of course, is afterwards discreetly adopted, preferably in another land.

'But you loved your dear friend, you wished to spare her

the pain of that discreet but irrevocable parting. You knew of one Annelise Stroop who had been a wet-nurse to your sister-in-law. This Frau Stroop – or Wolf – possessed three compelling virtues – she was eminently bribeable, perpetually in a delicate condition, and her children never lived. You waited for her latest confinement, then installed her with her infant in the royal nursery. The child would go the way of the others, of course, but who had any interest in some peasant wet-nurse's spawn? You would bury Nurse Wolf's brat as if it were your own pretended stillborn issue, and Aunt Helena's bastard would replace it and be brought up in the royal nursery with Tatiana's child. Aunt Helena would be able to watch her offspring grow and flourish. Very touching.'

I paused. Behind the grotesque leer, she seemed to survey me with surprising steadfastness, although the dribble still issued from her crooked mouth.

'As I say, my dear Winders, your secret appeared so transparent it seemed scarcely to require my genius to divine it. Of course Aunt Helena's bastard would resemble Sigismund – he would carry the same blood on both sides, would be more of a Hohenstaufen than Tatiana's son. Of course the boy who was brought up as Nurse Wolf's child would remember all those convincing little details about the Residenz, the gardeners and the flunkeys and the names of pets. And of course if he reappeared pretending to be my deluded Pater's longed-for Crown Prince he would have little difficulty carrying it off. After all, whose evidence would identify him? Oh there was Brother Jean from Mont Rémy, I admit, but here I agree with Vielfrass – in the transcripts he refers to "a prince" or "the prince" very loosely and inconclusively, he would have sworn the moon was made of Nordstadt cheese to help a man he considered his friend. Whose evidence, my dear old Winders, would prove the most telling? Why, that of the only two persons of consequence who had daily visited the nursery. Yourself and dear Aunt Helena.

'Yet there were still things that puzzled me, Winders, things that did not quite fit. The scar, for instance. The Crown Prince was scarred from a riding accident, other witnesses than you testified to that. But when you saw the stranger had such a scar it did not dismay you. On the contrary Aunt Helena fainted with rapture and you too appeared to suffer a positive paroxysm of delight. It niggled at me, flawed the simplicity of my thesis, left me something I could not explain. Until, that is, I had the pleasure of meeting the Countess von Blankenberg.'

She responded at last, gave a quite perceptible start.

'Oh yes, my dear Winders, you may think I am lazy, feckless, good for nothing, but I can be diligent when I have a mind. Determined to leave no stone unturned, I travelled to Vienna – and was rewarded by an account of the extraordinary incidents on the night after Tatiana's death. Incidents, my old Winders, in which you played the leading part.'

Her one functional hand was quivering so that she was obliged to grasp the edge of the workbench. I smiled.

'I have heard you say it yourself so many times – happy events do not always occur when they are expected. The day came for Aunt Helena to be confined – and passed without issue. Nurse Wolf's sickly infant, which had held on to life against the odds for two months, now gave up the struggle and died. Still, your feathers were not too much ruffled. After all, to guard against discrepancies of sex the child had been kept as much out of sight as possible, it would be a simple matter to pretend its continued existence. You had promised it a Christian burial. You kept your promise and waited. And then a quite remarkable coincidence occurred. Aunt Helena was delivered a fortnight late of a son. The next day your spy in the Royal Nursery sent word that Tatiana had been delivered a fortnight early – and also of a son. Two boy children by the same father, with a mere day between them . . .'

I paused for a second the better to register my effect then, like Vielfrass in his raven's mode, swooped upon her.

'What made you do it, Winders – respectable, God-fearing matron that you are? Revenge against Sigismund for slighting your dear friend? A sense perhaps that Aunt Helena's child was more rightly a Hohenstaufen than Tatiana's? Or simple gratitude to the woman who had translated you, an obscure minor nobleman's widow, to a position of influence and power? In any event, the temptation was too much, was it not? If ever you had served Princess Helena well, your devotion excelled itself that night at Schwanensee.'

A curious gargling noise came from her throat. 'No! N-n-no!'

'Tush! My dear old Winders, there is no point in denying it. You see I have at last spoken to Nurse Wolf.'

'Nurse Wolf is dead!'

'Nurse Wolf, or Stroop as she is once again known, is at present enjoying His Majesty's hospitality not three kilometres away in Rosenholm jail.'

'Dead. Dead. D-d-dead!'

I laughed. 'I had to forge all manner of documents, use my utmost ingenuity to see her. And a miserable old drunkard she is. But very much alive, I fear. I talked to her for nearly an hour. And, though they say she is mad, I must confess I found the conversation most instructive. How easy it must have seemed, my dear old Winders. Tatiana had succumbed in childbed. Sigismund was abroad. True, the Cabinet Secretary had dutifully inspected the new Crown Prince, but he was unlikely to be able to tell one new-born infant from another. You had only to expel from Tatiana's Household everyone who had been present during the confinement and you were safe. By the time Sigismund returned from Venice there were you, calmly dandling his so-called son and heir. And there in the nursery was another child, a disinherited child, a child condemned by you to live his life in obscurity as Dieter Wolf. "My son is a Prince, my son is a Prince!" Oh, she is not so mad, Nurse Wolf, not so mad at all.'

Her scrawny neck jerked, she appeared to be fighting for breath. 'Nurse Wolf is dead! Or why . . . ? Why hide the poor children? Why let us believe they were k-k-killed? No woman . . . no mother's heart could . . .'

'A mother's heart? The creature was far more interested in spending the money she had extracted from you in such lavish quantities. Her disappearance permitted her at last to fritter it away without attracting suspicion. And as for the children – she is not a woman overburdened with intelligence. When Uncle Gustav's regency fell and you all went into exile she believed they could serve her purposes no further, that their presence merely exposed her to danger. She imagined they would remain shut away at Mont Rémy for the rest of their lives. And so they should have – had it not been for dear old Max's insatiable ambition.' I smiled. 'It must have put you in the funk of all funks when you saw the photograph. You had neither of you ever been certain about Uncle Gustav – whether he had guessed, at least about Aunt Helena's child. And now you were faced with the possibility of the true Crown Prince returning and revealing how you had deprived him of his birthright. But your luck held, didn't it? When you saw the scar you knew you were looking at Sigismund's bastard. You knew it, and his mother knew it.'

She was gasping for air, tearing at the throat of her dress with quivering fingers. 'No! Not Her H-h-highness. I admit it . . . admit all of it . . . blame me! Not the dear Princess. She n-n-never . . . never knew.'

'Come now, Winders. Aunt Helena may not have been privy to the workings of your crafty old mind that night thirty years ago. But when she returned to Schwanensee she discovered what you had done and condoned it. As she has condoned it ever since.'

'Nothing. She knew n-n-nothing.'

'Tush! Do you hope to persuade me she did not recognise her own son from the first moment she set foot in the nursery?'

'She did not know . . . did not wish . . . My decision, mine. When she found out she was shocked . . . f-f-frightened. But too late. No going back then . . . May our B-b-blessed Lady pardon me . . . No going back . . . ever.'

'No going back indeed. When the imposter returned you welcomed him with open arms. You were both as eager as he to continue the deceit.'

Her goggle eye fixed me strangely. Her lips worked as if she were making a febrile effort to gain mastery of her tongue. 'You may blame me . . . You may blame the poor Princess . . . for keeping s-s-silent. But you cannot blame His Majesty. He . . . at least . . . has never known.'

'Oh, hasn't he? I should not, if I were you, be so certain of that.'

'How could he know? He was an innocent b-b-baby.'

'Nurse Wolf is not renowned for her reticence. Perhaps later on she told her charges the truth. In any event, he is not so innocent now. Otherwise why should Dieter Wolf's body have been found at Fontarelles, why should he have felt obliged to murder the real Crown Prince?'

'His Majesty is a good man . . . a good King—'

'Old Max is as ruthless and ambitious as the devil. What you stole for him he will never willingly surrender. He is as guilty as any of you – guiltier perhaps, my dear Winders, even than you.'

She was silent for a moment, staring at me behind the salacious mask with that fixed expression I could not perfectly construe. The tremor in her hand set her rings clattering against the workbench and it seemed that the spiders once more stirred in their cages, responding as if to some arcane signal.

'You will harm him,' she whispered. 'You will use your knowledge to harm His Majesty . . . destroy Her H-h-highness. I have given my honesty . . . my peace of mind, my immortal soul. But it is still not enough. You mean . . . to bring this down on us . . . for your own w-w-wicked ends.'

I glanced back at the little washstand and the towel hanging on its rail. Not perfect for the task but, *faute de mieux*, it must suffice. 'My dear woman, do stop squawking. I have told you a hundred times I have no intention of harming Max. On the contrary, in all my plans I hold his future happiness very much to heart.'

'Then why t-t-torment me? Why bring me here in the d-d-dead of night? You know . . . all there is. What more do you w-w-want?'

I turned casually towards the washstand. 'Perhaps, my dear Winders, I wish you simply to be impressed by my genius.'

'I have done your evil work. I will do no m-m-more!'

'I do not ask more.' It was confoundedly inconvenient that she had positioned herself behind the workbench and so close to the door while I, to reach the washstand, had been obliged to put the length of the room between us. But still, she had no strength, with her dragging leg she would have difficulty evading me. I put out a hand towards the towel. 'I have achieved what I desire, my old Winders, my plans have almost reached fruition. There is only one outstanding matter – the question of the Little Treaty, which my dear friend Count Vielfrass promises to deal with most satisfactorily. But in any case, what use could you be to me now? Tell me that, Winders. What use could I have for a pathetic old cripple? Particularly when she is prone to such dangerous attacks of conscience.'

I had the towel knotted around both hands. I turned with it. To my surprise she did not move or show any sign of fear. Her one eye glittered in the half-light from the spider cages, glassy and unblinking. I drew the towel taut, came on towards her slowly. She continued to stare at me as if transfixed. My feet moved softly over the marble, I was suddenly excited by the towelling taut in my hands, by this slow, deliberate stalking of my prey, by the sense of my body, fluid and powerful, every muscle of it co-ordinated by an Olympian control. I gave a little low laugh. For I was all at once aware of being violently aroused.

And then I saw her go for the microscope, struggling to lift it with her one good hand. Her face twisted, her shoulders heaved, I thought she would throw it at me and ducked – but instead she hurled it with all her strength at the tank containing the Black Widows. The glass of the tank shattered, the little glass-sided box was flung out upon the marble not a metre from my feet, there was a splintering, a tinkling, I saw something scuttle straight towards me. Then the room was plunged into darkness.

I froze. The hairs on the back of my neck stiffened. I felt my skin prickle, felt every centimetre of it acute and quivering, alive with movement. I waited, paralysed, in the darkness for that sudden, lethal stinging of my flesh.

I heard her moving, heard the drag of her lame leg. Something clattered to the floor and spilled its contents noisily. A box of slides from the workbench. She had thrown the switch on the generator and now she was feeling her way along the bench, making for the door. Oh God! – too late I remembered the missing key – she had planned it all along, the laboratory, the lights, her careful position near the doorway, she was going to turn the key on me and lock me in with them!

I let out a sob. From somewhere in the darkness laughter answered me. She was to my right, had reached the door perhaps. I must not let her reach it, must not, must not. Some instinct beyond thought of the spiders propelled me forward, my shoes crunched on broken glass, I hurled myself at the laughter, whimpering. My foot caught a stool, I staggered, crashed with force into a solid wall which sent me reeling. My hands touched wood – and, oh God, what else? – but no, only the nip of broken glass. The workbench. And after the workbench, oh pray I could reach the door in safety.

And then I heard the laughter turn suddenly to a gurgle. My groping hands touched something soft, a heavy mass that tottered towards me, toppling into my arms. My foot was tangled in her skirt, we fell, she clinging to me, gurgling, retching, clutching me rapaciously to her breast. I found her chin, pushed her face away from me, felt it slippery beneath my palm. She gave a strange bubbling sigh, then suddenly fell forward. There was a gust on my cheek like air hissing from a bellows, an infinite weight pinioned my chest. I lay for a second rigid. Then with a shriek I heaved her off me, struggled to my hands and knees. Crawling blindly, I clutched at velvet. The door curtain. With a sob of relief I tore at the handle. In the dim light I could just make out her inert body. But I did not stop, not to search her clothing for incriminating confessions, not even to make sure she was dead. Slamming the door fast behind me, I ran down the corridor for my life.

CHAPTER FIFTEEN

Marie Bathildis

I

Of all the barren hours I had endured at the Summer Palace, those interminable ten days before the elections were the worst. Yes, I might comfort myself with the thought that I was loved; but, however much I clung to the memory of Maximilian's tenderness, another image would force itself upon me, a vision of him alone in his study, his mouth grim, his hands restless, his face taut with fatigue and anxiety as he contemplated the approaching crisis. And I, who longed to take some part of his burden, was compelled to sit, impotently waiting, was expected to draw consolation from the careful provisions he had made for my safety when I was helpless to guard his or even to know the precise measure of his danger. Though I knew for the sake of the child I must remain calm, the long hours frittered away in needlepoint and novels and other anodine feminine pursuits brought me close to distraction. Even the weather seemed to mock my fear: in the West Gardens butterflies flirted and danced in the windless air, roses drooped with gorging bees, in an azure sky the sun shone imperturbably.

Although I understood Maximilian's need for secrecy, it was having no real information that was the hardest to bear. A letter came for Suzannah from Princess Helena on her journey homewards, but that was posted from Paris and was given over, besides, to her grief at hearing of Ursula von Windersdorf's death. Otherwise we were obliged to make do with the newspapers and, though we combed *Der Freie* every morning with particular care, we were rewarded only with the usual bland effusions of the censor. The inaugural ceremonies of the new railway were described over many columns, with a fulsome paeon to Sylvanian-Thalian co-operation and not a detail lacking, from the marches played

by the three military bands to the exact particulars of the
King's and the Grand Duke's decorations. There were carefully edited digests of election speeches, brief accounts of
Ursi's funeral, reports of His Majesty's departure for Rosenholm, but certainly no whisper of anything untoward.

And then, five days before the elections, as I was taking
a late breakfast upon the terrace, Suzannah appeared,
breathless and jubilant, brandishing the morning's edition
of *Der Freie*.

'ASSASSIN GRÜBER IN PAY OF LANDGRAFS', the head-
line read. 'Attempt on His Majesty's Life Plotted by Right.
Mystery Nobleman was Go-between.' The article spread over
three columns and was also taken up in the leader. Further
investigation of Grüber's background had revealed that far from
having connections with the Liberals he had been a vocal
supporter of Vielfrass and his party. Acquaintances testified
that he had boasted of numbering members of the aristocracy
amongst his friends and that even before the shooting he
had received money from a mysterious go-between known
only as Sebastian. Fellow tenants of Grüber's lodging house
also spoke of hearing the name of this sinister paymaster,
often coupled with drunken claims of influence over matters
of State. The true identity of Sebastian remained obscure,
although *Der Freie* speculated that the incognito concealed a
figure well-known in Court or political circles, possibly even
a minister in Vielfrass's government. Grüber had been absent
from Rosenholm two days before the assassination attempt
and had made no secret on his return of being flush with
money. He had been heard in his cups to ascribe his pros-
perity to the good offices of his mysterious benefactor.

I glanced up at Suzannah, remembering Maximilian's dry
little smile when he had mentioned his meeting with Drexler.
'Will it work, do you suppose? Or will it merely be dismissed
as yet more rumour?'

'Even if it is rumour, Ma'am, it must surely help Keller.'

'If only it is not too late.'

But it was not. The next morning it seemed suddenly as
if the censor had never existed. Even the right-wing papers
felt obliged to take up the story, while the Centre Party
organ, *Der Wachturm*, began to mutter darkly about the
involvement of right-wing provocateurs in the March rioting.

But the Liberal *Der Freie* now offered a new and yet more startling development: a mulatto maid at the Dacha Zelenska, a Rosenholm boarding house favoured by retired cavalry officers, had come forward to testify that the elusive Sebastian had often patronised the establishment's card-tables and had several times used its private rooms for meeting with someone who, despite his incognito, she was prepared to depose on oath was Chancellor Vielfrass himself.

The following day, the date predicted for my confinement, the scandal continued unabated. Though a writ served upon Drexler prevented further mention of Vielfrass's name, the association lingered resonantly behind each fresh speculation about Grüber and Sebastian. While election speeches were still assiduously reported, political issues took second place. The proprietress of the Dacha Zelenska had been arrested on the point of fleeing to Austria and further damaging revelations were expected from her interrogation. As to the identity and whereabouts of Sebastian rumour grew wild, although the man himself obstinately evaded capture. Two days before the polls Weber was forced to announce that the State Police, at the request of His Majesty's Cabinet Secretary, were to begin an enquiry into the Sebastian affair. There were rumours that Vielfrass would tender his resignation as leader of the Right the moment the vote was declared. Even while the count was in progress *Der Freie*, *Der Wachturm* and all but the extreme right-wing *Catholic Herald* were predicting a working majority for the Liberals. And on the morning of 25th May, *Der Freie* trumpeted confidently that Maximilian would have invited Keller to form a government by the afternoon.

Suzannah and I followed these accounts with mixed emotions. That Vielfrass was defeated, that against all odds the Liberals had gained power, was of course reason for jubilation. Yet I could not but remember the consequences Maximilian had predicted. Though the sun still blazed over lawn and box-tree, bleaching the orangery wall pale gold and misting the fountains with shimmering haze, I could feel no warmth.

Ursi had been right. The lying-in room stood prepared, nurses and midwife had already taken residence and

Professor Axel-Liebnitz, Court Physician-in-Chief, held himself in readiness at his estate near Helsingbad; but the day for my confinement had passed without event. Despite my discomfort, I found I was relieved. Safe in my womb the child could not be used as a bargaining counter, would serve, indeed, as insurance for Maximilian's life. Soothing the movement in my belly, I willed the baby to have patience for a while.

In the general anxiety there was one other source of relief too. I had frequently reproached myself with my failure to warn Maximilian of Anton, had felt shamefaced before Suzannah when I recalled my cowardice. But while the Sebastian scandal was at its height she had received a further letter from the Princess Helena recounting the details of Ursula von Windersdorf's funeral and reporting that Anton had departed unexpectedly for Heidelberg, with no definite date fixed for his return. Though the news did not absolve me of my guilt it lightened it a little. In Heidelberg Anton could play no more part in Vielfrass's plots nor otherwise harm Maximilian. Now there was only Vielfrass to contend with.

Though I retired early on the night of the twenty-fifth I could not sleep, could not shut out the image of Maximilian alone in his study, cigarette burning between his fingers, face strained with waiting. Towards morning, I fell into a half-sleep in which I dreamt I was in the Kirchengasse again. Yet this time there was no crowd, no procession, no choir, only a deep, cloistral silence in which even the gun made no sound as from an infinite distance I saw a tall black figure falling. Then I was in the White Room, yet it was not Maximilian who stood before the fire but Aubyn, and when he turned his face to me it was wet with tears and he kept repeating over and over: 'There was nothing I could do, dear girl, nothing, nothing I could do!' I woke screaming, not believing for some seconds that I was awake but hearing Aubyn's words, feeling the presence of the dream all about me. Then I saw the foot of the bed silhouetted in the half-light, became aware that my back ached and that I was sweating profusely. But the dream lingered with me like a palpable reality, even when my maids were putting me into my dressing-jacket.

The morning had dawned as perfect as all the preceding mornings; from a cloudless sky a pristine light spilled shadow over lawns silver with dew; in the silence tiny sounds carried with ringing clarity, a thrush warbling in the orangery, a clatter of pans from the kitchens, the distant bark of the sergeant of the guard. I remembered another morning, just as calm and bright, when I had looked out across the Residenz gardens and scarcely noticed at first the columns of smoke rising beyond the cedars.

The pain in my back seemed to have intensified and I was plagued by a renewed onslaught from the stomach cramps I had suffered periodically over the last month. I could not face the sun, nor any thought of breakfast, but lay on the chaise in my boudoir with the blinds drawn, waiting anxiously for the newspapers. By ten o'clock they still had not arrived.

'The night train from Rosenholm has been delayed, Ma'am,' said Suzannah soothingly. 'According to the station master there is some trouble on the line. Major von Pauling says the telegraph wires to the city are also down.'

I stared at her. 'Then he no longer has any contact with the Residenz?'

If she frowned she had covered it in an instant. 'It is probably nothing – a flock of birds, a high wind. Do you remember in the snows we were cut off for three days?' She looked at me narrowly. 'You seem unwell this morning, Ma'am. Forgive me, but do you—?'

'It is only that I am sick with worry,' I said, shifting to ease the niggle in my back. 'Let me rest for a while. And tell Major von Pauling he must inform me the moment he has re-established communication with Rosenholm.'

I lay for a while wishing I could have faith in Suzannah's calm, trying vainly to empty my mind of thought. But when, an hour or so later, I heard voices in the room beyond I could stand it no longer. Rising with difficulty I pulled open the connecting doors.

'Not now!' Suzannah was saying urgently. 'Besides, if I am correct it is in any case too late—' She swung round as I entered, biting her lip. Major von Pauling, the commander of my guard, and Count von Thaal, my Major Domo, drew to attention smartly and bowed. Suzannah had lost her calm,

I noticed, and the Count's pate glistened with a perspiration more excessive than the heat would warrant.

'You have had word from Rosenholm?' I asked.

Count von Thaal licked his lips delicately. 'Ahem – not precisely, Ma'am.'

The Major, a compact man with carefully trimmed side-whiskers, advanced a step and clicked his heels. 'I regret . . . I regret, Your Majesty, that we have received news which obliges us – in accordance with our orders, Ma'am, Count Thaal and myself must without delay expedite the removal of Your Majesty's Household to Schwanensee.'

'What news? You must tell me.'

I observed that Suzannah, despite protocol, knitted her brows in warning at the Major. He paused, selecting his words with care. 'Two hours ago we received word of an army rebellion in Karlottenberg. It now appears that Karlottenberg, Maar and Eugensberg – indeed most of the territories to the East stretching westward towards the River Jana – are under the control of rebels demanding the reinstatement of ex-Chancellor Vielfrass. We have no report yet from Nordstadt but it appears the Thalian border is calm, as is the mountain area—'

'And Rosenholm?'

'Our direct wires to the Residenz have been out of action since the telegraphists first attempted routine contact this morning.'

'But half an hour ago—' broke in Count von Thaal excitedly, to be silenced by another frown from Suzannah.

'Pray continue,' I said.

'Half an hour ago,' said the Major gravely, 'we received a telegram from Behrensdorf, dispatched upon information brought by a messenger from the capital. It seems – it seems, Ma'am, that at one o'clock this morning sustained gunfire was heard from the gardens around the Residenz and the Rosenpalast. And I am afraid shooting was also heard within the Residenz itself.'

I struggled with my voice. 'And my husband?'

'We pray, Ma'am, that His Majesty is unharmed. But under the circumstances, in view of his orders—'

'We have no choice,' broke in Count Thaal, 'but to

recommend Your Majesty's departure to Schwanensee immediately.'

I gazed at them, at the perspiration dripping in little beads from Thaal's nose, at Suzannah pale and glowering, at the Major, almost shamefacedly, avoiding my glance. I opened my mouth to speak, but was suddenly gripped by such a fierce wave of pain that the words died, I found myself clutching my belly, panting.

'Don't you see?' hissed Suzannah, rushing to take my hand. 'Don't you see why I begged you to say nothing of the dispatch from Behrensdorf? Her Majesty cannot travel to Schwanensee, cannot be moved anywhere at the moment!'

II

I had, weeks previously, decided upon Sigismund II's State Bedroom for my accouchement. It had appeared entirely fitting at the time – after all, not only had my baby been conceived in that massive gilded bed but so too, according to legend, had Sigismund got Tatiana with child there – although when I had mentioned it to Maximilian he had seemed curiously disconcerted by my desire for such symmetry. Now, while servants went in every direction to summon my doctors, the midwife, my Mistress of the Robes and my chaplain, I was taken to my dressing-room, put into a fresh white cambric nightgown and gently led there like a bride. But on the threshold I drew back. There was something all at once repugnant in the leering putti, the tasselled whisperings of primrose silk; I saw a cupid here with half a nose, there without a finger, nymphs mirrored in flyblown glass, locked not in wantonness but in the rigour of decay. The dream came to me once more, the echoing silence of the Kirchengasse, the dark figure falling, falling. Then the pain returned. Not now. The child must not, could not come now.

With soothing noises they led me past the *torchères* and the balustrade towards the bed. Here figures in white linen smocks hovered, on a painted commode the chloroform jar stood in readiness, round the posts at the foot of the bed a strong silk ribbon had been secured for me to ride like a jockey when the pains were in earnest. I submitted to their examinations, drank the camomile tea they gave me. I would not scream, I would not cry. His danger, his suffering was the greater. The cramps were still infrequent and, though my waters had broken, seemed less intense now. I lay staring up at the dusty swathes of the canopy, willing myself impervious, separate from my body.

I had asked Suzannah to be with me and for a while, to distract me, she recited passages from the translation of Mme de Sévigné we had been reading. But neither of our hearts was in it, our attention was drawn continually to the bustle in the anteroom. Pauling and Thaal had telegraphed Behrensdorf in the hope of sending word somehow to Rosenholm, for as well as the need to inform Maximilian – if he were not by now beyond all information – the law required that the King's Cabinet Secretary and the Minister of the Interior should attend the birth. In the palace grounds Pauling's Hussars stood at the alert. And all the while everyone waited tensely for some signal from the telegraph instrument which communicated directly with the Residenz. Twice, unable to master my fear, I sent Suzannah for news. But when she returned the second time I caught the suspicion of tears in her eyes, remembered that Aubyn too, as governor of the city, stood in equal danger, and regretted my selfishness. The pains came and went. They were slighter now and often with lengthy intervals between them.

By four o'clock they had ceased completely. Professor Axel-Liebnitz examined me again, the midwife administered castor oil, they clicked their tongues, urged me to rise and walk about to see what exercise might do.

Suzannah gazed at me pleadingly. 'I beg you, Ma'am, for the sake of the baby. His Majesty would wish it.'

I pressed my face to the pillow. I longed for this child desperately. But must I now choose – its life or Maximilian's?

We walked, turn and turn about, across the marble. The pains recommenced but not strongly. The *torchères* were lit, there was still no word from Rosenholm. By eleven my contractions had ceased again. They drew the curtains round the bed and let me doze.

I was in the Kirchengasse, I could see the gun, I wanted to

run to him, but I could not move. And then the shot came,
not silent this time but ringing out, a single shot with
answering fire. I rose up screaming, saw Axel-Liebnitz's
pince-nez glint through the parted curtains, heard Suzannah's voice soothing me. Then there were other voices in a
babble. 'An intruder on the roof! Pauling's men have him.
He won't bother us again, God be praised.' But I saw Aubyn
standing before the mantel in the White Room, his eyes
bright with tears, and knew they were lying. I filled my
lungs and screamed again. Then Suzannah was comforting
me, the midwife was gently twisting my fingers about the
silken reins. The pain came a second time, not discomfort
now but wrenching, tearing pain. And I began with urgency
to ride my race.

I was no longer riding against the pain but lying on my back
in a brief respite and it was daylight once more. I could see
everything around me with absolute precision, the silvery
moats of dust shivering in a sunbeam, the tallow congealed
upon the tapers, a dead moth lodged in the tester high above
me,• its wings dark and powdery as incense. I felt light-
headed, divorced from my body, as if, like the moth, my
essence too drifted amongst the gilded roses, powdery and
insubstantial. I moved my eyes and saw Anton von Tarn
sitting at my bedside, smiling. But no, it was Suzannah,
Suzannah's smile, and she was saying that the rebels had
surrendered and that Maximilian was safe and Aubyn too,
and that I must now think only of the baby. But I had heard
the shots and knew it was not true, knew it was Anton
speaking to me and that he was lying. Then the pain came
back worse than before and I vomited; and when my vision
cleared he was there again, holding my head, sponging my
brow with a flannel. I shrieked at him to go away but he
only smiled; and I saw it was my fault that he was smiling,
my fault that Maximilian lay dead and I had not warned
him. I tried to push the flannel aside, I howled in fear; but
the smile broadened, the hand pressed the chloroform pad
hard upon my lips.

It was twilight and they had lit the *torchères* once again and
I was riding from the Turkish Hunting Box to the Summer

Palace, riding so that the hair fell in my eyes and the reins
were slippery and my whole body shuddered with the effort.
The midwife was riding beside me, holding me in the saddle
and shouting instructions: 'Open your knees . . . chin
down . . . forgive me, Ma'am, but the knees still a little
wider.' And there was someone else too, someone else's
hand, not Suzannah's, on my forehead, someone saying
softly: 'Not much longer, my darling, you must not give up
now, not now when it is so nearly over.' And I looked up,
panting out my pain, and saw in the half-light a dark face,
gaunt and unshaven, and I screamed and the midwife
shouted: 'Knees wider . . . bear down . . . and again, Ma'am
– oh yes, that's the ticket!'

Then I fell back and there was all at once a high, irascible
wailing, and the dark face was there again, its usually cool
blue eyes unusually bright and glistening. 'Oh my darling
little Mouse, you have a son, you have given us a son!' Then
my hallucination vanished, I was aware only of the bundle
they put to my breast, of a very small, wizened face still
slimed with blood and mucus, its tiny eyelids closed and its
tiny mouth wide open, bawling fiercely. And I was still
wondering at the perfection of this creature as I drifted into
unconsciousness.

III

They had washed me and braided my hair and put me
between crisp sheets; it seemed from the light to be the
middle of the morning. I shifted, felt pain, a soreness in
my breasts, a leaden exhaustion. Yet I was gripped by an
inordinate longing to see my child; and there was a question
also, a question to which I now scarcely dared demand the
answer. I struggled to sit up and saw at once two figures
stir amongst the primrose hangings, Suzannah and the
nurse. They curtsied and the nurse, having plumped my
pillows, went immediately to fetch the baby.

Suzannah, although she too looked tired, was smiling
broadly. 'Our new Crown Prince is such a dear thing,
Ma'am. Professor Axel-Liebnitz has pronounced him the
model of health and sturdiness. And even the Cabinet

Secretary – though I think he is terrified of babies – was obliged to admit he is the image of His Majesty—'

I put my hand on her arm to silence this uncharacteristic burst of chatter. 'Suzannah, last night – last night I thought . . .' I hesitated, still hardly daring the question.

Her smile widened. 'Oh Ma'am, we tried so hard to convince you it truly was His Majesty, but you would have none of it. You insisted he was a delusion conjured up by the chloroform.'

I remembered my dream and Anton's face smiling, and shivered for an instant. 'Then he came. Despite everything he kept his promise.'

'He was here a full two hours before the Crown Prince was born, and he would not leave your side for an instant. Even at the last, when the Herr Professor suggested he should retire with the rest of us to the anteroom in case his sensibilities should be offended – I have never seen His Majesty lose his temper but for a second I feared greatly for the Herr Professor's pince-nez. When His Majesty came out afterwards to receive our congratulations he seemed so moved and proud. And then, when he had read the latest dispatches from Rosenholm and the East, we finally persuaded him to bed, for he has slept even less than we these past two days.'

'And Aubyn? I can see from your face there is good news of Aubyn too.'

'Rosenholm is peaceful apart from a few last pockets of resistance. His Majesty will tell you—'

But here we became aware of the nurse, who had been hovering respectfully in the dressing-room doorway. I took the bundle gingerly from her, staring in fresh wonder at the small red face beneath its thatch of dark fur. At once his mouth opened, he heaved in breath and let out an irate howl. The etiquette of the Hohenstaufen Court decreed a wet-nurse, but I had extracted a promise from Maximilian that I might so far break with tradition as to attempt to feed the child myself. Now the nurse assisted me in putting the baby to my breast; and we marvelled how the crying instantly ceased, how the small mouth, quite oblivious of etiquette and tradition, closed eagerly upon my nipple.

When, later, I glanced up, I thought I caught a wistfulness

in Suzannah's gaze. 'He is so very beautiful,' she said. 'I shall offer so many candles for his happiness. I hope he will always have a surfeit of it.'

Thinking of Aubyn, I smiled. 'Oh, my dear, I hope we all shall.'

We lapsed for a while into a roseate silence. Then suddenly the nurse was curtsying, Suzannah had risen from her chair. Looking up, I saw, framed in the doorway to the anteroom, a tall, still figure.

He was in his dressing-gown, as if he had left his apartments immediately on waking. At the foot of the bed he paused, his eyes once again suffused with emotion. When he bent to kiss me his lips brushed my forehead softly, almost tentatively.

'I did not mean to break in upon you. It was such an exquisite picture I was content simply to watch you both.'

I gazed up at him in silence for a moment, searching his face for signs of pain or injury and finding, beyond his exhaustion, only that look of uncontained joy. 'Oh, thank God, Maxim,' I whispered. 'Thank God, thank God.'

He took the chair that Suzannah had vacated and we remained for a while steeped in the peace of our son's contented suckling. He would be called Friedrich – on that we had no need for conference, although to it must eventually be appended the litany of other family names. In Rosenholm the salvo of one hundred and one guns had been fired but otherwise, out of respect for those who had lost their lives in the uprising, there would be no public celebration. As to Suzannah's view that Freddy was the image of his father – and indeed the baby's eyes were a very cool and startling blue – Maximilian was sardonic.

'Heaven forbid! No, my dear Mouse, he reminds me of one of the Chapter monks at Mont Rémy – wrinkled and toothless and silently possessed of the wisdom of ages. What a pity the poor little devil will spend the rest of his life unlearning it.'

Eventually I rang for the nurse, who winded the baby and took him away. Then Maximilian gathered me into his arms and we lay holding each other tightly, feeling our hearts beating, scarcely breathing.

'Oh, my dear brave, clever little Mouse. I am inordinately proud of you.'

I took his head in my hands, explored his face with my fingers. 'Did they tell you I was convinced you were dead?'

He laughed. 'Not this time, Mousie. Oh, it's true Olendorf's battle of conscience took a damnable while to resolve itself. He gave us a mere hour's warning. But we were prepared and it was enough.'

He began then to relate the events of the previous two days, from the time he had summoned Keller to the Residenz. It seemed that eight hours later the new Chancellor, along with most senior members of his party, had been hauled out of bed and summarily arrested. Simultaneously Vielfrass and some thirty of his supporters backed by a detachment of rebel troops from the 2nd Cuirassiers had seized the Parliament Building, while Baron von Menken, Maximilian's Cabinet Chief, had ordered the 1st Foot Guards to surround the Residenz and the Rosenpalast. The Post Office, the Defence Ministry and several other strategic buildings also came under attack, while Police Headquarters flew the *Landgrafs'* flag and the rebels, having previously cut the telegraph wires, now stormed the railway station in order to isolate the capital.

At the Residenz, however, Field Marshal von Olendorf's defection had left Maximilian apprised of the precise timing of the coup. The still-loyal Garde du Corps were waiting in readiness, while Maximilian, declining to seek sanctuary in the Thalian Embassy with Prince Gustav and Princess Helena, remained calmly in the White Room until the 1st Foot had been repulsed and Menken and his party were prisoners. At the City Governor's Headquarters in the Maria-Antonienburg Aubyn too was ready and had mobilised the remaining loyal troops. Even so, fighting had been fierce, particularly around the Parliament House and Police Headquarters and in the Old Town where the Cuirassiers were garrisoned. Most of the rebel strongholds had not fallen until the next day, and Vielfrass and his troops still held out, even now, in the besieged Parliament Building.

Meanwhile the struggle had begun to restore communication with the rest of the country. Messengers had already

brought news via Behrensdorf of the grave situation in the
East, but the mountain regions remained peaceful, and on
the Western border Uncle Berthold's troops were drawn up
in case of further army revolt at Jedburg. Lack of telegraph
and transport systems had always rendered news from the
North slow and difficult to assess, but it seemed from
dispatches Major von Pauling had received in the last few
hours that Nordstadt and the other Northern territories had
ignored the call to arms and that there was mercifully
no sign of Prussian aggression from the border. Matters had,
as Maximilian had predicted, turned upon the loyalty of
the army. Despite the rebel generals at Karlottenberg,
Eugensberg and Maar, the majority of senior officers had
chosen with Olendorf to abide by their oath. Most of the
crack regiments, apart from the 2nd and 4th Cuirassiers, had
remained loyal although a high proportion of their officers
were drawn from Eastern landowning families; and even the
detachment of Cuirassiers which had been dispatched to the
Summer Palace to relieve Major von Pauling of his command
had thought better of it and turned back at Aveling. Two-
thirds of the army now stood in Maximilian's defence, resistance at Eugensberg was said to be weakening, and the
Deathwatch and the Duke Louis were advancing on Maar.
Once the Parliament Building fell and Vielfrass was captured
it was hoped that the rebel generals would see the futility
of further resistance.

Again I surveyed Maximilian and was relieved to find him
whole and unharmed. 'But we were told there were shots
fired within the Residenz itself.'

'One of Menken's party began flourishing a revolver. I
think he was trying to shoot poor Olendorf. But apart from
taking a nick out of a Garde du Corps lieutenant and a crystal
or two off a chandelier he did no damage. I have told you,
Mouse, I was never in any real danger.' He touched my
cheek. 'Oh come now, I have been damnably, undeservedly
lucky. It seems my time has not come yet, that I am to be
spared until I have finished what I set out to do. Save your
compassion, if you will, for the decent young men who have
given their lives on both sides for a quarrel I wish to God
had never been necessary.'

I buried my face in his shoulder. 'Suzannah said there was

shooting here too, the night before last – but I was confused
and doubted her.'

'Two Hussars caught an agent of Vielfrass's trying to worm
in past the guard. One of your nurses has also been arrested.'

'But . . . why should—?'

He stroked my hair. 'No need to concern yourself with
that now, little one. You are safe, and the Count's spies will
soon be without a master.'

'And Keller is Chancellor, thanks be to your mysterious
Herr Sebastian. Did you and Drexler invent him?'

'My dear child, the constitution forbids me to act in any
way that would influence the outcome of an election. Oh, I
will admit Radek's initial information was scanty, that I may
have encouraged Drexler to embroider somewhat. But when
he investigated it transpired there truly was a connection
with Vielfrass.'

'So Sebastian does exist?'

I glanced up and saw with surprise that his face was
suddenly grim and guarded. 'Yes, he exists, confound him!'

'And do you know who he is? Will he ever be captured?'

'I think he is out of our reach by now, Mouse, in fact a
part of me almost hopes—' But here he broke off, for a
footman had appeared to announce that Major von Pauling
had just received urgent news from the telegraph office.

When he returned his relief was patent. 'The Parliament
Building has fallen, thank God. The rebels surrendered
three-quarters of an hour ago without further firing.'

'And Count Vielfrass?'

'Is dead. Swallowed cyanide rather than be taken
prisoner.'

I lay back against the pillows with a great sigh. 'Then at
last, Maxim, it is ended.'

'There are the generals in the East still, Mouse. And a
great many wounds to heal. And I must, sweet child, take
my leave of you once more – the troop train we commandeered will be ready within the hour for my return to
Rosenholm.'

'But it will be ended – there will be peace soon?'

'I pray so. But then our real work must begin. Keller will
be obliged to find a means of appeasing the *Landgrafs* if we
are ever to see the reforms he and I long for. And he must

find that means quickly, or the ordinary men, the poor and the unemployed who voted for him, will begin to believe they have been gulled yet again by empty promises. God knows, even then we may offer them too little, too late. Oh indeed, Mouse, there will be work enough ahead of us.'

Remembering the legend of the dragon I repressed a momentary shiver. 'But we shall have hope at last?'

He gathered me to him again. 'Yes, Mouse. We shall have the strongest hope. And you and I shall forswear these intolerable partings. The moment you are well enough, I want you beside me, using your instinct with the people and sharing the work, and putting me in pain with desire at Court Drawing-rooms when every aristocratic matron in Sylvania has her *lorgnette* trained upon us.'

In spite of myself I laughed. His arms tightened. 'Oh Mouse, and it will not all be work. We shall travel too when things are easier, make the honeymoon journey we denied ourselves – to England, perhaps, to your family, or to France – I should very much like you to know Paris. Oh Mouse, Mouse, we have lost so much time, but we shall make it up, I promise, every last minute of it.'

I lay drowsing in the crook of his shoulder while he expanded on all we should do and see. Despite his pessimism, I felt drained with relief. For, whatever might lie ahead of us, Freddy and Leo von Maar and even poor Ursi had justice at last; Count Vielfrass could torment us no longer. And then another thought was born in upon me, that my failure to voice my suspicions of Anton no longer mattered. He too was beyond hurting us, far off in Heidelberg, and now Vielfrass had committed suicide without coming to trial there would be no painful revelations, Maximilian need never learn of Anton's guilt. I knew I should have felt remorse that through my cowardice Anton had escaped punishment, but I was overwhelmed instead by a great and dizzying lightness. Between Maximilian and myself the final barrier had been lifted. Oh yes, we had indeed reached a new beginning and yes, I thought, echoing Suzannah's words, we should surely have such a surfeit of happiness.

CHAPTER SIXTEEN

Anton von Tarn

I

My friend Messinger is an ass. But then they are all fools, with their bloodless natures and earthbound desires, all pigs incapable of distinguishing truffles from their own ordure, Winders, the Paterfamilias, Grüber, the Dusky Maiden, whose laughable attempt at revenge has merely landed her back in jail where she belongs – even Vielfrass, who believed I was his creature and ended by sticking fast in his own web – oh yes, I stood – I stand – on my glittering pinnacle, above all of them. And I have stooped down only to overcome.

Not that I have been spared suffering. Indeed, these past weeks, shut up in this gloomy hovel Messinger is pleased to call a hunting box, I have sometimes wondered whether I should not have escaped to Heidelberg after all. But here I may watch, here Messinger, as well as his slobbering kisses, brings me news from Rosenholm so that I may tell when the time has come.

How do I live? Often in the day, as I toss upon this rank little bed, my head fills as if some insect were hatched there, feeding, growing, so that my skull must burst to let it out. Sometimes I beat my temples against the wall, gnaw my forearms with the pain of it. But then, at night, wandering with my candle behind closed shutters, moving amongst the white-sheeted furniture as stealthily and shrouded as a ghost myself, I feel my heart lift with a giddy elation, I see my affliction for the thing it is, no mere mortal pain but the exquisite agony of metamorphosis; and I throw my arms wide and gaze at my towering shadow upon the wall and laugh.

Justice, good, honour, duty? As the prophet says: 'Unchanging good and evil do not exist. From out of themselves they must overcome themselves again and again . . . And

he who has to be a creator in good and evil, truly, has first
to be a destroyer and break values.' I am the destroyer, I am
the creator. I have the power, the pure unquenchable will.
I shall create Max according to his true nature so that he
may stand with me upon my breathless height. And the time
has come. The time is now.

I reel with it; and yet I must be circumspect – Messinger
says the place is swarming with Hussars. But I have only to
shake the mothballs from my uniform – and who is to question one more officer keeping his distance and his head
averted? Besides, there is this, my journal, the proof of my
power. When the ink is dry on these last lines it shall be
parcelled up securely and sent to a safe place with instructions that it may be opened only in the event of my death.

Then my preparations are done, I am ready. '*Behold, it
comes, it is near, the great noontide!*'

CHAPTER SEVENTEEN

Marie Bathildis

I

'There is Venice too,' I said. 'I should so like to see the Doge's Palace and the Bridge of Sighs and everything just as Mr Ruskin describes it.'

Suzannah sighed wistfully. 'I have never been to Venice. Or to Paris or London. I believe I am as excited as if it were my own wedding trip.'

'Ah,' I said smiling, 'and who knows, perhaps . . .' But she blushed so furiously that I forbore to tease her further about the letter from Aubyn, the third she had received within a week.

Maximilian also wrote, daily – missives which, while they were sometimes scant of information, were always full of love. But tomorrow there would be no more breathless anticipation of the day's dispatches, for they would be here at the Summer Palace, both he and Aubyn – were expected to return from their tour of the pacified Eastern provinces this very afternoon, to disembark from the Royal Train in less than an hour. My excitement had made me fidgety, bored with gruel and cordials and my three-week existence as an invalid. I had sent for my maids to dress my hair and put me into a teagown and we had come downstairs to the library to pore over atlases and Baedeckers, to dream of the future and the European journey Maximilian had promised.

How clearly I remember it even now – although I have never since set foot in the library of the Summer Palace and never shall again – the peaceful ordinariness of that afternoon, so empty of warning; a green log hissing in the grate, Suzannah bending forward to show me engravings of St Mark's or the Rialto, the three o'clock sun hatching the faded blues and pinks of the rug with bars of gold. Freddy prospered and was learning to smile, for a whole glorious

fortnight I should have my husband to myself again. I
revolved this certainty of happiness, letting it play like
perfume upon my senses, nodding to Suzannah absently,
laying aside my volume of Ruskin with an indulgent sigh.
When the footman appeared in the doorway and Suzannah
rose to attend to the interruption I was content to remain
oblivious, caught up in my reverie. Even when the doors
were suddenly thrown open I felt no premonition, was
surprised, nothing more, by Suzannah's angry voice.

'I repeat, I forbid you! You may not burst in upon Her
Majesty just as you please!'

The intruder appeared to be a lieutenant of my guard. I
stared, puzzled by his disdain for protocol and by Suzannah's expression, in which anger seemed to mingle with
alarm. He closed the doors and came several paces towards
me across the marble. And it was still an instant before I
recognised him and understood.

In all the hours he had haunted me it had been his beauty
I had recalled, his blondness, his feminine delicacy of
feature, the long lashes shadowing golden skin. But now the
face that confronted me was sallow, fleshless, as if consumed
by fever. Only the smile was as I remembered, playing upon
his lips with insolent ease.

'My dear Marie,' he drawled, declining in a graceful bow,
'the prodigal returns to you after all these weeks. I trust you
will offer me a more civil welcome than my sister.'

I continued to stare at him, bewildered. Despite his
affected negligence there was a pent-up excitement quivering
in the blanched lips and hectic eyes. His Adam's apple
danced, his hands trembled visibly. I remembered my nightmare, and my cowardice.

'What do you mean by this, Anton? Why have you thrust
your way in here, crept past my guard like a thief? We were
told you had gone abroad. Why have you come back?'

Again the smile, at once affable and mocking. 'To pay my
respects to you, Marie. And, of course, to enjoy a word or
two with dear old Max.'

My throat was suddenly dry. 'His Majesty is not here, he
is away in the East.'

'Oh come, dearest cousin! Are the Court Circulars mere
fiction?'

'He is expected, but not until tomorrow. And now, since your intrusion has been pointless, I must request that you take your leave.'

'Not until tomorrow? With the carriages already sent to meet the train? Oh tush, Marie! I fancy if we have patience we shall be rewarded in minutes. And what an affecting reunion it will be! I have a proposition, d'you see, to put to old Max which he cannot but find eminently in his best interests. And there is another matter – a question of justice I require settled. You would not have me disappointed, would you, of such a fruitful meeting between old friends?'

'Suzannah,' I said quietly, 'instruct the footman to summon the guard.'

She moved instantly but he was faster, covering the distance to the doorway in seconds so that he stood directly in her path.

'These are difficult times, sister mine. A fellow may find himself arrested or offered up for target practice before he can utter a word in his own defence. I fancy we shall pursue this tête-a-tête more usefully without the company of a platoon of Hussars.'

'Anton, you are absurd and impertinent! Let me pass or I shall shout for the servant.'

'Through these heavy doors, dearest? I doubt your girlish cries would be to great avail.'

She surveyed him for a moment. Then she took two paces forward. 'Her Majesty has no taste for your play-acting, Anton. She orders you, I order you to stand aside!'

The change in him was instant, the smile twisting to a snarl, his whole body quivering with rage. 'You're very free with your orders, sister. Do this, do that, go to the school-room, do not pester dearest Papa! Well, I am no longer your baby brother to be chivied and humiliated. I have the power and I shall give the orders. Do you hear that, sister mine? It is you who will obey me! Or I shall drill a neat hole in your precious Majesty's empty head!'

His hand had gone to his belt before I had been able to take it in. I stared disbelievingly at the revolver barrel aimed at my temples and at the eyes beyond it glittering with rage. There was no trace in him now of the negligent fop. I saw his fingers tremble as he slid back the safety catch, heard the click, continued to stare, paralysed. Then I heard Suzannah whisper: 'No!' There was a distance of about six metres between Anton and myself while she stood no more than a few paces from him. Before I could find my voice to scream she had hurled herself into the line of fire so that the gun pointed directly at her throat.

'No, little brother,' she said quietly. 'You will not touch Her Majesty, you will not threaten her. You will cease this preposterous melodrama and give the revolver to me.'

'Please, Suzannah,' I said. 'Please, I beg of you . . .' But she paid no heed, merely taking a step closer to him.

'He will not shoot me,' she said in that same calm, quiet voice. 'He will not shoot either of us. He has been mortally afraid of firearms ever since he was a boy. And besides he has always used others to do his vile work, he lacks the courage to pull the trigger himself. Come now, Anton, give me the gun.'

She held out her hand to him. Beyond her shoulder I thought I saw hesitation in the blazing eyes. Though he did not give way he seemed to lower the gun a fraction. 'I have the courage,' he said, and his voice was suddenly high, almost childlike. 'I am the creator and the destroyer! I have already tasted the sublime power of the gods.'

'Please, Anton,' I pleaded, 'whatever you have done, I know His Majesty will deal fairly with you. I promise, I guarantee it. Please let us wait till he comes.'

'You promise, you guarantee?' He threw back his head all at once in a gale of laughter. 'Oh yes, Marie, you shall guarantee my safety, no doubt of that.'

'But when His Majesty comes,' said Suzannah coaxingly. 'If you harm either of us beforehand you have no hope of saving yourself. Come, little brother, give me the revolver. You must see how foolish this is.' And she too essayed a laugh.

The sound of the shot seemed to fill the room. I stared incredulously as Suzannah toppled forward and fell like an unstrung puppet at his feet. Almost immediately the door burst open upon the terrified face of the footman. Anton spun on his heel, firing wildly. Before I heard the doors slam shut again, before I was even aware of moving, I had gathered up my skirts and was running. The gallery stairs were directly in front of me and I took them blindly, regardless of the trap they offered, regardless of anything but the need to get away from him, to put myself as far as possible at the limit of his range. My ears rang, my nostrils burned with the stench of cordite, my skirts hobbled me. Half way up I stumbled and he was upon me, seizing me by the ankle. I thrashed out, managed to tear myself free, struggled frantically to gain the last few stairs. And I had reached the gallery, was hauling myself upright when he had hold of me again. I kicked, I screamed, but he held me by the waist, pinioned to him. I heard the doors crash open, heard shouts and running feet. But in that instant he had spun me round to face the doorway and had thrust the muzzle of the revolver under my chin.

'Hold your fire, all of you!' screamed a familiar voice. 'Dear God in Heaven, hold your fire!'

The ring of boots was immediately stilled.

The gun had forced my head backwards against Anton's shoulder and upwards, so that, straddled across him as a human shield, the steel of the revolver pressed hard up beneath my jaw, I could not, even with my eyes cast down, see the floor below or any further than the opposite gallery. Nevertheless as Anton had whirled me round I thought I had glimpsed the blue of the Garde du Corps and I sensed in the silence the presence of several men, their weapons aimed, their bodies stiffened. I wanted to scream that there was Suzannah too, that some of them must help Suzannah, but pain and fear strangled the words. Only that voice gave me comfort, a fragment of hope to which I clung numbly.

'Well,' said Anton from close to my ear, 'if it isn't dear old Max.'

'You have thirty seconds,' came the voice, like a knife. 'If, after that time, you have not thrown down your revolver I shall not hesitate to shoot.'

The laugh at my ear belied the quivering muscles strained against mine. 'My dear old thing, I'm only too aware you're a crack shot – you might well be capable of putting a bullet between my eyes without injuring the Little Treaty here. But I need scarcely point out that my dying act will be to pull this trigger. And besides, you cannot kill me. You cannot kill me, Max, before you have listened to me. Otherwise you will also destroy yourself.'

There was a pause. Then the voice came back sharply: 'If your threat is to me then you must make me your target. I repeat, you have thirty seconds to let Her Majesty go.'

'Do you take me for a fool, Max? Or are you perhaps under the same misapprehension as my dear sister – that I'm too pathetic a creature to use this thing? Well, do you?' And he jerked the steel up into my throat with such force that I could not prevent myself from crying out.

There was a sound from below like the drawing-in of breath. 'Very well,' said Maximilian quietly. 'What is it you want?'

'To talk to you, Max. Alone. Without Cousin Aubyn and six of your bodyguard training their Erfurts at my head.'

Again there was a stirring from the floor and I heard Aubyn's voice: 'No, Max. In God's name! Dammit, the boy is—'

'Leave us, Aubyn. For Marie's sake.'

'But the danger to both of you—'

'Leave us, damn you! Do as he asks! Anton,' – once more Maximilian's voice was raised towards us – 'everyone will withdraw as you have requested. I trust you will also permit us to remove your sister so that she can receive the attention of a doctor?'

From Aubyn's direction came a strange soft noise like a cough. 'I am afraid, Max, there is no longer any need for that.'

There was an instant's pause in which I felt a sob rising in my throat. The revolver muzzle jabbed my head back savagely, Anton's arm tightened, crushing me against him so that I could hear his heart pounding as if it were my own. The noise seemed suddenly to drown everything, booming above Maximilian's command to the Garde du Corps and the click of boots and the crashing of the doors, roaring above the sound of my sobs, vibrating obscenely within me as if my body were possessed by it. I screwed up my eyes with the effort not to retch. Maximilian's voice came again, echoing and indistinct. 'Very well, Anton. I have complied with your wishes, now you shall comply with mine. Let me at least see her face.'

'While you continue to point a gun at me?'

'Damn you to hell! You are breaking her neck!'

There was another pause, then Maximilian seemed to give way, for I felt a shudder of relief pass through Anton's body. The arm about my waist shifted, the steel goad travelled from my jaw to lodge itself sharply just above my right ear, jerking my head abruptly forward. The blood still roared in my temples, the repugnant heartbeat thundered. Then, gradually, the noise diminished.

Maximilian stood, alone and motionless, a little to the left of the foot of the stairs. Though he had lowered his revolver he had not returned it to his belt, I noticed, but held it along the line of his thigh with his finger still on the trigger. His eyes, too, and the angle of his body, were trained upon Anton's with the fixity of someone taking aim, so that when his glance moved, as it did now to meet mine, it travelled slowly, carefully, as if he were adjusting his sights. I stared down at the tall, still figure and felt, in its calm, its unwavering authority, a return of the comfort his voice had brought. Then I saw, beyond him, Suzannah's body huddled in its own blood. I closed my eyes.

'Mousie darling, look at me. Are you badly hurt?'

His eyes, his voice, were for an instant softened so that I was once more close to tears. 'No.' I bit my lip. 'No, Maxim. Please, have a care for yourself.'

'And Freddy? Is Freddy safe?'

From behind me, Anton laughed. 'Oh, never fear, Max, I haven't laid a finger on the child. After all, we shall need your heir, you and I – even if he is her spawn.'

Maximilian's eyes had left my face in a moment, had coldly, steadily taken aim again. He continued thus to survey Anton for some seconds. Then his lips twisted. 'God help me, I should have had you arrested weeks ago. Why, at least, since you had the advantage of my blind stupidity, did you not remain in Heidelberg?'

'Do you truly believe I ever went there? Did you seriously imagine I would sit twiddling my thumbs until your agents arrived to pick me off like a woodcock? Oh, don't deny it, Max. They are beating the groves of academe for me even now. So much for your solemn promise of friendship and protection!'

'A promise to which imbecility held me far too long. Yes, I could believe you had sent the letter, perhaps I even understood why – spite and petty jealousy are at least comprehensible, even though they may not always be forgiveable. But I could not believe – did not wish to believe – that you would conspire with Vielfrass to murder a sick and helpless man, much less Leo, your own father.'

'Yet you had me followed. A seedy specimen in a rusty bowler whom I took at first to be Vielfrass's familiar. That was scarcely within the terms of your promise.'

'And even then, dear God, I was not sure what I suspected. Even then, although Radek had trailed you to the Dacha Zelenska a score of times, it was not until that curious creature came forward with her statement that we made the connection.'

'Ah yes, the Dusky Maiden. Hell hath no fury . . . Not that you could ever have proved your case, of course. The Maiden is hardly the most credible witness, Mme Zelenska herself would die on the rack rather than sacrifice her reputation for discretion. And Grüber – who, I truly think, believed our promise of a luxurious existence in Austria – Grüber is dead. But all the same it seemed advisable for poor Sebastian to make himself scarce.'

'Until now.'

'Oh, don't sound so grim and unforgiving, Max. I can forgive you for breaking your promise, for treating me as if I were some mere creeping ordinary mortal and you had annexed the Godhead to yourself. Why can you not find it in you to pardon me? After all, you should be grateful to Sebastian. He has brought down Vielfrass, given you Keller to eat out of your hand, made you more powerful than ever you were. Oh yes, my friend, you owe poor loyal Sebastian at least a crumb of thanks. Instead of which you hound him with rusty bowlers and threaten to have him shot like a dog.'

Maximilian's jaw tightened, his eyes flickered briefly to my face. I clenched my teeth, fought to keep my expression steady, for the strain of remaining fixed in one position was beginning to tell on every muscle of my body. I could sense the pain in Anton too, despite his excitement, could feel, in our repugnant intimacy, his pelvis and thighs trembling with effort. He shifted me awkwardly so that my weight was disposed against his left leg and it seemed to me once again that his grasp around my waist slackened.

Maximilian had resumed his relentless, concentrated look. 'If that is what you wished to say to me, Anton, then we may now make an end to this. Let Her Majesty go and I undertake that no one will harm you. I guarantee you will have the benefit of a fair and proper trial.'

'Fair? Proper? Our old friends justice and honour again? Oh my dear Max, must we continue this pretence? Must we, who are gods, continue to debase our divinity with the small coin of small men—?'

'My patience, Anton, is at its limit. What is it you want?'

Again I felt the arm that held me shift its grasp, was certain this time that Maximilian also noticed it, noticed it and was waiting, probing Anton to lull him until the instant he saw his chance. Silently I drew in my breath.

'I have a proposal to make to you, dear old Max, which you will find irresistible.'

'I will not bargain with you.'

'Oh, but this, dear friend, is no commonplace bargain. This, if you value your power as I know you do, is – God damn you! You traitor, Max! Call them off, call them off or I fire—!'

I had seen it too, the flash of scarlet in the window of the gallery opposite, the glint of sunlight upon steel. Anton's grip tightened instantly, the revolver muzzle jabbed viciously at my skull.

'You promised me! You promised we should be alone! You said you would dismiss your guard! So much for your promises and your protection! Well, by God, I promise you this, Max – if that Hussar does not withdraw by the time I have counted to twenty I shall decorate the walls with the Little Treaty's brains!'

Shifting his glance from Anton for the first time, Maximilian turned and gestured at the window. The sniper vanished down his ladder as swiftly and silently as he had appeared. But our chance was gone. Anton's arm encircled my ribs so tightly that I fought to breathe. His own breath came in my ear, harsh and shallow, I heard the pounding of his heart again, I felt once more its sickening invasion of my own body.

'Well,' said Maximilian after a moment, 'the danger is past. Aubyn will understand he must not attempt any further surprises. You were about, I think, to make some outline of your proposal. Perhaps you will favour us with it now.'

The deliberate calm in his voice seemed to take its effect. Anton heaved in breath, the agonising pressure upon my temple subsided.

'My proposal? Oh, let us rather call it a gift, Max, the gift that delivers you from the fetters of the mean and the earthbound, that raises you up, reborn in your true nature, to rejoice in the glorious triumph of the will—'

'Speak to the point, Anton. What is it you ask of me?'

'Ask? I do not ask. I demand. And you shall not, may not, deny me. I am the creator, I am the liberator. But I warn you, dear old Max, I can also destroy—'

'Your point! Pray come to it.'

I felt Anton shiver against me like someone at the brink of a lake anticipating the exhilaration of the water.

'I require of you two things, Max. First, you are powerful and I require to share your power. You shall not cast me aside as you have these past months, you shall not deny all we are to each other, body and soul. Dear God, I have suffered, wretchedly, bitterly I have suffered, but through it all I have struggled and overcome, served my apprenticeship, made myself more than worthy of you. I wish to stand where you stand, above Keller, above cloddish Cousin Aubyn, above all of them, recognised and respected as your equal. Sebastian brought you to the apotheosis of your power. Sebastian now craves his reward.'

Maximilian stared up at him, his expression unchanging. 'And your second demand? You mentioned another.'

From behind me came a laugh that made my throat constrict. 'I require, my dear old Max, what you, pandering to the hypocrites, would call "justice".' I require the execution of the convicted murderess of my father.'

Again Maximilian surveyed him in silence for some moments. Then he said quietly, 'My dear Anton, you are madder than I thought.'

'This woman,' – another thrust of the revolver blinded me with pain – 'this creature here was found guilty by the tribunal and awaits sentence.'

'It will scarcely surprise you that after the Sebastian affair the tribunal was discredited and the verdict reversed.'

'A secret tribunal, a secret verdict and a secret reversal. Keller is your cypher, the State Police pipe to your tune now, you may have things fall as you wish. Someone must pay the debt for the dear Paterfamilias. And the tribunal found evidence enough against the Little Treaty at the time.'

'What of the evidence against Sebastian?'

'The fabrications of the gutter press? The hearsay of unreliable witnesses?'

'The body of your sister lies over there, Anton. The witnesses to her death will stand up in any court.'

'The Little Treaty could not have committed her crimes without an accomplice. That accomplice has now been discovered and brought to book. You possess the power, Max – *we* possess the power. The Treaty has given you your precious heir, what further use can she be to you? Look at her,' – the revolver stabbed at the angle of my jaw – 'look at this drab little whore of yours, quaking and snivelling with fear. How long will marriage bind you to her, Max? Twenty years, thirty? How long will you be forced to fawn upon her, listen to her brainless chatter, copulate for duty's sake in the stinking sewer of her bed? A man of your intellect, your ambition, your godgiven nature? Can such a man bear to defile himself so? When you and I stand together on the summit, Max, we must breathe the pure air unimpeded. There is no place in our triumph for such – such ordure. Let me liberate you, Max. Let me dispose of this taint, this encumbrance now, while my revolver is at her throat.'

Maximilian's eyes did not waver but his mouth hardened into a grim line. 'Your demands are rejected, of course. And for every hurt you give Her Majesty I shall make you answer. Of that alone you have my firm promise.'

'Oh, my dear old Max, very fine, very noble! The dutiful husband defends his wifey! But you will recall, dear friend, how little such platitudes tell with me. Have you forgotten our kinship, have you forgotten I know what is in your soul as if your lifeblood flowed in my veins? Oh, you may pretend for such insects as Keller and Aubyn, but I know what truly drives you, I know what you value most. You will agree to all I ask, Max, you will fall on your knees and beg me to rid you of the Little Treaty. For I hold your precious power like a *pfennig* piece in the palm of my hand. I know, don't you see, old Max. I know the truth about Dieter Wolf. I know all about your personal devil and the body at Fontarelles.'

I stared down uncomprehendingly at Maximilian and saw with amazement a change come over him. Though he remained motionless, though he still held Anton with that cold fixity of aim, something flickered in his eyes as if for an instant he were caught off-balance. Anton also observed it, I was certain; I heard him lick his lips.

'Oh yes, my dear old thing, I have been quite painstaking in my research. I have documentary evidence, dates, confessions. Pray don't imagine I condemn you for it – on the contrary I hope I should have possessed the same ruthless dedication. But I know, don't you see – and since I know I can't be gulled by all that claptrap about duty and justice. Your power is mine now, everything you've worked and schemed and lied for. So perhaps, my friend, it behoves you to attend to poor Sebastian a trifle more seriously. Oh and don't,' – again the chilling laughter – 'don't for a moment believe you may evade me. I am only too aware how your noble scruples desert you when it is a matter of retaining your spoils, how there is little you will hold back from, least of all murder. I have written out my evidence and sent it to Cousin Aubyn's office in the Maria-Antonienburg. Should I die, he is instructed to break the seal upon the parcel and read its contents. And he will, my dear old Max – whatever loyalty he feels to you, his tedious code of honour cannot but oblige him to do so. Despite your threats, you see, you cannot destroy poor Sebastian. But he can destroy you, he can take what you have slaved for, shed blood for, given your very soul for, and with one blow shatter it to fragments. You have my terms, Max. I wish only to be rid of the Little Treaty and to have all between us as it was. I am sure you will agree, the price is paltry.'

I fixed my gaze upon Maximilian, waiting for his contemptuous reply. But he said nothing. Behind me Anton sucked in his breath, I felt every muscle of him drawn taut. I searched Maximilian's face but it was impenetrable. And yet – and yet there was in his eyes that strangeness still, as if he were struggling with a calculation. To my seared temples and cramped limbs, to the consuming agony of physical endurance, was slowly added another pain, muted but inexorable – a twinge of doubt. Though my dress was sodden with perspiration, though the salt pricked my skin and stung my eyes, my mouth was so dry I could scarcely swallow. The silence seemed endless. I watched Maximilian dazedly, battling with my confusion, trying desperately to draw his glance to mine, willing him to speak. But he remained still as stone, his face opaque.

Then, so suddenly that I started, he laughed. It was a small, tight laugh. 'Very well,' he said.

I stared at him incredulously. Anton too seemed momentarily transfixed.

'My dear old Max—'

'I have said – very well.'

'You concede? You agree to my terms?'

'My dear Anton, it hardly seems you leave me great choice.'

'You concede even the Little Treaty here?'

'I concede what I must concede. I have my heir, as you remind me. And what sane man would face ruin for the sake of sentiment?'

I gazed down in horror at him, praying that I should understand from some hidden glance, some trick of the lips, that this was no more than a clever stratagem. But his eyes avoided mine, his expression seemed only to register defeat. His hand, where it had tensed upon the revolver, now hung at his side as if suddenly weighed down by its useless burden.

'It seems, my dear Anton, that I should congratulate you on your diligence – and your perspicacity. Perhaps we are fools to believe we may change, perhaps there is always one instant, one fatal choice that fixes the course of our lives for ever. I cannot deny your argument is compelling. All the same, what you ask of me – to deceive the Assembly, to suborn witnesses, bribe the police – it will not be easy.'

'Yet you will do it? On your oath? You swear?'

'I swear – I swear, Anton, that you leave me no alternative but to act as I must now.'

'Then . . . oh dear God . . . oh, God in Heaven . . . oh, my dear Max, you shall not regret it! I am worthy, I shall not fail you – remember I too have crossed the frontier which separates mere mortals from the highest state of man, I too am master of life and death. We shall be as we were to each other, two supreme beings, above good and evil, above all the swinish rot preached by the servile. Oh, when I have thought of this moment in all your cruelty to me, when sometimes I have even doubted – but how can one doubt what is ordained, gloriously, triumphantly inevitable . . . ?'

Maximilian had listened to this outpouring as if he were oblivious of my existence, had seemed even to nod his assent. But now, suddenly, his eyes were trained hard upon mine. 'Marie, are you faint?'

Though I tried to move my lips I could not answer.

'I asked if you were faint. You seemed close to fainting.'

Despite my confusion and the harshness of his tone, I was aware all at once of a purpose in his look, of the way he repeated and carefully laid emphasis on the word. And then I understood, then I became conscious of what, in my horror, I had been too numbed to perceive, that Anton from his relief and exhaustion had begun to tremble uncontrollably, that the muzzle of the revolver wavered, that the arm which had pinioned me by the waist was gradually drifting harmlessly towards my hip.

'Yes, Maxim. I believe I am a little faint.'

Maximilian's glance flashed back instantly to Anton, and there was in it now all its marksman's concentration. 'She will not faint yet. But she may very soon. Which brings us, my dear Anton, to the matter of her execution. Will you trust me to invoke all the official procedures or do you still insist on playing executioner yourself? If so, you must be hasty about it. I imagine even you might find some difficulty in shooting an unconscious woman.'

Anton seemed not to hear. His trembling increased, his chest heaved, his voice took on a high, crooning note as if he were entranced. 'Achilles and Patroclus, Nisus and Euryalus – did I not tell you, Max, how it must be? The two of us bound together until death – above the insects, the Common Good – above duty, honour, virtue, justice – the two of us, Max, warrior gods, obeying only the will, the pure creative will to power—'

'Will you shoot her now, Anton? Are you man enough not to bungle it?'

Anton paused as if the trance still held him. I could sense his bewilderment, feel him blind, dazed, like a sleepwalker.

'Do you remember our time in Switzerland? Do you remember our hours of target practice together?'

'Achilles and Patroclus, Max. David and Jonathan—'

'Show me you won't bungle it. Show me you remember all Herr Fischer taught us.'

'My dear old Max—'

'Show me, Anton. Show me how you will hold the gun.'

What happened next seemed to take place infinitely slowly as if we were all three swimming beneath a great weight of water, yet it must have occurred in a split second. I felt Anton struggle to respond, saw from the corner of my eye the hand with the revolver move, trembling, obedient as a schoolboy's, clear of my jaw. And in that same instant Maximilian screamed: 'Now!' and I fell, hurling myself leftwards to the gallery floor. I remember even as I was falling seeing Maximilian's gun go up, hearing the shot. There was a long-drawn-out animal howl, a second explosion; then the clack, clack, stair by stair, of steel clattering towards marble, and the sound of something heavy crashing, slithering after it. The doors thundered open upon a volley of running boots. The air was sulphurous with shot. Hardly daring to, very slowly and carefully, I lifted my head.

Maximilian stood, apparently unharmed, with his revolver still raised in both hands. His lips were white and he seemed to rock slightly as if from the recoil of the weapon. At the bottom of the stairs, about a metre from his feet, lay Anton's revolver, and halfway down the staircase, one arm hanging through the bannisters, his legs sprawled, lay Anton on his belly, head dangling. At first I saw only the sleek blond hair. Then I glimpsed the scarlet dripping from the step beneath, would have looked away – but in that instant the head raised itself and, seeming to peer at Maximilian, gave out a thick slobbering sound that might almost have been laughter. The prone torso shuddered with it, the pelvis jerked. All at once the head plunged forward and the body, slithering down a further step, was still.

Maximilian's eyes remained upon the staircase, transfixed,

for a second. Then the revolver fell to his side, his glance travelled upwards, I saw him put out his hand to me, saw his lips begin to form my name. Weak with relief, I groped for the bannisters. But I stopped, grew rigid; for suddenly he staggered and his mouth was full of blood.

II

I knew. I had known as Aubyn had rushed forward to catch him in his arms. I had seen then that the blood on the skirt of his tunic could not be Anton's, that it was only hope, love, foolishness which had made me assume the second shot had gone wide. I had understood then why Anton had reserved his last breath for laughter.

They had tried to make me lie down while my physician examined him, had offered me sedatives. But I had understood that my debility and pain were of no account, that there was worse, much worse to come and that my head must be clear, my body strong for it. I knew, oh yes, I knew before Aubyn came tiptoeing into my boudoir, closing the doors noiselessly behind him, and I saw his face as it had been in my dream, in the White Room, the jaw set squarely but the eyes glassy with tears.

'Please,' I said softly. 'I understand how difficult it is. But you must not concern yourself with trying to spare me.'

He stared briefly at his boots. 'They've sent for Axel-Liebnitz, of course. For a second opinion. But according to Dr Seisser the angle of the bullet – there is damage to both the liver and the bowel – Seisser's view is that surgery is impossible.'

'And without surgery?'

'Eight hours. Perhaps a little more. If he does not bleed to death, the peritonitis from the stomach wound will in itself prove fatal.'

'Yes. Yes, I see.'

'We have telegraphed Gustav and Helena in Rosenholm. And Keller, of course, and the Cardinal Archbishop and Max's Cabinet Chief. It seems unlikely that they will arrive in time but what can be done has been done.'

'Thank you. I am grateful.'

Silence fell between us for a moment, he again inspecting his boots, I examining my fingers. When we made to speak it was both at once.

'It was quite deliberate—'

'My dear girl, I—'

'He made Anton turn the gun on him. To save me. He risked himself deliberately.'

'My dear Marie, I wish to God . . . I am so damnably sorry . . .'

'And I, for Suzannah.'

'Yes.' He turned his head aside. 'Yes. Thank you.' Then, tugging at his moustache, he seemed to draw himself up, to put on every thread, every polished, punctilious button of his military rigour. He took my arm. 'Come – if you are strong enough – he is asking for you – for both of us.'

When I considered the events of the past months, I suppose it should not have surprised me that Maximilian was, in every minute practical detail, so coolly prepared for death. Yet it was with shock that I observed this preparedness, as if, in the carefully drawn-up bequests and dispositions, never once discussed, yet clearly often uppermost in his thoughts, I was reminded of that secret territory of his once again, the part of him to which no amount of love gave right of admission.

With unconscious and terrible irony they had carried him to Sigismund's bedroom, to that monstrous confection of a bed in which both he and his son had been conceived; and there, beneath the leers of the putti, in the presence of Seisser, Major von Pauling and senior members of both our Households, Aubyn and I heard ourselves named Regents for our new three-week old King. I sat at the head of the bed, Maximilian's hand in mine, watching the waxiness of approaching death invade his face. Though Seisser had contrived a cradle to spare his patient the weight of the bedclothes and though, to slow the haemorrhage, the wound had been packed with ice, the pain was evident in Maximilian's voice and he was twice obliged to desist while he vomited blood. Yet he refused morphia, continuing clearly and without emotion until every particular of his last duty had been discharged. Only then, while I wiped the sweat from his forehead, did he close his eyes, exhausted, for some moments until, finding a further reserve of strength, he asked that everyone should withdraw except for Aubyn and myself.

When the anteroom doors had closed he took my hand and, lifting it to his lips, laid it across his throat so that I could feel the life pulsing there still. 'My darling Mouse, how is our son?'

'He is well – sleeping. I shall bring him to you soon. And – and Father Arno waits in readiness to hear your confession.'

To my alarm his eyes darkened, his mouth took on that mordant twist which had so frightened me before. 'I shall not make confession.'

'But you must – you cannot—'

He brought his fingers up to stop my lips. 'Dear child, since I was eighteen I have not taken the sacraments unless it was on false pretences. I cannot now – now when there is no evasion – continue the falsehood. Yet I cannot freely and fully make confession.' He looked up at me gravely for a moment, then his glance moved to Aubyn at the other side of the bed. 'I do not know – my closest friend and my dearly-loved wife – how else but that I should trust you both to rule wisely for Freddy until he reaches his majority. But I do not know, even as I express the wish, whether my hopes for my son, for Sylvania, are no more than sinful conceit.'

Aubyn cleared his throat. 'My dear fellow, you must not distress yourself. We accept your trust as a sacred duty, we shall endeavour to make ourselves worthy—'

Maximilian smiled a small, dry smile. 'You mistake me. Marie, you will recall Anton's words – about Fontarelles.'

'When he attempted to blackmail you and I, Heaven forgive me, believed for an instant you had surrendered to him? I heard the words, yes. But they had no more meaning than anything else he said.'

'They are written down. He has left you a journal, Aubyn – he sent it to you in the Maria-Antonienburg.'

'Then I shall burn it, old fellow. We shall not trouble ourselves with the ravings of a madman.'

'No. No, you must read the journal. In that, at least, Anton was right. Its very existence obliges you to do so.'

'My dear Max – ' Aubyn shifted uncomfortably. 'I fear I don't follow you. Do you mean – do you know what is written in it?'

'Perhaps. I am not certain. But whatever it is, I ask this of you – judge me as you must, I deserve no better, but remember that Freddy is also Marie's child, that his blood is also her blood.'

Aubyn's eyes met mine across the bed, frowning in distress and bewilderment. 'My dear fellow, I'd much rather—'

'You will read it. You will read it because if you do not your conscience will always trouble you. And having read it, you must make a judgement. Please, old friend,' – he stretched out to touch Aubyn's wrist – 'promise me you will do as I ask.'

Aubyn tugged wretchedly at his moustache. 'Very well, Max, if it will make you easier – you have my promise.'

Maximilian pressed Aubyn's fingers for an instant, then his hand fell back, he closed his eyes as if some measure of his pain had been relieved. 'Forgive me for leaving you this burden. But whatever your judgement I know it will be fair and upright, that it will take account of the innocent as well as the guilty. I trust the future of my wife and son to your care.'

Once more Aubyn and I exchanged glances, once more I saw his perplexity reflect my own. I put my hand to Maximilian's cheek. 'My darling, I do not understand what troubles you. But I know you, I know it cannot be so very terrible that you must hazard your immortal soul. Please, let Father Arno come to you. Confession will give you comfort—'

He opened his eyes. 'No, Mouse,' he said gently.

'But whatever you fear, whatever is in the journal – surely you have expiated it, paid your debt long ago. Oh my darling, if there were nothing else, the fact that you are lying here – that to save me, you . . .' I bit my lip.

He stroked my face softly. 'I did not seek to die, Mousie. I had every intention of watching my son grow up, of continuing to live in the warmth of your love. I calculated the odds and lost. That is all.'

'And now – will you calculate the odds again, risk everlasting damnation? Please, Maxim, I beg of you—'

'I made a vow once, Mouse, which I may not break. And besides I would not willingly place such a weight on poor Father Arno's shoulders.'

'But to risk eternal hellfire—?'

He smiled. 'I did not think you believed in hellfire, Mousie.'

I stared at him, hearing the other Freddy's voice suddenly: 'He is a good man, Tilda. But he feels himself exiled from God.' For the first time, with force, I sensed the anguish of that exile. 'I may doubt, Maxim. But you do not. You know how you condemn yourself.'

'Perhaps. But I must accept it, Mouse. There is nothing else left to me.'

Afterwards, during our vigil, I tried to smother my apprehension, tried, as Aubyn did also, not to tire him with questions or further insistence upon the chaplain, but merely to make of these last precious hours the most we could. Besides, as my misery closed in upon me it pushed aside thought. I summoned the nurse to bring the baby and we laid him on the pillow beside his father, but he at once seemed to absorb our grief, setting up such an inconsolable wailing that I was compelled to instruct the nurse to return him to his crib. Later a telegram arrived from Rosenholm informing us that the train carrying Prince Gustav, Princess Helena and the Chancellor was on its way, and some twenty minutes afterwards Axel-Liebnitz was announced. But, though the Professor probed beneath the cradled bedcovers and felt the patient's pulse and went into a huddle with Seisser and his assistant, he eventually emerged only to shake his head.

The light began to fade and the tapers were lit in the *torchères*. Maximilian's breathing was shallow, his forehead burned, speech seemed to exhaust him and he was subject increasingly to spasms of intense pain. I begged him to relent, to permit Seisser to give him morphia, and at last he agreed. The injection appeared to ease him; he closed his eyes and after a while drifted into an uncertain sleep.

Despite myself, I too had begun to succumb to my exhaustion, when suddenly I heard him cry out. In the chair opposite Aubyn also was jolted from a doze. I held Maxim-

ilian as he tossed upon the pillows, we listened uncomprehendingly to what seemed at first a mere jumble of words,
part German, part French, part the gibberish of delirium.
Then, all at once, he let out three or four sentences of intelli-
gible French before subsiding again, insensible.

Aubyn looked across at me questioningly and I saw
rekindled in his eyes that spark of apprehension we had
both so determinedly struggled to extinguish. It made me
hesitate for some moments before I attempted a translation.

'It was about Dieter Wolf – something about fighting a
devil at Fontarelles. Then he – he said quite clearly: "Dieter
Wolf is dead, but I did not kill him." Just that. Nothing
more.'

'What does it mean, Marie? What, in God's name, does it
mean?'

'How can we know? Oh, my dear Aubyn, I think I pray
that we never shall.'

It was about two hours later, just after eleven, that the
change came. Maximilian had been drifting in and out of
consciousness, but now he woke and began vomiting again,
blood and brown bile. His face grew pinched, his eyes filmy,
and where he had burned with fever he was suddenly so
cold that his teeth chattered. Axel-Liebnitz and Seisser took
his pulse and administered a further injection of morphia,
and after a while the vomiting ceased and he lapsed into a
deep unconsciousness from which, both doctors reluctantly
averred, he was unlikely ever to emerge.

I took matters into my own hands then and summoned
Father Arno to give him the last rites for I felt certain that,
if there were a deity capable of mercy, he would read Maximilian's heart as we could not read it and forgive the lack of
a confession. After the final amens had been said and the
oil and candles put away I watched him, apparently sleeping
peacefully, and felt a little easier.

The clock above the West Gate had chimed two, the tapers
guttered and opposite me Aubyn was again nodding in his
chair when I became aware of a slight movement from the
bed and saw that Maximilian's eyes were open.

His voice came so faintly, below a whisper, that I had to
bend close to catch the words. 'Mousie, where are you?'

I took his hand and pressed it to my face. It was cold as
marble. 'Is the pain still very bad?'

'No. No pain.' With intense effort he widened his lips into
a smile. 'My dear, sweet Mouse, I have loved you so much.'

I kissed his hand. 'And I you, my darling.'

'I wish . . . I wish we had been given more time . . . that
I could have—' He stopped suddenly, the smile vanished,
his eyes appeared to fix on some point beyond me. Then all
at once he reared from the pillows, seemed to be struggling
to sit up. 'Oh, darling Mousie – put your arms around me!'

I gathered him to me and held his head against my breast,
held him long after I had ceased to feel my dress grow wet
with his blood, long after I had felt, with that last soft sigh,
the life go out of him.

                                III

I could not cry. The Princess Helena had wept without let
for two days, but to me no tears would come. I had been
twice to St Xaviersdom to see Maximilian lying in state: from
the Royal closet above the altar I had stared down at the
flickering tapers and the four sentries of the Garde du Corps
stiffly holding their swords reversed; I had watched the
endless human train shuffling past the catafalque and had
heard its stifled weeping almost as a reproach. But in the
reverent chill I shivered, was forced to draw away. Oh, it
was not that the pain still marked him; in the full dress of
the Deathwatch, lying amidst laurel branches, hands folded
upon his sword and with the crown beside his head, he
looked tranquil, impervious, as commandingly handsome as
he had in life. Yet it was the profile struck upon a coin I
saw now, the painter's image, the frigid perfection of the
sculptor's art. Three days ago Suzannah had been laid to
rest beside her father in the family mausoleum at Maar, and
tomorrow Maximilian too would make his last journey to the
Residenz chapel, his coffin draped in his personal standard
and bearing the crown with his insignia and medals, his
charger, Balthaazar, boots reversed in the stirrups, led behind
the gun carriage to the sob of muffled drums. And I, veiled
in my closed landau, would look out at the crape-decked

windows and the pale sea of faces and think it was an ideal we buried, an effigy upon a postage stamp that we mourned with all this pomp; and I would see then, as I did now, the flesh and blood being I had loved, that rare smile, his eyes as he had first felt the baby moving. Yet I could not cry.

I had taken to drifting bleakly about his apartments, wandering from room to room, hovering in his dressing-room or in that cool white cell of his, to which I had never before gained admission, dwelling upon his boot-trees, his razors, the strands of hair in his brushes, the mundane proofs of that humanity which the world now conspired to deny. But this afternoon, startling the duty adjutant, who was bent on some business connected with the funeral, I discovered I was not alone in my quest. Aubyn was in the study, working, so the adjutant said, on Maximilian's papers.

He was sitting in a chair beside the tiled stove reading something which, as I entered, he seemed guiltily to be trying to hide. I saw it was a cloth-covered exercise book, like a child's.

I stared at him, perplexed by the anguish that showed so transparently in his pink face. Then I understood.

'I promised him, you see, dear girl. Dammit, I put it off for as long as I was able. I wish to God I was not obliged even to touch the thing!'

I glanced down at the book, then back at his face. 'If you have finished, I too should like to read it.'

'My dear Marie, I hardly think— You know what the fellow was, a pervert, a madman. In common decency I should spare you—'

'Please, Aubyn,' I said.

He struggled with himself for a moment. Then, reluctantly, offering the book by one corner, at arm's length, flinching as if it would burn me, he gave it into my hands.

I sat huddled in shawls before my boudoir fire, staring for a time at the marbled covers, not daring to open them. Then, steeling myself, I began to read. I read on, past dinner, well into the evening, forcing myself to continue, for I knew nothing in the world would induce me to pick the journal up again if once I laid it aside. When I had finished, had watched the hated handwriting decline from the elegant Gothic script of the first entries to the smudged scrawl of the last, I put the book quickly away from me. I remained for a long while staring at the fire.

I did not believe it. I must perforce accept the account of Ursula von Windersdorf changing the children, for how else could Anton have established such a hold on her, how else were the enigmatic references in her confession explained? But I could not believe that Maximilian had known and deliberately sought to perpetuate the deception for, to believe that, I must acknowledge Anton's estimation of him as a liar, a fraud – and the murderer of the true Crown Prince at Fontarelles. No, it was as Aubyn had said; the journal was nothing more than the ravings of a madman. Anton's twisted mind had taken a thread of hearsay and coincidence and stretched it, with supposition, to breaking point.

But – oh, had not Maximilian as much as admitted his guilt before he died, refusing confession, talking of sin and his own damnation as if he had known too well what Anton had discovered? And were there not other things too, earlier memories, his self-disgust, his bitter references to the force of his ambition? Was that sense I had always had of the closed-away part of him perhaps, after all, no more than instinctive knowledge of his crime?

I confronted now the Maximilian I had first seen, the dark face with its duellist's scar, a cold man, a ruthless man capable of forcing me into an unwilling marriage, of threatening the other Freddy's life. But that had been Vielfrass's plot, built on Vielfrass's lies, and I had come to understand how wrong I had been, wrong as I had been later, too, about Anton's letter and Freddy's death and the depth of Maximilian's love for me. Wrong – or merely deluded by that love? Deluded by the scent of his skin, the touch of his lips upon my breast, the ache of my body for his? Could it be that, as he had once concealed his relationship with Anton, so he had hidden darker aspects of his character from me, cloaking with a pretence of integrity and honour a perverse pleasure in evil?

No, I would not, could not believe it. Anton had simply judged Maximilian according to his own nature. The man I knew, who had fought Vielfrass, who had cared so passionately for justice and freedom, who had in the end given his life to save mine, could not have been as the journal portrayed him. For – set aside the other accusations of fraud and impersonation – of one thing I was above all certain. Maximilian had been incapable of committing the act that Anton alleged had made the rest possible, the cold-blooded murder at Fontarelles. I remembered suddenly the words of his delirium, words we had not understood. 'Dieter Wolf is dead, but I did not kill him.' Oh, pray God, if that were true Anton must be wrong and the journal after all an insane delusion.

I glanced up from the fire, startled, for Hildegard von Saxe-Limbeck, one of my newly-appointed ladies, had appeared in the doorway to say that Aubyn begged admittance.

Aubyn? What did Aubyn believe – Aubyn who had been sworn by Maximilian to read the journal and make a judgement? For the first time I took in the full implication of Anton's accusations for Sylvania and for my poor baby Freddy. Even if Aubyn believed Maximilian innocent there was now a taint in Freddy's blood, a grave question over his right to the throne. And if Aubyn supported Anton's theory . . . ? I remembered our conversation at the Summer Palace after Vielfrass had told him that Anton and Maximilian had been lovers, remembered his revulsion, his disgust even for the uniform he wore. Oh, he had relented, had become once again his old, loyal, generous-hearted self. But how could he brush aside the suspicion of murder, how could his own unfailing sense of honour show any mercy towards a man he believed bore such guilt? I thought again of Freddy, lying oblivious and innocent in his crib, and clasped my hands tightly to control my shivering.

Aubyn came into the room very straight and stiff, looking first at me and then at the exercise book beside my chair. His brow was crinkled, his eyes grave. I could not bear to hold his glance for fear of what I should see in it.

'Well,' I said softly, 'what will you do? Whatever your decision, you know you may trust me to abide by it.'

He paused for an instant before the mantel. Then, bending to kiss my cheek, he took Anton's journal, and tearing it apart with his great, freckled hands, flung the pieces on the fire.

Epilogue

Today is the seventh anniversary of my beloved's death, and this morning I went to make my customary remembrances; first to the Lady Chapel of St Xaviersdom where, in a niche above the image of the Blessed Virgin, his heart, encased in a silver-gilt vase, stands with those of his father and other past Hohenstaufen kings; thence to the crypt of the Residenz Chapel, where his coffin is laid.

For seven years now I have taken my taper and a fresh wreath of laurels and, kneeling beside the coffin, my hand upon its lid, I have told Maximilian, if he is there to listen, that Freddy continues to grow strong and healthy, the picture of his father, that Aubyn and I endeavour to rule as wisely as we can – although Left and Right still squabble in the Assembly, although the harvest still fails, although there is still rioting and intrigue and corruption as if, true to the legend of the dragon, this country of ours is so far gone in decay that no medicine can heal her. For seven years I have begged him to hear me, advise me, so that all his work may not be squandered. And if I have thought of the allegations in Anton's journal, of the doubt which taints my son's blood, mocks the cypher on the coffin lid and threatens even my darling's memory, I have determinedly cast such thoughts aside. Until today.

It came upon me from the first, when my ladies had retired and the arched door had closed softly behind me, entombing me in shadow and silence. I had hesitated upon the steps, accustoming my lungs to the dank air, and had felt it suddenly: a strangeness, a stirring, as if, amongst the dark bulks of the coffins I was not the only living thing. I scanned the arcaded vault nervously with my taper; but no, there was only shadow, only the sound of my skirt rustling upon the flagstones, of a rat, perhaps, scuttling into hiding. I walked on between the twin rows of leaden caskets to where Maximilian lay, put out my hand to touch my last year's tribute of dried and crumbling leaves – and, oh yet there it came again. A little sound, the scrape of leather upon stone and, now that I stood frozen, the faint but undeniable rhythm of breathing.

I turned, my taper shuddering. And saw, beside the coffin of Sigismund II, half obscured by the shadow of a pillar, a robed and hooded figure, its arms doubled into the folds of its sleeves, its face mere darkness.

I stepped back, opened my mouth to scream, watched in terror the apparition decline in a low bow, then limp a pace or two out of the shadow of the arch towards me. A voice said softly: 'Pray, Ma'am, do not be alarmed.' And, when my taper steadied, its flame revealed the brown habit and cowl of a Franciscan friar.

I stared wordlessly at the figure. Though the cowl still shaded its face, the yellow nakedness of its sandalled feet, the dust upon its robes, its very stance, the apologetic hunch of physical frailty, all proclaimed it to be palpable and human. The voice too, reedy, self-deprecating and with a foreign inflection, scarcely betokened the supernatural. Indeed, the apparition seemed as much perturbed as I by our confrontation.

My terror turned to anger. 'How dare you, Brother! By what right do you presume to trespass here? Your cloth alone should render you sensible to the offence in such an intrusion.'

The hooded head was lowered humbly. 'Forgive me, Ma'am. I crave pardon for frightening Your Majesty. I wished only, as Your Majesty does, to pay my respects to our late King.'

'I repeat, Brother, you have no right.'

'No right, perhaps. And yet, though I have travelled most of my life and lately spent many years in the Holy Land, I am a Sylvanian by birth. And besides – besides, I owe His Majesty a great debt.'

I could not help but be softened by both his humility and his pathetic appearance. 'A debt, Brother?'

'My life. My freedom. Oh, it was wrong, I know but – they say he was a good King.'

'Yes, he was a good King. A good King and a good man.'

'It is true he was always the stronger, always fought my battles for me, protected me against Brother Ignatius. Perhaps God, in His mercy, will forgive . . .'

Once more my taper trembled. 'Forgive what, Brother? What must God forgive?'

'I – I meant only, Ma'am, that we are all sinners.'

I stared at him. Though I had assumed his feebleness to b the burden of age I realised now from the timbre of his voice, from the hands that plucked the cord at his waist, slender, pale, as yet unblemished by knotted joints or veins, that he could not be beyond middle years. My lips were dry. I was seized by an urgent need to see his face.

'Who are you? Why have you come here?'

He mumbled something, shuffled back a pace or two.

'I must know, Brother. You must tell me at once.'

'I – I cannot, Ma'am. I beg you, forgive me.'

'I order you, command you!'

'I cannot, Ma'am. I have made a vow.'

'My husband used those words when he refused – when he was close to death. Did your vow bind him too? I do not command – I implore you, Brother – tell me who you are and what you owe him?'

Though I could not see his face I felt him flinch before my taper. His head craned longingly towards the concealing shadows of the arch. 'You would not wish it, Ma'am. Could I speak, you would not wish it.'

I thought of all the years of doubt, of my uncertainty for Freddy, of the stain upon Maximilian's memory which, though the flames had consumed the journal in minutes, could not be so quickly and easily wiped out. 'I wish only for the truth. Whatever your vow, my husband's death must surely release you. I beg you, Brother, if you have any heart, any feeling, tell me who you are?'

He had regained the safety of the shadow so that he seemed, beside the dark bulk of Sigismund's coffin, insubstantial once more. I heard his feet shuffle. Then he said slowly: 'My name is Dieter Wolf. Yet Dieter Wolf is dead.'

I was for an instant faint, feared I should drop the taper 'But the body – there was a body at Fontarelles – a murder.'

'Four carters set upon one another in a drunken brawl. Though we – he – tried to stop the fighting, one of them was beaten so badly his comrades took flight and left him to die. The victim was scarcely more than a boy, near our age and not unlike in build . . .'

The disembodied voice hesitated, I sensed his lips move soundlessly as though in prayer. When he spoke again it was indistinctly and with all the effort of pain. 'Eighteen we were – mere boys, as I say – green in judgement. It did not seem such a great wrong then. And yet we sinned, both of us But I, in my weakness, was the greater sinner.'

While I heard his pain, I felt only lightheaded with relief. Had I not known that Anton's allegations were false, that Maximilian could not have taken life in cold blood, even if he had discovered that he was merely Helena's bastard and that Dieter Wolf was the true Crown Prince? Beyond any other consideration, any other significance in the stranger's presence, the fact of it held me transfixed. 'But if you are Dieter Wolf – if Dieter Wolf was not murdered – then neither of you did wrong.'

He seemed not to hear me. 'Oh, I have tried to do penance all these years, I have fasted, prayed, mortified my body. But what good are penances when God knows I cannot truly repent? The devil, he said. But it was Satan in me, Satan speaking to him through my mouth, my weakness. If he sinned it was my greater sinfulness that drove him to it . . .'

He paused, sighing, apparently disinclined to continue. I peered in perplexity at his shadow, thinking of Ursula von Windersdorf's transgression and wondering anew how much Nurse Wolf had revealed to her charges, whether perhaps Ursi's was the wrong-doing he meant.

'But was it truly your sin – or Maximilian's?' I asked tentatively. 'Should you not rather blame fate?'

'Fate?' The word seemed to galvanise him, he gave a sudden sour laugh. 'Yes, it is a cruel fate that makes one man weak, unworldly, afraid of his own shadow, the other brave, clever and strong – then decrees that, while the strong man is born to obscurity, the weak must inherit all the burdens of earthly power. Even as a child I was unfitted, terrified of my father with his guns and his horses and his rages, frightened of the pony he gave me and the beatings my tears earned every time I took a fall. But Dieter was never frightened – never cried when he was given the strap—'

'Dieter?' I stared uncomprehendingly. 'But you told me—'

'And yet what is fate but God's will? But it was Him I wished to serve. I loved the cloister, longed to remain for the rest of my days out of the world. The world, however, would have none of it. The world pursued me, even in the Enclosure, with its spies and its informers until I was in terror for my life.'

'But if you now call Maximilian Dieter,' I persisted, 'if it was as Dieter he was known as a child, then you – you were—'

He cut across me, oblivious, talking rapidly now as if swept away by the flood of his confession. 'I think the temptation visited me even before I knew I must run away, even before I begged Dieter to come with me. The life I loved stifled him. As I longed to dedicate myself to God so he longed for the world, the flesh and the devil. Why should we not both have what we desired? After all, no one in Sylvania had seen either of us since we were children and we had often speculated that he must be my father's offspring on the sinister side, for he looked more like Sigismund than I did. He could easily pass for me with the addition of one small distinguishing mark—'

'A scar?' I asked softly. 'A scar on the left temple?'

'The temptation grew and took hold. There was not a day on the road to Paris that I did not pester him with it, whisper it in his ear like the Serpent. He would not listen. But I knew in his heart he wanted it, that sooner or later he would weaken. And then came the dying boy at Fontarelles. Since we were neither of us ordained we could not give absolution and Dieter said he would fetch a priest. But I – may God forgive me – was frightened, knew if the priest came there would be questions, investigations, that I should be delivered up to the spies on my trail. I implored Dieter not to go, wept, clung to him, even – how it shames me to recall it! – threatened to kill myself rather than face discovery. While I was wallowing thus, the boy died. I remember how

Dieter looked at me then – very cold and hard and thoughtful. He went away by himself for a long while. And at dawn when he returned he said, with that same hard look, that he would agree to my plan.'

'He agreed,' I said slowly and wonderingly, 'to change places with you?'

'I made him swear before God that he would not go back on his decision or ever, while I lived, reveal our deception. I took the same oath. Then we exchanged baptismal certificates.'

'And you – Dieter Wolf as you had now become – put your papers on the carter's body?'

'The boy was badly beaten about the face and near my height. I was Dieter Wolf, and yet Dieter Wolf was dead. No one would question it as they would a dead Crown Prince. I could vanish into the obscurity I craved. We buried the corpse in a nearby midden and parted company at the next crossroads, never to see each other again.'

He paused, and for a moment there was a silence in which I could hear my own unsteady breathing.

'So,' I said at last, carefully, 'you were brought up as the Crown Prince and my husband as Dieter Wolf. And at Fontarelles you simply changed places.'

The shadow bowed its head in assent.

'Then neither of you knew – Nurse Wolf never told you . . . ?' I hesitated. 'Please, come nearer so I may see your face.'

At first he still hung back in the gloom of the arch, but then, reluctantly, his sandals scuffling upon the flags, he hobbled towards me, a tall man prematurely bowed, his shoulders bony beneath his habit, his pale hands twitching nervously. I raised my taper and he drew back the cowl and I saw a white face, long and emaciated, saw, not the dark sensual arrogance of Sigismund, but the pale hair and eyes, the irresolute jaw of the Friedrichite side of the family.

'Your forehead?' I said softly.

He pushed up the spiky fringe of his tonsure to reveal a thin, red, horseshoe-shaped cicatrice on his left temple.

The brightness of the flame made him blink. Lowering his eyes he smiled sadly. 'He served his country well,' he said. 'And I have tried as best I can to serve God. I cannot truly repent of what we did. All the same, it was a mortal sin I led us into. There is not a day but my conscience burns for it.'

I glanced from the face of Helena's bastard to the coffin of Maximilian von Hohenstaufen, son of Tatiana, rightful heir to His Majesty King Sigismund II, and considered the last ironic trick Sylvania had played us.

'Your conscience may rest easy,' I said. Then I began, bitterly, to laugh.